The Editor

DONALD PIZER is Pierce Butler Professor of English Emeritus at Tulane University. He is the author of *The Novels of Theodore Dreiser, Realism and Naturalism in Nineteenth-Century American Literature,* and *The Novels of Frank Norris.* He is the editor of the Norton Critical Editions of *McTeague* and *The Red Badge of Courage* as well as numerous volumes of the works of Theodore Dreiser, Frank Norris, Stephen Crane, Jack London, John Dos Passos, and Hamlin Garland.

W. W. NORTON & COMPANY, INC.
Also Publishes

ENGLISH RENAISSANCE DRAMA: A NORTON ANTHOLOGY
edited by David Bevington et al.

THE NORTON ANTHOLOGY OF AFRICAN AMERICAN LITERATURE
edited by Henry Louis Gates Jr. and Nellie Y. McKay et al.

THE NORTON ANTHOLOGY OF AMERICAN LITERATURE
edited by Nina Baym et al.

THE NORTON ANTHOLOGY OF CHILDREN'S LITERATURE
edited by Jack Zipes et al.

THE NORTON ANTHOLOGY OF DRAMA
edited by J. Ellen Gainor, Stanton B. Garner Jr., and Martin Puchner

THE NORTON ANTHOLOGY OF ENGLISH LITERATURE
edited by M. H. Abrams and Stephen Greenblatt et al.

THE NORTON ANTHOLOGY OF LITERATURE BY WOMEN
edited by Sandra M. Gilbert and Susan Gubar

THE NORTON ANTHOLOGY OF MODERN AND CONTEMPORARY POETRY
edited by Jahan Ramazani, Richard Ellmann, and Robert O'Clair

THE NORTON ANTHOLOGY OF POETRY
edited by Margaret Ferguson, Mary Jo Salter, and Jon Stallworthy

THE NORTON ANTHOLOGY OF SHORT FICTION
edited by R. V. Cassill and Richard Bausch

THE NORTON ANTHOLOGY OF THEORY AND CRITICISM
edited by Vincent B. Leitch et al.

THE NORTON ANTHOLOGY OF WORLD LITERATURE
edited by Sarah Lawall et al.

THE NORTON FACSIMILE OF THE FIRST FOLIO OF SHAKESPEARE
prepared by Charlton Hinman

THE NORTON INTRODUCTION TO LITERATURE
edited by Alison Booth and Kelly J. Mays

THE NORTON READER
edited by Linda H. Peterson and John C. Brereton

THE NORTON SAMPLER
edited by Thomas Cooley

THE NORTON SHAKESPEARE, BASED ON THE OXFORD EDITION
edited by Stephen Greenblatt et al.

For a complete list of Norton Critical Editions, visit
www.wwnorton.com/college/English/nce_home.htm

A NORTON CRITICAL EDITION

Theodore Dreiser

SISTER CARRIE

AN AUTHORITATIVE TEXT
BACKGROUNDS AND SOURCES
CRITICISM

Third Edition

Edited by

DONALD PIZER
TULANE UNIVERSITY

W. W. NORTON & COMPANY • *New York* • *London*

W. W. Norton & Company has been independent since its founding in 1923, when William Warder Norton and Mary D. Herter Norton first published lectures delivered at the People's Institute, the adult education division of New York City's Cooper Union. The Nortons soon expanded their program beyond the Institute, publishing books by celebrated academics from America and abroad. By mid-century, the two major pillars of Norton's publishing program—trade books and college texts—were firmly established. In the 1950s, the Norton family transferred control of the company to its employees, and today—with a staff of four hundred and a comparable number of trade, college, and professional titles published each year—W. W. Norton & Company stands as the largest and oldest publishing house owned wholly by its employees.

The text of this book is composed in Fairfield Medium
with the display set in Bernhard Modern.
Composition by Binghamton Valley Composition.
Manufacturing by the Courier Companies—Westford Division.
Production manager: Benjamin Reynolds.

Library of Congress Cataloging-in-Publication Data

Dreiser, Theodore, 1871–1945.
Sister Carrie: an authoritative text, backgrounds, and sources criticism /
Theodore Dreiser; edited by Donald Pizer.—3rd ed.
p. cm. — (A Norton critical edition)
Includes bibliographical references.

ISBN 0-393-92773-3 (pbk.)

1. Actresses—Fiction.   2. Mistresses—Fiction.   3. Young women—Fiction.
4. Chicago (Ill.)—Fiction.   5. New York (N.Y.)—Fiction.   6. Dreiser,
Theodore, 1871–1945. Sister Carrie.   I. Pizer, Donald.   II. Title.   III. Series.

PS3507.R55S5 2005
813'.52—dc22   2005053415

W. W. Norton & Company, Inc., 500 Fifth Avenue, New York, N.Y. 10110
www.wwnorton.com

W. W. Norton & Company Ltd., Castle House,
75/76 Wells Street, London W1T 3QT

7 8 9 0

Contents

Preface to the Third Edition   ix
A Note on the Text   xi

The Text of *Sister Carrie*   1
  Appendix: Passages Cut by Dreiser and Arthur Henry in the
    Typescript Version of *Sister Carrie*   356

Backgrounds and Sources I
  CARRIE
    Photograph of Emma Dreiser   374
    Chicago Mail • He Cleaned Out the Safe   375
    Chicago Tribune • Clerk and Cash   375
    Chicago Mail • A Woman in the Case   376
    Chicago Mail • A Dashing Blonde   378
    Chicago Tribune • Hopkins Is Sorry   379
    Theodore Dreiser • [Sisters and Suitors]   380
    • [Emma's Elopement]   384
  HURSTWOOD
    Theodore Dreiser • [Downfall in the City]   387
  DROUET
    George Ade • The Fable of the Two Mandolin Players
    and the Willing Performer   391
  THE CITY
    Theodore Dreiser • [Chicago]   395
    • [New York]   397
    • Reflections   399
    • Curious Shifts of the Poor   403
  THE STRIKE
    Theodore Dreiser • [A Street-Car Strike]   413
    • The Strike To-day   414

Backgrounds and Sources II
  COMPOSITION
    Theodore Dreiser • To H. L. Mencken (May 13, 1916)   424
    Dorothy Dudley • [The Composition of *Sister Carrie*]   427
    New York Herald • "Sister Carrie": Theodore Dreiser   428

PUBLICATION

Frank Norris • To Theodore Dreiser (May 28, 1900)   430
  • To Theodore Dreiser (June 8, 1900)   430
Walter H. Page • To Theodore Dreiser (June 9, 1900)   431
Arthur Henry • To Theodore Dreiser (July 14, 1900)   431
Frank Norris • To Arthur Henry (July 18, 1900)   433
Arthur Henry • To Theodore Dreiser (July 19, 1900)   433
Walter H. Page • To Theodore Dreiser (July 19, 1900)   435
Theodore Dreiser • To Arthur Henry (July 23, 1900)   436
  • To Walter H. Page (July 23, 1900)   439
Arthur Henry • To Theodore Dreiser (July 26, 1900)   441
  • To Theodore Dreiser (July 1900)   442
Walter H. Page • To Theodore Dreiser (August 2, 1900)   443
Theodore Dreiser • To Walter H. Page (August 6, 1900)   444
Arthur Henry • To Theodore Dreiser (August 1900?)   446
Walter H. Page • To Theodore Dreiser (August 15, 1900)   447
F. N. Doubleday • To Theodore Dreiser (Sept. 4, 1900)   447
Theodore Dreiser • To F. N. Doubleday
  (after Sept. 4, 1900)   448
  • To Frank Norris (December 1900)   449
Frank Norris • To Theodore Dreiser (January 28, 1901)   450

LEGEND

St. Louis Post-Dispatch • Author of Sister Carrie   452
S. A. Everitt • To Theodore Dreiser (February 9, 1905)   454
Theodore Dreiser • To Fremont Older (Nov. 27, 1923)   455
F. N. Doubleday • To Franklin Walker (May 4, 1931)   459
Theodore Dreiser • The Early Adventures of Sister Carrie   459
Dorothy Dudley • [The "Suppression" Controversy]   461

Criticism

Theodore Dreiser • True Art Speaks Plainly   469
Otis Notman • Mr. Dreiser   470
Theodore Dreiser • To John Howard Lawson
  (Oct. 10, 1928)   471
Julian Markels • Dreiser and the Plotting of Inarticulate
  Experience   472
Ellen Moers • The Finesse of Dreiser   479
Robert Penn Warren • [Sister Carrie]   488
Philip Fisher • The Life History of Objects: The
  Naturalist Novel and the City   497
Amy Kaplan • The Sentimental Revolt of Sister Carrie   510
Alan Trachtenberg • Who Narrates? Dreiser's Presence in
  Sister Carrie   521
Kevin R. McNamara • The Ames of The Good Society:
  Sister Carrie and Social Engineering   537

Blanche H. Gelfant • What More Can Carrie Want?
    Naturalistic Ways of Consuming Women   554
Donald Pizer • The Problem of American Literary
    Naturalism and Theodore Dreiser's *Sister Carrie*   573
Cristina Ruotolo • "Whence the Song:" Voice and
    Audience in Dreiser's *Sister Carrie*   584

The Chronology of *Sister Carrie*   605
Selected Bibliography   607

Preface to the Third Edition

Theodore Dreiser (1871–1945) is one of the most controversial figures in American literary history. His life, as told by W. A. Swanberg in his *Dreiser* (1965), is a case study in how to disenchant friends and alienate almost everyone else. Embittered by his youthful poverty and often made cynical by his years as a newspaperman and magazine editor, Dreiser endeared himself to few and angered many. He was suspicious of most men and desired most women, and though he questioned the motives of others he seldom questioned his own. Dreiser's novels shared with the man a capacity to affront. From *Sister Carrie* (1900) to *An American Tragedy* (1925) they grew longer and seemingly more shapeless. The efforts of friends and editors had little effect on Dreiser's awkward, frequently clichéd verbiage. But despite these stylistic inadequacies, his best novels express a brooding insistence on the essential tragedy of life that has absorbed readers and critics for over a century.

Sister Carrie is universally recognized as a major American novel. My intent in this Norton Critical Edition is to provide an annotated text, a core of background and source material, and significant essays in criticism. The text is that of the 1900 Doubleday, Page and Company first edition. The basis for this choice is discussed in the Note on the Text at the end of this preface. In addition, a number of passages that Dreiser and his friend Arthur Henry cut from *Sister Carrie* before publication are provided in an Appendix to the text of the novel.

The footnotes to the text describe the location and nature of Chicago and New York theaters, restaurants, hotels, and so on, when this information is not apparent from the text, when it is historically or fictionally important, and when it does not involve a well-known landmark. It can be assumed that all places are actual places and that all names of persons are fictional, unless I note otherwise. Also, I have pointed out the sources of a few passages, though for the most part I have reserved such commentary for the Backgrounds and Sources sections of this Norton Critical Edition.

The emphasis in the Backgrounds and Sources sections is on Dreiser's sources for the principal characters and events of *Sister Carrie* and on the composition and publication history of the first edition.

The relationship of the novel to Dreiser's life and times is of great interest, as he was profoundly indebted in the themes of the work both to the circumstances of his own life and to the character of turn-of-the-century American experience. And Dreiser's difficulties with his publisher over the publication of *Sister Carrie* is one of the most infamous and iconographic events in early twentieth-century American literary history.

Much of the criticism of *Sister Carrie* that appeared during Dreiser's lifetime is primarily of historical importance. From the publication of the novel until his death in late 1945, discussion of Dreiser and his work was deeply colored by his symbolic role in the American cultural scene as he was either attacked as a prime example of "barbaric naturalism" or celebrated as a champion of artistic freedom. In addition, his radical social and political views often encouraged a polemical response to his work, especially during the last two decades of his life. It was not until Robert H. Elias's pioneering biography, *Theodore Dreiser: Apostle of Nature* (1949), and F. O. Mathiessen's critical study, *Theodore Dreiser* (1951), that Dreiser's life and fiction began to be viewed in perspective and with scholarly accuracy and detachment.

The Criticism section of the third Norton Critical Edition of *Sister Carrie* begins with three brief selections in which Dreiser himself comments on his intent in the novel. The four essays that follow, by Julian Markels, Ellen Moers, Robert Penn Warren, and Philip Fisher, all of which also appeared in the second edition, deal with such long-standing issues in *Sister Carrie* criticism as Dreiser's fictional artistry, his tragic conception of life, and his portrait of the modern American city. The final six essays are new to the third edition. Donald Pizer reviews the century-long critical preoccupation with *Sister Carrie* as naturalist fiction and offers a possible resolution of the issue, and Alan Trachtenberg explores the complex matter of Dreiser's "looming presence" in the work. The essays by Amy Kaplan, Kevin McNamara, Blanche H. Gelfant, and Cristina Ruotolo are related, each in its own way, to the contemporary critical emphasis on the writer's immersion in the beliefs, values, and cultural practices of his historical moment and thus his reflection of them, often unconsciously, in his work. Common to several of these essays is the issue of the nature and extent of Dreiser's endorsement of the consumerist ethos emerging out of the late-nineteenth-century industrialization and urbanization of American life. The extraordinary responsiveness of *Sister Carrie* to this major concern of recent critics is further testimony to the enduring significance of the novel.

A Note on the Text

Until the early 1980s, the text for new editions of *Sister Carrie* was invariably that of the Doubleday, Page first edition of 1900, since Dreiser during his life made only one change in this edition, in 1907, when he revised a passage in chapter 1 (see p. 3 below). The editors of the Pennsylvania Edition of *Sister Carrie* (Philadelphia: University of Pennsylvania Press, 1981), however, believe that Dreiser in his role as reviser of the prepublication typescript version of *Sister Carrie* censored the novel to make it more acceptable to a late Victorian audience. The text of the Pennsylvania Edition is therefore principally that of the handwritten first draft before Dreiser revised its conclusion (see p. 423 below) and before he and his friend Arthur Henry cut about thirty-six thousand words from the typescript. Both the interpretation of the prepublication history of *Sister Carrie* by the editors of the Pennsylvania Edition and their decision to substitute Dreiser's uncut holograph version for the first edition as the authoritative text of the novel were challenged by a number of reviewers of the Pennsylvania Edition. For a list of essays on the issue, see "*Sister Carrie*: The Textual Controversy" in the Selected Bibliography, pp. 607–11 below.

Despite the questionable claims of the Pennsylvania Edition, it does provide, in its text and apparatus, a valuable record of Dreiser's process of revision. In particular, it makes available the block cuts that Dreiser and Henry made in the typescript. Their intent in cutting the novel appears to have been principally to make a very long novel shorter. (Even in its cut form, *Sister Carrie* was 557 pages in its first edition.) Much of this omitted material therefore consists of commentary and scenes (largely in the Chicago portion) that duplicate or add little to themes present elsewhere in the novel. Nevertheless, because this cut material is indeed often fuller and therefore more explicit in its expression of these themes, it is of some interest to the critical reader of the novel. A generous sampling of the cuts made by Dreiser and Henry is provided in the Appendix that follows the text of *Sister Carrie*.

The Text of
SISTER CARRIE

TO MY FRIEND
Arthur Henry
WHOSE STEADFAST IDEALS AND SERENE
DEVOTION TO TRUTH AND BEAUTY
HAVE SERVED TO LIGHTEN THE METHOD
AND STRENGTHEN THE PURPOSE OF
THIS VOLUME.

Chapter I

THE MAGNET ATTRACTING: A WAIF AMID FORCES

When Caroline Meeber boarded the afternoon train for Chicago, her total outfit consisted of a small trunk, a cheap imitation alligator-skin satchel, a small lunch in a paper box, and a yellow leather snap purse, containing her ticket, a scrap of paper with her sister's address in Van Buren Street, and four dollars in money. It was in August, 1889.[1] She was eighteen years of age, bright, timid, and full of the illusions of ignorance and youth. Whatever touch of regret at parting characterised her thoughts, it was certainly not for advantages now being given up. A gush of tears at her mother's farewell kiss, a touch in her throat when the cars clacked by the flour mill where her father worked by the day, a pathetic sigh as the familiar green environs of the village passed in review, and the threads which bound her so lightly to girlhood and home were irretrievably broken.

To be sure there was always the next station, where one might descend and return. There was the great city, bound more closely by these very trains which came up daily. Columbia City was not so very far away, even once she was in Chicago.[2] What, pray, is a few hours—a few hundred miles? She looked at the little slip bearing her sister's address and wondered. She gazed at the green landscape, now passing in swift review, until her swifter thoughts replaced its impression with vague conjectures of what Chicago might be.

When a girl leaves her home at eighteen, she does one of two things. Either she falls into saving hands and becomes better, or she rapidly assumes the cosmopolitan standard of virtue and becomes worse. Of an intermediate balance, under the circumstances, there is no possibility. The city has its cunning wiles, no less than the infinitely smaller and more human tempter. There are large forces which allure with all the soulfulness of expression possible in the most cultured human. The gleam of a thousand lights is often as effective as the persuasive light in a wooing and fascinating eye. Half the undoing of the unsophisticated and natural mind is accomplished by forces wholly superhuman. A blare of sound, a roar of life, a vast array of human hives, appeal to the astonished senses in equivocal terms. Without a counsellor at hand to whisper cautious interpretations, what falsehoods may not these things breathe into the unguarded ear! Unrecognised for what they are, their beauty, like music, too often relaxes, then weakens, then perverts the simpler human perceptions.

1. See The Chronology of *Sister Carrie*, pp. 605–06.
2. There is no Columbia City, Wisconsin. However, when Dreiser himself came to Chicago in the summer of 1887 to look for work, he left from Warsaw, Indiana. Columbia City, Indiana, is approximately twenty miles east of Warsaw.

1

Caroline, or Sister Carrie, as she had been half affectionately termed by the family, was possessed of a mind rudimentary in its power of observation and analysis. Self-interest with her was high, but not strong. It was, nevertheless, her guiding characteristic. Warm with the fancies of youth, pretty with the insipid prettiness of the formative period, possessed of a figure promising eventual shapeliness and an eye alight with certain native intelligence, she was a fair example of the middle American class—two generations removed from the emigrant. Books were beyond her interest— knowledge a sealed book. In the intuitive graces she was still crude. She could scarcely toss her head gracefully. Her hands were almost ineffectual. The feet, though small, were set flatly. And yet she was interested in her charms, quick to understand the keener pleasures of life, ambitious to gain in material things. A half-equipped little knight she was, venturing to reconnoitre the mysterious city and dreaming wild dreams of some vague, far-off supremacy, which should make it prey and subject—the proper penitent, grovelling at a woman's slipper.

"That," said a voice in her ear, "is one of the prettiest little resorts in Wisconsin."

"Is it?" she answered nervously.

The train was just pulling out of Waukesha.[3] For some time she had been conscious of a man behind. She felt him observing her mass of hair. He had been fidgetting, and with natural intuition she felt a certain interest growing in that quarter. Her maidenly reserve, and a certain sense of what was conventional under the circumstances, called her to forestall and deny this familiarity, but the daring and magnetism of the individual, born of past experiences and triumphs, prevailed. She answered.

He leaned forward to put his elbows upon the back of her seat and proceeded to make himself volubly agreeable.

"Yes, that is a great resort for Chicago people. The hotels are swell. You are not familiar with this part of the country, are you?"

"Oh, yes, I am," answered Carrie. "That is, I live at Columbia City. I have never been through here, though."

"And so this is your first visit to Chicago," he observed.

All the time she was conscious of certain features out of the side of her eye. Flush, colourful cheeks, a light moustache, a grey fedora hat. She now turned and looked upon him in full, the instincts of self-protection and coquetry mingling confusedly in her brain.

"I didn't say that," she said.

"Oh," he answered, in a very pleasing way and with an assumed air of mistake, "I thought you did."

---

3. About fifty miles north of Chicago; the resort was noted for its mineral springs.

Here was a type of the travelling canvasser for a manufacturing house—a class which at that time was first being dubbed by the slang of the day "drummers." He came within the meaning of a still newer term, which had sprung into general use among Americans in 1880, and which concisely expressed the thought of one whose dress or manners are calculated to elicit the admiration of susceptible young women—a "masher." His suit was of a striped and crossed pattern of brown wool, new at that time, but since become familiar as a business suit. The low crotch of the vest revealed a stiff shirt bosom of white and pink stripes. From his coat sleeves protruded a pair of linen cuffs of the same pattern, fastened with large, gold plate buttons, set with the common yellow agates known as "cat's-eyes." His fingers bore several rings—one, the ever-enduring heavy seal—and from his vest dangled a neat gold watch chain, from which was suspended the secret insignia of the Order of Elks. The whole suit was rather tight-fitting, and was finished off with heavy-soled tan shoes, highly polished, and the grey fedora hat. He was, for the order of intellect represented, attractive, and whatever he had to recommend him, you may be sure was not lost upon Carrie, in this, her first glance.

Lest this order of individual should permanently pass, let me put down some of the most striking characteristics of his most successful manner and method. Good clothes, of course, were the first essential, the things without which he was nothing. A strong physical nature, actuated by a keen desire for the feminine, was the next. A mind free of any consideration of the problems or forces of the world and actuated not by greed, but an insatiable love of variable pleasure. His method was always simple. Its principal element was daring, backed, of course, by an intense desire and admiration for the sex. Let him meet with a young woman twice and he would straighten her necktie for her and perhaps address her by her first name.[4] In the great department stores he was at his ease. If he caught the attention of some young woman while waiting for the cash boy to

---

4. From this sentence to the end of the paragraph, Dreiser borrowed much of his wording from George Ade's "The Fable of the Two Mandolin Players and the Willing Performer" (see pp. 391–94). In 1907 Dreiser revised the passage to read as follows:

Let him meet with a young woman once and he would approach her with an air of kindly familiarity, not unmixed with pleading, which would result in most cases in a tolerant acceptance. If she showed any tendency to coquetry he would be apt to straighten her tie, or if she "took up" with him at all, to call her by her first name. If he visited a department store it was to lounge familiarly over the counter and ask some leading questions. In more exclusive circles, on the train or in waiting stations, he went slower. If some seemingly vulnerable object appeared he was all attention—to pass the compliments of the day, to lead the way to the parlor car, carrying her grip, or, failing that, to take a seat next her with the hope of being able to court her to her destination. Pillows, books, a foot-stool, the shade lowered; all these figured in the things which he could do. If, when she reached her destination, he did not alight and attend her baggage for her, it was because, in his own estimation, he had signally failed.

come back with his change, he would find out her name, her favourite flower, where a note would reach her, and perhaps pursue the delicate task of friendship until it proved unpromising, when it would be relinquished. He would do very well with more pretentious women, though the burden of expense was a slight deterrent. Upon entering a parlour car, for instance, he would select a chair next to the most promising bit of femininity and soon enquire if she cared to have the shade lowered. Before the train cleared the yards he would have the porter bring her a footstool. At the next lull in his conversational progress he would find her something to read, and from then on, by dint of compliment gently insinuated, personal narrative, exaggeration and service, he would win her tolerance, and, mayhap, regard.

A woman should some day write the complete philosophy of clothes. No matter how young, it is one of the things she wholly comprehends. There is an indescribably faint line in the matter of man's apparel which somehow divides for her those who are worth glancing at and those who are not. Once an individual has passed this faint line on the way downward he will get no glance from her. There is another line at which the dress of a man will cause her to study her own. This line the individual at her elbow now marked for Carrie. She became conscious of an inequality. Her own plain blue dress, with its black cotton tape trimmings, now seemed to her shabby. She felt the worn state of her shoes.

"Let's see," he went on, "I know quite a number of people in your town. Morgenroth the clothier and Gibson the dry goods man."

"Oh, do you?" she interrupted, aroused by memories of longings their show windows had cost her.

At last he had a clew to her interest, and followed it deftly. In a few minutes he had come about into her seat. He talked of sales of clothing, his travels, Chicago, and the amusements of that city.

"If you are going there, you will enjoy it immensely. Have you relatives?"

"I am going to visit my sister," she explained.

"You want to see Lincoln Park," he said, "and Michigan Boulevard. They are putting up great buildings there. It's a second New York—great. So much to see—theatres, crowds, fine houses—oh, you'll like that."

There was a little ache in her fancy of all he described. Her insignificance in the presence of so much magnificence faintly affected her. She realised that hers was not to be a round of pleasure, and yet there was something promising in all the material prospect he set forth. There was something satisfactory in the attention of this individual with his good clothes. She could not help smiling as he told her of some popular actress of whom she reminded him. She was not silly, and yet attention of this sort had its weight.

"You will be in Chicago some little time, won't you?" he observed at one turn of the now easy conversation.

"I don't know," said Carrie vaguely—a flash vision of the possibility of her not securing employment rising in her mind.

"Several weeks, anyhow," he said, looking steadily into her eyes.

There was much more passing now than the mere words indicated. He recognised the indescribable thing that made up for fascination and beauty in her. She realised that she was of interest to him from the one standpoint which a woman both delights in and fears. Her manner was simple, though for the very reason that she had not yet learned the many little affectations with which women conceal their true feelings. Some things she did appeared bold. A clever companion—had she ever had one—would have warned her never to look a man in the eyes so steadily.

"Why do you ask?" she said.

"Well, I'm going to be there several weeks. I'm going to study stock at our place and get new samples. I might show you 'round."

"I don't know whether you can or not. I mean I don't know whether I can. I shall be living with my sister, and—"

"Well, if she minds, we'll fix that." He took out his pencil and a little pocket note-book as if it were all settled. "What is your address there?"

She fumbled her purse which contained the address slip.

He reached down in his hip pocket and took out a fat purse. It was filled with slips of paper, some mileage books, a roll of greenbacks. It impressed her deeply. Such a purse had never been carried by any one attentive to her. Indeed, an experienced traveller, a brisk man of the world, had never come within such close range before. The purse, the shiny tan shoes, the smart new suit, and the *air* with which he did things, built up for her a dim world of fortune, of which he was the centre. It disposed her pleasantly toward all he might do.

He took out a neat business card, on which was engraved Bartlett, Caryoe & Company, and down in the lefthand corner, Chas. H. Drouet.

"That's me," he said, putting the card in her hand and touching his name. "It's pronounced Drew-eh. Our family was French, on my father's side."

She looked at it while he put up his purse. Then he got out a letter from a bunch in his coat pocket. "This is the house I travel for," he went on, pointing to a picture on it, "corner of State and Lake." There was pride in his voice. He felt that it was something to be connected with such a place, and he made her feel that way.

"What is your address?" he began again, fixing his pencil to write. She looked at his hand.

"Carrie Meeber," she said slowly. "Three hundred and fifty-four West Van Buren Street, care S. C. Hanson."

He wrote it carefully down and got out the purse again. "You'll be at home if I come around Monday night?" he said.

"I think so," she answered.

How true it is that words are but the vague shadows of the volumes we mean. Little audible links, they are, chaining together great inaudible feelings and purposes. Here were these two, bandying little phrases, drawing purses, looking at cards, and both unconscious of how inarticulate all their real feelings were. Neither was wise enough to be sure of the working of the mind of the other. He could not tell how his luring succeeded. She could not realise that she was drifting, until he secured her address. Now she felt that she had yielded something—he, that he had gained a victory. Already they felt that they were somehow associated. Already he took control in directing the conversation. His words were easy. Her manner was relaxed.

They were nearing Chicago. Signs were everywhere numerous. Trains flashed by them. Across wide stretches of flat, open prairie they could see lines of telegraph poles stalking across the fields toward the great city. Far away were indications of suburban towns, some big smoke-stacks towering high in the air.

Frequently there were two-story frame houses standing out in the open fields, without fence or trees, lone outposts of the approaching army of homes.

To the child, the genius with imagination, or the wholly untravelled, the approach to a great city for the first time is a wonderful thing. Particularly if it be evening—that mystic period between the glare and gloom of the world when life is changing from one sphere or condition to another. Ah, the promise of the night. What does it not hold for the weary! What old illusion of hope is not here forever repeated! Says the soul of the toiler to itself, "I shall soon be free. I shall be in the ways and the hosts of the merry. The streets, the lamps, the lighted chamber set for dining, are for me. The theatre, the halls, the parties, the ways of rest and the paths of song—these are mine in the night." Though all humanity be still enclosed in the shops, the thrill runs abroad. It is in the air. The dullest feel something which they may not always express or describe. It is the lifting of the burden of toil.

Sister Carrie gazed out of the window. Her companion, affected by her wonder, so contagious are all things, felt anew some interest in the city and pointed out its marvels.

"This is Northwest Chicago," said Drouet. "This is the Chicago River," and he pointed to a little muddy creek, crowded with the huge masted wanderers from far-off waters nosing the black-posted banks. With a puff, a clang, and a clatter of rails it was gone. "Chicago is getting to be a great town," he went on. "It's a wonder. You'll find lots to see here."

She did not hear this very well. Her heart was troubled by a kind of terror. The fact that she was alone, away from home, rushing into a great sea of life and endeavour, began to tell. She could not help but feel a little choked for breath—a little sick as her heart beat so fast. She half closed her eyes and tried to think it was nothing, that Columbia City was only a little way off.

"Chicago! Chicago!" called the brakeman, slamming open the door. They were rushing into a more crowded yard, alive with the clatter and clang of life. She began to gather up her poor little grip and closed her hand firmly upon her purse. Drouet arose, kicked his legs to straighten his trousers, and seized his clean yellow grip.

"I suppose your people will be here to meet you?" he said. "Let me carry your grip."

"Oh, no," she said. "I'd rather you wouldn't. I'd rather you wouldn't be with me when I meet my sister."

"All right," he said in all kindness. "I'll be near, though, in case she isn't here, and take you out there safely."

"You're so kind," said Carrie, feeling the goodness of such attention in her strange situation.

"Chicago!" called the brakeman, drawing the word out long. They were under a great shadowy train shed, where the lamps were already beginning to shine out, with passenger cars all about and the train moving at a snail's pace. The people in the car were all up and crowding about the door.

"Well, here we are," said Drouet, leading the way to the door. "Good-bye, till I see you Monday."

"Good-bye," she answered, taking his proffered hand.

"Remember, I'll be looking till you find your sister."

She smiled into his eyes.

They filed out, and he affected to take no notice of her. A lean-faced, rather commonplace woman recognised Carrie on the platform and hurried forward.

"Why, Sister Carrie!" she began, and there was a perfunctory embrace of welcome.

Carrie realised the change of affectional atmosphere at once. Amid all the maze, uproar, and novelty she felt cold reality taking her by the hand. No world of light and merriment. No round of amusement. Her sister carried with her most of the grimness of shift and toil.

"Why, how are all the folks at home?" she began; "how is father, and mother?"

Carrie answered, but was looking away. Down the aisle, toward the gate leading into the waiting-room and the street, stood Drouet. He was looking back. When he saw that she saw him and was safe with her sister he turned to go, sending back the shadow of a smile. Only Carrie saw it. She felt something lost to her when he moved away. When he disappeared she felt his absence thoroughly. With her sister she was much alone, a lone figure in a tossing, thoughtless sea.

Chapter II

WHAT POVERTY THREATENED: OF GRANITE AND BRASS

Minnie's flat, as the one-floor resident apartments were then being called, was in a part of West Van Buren Street inhabited by families of labourers and clerks, men who had come, and were still coming, with the rush of population pouring in at the rate of 50,000 a year.[1] It was on the third floor, the front windows looking down into the street, where, at night, the lights of grocery stores were shining and children were playing. To Carrie, the sound of the little bells upon the horse-cars, as they tinkled in and out of hearing, was as pleasing as it was novel. She gazed into the lighted street when Minnie brought her into the front room, and wondered at the sounds, the movement, the murmur of the vast city which stretched for miles and miles in every direction.

Mrs. Hanson, after the first greetings were over, gave Carrie the baby and proceeded to get supper. Her husband asked a few questions and sat down to read the evening paper. He was a silent man, American born, of a Swede father, and now employed as a cleaner of refrigerator cars at the stock-yards. To him the presence or absence of his wife's sister was a matter of indifference. Her personal appearance did not affect him one way or the other. His one observation to the point was concerning the chances of work in Chicago.

"It's a big place," he said. "You can get in somewhere in a few days. Everybody does."

It had been tacitly understood beforehand that she was to get work and pay her board. He was of a clean, saving disposition, and had already paid a number of monthly instalments on two lots far out on the West Side. His ambition was some day to build a house on them.

In the interval which marked the preparation of the meal Carrie found time to study the flat. She had some slight gift of observation and that sense, so rich in every woman—intuition.

She felt the drag of a lean and narrow life. The walls of the rooms

---

1. In general, the South Side of Chicago was devoted to heavy industry, the West Side to light industry and to working-class and lower-middle-class homes and flats, and the North Side to middle- and upper-middle-class homes. The Hansons' flat is on the near West Side, close to the Chicago River.

were discordantly papered. The floors were covered with matting and the hall laid with a thin rag carpet. One could see that the furniture was of that poor, hurriedly patched together quality sold by the instalment houses.

She sat with Minnie, in the kitchen, holding the baby until it began to cry. Then she walked and sang to it, until Hanson, disturbed in his reading, came and took it. A pleasant side to his nature came out here. He was patient. One could see that he was very much wrapped up in his offspring.

"Now, now," he said, walking. "There, there," and there was a certain Swedish accent noticeable in his voice.

"You'll want to see the city first, won't you?" said Minnie, when they were eating. "Well, we'll go out Sunday and see Lincoln Park."

Carrie noticed that Hanson had said nothing to this. He seemed to be thinking of something else.

"Well," she said, "I think I'll look around to-morrow. I've got Friday and Saturday, and it won't be any trouble. Which way is the business part?"

Minnie began to explain, but her husband took this part of the conversation to himself.

"It's that way," he said, pointing east. "That's east." Then he went off into the longest speech he had yet indulged in, concerning the lay of Chicago. "You'd better look in those big manufacturing houses along Franklin Street and just the other side of the river," he concluded. "Lots of girls work there. You could get home easy, too. It isn't very far."

Carrie nodded and asked her sister about the neighbourhood. The latter talked in a subdued tone, telling the little she knew about it, while Hanson concerned himself with the baby. Finally he jumped up and handed the child to his wife.

"I've got to get up early in the morning, so I'll go to bed," and off he went, disappearing into the dark little bedroom off the hall, for the night.

"He works way down at the stock-yards," explained Minnie, "so he's got to get up at half-past five."

"What time do you get up to get breakfast?" asked Carrie.

"At about twenty minutes of five."

Together they finished the labour of the day, Carrie washing the dishes while Minnie undressed the baby and put it to bed. Minnie's manner was one of trained industry, and Carrie could see that it was a steady round of toil with her.

She began to see that her relations with Drouet would have to be abandoned. He could not come here. She read from the manner of Hanson, in the subdued air of Minnie, and, indeed, the whole atmosphere of the flat, a settled opposition to anything save a conservative round of toil. If Hanson sat every evening in the front room and read his paper, if he went to bed at nine, and Minnie a little later, what would they expect of her? She saw that she would first need to get work and establish herself on a paying basis before she could think of having company of any sort. Her little flirtation with Drouet seemed now an extraordinary thing.

"No," she said to herself, "he can't come here."

She asked Minnie for ink and paper, which were upon the mantel in the dining-room, and when the latter had gone to bed at ten, got out Drouet's card and wrote him.

"I cannot have you call on me here. You will have to wait until you hear from me again. My sister's place is so small."

She troubled herself over what else to put in the letter. She wanted to make some reference to their relations upon the train, but was too timid. She concluded by thanking him for his kindness in a crude way, then puzzled over the formality of signing her name, and finally decided upon the severe, winding up with a "Very truly," which she subsequently changed to "Sincerely." She sealed and addressed the letter, and going in the front room, the alcove of which contained her bed, drew the one small rocking-chair up to the open window, and sat looking out upon the night and streets in silent wonder. Finally, wearied by her own reflections, she began to grow dull in her chair, and feeling the need of sleep, arranged her clothing for the night and went to bed.

When she awoke at eight the next morning, Hanson had gone. Her sister was busy in the dining-room, which was also the sitting-room, sewing. She worked, after dressing, to arrange a little breakfast for herself, and then advised with Minnie as to which way to look. The latter had changed considerably since Carrie had seen her. She was now a thin, though rugged, woman of twenty-seven, with ideas of life coloured by her husband's, and fast hardening into narrower conceptions of pleasure and duty than had ever been hers in a thoroughly circumscribed youth. She had invited Carrie, not because she longed for her presence, but because the latter was dissatisfied at home, and could probably get work and pay her board here. She was pleased to see her in a way, but reflected her husband's point of view in the matter of work. Anything was good enough so long as it paid—say, five dollars a week to begin with. A shop girl was the destiny prefigured for the newcomer. She would get in one of the great shops and do well enough until—well, until something happened. Neither of them knew exactly what. They did not figure on promotion. They did not exactly count on marriage. Things would go on, though, in a dim kind of way until the better thing would eventuate, and Carrie would be rewarded for coming and toiling in the city. It was under such auspicious circumstances that she started out this morning to look for work.

Before following her in her round of seeking, let us look at the sphere in which her future was to lie. In 1889 Chicago had the peculiar qualifications of growth which made such adventuresome pilgrimages even on the part of young girls plausible. Its many and growing commercial opportunities gave it widespread fame, which made of it a giant magnet, drawing to itself, from all quarters, the hopeful and the hopeless—those who had their fortune yet to make and those whose fortunes and affairs had reached a disastrous climax elsewhere. It was a city of over 500,000[2] with the ambition, the daring, the activity of a metropolis of a million. Its streets and houses were already scattered over an area of seventy-five square miles. Its population was not so much thriving upon established commerce as upon the industries which prepared for the arrival of others. The sound of the hammer engaged upon the erection of new structures was everywhere heard. Great industries were moving in. The huge railroad corporations which had long before recognised the prospects of the place had seized upon vast tracts of land for transfer and shipping purposes. Street-car lines had been extended far out into the open country in anticipation of rapid growth. The city had laid miles and miles of streets and sewers through regions where, perhaps, one solitary house stood out alone—a pioneer of the populous ways to be. There were regions open to the sweeping winds and rain, which were yet lighted throughout the night with long, blinking lines of gas-lamps, fluttering in the wind. Narrow board walks extended out, passing here a house, and there a store, at far intervals, eventually ending on the open prairie.

In the central portion was the vast wholesale and shopping district, to which the uninformed seeker for work usually drifted. It was a characteristic of Chicago then, and one not generally shared by other cities, that individual firms of any pretension occupied individual buildings. The presence of ample ground made this possible. It gave an imposing appearance to most of the wholesale houses, whose offices were upon the ground floor and in plain view of the street. The large plates of window glass, now so common, were then rapidly coming into use, and gave to the ground floor offices a distinguished and prosperous look. The casual wanderer could see as he passed a polished array of office fixtures, much frosted glass, clerks hard at work, and genteel business men in "nobby" suits[3] and clean linen lounging about or sitting in groups. Polished brass or nickel signs at

2. Dreiser is referring to the census count of 1880. By 1890, with additional growth and annexations, the population of Chicago was over 1 million.
3. An elegant or flashy suit.

the square stone entrances announced the firm and the nature of the business in rather neat and reserved terms. The entire metropolitan centre possessed a high and mighty air calculated to overawe and abash the common applicant, and to make the gulf between poverty and success seem both wide and deep.

Into this important commercial region the timid Carrie went. She walked east along Van Buren Street through a region of lessening importance, until it deteriorated into a mass of shanties and coalyards, and finally verged upon the river. She walked bravely forward, led by an honest desire to find employment and delayed at every step by the interest of the unfolding scene, and a sense of helplessness amid so much evidence of power and force which she did not understand. These vast buildings, what were they? These strange energies and huge interests, for what purposes were they there? She could have understood the meaning of a little stone-cutter's yard at Columbia City, carving little pieces of marble for individual use, but when the yards of some huge stone corporation came into view, filled with spur tracks and flat cars, transpierced by docks from the river and traversed overhead by immense trundling cranes of wood and steel, it lost all significance in her little world.

It was so with the vast railroad yards, with the crowded array of vessels she saw at the river, and the huge factories over the way, lining the water's edge. Through the open windows she could see the figures of men and women in working aprons, moving busily about. The great streets were wall-lined mysteries to her; the vast offices, strange mazes which concerned far-off individuals of importance. She could only think of people connected with them as counting money, dressing magnificently, and riding in carriages. What they dealt in, how they laboured, to what end it all came, she had only the vaguest conception. It was all wonderful, all vast, all far removed, and she sank in spirit inwardly and fluttered feebly at the heart as she thought of entering any one of these mighty concerns and asking for something to do—something that she could do—anything.

Chapter III

WE QUESTION OF FORTUNE: FOUR-FIFTY A WEEK

Once across the river and into the wholesale district, she glanced about her for some likely door at which to apply. As she contemplated the wide windows and imposing signs, she became conscious of being gazed upon and understood for what she was—a wage-seeker. She had never done this thing before, and lacked courage. To avoid a certain indefinable shame she felt at being caught spying about for a position, she quickened her steps and assumed an air of indifference supposedly common to one upon an errand. In this way she passed many manufacturing and wholesale houses without once glancing in. At last, after several blocks of walking, she felt that this would not do, and began to look about again; though without relaxing her pace. A little way on she saw a great door which, for some reason, attracted her attention. It was ornamented by a small brass sign, and seemed to be the entrance to a vast hive of six or seven floors. "Perhaps," she thought, "they may want some one," and crossed over to enter. When she came within a score of feet of the desired goal, she saw through the window a young man in a grey checked suit. That he had anything to do with the concern, she could not tell, but because he happened to be looking in her direction her weakening heart misgave her and she hurried by, too overcome with shame to enter. Over the way stood a great six-story structure, labelled Storm and King,[1] which she viewed with rising hope. It was a wholesale dry goods concern and employed women. She could see them moving about now and then upon the upper floors. This place she decided to enter, no matter what. She crossed over and walked directly toward the entrance. As she did so, two men came out and paused in the door. A telegraph messenger in blue dashed past her and up the few steps that led to the entrance and disappeared. Several pedestrians out of the hurrying throng which filled the sidewalks passed about her as she paused, hesitating. She looked helplessly around, and then, seeing herself observed, retreated. It was too difficult a task. She could not go past them.

So severe a defeat told sadly upon her nerves. Her feet carried her mechanically forward, every foot of her progress being a satisfactory portion of a flight which she gladly made. Block after block passed by. Upon street-lamps at the various corners she read names such as Madison, Monroe, La Salle, Clark, Dearborn, State, and still she went, her feet beginning to tire upon the broad stone flagging. She was pleased in part that the streets were bright and clean. The morning sun, shining down with steadily increasing warmth, made the shady side of the streets pleasantly cool. She looked at the blue sky overhead with more realisation of its charm than had ever come to her before.

Her cowardice began to trouble her in a way. She turned back, resolving to hunt up Storm and King and enter. On the way she encountered a great wholesale shoe company, through the broad plate windows of which she saw an enclosed executive department, hidden by frosted glass. Without this enclosure, but just within the street entrance, sat a grey-haired gentleman at a small table, with a

---

1. A fictitious name.

large open ledger before him. She walked by this institution several times hesitating, but, finding herself unobserved, faltered past the screen door and stood humbly waiting.

"Well, young lady," observed the old gentleman, looking at her somewhat kindly, "what is it you wish?"

"I am, that is, do you—I mean, do you need any help?" she stammered.

"Not just at present," he answered smiling. "Not just at present. Come in some time next week. Occasionally we need some one."

She received the answer in silence and backed awkwardly out. The pleasant nature of her reception rather astonished her. She had expected that it would be more difficult, that something cold and harsh would be said—she knew not what. That she had not been put to shame and made to feel her unfortunate position, seemed remarkable.

Somewhat encouraged, she ventured into another large structure. It was a clothing company, and more people were in evidence—well-dressed men of forty and more, surrounded by brass railings.

An office boy approached her.

"Who is it you wish to see?" he asked.

"I want to see the manager," she said.

He ran away and spoke to one of a group of three men who were conferring together. One of these came towards her.

"Well?" he said coldly. The greeting drove all courage from her at once.

"Do you need any help?" she stammered.

"No," he replied abruptly, and turned upon his heel.

She went foolishly out, the office boy deferentially swinging the door for her, and gladly sank into the obscuring crowd. It was a severe setback to her recently pleased mental state.

Now she walked quite aimlessly for a time, turning here and there, seeing one great company after another, but finding no courage to prosecute her single inquiry. High noon came, and with it hunger. She hunted out an unassuming restaurant and entered, but was disturbed to find that the prices were exorbitant for the size of her purse. A bowl of soup was all that she could afford, and, with this quickly eaten, she went out again. It restored her strength somewhat and made her moderately bold to pursue the search.

In walking a few blocks to fix upon some probable place, she again encountered the firm of Storm and King, and this time managed to get in. Some gentlemen were conferring close at hand, but took no notice of her. She was left standing, gazing nervously upon the floor. When the limit of her distress had been nearly reached, she was beckoned to by a man at one of the many desks within the near-by railing.

"Who is it you wish to see?" he inquired.

"Why, any one, if you please," she answered. "I am looking for something to do."

"Oh, you want to see Mr. McManus," he returned. "Sit down," and he pointed to a chair against the neighbouring wall. He went on leisurely writing, until after a time a short, stout gentleman came in from the street.

"Mr. McManus," called the man at the desk, "this young woman wants to see you."

The short gentleman turned about towards Carrie, and she arose and came forward.

"What can I do for you, miss?" he inquired, surveying her curiously.

"I want to know if I can get a position," she inquired.

"As what?" he asked.

"Not as anything in particular," she faltered.

"Have you ever had any experience in the wholesale dry goods business?" he questioned.

"No, sir," she replied.

"Are you a stenographer or typewriter?"

"No, sir."

"Well, we haven't anything here," he said. "We employ only experienced help."

She began to step backward toward the door, when something about her plaintive face attracted him.

"Have you ever worked at anything before?" he inquired.

"No, sir," she said.

"Well, now, it's hardly possible that you would get anything to do in a wholesale house of this kind. Have you tried the department stores?"

She acknowledged that she had not.

"Well, if I were you," he said, looking at her rather genially, "I would try the department stores. They often need young women as clerks."

"Thank you," she said, her whole nature relieved by this spark of friendly interest.

"Yes," he said, as she moved toward the door, "you try the department stores," and off he went.

At that time the department store was in its earliest form of successful operation, and there were not many. The first three in the United States, established about 1884, were in Chicago.[2] Carrie was

2. Dreiser is perhaps thinking of Marshall Field's, The Fair, and the Boston Store. Although department stores had their origin in the East, they developed with particular rapidity in Chicago as a result of the commercial reorganization of the city after the 1871 fire. The year before beginning *Sister Carrie*, Dreiser wrote an article about Marshall Field:

familiar with the names of several through the advertisements in the "Daily News," and now proceeded to seek them. The words of Mr. McManus had somehow managed to restore her courage, which had fallen low, and she dared to hope that this new line would offer her something. Some time she spent in wandering up and down, thinking to encounter the buildings by chance, so readily is the mind, bent upon prosecuting a hard but needful errand, eased by that self-deception which the semblance of search, without the reality, gives. At last she inquired of a police officer, and was directed to proceed "two blocks up," where she would find "The Fair."

The nature of these vast retail combinations, should they ever permanently disappear, will form an interesting chapter in the commercial history of our nation. Such a flowering out of a modest trade principle the world had never witnessed up to that time. They were along the line of the most effective retail organisation, with hundreds of stores coordinated into one and laid out upon the most imposing and economic basis. They were handsome, bustling, successful affairs, with a host of clerks and a swarm of patrons. Carrie passed along the busy aisles, much affected by the remarkable displays of trinkets, dress goods, stationery, and jewelry. Each separate counter was a show place of dazzling interest and attraction. She could not help feeling the claim of each trinket and valuable upon her personally, and yet she did not stop. There was nothing there which she could not have used—nothing which she did not long to own. The dainty slippers and stockings, the delicately frilled skirts and petticoats, the laces, ribbons, hair-combs, purses, all touched her with individual desire, and she felt keenly the fact that not any of these things were in the range of her purchase. She was a work-seeker, an outcast without employment, one whom the average employee could tell at a glance was poor and in need of a situation.

It must not be thought that any one could have mistaken her for a nervous, sensitive, high-strung nature, cast unduly upon a cold, calculating, and unpoetic world. Such certainly she was not. But women are peculiarly sensitive to their adornment.

Not only did Carrie feel the drag of desire for all which was new and pleasing in apparel for women, but she noticed too, with a touch at the heart, the fine ladies who elbowed and ignored her, brushing past in utter disregard of her presence, themselves eagerly enlisted in the materials which the store contained. Carrie was not familiar with the appearance of her more fortunate sisters of the city. Neither had she before known the nature and appearance of the shop girls with whom she now compared poorly. They were pretty in the main,

---

"Life Stories of Successful Men—No. 12, Marshall Field," *Success* 2 (December 8, 1898): 7–8.

some even handsome, with an air of independence and indifference which added, in the case of the more favoured, a certain piquancy. Their clothes were neat, in many instances fine, and wherever she encountered the eye of one it was only to recognise in it a keen analysis of her own position—her individual shortcomings of dress and that shadow of *manner* which she thought must hang about her and make clear to all who and what she was. A flame of envy lighted in her heart. She realised in a dim way how much the city held— wealth, fashion, ease—every adornment for women, and she longed for dress and beauty with a whole heart.

On the second floor were the managerial offices, to which, after some inquiry, she was now directed. There she found other girls ahead of her, applicants like herself, but with more of that self-satisfied and independent air which experience of the city lends; girls who scrutinised her in a painful manner. After a wait of perhaps three-quarters of an hour, she was called in turn.

"Now," said a sharp, quick-mannered Jew, who was sitting at a roll-top desk near the window, "have you ever worked in any other store?"

"No, sir," said Carrie.

"Oh, you haven't," he said, eyeing her keenly.

"No, sir," she replied.

"Well, we prefer young women just now with some experience. I guess we can't use you."

Carrie stood waiting a moment, hardly certain whether the interview had terminated.

"Don't wait!" he exclaimed. "Remember we are very busy here."

Carrie began to move quickly to the door.

"Hold on," he said, calling her back. "Give me your name and address. We want girls occasionally."

When she had gotten safely into the street, she could scarcely restrain the tears. It was not so much the particular rebuff which she had just experienced, but the whole abashing trend of the day. She was tired and nervous. She abandoned the thought of appealing to the other department stores and now wandered on, feeling a certain safety and relief in mingling with the crowd.

In her indifferent wandering she turned into Jackson Street, not far from the river, and was keeping her way along the south side of that imposing thoroughfare, when a piece of wrapping paper, written on with marking ink and tacked up on the door, attracted her attention. It read, "Girls wanted—wrappers & stitchers." She hesitated a moment, then entered.

The firm of Speigelheim & Co.,[3] makers of boys' caps, occupied

---

3. A fictitious name.

one floor of the building, fifty feet in width and some eighty feet in depth. It was a place rather dingily lighted, the darkest portions having incandescent lights, filled with machines and work benches. At the latter laboured quite a company of girls and some men. The former were drabby-looking creatures, stained in face with oil and dust, clad in thin, shapeless, cotton dresses and shod with more or less worn shoes. Many of them had their sleeves rolled up, revealing bare arms, and in some cases, owing to the heat, their dresses were open at the neck. They were a fair type of nearly the lowest order of shop-girls—careless, slouchy, and more or less pale from confinement. They were not timid, however; were rich in curiosity, and strong in daring and slang.

Carrie looked about her, very much disturbed and quite sure that she did not want to work here. Aside from making her uncomfortable by sidelong glances, no one paid her the least attention. She waited until the whole department was aware of her presence. Then some word was sent around, and a foreman, in an apron and shirt sleeves, the latter rolled up to his shoulders, approached.

"Do you want to see me?" he asked.

"Do you need any help?" said Carrie, already learning directness of address.

"Do you know how to stitch caps?" he returned.

"No, sir," she replied.

"Have you ever had any experience at this kind of work?" he inquired.

She answered that she had not.

"Well," said the foreman, scratching his ear meditatively, "we do need a stitcher. We like experienced help, though. We've hardly got time to break people in." He paused and looked away out of the window. "We might, though, put you at finishing," he concluded reflectively.

"How much do you pay a week?" ventured Carrie, emboldened by a certain softness in the man's manner and his simplicity of address.

"Three and a half," he answered.

"Oh," she was about to exclaim, but checked herself and allowed her thoughts to die without expression.

"We're not exactly in need of anybody," he went on vaguely, looking her over as one would a package. "You can come on Monday morning, though," he added, "and I'll put you to work."

"Thank you," said Carrie weakly.

"If you come, bring an apron," he added.

He walked away and left her standing by the elevator, never so much as inquiring her name.

While the appearance of the shop and the announcement of the price paid per week operated very much as a blow to Carrie's fancy, the fact that work of any kind was offered after so rude a round of experience was gratifying. She could not begin to believe that she would take the place, modest as her aspirations were. She had been used to better than that. Her mere experience and the free out-of-door life of the country caused her nature to revolt at such confinement. Dirt had never been her share. Her sister's flat was clean. This place was grimy and low, the girls were careless and hardened. They must be bad-minded and hearted, she imagined. Still, a place had been offered her. Surely Chicago was not so bad if she could find one place in one day. She might find another and better later.

Her subsequent experiences were not of a reassuring nature, however. From all the more pleasing or imposing places she was turned away abruptly with the most chilling formality. In others where she applied only the experienced were required. She met with painful rebuffs, the most trying of which had been in a manufacturing cloak house, where she had gone to the fourth floor to inquire.

"No, no," said the foreman, a rough, heavily built individual, who looked after a miserably lighted workshop, "we don't want any one. Don't come here."

With the wane of the afternoon went her hopes, her courage, and her strength. She had been astonishingly persistent. So earnest an effort was well deserving of a better reward. On every hand, to her fatigued senses, the great business portion grew larger, harder, more stolid in its indifference. It seemed as if it was all closed to her, that the struggle was too fierce for her to hope to do anything at all. Men and women hurried by in long, shifting lines. She felt the flow of the tide of effort and interest—felt her own helplessness without quite realising the wisp on the tide that she was. She cast about vainly for some possible place to apply, but found no door which she had the courage to enter. It would be the same thing all over. The old humiliation of her plea, rewarded by curt denial. Sick at heart and in body, she turned to the west, the direction of Minnie's flat, which she had now fixed in mind, and began that wearisome, baffled retreat which the seeker for employment at nightfall too often makes. In passing through Fifth Avenue, south towards Van Buren Street, where she intended to take a car, she passed the door of a large wholesale shoe house, through the plate-glass window of which she could see a middle-aged gentleman sitting a a small desk. One of those forlorn impulses which often grow out of a fixed sense of defeat, the last sprouting of a baffled and uprooted growth of ideas, seized upon her. She walked deliberately through the door and up to the gentleman, who looked at her weary face with partially awakened interest.

"What is it?" he said.

"Can you give me something to do?" said Carrie.

"Now, I really don't know," he said kindly. "What kind of work is it you want—you're not a typewriter, are you?"

"Oh, no," answered Carrie.

"Well, we only employ book-keepers and typewriters here. You might go around to the side and inquire upstairs. They did want some help upstairs a few days ago. Ask for Mr. Brown."

She hastened around to the side entrance and was taken up by the elevator to the fourth floor.

"Call Mr. Brown, Willie," said the elevator man to a boy near by.

Willie went off and presently returned with the information that Mr. Brown said she should sit down and that he would be around in a little while.

It was a portion of the stock room which gave no idea of the general character of the place, and Carrie could form no opinion of the nature of the work.

"So you want something to do," said Mr. Brown, after he inquired concerning the nature of her errand. "Have you ever been employed in a shoe factory before?"

"No, sir," said Carrie.

"What is your name?" he inquired, and being informed, "Well, I don't know as I have anything for you. Would you work for four and a half a week?"

Carrie was too worn by defeat not to feel that it was considerable. She had not expected that he would offer her less than six. She acquiesced, however, and he took her name and address.

"Well," he said, finally, "you report here at eight o'clock Monday morning. I think I can find something for you to do."

He left her revived by the possibilities, sure that she had found something at last. Instantly the blood crept warmly over her body. Her nervous tension relaxed. She walked out into the busy street and discovered a new atmosphere. Behold, the throng was moving with a lightsome step. She noticed that men and women were smiling. Scraps of conversation and notes of laughter floated to her. The air was light. People were already pouring out of the buildings, their labour ended for the day. She noticed that they were pleased, and thoughts of her sister's home and the meal that would be awaiting her quickened her steps. She hurried on, tired perhaps, but no longer weary of foot. What would not Minnie say! Ah, the long winter in Chicago—the lights, the crowd, the amusement! This was a great, pleasing metropolis after all. Her new firm was a goodly institution. Its windows were of huge plate glass. She could probably do well there. Thoughts of Drouet returned—of the things he had told her. She now felt that life was better, that it was livelier, sprightlier. She boarded a car in the best of spirits, feeling her blood still flowing pleasantly. She would live in Chicago, her mind kept saying to itself. She would have a better time than she had ever had before—she would be happy.

Chapter IV

THE SPENDINGS OF FANCY: FACTS ANSWER WITH SNEERS

For the next two days Carrie indulged in the most high-flown speculations.

Her fancy plunged recklessly into privileges and amusements which would have been much more becoming had she been cradled a child of fortune. With ready will and quick mental selection she scattered her meagre four-fifty per week with a swift and graceful hand. Indeed, as she sat in her rocking-chair these several evenings before going to bed and looked out upon the pleasantly lighted street, this money cleared for its prospective possessor the way to every joy and every bauble which the heart of woman may desire. "I will have a fine time," she thought.

Her sister Minnie knew nothing of these rather wild cerebrations, though they exhausted the markets of delight. She was too busy scrubbing the kitchen woodwork and calculating the purchasing power of eighty cents for Sunday's dinner. When Carrie had returned home, flushed with her first success and ready, for all her weariness, to discuss the now interesting events which led up to her achievement, the former had merely smiled approvingly and inquired whether she would have to spend any of it for car fare. This consideration had not entered in before, and it did not now for long affect the glow of Carrie's enthusiasm. Disposed as she then was to calculate upon that vague basis which allows the subtraction of one sum from another without any perceptible diminution, she was happy.

When Hanson came home at seven o'clock, he was inclined to be a little crusty—his usual demeanour before supper. This never showed so much in anything he said as in a certain solemnity of countenance and the silent manner in which he slopped about. He had a pair of yellow carpet slippers which he enjoyed wearing, and these he would immediately substitute for his solid pair of shoes. This, and washing his face with the aid of common washing soap until it glowed a shiny red, constituted his only preparation for his evening meal. He would then get his evening paper and read in silence.

For a young man, this was rather a morbid turn of character, and so affected Carrie. Indeed, it affected the entire atmosphere of the flat, as such things are inclined to do, and gave to his wife's mind its subdued and tactful turn, anxious to avoid taciturn replies. Under the influence of Carrie's announcement he brightened up somewhat.

"You didn't lose any time, did you?" he remarked, smiling a little.

"No," returned Carrie with a touch of pride.

He asked her one or two more questions and then turned to play with the baby, leaving the subject until it was brought up again by Minnie at the table.

Carrie, however, was not to be reduced to the common level of observation which prevailed in the flat.

"It seems to be such a large company," she said at one place. "Great big plate-glass windows and lots of clerks. The man I saw said they hired ever so many people."

"It's not very hard to get work now," put in Hanson, "if you look right."

Minnie, under the warming influence of Carrie's good spirits and her husband's somewhat conversational mood, began to tell Carrie of some of the well-known things to see—things the enjoyment of which cost nothing.

"You'd like to see Michigan Avenue. There are such fine houses. It is such a fine street."

"Where is 'H. R. Jacob's'?" interrupted Carrie, mentioning one of the theatres devoted to melodrama which went by that name at the time.[1]

"Oh, it's not very far from here," answered Minnie. "It's in Halstead Street, right up here."

"How I'd like to go there. I crossed Halstead Street to-day, didn't I?"

At this there was a slight halt in the natural reply. Thoughts are a strangely permeating factor. At her suggestion of going to the theatre, the unspoken shade of disapproval to the doing of those things which involved the expenditure of money—shades of feeling which arose in the mind of Hanson and then in Minnie—slightly affected the atmosphere of the table. Minnie answered "yes," but Carrie could feel that going to the theatre was poorly advocated here. The subject was put off for a little while until Hanson, through with his meal, took his paper and went into the front room.

When they were alone, the two sisters began a somewhat freer conversation, Carrie interrupting it to hum a little, as they worked at the dishes.

"I should like to walk up and see Halstead Street, if it isn't too far," said Carrie, after a time. "Why don't we go to the theatre to-night?"

"Oh, I don't think Sven would want to go to-night," returned Minnie. "He has to get up so early."

"He wouldn't mind—he'd enjoy it," said Carrie.

1. H. R. Jacob's Theatre was on Halstead (then and now often spelled Halsted) and Madison, a few blocks from the Hansons' Van Buren Street flat.

"No, he doesn't go very often," returned Minnie.

"Well, I'd like to go," rejoined Carrie. "Let's you and me go."

Minnie pondered a while, not upon whether she could or would go—for that point was already negatively settled with her—but upon some means of diverting the thoughts of her sister to some other topic.

"We'll go some other time," she said at last, finding no ready means of escape.

Carrie sensed the root of the opposition at once.

"I have some money," she said. "You go with me."

Minnie shook her head.

"He could go along," said Carrie.

"No," returned Minnie softly, and rattling the dishes to drown the conversation. "He wouldn't."

It had been several years since Minnie had seen Carrie, and in that time that latter's character had developed a few shades. Naturally timid in all things that related to her own advancement, and especially so when without power or resource, her craving for pleasure was so strong that it was the one stay of her nature. She would speak for that when silent on all else.

"Ask him," she pleaded softly.

Minnie was thinking of the resource which Carrie's board would add. It would pay the rent and would make the subject of expenditure a little less difficult to talk about with her husband. But if Carrie was going to think of running around in the beginning there would be a hitch somewhere. Unless Carrie submitted to a solemn round of industry and saw the need of hard work without longing for play, how was her coming to the city to profit them? These thoughts were not those of a cold, hard nature at all. They were the serious reflections of a mind which invariably adjusted itself, without much complaining, to such surroundings as its industry could make for it.

At last she yielded enough to ask Hanson. It was a half-hearted procedure without a shade of desire on her part.

"Carrie wants us to go to the theatre," she said, looking in upon her husband. Hanson looked up from his paper, and they exchanged a mild look, which said as plainly as anything: "This isn't what we expected."

"I don't care to go," he returned. "What does she want to see?"

"H. R. Jacob's," said Minnie.

He looked down at his paper and shook his head negatively.

When Carrie saw how they looked upon her proposition, she gained a still clearer feeling of their way of life. It weighed on her, but took no definite form of opposition.

"I think I'll go down and stand at the foot of the stairs," she said, after a time.

Minnie made no objection to this, and Carrie put on her hat and went below.

"Where has Carrie gone?" asked Hanson, coming back into the dining-room when he heard the door close.

"She said she was going down to the foot of the stairs," answered Minnie. "I guess she just wants to look out a while."

"She oughtn't to be thinking about spending her money on theatres already, do you think?" he said.

"She just feels a little curious, I guess," ventured Minnie. "Everything is so new."

"I don't know," said Hanson, and went over to the baby, his forehead slightly wrinkled.

He was thinking of a full career of vanity and wastefulness which a young girl might indulge in, and wondering how Carrie could contemplate such a course when she had so little, as yet, with which to do.

On Saturday Carrie went out by herself—first toward the river, which interested her, and then back along Jackson Street, which was then lined by the pretty houses and fine lawns which subsequently caused it to be made into a boulevard. She was struck with the evidences of wealth, although there was, perhaps, not a person on the street worth more than a hundred thousand dollars. She was glad to be out of the flat, because already she felt that it was a narrow, humdrum place, and that interest and joy lay elsewhere. Her thoughts now were of a more liberal character, and she punctuated them with speculations as to the whereabouts of Drouet. She was not sure but that he might call anyhow Monday night, and, while she felt a little disturbed at the possibility, there was, nevertheless, just the shade of a wish that be would.

On Monday she arose early and prepared to go to work. She dressed herself in a worn shirt-waist, of dotted blue percale, a skirt of light brown serge rather faded, and a small straw hat which she had worn all summer at Columbia City. Her shoes were old, and her necktie was in that crumpled, flattened state which time and much wearing impart. She made a very average looking shop-girl with the exception of her features. These were slightly more even than common, and gave her a sweet, reserved, and pleasing appearance.

It is no easy thing to get up early in the morning when one is used to sleeping until seven and eight, as Carrie had been at home. She gained some inkling of the character of Hanson's life when, half asleep, she looked out into the dining-room at six o'clock and saw him silently finishing his breakfast. By the time she was dressed he was gone, and she, Minnie, and the baby ate together, the latter being just old enough to sit in a high chair and disturb the dishes with a spoon. Her spirits were greatly subdued now when the fact of entering upon strange and untried duties confronted her. Only the ashes of all her fine fancies were remaining—ashes still concealing, nevertheless, a few red embers of hope. So subdued was she by her weakening nerves, that she ate quite in silence, going over imaginary conceptions of the character of the shoe company, the nature of the work, her employer's attitude. She was vaguely feeling that she would come in contact with the great owners, that her work would be where grave, stylishly dressed men occasionally look on.

"Well, good luck," said Minnie, when she was ready to go. They had agreed it was best to walk, that morning at least, to see if she could do it every day—sixty cents a week for car fare being quite an item under the circumstances.

"I'll tell you how it goes to-night," said Carrie.

Once in the sunlit street, with labourers tramping by in either direction, the horse-cars passing crowded to the rails with the small clerks and floor help in the great wholesale houses, and men and women generally coming out of doors and passing about the neighbourhood, Carrie felt slightly reassured. In the sunshine of the morning, beneath the wide, blue heavens, with a fresh wind astir, what fears, except the most desperate, can find a harbourage? In the night, or the gloomy chambers of the day, fears and misgivings wax strong, but out in the sunlight there is, for a time, cessation even of the terror of death.

Carrie went straight forward until she crossed the river, and then turned into Fifth Avenue. The thoroughfare, in this part, was like a walled cañon of brown stone and dark red brick. The big windows looked shiny and clean. Trucks were rumbling in increasing numbers; men and women, girls and boys were moving onward in all directions. She met girls of her own age, who looked at her as if with contempt for her diffidence. She wondered at the magnitude of this life and at the importance of knowing much in order to do anything in it at all. Dread at her own inefficiency crept upon her. She would not know how, she would not be quick enough. Had not all the other places refused her because she did not know something or other? She would be scolded, abused, ignominiously discharged.

It was with weak knees and a slight catch in her breathing that she came up to the great shoe company at Adams and Fifth Avenue and entered the elevator. When she stepped out on the fourth floor there was no one at hand, only great aisles of boxes piled to the ceiling. She stood, very much frightened, awaiting some one.

Presently Mr. Brown came up. He did not seem to recognise her.

"What is it you want?" he inquired.

Carrie's heart sank.

"You said I should come this morning to see about work—"

"Oh," he interrupted. "Um—yes. What is your name?"

"Carrie Meeber."

"Yes," said he. "You come with me."

He led the way through dark, box-lined aisles which had the smell of new shoes, until they came to an iron door which opened into the factory proper. There was a large, low-ceiled room, with clacking, rattling machines at which men in white shirt sleeves and blue gingham aprons were working. She followed him diffidently through the clattering automatons, keeping her eyes straight before her, and flushing slightly. They crossed to a far corner and took an elevator to the sixth floor. Out of the array of machines and benches, Mr. Brown signalled a foreman.

"This is the girl," he said, and turning to Carrie, "You go with him." He then returned, and Carrie followed her new superior to a little desk in a corner, which he used as a kind of official centre.

"You've never worked at anything like this before, have you?" he questioned, rather sternly.

"No, sir," she answered.

He seemed rather annoyed at having to bother with such help, but put down her name and then led her across to where a line of girls occupied stools in front of clacking machines. On the shoulder of one of the girls who was punching eye-holes in one piece of the upper, by the aid of the machine, he put his hand.

"You," he said, "show this girl how to do what you're doing. When you get through, come to me."

The girl so addressed rose promptly and gave Carrie her place.

"It isn't hard to do," she said, bending over. "You just take this so, fasten it with this clamp, and start the machine."

She suited action to word, fastened the piece of leather, which was eventually to form the right half of the upper of a man's shoe, by little adjustable clamps, and pushed a small steel rod at the side of the machine. The latter jumped to the task of punching, with sharp, snapping clicks, cutting circular bits of leather out of the side of the upper, leaving the holes which were to hold the laces. After observing a few times, the girl let her work at it alone. Seeing that it was fairly well done, she went away.

The pieces of leather came from the girl at the machine to her right, and were passed on to the girl at her left. Carrie saw at once that an average speed was necessary or the work would pile up on her and all those below would be delayed. She had no time to look about, and bent anxiously to her task. The girls at her left and right realised her predicament and feelings, and, in a way, tried to aid her, as much as they dared, by working slower.

At this task she laboured incessantly for some time, finding relief from her own nervous fears and imaginings in the humdrum, mechanical movement of the machine. She felt, as the minutes passed, that the room was not very light. It had a thick odour of fresh leather, but that did not worry her. She felt the eyes of the other help upon her, and troubled lest she was not working fast enough.

Once, when she was fumbling at the little clamp, having made a slight error in setting in the leather, a great hand appeared before her eyes and fastened the clamp for her. It was the foreman. Her heart thumped so that she could scarcely see to go on.

"Start your machine," he said, "start your machine. Don't keep the line waiting."

This recovered her sufficiently and she went excitedly on, hardly breathing until the shadow moved away from behind her. Then she heaved a great breath.

As the morning wore on the room became hotter. She felt the need of a breath of fresh air and a drink of water, but did not venture to stir. The stool she sat on was without a back or foot-rest, and she began to feel uncomfortable. She found, after a time, that her back was beginning to ache. She twisted and turned from one position to another slightly different, but it did not ease her for long. She was beginning to weary.

"Stand up, why don't you?" said the girl at her right, without any form of introduction. "They won't care."

Carrie looked at her gratefully. "I guess I will," she said.

She stood up from her stool and worked that way for a while, but it was a more difficult position. Her neck and shoulders ached in bending over.

The spirit of the place impressed itself on her in a rough way. She did not venture to look around, but above the clack of the machine she could hear an occasional remark. She could also note a thing or two out of the side of her eye.

"Did you see Harry last night?" said the girl at her left, addressing her neighbour.

"No."

"You ought to have seen the tie he had on. Gee, but he was a mark."

"S-s-t," said the other girl, bending over her work. The first, silenced, instantly assumed a solemn face. The foreman passed slowly along, eyeing each worker distinctly. The moment he was gone, the conversation was resumed again.

"Say," began the girl at her left, "what jeh think he said?"

"I don't know."

"He said he saw us with Eddie Harris at Martin's last night."

"No!" They both giggled.

A youth with tan-coloured hair, that needed clipping very badly, came shuffling along between the machines, bearing a basket of leather findings under his left arm, and pressed against his stomach.

When near Carrie, he stretched out his right hand and gripped one girl under the arm.

"Aw, let me go," she exclaimed angrily. "Duffer."

He only grinned broadly in return.

"Rubber!" he called back as she looked after him. There was nothing of the gallant in him.

Carrie at last could scarcely sit still. Her legs began to tire and she wanted to get up and stretch. Would noon never come? It seemed as if she had worked an entire day. She was not hungry at all, but weak, and her eyes were tired, straining at the one point where the eye-punch came down. The girl at the right noticed her squirmings and felt sorry for her. She was concentrating herself too thoroughly—what she did really required less mental and physical strain. There was nothing to be done, however. The halves of the uppers came piling steadily down. Her hands began to ache at the wrists and then in the fingers, and towards the last she seemed one mass of dull, complaining muscles, fixed in an eternal position and performing a single mechanical movement which became more and more distasteful, until at last it was absolutely nauseating. When she was wondering whether the strain would ever cease, a dull-sounding bell clanged somewhere down an elevator shaft, and the end came. In an instant there was a buzz of action and conversation. All the girls instantly left their stools and hurried away in an adjoining room, men passed through, coming from some department which opened on the right. The whirling wheels began to sing in a steadily modifying key, until at last they died away in a low buzz. There was an audible stillness, in which the common voice sounded strange.

Carrie got up and sought her lunch box. She was stiff, a little dizzy, and very thirsty. On the way to the small space portioned off by wood, where all the wraps and lunches were kept, she encountered the foreman, who stared at her hard.

"Well," he said, "did you get along all right?"

"I think so," she replied, very respectfully.

"Um," he replied, for want of something better, and walked on.

Under better material conditions, this kind of work would not have been so bad, but the new socialism which involves pleasant working conditions for employees had not then taken hold upon manufacturing companies.[2]

The place smelled of the oil of the machines and the new leather—a combination which, added to the stale odours of the building, was not pleasant even in cold weather. The floor, though regularly swept every evening, presented a littered surface. Not the slightest provi-

2. Dreiser had recently written an article about John H. Patterson, a manufacturer who practiced the "new socialism" of pleasant working conditions for his employees. See Dreiser's "It Pays to Treat Workers Generously," Success 2 (September, 16, 1899): 691–92.

sion had been made for the comfort of the employees, the idea being that something was gained by giving them as little and making the work as hard and unremunerative as possible. What we know of footrests, swivel-back chairs, dining-rooms for the girls, clean aprons and curling irons supplied free, and a decent cloak room, were unthought of. The washrooms were disagreeable, crude, if not foul places, and the whole atmosphere was sordid.

Carrie looked about her, after she had drunk a tinful of water from a bucket in one corner, for a place to sit and eat. The other girls had ranged themselves about the windows or the work-benches of those of the men who had gone out. She saw no place which did not hold a couple or a group of girls, and being too timid to think of intruding herself, she sought out her machine and, seated upon her stool, opened her lunch on her lap. There she sat listening to the chatter and comment about her. It was, for the most part, silly and graced by the current slang. Several of the men in the room exchanged compliments with the girls at long range.

"Say, Kitty," called one to a girl who was doing a waltz step in a few feet of space near one of the windows, "are you going to the ball with me?"

"Look out, Kitty," called another, "you'll jar your back hair."

"Go on, Rubber," was her only comment.

As Carrie listened to this and much more of similar familiar badinage among the men and girls, she instinctively withdrew into herself. She was not used to this type, and felt that there was something hard and low about it all. She feared that the young boys about would address such remarks to her—boys who, beside Drouet, seemed uncouth and ridiculous. She made the average feminine distinction between clothes, putting worth, goodness, and distinction in a dress suit, and leaving all the unlovely qualities and those beneath notice in overalls and jumper.

She was glad when the short half hour was over and the wheels began to whirr again. Though wearied, she would be inconspicuous. This illusion ended when another young man passed along the aisle and poked her indifferently in the ribs with his thumb. She turned about, indignation leaping to her eyes, but he had gone on and only once turned to grin. She found it difficult to conquer an inclination to cry.

The girl next her noticed her state of mind. "Don't you mind," she said. "He's too fresh."

Carrie said nothing, but bent over her work. She felt as though she could hardly endure such a life. Her idea of work had been so entirely different. All during the long afternoon she thought of the city outside and its imposing show, crowds, and fine buildings. Columbia City and the better side of her home life came back. By three o'clock she was sure it must be six, and by four it seemed as if they had forgotten to note the hour and were letting all work overtime. The foreman became a true ogre, prowling constantly about, keeping her tied down to her miserable task. What she heard of the conversation about her only made her feel sure that she did not want to make friends with any of these. When six o'clock came she hurried eagerly away, her arms aching and her limbs stiff from sitting in one position.

As she passed out along the hall after getting her hat, a young machine hand, attracted by her looks, made bold to jest with her.

"Say, Maggie," he called, "if you wait, I'll walk with you."

It was thrown so straight in her direction that she knew who was meant, but never turned to look.

In the crowded elevator, another dusty, toil-stained youth tried to make an impression on her by leering in her face.

One young man, waiting on the walk outside for the appearance of another, grinned at her as she passed.

"Ain't going my way, are you?" he called jocosely.

Carrie turned her face to the west with a subdued heart. As she turned the corner, she saw through the great shiny window the small desk at which she had applied. There were the crowds, hurrying with the same buzz and energy-yielding enthusiasm. She felt a slight relief, but it was only at her escape. She felt ashamed in the face of better dressed girls who went by. She felt as though she should be better served, and her heart revolted.

Chapter V

A GLITTERING NIGHT FLOWER: THE USE OF A NAME

Drouet did not call that evening. After receiving the letter, he had laid aside all thought of Carrie for the time being and was floating around having what he considered a gay time. On this particular evening he dined at "Rector's," a restaurant of some local fame, which occupied a basement at Clark and Monroe Streets. Thereafter he visited the resort of Fitzgerald and Moy's in Adams Street, opposite the imposing Federal Building.[1] There he leaned over the splendid bar and swallowed a glass of plain whiskey and purchased a couple of cigars, one of which he lighted. This to him represented in part high life—a fair sample of what the whole must be.

Drouet was not a drinker in excess. He was not a moneyed man. He only craved the best, as his mind conceived it, and such doings seemed to him a part of the best. Rector's, with its polished marble

1. Dreiser places Fitzgerald and Moy's in the heart of downtown Chicago, on Adams between State and Clark.

walls and floor, its profusion of lights, its show of china and silver-ware, and, above all, its reputation as a resort for actors and profes-sional men, seemed to him the proper place for a successful man to go. He loved fine clothes, good eating, and particularly the company and acquaintanceship of successful men. When dining, it was a source of keen satisfaction to him to know that Joseph Jefferson was wont to come to this same place, or that Henry E. Dixie, a well-known performer of the day, was then only a few tables off.[2] At Rector's he could always obtain this satisfaction, for there one could encounter politicians, brokers, actors, some rich young "rounders" of the town, all eating and drinking amid a buzz of popular com-monplace conversation.

"That's So-and-so over there," was a common remark of these gen-tlemen among themselves, particularly among those who had not yet reached, but hoped to do so, the dazzling height which money to dine here lavishly represented.

"You don't say so," would be the reply.

"Why, yes, didn't you know that? Why, he's manager of the Grand Opera House."

When these things would fall upon Drouet's ears, he would straighten himself a little more stiffly and eat with solid comfort. If he had any vanity, this augmented it, and if he had any ambition, this stirred it. He would be able to flash a roll of greenbacks too some day. As it was, he could eat where *they* did.

His preference for Fitzgerald and Moy's Adams Street place was another yard off the same cloth. This was really a gorgeous saloon from a Chicago standpoint. Like Rector's, it was also ornamented with a blaze of incandescent lights, held in handsome chandeliers. The floors were of brightly coloured tiles, the walls a composition of rich, dark, polished wood, which reflected the light, and coloured stucco-work, which gave the place a very sumptuous appearance. The long bar was a blaze of lights, polished wood-work, coloured and cut glassware, and many fancy bottles. It was a truly swell saloon, with rich screens, fancy wines, and a line of bar goods unsurpassed in the country.

At Rector's, Drouet had met Mr. G. W. Hurstwood, manager of Fitzgerald and Moy's. He had been pointed out as a very successful and well-known man about town. Hurstwood looked the part, for, besides being slightly under forty, he had a good, stout constitution, an active manner, and a solid, substantial air, which was composed in part of his fine clothes, his clean linen, his jewels, and, above all, his own sense of his importance. Drouet immediately conceived a

2. Joseph Jefferson was famous for his portrayal of Rip Van Winkle (see p. 81). Henry E. Dixey is the correct spelling.

notion of him as being some one worth knowing, and was glad not only to meet him, but to visit the Adams Street bar thereafter whenever he wanted a drink or a cigar.

Hurstwood was an interesting character after his kind. He was shrewd and clever in many little things, and capable of creating a good impression. His managerial position was fairly important—a kind of stewardship which was imposing, but lacked financial control. He had risen by perseverance and industry, through long years of service, from the position of barkeeper in a commonplace saloon to his present altitude. He had a little office in the place, set off in polished cherry and grill-work, where he kept, in a roll-top desk, the rather simple accounts of the place—supplies ordered and needed. The chief executive and financial functions devolved upon the owners—Messrs. Fitzgerald and Moy—and upon a cashier who looked after the money taken in.

For the most part he lounged about, dressed in excellent tailored suits of imported goods, a solitaire ring, a fine blue diamond in his tie, a striking vest of some new pattern, and a watch-chain of solid gold, which held a charm of rich design, and a watch of the latest make and engraving. He knew by name, and could greet personally with a "Well, old fellow," hundreds of actors, merchants, politicians, and the general run of successful characters about town, and it was part of his success to do so. He had a finely graduated scale of informality and friendship, which improved from the "How do you do?" addressed to the fifteen-dollar-a-week clerks and office attachés, who, by long frequenting of the place, became aware of his position, to the "Why, old man, how are you?" which he addressed to those noted or rich individuals who knew him and were inclined to be friendly. There was a class, however, too rich, too famous, or too successful, with whom he could not attempt any familiarity of address, and with these he was professionally tactful, assuming a grave and dignified attitude, paying them the deference which would win their good feeling without in the least compromising his own bearing and opinions. There were, in the last place, a few good followers, neither rich nor poor, famous, nor yet remarkably successful, with whom he was friendly on the score of good-fellowship. These were the kind of men with whom he would converse longest and most seriously. He loved to go out and have a good time once in a while—to go to the races, the theatres, the sporting entertainments at some of the clubs. He kept a horse and neat trap, had his wife and two children, who were well established in a neat house on the North Side near Lincoln Park, and was altogether a very acceptable individual of our great American upper class—the first grade below the luxuriously rich.

Hurstwood liked Drouet. The latter's genial nature and dressy appearance pleased him. He knew that Drouet was only a travelling salesman—and not one of many years at that—but the firm of Bartlett, Caryoe & Company was a large and properous house, and Drouet stood well. Hurstwood knew Caryoe quite well, having drunk a glass now and then with him, in company with several others, when the conversation was general. Drouet had what was a help in his business, a moderate sense of humour, and could tell a good story when the occasion required. He could talk races with Hurstwood, tell interesting incidents concerning himself and his experiences with women, and report the state of trade in the cities which he visited, and so managed to make himself almost invariably agreeable. To-night he was particularly so, since his report to the company had been favourably commented upon, his new samples had been satisfactorily selected, and his trip marked out for the next six weeks.

"Why, hello, Charlie, old man," said Hurstwood, as Drouet came in that evening about eight o'clock. "How goes it?" The room was crowded.

Drouet shook hands, beaming good nature, and they strolled towards the bar.

"Oh, all right."

"I haven't seen you in six weeks. When did you get in?"

"Friday," said Drouet. "Had a fine trip."

"Glad of it," said Hurstwood, his black eyes lit with a warmth which half displaced the cold make-believe that usually dwelt in them. "What are you going to take?" he added, as the barkeeper, in snowy jacket and tie, leaned toward them from behind the bar.

"Old Pepper," said Drouet.

"A little of the same for me," put in Hurstwood.

"How long are you in town this time?" inquired Hurstwood.

"Only until Wednesday. I'm going up to St. Paul."

"George Evans was in here Saturday and said he saw you in Milwaukee last week."

"Yes, I saw George," returned Drouet. "Great old boy, isn't he? We had quite a time there together."

The barkeeper was setting out the glasses and bottle before them, and they now poured out the draught as they talked, Drouet filling his to within a third of full, as was considered proper, and Hurstwood taking the barest suggestion of whiskey and modifying it with seltzer.

"What's become of Caryoe?" remarked Hurstwood. "I haven't seen him around here in two weeks."

"Laid up, they say," exclaimed Drouet. "Say, he's a gouty old boy!"

"Made a lot of money in his time, though, hasn't he?"

"Yes, wads of it," returned Drouet. "He won't live much longer. Barely comes down to the office now."

"Just one boy, hasn't he?" asked Hurstwood.

"Yes, and a swift-pacer," laughed Drouet.

"I guess he can't hurt the business very much, though, with the other members all there."

"No, he can't injure that any, I guess."

Hurstwood was standing, his coat open, his thumbs in his pockets, the light on his jewels and rings relieving them with agreeable distinctness. He was the picture of fastidious comfort.

To one not inclined to drink, and gifted with a more serious turn of mind, such a bubbling, chattering, glittering chamber must ever seem an anomaly, a strange commentary on nature and life. Here come the moths, in endless procession, to bask in the light of the flame. Such conversation as one may hear would not warrant a commendation of the scene upon intellectual grounds. It seems plain that schemers would choose more sequestered quarters to arrange their plans, that politicians would not gather here in company to discuss anything save formalities, where the sharp-eared may hear, and it would scarcely be justified on the score of thirst, for the majority of those who frequent these more gorgeous places have no craving for liquor. Nevertheless, the fact that here men gather, here chatter, here love to pass and rub elbows, must be explained upon some grounds. It must be that a strange bundle of passions and vague desires give rise to such a curious social institution or it would not be.

Drouet, for one, was lured as much by his longing for pleasure as by his desire to shine among his betters. The many friends he met here dropped in because they craved, without, perhaps, consciously analysing it, the company, the glow, the atmosphere which they found. One might take it, after all, as an augur of the better social order, for the things which they satisfied here, though sensory, were not evil. No evil could come out of the contemplation of an expensively decorated chamber. The worst effect of such a thing would be, perhaps, to stir up in the material-minded an ambition to arrange their lives upon a similarly splendid basis. In the last analysis, that would scarcely be called the fault of the decorations, but rather of the innate trend of the mind. That such a scene might stir the less expensively dressed to emulate the more expensively dressed could scarcely be laid at the door of anything save the false ambition of the minds of those so affected. Remove the element so thoroughly and solely complained of—liquor—and there would not be one to gainsay the qualities of beauty and enthusiasm which would remain. The pleased eye with which our modern restaurants of fashion are looked upon is proof of this assertion.

Yet, here is the fact of the lighted chamber, the dressy, greedy company, the small, self-interested palaver, the disorganized, aimless, wandering mental action which it represents—the love of light and show and finery which, to one outside, under the serene light of the eternal stars, must seem a strange and shiny thing. Under the stars and sweeping night winds, what a lamp-flower it must bloom; a strange, glittering night-flower, odour-yielding, insect-drawing, insect-infested rose of pleasure.

"See that fellow coming in there?" said Hurstwood, glancing at a gentleman just entering, arrayed in a high hat and Prince Albert coat, his fat cheeks puffed and red as with good eating.

"No, where?" said Drouet.

"There," said Hurstwood, indicating the direction by a cast of his eye, "the man with the silk hat."

"Oh, yes," said Drouet, now affecting not to see. "Who is he?"

"That's Jules Wallace, the spiritualist."[3]

Drouet followed him with his eyes, much interested.

"Doesn't look much like a man who sees spirits, does he?" said Drouet.

"Oh, I don't know," returned Hurstwood. "He's got the money, all right," and a little twinkle passed over his eyes.

"I don't go much on those things, do you?" asked Drouet.

"Well, you never can tell," said Hurstwood. "There may be something to it. I wouldn't bother about it myself, though. By the way," he added, "are you going anywhere to-night?"

" 'The Hole in the Ground,' " said Drouet, mentioning the popular farce of the time.[4]

"Well, you'd better be going. It's half after eight already," and he drew out his watch.

The crowd was already thinning out considerably—some bound for the theatres, some to their clubs, and some to that most fascinating of all the pleasures—for the type of man there represented, at least—the ladies.

"Yes, I will," said Drouet.

"Come around after the show. I have something I want to show you," said Hurstwood.

"Sure," said Drouet, elated.

"You haven't anything on hand for the night, have you?" added Hurstwood.

"Not a thing."

"Well, come round, then."

"I struck a little peach coming in on the train Friday," remarked Drouet, by way of parting. "By George, that's so, I must go and call on her before I go away."

---

3. While a reporter for the *St. Louis Republic* in 1893, Dreiser had written a series of articles about Jules Wallace, who was "performing" in St. Louis at the time. See, for example, his "Jules Wallace, Fake, Fraud, Medium, Healer," *St. Louis Republic* 9 Sept. 1893:1–2.
4. *A Hole in the Ground* (1887) was one of seventeen farces by Charles H. Hoyt.

"Oh, never mind her," Hurstwood remarked.

"Say, she was a little dandy, I tell you," went on Drouet confiden-tially, and trying to impress his friend.

"Twelve o'clock," said Hurstwood.

"That's right," said Drouet, going out.

Thus was Carrie's name bandied about in the most frivolous and gay of places, and that also when the little toiler was bemoaning her narrow lot, which was almost inseparable from the early stages of this, her unfolding fate.

Chapter VI

THE MACHINE AND THE MAIDEN: A KNIGHT OF TO-DAY

At the flat that evening Carrie felt a new phase of its atmosphere. The fact that it was unchanged, while her feelings were different, increased her knowledge of its character. Minnie, after the good spir-its Carrie manifested at first, expected a fair report. Hanson sup-posed that Carrie would be satisfied.

"Well," he said, as he came in from the hall in his working clothes, and looked at Carrie through the dining-room door, "how did you make out?"

"Oh," said Carrie, "it's pretty hard. I don't like it."

There was an air about her which showed plainer than any words that she was both weary and disappointed.

"What sort of work is it?" he asked, lingering a moment as he turned upon his heel to go into the bathroom.

"Running a machine," answered Carrie.

It was very evident that it did not concern him much, save from the side of the flat's success. He was irritated a shade because it could not have come about in the throw of fortune for Carrie to be pleased.

Minnie worked with less elation than she had just before Carrie arrived. The sizzle of the meat frying did not sound quite so pleasing now that Carrie had reported her discontent. To Carrie, the one relief of the whole day would have been a jolly home, a sympathetic reception, a bright supper table, and some one to say: "Oh, well, stand it a little while. You will get something better," but now this was ashes. She began to see that they looked upon her complaint as unwarranted, and that she was supposed to work on and say nothing. She knew that she was to pay four dollars for her board and room, and now she felt that it would be an exceedingly gloomy round, living with these people.

Minnie was no companion for her sister—she was too old. Her thoughts were staid and solemnly adapted to a condition. If Hanson had any pleasant thoughts or happy feelings he concealed them. He seemed to do all his mental operations without the aid of physical expression. He was as still as a deserted chamber. Carrie, on the other hand, had the blood of youth and some imagination. Her day of love and the mysteries of courtship were still ahead. She could think of things she would like to do, of clothes she would like to wear, and of places she would like to visit. These were the things upon which her mind ran, and it was like meeting with opposition at every turn to find no one here to call forth or respond to her feelings.

She had forgotten, in considering and explaining the result of her day, that Drouet might come. Now, when she saw how unreceptive these two people were, she hoped he would not. She did not know exactly what she would do or how she would explain to Drouet, if he came. After supper she changed her clothes. When she was trimly dressed she was rather a sweet little being, with large eyes and a sad mouth. Her face expressed the mingled expectancy, dissatisfaction and depression she felt. She wandered about after the dishes were put away, talked a little with Minnie, and then decided to go down and stand in the door at the foot of the stairs. If Drouet came, she could meet him there. Her face took on the semblance of a look of happiness as she put on her hat to go below.

"Carrie doesn't seem to like her place very well," said Minnie to her husband when the latter came out, paper in hand, to sit in the dining-room a few minutes.

"She ought to keep it for a time, anyhow," said Hanson. "Has she gone downstairs?"

"Yes," said Minnie.

"I'd tell her to keep it if I were you. She might be here weeks without getting another one."

Minnie said she would, and Hanson read his paper.

"If I were you," he said a little later, "I wouldn't let her stand in the door down there. It don't look good."

"I'll tell her," said Minnie.

The life of the streets continued for a long time to interest Carrie. She never wearied of wondering where the people in the cars were going or what their enjoyments were. Her imagination trod a very narrow round, always winding up at points which concerned money, looks, clothes, or enjoyment. She would have a far-off thought of Columbia City now and then, or an irritating rush of feeling concerning her experiences of the present day, but, on the whole, the little world about her enlisted her whole attention.

The first floor of the building, of which Hanson's flat was the third, was occupied by a bakery, and to this, while she was standing there, Hanson came down to buy a loaf of bread. She was not aware of his presence until he was quite near her.

"I'm after bread," was all he said as he passed.

The contagion of thought here demonstrated itself. While Hanson really came for bread, the thought dwelt with him that now he would see what Carrie was doing. No sooner did he draw near her with that in mind than she felt it. Of course, she had no understanding of what put it into her head, but, nevertheless, it aroused in her the first shade of real antipathy to him. She knew now that she did not like him. He was suspicious.

A thought will colour a world for us. The flow of Carrie's meditations had been disturbed, and Hanson had not long gone upstairs before she followed. She had realised with the lapse of the quarter hours that Drouet was not coming, and somehow she felt a little resentful, a little as if she had been forsaken—was not good enough. She went upstairs, where everything was silent. Minnie was sewing by a lamp at the table. Hanson had already turned in for the night. In her weariness and disappointment Carrie did no more than announce that she was going to bed.

"Yes you'd better," returned Minnie. "You've got to get up early, you know."

The morning was no better. Hanson was just going out the door as Carrie came from her room. Minnie tried to talk with her during breakfast, but there was not much of interest which they could mutually discuss. As on the previous morning, Carrie walked down town, for she began to realise now that her four-fifty would not even allow her car fare after she paid her board. This seemed a miserable arrangement. But the morning light swept away the first misgivings of the day, as morning light is ever wont to do.

At the shoe factory she put in a long day, scarcely so wearisome as the preceding, but considerably less novel. The head foreman, on his round, stopped by her machine.

"Where did you come from?" he inquired.

"Mr. Brown hired me," she replied.

"Oh, he did, eh!" and then, "See that you keep things going."

The machine girls impressed her even less favourably. They seemed satisfied with their lot, and were in a sense "common." Carrie had more imagination than they. She was not used to slang. Her instinct in the matter of dress was naturally better. She disliked to listen to the girl next to her, who was rather hardened by experience.

"I'm going to quit this," she heard her remark to her neighbour. "What with the stipend and being up late, it's too much for me health."

They were free with the fellows, young and old, about the place, and exchanged banter in rude phrases, which at first shocked her. She saw that she was taken to be of the same sort and addressed accordingly.

"Hello," remarked one of the stout-wristed sole-workers to her at noon. "You're a daisy." He really expected to hear the common "Aw! go chase yourself!" in return, and was sufficiently abashed, by Carrie's silently moving away, to retreat, awkwardly grinning.

That night at the flat she was even more lonely—the dull situation was becoming harder to endure. She could see that the Hansons seldom or never had any company. Standing at the street door looking out, she ventured to walk out a little way. Her easy gait and idle manner attracted attention of an offensive but common sort. She was slightly taken back at the overtures of a well-dressed man of thirty, who in passing looked at her, reduced his pace, turned back, and said:

"Out for a little stroll, are you, this evening?"

Carrie looked at him in amazement, and then summoned sufficient thought to reply: "Why, I don't know you," backing away as she did so.

"Oh, that don't matter," said the other affably.

She bandied no more words with him, but hurried away, reaching her own door quite out of breath. There was something in the man's look which frightened her.

During the remainder of the week it was very much the same. One or two nights she found herself too tired to walk home and expended car fare. She was not very strong, and sitting all day affected her back. She went to bed one night before Hanson.

Transplantation is not always successful in the matter of flowers or maidens. It requires sometimes a richer soil, a better atmosphere to continue even a natural growth. It would have been better if her acclimatization had been more gradual—less rigid. She would have done better if she had not secured a position so quickly, and had seen more of the city which she constantly troubled to know about.

On the first morning it rained she found that she had no umbrella. Minnie loaned her one of hers, which was worn and faded. There was the kind of vanity in Carrie that troubled at this. She went to one of the great department stores and bought herself one, using a dollar and a quarter of her small store to pay for it.

"What did you do that for, Carrie?" asked Minnie when she saw it.

"Oh, I need one," said Carrie.

"You foolish girl."

Carrie resented this, though she did not reply. She was not going to be a common shop-girl, she thought; they need not think it, either.

On the first Saturday night Carrie paid her board, four dollars. Minnie had a quaver of conscience as she took it, but did not know how to explain to Hanson if she took less. That worthy gave up just four dollars less toward the household expenses with a smile of satisfaction. He contemplated increasing his Building and Loan payments. As for Carrie, she studied over the problem of finding clothes and amusement on fifty cents a week. She brooded over this until she was in a state of mental rebellion.

"I'm going up the street for a walk," she said after supper.

"Not alone are you?" asked Hanson.

"Yes," returned Carrie.

"I wouldn't," said Minnie.

"I want to see *something*," said Carrie, and by the tone she put into the last word they realised for the first time she was not pleased with them.

"What's the matter with her?" asked Hanson, when she went into the front room to get her hat.

"I don't know," said Minnie.

"Well, she ought to know better than to want to go out alone."

Carrie did not go very far, after all. She returned and stood in the door. The next day they went out to Garfield Park, but it did not please her. She did not look well enough. In the shop next day she heard the highly coloured reports which girls give of their trivial amusements. They had been happy. On several days it rained and she used up car fare. One night she got thoroughly soaked, going to catch the car at Van Buren Street. All that evening she sat alone in the front room looking out upon the street, where the lights were reflected on the wet pavements, thinking. She had imagination enough to be moody.

On Saturday she paid another four dollars and pocketed her fifty cents in despair. The speaking acquaintanceship which she formed with some of the girls at the shop discovered to her the fact that they had more of their earnings to use for themselves than she did. They had young men of the kind whom she, since her experience with Drouet, felt above, who took them about. She came to thoroughly dislike the light-headed young fellows of the shop. Not one of them had a show of refinement. She saw only their workday side.

There came a day when the first premonitory blast of winter swept over the city. It scudded the fleecy clouds in the heavens, trailed long, thin streamers of smoke from the tall stacks, and raced about the streets and corners in sharp and sudden puffs. Carrie now felt the problem of winter clothes. What was she to do? She had no winter jacket, no hat, no shoes. It was difficult to speak to Minnie about this, but at last she summoned the courage.

"I don't know what I'm going to do about clothes," she said one evening when they were together. "I need a hat."

Minnie looked serious.

"Why don't you keep part of your money and buy yourself one?" she suggested, worried over the situation which the withholding of Carrie's money would create.

"I'd like to for a week or so, if you don't mind," ventured Carrie.

"Could you pay two dollars?" asked Minnie.

Carrie readily acquiesced, glad to escape the trying situation, and liberal now that she saw a way out. She was elated and began figuring at once. She needed a hat first of all. How Minnie explained to Hanson she never knew. He said nothing at all, but there were thoughts in the air which left disagreeable impressions.

The new arrangement might have worked if sickness had not intervened. It blew up cold after a rain one afternoon when Carrie was still without a jacket. She came out of the warm shop at six and shivered as the wind struck her. In the morning she was sneezing, and going down town made it worse. That day her bones ached and she felt light-headed. Towards evening she felt very ill, and when she reached home was not hungry. Minnie noticed her drooping actions and asked her about herself.

"I don't know," said Carrie. "I feel real bad."

She hung about the stove, suffered a chattering chill, and went to bed sick. The next morning she was thoroughly feverish.

Minnie was truly distressed at this, but maintained a kindly demeanour. Hanson said perhaps she had better go back home for a while. When she got up after three days, it was taken for granted that her position was lost. The winter was near at hand, she had no clothes and now she was out of work.

"I don't know," said Carrie; "I'll go down Monday and see if I can't get something."

If anything, her efforts were more poorly rewarded on this trial than the last. Her clothes were nothing suitable for fall wearing. Her last money she had spent for a hat. For three days she wandered about, utterly dispirited. The attitude of the flat was fast becoming unbearable. She hated to think of going back there each evening. Hanson was so cold. She knew it could not last much longer. Shortly she would have to give up and go home.

On the fourth day she was down town all day, having borrowed ten cents for lunch from Minnie. She had applied in the cheapest kind of places without success. She even answered for a waitress in a small restaurant where she saw a card in the window, but they wanted an experienced girl. She moved through the thick throng of strangers, utterly subdued in spirit. Suddenly a hand pulled her arm and turned her about.

"Well, well!" said a voice. In the first glance she beheld Drouet. He was not only rosy-cheeked, but radiant. He was the essence of sunshine and good-humour. "Why, how are you, Carrie?" he said. "You're a daisy. Where have you been?"

Carrie smiled under his irresistible flood of geniality.

"I've been out home," she said.

"Well," he said, "I saw you across the street there. I thought it was you. I was just coming out to your place. How are you, anyhow?"

"I'm all right," said Carrie, smiling.

Drouet looked her over and saw something different.

"Well," he said, "I want to talk to you. You're not going anywhere in particular, are you?"

"Not just now," said Carrie.

"Let's go up here and have something to eat. George! but I'm glad to see you again."

She felt so relieved in his radiant presence, so much looked after and cared for, that she assented gladly, though with the slightest air of holding back.

"Well," he said as he took her arm—and there was an exuberance of good-fellowship in the word which fairly warmed the cockles of her heart.

They went through Monroe Street to the old Windsor dining-room, which was then a large, comfortable place, with an excellent cuisine and substantial service.[1] Drouet selected a table close by the window, where the busy rout of the street could be seen. He loved the changing panorama of the street—to see and be seen as he dined.

"Now," he said, getting Carrie and himself comfortably settled, "what will you have?"

Carrie looked over the large bill of fare which the waiter handed her without really considering it. She was very hungry, and the things she saw there awakened her desires, but the high prices held her attention. "Half broiled spring chicken—seventy-five. Sirloin steak with mushrooms—one twenty-five." She had dimly heard of these things, but it seemed strange to be called to order from the list.

"I'll fix this," exclaimed Drouet. "Sst! waiter."

That officer of the board, a full-chested, round-faced negro, approached, and inclined his ear.

"Sirloin with mushrooms," said Drouet. "Stuffed tomatoes."

"Yassah," assented the negro, nodding his head.

"Hashed brown potatoes."

"Yassah."

"Asparagus."

"Yassah."

"And a pot of coffee."

Drouet turned to Carrie. "I haven't had a thing since breakfast. Just got in from Rock Island. I was going off to dine when I saw you."

Carrie smiled and smiled.

"What have you been doing?" he went on. "Tell me all about yourself. How is your sister?"

1. In the Windsor House Hotel, at Washington and Dearborn.

"She's well," returned Carrie, answering the last query.

He looked at her hard.

"Say," he said, "you haven't been sick, have you?"

Carrie nodded.

"Well, now, that's a blooming shame, isn't it? You don't look very well. I thought you looked a little pale. What have you been doing?"

"Working," said Carrie.

"You don't say so! At what?"

She told him.

"Rhodes, Morgenthau and Scott[2]—why, I know that house. Over here on Fifth Avenue, isn't it? They're a close-fisted concern. What made you go there?"

"I couldn't get anything else," said Carrie frankly.

"Well, that's an outrage," said Drouet. "You oughtn't to be working for those people. Have the factory right back of the store, don't they?"

"Yes," said Carrie.

"That isn't a good house," said Drouet. "You don't want to work at anything like that, anyhow."

He chattered on at a great rate, asking questions, explaining things about himself, telling her what a good restaurant it was, until the waiter returned with an immense tray, bearing the hot savoury dishes which had been ordered. Drouet fairly shone in the matter of serving. He appeared to great advantage behind the white napery and silver platters of the table and displaying his arms with a knife and fork. As he cut the meat his rings almost spoke. His new suit creaked as he stretched to reach the plates, break the bread, and pour the coffee. He helped Carrie to a rousing plateful and contributed the warmth of his spirit to her body until she was a new girl. He was a splendid fellow in the true popular understanding of the term, and captivated Carrie completely.

That little soldier of fortune took her good turn in an easy way. She felt a little out of place, but the great room soothed her and the view of the well-dressed throng outside seemed a splendid thing. Ah, what was it not to have money! What a thing it was to be able to come in here and dine! Drouet must be fortunate. He rode on trains, dressed in such nice clothes, was so strong, and ate in these fine places. He seemed quite a figure of a man, and she wondered at his friendship and regard for her.

"So you lost your place because you got sick, eh?" he said. "What are you going to do now?"

"Look around," she said, a thought of the need that hung outside this fine restaurant like a hungry dog at her heels passing into her eyes.

2. A fictitious name.

"Oh, no," said Drouet, "that won't do. How long have you been looking?"

"Four days," she answered.

"Think of that!" he said, addressing some problematical individual. "You oughtn't to be doing anything like that. These girls," and he waved an inclusion of all shop and factory girls, "don't get anything. Why, you can't live on it, can you?"

He was a brotherly sort of creature in his demeanour. When he had scouted the idea of that kind of toil, he took another tack. Carrie was really very pretty. Even then, in her commonplace garb, her figure was evidently not bad, and her eyes were large and gentle. Drouet looked at her and his thoughts reached home. She felt his admiration. It was powerfully backed by his liberality and good-humour. She felt that she liked him—that she could continue to like him ever so much. There was something even richer than that, running as a hidden strain, in her mind. Every little while her eyes would meet his, and by that means the interchanging current of feeling would be fully connected.

"Why don't you stay down town and go to the theatre with me?" he said, hitching his chair closer. The table was not very wide.

"Oh, I can't," she said.

"What are you going to do to-night?"

"Nothing" she answered, a little drearily.

"You don't like out there where you are, do you?"

"Oh, I don't know."

"What are you going to do if you don't get work?"

"Go back home, I guess."

There was the least quaver in her voice as she said this. Somehow, the influence he was exerting was powerful. They came to an understanding of each other without words—he of her situation, she of the fact that he realised it.

"No," he said, "you can't make it!" genuine sympathy filling his mind for the time. "Let me help you. You take some of my money."

"Oh, no!" she said, leaning back.

"What are you going to do?" he said.

She sat meditating, merely shaking her head.

He looked at her quite tenderly for his kind. There were some loose bills in his vest pocket—greenbacks. They were soft and noiseless, and he got his fingers about them and crumpled them up in his hand.

"Come on" he said, "I'll see you through all right. Get yourself some clothes."

It was the first reference he had made to that subject, and now she realised how bad off she was. In his crude way he had struck the key-note. Her lips trembled a little.

She had her hand out on the table before her. They were quite alone in their corner, and he put his larger, warmer hand over it.

"Aw, come, Carrie," he said, "what can you do alone? Let me help you."

He pressed her hand gently and she tried to withdraw it. At this he held it fast, and she no longer protested. Then he slipped the greenbacks he had into her palm, and when she began to protest, he whispered.

"I'll loan it to you—that's all right. I'll loan it to you."

He made her take it. She felt bound to him by a strange tie of affection now. They went out, and he walked with her far out south toward Polk Street, talking.

"You don't want to live with those people?" he said in one place, abstractedly. Carrie heard it, but it made only a slight impression.

"Come down and meet me to-morrow," he said, "and we'll go to the matineé. Will you?"

Carrie protested a while, but acquiesced.

"You're not doing anything. Get yourself a nice pair of shoes and a jacket."

She scarcely gave a thought to the complication which would trouble her when he was gone. In his presence, she was of his own hopeful, easy-way-out mood.

"Don't you bother about those people out there," he said at parting. "I'll help you."

Carrie left him, feeling as though a great arm had slipped out before her to draw off trouble. The money she had accepted was two soft, green, handsome ten-dollar bills.

Chapter VII

THE LURE OF THE MATERIAL: BEAUTY SPEAKS FOR ITSELF

The true meaning of money yet remains to be popularly explained and comprehended. When each individual realises for himself that this thing primarily stands for and should only be accepted as a moral due—that it should be paid out as honestly stored energy, and not as a usurped privilege—many of our social, religious, and political troubles will have permanently passed. As for Carrie, her understanding of the moral significance of money was the popular understanding, nothing more. The old definition: "Money: something everybody else has and I must get," would have expressed her understanding of it thoroughly. Some of it she now held in her hand—two soft, green ten-dollar bills—and she felt that she was immensely better off for the having of them. It was something that was power in itself. One of her order of mind would have been content to be cast away upon a desert island with a bundle of money, and only the long strain of starvation would have taught her that in some cases it could have no value. Even then she would have had no conception of the relative value of the thing; her one thought would, undoubtedly, have concerned the pity of having so much power and the inability to use it.

The poor girl thrilled as she walked away from Drouet. She felt ashamed in part because she had been weak enough to take it, but her need was so dire, she was still glad. Now she would have a nice new jacket! Now she would buy a nice pair of pretty button shoes. She would get stockings, too, and a skirt, and, and—until already, as in the matter of her prospective salary, she had got beyond, in her desires, twice the purchasing power of her bills.

She conceived a true estimate of Drouet. To her, and indeed to all the world, he was a nice, good-hearted man. There was nothing evil in the fellow. He gave her the money out of a good heart—out of a realisation of her want. He would not have given the same amount to a poor young man, but we must not forget that a poor young man could not, in the nature of things, have appealed to him like a poor young girl. Femininity affected his feelings. He was the creature of an inborn desire. Yet no beggar could have caught his eye and said, "My God, mister, I'm starving," but he would gladly have handed out what was considered the proper portion to give beggars and thought no more about it. There would have been no speculation, no philosophising. He had no mental process in him worthy the dignity of either of those terms. In his good clothes and fine health, he was a merry, unthinking moth of the lamp. Deprived of his position, and struck by a few of the involved and baffling forces which sometimes play upon man he would have been as helpless as Carrie—as helpless, as non-understanding, as pitiable, if you will, as she.

Now, in regard to his pursuit of women, he meant them no harm, because he did not conceive of the relation which he hoped to hold with them as being harmful. He loved to make advances to women, to have them succumb to his charms, not because he was a cold-blooded, dark, scheming villain, but because his inborn desire urged him to that as a chief delight. He was vain, he was boastful, he was as deluded by fine clothes as any silly-headed girl. A truly deep-dyed villain could have hornswaggled him as readily as he could have flattered a pretty shop-girl. His fine success as a salesman lay in his geniality and the thoroughly reputable standing of his house. He bobbed about among men, a veritable bundle of enthusiasm—no power worthy the name of intellect, no thoughts worthy the adjective noble, no feelings long continued in one strain. A Madame Sappho would have called him a pig; a Shakespeare would have said "my merry child;" old, drinking Caryoe thought him a clever, successful business man. In short, he was as good as his intellect conceived.

The best proof that there was something open and commendable about the man was the fact that Carrie took the money. No deep, sinister soul with ulterior motives could have given her fifteen cents under the guise of friendship. The unintellectual are not so helpless. Nature has taught the beasts of the field to fly when some unheralded danger threatens. She has put into the small, unwise head of the chipmunk the untutored fear of poisons. "He keepeth His creatures whole," was not written of beasts alone. Carrie was unwise, and, therefore, like the sheep in its unwisdom, strong in feeling. The instinct of self-protection, strong in all such natures, was roused but feebly, if at all, by the overtures of Drouet.

When Carrie had gone, he felicitated himself upon her good opinion. By George, it was a shame young girls had to be knocked around like that. Cold weather coming on and no clothes. Tough. He would go around to Fitzgerald and Moy's and get a cigar. It made him feel light of foot as he thought about her.

Carrie reached home in high good spirits, which she could scarcely conceal. The possession of the money involved a number of points which perplexed her seriously. How should she buy any clothes when Minnie knew that she had no money? She had no sooner entered the flat than this point was settled for her. It could not be done. She could think of no way of explaining.

"How did you come out?" asked Minnie, referring to the day.

Carrie had none of the small deception which could feel one thing and say something directly opposed. She would prevaricate, but it would be in the line of her feelings at least. So instead of complaining when she felt so good, she said:

"I have the promise of something."

"Where?"

"At the Boston Store."

"Is it sure promised?" questioned Minnie.

"Well, I'm to find out to-morrow," returned Carrie, disliking to draw out a lie any longer than was necessary.

Minnie felt the atmosphere of good feeling which Carrie brought with her. She felt now was the time to express to Carrie the state of Hanson's feeling about her entire Chicago venture.

"If you shouldn't get it—" she paused, troubled for an easy way.

"If I don't get something pretty soon, I think I'll go home."

Minnie saw her chance.

"Sven thinks it might be best for the winter, anyhow."

The situation flashed on Carrie at once. They were unwilling to keep her any longer, out of work. She did not blame Minnie, she did not blame Hanson very much. Now, as she sat there digesting the remark, she was glad she had Drouet's money.

"Yes," she said after a few moments, "I thought of doing that."

She did not explain that the thought, however, had aroused all the antagonism of her nature. Columbia City, what was there for her? She knew its dull, little round by heart. Here was the great, mysterious city which was still a magnet for her. What she had seen only suggested its possibilities. Now to turn back on it and live the little old life out there—she almost exclaimed against the thought.

She had reached home early and went in the front room to think. What could she do? She could not buy new shoes and wear them here. She would need to save part of the twenty to pay her fare home. She did not want to borrow of Minnie for that. And yet, how could she explain where she even got that money? If she could only get enough to let her out easy.

She went over the tangle again and again. Here, in the morning, Drouet would expect to see her in a new jacket, and that couldn't be. The Hansons expected her to go home, and she wanted to get away, and yet she did not want to go home. In the light of the way they would look on her getting money without work, the taking of it now seemed dreadful. She began to be ashamed. The whole situation depressed her. It was all so clear when she was with Drouet. Now it was all so tangled, so hopeless—much worse than it was before, because she had the semblance of aid in her hand which she could not use.

Her spirits sank so that at supper Minnie felt that she must have had another hard day. Carrie finally decided that she would give the money back. It was wrong to take it. She would go down in the morning and hunt for work. At noon she would meet Drouet as agreed and tell him. At this decision her heart sank, until she was the old Carrie of distress.

Curiously, she could not hold the money in her hand without feeling some relief. Even after all her depressing conclusions, she could sweep away all thought about the matter and then the twenty dollars seemed a wonderful and delightful thing. Ah, money, money, money! What a thing it was to have. How plenty of it would clear away all these troubles.

In the morning she got up and started out a little early. Her decision to hunt for work was moderately strong, but the money in her pocket, after all her troubling over it, made the work question the least shade less terrible. She walked into the wholesale district, but as the thought of applying came with each passing concern, her heart shrank. What a coward she was, she thought to herself. Yet she had applied so often. It would be the same old story. She walked on and

on, and finally did go into one place, with the old result. She came
out feeling that luck was against her. It was no use.

Without much thinking, she reached Dearborn Street. Here was
the great Fair store with its multitude of delivery wagons about, its
long window display, its crowd of shoppers. It readily changed her
thoughts, she who was so weary of them. It was here that she had
intended to come and get her new things. Now for relief from distress, she thought she would go in and see. She would look at the
jackets.

There is nothing in this world more delightful than that middle
state in which we mentally balance at times, possessed of the means,
lured by desire, and yet deterred by conscience or want of decision.
When Carrie began wandering around the store amid the fine displays she was in this mood. Her original experience in this same place
had given her a high opinion of its merits. Now she paused at each
individual bit of finery, where before she had hurried on. Her
woman's heart was warm with desire for them. How would she look
in this, how charming that would make her! She came upon the
corset counter and paused in rich reverie as she noted the dainty
concoctions of colour and lace there displayed. If she would only
make up her mind, she could have one of those now. She lingered
in the jewelry department. She saw the earrings, the bracelets, the
pins, the chains. What would she not have given if she could have
had them all! She would look fine too, if only she had some of these
things.

The jackets were the greatest attraction. When she entered the
store, she already had her heart fixed upon the peculiar little tan
jacket with large mother-of-pearl buttons which was all the rage that
fall. Still she delighted to convince herself that there was nothing
she would like better. She went about among the glass cases and
racks where these things were displayed, and satisfied herself that
the one she thought of was the proper one. All the time she wavered
in mind, now persuading herself that she could buy it right away if
she chose, now recalling to herself the actual condition. At last the
noon hour was dangerously near, and she had done nothing. She
must go now and return the money.

Drouet was on the corner when she came up.

"Hello," he said, "where is the jacket and"—looking down—"the
shoes?"

Carrie had thought to lead up to her decision in some intelligent
way, but this swept the whole fore-schemed situation by the board.

"I came to tell you that—that I can't take the money."

"Oh, that's it, is it?" he returned. "Well, you come on with me.
Let's go over here to Partridge's."

Carrie walked with him. Behold, the whole fabric of doubt and impossibility had slipped from her mind. She could not get at the points that were so serious, the things she was going to make plain to him.

"Have you had lunch yet? Of course you haven't. Let's go in here," and Drouet turned into one of the very nicely furnished restaurants off State Street, in Monroe.

"I mustn't take the money," said Carrie, after they were settled in a cosey corner, and Drouet had ordered the lunch. "I can't wear those things out there. They—they wouldn't know where I got them."

"What do you want to do," he smiled, "go without them?"

"I think I'll go home," she said, wearily.

"Oh, come," he said, "you've been thinking it over too long. I'll tell you what you do. You say you can't wear them out there. Why don't you rent a furnished room and leave them in that for a week?"

Carrie shook her head. Like all women, she was there to object and be convinced. It was for him to brush the doubts away and clear the path if he could.

"Why are you going home?" he asked.

"Oh, I can't get anything here."

"They won't keep you?" he remarked, intuitively.

"They can't," said Carrie.

"I'll tell you what you do," he said. "You come with me. I'll take care of you."

Carrie heard this passively. The peculiar state which she was in made it sound like the welcome breath of an open door. Drouet seemed of her own spirit and pleasing. He was clean, handsome, well-dressed, and sympathetic. His voice was the voice of a friend.

"What can you do back at Columbia City?" he went on, rousing by the words in Carrie's mind a picture of the dull world she had left. "There isn't anything down there. Chicago's the place. You can get a nice room here and some clothes, and then you can do something."

Carrie looked out through the window into the busy street. There it was, the admirable, great city, so fine when you are not poor. An elegant coach, with a prancing pair of bays, passed by, carrying in its upholstered depths a young lady.

"What will you have if you go back?" asked Drouet. There was no subtle undercurrent to the question. He imagined that she would have nothing at all of the things he thought worth while.

Carrie sat still, looking out. She was wondering what she could do. They would be expecting her to go home this week.

Drouet turned to the subject of the clothes she was going to buy.

"Why not get yourself a nice little jacket? You've got to have it. I'll loan you the money. You needn't worry about taking it. You can get yourself a nice room by yourself. I won't hurt you."

Carrie saw the drift, but could not express her thoughts. She felt more than ever the helplessness of her case.

"If I could only get something to do," she said.

"Maybe you can," went on Drouet, "if you stay here. You can't if you go away. They won't let you stay out there. Now, why not let me get you a nice room? I won't bother you—you needn't be afraid. Then, when you get fixed up, maybe you could get something."

He looked at her pretty face and it vivified his mental resources. She was a sweet little mortal to him—there was no doubt of that. She seemed to have some power back of her actions. She was not like the common run of store-girls. She wasn't silly.

In reality, Carrie had more imagination than he—more taste. It was a finer mental strain in her that made possible her depression and loneliness. Her poor clothes were neat, and she held her head unconsciously in a dainty way.

"Do you think I could get something?" she asked.

"Sure," he said, reaching over and filling her cup with tea. "I'll help you."

She looked at him, and he laughed reassuringly.

"Now I'll tell you what we'll do. We'll go over here to Partridge's[1] and you pick out what you want. Then we'll look around for a room for you. You can leave the things there. Then we'll go to the show to-night."

Carrie shook her head.

"Well, you can go out to the flat then, that's all right. You don't need to stay in the room. Just take it and leave your things there."

She hung in doubt about this until the dinner was over.

"Let's go over and look at the jackets," he said.

Together they went. In the store they found that shine and rustle of new things which immediately laid hold of Carrie's heart. Under the influence of a good dinner and Drouet's radiating presence, the scheme proposed seemed feasible. She looked about and picked a jacket like the one which she had admired at The Fair. When she got it in her hand it seemed so much nicer. The saleswoman helped her on with it, and, by accident, it fitted perfectly. Drouet's face lightened as he saw the improvement. She looked quite smart.

"That's the thing," he said.

Carrie turned before the glass. She could not help feeling pleased as she looked at herself. A warm glow crept into her cheeks.

"That's the thing," said Drouet. "Now pay for it."

"It's nine dollars," said Carrie.

"That's all right—take it," said Drouet.

She reached in her purse and took out one of the bills. The woman

---

1. Pardridge's (not Partridge's) was a well-known State Street clothing store.

asked if she would wear the coat and went off. In a few minutes she was back and the purchase was closed.

From Partridge's they went to a shoe store, where Carrie was fitted for shoes. Drouet stood by, and when he saw how nice they looked, said, "Wear them." Carrie shook her head, however. She was thinking of returning to the flat. He bought her a purse for one thing, and a pair of gloves for another, and let her buy the stockings.

"To-morrow," he said, "you come down here and buy yourself a skirt."

In all of Carrie's actions there was a touch of misgiving. The deeper she sank into the entanglement, the more she imagined that the thing hung upon the few remaining things she had not done. Since she had not done these, there was a way out.

Drouet knew a place in Wabash Avenue where there were rooms. He showed Carrie the outside of these, and said: "Now, you're my sister." He carried the arrangement off with an easy hand when it came to the selection, looking around, criticising, opining. "Her trunk will be here in a day or so," he observed to the landlady, who was very pleased.

When they were alone, Drouet did not change in the least. He talked in the same general way as if they were out in the street. Carrie left her things.

"Now," said Drouet, "why don't you move to-night?"

"Oh, I can't," said Carrie.

"Why not?"

"I don't want to leave them so."

He took that up as they walked along the avenue. It was a warm afternoon. The sun had come out and the wind had died down. As he talked with Carrie, he secured an accurate detail of the atmosphere of the flat.

"Come out of it," he said, "they won't care. I'll help you get along."

She listened until her misgivings vanished. He would show her about a little and then help her get something. He really imagined that he would. He would be out on the road and she could be working.

"Now, I'll tell you what you do," he said, "you go out there and get whatever you want and come away."

She thought a long time about this. Finally she agreed. He would come out as far as Peoria Street and wait for her. She was to meet him at half-past eight. At half-past five she reached home, and at six her determination was hardened.

"So you didn't get it?" said Minnie, referring to Carrie's story of the Boston Store.

Carrie looked at her out of the corner of her eye. "No," she answered.

"I don't think you'd better try any more this fall," said Minnie.
Carrie said nothing.

When Hanson came home he wore the same inscrutable demeanour. He washed in silence and went off to read his paper. At dinner Carrie felt a little nervous. The strain of her own plans was considerable, and the feeling that she was not welcome here was strong.

"Didn't find anything, eh?" said Hanson.

"No."

He turned to his eating again, the thought that it was a burden to have her here dwelling in his mind. She would have to go home, that was all. Once she was away, there would be no more coming back in the spring.

Carrie was afraid of what she was going to do, but she was relieved to know that this condition was ending. They would not care. Hanson particularly would be glad when she went. He would not care what became of her.

After dinner she went into the bathroom, where they could not disturb her, and wrote a little note.

"Good-bye, Minnie," it read. "I'm not going home. I'm going to stay in Chicago a little while and look for work. Don't worry. I'll be all right."

In the front room Hanson was reading his paper. As usual, she helped Minnie clear away the dishes and straighten up. Then she said:

"I guess I'll stand down at the door a little while." She could scarcely prevent her voice from trembling.

Minnie remembered Hanson's remonstrance.

"Sven doesn't think it looks good to stand down there," she said.

"Doesn't he?" said Carrie. "I won't do it any more after this."

She put on her hat and fidgeted around the table in the little bedroom, wondering where to slip the note. Finally she put it under Minnie's hair-brush.

When she had closed the hall-door, she paused a moment and wondered what they would think. Some thought of the queerness of her deed affected her. She went slowly down the stairs. She looked back up the lighted step, and then affected to stroll up the street. When she reached the corner she quickened her pace.

As she was hurrying away, Hanson came back to his wife.

"Is Carrie down at the door again?" he asked.

"Yes," said Minnie; "she said she wasn't going to do it any more."

He went over to the baby where it was playing on the floor and began to poke his finger at it.

Drouet was on the corner waiting, in good spirits.

"Hello, Carrie," he said, as a sprightly figure of a girl drew near him. "Got here safe, did you? Well, we'll take a car."

Chapter VIII

INTIMATIONS BY WINTER: AN AMBASSADOR SUMMONED

Among the forces which sweep and play throughout the universe, untutored man is but a wisp in the wind. Our civilisation is still in a middle stage, scarcely beast, in that it is no longer wholly guided by instinct; scarcely human, in that it is not yet wholly guided by reason. On the tiger no responsibility rests. We see him aligned by nature with the forces of life—he is born into their keeping and without thought he is protected. We see man far removed from the lairs of the jungles, his innate instincts dulled by too near an approach to free-will, his free-will not sufficiently developed to replace his instincts and afford him perfect guidance. He is becoming too wise to hearken always to instincts and desires; he is still too weak to always prevail against them. As a beast, the forces of life aligned him with them; as a man, he has not yet wholly learned to align himself with the forces. In this intermediate stage he wavers—neither drawn in harmony with nature by his instincts nor yet wisely putting himself into harmony by his own free-will. He is even as a wisp in the wind, moved by every breath of passion, acting now by his will and now by his instincts, erring with one, only to retrieve by the other, falling by one, only to rise by the other—a creature of incalculable variability. We have the consolation of knowing that evolution is ever in action, that the ideal is a light that cannot fail. He will not forever balance thus between good and evil. When this jangle of free-will and instinct shall have been adjusted, when perfect understanding has given the former the power to replace the latter entirely, man will no longer vary. The needle of understanding will yet point steadfast and unwavering to the distant pole of truth.

In Carrie—as in how many of our worldlings do they not?— instinct and reason, desire and understanding, were at war for the mastery. She followed whither her craving led. She was as yet more drawn than she drew.

When Minnie found the note next morning, after a night of mingled wonder and anxiety, which was not exactly touched by yearning, sorrow, or love, she exclaimed: "Well, what do you think of that?"

"What?" said Hanson.

"Sister Carrie has gone to live somewhere else."

Hanson jumped out of bed with more celerity than he usually displayed and looked at the note. The only indication of his thoughts came in the form of a little clicking sound made by his tongue; the sound some people make when they wish to urge on a horse.

"Where do you suppose she's gone to?" said Minnie, thoroughly aroused.

"I don't know," a touch of cynicism lighting his eye. "Now she has gone and done it."

Minnie moved her head in a puzzled way.

"Oh, oh," she said, "she doesn't know what she has done."

"Well," said Hanson, after a while, sticking his hands out before him, "what can you do?"

Minnie's womanly nature was higher than this. She figured the possibilities in such cases.

"Oh," she said at last, "poor Sister Carrie!"

At the time of this particular conversation, which occurred at 5 A.M., that little soldier of fortune was sleeping a rather troubled sleep in her new room, alone.

Carrie's new state was remarkable in that she saw possibilities in it. She was no sensualist, longing to drowse sleepily in the lap of luxury. She turned about, troubled by her daring, glad of her release, wondering whether she would get something to do, wondering what Drouet would do. That worthy had his future fixed for him beyond a peradventure. He could not help what he was going to do. He could not see clearly enough to wish to do differently. He was drawn by his innate desire to act the old pursuing part. He would need to delight himself with Carrie as surely as he would need to eat his heavy breakfast. He might suffer the least rudimentary twinge of conscience in whatever he did, and in just so far he was evil and sinning. But whatever twinges of conscience he might have would be rudimentary, you may be sure.

The next day he called upon Carrie, and she saw him in her chamber. He was the same jolly, enlivening soul.

"Aw," he said, "what are you looking so blue about? Come on out to breakfast. You want to get your other clothes to-day."

Carrie looked at him with the hue of shifting thought in her large eyes.

"I wish I could get something to do," she said.

"You'll get that all right," said Drouet. "What's the use worrying right now? Get yourself fixed up. See the city. I won't hurt you."

"I know you won't," she remarked, half truthfully.

"Got on the new shoes, haven't you? Stick 'em out. George, they look fine. Put on your jacket."

Carrie obeyed.

"Say, that fits like a T, don't it?" he remarked, feeling the set of it at the waist and eyeing it from a few paces with real pleasure. "What you need now is a new skirt. Let's go to breakfast."

Carrie put on her hat.

"Where are the gloves?" he inquired.

"Here," she said, taking them out of the bureau drawer.

"Now, come on," he said.

Thus the first hour of misgiving was swept away.

It went this way on every occasion. Drouet did not leave her much alone. She had time for some lone wanderings, but mostly he filled her hours with sight-seeing. At Carson, Pirie's he bought her a nice skirt and shirt waist.[1] With his money she purchased the little necessaries of toilet, until at last she looked quite another maiden. The mirror convinced her of a few things which she had long believed. She was pretty, yes, indeed! How nice her hat set, and weren't her eyes pretty. She caught her little red lip with her teeth and felt her first thrill of power. Drouet was so good.

They went to see "The Mikado" one evening, an opera which was hilariously popular at that time.[2] Before going, they made off for the Windsor dining-room, which was in Dearborn Street, a considerable distance from Carrie's room. It was blowing up cold, and out of her window Carrie could see the western sky, still pink with the fading light, but steely blue at the top where it met the darkness. A long, thin cloud of pink hung in midair, shaped like some island in a far-off sea. Somehow the swaying of some dead branches of trees across the way brought back the picture with which she was familiar when she looked from their front window in December days at home.

She paused and wrung her little hands.

"What's the matter?" said Drouet.

"Oh, I don't know," she said, her lip trembling.

He sensed something, and slipped his arm over her shoulder, patting her arm.

"Come on," he said gently, "you're all right."

She turned to slip on her jacket.

"Better wear that boa about your throat to-night."

They walked north on Wabash to Adams Street and then west. The lights in the stores were already shining out in gushes of golden hue. The arc lights were sputtering overhead, and high up were the lighted windows of the tall office buildings. The chill wind whipped in and out in gusty breaths. Homeward bound, the six o'clock throng bumped and jostled. Light overcoats were turned up about the ears, hats were pulled down. Little shop-girls went fluttering by in pairs and fours, chattering, laughing. It was a spectacle of warm-blooded humanity.

Suddenly a pair of eyes met Carrie's in recognition. They were looking out from a group of poorly dressed girls. Their clothes were faded and loose-hanging, their jackets old, their general make-up shabby.

1. Carson, Pirie's, on Madison, was a major Chicago clothing store.
2. This Gilbert and Sullivan operetta had opened in New York in 1885 and was soon a great success throughout the country.

Carrie recognised the glance and the girl. She was one of those who worked at the machines in the shoe factory. The latter looked, not quite sure, and then turned her head and looked. Carrie felt as if some great tide had rolled between them. The old dress and the old machine came back. She actually started. Drouet didn't notice until Carrie bumped into a pedestrian.

"You must be thinking," he said.

They dined and went to the theatre. That spectacle pleased Carrie immensely. The colour and grace of it caught her eye. She had vain imaginings about place and power, about far-off lands and magnificent people. When it was over, the clatter of coaches and the throng of fine ladies made her stare.

"Wait a minute," said Drouet, holding her back in the showy foyer where ladies and gentlemen were moving in a social crush, skirts rustling, lace-covered heads nodding, white teeth showing through parted lips. "Let's see."

"Sixty-seven," the coach-caller was saying, his voice lifted in a sort of euphonious cry. "Sixty-seven."

"Isn't it fine?" said Carrie.

"Great," said Drouet. He was as much affected by this show of finery and gayety as she. He pressed her arm warmly. Once she looked up, her even teeth glistening through her smiling lips, her eyes alight. As they were moving out he whispered down to her, "You look lovely!" They were right where the coach-caller was swinging open a coach-door and ushering in two ladies.

"You stick to me and we'll have a coach," laughed Drouet.

Carrie scarcely heard, her head was so full of the swirl of life.

They stopped in at a restaurant for a little after-theatre lunch. Just a shade of a thought of the hour entered Carrie's head, but there was no household law to govern her now. If any habits ever had time to fix upon her, they would have operated here. Habits are peculiar things. They will drive the really non-religious mind out of bed to say prayers that are only a custom and not a devotion. The victim of habit, when he has neglected the thing which it was his custom to do, feels a little scratching in the brain, a little irritating something which comes of being out of the rut, and imagines it to be the prick of conscience, the still, small voice that is urging him ever to righteousness. If the digression is unusual enough, the drag of habit will be heavy enough to cause the unreasoning victim to return and perform the perfunctory thing. "Now, bless me," says such a mind, "I have done my duty," when, as a matter of fact, it has merely done its old, unbreakable trick once again.

Carrie had no excellent home principles fixed upon her. If she had, she would have been more consciously distressed. Now the lunch went off with considerable warmth. Under the influence of the varied occurrences, the fine, invisible passion which was emanating from Drouet, the food, the still unusual luxury, she relaxed and heard with open ears. She was again the victim of the city's hypnotic influence.

"Well," said Drouet at last, "we had better be going."

They had been dawdling over the dishes, and their eyes had frequently met. Carrie could not help but feel the vibration of force which followed, which, indeed, was his gaze. He had a way of touching her hand in explanation, as if to impress a fact upon her. He touched it now as he spoke of going.

They arose and went out into the street. The downtown section was now bare, save for a few whistling strollers, a few *owl* cars, a few open resorts whose windows were still bright. Out Wabash Avenue they strolled, Drouet still pouring forth his volume of small information. He had Carrie's arm in his, and held it closely as he explained. Once in a while, after some witticism, he would look down, and his eyes would meet hers. At last they came to the steps, and Carrie stood up on the first one, her head now coming even with his own. He took her hand and held it genially. He looked steadily at her as she glanced about, warmly musing.

At about that hour, Minnie was soundly sleeping, after a long evening of troubled thought. She had her elbow in an awkward position under her side. The muscles so held irritated a few nerves, and now a vague scene floated in on the drowsy mind. She fancied she and Carrie were somewhere beside an old coal-mine. She could see the tall runway and the heap of earth and coal cast out. There was a deep pit, into which they were looking; they could see the curious wet stones far down where the wall disappeared in vague shadows. An old basket, used for descending, was hanging there, fastened by a worn rope.

"Let's get in," said Carrie.

"Oh, no," said Minnie.

"Yes, come on" said Carrie.

She began to pull the basket over, and now, in spite of all protest, she had swung over and was going down.

"Carrie," she called, "Carrie, come back"; but Carrie was far down now and the shadow had swallowed her completely.

She moved her arm.

Now the mystic scenery merged queerly and the place was by waters she had never seen. They were upon some board or ground or something that reached far out, and at the end of this was Carrie. They looked about, and now the thing was sinking, and Minnie heard the low sip of the encroaching water.

"Come on, Carrie," she called, but Carrie was reaching farther out. She seemed to recede, and now it was difficult to call to her.

"Carrie," she called, "Carrie," but her own voice sounded far away, and the strange waters were blurring everything. She came away suffering as though she had lost something. She was more inexpressibly sad than she had even been in life.

It was this way through many shifts of the tired brain, those curious phantoms of the spirit slipping in, blurring strange scenes, one with the other. The last one made her cry out, for Carrie was slipping away somewhere over a rock, and her fingers had let loose and she had seen her falling.

"Minnie! What's the matter? Here, wake up," said Hanson, disturbed, and shaking her by the shoulder.

"Wha—what's the matter?" said Minnie, drowsily.

"Wake up," he said, "and turn over. You're talking in your sleep."

A week or so later Drouet strolled into Fitzgerald and Moy's, spruce in dress and manner.

"Hello, Charley," said Hurstwood, looking out from his office door.

Drouet strolled over and looked in upon the manager at his desk.

"When do you go out on the road again?" he inquired.

"Pretty soon," said Drouet.

"Haven't seen much of you this trip," said Hurstwood.

"Well, I've been busy," said Drouet.

They talked some few minutes on general topics.

"Say," said Drouet, as if struck by a sudden idea, "I want you to come out some evening."

"Out where?" inquired Hurstwood.

"Out to my house, of course," said Drouet, smiling.

Hurstwood looked up quizzically, the least suggestion of a smile hovering about his lips. He studied the face of Drouet in his wise way, and then with the demeanour of a gentleman, said: "Certainly; glad to."

"We'll have a nice game of euchre."[3]

"May I bring a nice little bottle of Sec?"[4] asked Hurstwood.

"Certainly," said Drouet. "I'll introduce you."

Chapter IX

CONVENTION'S OWN TINDER-BOX: THE EYE THAT IS GREEN

Hurstwood's residence on the North Side, near Lincoln Park, was a brick building of a very popular type then, a three-story affair with the first floor sunk a very little below the level of the street. It had a large bay window bulging out from the second floor, and was graced in front by a small grassy plot, twenty-five feet wide and ten feet

3. A card game that requires from two to four players.
4. A dry wine.

deep. There was also a small rear yard, walled in by the fences of the neighbours and holding a stable where he kept his horse and trap.

The ten rooms of the house were occupied by himself, his wife Julia, and his son and daughter, George, Jr., and Jessica. There were besides these a maid-servant, represented from time to time by girls of various extraction, for Mrs. Hurstwood was not always easy to please.

"George, I let Mary go yesterday," was not an unfrequent salutation at the dinner table.

"All right," was his only reply. He had long since wearied of discussing the rancorous subject.

A lovely home atmosphere is one of the flowers of the world, than which there is nothing more tender, nothing more delicate, nothing more calculated to make strong and just the natures cradled and nourished within it. Those who have never experienced such a beneficent influence will not understand wherefore the tear springs glistening to the eyelids at some strange breath in lovely music. The mystic chords which bind and thrill the heart of the nation, they will never know.

Hurstwood's residence could scarcely be said to be infused with this home spirit. It lacked that toleration and regard without which the home is nothing. There was fine furniture, arranged as soothingly as the artistic perception of the occupants warranted. There were soft rugs, rich, upholstered chairs and divans, a grand piano, a marble carving of some unknown Venus by some unknown artist, and a number of small bronzes gathered from heaven knows where, but generally sold by the large furniture houses along with everything else which goes to make the "perfectly appointed house."

In the dining-room stood a sideboard laden with glistening decanters and other utilities and ornaments in glass, the arrangement of which could not be questioned. Here was something Hurstwood knew about. He had studied the subject for years in his business. He took no little satisfaction in telling each Mary, shortly after she arrived, something of what the art of the thing required. He was not garrulous by any means. On the contrary, there was a fine reserve in his manner toward the entire domestic economy of his life which was all that is comprehended by the popular term, gentlemanly. He would not argue, he would not talk freely. In his manner was something of the dogmatist. What he could not correct, he would ignore. There was a tendency in him to walk away from the impossible thing.

There was a time when he had been considerably enamoured of his Jessica, especially when he was younger and more confined in his success. Now, however, in her seventeenth year, Jessica had developed a certain amount of reserve and independence which was not inviting to the richest form of parental devotion. She was in the high school, and had notions of life which were decidedly those of a patrician. She liked nice clothes and urged for them constantly. Thoughts of love and elegant individual establishments were running in her head. She met girls at the high school whose parents were truly rich and whose fathers had standing locally as partners or owners of solid businesses. These girls gave themselves the airs befitting the thriving domestic establishments from whence they issued. They were the only ones of the school about whom Jessica concerned herself.

Young Hurstwood, Jr., was in his twentieth year, and was already connected in a promising capacity with a large real estate firm. He contributed nothing for the domestic expenses of the family, but was thought to be saving his money to invest in real estate. He had some ability, considerable vanity, and a love of pleasure that had not, as yet, infringed upon his duties, whatever they were. He came in and went out, pursuing his own plans and fancies, addressing a few words to his mother occasionally, relating some little incident to his father, but for the most part confining himself to those generalities with which most conversation concerns itself. He was not laying bare his desires for any one to see. He did not find any one in the house who particularly cared to see.

Mrs. Hurstwood was the type of the woman who has ever endeavoured to shine and has been more or less chagrined at the evidences of superior capability in this direction elsewhere. Her knowledge of life extended to that little conventional round of society of which she was not—but longed to be—a member. She was not without realisation already that this thing was impossible, so far as she was concerned. For her daughter, she hoped better things. Through Jessica she might rise a little. Through George, Jr.'s, possible success she might draw to herself the privilege of pointing proudly. Even Hurstwood was doing well enough, and she was anxious that his small real estate adventures should prosper. His property holdings, as yet, were rather small, but his income was pleasing and his position with Fitzgerald and Moy was fixed. Both those gentlemen were on pleasant and rather informal terms with him.

The atmosphere which such personalities would create must be apparent to all. It worked out in a thousand little conversations, all of which were of the same calibre.

"I'm going up to Fox Lake[1] to-morrow," announced George. Jr., at the dinner table one Friday evening.

"What's going on up there?" queried Mrs. Hurstwood.

"Eddie Fahrway's got a new steam launch, and he wants me to come up and see how it works."

1. A resort about thirty-five miles northwest of Chicago.

"How much did it cost him?" asked his mother.

"Oh, over two thousand dollars. He says it's a dandy."

"Old Fahrway must be making money," put in Hurstwood.

"He is, I guess. Jack told me they were shipping Vega-cura[2] to Australia now—said they sent a whole box to Cape Town last week."

"Just think of that!" said Mrs. Hurstwood, "and only four years ago they had that basement in Madison Street."

"Jack told me they were going to put up a six-story building next spring in Robey Street."

"Just think of that!" said Jessica.

On this particular occasion Hurstwood wished to leave early.

"I guess I'll be going down town," he remarked, rising.

"Are we going to McVicker's[3] Monday?" questioned Mrs. Hurstwood, without rising.

"Yes," he said indifferently.

They went on dining, while he went upstairs for his hat and coat. Presently the door clicked.

"I guess papa's gone," said Jessica.

The latter's school news was of a particular stripe.

"They're going to give a performance in the Lyceum, upstairs," she reported one day, "and I'm going to be in it."

"Are you?" said her mother.

"Yes, and I'll have to have a new dress. Some of the nicest girls in the school are going to be in it. Miss Palmer is going to take the part of Portia."

"Is she?" said Mrs. Hurstwood.

"They've got that Martha Griswold in it again. She thinks she can act."

"Her family doesn't amount to anything, does it?" said Mrs. Hurstwood sympathetically. "They haven't anything, have they?"

"No," returned Jessica, "they're poor as church mice."

She distinguished very carefully between the young boys of the school, many of whom were attracted by her beauty.

"What do you think?" she remarked to her mother one evening; "that Herbert Crane tried to make friends with me."

"Who is he, my dear?" inquired Mrs. Hurstwood.

"Oh, no one," said Jessica, pursing her pretty lips. "He's just a student there. He hasn't anything."

The other half of this picture came when young Blyford, son of Blyford, the soap manufacturer, walked home with her. Mrs. Hurstwood was on the third floor, sitting in a rocking-chair reading, and happened to look out at the time.

2. A patent medicine.
3. The principal Chicago theater of the 1880s and 1890s, on Madison between State and Dearborn. Elsewhere in *Sister Carrie* it is incorrectly spelled McVickar's.

"Who was that with you, Jessica?" she inquired, as Jessica came upstairs.

"It's Mr. Blyford, mamma," she replied.

"Is it?" said Mrs. Hurstwood.

"Yes, and he wants me to stroll over into the park with him," explained Jessica, a little flushed with running up the stairs.

"All right, my dear," said Mrs. Hurstwood. "Don't be gone long."

As the two went down the street, she glanced interestedly out of the window. It was a most satisfactory spectacle indeed, most satisfactory.

In this atmosphere Hurstwood had moved for a number of years, not thinking deeply concerning it. His was not the order of nature to trouble for something better, unless the better was immediately and sharply contrasted. As it was, he received and gave, irritated sometimes by the little displays of selfish indifference, pleased at times by some show of finery which supposedly made for dignity and social distinction. The life of the resort which he managed was his life. There he spent most of his time. When he went home evenings the house looked nice. With rare exceptions the meals were acceptable, being the kind that an ordinary servant can arrange. In part, he was interested in the talk of his son and daughter, who always looked well. The vanity of Mrs. Hurstwood caused her to keep her person rather showily arrayed, but to Hurstwood this was much better than plainness. There was no love lost between them. There was no great feeling of dissatisfaction. Her opinion on any subject was not startling. They did not talk enough together to come to the argument of any one point. In the accepted and popular phrase, she had her ideas and he had his. Once in a while he would meet a woman whose youth, sprightliness, and humour would make his wife seem rather deficient by contrast, but the temporary dissatisfaction which such an encounter might arouse would be counterbalanced by his social position and a certain matter of policy. He could not complicate his home life, because it might affect his relations with his employers. They wanted no scandals. A man, to hold his position, must have a dignified manner, a clean record, a respectable home anchorage. Therefore he was circumspect in all he did, and whenever he appeared in the public ways in the afternoon, or on Sunday, it was with his wife, and sometimes his children. He would visit the local resorts, or those near by in Wisconsin, and spend a few stiff, polished days strolling about conventional places doing conventional things. He knew the need of it.

When some one of the many middle-class individuals whom he knew, who had money, would get into trouble, he would shake his head. It didn't do to talk about those things. If it came up for discussion among such friends as with him passed for close, he would deprecate the folly of the thing. "It was all right to do it—all men do those things—but why wasn't he careful? A man can't be too careful." He lost sympathy for the man that made a mistake and was found out.

On this account he still devoted some time to showing his wife about—time which would have been wearisome indeed if it had not been for the people he would meet and the little enjoyments which did not depend upon her presence or absence. He watched her with considerable curiosity at times, for she was still attractive in a way and men looked at her. She was affable, vain, subject to flattery, and this combination, he knew quite well, might produce a tragedy in a woman of her home position. Owing to his order of mind, his confidence in the sex was not great. His wife never possessed the virtues which would win the confidence and admiration of a man of his nature. As long as she loved him vigorously he could see how confidence could be, but when that was no longer the binding chain—well, something might happen.

During the last year or two the expenses of the family seemed a large thing. Jessica wanted fine clothes, and Mrs. Hurstwood, not to be outshone by her daughter, also frequently enlivened her apparel. Hurstwood had said nothing in the past, but one day he murmured.

"Jessica must have a new dress this month," said Mrs. Hurstwood one morning.

Hurstwood was arraying himself in one of his perfection vests before the glass at the time.

"I thought she just bought one," he said.

"That was just something for evening wear," returned his wife complacently.

"It seems to me," returned Hurstwood, "that she's spending a good deal for dresses of late."

"Well, she's going out more," concluded his wife, but the tone of his voice impressed her as containing something she had not heard there before.

He was not a man who travelled much, but when he did, he had been accustomed to take her along. On one occasion recently a local aldermanic junket had been arranged to visit Philadelphia—a junket that was to last ten days. Hurstwood had been invited.

"Nobody knows us down there," said one, a gentleman whose face was a slight improvement over gross ignorance and sensuality. He always wore a silk hat of most imposing proportions. "We can have a good time." His left eye moved with just the semblance of a wink. "You want to come along, George."

The next day Hurstwood announced his intention to his wife.

"I'm going away, Julia," he said, "for a few days."

"Where?" she asked, looking up.

"To Philadelphia, on business."

She looked at him consciously, expecting something else.

"I'll have to leave you behind this time."

"All right," she replied, but he could see that she was thinking that it was a curious thing. Before he went she asked him a few more questions, and that irritated him. He began to feel that she was a disagreeable attachment.

On this trip he enjoyed himself thoroughly, and when it was over he was sorry to get back. He was not willingly a prevaricator, and hated thoroughly to make explanations concerning it. The whole incident was glossed over with general remarks, but Mrs. Hurstwood gave the subject considerable thought. She drove out more, dressed better, and attended theatres freely to make up for it.

Such an atmosphere could hardly come under the category of home life. It ran along by force of habit, by force of conventional opinion. With the lapse of time it must necessarily become dryer and dryer—must eventually be tinder, easily lighted and destroyed.

Chapter X

THE COUNSEL OF WINTER: FORTUNE'S AMBASSADOR CALLS

In the light of the world's attitude toward woman and her duties, the nature of Carrie's mental state deserves consideration. Actions such as hers are measured by an arbitrary scale. Society possesses a conventional standard whereby it judges all things. All men should be good, all women virtuous. Wherefore, villain, hast thou failed?

For all the liberal analysis of Spencer and our modern naturalistic philosophers, we have but an infantile perception of morals.[1] There is more in the subject than mere conformity to a law of evolution. It is yet deeper than conformity to things of earth alone. It is more involved than we, as yet, perceive. Answer, first, why the heart thrills; explain wherefore some plaintive note goes wandering about the world, undying; make clear the rose's subtle alchemy evolving its ruddy lamp in light and rain. In the essence of these facts lie the first principles of morals.

"Oh," thought Drouet, "how delicious is my conquest."

"Ah," thought Carrie, with mournful misgivings, "what is it I have lost?"

Before this world-old proposition we stand, serious, interested, confused; endeavouring to evolve the true theory of morals—the true answer to what is right.

---

1. Dreiser had read the works of Herbert Spencer, T. H. Huxley, and John Tyndall while a Pittsburgh reporter in 1894. The "naturalistic" or evolutionary position was that morality was not a static, absolute phenomenon but rather advanced progressively as first the race and then society evolved.

In the view of a certain stratum of society, Carrie was comfortably established—in the eyes of the starveling, beaten by every wind and gusty sheet of rain, she was safe in a halcyon harbour. Drouet had taken three rooms, furnished, in Ogden Place, facing Union Park, on the West Side.[2] That was a little, green-carpeted breathing spot, than which, to-day, there is nothing more beautiful in Chicago. It afforded a vista pleasant to contemplate. The best room looked out upon the lawn of the park, now sear and brown, where a little lake lay sheltered. Over the bare limbs of the trees, which now swayed in the wintry wind, rose the steeple of the Union Park Congregational Church, and far off the towers of several others.

The rooms were comfortably enough furnished. There was a good Brussels carpet on the floor, rich in dull red and lemon shades, and representing large jardinières filled with gorgeous, impossible flowers. There was a large pier-glass mirror between the two windows. A large, soft, green, plush-covered couch occupied one corner, and several rocking-chairs were set about. Some pictures, several rugs, a few small pieces of bric-à-brac, and the tale of contents is told.

In the bedroom, off the front room, was Carrie's trunk, bought by Drouet, and in the wardrobe built into the wall quite an array of clothing—more than she had ever possessed before, and of very becoming designs. There was a third room for possible use as a kitchen, where Drouet had Carrie establish a little portable gas stove for the preparation of small lunches, oysters, Welsh rarebits, and the like, of which he was exceedingly fond; and, lastly, a bath. The whole place was cosey, in that it was lighted by gas and heated by furnace registers, possessing also a small grate, set with an asbestos back, a method of cheerful warming which was then first coming into use. By her industry and natural love of order, which now developed, the place maintained an air pleasing in the extreme.

Here, then, was Carrie, established in a pleasant fashion, free of certain difficulties which most ominously confronted her, laden with many new ones which were of a mental order, and altogether so turned about in all of her earthly relationships that she might well have been a new and different individual. She looked into her glass and saw a prettier Carrie than she had seen before; she looked into her mind, a mirror prepared of her own and the world's opinions, and saw a worse. Between these two images she wavered, hesitating which to believe.

"My, but you're a little beauty," Drouet was wont to exclaim to her.

She would look at him with large, pleased eyes.

2. One of the smallest Chicago parks, Union Park was about two miles directly west of downtown Chicago. Dreiser himself had lived in Ogden Place in the summer of 1892 while working on the *Chicago Globe*.

"You know it, don't you?" he would continue.

"Oh, I don't know," she would reply, feeling delight in the fact that one should think so, hesitating to believe, though she really did, that she was vain enough to think so much of herself.

Her conscience, however, was not a Drouet, interested to praise. There she heard a different voice, with which she argued, pleaded, excused. It was no just and sapient counsellor, in its last analysis. It was only an average little conscience, a thing which represented the world, her past environment, habit, convention, in a confused way. With it, the voice of the people was truly the voice of God.

"Oh, thou failure!" said the voice.

"Why?" she questioned.

"Look at those about," came the whispered answer. "Look at those who are good. How would they scorn to do what you have done. Look at the good girls; how will they draw away from such as you when they know you have been weak. You had not tried before you failed."

It was when Carrie was alone, looking out across the park, that she would be listening to this. It would come infrequently—when something else did not interfere, when the pleasant side was not too apparent, when Drouet was not there. It was somewhat clear in utterance at first, but never wholly convincing. There was always an answer, always the December days threatened. She was alone; she was desireful; she was fearful of the whistling wind. The voice of want made answer for her.

Once the bright days of summer pass by, a city takes on that sombre garb of grey, wrapt in which it goes about its labours during the long winter. Its endless buildings look grey, its sky and its streets assume a sombre hue; the scattered, leafless trees and wind blown dust and paper but add to the general solemnity of colour. There seems to be something in the chill breezes which scurry through the long, narrow thoroughfares productive of rueful thoughts. Not poets alone, nor artists, nor that superior order of mind which arrogates to itself all refinement, feel this, but dogs and all men. These feel as much as the poet, though they have not the same power of expression. The sparrow upon the wire, the cat in the doorway, the dray horse tugging his weary load, feel the long, keen breaths of winter. It strikes to the heart of all life, animate and inanimate. If it were not for the artificial fires of merriment, the rush of profit-seeking trade, and pleasure-selling amusements; if the various merchants failed to make the customary display within and without their establishments; if our streets were not strung with signs of gorgeous hues and thronged with hurrying purchasers, we would quickly discover how firmly the chill hand of winter lays upon the heart; how dispiriting are the days during which the sun withholds a portion of our allowance of light and warmth. We are more dependent upon these things than is often thought. We are insects produced by heat, and pass without it.

In the drag of such a grey day the secret voice would reassert itself, feebly and more feebly.

Such mental conflict was not always uppermost. Carrie was not by any means a gloomy soul. More, she had not the mind to get firm hold upon a definite truth. When she could not find her way out of the labyrinth of ill-logic which thought upon the subject created, she would turn away entirely.

Drouet, all the time, was conducting himself in a model way for one of his sort. He took her about a great deal, spent money upon her, and when he travelled took her with him. There were times when she would be alone for two or three days, while he made the shorter circuits of his business, but, as a rule, she saw a great deal of him.

"Say, Carrie," he said one morning, shortly after they had so established themselves, "I've invited my friend Hurstwood to come out some day and spend the evening with us."

"Who is he?" asked Carrie, doubtfully.

"Oh, he's a nice man. He's manager of Fitzgerald and Moy's."

"What's that?" said Carrie.

"The finest resort in town. It's a way-up, swell place."

Carrie puzzled a moment. She was wondering what Drouet had told him, what her attitude would be.

"That's all right," said Drouet, feeling her thought. "He doesn't know anything. You're Mrs. Drouet now."

There was something about this which struck Carrie as slightly inconsiderate. She could see that Drouet did not have the keenest sensibilities.

"Why don't we get married?" she inquired, thinking of the voluble promises he had made.

"Well, we will," he said, "just as soon as I get this little deal of mine closed up."

He was referring to some property which he said he had, and which required so much attention, adjustment, and what not, that somehow or other it interfered with his free moral, personal actions.

"Just as soon as I get back from my Denver trip in January we'll do it."

Carrie accepted this as basis for hope—it was a sort of salve to her conscience, a pleasant way out. Under the circumstances, things would be righted. Her actions would be justified.

She really was not enamoured of Drouet. She was more clever than he. In a dim way, she was beginning to see where he lacked. If it had not been for this, if she had not been able to measure and judge him in a way, she would have been worse off than she was.

She would have adored him. She would have been utterly wretched in her fear of not gaining his affection, of losing his interest, of being swept away and left without an anchorage. As it was, she wavered a little, slightly anxious, at first, to gain him completely, but later feeling at ease in waiting. She was not exactly sure what she thought of him—what she wanted to do.

When Hurstwood called, she met a man who was more clever than Drouet in a hundred ways. He paid that peculiar deference to women which every member of the sex appreciates. He was not overawed, he was not overbold. His great charm was attentiveness. Schooled in winning those birds of fine feather among his own sex, the merchants and professionals who visited his resort, he could use even greater tact when endeavouring to prove agreeable to some one who charmed him. In a pretty woman of any refinement of feeling whatsoever he found his greatest incentive. He was mild, placid, assured, giving the impression that he wished to be of service only—to do something which would make the lady more pleased.

Drouet had ability in this line himself when the game was worth the candle, but he was too much the egotist to reach the polish which Hurstwood possessed. He was too buoyant, too full of ruddy life, too assured. He succeeded with many who were not quite schooled in the art of love. He failed dismally where the woman was slightly experienced and possessed innate refinement. In the case of Carrie he found a woman who was all of the latter, but none of the former. He was lucky in the fact that opportunity tumbled into his lap, as it were. A few years later, with a little more experience, the slightest tide of success, and he had not been able to approach Carrie at all.

"You ought to have a piano here, Drouet," said Hurstwood, smiling at Carrie, on the evening in question, "so that your wife could play."

Drouet had not thought of that.

"So we ought," he observed readily.

"Oh, I don't play," ventured Carrie.

"It isn't very difficult," returned Hurstwood. "You could do very well in a few weeks."

He was in the best form for entertaining this evening. His clothes were particularly new and rich in appearance. The coat lapels stood out with that medium stiffness which excellent cloth possesses. The vest was of a rich Scotch plaid, set with a double row of round mother-of-pearl buttons. His cravat was a shiny combination of silken threads, not loud, not inconspicuous. What he wore did not strike the eye so forcibly as that which Drouet had on, but Carrie could see the elegance of the material. Hurstwood's shoes were of soft, black calf, polished only to a dull shine. Drouet wore patent leather, but Carrie could not help feeling that there was a distinction in favour of the soft leather, where all else was so rich. She noticed these things almost unconsciously. They were things which would naturally flow from the situation. She was used to Drouet's appearance.

"Suppose we have a little game of euchre?" suggested Hurstwood, after a light round of conversation. He was rather dexterous in avoiding everything that would suggest that he knew anything of Carrie's past. He kept away from personalities altogether, and confined himself to those things which did not concern individuals at all. By his manner, he put Carrie at her ease, and by his deference and pleasantries he amused her. He pretended to be seriously interested in all she said.

"I don't know how to play," said Carrie.

"Charlie, you are neglecting a part of your duty," he observed to Drouet most affably. "Between us, though," he went on, "we can show you."

By his tact he made Drouet feel that he admired his choice. There was something in his manner that showed that he was pleased to be there. Drouet felt really closer to him than ever before. It gave him more respect for Carrie. Her appearance came into a new light, under Hurstwood's appreciation. The situation livened considerably.

"Now, let me see," said Hurstwood, looking over Carrie's shoulder very deferentially. "What have you?" He studied for a moment. "That's rather good," he said.

"You're lucky. Now, I'll show you how to trounce your husband. You take my advice."

"Here," said Drouet, "if you two are going to scheme together, I won't stand a ghost of a show. Hurstwood's a regular sharp."

"No, it's your wife. She brings me luck. Why shouldn't she win?"

Carrie looked gratefully at Hurstwood, and smiled at Drouet. The former took the air of a mere friend. He was simply there to enjoy himself. Anything that Carrie did was pleasing to him, nothing more.

"There," he said, holding back one of his own good cards, and giving Carrie a chance to take a trick. "I count that clever playing for a beginner."

The latter laughed gleefully as she saw the hand coming her way. It was as if she were invincible when Hurstwood helped her.

He did not look at her often. When he did, it was with a mild light in his eye. Not a shade was there of anything save geniality and kindness. He took back the shifty, clever gleam, and replaced it with one of innocence. Carrie could not guess but that it was pleasure with him in the immediate thing. She felt that he considered she was doing a great deal.

"It's unfair to let such playing go without earning something," he said after a time, slipping his finger into the little coin pocket of his coat. "Let's play for dimes."

"All right," said Drouet, fishing for bills.

Hurstwood was quicker. His fingers were full of new ten-cent pieces. "Here we are," he said, supplying each one with a little stack.

"Oh, this is gambling," smiled Carrie. "It's bad."

"No," said Drouet, "only fun. If you never play for more than that, you will go to Heaven."

"Don't you moralise," said Hurstwood to Carrie gently, "until you see what becomes of the money."

Drouet smiled.

"If your husband gets them, he'll tell you how bad it is."

Drouet laughed loud.

There was such an ingratiating tone about Hurstwood's voice, the insinuation was so perceptible that even Carrie got the humour of it.

"When do you leave?" said Hurstwood to Drouet.

"On Wednesday," he replied.

"It's rather hard to have your husband running about like that, isn't it?" said Hurstwood, addressing Carrie.

"She's going along with me this time," said Drouet.

"You must both go with me to the theatre before you go."

"Certainly," said Drouet. "Eh, Carrie?"

"I'd like it ever so much," she replied.

Hurstwood did his best to see that Carrie won the money. He rejoiced in her success, kept counting her winnings, and finally gathered and put them in her extended hand. They spread a little lunch, at which he served the wine, and afterwards he used fine tact in going.

"Now," he said, addressing first Carrie and then Drouet with his eyes, "you must be ready at 7:30. I'll come and get you."

They went with him to the door and there was his cab waiting, its red lamps gleaming cheerfully in the shadow.

"Now," he observed to Drouet, with a tone of good-fellowship, "when you leave your wife alone, you must let me show her around a little. It will break up her loneliness."

"Sure," said Drouet, quite pleased at the attention shown.

"You're so kind," observed Carrie.

"Not at all," said Hurstwood, "I would want your husband to do as much for me."

He smiled and went lightly away. Carrie was thoroughly impressed. She had never come in contact with such grace. As for Drouet, he was equally pleased.

"There's a nice man," he remarked to Carrie, as they returned to their cosey chamber. "A good friend of mine, too."

"He seems to be," said Carrie.

Chapter XI

THE PERSUASION OF FASHION: FEELING GUARDS O'ER ITS OWN

Carrie was an apt student of fortune's ways—of fortune's super-ficialities. Seeing a thing, she would immediately set to inquiring how she would look, properly related to it. Be it known that this is not fine feeling, it is not wisdom. The greatest minds are not so afflicted; and, on the contrary, the lowest order of mind is not so disturbed. Fine clothes to her were a vast persuasion; they spoke tenderly and Jesuitically for themselves. When she came within earshot of their pleading, desire in her bent a willing ear. The voice of the so-called inanimate! Who shall translate for us the language of the stones?

"My dear," said the lace collar she secured from Partridge's, "I fit you beautifully; don't give me up."

"Ah, such little feet," said the leather of the soft new shoes; "how effectively I cover them. What a pity they should ever want my aid."

Once these things were in her hand, on her person, she might dream of giving them up; the method by which they came might intrude itself so forcibly that she would ache to be rid of the thought of it, but she would not give them up. "Put on the old clothes—that torn pair of shoes," was called to her by her conscience in vain. She could possibly have conquered the fear of hunger and gone back; the thought of hard work and a narrow round of suffering would, under the last pressure of conscience, have yielded, but spoil her appearance?—be old-clothed and poor-appearing?—never!

Drouet heightened her opinion on this and allied subjects in such a manner as to weaken her power of resisting their influence. It is so easy to do this when the thing opined is in the line of what we desire. In his hearty way, he insisted upon her good looks. He looked at her admiringly, and she took it at its full value. Under the circum-stances, she did not need to carry herself as pretty women do. She picked that knowledge up fast enough for herself. Drouet had a habit, characteristic of his kind, of looking after stylishly dressed or pretty women on the street and remarking upon them. He had just enough of the feminine love of dress to be a good judge—not of intellect, but of clothes. He saw how they set their little feet, how they carried their chins, with what grace and sinuosity they swung their bodies. A dainty, self-conscious swaying of the hips by a woman was to him as alluring as the glint of rare wine to a toper. He would turn and follow the disappearing vision with his eyes. He would thrill as a child with the unhindered passion that was in him. He loved the thing that women love in themselves, grace. At this, their own shrine, he knelt with them, an ardent devotee.

"Did you see that woman who went by just now?" he said to Carrie on the first day they took a walk together. "Fine stepper, wasn't she?"

Carrie looked, and observed the grace commended.

"Yes, she is," she returned, cheerfully, a little suggestion of possible defect in herself awakening in her mind. If that was so fine, she must look at it more closely. Instinctively, she felt a desire to imitate it. Surely she could do that too.

When one of her mind sees many things emphasized and reemphasized and admired, she gathers the logic of it and applies accordingly. Drouet was not shrewd enough to see that this was not tactful. He could not see that it would be better to make her feel that she was competing with herself, not others better than herself. He would not have done it with an older, wiser woman, but in Carrie he saw only the novice. Less clever than she, he was naturally unable to comprehend her sensibility. He went on educating and wounding her, a thing rather foolish in one whose admiration for his pupil and victim was apt to grow.

Carrie took the instructions affably. She saw what Drouet liked; in a vague way she saw where he was weak. It lessens a woman's opinion of a man when she learns that his admiration is so pointedly and generously distributed. She sees but one object of supreme compliment in this world, and that is herself. If a man is to succeed with many women, he must be all in all to each.

In her own apartments Carrie saw things which were lessons in the same school.

In the same house with her lived an official of one of the theatres, Mr. Frank A. Hale, manager of the Standard,[1] and his wife, a pleasing-looking brunette of thirty-five. They were people of a sort very common in America today, who live respectably from hand to mouth. Hale received a salary of forty-five dollars a week. His wife, quite attractive, affected the feeling of youth, and objected to that sort of home life which means the care of a house and the raising of a family. Like Drouet and Carrie, they also occupied three rooms on the floor above.

Not long after she arrived Mrs. Hale established social relations with her, and together they went about. For a long time this was her only companionship, and the gossip of the manager's wife formed the medium through which she saw the world. Such trivialities, such praises of wealth, such conventional expression of morals as sifted through this passive creature's mind, fell upon Carrie and for the while confused her.

On the other hand, her own feelings were a corrective influence. The constant drag to something better was not to be denied. By those things which address the heart was she steadily recalled. In the apartments across the hall were a young girl and her mother. They were

---

1. A theater at Jackson and Halsted.

from Evansville, Indiana, the wife and daughter of a railroad treasurer. The daughter was here to study music, the mother to keep her
company.

Carrie did not make their acquaintance, but she saw the daughter
coming in and going out. A few times she had seen her at the piano
in the parlour, and not infrequently had heard her play. This young
woman was particularly dressy for her station, and wore a jewelled
ring or two which flashed upon her white fingers as she played.

Now Carrie was affected by music. Her nervous composition
responded to certain strains, much as certain strings of a harp vibrate
when a corresponding key of a piano is struck. She was delicately
moulded in sentiment, and answered with vague ruminations to certain wistful chords. They awoke longings for those things which she
did not have. They caused her to cling closer to things she possessed.
One short song the young lady played in a most soulful and tender
mood. Carrie heard it through the open door from the parlour below.
It was at that hour between afternoon and night when, for the idle,
the wanderer, things are apt to take on a wistful aspect. The mind
wanders forth on far journeys and returns with sheaves of withered
and departed joys. Carrie sat at her window looking out. Drouet had
been away since ten in the morning. She had amused herself with a
walk, a book by Bertha M. Clay[2] which Drouet had left there, though
she did not wholly enjoy the latter, and by changing her dress for the
evening. Now she sat looking out across the park as wistful and
depressed as the nature which craves variety and life can be under
such circumstances. As she contemplated her new state, the strain
from the parlour below stole upward. With it her thoughts became
coloured and enmeshed. She reverted to the things which were best
and saddest within the small limit of her experience. She became for
the moment a repentant.

While she was in this mood Drouet came in, bringing with him an
entirely different atmosphere. It was dusk and Carrie had neglected
to light the lamp. The fire in the grate, too, had burned low.

"Where are you, Cad?" he said, using a pet name he had given
her.

"Here," she answered.

There was something delicate and lonely in her voice, but he could
not hear it. He had not the poetry in him that would seek a woman

2. Bertha M. Clay was the pseudonym of Charlotte M. Brame (1836–84), a prolific writer
of sentimental romances. Her plots often centered on a fatal love between a nobleman
and a lowborn girl. After her death, her pseudonym was used by a number of writers who
worked for the Street and Smith Publishing Company, and books under her name
appeared as late as 1900. Her most popular work was *Dora Thorne* (1883), which is
perhaps the novel that Carrie is reading, since she recalls having read it on p. 227 below.
Throughout his career Dreiser used the popularity of Bertha Clay's novels to indicate the
low level of American literary taste. See, for example, his "Why Not Tell Europe About
Bertha Clay," *New York Call* 24 Oct. 1921: 6.

out under such circumstances and console her for the tragedy of life. Instead, he struck a match and lighted the gas.

"Hello," he exclaimed, "you've been crying."

Her eyes were still wet with a few vague tears.

"Pshaw," he said, "you don't want to do that."

He took her hand, feeling in his good-natured egotism that it was probably lack of his presence which had made her lonely.

"Come on, now," he went on; "it's all right. Let's waltz a little to that music."

He could not have introduced a more incongruous proposition. It made clear to Carrie that he could not sympathise with her. She could not have framed thoughts which would have expressed his defect or made clear the difference between them, but she felt it. It was his first great mistake.

What Drouet said about the girl's grace, as she tripped out evenings accompanied by her mother, caused Carrie to perceive the nature and value of those little modish ways which women adopt when they would presume to be something. She looked in the mirror and pursed up her lips, accompanying it with a little toss of the head, as she had seen the railroad treasurer's daughter do. She caught up her skirts with an easy swing, for had not Drouet remarked that in her and several others, and Carrie was naturally imitative. She began to get the hang of those little things which the pretty woman who has vanity invariably adopts. In short, her knowledge of grace doubled, and with it her appearance changed. She became a girl of considerable taste.

Drouet noticed this. He saw the new bow in her hair and the new way of arranging her locks which she affected one morning.

"You look fine that way, Cad," he said.

"Do I?" she replied, sweetly. It made her try for other effects that selfsame day.

She used her feet less heavily, a thing that was brought about by her attempting to imitate the treasurer's daughter's graceful carriage. How much influence the presence of that young woman in the same house had upon her it would be difficult to say. But, because of all these things, when Hurstwood called he had found a young woman who was much more than the Carrie to whom Drouet had first spoken. The primary defects of dress and manner had passed. She was pretty, graceful, rich in the timidity born of uncertainty, and with a something childlike in her large eyes which captured the fancy of this starched and conventional poser among men. It was the ancient attraction of the fresh for the stale. If there was a touch of appreciation left in him for the bloom and unsophistication which is the charm of youth, it rekindled now. He looked into her pretty face and felt the subtle waves of young life radiating therefrom. In that large clear eye he could see nothing that his *blasé* nature could understand as guile. The little vanity, if he could have perceived it there, would have touched him as a pleasant thing.

"I wonder," he said, as he rode away in his cab, "how Drouet came to win her."

He gave her credit for feelings superior to Drouet at the first glance.

The cab plopped along between the far-receding lines of gas lamps on either hand. He folded his gloved hands and saw only the lighted chamber and Carrie's face. He was pondering over the delight of youthful beauty.

"I'll have a bouquet for her," he thought. "Drouet won't mind."

He never for a moment concealed the fact of her attraction for himself. He troubled himself not at all about Drouet's priority. He was merely floating those gossamer threads of thought which, like the spider's, he hoped would lay hold somewhere. He did not know, he could not guess, what the result would be.

A few weeks later Drouet, in his peregrinations, encountered one of his well-dressed lady acquaintances in Chicago on his return from a short trip to Omaha. He had intended to hurry out to Ogden Place and surprise Carrie, but now he fell into an interesting conversation and soon modified his original intention.

"Let's go to dinner," he said, little recking any chance meeting which might trouble his way.

"Certainly," said his companion.

They visited one of the better restaurants for a social chat. It was five in the afternoon when they met; it was seven-thirty before the last bone was picked.

Drouet was just finishing a little incident he was relating, and his face was expanding into a smile, when Hurstwood's eye caught his own. The latter had come in with several friends, and, seeing Drouet and some woman, not Carrie, drew his own conclusion.

"Ah, the rascal," he thought, and then, with a touch of righteous sympathy, "that's pretty hard on the little girl."

Drouet jumped from one easy thought to another as he caught Hurstwood's eye. He felt but very little misgiving, until he saw that Hurstwood was cautiously pretending not to see. Then some of the latter's impression forced itself upon him. He thought of Carrie and their last meeting. By George, he would have to explain this to Hurstwood. Such a chance half-hour with an old friend must not have anything more attached to it than it really warranted.

For the first time he was troubled. Here was a moral complication of which he could not possibly get the ends. Hurstwood would laugh at him for being a fickle boy. He would laugh with Hurstwood. Carrie would never hear, his present companion at table would never know,

and yet he could not help feeling that he was getting the worst of
it—there was some faint stigma attached, and he was not guilty. He
broke up the dinner by becoming dull, and saw his companion on
her car. Then he went home.

"He hasn't talked to me about any of these later flames," thought
Hurstwood to himself. "He thinks I think he cares for the girl out
there."

"He ought not to think I'm knocking around, since I have just
introduced him out there," thought Drouet.

"I saw you," Hurstwood said, genially, the next time Drouet drifted
in to his polished resort, from which he could not stay away. He
raised his forefinger indicatively, as parents do to children.

"An old acquaintance of mine that I ran into just as I was coming
up from the station," explained Drouet. "She used to be quite a
beauty."

"Still attracts a little, eh?" returned the other, affecting to jest.

"Oh, no," said Drouet, "just couldn't escape her this time."

"How long are you here?" asked Hurstwood.

"Only a few days."

"You must bring the girl down and take dinner with me," he said.
"I'm afraid you keep her cooped up out there. I'll get a box for Joe
Jefferson."

"Not me," answered the drummer. "Sure I'll come."

This pleased Hurstwood immensely. He gave Drouet no credit for
any feelings toward Carrie whatever. He envied him, and now, as he
looked at the well-dressed, jolly salesman, whom he so much liked,
the gleam of the rival glowed in his eye. He began to "size up" Drouet
from the standpoints of wit and fascination. He began to look to see
where he was weak. There was no disputing that, whatever he might
think of him as a good fellow, he felt a certain amount of contempt
for him as a lover. He could hood-wink him all right. Why, if he
would just let Carrie see one such little incident as that of Thursday,
it would settle the matter. He ran on in thought, almost exulting, the
while he laughed and chatted, and Drouet felt nothing. He had no
power of analysing the glance and the atmosphere of a man like
Hurstwood. He stood and smiled and accepted the invitation while
his friend examined him with the eye of a hawk.

The object of this peculiarly involved comedy was not thinking of
either. She was busy adjusting her thoughts and feelings to newer
conditions, and was not in danger of suffering disturbing pangs from
either quarter.

One evening Drouet found her dressing herself before the glass.

"Cad," said he, catching her, "I believe you're getting vain."

"Nothing of the kind," she returned, smiling.

"Well, you're mighty pretty," he went on, slipping his arm around her. "Put on that navy-blue dress of yours and I'll take you to the show."

"Oh, I've promised Mrs. Hale to go with her to the Exposition to-night,"[3] she returned, apologetically.

"You did, eh?" he said, studying the situation abstractedly. "I wouldn't care to go to that myself."

"Well, I don't know," answered Carrie, puzzling, but not offering to break her promise in his favour.

Just then a knock came at their door and the maid-servant handed a letter in.

"He says there's an answer expected," she explained.

"It's from Hurstwood," said Drouet, noting the superscription as he tore it open.

"You are to come down and see Joe Jefferson with me tonight," it ran in part. "It's my turn, as we agreed the other day. All other bets are off."

"Well, what do you say to this?" asked Drouet, innocently, while Carrie's mind bubbled with favourable replies.

"You had better decide, Charlie," she said, reservedly.

"I guess we had better go, if you can break that engagement upstairs," said Drouet.

"Oh, I can," returned Carrie without thinking.

Drouet selected writing paper while Carrie went to change her dress. She hardly explained to herself why this latest invitation appealed to her most.

"Shall I wear my hair as I did yesterday?" she asked, as she came out with several articles of apparel pending.

"Sure," he returned, pleasantly.

She was relieved to see that he felt nothing. She did not credit her willingness to go to any fascination Hurstwood held for her. It seemed that the combination of Hurstwood, Drouet, and herself was more agreeable than anything else that had been suggested. She arrayed herself most carefully and they started off, extending excuses upstairs.

"I say," said Hurstwood, as they came up the theatre lobby, "we are exceedingly charming this evening."

Carrie fluttered under his approving glance.

"Now, then," he said, leading the way up the foyer into the theatre.

If ever there was dressiness it was here. It was the personification of the old term spick and span.

"Did you ever see Jefferson?" he questioned, as he leaned toward Carrie in the box.

"I never did," she returned.

---

3. The Inter-State Industrial Exposition was a permanent fair that was housed in the Exposition Building on Michigan Avenue.

"He's delightful, delightful," he went on, giving the commonplace rendition of approval which such men know. He sent Drouet after a programme, and then discoursed to Carrie concerning Jefferson as he had heard of him. The former was pleased beyond expression, and was really hypnotised by the environment, the trappings of the box, the elegance of her companion. Several times their eyes accidentally met, and then there poured into hers such a flood of feeling as she had never before experienced. She could not for the moment explain it, for in the next glance or the next move of the hand there was seeming indifference, mingled only with the kindest attention.

Drouet shared in the conversation, but he was almost dull in comparison. Hurstwood entertained them both, and now it was driven into Carrie's mind that here was the superior man. She instinctively felt that he was stronger and higher, and yet withal so simple. By the end of the third act she was sure that Drouet was only a kindly soul, but otherwise defective. He sank every moment in her estimation by the strong comparison.

"I have had such a nice time," said Carrie, when it was all over and they were coming out.

"Yes, indeed," added Drouet, who was not in the least aware that a battle had been fought and his defences weakened. He was like the Emperor of China, who sat glorying in himself, unaware that his fairest provinces were being wrested from him.

"Well, you have saved me a dreary evening," returned Hurstwood. "Good-night."

He took Carrie's little hand, and a current of feeling swept from one to the other.

"I'm so tired," said Carrie, leaning back in the car when Drouet began to talk.

"Well, you rest a little while I smoke," he said, rising, and then he foolishly went to the forward platform of the car and left the game as it stood.

Chapter XII

OF THE LAMPS OF THE MANSIONS: THE AMBASSADOR'S PLEA

Mrs. Hurstwood was not aware of any of her husband's moral defections, though she might readily have suspected his tendencies, which she well understood. She was a woman upon whose action under provocation you could never count. Hurstwood, for one, had not the slightest idea of what she would do under certain circumstances. He had never seen her thoroughly aroused. In fact, she was not a woman who would fly into a passion. She had too little faith in mankind not to know that they were erring. She was too calculating to jeopardise any advantage she might gain in the way of information by fruitless clamour. Her wrath would never wreak itself in one fell blow. She would wait and brood, studying the details and adding to them until her power might be commensurate with her desire for revenge. At the same time, she would not delay to inflict any injury, big or little, which would wound the object of her revenge and still leave him uncertain as to the source of the evil. She was a cold, self-centered woman, with many a thought of her own which never found expression, not even by so much as the glint of an eye.

Hurstwood felt some of this in her nature, though he did not actually perceive it. He dwelt with her in peace and some satisfaction. He did not fear her in the least—there was no cause for it. She still took a faint pride in him, which was augmented by her desire to have her social integrity maintained. She was secretly somewhat pleased by the fact that much of her husband's property was in her name, a precaution which Hurstwood had taken when his home interests were somewhat more alluring than at present. His wife had not the slightest reason to feel that anything would ever go amiss with their household, and yet the shadows which run before gave her a thought of the good of it now and then. She was in a position to become refractory with considerable advantage, and Hurstwood conducted himself circumspectly because he felt that he could not be sure of anything once she became dissatisfied.

It so happened that on the night when Hurstwood, Carrie, and Drouet were in the box at McVickar's, George, Jr., was in the sixth row of the parquet with the daughter of H. B. Carmichael, the third partner of a wholesale drygoods house of that city. Hurstwood did not see his son, for he sat, as was his wont, as far back as possible, leaving himself just partially visible, when he bent forward, to those within the first six rows in question. It was his wont to sit this way in every theatre—to make his personality as inconspicuous as possible where it would be no advantage to him to have it otherwise.

He never moved but what, if there was any danger of his conduct being misconstrued or ill-reported, he looked carefully about him and counted the cost of every inch of conspicuity.

The next morning at breakfast his son said:

"I saw you, Governor, last night."

"Were you at McVickar's?" said Hurstwood, with the best grace in the world.

"Yes," said young George.

"Who with?"

"Miss Carmichael."

Mrs. Hurstwood directed an inquiring glance at her husband, but could not judge from his appearance whether it was any more than a casual look into the theatre which was referred to.

"How was the play?" she inquired.

"Very good," returned Hurstwood, "only it's the same old thing, 'Rip Van Winkle'."[1]

"Whom did you go with?" queried his wife, with assumed indifference.

"Charlie Drouet and his wife. They are friends of Moy's, visiting here."

Owing to the peculiar nature of his position, such a disclosure as this would ordinarily create no difficulty. His wife took it for granted that his situation called for certain social movements in which she might not be included. But of late he had pleaded office duty on several occasions when his wife asked for his company to any evening entertainment. He had done so in regard to the very evening in question only the morning before.

"I thought you were going to be busy," she remarked, very carefully.

"So I was," he exclaimed, "I couldn't help the interruption, but I made up for it afterward by working until two."

This settled the discussion for the time being, but there was a residue of opinion which was not satisfactory. There was no time at which the claims of his wife could have been more unsatisfactorily pushed. For years he had been steadily modifying his matrimonial devotion, and found her company dull. Now that a new light shone upon the horizon, this older luminary paled in the west. He was satisfied to turn his face away entirely, and any call to look back was irksome.

She, on the contrary, was not at all inclined to accept anything less than a complete fulfilment of the letter of their relationship, though the spirit might be wanting.

"We are coming down town this afternoon," she remarked, a few days later. "I want you to come over to Kinsley's and meet Mr. Phillips and his wife. They're stopping at the Tremont, and we're going to show them around a little."[2]

After the occurrence of Wednesday, he could not refuse, though the Phillips were about as uninteresting as vanity and ignorance could make them. He agreed, but it was with short grace. He was angry when he left the house.

"I'll put a stop to this," he thought. "I'm not going to be bothered fooling around with visitors when I have work to do."

Not long after this Mrs. Hurstwood came with a similar proposition, only it was to a matinée this time.

1. Jefferson had begun appearing in *Rip Van Winkle* in 1865.
2. Kinsley's was a restaurant on West Adams, close to where Dreiser locates Fitzgerald and Moy's; the Tremont was an old but still-fashionable hotel on Lake and Dearborn.

"My dear," he returned, "I haven't time. I'm too busy."

"You find time to go with other people, though," she replied, with considerable irritation.

"Nothing of the kind," he answered. "I can't avoid business relations, and that's all there is to it."

"Well, never mind," she exclaimed. Her lips tightened. The feeling of mutual antagonism was increased.

On the other hand, his interest in Drouet's little shop-girl grew in an almost evenly balanced proportion. That young lady, under the stress of her situation and the tutelage of her new friend, changed effectively. She had the aptitude of the struggler who seeks emancipation. The glow of a more showy life was not lost upon her. She did not grow in knowledge so much as she awakened in the matter of desire. Mrs. Hale's extended harangues upon the subjects of wealth and position taught her to distinguish between degrees of wealth.

Mrs. Hale loved to drive in the afternoon in the sun when it was fine, and to satisfy her soul with a sight of those mansions and lawns which she could not afford. On the North Side had been erected a number of elegant mansions along what is now known as the North Shore Drive. The present lake wall of stone and granitoid was not then in place, but the road had been well laid out, the intermediate spaces of lawn were lovely to look upon, and the houses were thoroughly new and imposing. When the winter season had passed and the first fine days of the early spring appeared, Mrs. Hale secured a buggy for an afternoon and invited Carrie. They rode first through Lincoln Park and on far out towards Evanston, turning back at four and arriving at the north end of the Shore Drive at about five o'clock. At this time of year the days are still comparatively short, and the shadows of the evening were beginning to settle down upon the great city. Lamps were beginning to burn with that mellow radiance which seems almost watery and translucent to the eye. There was a softness in the air which speaks with an infinite delicacy of feeling to the flesh as well as to the soul. Carrie felt that it was a lovely day. She was ripened by it in spirit for many suggestions. As they drove along the smooth pavement an occasional carriage passed. She saw one stop and the footman dismount, opening the door for a gentleman who seemed to be leisurely returning from some afternoon pleasure. Across the broad lawns, now first freshening into green, she saw lamps faintly glowing upon rich interiors. Now it was but a chair, now a table, now an ornate corner, which met her eye, but it appealed to her as almost nothing else could. Such childish fancies as she had had of fairy palaces and kingly quarters now came back. She imagined that across these richly carved entrance-ways, where the globed and crystalled lamps shone upon panelled doors set with stained and designed panes of glass, was neither care nor unsatisfied desire. She was perfectly certain that here was happiness. If she could but stroll up yon broad walk, cross that rich entrance-way, which to her was of the beauty of a jewel, and sweep in grace and luxury to possession and command—oh! how quickly would sadness flee; how, in an instant, would the heartache end. She gazed and gazed, wondering, delighting, longing, and all the while the siren voice of the unrestful was whispering in her ear.

"If we could have such a home as that," said Mrs. Hale sadly, "how delightful it would be."

"And yet they do say," said Carrie, "that no one is ever happy."

She had heard so much of the canting philosophy of the grapeless fox.

"I notice," said Mrs. Hale, "that they all try mighty hard, though, to take their misery in a mansion."

When she came to her own rooms, Carrie saw their comparative insignificance. She was not so dull but that she could perceive they were but three small rooms in a moderately well-furnished boarding-house. She was not contrasting it now with what she had had, but what she had so recently seen. The glow of the palatial doors was still in her eye, the roll of cushioned carriages still in her ears. What, after all, was Drouet? What was she? At her window, she thought it over, rocking to and fro, and gazing out across the lamp-lit park toward the lamp-lit houses on Warren and Ashland avenues. She was too wrought up to care to go down to eat, too pensive to do aught but rock and sing. Some old tunes crept to her lips, and, as she sang them, her heart sank. She longed and longed and longed. It was now for the old cottage room in Columbia City, now the mansion upon the Shore Drive, now the fine dress of some lady, now the elegance of some scene. She was sad beyond measure, and yet uncertain, wishing, fancying. Finally, it seemed as if all her state was one of loneliness and forsakenness, and she could scarce refrain from trembling at the lip. She hummed and hummed as the moments went by, sitting in the shadow by the window, and was therein as happy, though she did not perceive it, as she ever would be.

While Carrie was still in this frame of mind, the house-servant brought up the intelligence that Mr. Hurstwood was in the parlour asking to see Mr. and Mrs. Drouet.

"I guess he doesn't know that Charlie is out of town," thought Carrie.

She had seen comparatively little of the manager during the winter, but had been kept constantly in mind of him by one thing and another, principally by the strong impression he had made. She was quite disturbed for the moment as to her appearance, but soon satisfied herself by the aid of the mirror, and went below.

Hurstwood was in his best form, as usual. He hadn't heard that Drouet was out of town. He was but slightly affected by the intelligence, and devoted himself to the more general topics which would interest Carrie. It was surprising—the ease with which he conducted a conversation. He was like every man who has had the advantage of practice and knows he has sympathy. He knew that Carrie listened to him pleasurably, and, without the least effort, he fell into a train of observation which absorbed her fancy. He drew up his chair and modulated his voice to such a degree that what he said seemed wholly confidential. He confined himself almost exclusively to his observation of men and pleasures. He had been here and there, he had seen this and that. Somehow he made Carrie wish to see similar things, and all the while kept her aware of himself. She could not shut out the consciousness of his individuality and presence for a moment. He would raise his eyes slowly in smiling emphasis of something, and she was fixed by their magnetism. He would draw out, with the easiest grace, her approval. Once he touched her hand for emphasis and she only smiled. He seemed to radiate an atmosphere which suffused her being. He was never dull for a minute, and seemed to make her clever. At least, she brightened under his influence until all her best side was exhibited. She felt that she was more clever with him than with others. At least, he seemed to find so much in her to applaud. There was not the slightest touch of patronage. Drouet was full of it.

There had been something so personal, so subtle, in each meeting between them, both when Drouet was present and when he was absent, that Carrie could not speak of it without feeling a sense of difficulty. She was no talker. She could never arrange her thoughts in fluent order. It was always a matter of feeling with her, strong and deep. Each time there had been no sentence of importance which she could relate, and as for the glances and sensations, what woman would reveal them? Such things had never been between her and Drouet. As a matter of fact, they could never be. She had been dominated by distress and the enthusiastic forces of relief which Drouet represented at an opportune moment when she yielded to him. Now she was persuaded by secret current feelings which Drouet had never understood. Hurstwood's glance was as effective as the spoken words of a lover, and more. They called for no immediate decision, and could not be answered.

People in general attach too much importance to words. They are under the illusion that talking effects great results. As a matter of fact, words are, as a rule, the shallowest portion of all the argument. They but dimly represent the great surging feelings and desires which lie behind. When the distraction of the tongue is removed, the heart listens.

In this conversation she heard, instead of his words, the voices of the things which he represented. How suave was the counsel of his appearance! How feelingly did his superior state speak for itself! The growing desire he felt for her lay upon her spirit as a gentle hand. She did not need to tremble at all, because it was invisible; she did not need to worry over what other people would say—what she herself would say—because it had no tangibility. She was being pleaded with, persuaded, led into denying old rights and assuming new ones, and yet there were no words to prove it. Such conversation as was indulged in held the same relationship to the actual mental enactments of the twain that the low music of the orchestra does to the dramatic incident which it is used to cover.

"Have you ever seen the houses along the Lake Shore on the North Side?" asked Hurstwood.

"Why, I was just over there this afternoon—Mrs. Hale and I. Aren't they beautiful?"

"They're very fine," he answered.

"Oh, me," said Carrie, pensively. "I wish I could live in such a place."

"You're not happy," said Hurstwood, slowly, after a slight pause.

He had raised his eyes solemnly and was looking into her own. He assumed that he had struck a deep chord. Now was a slight chance to say a word in his own behalf. He leaned over quietly and continued his steady gaze. He felt the critical character of the period. She endeavoured to stir, but it was useless. The whole strength of a man's nature was working. He had good cause to urge him on. He looked and looked, and the longer the situation lasted the more difficult it became. The little shop-girl was getting into deep water. She was letting her few supports float away from her.

"Oh," she said at last, "you mustn't look at me like that."

"I can't help it," he answered.

She relaxed a little and let the situation endure, giving him strength.

"You are not satisfied with life, are you?"

"No," she answered, weakly.

He saw he was the master of the situation—he felt it. He reached over and touched her hand.

"You mustn't," she exclaimed, jumping up.

"I didn't intend to," he answered, easily.

She did not run away, as she might have done. She did not terminate the interview, but he drifted off into a pleasant field of thought with the readiest grace. Not long after he rose to go, and she felt that he was in power.

"You mustn't feel bad," he said, kindly; "things will straighten out in the course of time."

She made no answer, because she could think of nothing to say.

"We are good friends, aren't we?" he said, extending his hand.

"Yes," she answered.

"Not a word, then, until I see you again."

He retained a hold on her hand.

"I can't promise," she said, doubtfully.

"You must be more generous than that," he said, in such a simple way that she was touched.

"Let's not talk about it any more," she returned.

"All right," he said, brightening.

He went down the steps and into his cab. Carrie closed the door and ascended into her room. She undid her broad lace collar before the mirror and unfastened her pretty alligator belt which she had recently bought.

"I'm getting terrible," she said, honestly affected by a feeling of trouble and shame. "I don't seem to do anything right."

She unloosed her hair after a time, and let it hang in loose brown waves. Her mind was going over the events of the evening.

"I don't know," she murmured at last, "what I can do."

"Well," said Hurstwood as he rode away, "she likes me all right; that I know."

The aroused manager whistled merrily for a good four miles to his office an old melody that he had not recalled for fifteen years.

Chapter XIII

HIS CREDENTIALS ACCEPTED: A BABEL OF TONGUES

It was not quite two days after the scene between Carrie and Hurstwood in the Ogden Place parlour before he again put in his appearance. He had been thinking almost uninterruptedly of her. Her leniency had, in a way, inflamed his regard. He felt that he must succeed with her, and that speedily.

The reason for his interest, not to say fascination, was deeper than mere desire. It was a flowering out of feelings which had been withering in dry and almost barren soil for many years. It is probable that Carrie represented a better order of woman than had ever attracted him before. He had had no love affair since that which culminated in his marriage, and since then time and the world had taught him how raw and erroneous was his original judgment. Whenever he thought of it, he told himself that, if he had it to do over again, he would never marry such a woman. At the same time, his experience with women in general had lessened his respect for the sex. He maintained a cynical attitude, well grounded on numerous experiences. Such women as he had known were of nearly one type, selfish, ignorant, flashy. The wives of his friends were not inspiring to look upon.

His own wife had developed a cold, commonplace nature which to him was anything but pleasing. What he knew of that under-world where grovel the beast-men of society (and he knew a great deal) had hardened his nature. He looked upon most women with suspicion—a single eye to the utility of beauty and dress. He followed them with a keen, suggestive glance. At the same time, he was not so dull but that a good woman commanded his respect. Personally, he did not attempt to analyse the marvel of a saintly woman. He would take off his hat, and would silence the light-tongued and the vicious in her presence—much as the Irish keeper of a Bowery hall will humble himself before a Sister of Mercy, and pay toll to charity with a willing and reverent hand. But he would not think much upon the question of why he did so.

A man in his situation who comes, after a long round of worthless or hardening experiences, upon a young, unsophisticated, innocent soul, is apt either to hold aloof, out of a sense of his own remoteness, or to draw near and become fascinated and elated by his discovery. It is only by a roundabout process that such men ever do draw near such a girl. They have no method, no understanding of how to ingratiate themselves in youthful favour, save when they find virtue in the toils. If, unfortunately, the fly has got caught in the net, the spider can come forth and talk business upon its own terms. So when maidenhood has wandered into the moil of the city, when it is brought within the circle of the "rounder" and the roué, even though it be at the outermost rim, they can come forth and use their alluring arts.

Hurstwood had gone, at Drouet's invitation, to meet a new baggage of fine clothes and pretty features. He entered, expecting to indulge in an evening of lightsome frolic, and then lose track of the newcomer forever. Instead he found a woman whose youth and beauty attracted him. In the mild light of Carrie's eye was nothing of the calculation of the mistress. In the diffident manner was nothing of the art of the courtesan. He saw at once that a mistake had been made, that some difficult conditions had pushed this troubled creature into his presence, and his interest was enlisted. Here sympathy sprang to the rescue, but it was not unmixed with selfishness. He wanted to win Carrie because he thought her fate mingled with his was better than if it were united with Drouet's. He envied the drummer his conquest as he had never envied any man in all the course of his experience.

Carrie was certainly better than this man, as she was superior, mentally, to Drouet. She came fresh from the air of the village, the light of the country still in her eye. Here was neither guile nor rapacity. There were slight inherited traits of both in her, but they were rudimentary. She was too full of wonder and desire to be greedy. She still looked about her upon the great maze of the city without understanding. Hurstwood felt the bloom and the youth. He picked her as he would the fresh fruit of a tree. He felt as fresh in her presence as one who is taken out of the flash of summer to the first cool breath of spring.

Carrie, left alone since the scene in question, and having no one with whom to counsel, had at first wandered from one strange mental conclusion to another, until at last, tired out, she gave it up. She owed something to Drouet, she thought. It did not seem more than yesterday that he had aided her when she was worried and distressed. She had the kindliest feelings for him in every way. She gave him credit for his good looks, his generous feelings, and even, in fact, failed to recollect his egotism when he was absent; but she could not feel any binding influence keeping her for him as against all others. In fact, such a thought had never had any grounding, even in Drouet's desires.

The truth is, that this goodly drummer carried the doom of all enduring relationships in his own lightsome manner and unstable fancy. He went merrily on, assured that he was alluring all, that affection followed tenderly in his wake, that things would endure unchangingly for his pleasure. When he missed some old face, or found some door finally shut to him, it did not grieve him deeply. He was too young, too successful. He would remain thus young in spirit until he was dead.

As for Hurstwood, he was alive with thoughts and feelings concerning Carrie. He had no definite plans regarding her, but he was determined to make her confess an affection for him. He thought he saw in her drooping eye, her unstable glance, her wavering manner, the symptoms of a budding passion. He wanted to stand near her and make her lay her hand in his—he wanted to find out what her next step would be—what the next sign of feeling for him would be. Such anxiety and enthusiasm had not affected him for years. He was a youth again in feeling—a cavalier in action.

In his position opportunity for taking his evenings out was excellent. He was a most faithful worker in general, and a man who commanded the confidence of his employers in so far as the distribution of his time was concerned. He could take such hours off as he chose, for it was well known that he fulfilled his managerial duties successfully, whatever time he might take. His grace, tact, and ornate appearance gave the place an air which was most essential, while at the same time his long experience made him a most excellent judge of its stock necessities. Bartenders and assistants might come and go, singly or in groups, but, so long as he was present, the host of old-time customers would barely notice the change. He gave the place the atmosphere to which they were used. Consequently, he arranged his hours very much to suit himself, taking now an afternoon, now an evening, but invariably returning between eleven and twelve to witness the last hour or two of the day's business and look after the closing details.

"You see that things are safe and all the employees are out when you go home, George," Moy had once remarked to him, and he never once, in all the period of his long service, neglected to do this. Neither of the owners had for years been in the resort after five in the afternoon, and yet their manager as faithfully fulfilled this request as if they had been there regularly to observe.

On this Friday afternoon, scarcely two days after his previous visit, he made up his mind to see Carrie. He could not stay away longer.

"Evans," he said, addressing the head barkeeper, "if any one calls, I will be back between four and five."

He hurried to Madison Street and boarded a horse-car, which carried him to Ogden Place in half an hour.[1]

Carrie had thought of going for a walk, and had put on a light grey woollen dress with a jaunty double-breasted jacket. She had out her hat and gloves, and was fastening a white lace tie about her throat when the housemaid brought up the information that Mr. Hurstwood wished to see her.

She started slightly at the announcement, but told the girl to say that she would come down in a moment, and proceeded to hasten her dressing.

Carrie could not have told herself at this moment whether she was glad or sorry that the impressive manager was awaiting her presence. She was slightly flurried and tingling in the cheeks, but it was more nervousness than either fear or favour. She did not try to conjecture what the drift of the conversation would be. She only felt that she must be careful, and that Hurstwood had an indefinable fascination for her. Then she gave her tie its last touch with her fingers and went below.

The deep-feeling manager was himself a little strained in the nerves by the thorough consciousness of his mission. He felt that he must make a strong play on this occasion, but now that the hour was come, and he heard Carrie's feet upon the stair, his nerve failed him. He sank a little in determination, for he was not so sure, after all, what her opinion might be.

When she entered the room, however, her appearance gave him courage. She looked simple and charming enough to strengthen the daring of any lover. Her apparent nervousness dispelled his own.

"How are you?" he said, easily. "I could not resist the temptation to come out this afternoon, it was so pleasant."

1. Hurstwood should have been able to take a cable rather than a horse car on West Madison in 1889. Charles T. Yerkes (the prototype of Dreiser's Frank A. Cowperwood in *The Titan* [1914]) had introduced the cable car on the West Side lines in the mid-1880s.

"Yes," said Carrie, halting before him, "I was just preparing to go for a walk myself."

"Oh, were you?" he said. "Supposing, then, you get your hat and we both go?"

They crossed the park and went west along Washington Boulevard, beautiful with its broad macadamised road, and large frame houses set back from the sidewalks. It was a street where many of the more prosperous residents of the West Side lived, and Hurstwood could not help feeling nervous over the publicity of it. They had gone but a few blocks when a livery stable sign in one of the side streets solved the difficulty for him. He would take her to drive along the new Boulevard.

The Boulevard at that time was little more than a country road. The part he intended showing her was much farther out on this same West Side, where there was scarcely a house. It connected Douglas Park with Washington or South Park, and was nothing more than a neatly *made* road, running due south for some five miles over an open, grassy prairie, and then due east over the same kind of prairie for the same distance.[2] There was not a house to be encountered anywhere along the larger part of the route, and any conversation would be pleasantly free of interruption.

At the stable he picked a gentle horse, and they were soon out of range of either public observation or hearing.

"Can you drive?" he said, after a time.

"I never tried," said Carrie.

He put the reins in her hand, and folded his arms.

"You see there's nothing to it much," he said, smilingly.

"Not when you have a gentle horse," said Carrie.

"You can handle a horse as well as any one, after a little practice," he added, encouragingly.

He had been looking for some time for a break in the conversation when he could give it a serious turn. Once or twice he had held his peace, hoping that in silence her thoughts would take the colour of his own, but she had lightly continued the subject. Presently, however, his silence controlled the situation. The drift of his thoughts began to tell. He gazed fixedly at nothing in particular, as if he were thinking of something which concerned her not at all. His thoughts, however, spoke for themselves. She was very much aware that a climax was pending.

"Do you know," he said, "I have spent the happiest evenings in years since I have known you?"

"Have you?" she said, with assumed airiness, but still excited by the conviction which the tone of his voice carried.

2. The various portions of Washington Boulevard have since been renamed. In the late 1880s the boulevard was over a hundred feet wide.

"I was going to tell you the other evening," he added, "but some-how the opportunity slipped away."

Carrie was listening without attempting to reply. She could think of nothing worth while to say. Despite all the ideas concerning right which had troubled her vaguely since she had last seen him, she was now influenced again strongly in his favour.

"I came out here to-day," he went on, solemnly, "to tell you just how I feel—to see if you wouldn't listen to me."

Hurstwood was something of a romanticist after his kind. He was capable of strong feelings—often poetic ones—and under a stress of desire, such as the present, he waxed eloquent. That is, his feelings and his voice were coloured with that seeming repression and pathos which is the essence of eloquence.

"You know," he said, putting his hand on her arm, and keeping a strange silence while he formulated words, "that I love you?"

Carrie did not stir at the words. She was bound up completely in the man's atmosphere. He would have church-like silence in order to express his feelings, and she kept it. She did not move her eyes from the flat, open scene before her. Hurstwood waited for a few moments, and then repeated the words.

"You must not say that," she said, weakly.

Her words were not convincing at all. They were the result of a feeble thought that something ought to be said. He paid no attention to them whatever.

"Carrie," he said, using her first name with sympathetic familiarity, "I want you to love me. You don't know how much I need some one to waste a little affection on me. I am practically alone. There is nothing in my life that is pleasant or delightful. It's all work and worry with people who are nothing to me."

As he said this, Hurstwood really imagined that his state was pit-iful. He had the ability to get off at a distance and view himself objectively—of seeing what he wanted to see in the things which made up his existence. Now, as he spoke, his voice trembled with that peculiar vibration which is the result of tensity. It went ringing home to his companion's heart.

"Why, I should think," she said, turning upon him large eyes which were full of sympathy and feeling, "that you would be very happy. You know so much of the world."

"That is it," he said, his voice dropping to a soft minor, "I know too much of the world."

It was an important thing to her to hear one so well-positioned and powerful speaking in this manner. She could not help feeling the strangeness of her situation. How was it that, in so little a while, the narrow life of the country had fallen from her as a garment, and the city, with all its mystery, taken its place? Here was this greatest mystery, the man of money and affairs sitting beside her, appealing to her. Behold, he had ease and comfort, his strength was great, his position high, his clothing rich, and yet he was appealing to her. She could formulate no thought which would be just and right. She troubled herself no more upon the matter. She only basked in the warmth of his feeling, which was as a grateful blaze to one who is cold. Hurstwood glowed with his own intensity, and the heat of his passion was already melting the wax of his companion's scruples.

"You think," he said, "I am happy; that I ought not to complain? If you were to meet all day with people who care absolutely nothing about you, if you went day after day to a place where there was nothing but show and indifference, if there was not one person in all those you knew to whom you could appeal for sympathy or talk to with pleasure, perhaps you would be unhappy too."

He was striking a chord now which found sympathetic response in her own situation. She knew what it was to meet with people who were indifferent, to walk alone amid so many who cared absolutely nothing about you. Had not she? Was not she at this very moment quite alone? Who was there among all whom she knew to whom she could appeal for sympathy? Not one. She was left to herself to brood and wonder.

"I could be content," went on Hurstwood, "if I had you to love me. If I had you to go to; you for a companion. As it is, I simply move about from place to place without any satisfaction. Time hangs heavily on my hands. Before you came I did nothing but idle and drift into anything that offered itself. Since you came—well, I've had you to think about."

The old illusion that here was some one who needed her aid began to grow in Carrie's mind. She truly pitied this sad, lonely figure. To think that all his fine state should be so barren for want of her; that he needed to make such an appeal when she herself was lonely and without anchor. Surely, this was too bad.

"I am not very bad," he said, apologetically, as if he owed it to her to explain on this score. "You think, probably, that I roam around, and get into all sorts of evil? I have been rather reckless, but I could easily come out of that. I need you to draw me back, if my life ever amounts to anything."

Carrie looked at him with the tenderness which virtue ever feels in its hope of reclaiming vice. How could such a man need reclaiming? His errors, what were they, that she could correct? Small they must be, where all was so fine. At worst, they were gilded affairs, and with what leniency are gilded errors viewed.

He put himself in such a lonely light that she was deeply moved.

"Is it that way?" she mused.

He slipped his arm about her waist, and she could not find the heart to draw away. With his free hand he seized upon her fingers. A breath of soft spring wind went bounding over the road, rolling some brown twigs of the previous autumn before it. The horse paced leisurely on, unguided.

"Tell me," he said, softly, "that you love me."

Her eyes fell consciously.

"Own to it, dear," he said, feelingly; "you do, don't you?"

She made no answer, but he felt his victory.

"Tell me," he said, richly, drawing her so close that their lips were near together. He pressed her hand warmly, and then released it to touch her cheek.

"You do?" he said, pressing his lips to her own.

For answer, her lips replied.

"Now," he said, joyously, his fine eyes ablaze, "you're my own girl, aren't you?"

By way of further conclusion, her head lay softly upon his shoulder.

Chapter XIV

WITH EYES AND NOT SEEING: ONE INFLUENCE WANES

Carrie in her rooms that evening was in a fine glow, physically and mentally. She was deeply rejoicing in her affection for Hurstwood and his love, and looked forward with fine fancy to their next meeting Sunday night. They had agreed, without any feeling of enforced secrecy, that she should come down town and meet him, though, after all, the need of it was the cause.

Mrs. Hale, from her upper window, saw her come in.

"Um," she thought to herself, "she goes riding with another man when her husband is out of the city. He had better keep an eye on her."

The truth is that Mrs. Hale was not the only one who had a thought on this score. The house-maid who had welcomed Hurstwood had her opinion also. She had no particular regard for Carrie, whom she took to be cold and disagreeable. At the same time, she had a fancy for the merry and easy-mannered Drouet, who threw her a pleasant remark now and then, and in other ways extended her the evidence of that regard which he had for all members of the sex. Hurstwood was more reserved and critical in his manner. He did not appeal to this bodiced functionary in the same pleasant way. She wondered that he came so frequently, that Mrs. Drouet should go out with him this afternoon when Mr. Drouet was absent. She gave vent to her opinions in the kitchen where the cook was. As a result, a hum of gossip was set going which moved about the house in that secret manner common to gossip.

Carrie, now that she had yielded sufficiently to Hurstwood to confess her affection, no longer troubled about her attitude towards him. Temporarily she gave little thought to Drouet, thinking only of the dignity and grace of her lover and of his consuming affection for her. On the first evening, she did little but go over the details of the afternoon. It was the first time her sympathies had ever been thoroughly aroused, and they threw a new light on her character. She had some power of initiative, latent before, which now began to exert itself. She looked more practically upon her state and began to see glimmerings of a way out. Hurstwood seemed a drag in the direction of honour. Her feelings were exceedingly creditable, in that they constructed out of these recent developments something which conquered freedom from dishonour. She had no idea what Hurstwood's next word would be. She only took his affection to be a fine thing, and appended better, more generous results accordingly.

As yet, Hurstwood had only a thought of pleasure without responsibility. He did not feel that he was doing anything to complicate his life. His position was secure, his home-life, if not satisfactory, was at least undisturbed, his personal liberty rather untrammelled. Carrie's love represented only so much added pleasure. He would enjoy this new gift over and above his ordinary allowance of pleasure. He would be happy with her and his own affairs would go on as they had, undisturbed.

On Sunday evening Carrie dined with him at a place he had selected in East Adams Street, and thereafter they took a cab to what was then a pleasant evening resort out on Cottage Grove Avenue near 39th Street. In the process of his declaration he soon realised that Carrie took his love upon a higher basis than he had anticipated. She kept him at a distance in a rather earnest way, and submitted only to those tender tokens of affection which better become the inexperienced lover. Hurstwood saw that she was not to be possessed for the asking, and deferred pressing his suit too warmly.

Since he feigned to believe in her married state he found that he had to carry out the part. His triumph, he saw, was still at a little distance. How far he could not guess.

They were returning to Ogden Place in the cab, when he asked:

"When will I see you again?"

"I don't know," she answered, wondering herself.

"Why not come down to The Fair," he suggested, "next Tuesday?" She shook her head.

"Not so soon," she answered.

"I'll tell you what I'll do," he added. "I'll write you, care of this West Side Post-office. Could you call next Tuesday?"

Carrie assented.

The cab stopped one door out of the way according to his call.

"Good-night," he whispered, as the cab rolled away.

Unfortunately for the smooth progression of this affair, Drouet returned. Hurstwood was sitting in his imposing little office the next afternoon when he saw Drouet enter.

"Why, hello, Charles," he called affably; "back again?"

"Yes," smiled Drouet, approaching and looking in at the door. Hurstwood arose.

"Well," he said, looking the drummer over, "rosy as ever, eh?"

They began talking of the people they knew and things that had happened.

"Been home yet?" finally asked Hurstwood.

"No, I am going, though," said Drouet.

"I remembered the little girl out there," said Hurstwood, "and called once. Thought you wouldn't want her left quite alone."

"Right you are," agreed Drouet. "How is she?"

"Very well," said Hurstwood. "Rather anxious about you, though. You'd better go out now and cheer her up."

"I will," said Drouet, smilingly.

"Like to have you both come down and go to the show with me Wednesday," concluded Hurstwood at parting.

"Thanks, old man," said his friend, "I'll see what the girl says and let you know."

They separated in the most cordial manner.

"There's a nice fellow," Drouet thought to himself as he turned the corner towards Madison.

"Drouet is a good fellow," Hurstwood thought to himself as he went back into his office, "but he's no man for Carrie."

The thought of the latter turned his mind into a most pleasant vein, and he wondered how he would get ahead of the drummer.

When Drouet entered Carrie's presence, he caught her in his arms as usual, but she responded to his kiss with a tremour of opposition.

"Well," he said, "I had a great trip."

"Did you? How did you come out with that La Crosse man you were telling me about?"

"Oh, fine; sold him a complete line. There was another fellow there, representing Burnstein, a regular hook-nosed sheeny, but he wasn't in it. I made him look like nothing at all."

As he undid his collar and unfastened his studs, preparatory to washing his face and changing his clothes, he dilated upon his trip. Carrie could not help listening with amusement to his animated descriptions.

"I tell you," he said, "I surprised the people at the office. I've sold more goods this last quarter than any other man of our house on the road. I sold three thousand dollars' worth in La Crosse."

He plunged his face in a basin of water, and puffed and blew as he rubbed his neck and ears with his hands, while Carrie gazed upon him with mingled thoughts of recollection and present judgment. He was still wiping his face, when he continued:

"I'm going to strike for a raise in June. They can afford to pay it, as much business as I turn in. I'll get it too, don't you forget."

"I hope you do," said Carrie.

"And then if that little real estate deal I've got on goes through, we'll get married," he said with a great show of earnestness, the while he took his place before the mirror and began brushing his hair.

"I don't believe you ever intend to marry me, Charlie," Carrie said ruefully. The recent protestations of Hurstwood had given her courage to say this.

"Oh, yes I do—course I do—what put that into your head?"

He had stopped his trifling before the mirror now and crossed over to her. For the first time Carrie felt as if she must move away from him.

"But you've been saying that so long," she said, looking with her pretty face upturned into his.

"Well, and I mean it too, but it takes money to live as I want to. Now, when I get this increase, I can come pretty near fixing things all right, and I'll do it. Now, don't you worry, girlie."

He patted her reassuringly upon the shoulder, but Carrie felt how really futile had been her hopes. She could clearly see that this easy-going soul intended no move in her behalf. He was simply letting things drift because he preferred the free round of his present state to any legal trammellings.

In contrast, Hurstwood appeared strong and sincere. He had no easy manner of putting her off. He sympathised with her and showed her what her true value was. He needed her, while Drouet did not care.

"Oh, no," she said remorsefully, her tone reflecting some of her own success and more of her helplessness, "you never will."

"Well, you wait a little while and see," he concluded. "I'll marry you all right."

Carrie looked at him and felt justified. She was looking for something which would calm her conscience, and here it was, a light, airy disregard of her claims upon his justice. He had faithfully promised to marry her, and this was the way he fulfilled his promise.

"Say," he said, after he had, as he thought, pleasantly disposed of the marriage question, "I saw Hurstwood to-day, and he wants us to go to the theatre with him."

Carrie started at the name, but recovered quickly enough to avoid notice.

"When?" she asked, with assumed indifference.

"Wednesday. We'll go, won't we?"

"If you think so," she answered, her manner being so enforcedly reserved as to almost excite suspicion. Drouet noticed something, but he thought it was due to her feelings concerning their talk about marriage.

"He called once, he said."

"Yes," said Carrie, "he was out here Sunday evening."

"Was he?" said Drouet. "I thought from what he said that he had called a week or so ago."

"So he did," answered Carrie, who was wholly unaware of what conversation her lovers might have held. She was all at sea mentally, and fearful of some entanglement which might ensue from what she would answer.

"Oh, then he called twice?" said Drouet, the first shade of misunderstanding showing in his face.

"Yes," said Carrie innocently, feeling now that Hurstwood must have mentioned but one call.

Drouet imagined that he must have misunderstood his friend. He did not attach particular importance to the information, after all.

"What did he have to say?" he queried, with slightly increased curiosity.

"He said he came because he thought I might be lonely. You hadn't been in there so long he wondered what had become of you."

"George is a fine fellow," said Drouet, rather gratified by his conception of the manager's interest. "Come on and we'll go out to dinner."

When Hurstwood saw that Drouet was back he wrote at once to Carrie, saying:

"I told him I called on you, dearest, when he was away. I did not say how often, but he probably thought once. Let me know of anything you may have said. Answer by special messenger when you get this, and, darling, I must see you. Let me know if you can't meet me at Jackson and Throop Streets Wednesday afternoon at two o'clock.[1] I want to speak with you before we meet at the theatre."

Carrie received this Tuesday morning when she called at the West Side branch of the post-office, and answered at once.

"I said you called twice," she wrote. "He didn't seem to mind. I will try and be at Throop Street if nothing interferes. I seem to be getting very bad. It's wrong to act as I do, I know."

Hurstwood, when he met her as agreed, reassured her on this score.

"You mustn't worry, sweetheart," he said. "Just as soon as he goes on the road again we will arrange something. We'll fix it so that you won't have to deceive any one."

1. This meeting place would require a short walk by Carrie from Ogden Place and a car ride by Hurstwood from Fitzgerald and Moy's.

Carrie imagined that he would marry her at once, though he had not directly said so, and her spirits rose. She proposed to make the best of the situation until Drouet left again.

"Don't show any more interest in me than you ever have," Hurstwood counselled concerning the evening at the theatre.

"You mustn't look at me steadily then," she answered, mindful of the power of his eyes.

"I won't," he said, squeezing her hand at parting and giving the glance she had just cautioned against.

"There," she said playfully, pointing a finger at him.

"The show hasn't begun yet," he returned.

He watched her walk from him with tender solicitation. Such youth and prettiness reacted upon him more subtly than wine.

At the theatre things passed as they had in Hurstwood's favour. If he had been pleasing to Carrie before, how much more so was he now. His grace was more permeating because it found a readier medium. Carrie watched his every movement with pleasure. She almost forgot poor Drouet, who babbled on as if he were the host.

Hurstwood was too clever to give the slightest indication of a change. He paid, if anything, more attention to his old friend than usual, and yet in no way held him up to that subtle ridicule which a lover in favour may so secretly practise before the mistress of his heart. If anything, he felt the injustice of the game as it stood, and was not cheap enough to add to it the slightest mental taunt.

Only the play produced an ironical situation, and this was due to Drouet alone.

The scene was one in "The Covenant," in which the wife listened to the seductive voice of a lover in the absence of her husband.[2]

"Served him right," said Drouet afterward, even in view of her keen expiation of her error. "I haven't any pity for a man who would be such a chump as that."

"Well, you never can tell," returned Hurstwood gently. "He probably thought he was right."

"Well, a man ought to be more attentive than that to his wife if he wants to keep her."

They had come out of the lobby and made their way through the showy crush about the entrance way.

"Say, mister," said a voice at Hurstwood's side, "would you mind giving me the price of a bed?"

Hurstwood was interestedly remarking to Carrie.

"Honest to God, mister, I'm without a place to sleep."

The plea was that of a gaunt-faced man of about thirty, who looked the picture of privation and wretchedness. Drouet was the first to

2. One of the few plays named in *Sister Carrie* for which there is no source.

see. He handed over a dime with an upwelling feeling of pity in his heart. Hurstwood scarcely noticed the incident. Carrie quickly forgot.

Chapter XV

THE IRK OF THE OLD TIES: THE MAGIC OF YOUTH

The complete ignoring by Hurstwood of his own home came with the growth of his affection for Carrie. His actions, in all that related to his family, were of the most perfunctory kind. He sat at breakfast with his wife and children, absorbed in his own fancies, which reached far without the realm of their interests. He read his paper, which was heightened in interest by the shallowness of the themes discussed by his son and daughter. Between himself and his wife ran a river of indifference.

Now that Carrie had come, he was in a fair way to be blissful again. There was delight in going down town evenings. When he walked forth in the short days, the street lamps had a merry twinkle. He began to experience the almost forgotten feeling which hastens the lover's feet. When he looked at his fine clothes, he saw them with her eyes—and her eyes were young.

When in the flush of such feelings he heard his wife's voice, when the insistent demands of matrimony recalled him from dreams to a stale practice, how it grated. He then knew that this was a chain which bound his feet.

"George," said Mrs. Hurstwood, in that tone of voice which had long since come to be associated in his mind with demands, "we want you to get us a season ticket to the races."

"Do you want to go to all of them?" he said with a rising inflection.

"Yes," she answered.

The races in question were soon to open at Washington Park, on the South Side, and were considered quite society affairs among those who did not affect religious rectitude and conservatism. Mrs. Hurstwood had never asked for a whole season ticket before, but this year certain considerations decided her to get a box. For one thing, one of her neighbours, a certain Mr. and Mrs. Ramsey, who were possessors of money, made out of the coal business, had done so. In the next place, her favourite physician, Dr. Beale, a gentleman inclined to horses and betting, had talked with her concerning his intention to enter a two-year-old in the Derby. In the third place, she wished to exhibit Jessica, who was gaining in maturity and beauty, and whom she hoped to marry to a man of means. Her own desire to be about in such things and parade among her acquaintances and the common throng was as much an incentive as anything.

Hurstwood thought over the proposition a few moments without answering. They were in the sitting-room on the second floor, waiting for supper. It was the evening of his engagement with Carrie and Drouet to see "The Covenant," which had brought him home to make some alterations in his dress.

"You're sure separate tickets wouldn't do as well?" he asked, hesitating to say anything more rugged.

"No," she replied impatiently.

"Well," he said, taking offence at her manner, "you needn't get mad about it. I'm just asking you."

"I'm not mad," she snapped. "I'm merely asking you for a season ticket."

"And I'm telling you," he returned, fixing a clear, steady eye on her, "that it's no easy thing to get. I'm not sure whether the manager will give it to me."

He had been thinking all the time of his "pull" with the race-track magnates.

"We can buy it then," she exclaimed sharply.

"You talk easy," he said. "A season family ticket costs one hundred and fifty dollars."

"I'll not argue with you," she replied with determination. "I want the ticket and that's all there is to it."

She had risen, and now walked angrily out of the room.

"Well, you get it then," he said grimly, though in a modified tone of voice.

As usual, the table was one short that evening.

The next morning he had cooled down considerably, and later the ticket was duly secured, though it did not heal matters. He did not mind giving his family a fair share of all that he earned, but he did not like to be forced to provide against his will.

"Did you know, mother," said Jessica another day, "the Spencers are getting ready to go away?"

"No. Where. I wonder?"

"Europe," said Jessica. "I met Georgine yesterday and she told me. She just put on more airs about it."

"Did she say when?"

"Monday, I think. They'll get a notice in the papers again—they always do."

"Never mind," said Mrs. Hurstwood consolingly, "we'll go one of these days."

Hurstwood moved his eyes over the paper slowly, but said nothing.

" 'We sail for Liverpool from New York,' " Jessica exclaimed, mocking her acquaintance. " 'Expect to spend most of the "summah" in France,'—vain thing. As if it was anything to go to Europe."

"It must be if you envy her so much," put in Hurstwood.

It grated upon him to see the feeling his daughter displayed.

"Don't worry over them, my dear," said Mrs. Hurstwood.

"Did George get off?" asked Jessica of her mother another day, thus revealing something that Hurstwood had heard nothing about.

"Where has he gone?" he asked, looking up. He had never before been kept in ignorance concerning departures.

"He was going to Wheaton,"[1] said Jessica, not noticing the slight put upon her father.

"What's out there?" he asked, secretly irritated and chagrined to think that he should be made to pump for information in this manner.

"A tennis match," said Jessica.

"He didn't say anything to me," Hurstwood concluded, finding it difficult to refrain from a bitter tone.

"I guess he must have forgotten," exclaimed his wife blandly.

In the past he had always commanded a certain amount of respect, which was a compound of appreciation and awe. The familiarity which in part still existed between himself and his daughter he had courted. As it was, it did not go beyond the light assumption of words. The *tone* was always modest. Whatever had been, however, had lacked affection, and now he saw that he was losing track of their doings. His knowledge was no longer intimate. He sometimes saw them at table, and sometimes did not. He heard of their doings occasionally, more often not. Some days he found that he was all at sea as to what they were talking about—things they had arranged to do or that they had done in his absence. More affecting was the feeling that there were little things going on of which he no longer heard. Jessica was beginning to feel that her affairs were her own. George, Jr., flourished about as if he were a man entirely and must needs have private matters. All this Hurstwood could see, and it left a trace of feeling, for he was used to being considered—in his official position, at least —and felt that his importance should not begin to wane here. To darken it all, he saw the same indifference and independence growing in his wife, while he looked on and paid the bills.

He consoled himself with the thought, however, that, after all, he was not without affection. Things might go as they would at his house, but he had Carrie outside of it. With his mind's eye he looked into her comfortable room in Ogden Place, where he had spent several such delightful evenings, and thought how charming it would be when Drouet was disposed of entirely and she was waiting evenings in cosey little quarters for him. That no cause would come up whereby Drouet would be led to inform Carrie concerning his married state, he felt hopeful. Things were going so smoothly that he

1. A town some ten miles west of downtown Chicago.

believed they would not change. Shortly now he would persuade Carrie and all would be satisfactory.

The day after their theatre visit he began writing her regularly—a letter every morning, and begging her to do as much for him. He was not literary by any means, but experience of the world and his growing affection gave him somewhat of a style. This he exercised at his office desk with perfect deliberation. He purchased a box of delicately coloured and scented writing paper in monogram, which he kept locked in one of the drawers. His friends now wondered at the cleric and very official-looking nature of his position. The five bartenders viewed with respect the duties which could call a man to do so much desk-work and penmanship.

Hurstwood surprised himself with his fluency. By the natural law which governs all effort, what he wrote reacted upon him. He began to feel those subtleties which he could find words to express. With every expression came increased conception. Those inmost breathings which there found words took hold upon him. He thought Carrie worthy of all the affection he could there express.

Carrie was indeed worth loving if ever youth and grace are to command that token of acknowledgment from life in their bloom. Experience had not yet taken away that freshness of the spirit which is the charm of the body. Her soft eyes contained in their liquid lustre no suggestion of the knowledge of disappointment. She had been troubled in a way by doubt and longing, but these had made no deeper impression than could be traced in a certain open wistfulness of glance and speech. The mouth had the expression at times, in talking and in repose, of one who might be upon the verge of tears. It was not that grief was thus ever present. The pronunciation of certain syllables gave to her lips this peculiarity of formation—a formation as suggestive and moving as pathos itself.

There was nothing bold in her manner. Life had not taught her domination—superciliousness of grace, which is the lordly power of some women. Her longing for consideration was not sufficiently powerful to move her to demand it. Even now she lacked self-assurance, but there was that in what she had already experienced which left her a little less than timid. She wanted pleasure, she wanted position, and yet she was confused as to what these things might be. Every hour the kaleidoscope of human affairs threw a new lustre upon something, and therewith it became for her the desired—the all. Another shift of the box, and some other had become the beautiful, the perfect.

On her spiritual side, also, she was rich in feeling, as such a nature well might be. Sorrow in her was aroused by many a spectacle—an uncritical upwelling of grief for the weak and the helpless. She was constantly pained by the sight of the white-faced, ragged men who slopped desperately by her in a sort of wretched mental stupor. The poorly clad girls who went blowing by her window evenings, hurrying home from some of the shops of the West Side, she pitied from the depths of her heart. She would stand and bite her lips as they passed, shaking her little head and wondering. They had so little, she thought. It was so sad to be ragged and poor. The hang of faded clothes pained her eyes.

"And they have to work so hard!" was her only comment.

On the street sometimes she would see men working—Irishmen with picks, coal-heavers with great loads to shovel, Americans busy about some work which was a mere matter of strength—and they touched her fancy. Toil, now that she was free of it, seemed even a more desolate thing than when she was part of it. She saw it through a mist of fancy—a pale, sombre half-light, which was the essence of poetic feeling. Her old father, in his flour-dusted miller's suit, sometimes returned to her in memory, revived by a face in a window. A shoemaker pegging at his last, a blastman seen through a narrow window in some basement where iron was being melted, a bench-worker seen high aloft in some window, his coat off, his sleeves rolled up; these took her back in fancy to the details of the mill. She felt, though she seldom expressed them, sad thoughts upon this score. Her sympathies were ever with that under-world of toil from which she had so recently sprung, and which she best understood.

Though Hurstwood did not know it, he was dealing with one whose feelings were as tender and as delicate as this. He did not know, but it was this in her, after all, which attracted him. He never attempted to analyse the nature of his affection. It was sufficient that there was tenderness in her eye, weakness in her manner, good-nature and hope in her thoughts. He drew near this lily, which had sucked its waxen beauty and perfume from below a depth of waters which he had never penetrated, and out of ooze and mould which he could not understand. He drew near because it was waxen and fresh. It lightened his feelings for him. It made the morning worth while.

In a material way, she was considerably improved. Her awkwardness had all but passed, leaving, if anything, a quaint residue which was as pleasing as perfect grace. Her little shoes now fitted her smartly and had high heels. She had learned much about laces and those little neck-pieces which add so much to a woman's appearance. Her form had filled out until it was admirably plump and well-rounded.

Hurstwood wrote her one morning, asking her to meet him in Jefferson Park, Monroe Street.[2] He did not consider it policy to call any more, even when Drouet was at home.

2. Jefferson Park, at Monroe and Loomis, was a short distance from Ogden Place. It is now called Skinner Park.

The next afternoon he was in the pretty little park by one, and had found a rustic bench beneath the green leaves of a lilac bush which bordered one of the paths. It was at that season of the year when the fulness of spring had not yet worn quite away. At a little pond near by some cleanly dressed children were sailing white canvas boats. In the shade of a green pagoda a bebuttoned officer of the law was resting, his arms folded, his club at rest in his belt. An old gardener was upon the lawn, with a pair of pruning shears, looking after some bushes. High overhead was the clear blue sky of the new summer, and in the thickness of the shiny green leaves of the trees hopped and twittered the busy sparrows.

Hurstwood had come out of his own home that morning feeling much of the same old annoyance. At his store he had idled, there being no need to write. He had come away to this place with the lightness of heart which characterises those who put weariness behind. Now, in the shade of this cool, green bush, he looked about him with the fancy of the lover. He heard the carts go lumbering by upon the neighbouring streets, but they were far off, and only buzzed upon his ear. The hum of the surrounding city was faint, the clang of an occasional bell was as music. He looked and dreamed a new dream of pleasure which concerned his present fixed condition not at all. He got back in fancy to the old Hurstwood, who was neither married nor fixed in a solid position for life. He remembered the light spirit in which he once looked after the girls—how he had danced, escorted them home, hung over their gates. He almost wished he was back there again—here in this pleasant scene he felt as if he were wholly free.

At two Carrie came tripping along the walk toward him, rosy and clean. She had just recently donned a sailor hat for the season with a band of pretty white-dotted blue silk. Her skirt was of a rich blue material, and her shirt waist matched it, with a thin stripe of blue upon a snow-white ground—stripes that were as fine as hairs. Her brown shoes peeped occasionally from beneath her skirt. She carried her gloves in her hand.

Hurstwood looked up at her with delight.

"You came, dearest," he said eagerly, standing to meet her and taking her hand.

"Of course," she said, smiling; "did you think I wouldn't?"

"I didn't know," he replied.

He looked at her forehead, which was moist from her brisk walk. Then he took out one of his own soft, scented silk handkerchiefs and touched her face here and there.

"Now," he said affectionately, "you're all right."

They were happy in being near one another—in looking into each other's eyes. Finally, when the long flush of delight had subsided, he said:

"When is Charlie going away again?"

"I don't know," she answered. "He says he has some things to do for the house here now."

Hurstwood grew serious, and he lapsed into quiet thought. He looked up after a time to say:

"Come away and leave him."

He turned his eyes to the boys with the boats, as if the request were of little importance.

"Where would we go?" she asked in much the same manner, rolling her gloves, and looking into a neighbouring tree.

"Where do you want to go?" he enquired.

There was something in the tone in which he said this which made her feel as if she must record her feelings against any local habitation.

"We can't stay in Chicago," she replied.

He had no thought that this was in her mind—that any removal would be suggested.

"Why not?" he asked softly.

"Oh, because," she said, "I wouldn't want to."

He listened to this with but dull perception of what it meant. It had no serious ring to it. The question was not up for immediate decision.

"I would have to give up my position," he said.

The tone he used made it seem as if the matter deserved only slight consideration. Carrie thought a little, the while enjoying the pretty scene.

"I wouldn't like to live in Chicago and him here," she said, thinking of Drouet.

"It's a big town, dearest," Hurstwood answered. "It would be as good as moving to another part of the country to move to the South Side."

He had fixed upon that region as an objective point.

"Anyhow," said Carrie, "I shouldn't want to get married as long as he is here. I wouldn't want to run away."

The suggestion of marriage struck Hurstwood forcibly. He saw clearly that this was her idea—he felt that it was not to be gotten over easily. Bigamy lightened the horizon of his shadowy thoughts for a moment. He wondered for the life of him how it would all come out. He could not see that he was making any progress save in her regard. When he looked at her now, he thought her beautiful. What a thing it was to have her love him, even if it be entangling! She increased in value in his eyes because of her objection. She was something to struggle for, and that was everything. How different from the women who yielded willingly! He swept the thought of them from his mind.

"And you don't know when he'll go away?" asked Hurstwood, quietly.

She shook her head.

He sighed.

"You're a determined little miss, aren't you?" he said, after a few moments, looking up into her eyes.

She felt a wave of feeling sweep over her at this. It was pride at what seemed his admiration—affection for the man who could feel this concerning her.

"No," she said coyly, "but what can I do?"

Again he folded his hands and looked away over the lawn into the street.

"I wish," he said pathetically, "you would come to me. I don't like to be away from you this way. What good is there in waiting? You're not any happier, are you?"

"Happier!" she exclaimed softly, "you know better than that."

"Here we are then," he went on in the same tone, "wasting our days. If you are not happy, do you think I am? I sit and write to you the biggest part of the time. I'll tell you what, Carrie," he exclaimed, throwing sudden force of expression into his voice and fixing her with his eyes, "I can't live without you, and that's all there is to it. Now," he concluded, showing the palm of one of his white hands in a sort of at-an-end, helpless expression, "what shall I do?"

This shifting of the burden to her appealed to Carrie. The semblance of the load without the weight touched the woman's heart.

"Can't you wait a little while yet?" she said tenderly. "I'll try and find out when he's going."

"What good will it do?" he asked, holding the same strain of feeling.

"Well, perhaps we can arrange to go somewhere."

She really did not see anything clearer than before, but she was getting into that frame of mind where, out of sympathy, a woman yields.

Hurstwood did not understand. He was wondering how she was to be persuaded—what appeal would move her to forsake Drouet. He began to wonder how far her affection for him would carry her. He was thinking of some question which would make her tell.

Finally he hit upon one of those problematical propositions which often disguise our own desires while leading us to an understanding of the difficulties which others make for us, and so discover for us a way. It had not the slightest connection with anything intended on his part, and was spoken at random before he had given it a moment's serious thought.

"Carrie," he said, looking into her face and assuming a serious look which he did not feel, "suppose I were to come to you next week, or this week for that matter—tonight say—and tell you I had to go away—that I couldn't stay another minute and wasn't coming back any more—would you come with me?"

His sweetheart viewed him with the most affectionate glance, her answer ready before the words were out of his mouth.

"Yes," she said.

"You wouldn't stop to argue or arrange?"

"Not if you couldn't wait."

He smiled when he saw that she took him seriously, and he thought what a chance it would afford for a possible junket of a week or two. He had a notion to tell her that he was joking and so brush away her sweet seriousness, but the effect of it was too delightful. He let it stand.

"Suppose we didn't have time to get married here?" he added, an afterthought striking him.

"If we got married as soon as we got to the other end of the journey it would be all right."

"I meant that," he said.

"Yes."

The morning seemed peculiarly bright to him now. He wondered whatever could have put such a thought into his head. Impossible as it was, he could not help smiling at its cleverness. It showed how she loved him. There was no doubt in his mind now, and he would find a way to win her.

"Well," he said, jokingly, "I'll come and get you one of these evenings," and then he laughed.

"I wouldn't stay with you, though, if you didn't marry me," Carrie added reflectively.

"I don't want you to," he said tenderly, taking her hand.

She was extremely happy now that she understood. She loved him the more for thinking that he would rescue her so. As for him, the marriage clause did not dwell in his mind. He was thinking that with such affection there could be no bar to his eventual happiness.

"Let's stroll about," he said gayly, rising and surveying all the lovely park.

"All right," said Carrie.

They passed the young Irishman, who looked after them with envious eyes.

" 'Tis a foine couple," he observed to himself. "They must be rich."

Chapter XVI

A WITLESS ALADDIN: THE GATE TO THE WORLD

In the course of his present stay in Chicago, Drouet paid some slight attention to the secret order to which he belonged. During his last trip he had received a new light on its importance.

"I tell you," said another drummer to him, "it's a great thing. Look at Hazenstab. He isn't so deuced clever. Of course he's got a good house behind him, but that won't do alone. I tell you it's his degree. He's a way-up Mason,[1] and that goes a long way. He's got a secret sign that stands for something."

Drouet resolved then and there that he would take more interest in such matters. So when he got back to Chicago he repaired to his local lodge headquarters.

"I say, Drouet," said Mr. Harry Quincel, an individual who was very prominent in this local branch of the Elks,[2] "you're the man that can help us out."

It was after the business meeting and things were going socially with a hum. Drouet was bobbing around chatting and joking with a score of individuals whom he knew.

"What are you up to?" he inquired genially, turning a smiling face upon his secret brother.

"We're trying to get up some theatricals for two weeks from to-day, and we want to know if you don't know some young lady who could take a part—it's an easy part."

"Sure," said Drouet, "what is it?" He did not trouble to remember that he knew no one to whom he could appeal on this score. His innate good-nature, however, dictated a favourable reply.

"Well, now, I'll tell you what we are trying to do," went on Mr. Quincel. "We are trying to get a new set of furniture for the lodge. There isn't enough money in the treasury at the present time, and we thought we would raise it by a little entertainment."

"Sure," interrupted Drouet, "that's a good idea."

"Several of the boys around here have got talent. There's Harry Burbeck, he does a fine black-face turn. Mac Lewis is all right at heavy dramatics. Did you ever hear him recite 'Over the Hills'?"[3]

---

1. A member of the order of Masons, a secret society founded in England in the early eighteenth century to aid in the spread of liberal, democratic, and anticlerical beliefs. (Many of the leaders of the American Revolution were Masons.) By the close of the nineteenth century, however, except for its still-secret rituals, the Masons differed little from other fraternal orders. By "way-up Mason," Drouet's friend means someone who has achieved high rank in the Masonic hierarchy.
2. Established in America in the mid-nineteenth century, the Benevolent and Protective Order of Elks were a fraternal organization whose branches (or "lodges") were devoted principally to activities benefiting local communities and charities.
3. Probably Will Carleton's "Over the Hills to the Poorhouse" (1873), a popular sentimental poem.

"Never did."

"Well, I tell you, he does it fine."

"And you want me to get some woman to take a part?" questioned Drouet, anxious to terminate the subject and get on to something else. "What are you going to play?"

" 'Under the Gaslight,' " said Mr. Quincel, mentioning Augustin Daly's famous production, which had worn from a great public success down to an amateur theatrical favourite, with many of the troublesome accessories cut out and the *dramatis personæ* reduced to the smallest possible number.[4]

Drouet had seen this play some time in the past.

"That's it," he said; "that's a fine play. It will go all right. You ought to make a lot of money out of that."

"We think we'll do very well," Mr. Quincel replied. "Don't you forget now," he concluded, Drouet showing signs of restlessness; "some young woman to take the part of Laura."

"Sure, I'll attend to it."

He moved away, forgetting almost all about it the moment Mr. Quincel had ceased talking. He had not even thought to ask the time or place.

Drouet was reminded of his promise a day or two later by the receipt of a letter announcing that the first rehearsal was set for the following Friday evening, and urging him to kindly forward the young lady's address at once, in order that the part might be delivered to her.

"Now, who the deuce do I know?" asked the drummer reflectively, scratching his rosy ear. "I don't know any one that knows anything about amateur theatricals."

He went over in memory the names of a number of women he knew, and finally fixed on one, largely because of the convenient location of her home on the West Side, and promised himself that as he came out that evening he would see her. When, however, he started west on the car he forgot, and was only reminded of his delinquency by an item in the "Evening News"—a small three-line affair

---

4. First produced in 1867, Daly's play had been one of the great popular successes of the American stage for almost two decades. It included a climactic scene in which the heroine, Laura, chops her way out of a railway shed with an axe in order to rescue a character who has been tied to the tracks by the villain. Dreiser undoubtedly knew of the play from his experience as a dramatic reviewer for the *St. Louis Globe-Democrat* during 1892–93, though he had perhaps seen it as early as the mid-1880s in Chicago. He was probably reminded of it by the widely noted death of Daly in June 1899.

In his use of the play, Dreiser eliminated all of its melodrama and comedy and concentrated on the situation of Laura as a noble-minded, self-sacrificing woman who, because of her suddenly disclosed low birth, is hounded by society and is forced to give up her fiancé Ray. Dreiser also omitted from *Sister Carrie* the play's "happy ending" at which Laura is revealed to be truly highborn and is reunited with Ray.

Dreiser's quotes from *Under the Gaslight* are taken verbatim from the 1895 acting version published by Samuel French of New York.

under the head of Secret Society Notes—which stated the Custer Lodge of the Order of Elks would give a theatrical performance in Avery Hall[5] on the 16th, when "Under the Gaslight" would be produced.

"George!" exclaimed Drouet, "I forgot that."

"What?" inquired Carrie.

They were at their little table in the room which might have been used for a kitchen, where Carrie occasionally served a meal. To-night the fancy had caught her, and the little table was spread with a pleasing repast.

"Why, my lodge entertainment. They're going to give a play, and they wanted me to get them some young lady to take a part."

"What is it they're going to play?"

" 'Under the Gaslight.' "

"When?"

"On the 16th."

"Well, why don't you?" asked Carrie.

"I don't know any one," he replied.

Suddenly he looked up.

"Say," he said, "how would you like to take the part?"

"Me?" said Carrie. "I can't act."

"How do you know?" questioned Drouet reflectively.

"Because," answered Carrie, "I never did."

Nevertheless, she was pleased to think he would ask. Her eyes brightened, for if there was anything that enlisted her sympathies it was the art of the stage.

True to his nature, Drouet clung to this idea as an easy way out.

"That's nothing. You can act all you have to down there."

"No, I can't," said Carrie weakly, very much drawn toward the proposition and yet fearful.

"Yes, you can. Now, why don't you do it? They need some one, and it will be lots of fun for you."

"Oh, no, it won't," said Carrie seriously.

"You'd like that. I know you would. I've seen you dancing around here and giving imitations and that's why I asked you. You're clever enough, all right."

"No, I'm not," said Carrie shyly.

"Now, I'll tell you what you do. You go down and see about it. It'll be fun for you. The rest of the company isn't going to be any good. They haven't any experience. What do they know about theatricals?"

He frowned as he thought of their ignorance.

"Hand me the coffee," he added.

---

5. Dreiser appears to have based Avery Hall on the Waverly Theatre, on Madison and Throop, near which he and his family had lived in the summer of 1884. This location is only a few blocks from Carrie's Ogden Place flat.

"I don't believe I could act, Charlie," Carrie went on pettishly. "You don't think I could, do you?"

"Sure. Out o' sight. I bet you make a hit. Now you want to go, I know you do. I knew it when I came home. That's why I asked you."

"What is the play, did you say?"

" 'Under the Gaslight.' "

"What part would they want me to take?"

"Oh, one of the heroines—I don't know."

"What sort of a play is it?"

"Well," said Drouet, whose memory for such things was not the best, "it's about a girl who gets kidnapped by a couple of crooks—a man and a woman that live in the slums. She had some money or something and they wanted to get it. I don't know now how it did go exactly."

"Don't you know what part I would have to take?"

"No, I don't, to tell the truth." He thought a moment. "Yes, I do, too. Laura, that's the thing—you're to be Laura."

"And you can't remember what the part is like?"

"To save me, Cad, I can't," he answered. "I ought to, too; I've seen the play enough. There's a girl in it that was stolen when she was an infant—was picked off the street or something—and she's the one that's hounded by the two old criminals I was telling you about." He stopped with a mouthful of pie poised on a fork before his face. "She comes very near getting drowned—no, that's not it. I'll tell you what I'll do," he concluded hopelessly, "I'll get you the book. I can't remember now for the life of me."

"Well, I don't know," said Carrie, when he had concluded, her interest and desire to shine dramatically struggling with her timidity for the mastery. "I might go if you thought I'd do all right."

"Of course, you'll do," said Drouet, who, in his efforts to enthuse Carrie, had interested himself. "Do you think I'd come home here and urge you to do something that I didn't think you would make a success of? You can act all right. It'll be good for you."

"When must I go?" said Carrie, reflectively.

"The first rehearsal is Friday night. I'll get the part for you to-night."

"All right," said Carrie resignedly, "I'll do it, but if I make a failure now it's your fault."

"You won't fail," assured Drouet. "Just act as you do around here. Be natural. You're all right. I've often thought you'd make a corking good actress."

"Did you really?" asked Carrie.

"That's right," said the drummer.

He little knew as he went out of the door that night what a secret flame he had kindled in the bosom of the girl he left behind. Carrie was possessed of that sympathetic, impressionable nature which, ever in the most developed form, has been the glory of the drama. She was created with that passivity of soul which is always the mirror of the active world. She possessed an innate taste for imitation and no small ability. Even without practice, she could sometimes restore dramatic situations she had witnessed by re-creating, before her mirror, the expressions of the various faces taking part in the scene. She loved to modulate her voice after the conventional manner of the distressed heroine, and repeat such pathetic fragments as appealed most to her sympathies. Of late, seeing the airy grace of the *ingenue* in several well-constructed plays, she had been moved to secretly imitate it, and many were the little movements and expressions of the body in which she indulged from time to time in the privacy of her chamber. On several occasions, when Drouet had caught her admiring herself, as he imagined, in the mirror, she was doing nothing more than recalling some little grace of the mouth or the eyes which she had witnessed in another. Under his airy accusation she mistook this for vanity and accepted the blame with a faint sense of error, though, as a matter of fact, it was nothing more than the first subtle outcroppings of an artistic nature, endeavouring to re-create the perfect likeness of some phase of beauty which appealed to her. In such feeble tendencies, be it known, such outworking of desire to reproduce life, lies the basis of all dramatic art.

Now, when Carrie heard Drouet's laudatory opinion of her dramatic ability, her body tingled with satisfaction. Like the flame which welds the loosened particles into a solid mass, his words united those floating wisps of feeling which she had felt, but never believed, concerning her possible ability, and made them into a gaudy shred of hope. Like all human beings, she had a touch of vanity. She felt that she could do things if she only had a chance. How often had she looked at the well-dressed actresses on the stage and wondered how she would look, how delightful she would feel if only she were in their place. The glamour, the tense situation, the fine clothes, the applause, these had lured her until she felt that she, too, could act— that she, too, could compel acknowledgment of power. Now she was told that she really could—that little things she had done about the house had made even him feel her power. It was a delightful sensation while it lasted.

When Drouet was gone, she sat down in her rocking-chair by the window to think about it. As usual, imagination exaggerated the possibilities for her. It was as if he had put fifty cents in her hand and she had exercised the thoughts of a thousand dollars. She saw herself in a score of pathetic situations in which she assumed a tremulous voice and suffering manner. Her mind delighted itself with scenes of luxury and refinement, situations in which she was the cynosure of all eyes, the arbiter of all fates. As she rocked to and fro she felt the tensity of woe in abandonment, the magnificence of wrath after deception, the languour of sorrow after defeat. Thoughts of all the charming women she had seen in plays—every fancy, every illusion which she had concerning the stage—now came back as a returning tide after the ebb. She built up feelings and a determination which the occasion did not warrant.

Drouet dropped in at the lodge when he went down town, and swashed around with a great *air*, as Quincel met him.

"Where is that young lady you were going to get for us?" asked the latter.

"I've got her," said Drouet.

"Have you?" said Quincel, rather surprised by his promptness; "that's good. What's her address?" and he pulled out his note-book in order to be able to send her part to her.

"You want to send her her part?" asked the drummer.

"Yes."

"Well, I'll take it. I'm going right by her house in the morning."

"What did you say her address was? We only want it in case we have any information to send her."

"Twenty-nine Ogden Place."

"And her name?"

"Carrie Madenda," said the drummer, firing at random. The lodge members knew him to be single.

"That sounds like somebody that can act, doesn't it?" said Quincel.

"Yes, it does."

He took the part home to Carrie and handed it to her with the manner of one who does a favour.

"He says that's the best part. Do you think you can do it?"

"I don't know until I look it over. You know I'm afraid, now that I've said I would."

"Oh, go on. What have you got to be afraid of? It's a cheap company. The rest of them aren't as good as you are."

"Well, I'll see," said Carrie, pleased to have the part, for all her misgivings.

He sidled around, dressing and fidgeting before he arranged to make his next remark.

"They were getting ready to print the programmes," he said, "and I gave them the name of Carrie Madenda. Was that all right?"

"Yes, I guess so," said his companion, looking up at him. She was thinking it was slightly strange.

"If you didn't make a hit, you know," he went on.

"Oh, yes," she answered, rather pleased now with his caution. It was clever for Drouet.

"I didn't want to introduce you as my wife, because you'd feel worse then if you didn't *go*. They all know me so well. But you'll go all right. Anyhow, you'll probably never meet any of them again."

"Oh, I don't care," said Carrie desperately. She was determined now to have a try at the fascinating game.

Drouet breathed a sigh of relief. He had been afraid that he was about to precipitate another conversation upon the marriage question.

The part of Laura, as Carrie found out when she began to examine it, was one of suffering and tears. As delineated by Mr. Daly, it was true to the most sacred traditions of melodrama as he found it when he began his career. The sorrowful demeanour, the tremolo music, the long, explanatory, cumulative addresses, all were there.

"Poor fellow," read Carrie, consulting the text and drawing her voice out pathetically. "Martin, be sure and give him a glass of wine before he goes."

She was surprised at the briefness of the entire part, not knowing that she must be on the stage while others were talking, and not only be there, but also keep herself in harmony with the dramatic movement of the scenes.

"I think I can do that, though," she concluded.

When Drouet came the next night, she was very much satisfied with her day's study.

"Well, how goes it, Caddie?" he said.

"All right," she laughed. "I think I have it memorised nearly."

"That's good," he said. "Let's hear some of it."

"Oh, I don't know whether I can get up and say it off here." she said bashfully.

"Well, I don't know why you shouldn't. It'll be easier here than it will there."

"I don't know about that," she answered.

Eventually she took off the ball-room episode with considerable feeling, forgetting, as she got deeper in the scene, all about Drouet, and letting herself rise to a fine state of feeling.

"Good," said Drouet; "fine; out o' sight! You're all right, Caddie, I tell you."

He was really moved by her excellent representation and the general appearance of the pathetic little figure as it swayed and finally fainted to the floor. He had bounded up to catch her, and now held her laughing in his arms.

"Ain't you afraid you'll hurt yourself?" he asked.

"Not a bit."

"Well, you're a wonder. Say, I never knew you could do anything like that."

"I never did, either," said Carrie merrily, her face flushed with delight.

"Well, you can bet that you're all right," said Drouet. "You can take my word for that. You won't fail."

Chapter XVII

A GLIMPSE THROUGH THE GATEWAY: HOPE LIGHTENS THE EYE

The, to Carrie, very important theatrical performance was to take place at the Avery on conditions which were to make it more noteworthy than was at first anticipated. The little dramatic student had written to Hurstwood the very morning her part was brought her that she was going to take part in a play.

"I really am," she wrote, feeling that he might take it as a jest; "I have my part now, honest, truly."

Hurstwood smiled in an indulgent way as he read this.

"I wonder what it is going to be? I must see that."

He answered at once, making a pleasant reference to her ability. "I haven't the slightest doubt you will make a success. You must come to the park to-morrow morning and tell me all about it."

Carrie gladly complied, and revealed all the details of the undertaking as she understood it.

"Well," he said, "that's fine. I'm glad to hear it. Of course, you will do well, you're so clever."

He had truly never seen so much spirit in the girl before. Her tendency to discover a touch of sadness had for the nonce disappeared. As she spoke her eyes were bright, her cheeks red. She radiated much of the pleasure which her undertakings gave her. For all her misgivings—and they were as plentiful as the moments of the day—she was still happy. She could not repress her delight in doing this little thing which, to an ordinary observer, had no importance at all.

Hurstwood was charmed by the development of the fact that the girl had capabilities. There is nothing so inspiring in life as the sight of a legitimate ambition, no matter how incipient. It gives colour, force, and beauty to the possessor.

Carrie was now lightened by a touch of this divine afflatus. She drew to herself commendation from her two admirers which she had not earned. Their affection for her naturally heightened their perception of what she was trying to do and their approval of what she did. Her inexperience conserved her own exuberant fancy, which ran riot with every straw of opportunity, making of it a golden divining rod whereby the treasure of life was to be discovered.

"Let's see," said Hurstwood, "I ought to know some of the boys in the lodge. I'm an Elk myself."

"Oh, you mustn't let him know I told you."

"That's so," said the manager.

"I'd like for you to be there, if you want to come, but I don't see how you can unless he asks you."

"I'll be there," said Hurstwood affectionately. "I can fix it so he won't know you told me. You leave it to me."

This interest of the manager was a large thing in itself for the performance, for his standing among the Elks was something worth talking about. Already he was thinking of a box with some friends, and flowers for Carrie. He would make it a dress-suit affair and give the little girl a chance.

Within a day or two, Drouet dropped into the Adams Street resort, and he was at once spied by Hurstwood. It was at five in the afternoon and the place was crowded with merchants, actors, managers, politicians, a goodly company of rotund, rosy figures, silk-hatted, starchy-bosomed, beringed and bescarfpinned to the queen's taste. John L. Sullivan, the pugilist, was at one end of the glittering bar, surrounded by a company of loudly dressed sports, who were holding a most animated conversation.[1] Drouet came across the floor with a festive stride, a new pair of tan shoes squeaking audibly at his progress.

"Well, sir," said Hurstwood, "I was wondering what had become of you. I thought you had gone out of town again."

Drouet laughed.

"If you don't report more regularly we'll have to cut you off the list."

"Couldn't help it," said the drummer, "I've been busy."

They strolled over toward the bar amid the noisy, shifting company of notables. The dressy manager was shaken by the hand three times in as many minutes.

"I hear your lodge is going to give a performance," observed Hurstwood, in the most offhand manner.

"Yes, who told you?"

"No one," said Hurstwood. "They just sent me a couple of tickets, which I can have for two dollars. Is it going to be any good?"

"I don't know," replied the drummer. "They've been trying to get me to get some woman to take a part."

"I wasn't intending to go," said the manager easily. "I'll subscribe, of course. How are things over there?"

"All right. They're going to fit things up out of the proceeds."

"Well," said the manager, "I hope they make a success of it. Have another?"

He did not intend to say any more. Now, if he should appear on the scene with a few friends, he could say that he had been urged

---

1. Dreiser had interviewed Sullivan for the St. Louis Globe-Democrat in 1893 and had liked him.

to come along. Drouet had a desire to wipe out the possibility of confusion.

"I think the girl is going to take a part in it," he said abruptly, after thinking it over.

"You don't say so! How did that happen?"

"Well, they were short and wanted me to find them some one. I told Carrie, and she seems to want to try."

"Good for her," said the manager. "It'll be a real nice affair. Do her good, too. Has she ever had any experience?"

"Not a bit."

"Oh, well, it isn't anything very serious."

"She's clever, though," said Drouet, casting off any imputation against Carrie's ability. "She picks up her part quick enough."

"You don't say so!" said the manager.

"Yes, sir; she surprised me the other night. By George, if she didn't."

"We must give her a nice little send-off," said the manager. "I'll look after the flowers."

Drouet smiled at his good-nature.

"After the show you must come with me and we'll have a little supper."

"I think she'll do all right," said Drouet.

"I want to see her. She's got to do all right. We'll make her," and the manager gave one of his quick, steely half-smiles, which was a compound of good-nature and shrewdness.

Carrie, meanwhile, attended the first rehearsal. At this performance Mr. Quincel presided, aided by Mr. Millice, a young man who had some qualifications of past experience, which were not exactly understood by any one. He was so experienced and so business-like, however, that he came very near being rude—failing to remember, as he did, that the individuals he was trying to instruct were volunteer players and not salaried underlings.

"Now, Miss Madenda," he said, addressing Carrie, who stood in one part uncertain as to what move to make, "you don't want to stand like that. Put expression in your face. Remember, you are troubled over the intrusion of the stranger. Walk so," and he struck out across the Avery stage in a most drooping manner.

Carrie did not exactly fancy the suggestion, but the novelty of the situation, the presence of strangers, all more or less nervous, and the desire to do anything rather than make a failure, made her timid. She walked in imitation of her mentor as requested, inwardly feeling that there was something strangely lacking.

"Now, Mrs. Morgan," said the director to one young married woman who was to take the part of Pearl, "you sit here. Now, Mr. Bamberger, you stand here, so. Now, what is it you say?"

"Explain," said Mr. Bamberger feebly. He had the part of Ray, Laura's lover, the society individual who was to waver in his thoughts of marrying her, upon finding that she was a waif and a nobody by birth.

"How is that—what does your text say?"

"Explain," repeated Mr. Bamberger, looking intently at his part.

"Yes, but it also says," the director remarked, "that you are to look shocked. Now, say it again, and see if you can't look shocked."

"Explain!" demanded Mr. Bamberger vigorously.

"No, no, that won't do! Say it this way—*explain*."

"Explain," said Mr. Bamberger, giving a modified imitation.

"That's better. Now go on."

"One night," resumed Mrs. Morgan, whose lines came next, "father and mother were going to the opera. When they were crossing Broadway, the usual crowd of children accosted them for alms—"

"Hold on," said the director, rushing forward, his arm extended. "Put more feeling into what you are saying."

Mrs. Morgan looked at him as if she feared a personal assault. Her eye lightened with resentment.

"Remember, Mrs. Morgan," he added, ignoring the gleam, but modifying his manner, "that you're detailing a pathetic story. You are now supposed to be telling something that is a grief to you. It requires feeling, repression, thus: 'The usual crowd of children accosted them for alms.' "

"All right," said Mrs. Morgan.

"Now, go on."

"As mother felt in her pocket for some change, her fingers touched a cold and trembling hand which had clutched her purse."

"Very good," interrupted the director, nodding his head significantly.

"A pickpocket! Well!" exclaimed Mr. Bamberger, speaking the lines that here fell to him.

"No, no, Mr. Bamberger," said the director, approaching, "not that way. 'A pickpocket—well?' so. That's the idea."

"Don't you think," said Carrie weakly, noticing that it had not been proved yet whether the members of the company knew their lines, let alone the details of expression, "that it would be better if we just went through our lines once to see if we know them? We might pick up some points."

"A very good idea, Miss Madenda," said Mr. Quincel, who sat at the side of the stage, looking serenely on and volunteering opinions which the director did not heed.

"All right," said the latter, somewhat abashed, "it might be well to do it." Then brightening, with a show of authority, "Suppose we run right through, putting in as much expression as we can."

"Good," said Mr. Quincel.

"This hand," resumed Mrs. Morgan, glancing up at Mr. Bamberger and down at her book, as the lines proceeded, "my mother grasped in her own, and so tight that a small, feeble voice uttered an exclamation of pain. Mother looked down, and there beside her was a little ragged girl."

"Very good," observed the director, now hopelessly idle.

"The thief!" exclaimed Mr. Bamberger.

"Louder," put in the director, finding it almost impossible to keep his hands off.

"The thief!" roared poor Bamberger.

"Yes, but a thief hardly six years old, with a face like an angel's. 'Stop,' said my mother. 'What are you doing?'

" 'Trying to steal,' said the child.

" 'Don't you know that it is wicked to do so?' asked my father.

" 'No,' said the girl, 'but it is dreadful to be hungry.'

" 'Who told you to steal?' asked my mother.

" 'She—there,' said the child, pointing to a squalid woman in a doorway opposite, who fled suddenly down the street. 'That is old Judas,' said the girl."

Mrs. Morgan read this rather flatly, and the director was in despair. He fidgeted around, and then went over to Mr. Quincel.

"What do you think of them?" he asked.

"Oh, I guess we'll be able to whip them into shape," said the latter, with an air of strength under difficulties.

"I don't know," said the director. "That fellow Bamberger strikes me as being a pretty poor shift for a lover."

"He's all we've got," said Quincel, rolling up his eyes. "Harrison went back on me at the last minute. Who else can we get?"

"I don't know," said the director. "I'm afraid he'll never pick up."

At this moment Bamberger was exclaiming, "Pearl, you are joking with me."

"Look at that now," said the director, whispering behind his hand. "My Lord! what can you do with a man who drawls out a sentence like that?"

"Do the best you can," said Quincel consolingly.

The rendition ran on in this wise until it came to where Carrie, as Laura, comes into the room to explain to Ray, who, after hearing Pearl's statement about her birth, had written the letter repudiating her, which, however, he did not deliver. Bamberger was just concluding the words of Ray, "I must go before she returns. Her step! Too late," and was cramming the letter in his pocket, when she began sweetly with:

"Ray!"

"Miss—Miss Courtland," Bamberger faltered weakly.

Carrie looked at him a moment and forgot all about the company present. She began to feel the part, and summoned an indifferent smile to her lips, turning as the lines directed and going to a window, as if he were not present. She did it with a grace which was fascinating to look upon.

"Who is that woman?" asked the director, watching Carrie in her little scene with Bamberger.

"Miss Madenda," said Quincel.

"I know her name," said the director, "but what does she do?"

"I don't know," said Quincel. "She's a friend of one of our members."

"Well, she's got more gumption than any one I've seen here so far—seems to take an interest in what she's doing."

"Pretty, too, isn't she?" said Quincel.

The director strolled away without answering.

In the second scene, where she was supposed to face the company in the ball-room, she did even better, winning the smile of the director, who volunteered, because of her fascination for him, to come over and speak with her.

"Were you ever on the stage?" he asked insinuatingly.

"No," said Carrie.

"You do so well, I thought you might have had some experience."

Carrie only smiled consciously.

He walked away to listen to Bamberger, who was feebly spouting some ardent line.

Mrs. Morgan saw the drift of things and gleamed at Carrie with envious and snapping black eyes.

"She's some cheap professional," she gave herself the satisfaction of thinking, and scorned and hated her accordingly.

The rehearsal ended for one day, and Carrie went home feeling that she had acquitted herself satisfactorily. The words of the director were ringing in her ears, and she longed for an opportunity to tell Hurstwood. She wanted him to know just how well she was doing. Drouet, too, was an object for her confidences. She could hardly wait until he should ask her, and yet she did not have the vanity to bring it up. The drummer, however, had another line of thought to-night and her little experience did not appeal to him as important. He let the conversation drop, save for what she chose to recite without solicitation, and Carrie was not good at that. He took it for granted that she was doing very well and he was relieved of further worry. Consequently he threw Carrie into repression, which was irritating. She felt his indifference keenly and longed to see Hurstwood. It was as if he were now the only friend she had on earth. The next morning Drouet was interested again, but the damage had been done.

She got a pretty letter from the manager, saying that by the time she got it he would be waiting for her in the park. When she came, he shone upon her as the morning sun.

"Well, my dear," he asked, "how did you come out?"

"Well enough," she said, still somewhat reduced after Drouet.

"Now, tell me just what you did. Was it pleasant?"

Carrie related the incidents of the rehearsal, warming up as she proceeded.

"Well, that's delightful," said Hurstwood. "I'm so glad. I must get over there to see you. When is the next rehearsal?"

"Tuesday," said Carrie, "but they don't allow visitors."

"I imagine I could get in," said Hurstwood significantly.

She was completely restored and delighted by his consideration, but she made him promise not to come around.

"Now you must do your best to please me," he said encouragingly. "Just remember that I want you to succeed. We will make the performance worth while. You do that now."

"I'll try," said Carrie, brimming with affection and enthusiasm.

"That's the girl," said Hurstwood fondly. "Now, remember," shaking an affectionate finger at her, "your best."

"I will," she answered, looking back.

The whole earth was brimming sunshine that morning. She tripped along, the clear sky pouring liquid blue into her soul. Oh, blessed are the children of endeavour in this, that they try and are hopeful. And blessed also are they who, knowing, smile and approve.

Chapter XVIII

JUST OVER THE BORDER: A HAIL AND FAREWELL

By the evening of the 16th the subtle hand of Hurstwood had made itself apparent. He had given the word among his friends—and they were many and influential—that here was something which they ought to attend, and, as a consequence, the sale of tickets by Mr. Quincel, acting for the lodge, had been large. Small four-line notes had appeared in all of the daily newspapers. These he had arranged for by the aid of one of his newspaper friends on the "Times," Mr. Harry McGarren, the managing editor.

"Say, Harry," Hurstwood said to him one evening, as the latter stood at the bar drinking before wending his belated way homeward, "you can help the boys out, I guess."

"What is it?" said McGarren, pleased to be consulted by the opulent manager.

"The Custer Lodge is getting up a little entertainment for their own good, and they'd like a little newspaper notice. You know what I mean—a squib or two saying that it's going to take place."

"Certainly," said McGarren, "I can fix that for you, George."

At the same time Hurstwood kept himself wholly in the background. The members of Custer Lodge could scarcely understand why their little affair was taking so well. Mr. Harry Quincel was looked upon as quite a star for this sort of work.

By the time the 16th had arrived Hurstwood's friends had rallied like Romans to a senator's call. A well-dressed, good-natured, flatteringly-inclined audience was assured from the moment he thought of assisting Carrie.

That little student had mastered her part to her own satisfaction, much as she trembled for her fate when she should once face the gathered throng, behind the glare of the footlights. She tried to console herself with the thought that a score of other persons, men and women, were equally tremulous concerning the outcome of their efforts, but she could not disassociate the general danger from her own individual liability. She feared that she would forget her lines, that she might be unable to master the feeling which she now felt concerning her own movements in the play. At times she wished that she had never gone into the affair; at others, she trembled lest she should be paralysed with fear and stand white and gasping, not knowing what to say and spoiling the entire performance.

In the matter of the company, Mr. Bamberger had disappeared. That hopeless example had fallen under the lance of the director's criticism. Mrs. Morgan was still present, but envious and determined, if for nothing more than spite, to do as well as Carrie at least. A loafing professional had been called in to assume the rôle of Ray, and, while he was a poor stick of his kind, he was not troubled by any of those qualms which attack the spirit of those who have never faced an audience. He swashed about (cautioned though he was to maintain silence concerning his past theatrical relationships) in such a self-confident manner that he was like to convince every one of his identity by mere matter of circumstantial evidence.

"It is so easy," he said to Mrs. Morgan, in the usual affected stage voice. "An audience would be the last thing to trouble me. It's the spirit of the part, you know, that is difficult."

Carrie disliked his appearance, but she was too much the actress not to swallow his qualities with complaisance, seeing that she must suffer his fictitious love for the evening.

At six she was ready to go. Theatrical paraphernalia had been provided over and above her care. She had practised her make-up in the morning, had rehearsed and arranged her material for the evening by one o'clock, and had gone home to have a final look at her part, waiting for the evening to come.

On this occasion the lodge sent a carriage. Drouet rode with her as far as the door, and then went about the neighbouring stores, looking for some good cigars. The little actress marched nervously into her dressing-room and began that painfully anticipated matter of make-up which was to transform her, a simple maiden, to Laura, The Belle of Society.

The flare of the gas-jets, the open trunks, suggestive of travel and display, the scattered contents of the make-up box—rouge, pearl powder, whiting, burnt cork, India ink, pencils for the eye-lids, wigs, scissors, looking-glasses, drapery—in short, all the nameless paraphernalia of disguise, have a remarkable atmosphere of their own. Since her arrival in the city many things had influenced her, but always in a far-removed manner. This new atmosphere was more friendly. It was wholly unlike the great brilliant mansions which waved her coldly away, permitting her only awe and distant wonder. This took her by the hand kindly, as one who says, "My dear, come in." It opened for her as if for its own. She had wondered at the greatness of the names upon the bill-boards, the marvel of the long notices in the papers, the beauty of the dresses upon the stage, the atmosphere of carriages, flowers, refinement. Here was no illusion. Here was an open door to see all of that. She had come upon it as one who stumbles upon a secret passage, and, behold, she was in the chamber of diamonds and delight!

As she dressed with a flutter, in her little stage room, hearing the voices outside, seeing Mr. Quincel hurrying here and there, noting Mrs. Morgan and Mrs. Hoagland at their nervous work of preparation, seeing all the twenty members of the cast moving about and worrying over what the result would be, she could not help thinking what a delight this would be if it would endure; how perfect a state, if she could only do well now, and then some time get a place as a real actress. The thought had taken a mighty hold upon her. It hummed in her ears as the melody of an old song.

Outside in the little lobby another scene was being enacted. Without the interest of Hurstwood, the little hall would probably have been comfortably filled, for the members of the lodge were moderately interested in its welfare. Hurstwood's word, however, had gone the rounds. It was to be a full-dress affair. The four boxes had been taken. Dr. Norman McNeill Hale and his wife were to occupy one. This was quite a card. C. R. Walker, dry-goods merchant and possessor of at least two hundred thousand dollars, had taken another; a well-known coal merchant had been induced to take the third, and Hurstwood and his friends the fourth. Among the latter was Drouet. The people who were now pouring here were not celebrities, nor even local notabilities, in a general sense. They were the lights of a certain circle—the circle of small fortunes and secret order distinctions. These gentlemen Elks knew the standing of one another. They had regard for the ability which could amass a small fortune, own a nice home, keep a barouche or carriage, perhaps, wear fine clothes, and maintain a good mercantile position. Naturally, Hurstwood, who was a little above the order of mind which accepted this standard as perfect, who had shrewdness and much assumption of dignity, who held an imposing and authoritative position, and commanded friendship by intuitive tact in handling people, was quite a figure. He was more generally known than most others in the same circle, and was looked upon as some one whose reserve covered a mine of influence and solid financial prosperity.

To-night he was in his element. He came with several friends directly from Rector's in a carriage. In the lobby he met Drouet, who was just returning from a trip for more cigars. All five now joined in an animated conversation concerning the company present and the general drift of lodge affairs.

"Who's here?" said Hurstwood, passing into the theatre proper, where the lights were turned up and a company of gentlemen were laughing and talking in the open space back of the seats.

"Why, how do you do, Mr. Hurstwood?" came from the first individual recognised.

"Glad to see you," said the latter, grasping his hand lightly.

"Looks quite an affair, doesn't it?"

"Yes, indeed," said the manager.

"Custer seems to have the backing of its members," observed the friend.

"So it should," said the knowing manager. "I'm glad to see it."

"Well, George," said another rotund citizen, whose avoirdupois made necessary an almost alarming display of starched shirt bosom, "how goes it with you?"

"Excellent," said the manager.

"What brings you over here? You're not a member of Custer."

"Good-nature," returned the manager. "Like to see the boys, you know."

"Wife here?"

"She couldn't come to-night. She's not well."

"Sorry to hear it—nothing serious, I hope."

"No, just feeling a little ill."

"I remember Mrs. Hurstwood when she was travelling once with you over to St. Joe—" and here the newcomer launched off in a trivial recollection, which was terminated by the arrival of more friends.

"Why, George, how are you?" said another genial West Side politician and lodge member. "My, but I'm glad to see you again; how are things, anyhow?"

"Very well; I see you got that nomination for alderman."

"Yes, we whipped them out over there without much trouble."

"What do you suppose Hennessy will do now?"

"Oh, he'll go back to his brick business. He has a brick-yard, you know."

"I didn't know that," said the manager. "Felt pretty sore, I suppose, over his defeat."

"Perhaps," said the other, winking shrewdly.

Some of the more favoured of his friends whom he had invited began to roll up in carriages now. They came shuffling in with a great show of finery and much evident feeling of content and importance.

"Here we are," said Hurstwood, turning to one from a group with whom he was talking.

"That's right," returned the newcomer, a gentleman of about forty-five.

"And say," he whispered, jovially, pulling Hurstwood over by the shoulder so that he might whisper in his ear, "if this isn't a good show, I'll punch your head."

"You ought to pay for seeing your old friends. Bother the show!"

To another who inquired, "Is it something really good?" the manager replied:

"I don't know. I don't suppose so." Then, lifting his hand graciously, "For the lodge."

"Lots of boys out, eh?"

"Yes, look up Shanahan. He was just asking for you a moment ago."

It was thus that the little theatre resounded to a babble of successful voices, the creak of fine clothes, the commonplace of good-nature, and all largely because of this man's bidding. Look at him any time within the half hour before the curtain was up, he was a member of an eminent group—a rounded company of five or more whose stout figures, large white bosoms, and shining pins bespoke the character of their success. The gentlemen who brought their wives called him out to shake hands. Seats clicked, ushers bowed while he looked blandly on. He was evidently a light among them, reflecting in his personality the ambitions of those who greeted him. He was acknowledged, fawned upon, in a way lionised. Through it all one could see the standing of the man. It was greatness in a way, small as it was.

Chapter XIX

AN HOUR IN ELFLAND: A CLAMOUR HALF HEARD

At last the curtain was ready to go up. All the details of the make-up had been completed, and the company settled down as the leader of the small, hired orchestra tapped significantly upon his music rack with his baton and began the soft curtain-raising strain. Hurstwood ceased talking, and went with Drouet and his friend Sagar Morrison around to the box.

"Now, we'll see how the little girl does," he said to Drouet, in a tone which no one else could hear.

On the stage, six of the characters had already appeared in the opening parlour scene. Drouet and Hurstwood saw at a glance that Carrie was not among them, and went on talking in a whisper. Mrs. Morgan, Mrs. Hoagland, and the actor who had taken Bamberger's part were representing the principal rôles in this scene. The professional, whose name was Patton, had little to recommend him outside of his assurance, but this at the present moment was most palpably needed. Mrs. Morgan, as Pearl, was stiff with fright. Mrs. Hoagland was husky in the throat. The whole company was so weak-kneed that the lines were merely spoken, and nothing more. It took all the hope and uncritical good-nature of the audience to keep from manifesting pity by that unrest which is the agony of failure.

Hurstwood was perfectly indifferent. He took it for granted that it would be worthless. All he cared for was to have it endurable enough to allow for pretension and congratulation afterward.

After the first rush of fright, however, the players got over the danger of collapse. They rambled weakly forward, losing nearly all the expression which was intended, and making the thing dull in the extreme, when Carrie came in.

One glance at her, and both Hurstwood and Drouet saw plainly that she also was weak-kneed. She came faintly across the stage, saying:

"And you, sir; we have been looking for you since eight o'clock," but with so little colour and in such a feeble voice that it was positively painful.

"She's frightened," whispered Drouet to Hurstwood.

The manager made no answer.

She had a line presently which was supposed to be funny.

"Well, that's as much as to say that I'm a sort of life pill."

It came out so flat, however, that it was a deathly thing. Drouet fidgeted. Hurstwood moved his toe the least bit.

There was another place in which Laura was to rise and, with a sense of impending disaster, say, sadly:

"I wish you hadn't said that, Pearl. You know the old proverb, 'Call a maid by a married name.' "

The lack of feeling in the thing was ridiculous. Carrie did not get it at all. She seemed to be talking in her sleep. It looked as if she were certain to be a wretched failure. She was more hopeless than Mrs. Morgan, who had recovered somewhat, and was now saying her lines clearly at least. Drouet looked away from the stage at the audience. The latter held out silently, hoping for a general change, of course. Hurstwood fixed his eye on Carrie, as if to hypnotise her into doing better. He was pouring determination of his own in her direction. He felt sorry for her.

In a few more minutes it fell to her to read the letter sent in by the strange villain. The audience had been slightly diverted by a conversation between the professional actor and a character called Snorky, impersonated by a short little American, who really developed some humour as a half-crazed, one-armed soldier, turned messenger for a living. He bawled his lines out with such defiance that, while they really did not partake of the humour intended, they were funny. Now he was off, however, and it was back to pathos, with Carrie as the chief figure. She did not recover. She wandered through the whole scene between herself and the intruding villain, straining the patience of the audience, and finally exiting, much to their relief.

"She's too nervous," said Drouet, feeling in the mildness of the remark that he was lying for once.

"Better go back and say a word to her."

Drouet was glad to do anything for relief. He fairly hustled around to the side entrance, and was let in by the friendly door-keeper. Carrie was standing in the wings, weakly waiting her next cue, all the snap and nerve gone out of her.

"Say, Cad," he said, looking at her, "you mustn't be nervous. Wake up. Those guys out there don't amount to anything. What are you afraid of?"

"I don't know," said Carrie. "I just don't seem to be able to do it."

She was grateful for the drummer's presence, though. She had found the company so nervous that her own strength had gone.

"Come on," said Drouet. "Brace up. What are you afraid of? Go on out there now, and do the trick. What do you care?"

Carrie revived a little under the drummer's electrical, nervous condition.

"Did I do so very bad?"

"Not a bit. All you need is a little more ginger. Do it as you showed me. Get that toss of your head you had the other night."

Carrie remembered her triumph in the room. She tried to think she could do it.

"What's next?" he said, looking at her part, which she had been studying.

"Why, the scene between Ray and me when I refuse him."

"Well, now you do that lively," said the drummer. "Put in snap, that's the thing. Act as if you didn't care."

"Your turn next, Miss Madenda," said the prompter.

"Oh, dear," said Carrie.

"Well, you're a chump for being afraid," said Drouet. "Come on now, brace up. I'll watch you from right here."

"Will you?" said Carrie.

"Yes, now go on. Don't be afraid."

The prompter signalled her.

She started out, weak as ever, but suddenly her nerve partially returned. She thought of Drouet looking.

"Ray," she said, gently, using a tone of voice much more calm than when she had last appeared. It was the scene which had pleased the director at the rehearsal.

"She's easier," thought Hurstwood to himself.

She did not do the part as she had at rehearsal, but she was better. The audience was at least not irritated. The improvement of the work of the entire company took away direct observation from her. They were making very fair progress, and now it looked as if the play would be passable, in the less trying parts at least.

Carrie came off warm and nervous.

"Well," she said, looking at him, "was it any better?"

"Well, I should say so. That's the way. Put life into it. You did that about a thousand per cent, better than you did the other scene. Now go on and fire up. You can do it. Knock 'em."

"Was it really better?"

"Better, I should say so. What comes next?"

"That ballroom scene."

"Well, you can do that all right," he said.

"I don't know," answered Carrie.

"Why, woman," he exclaimed, "you did it for me! Now you go out there and do it. It'll be fun for you. Just do as you did in the room. If you'll reel it off that way, I'll bet you make a hit. Now, what'll you bet? You do it."

The drummer usually allowed his ardent good-nature to get the better of his speech. He really did think that Carrie had acted this particular scene very well, and he wanted her to repeat it in public. His enthusiasm was due to the mere spirit of the occasion.

When the time came, he buoyed Carrie up most effectually. He began to make her feel as if she had done very well. The old melancholy of desire began to come back as he talked at her, and by the time the situation rolled around she was running high in feeling.

"I think I can do this."

"Sure you can. Now you go ahead and see."

On the stage, Mrs. Van Dam was making her cruel insinuation against Laura.

Carrie listened, and caught the infection of something—she did not know what. Her nostrils sniffed thinly.

"It means," the professional actor began, speaking as Ray, "that society is a terrible avenger of insult. Have you ever heard of the Siberian wolves? When one of the pack falls through weakness, the others devour him. It is not an elegant comparison, but there is something wolfish in society. Laura has mocked it with a pretence, and society, which is made up of pretence, will bitterly resent the mockery."

At the sound of her stage name Carrie started. She began to feel the bitterness of the situation. The feelings of the outcast descended upon her. She hung at the wing's edge, wrapt in her own mounting thoughts. She hardly heard anything more, save her own rumbling blood.

"Come, girls," said Mrs. Van Dam, solemnly, "let us look after our things. They are no longer safe when such an accomplished thief enters."

"Cue," said the prompter, close to her side, but she did not hear. Already she was moving forward with a steady grace, born of inspiration. She dawned upon the audience, handsome and proud, shifting, with the necessity of the situation, to a cold, white, helpless object, as the social pack moved away from her scornfully.

Hurstwood blinked his eyes and caught the infection. The radiating waves of feeling and sincerity were already breaking against the farthest walls of the chamber. The magic of passion, which will yet dissolve the world, was here at work.

There was a drawing, too, of attention, a riveting of feeling, heretofore wandering.

"Ray! Ray! Why do you not come back to her?" was the cry of Pearl.

Every eye was fixed on Carrie, still proud and scornful. They moved as she moved. Their eyes were with her eyes.

Mrs. Morgan, as Pearl, approached her.

"Let us go home," she said.

"No," answered Carrie, her voice assuming for the first time a penetrating quality which it had never known. "Stay with him!"

She pointed an almost accusing hand toward her lover. Then, with a pathos which struck home because of its utter simplicity, "He shall not suffer long."

Hurstwood realised that he was seeing something extraordinarily good. It was heightened for him by the applause of the audience as the curtain descended and the fact that it was Carrie. He thought now that she was beautiful. She had done something which was above his sphere. He felt a keen delight in realising that she was his.

"Fine," he said, and then, seized by a sudden impulse, arose and went about to the stage door.

When he came in upon Carrie she was still with Drouet. His feelings for her were most exuberant. He was almost swept away by the strength and feeling she exhibited. His desire was to pour forth his praise with the unbounded feelings of a lover, but here was Drouet, whose affection was also rapidly reviving. The latter was more fascinated, if anything, than Hurstwood. At least, in the nature of things, it took a more ruddy form.

"Well, well," said Drouet, "you did out of sight. That was simply great. I knew you could do it. Oh, but you're a little daisy!"

Carrie's eyes flamed with the light of achievement.

"Did I do all right?"

"Did you? Well, I guess. Didn't you hear the applause?"

There was some faint sound of clapping yet.

"I thought I got it something like—I felt it."

Just then Hurstwood came in. Instinctively he felt the change in Drouet. He saw that the drummer was near to Carrie, and jealousy leaped alight in his bosom. In a flash of thought, he reproached himself for having sent him back. Also, he hated him as an intruder. He could scarcely pull himself down to the level where he would have to congratulate Carrie as a friend. Nevertheless, the man mastered himself, and it was a triumph. He almost jerked the old subtle light to his eyes.

"I thought," he said, looking at Carrie, "I would come around and tell you how well you did, Mrs. Drouet. It was delightful."

Carrie took the cue, and replied:

"Oh, thank you."

"I was just telling her," put in Drouet, now delighted with his possession, "that I thought she did fine."

"Indeed you did," said Hurstwood, turning upon Carrie eyes in which she read more than the words.

Carrie laughed luxuriantly.

"If you do as well in the rest of the play, you will make us all think you are a born actress."

Carrie smiled again. She felt the acuteness of Hurstwood's position, and wished deeply that she could be alone with him, but she did not understand the change in Drouet. Hurstwood found that he could not talk, repressed as he was, and grudging Drouet every moment of his presence, he bowed himself out with the elegance of a Faust. Outside he set his teeth with envy.

"Damn it!" he said, "is he always going to be in the way?" He was moody when he got back to the box, and could not talk for thinking of his wretched situation.

As the curtain for the next act arose, Drouet came back. He was very much enlivened in temper and inclined to whisper, but Hurstwood pretended interest. He fixed his eyes on the stage, although Carrie was not there, a short bit of melodramatic comedy preceding her entrance. He did not see what was going on, however. He was thinking his own thoughts, and they were wretched.

The progress of the play did not improve matters for him. Carrie, from now on, was easily the centre of interest. The audience, which had been inclined to feel that nothing could be good after the first gloomy impression, now went to the other extreme and saw power where it was not. The general feeling reacted on Carrie. She presented her part with some felicity, though nothing like the intensity which had aroused the feeling at the end of the long first act.

Both Hurstwood and Drouet viewed her pretty figure with rising feelings. The fact that such ability should reveal itself in her, that they should see it set forth under such effective circumstances, framed almost in massy gold and shone upon by the appropriate lights of sentiment and personality, heightened her charm for them. She was more than the old Carrie to Drouet. He longed to be at home with her until he could tell her. He awaited impatiently the end, when they should go home alone.

Hurstwood, on the contrary, saw in the strength of her new attractiveness his miserable predicament. He could have cursed the man beside him. By the Lord, he could not even applaud feelingly as he would. For once he must simulate when it left a taste in his mouth.

It was in the last act that Carrie's fascination for her lovers assumed its most effective character.

Hurstwood listened to its progress, wondering when Carrie would come on. He had not long to wait. The author had used the artifice of sending all the merry company for a drive, and now Carrie came in alone. It was the first time that Hurstwood had had a chance to see her facing the audience quite alone, for nowhere else had she been without a foil of some sort. He suddenly felt, as she entered, that her old strength—the power that had grasped him at the end of the first act—had come back. She seemed to be gaining feeling, now that the play was drawing to a close and the opportunity for great action was passing.

"Poor Pearl," she said, speaking with natural pathos. "It is a sad thing to want for happiness, but it is a terrible thing to see another groping about blindly for it, when it is almost within the grasp."

She was gazing now sadly out upon the open sea, her arm resting listlessly upon the polished door-post.

Hurstwood began to feel a deep sympathy for her and for himself. He could almost feel that she was talking to him. He was, by a combination of feelings and entanglements, almost deluded by that quality of voice and manner which, like a pathetic strain of music, seems ever a personal and intimate thing. Pathos has this quality, that it seems ever addressed to one alone.

"And yet, she can be very happy with him," went on the little actress. "Her sunny temper, her joyous face will brighten any home."

She turned slowly toward the audience without seeing. There was so much simplicity in her movements that she seemed wholly alone. Then she found a seat by a table, and turned over some books, devoting a thought to them.

"With no longings for what I may not have," she breathed in conclusion—and it was almost a sigh—"my existence hidden from all save two in the wide world, and making my joy out of the joy of that innocent girl who will soon be his wife."

Hurstwood was sorry when a character, known as Peach Blossom, interrupted her. He stirred irritably, for he wished her to go on. He was charmed by the pale face, the lissome figure, draped in pearl grey, with a coiled string of pearls at the throat. Carrie had the air of one who was weary and in need of protection, and, under the fascinating make-believe of the moment, he rose in feeling until he was ready in spirit to go to her and ease her out of her misery by adding to his own delight.

In a moment Carrie was alone again, and was saying, with animation:

"I must return to the city, no matter what dangers may lurk here. I must go, secretly if I can; openly, if I must."

There was a sound of horses' hoofs outside, and then Ray's voice saying:

"No, I shall not ride again. Put him up."

He entered, and then began a scene which had as much to do with the creation of the tragedy of affection in Hurstwood as anything in his peculiar and involved career. For Carrie had resolved to make something of this scene, and, now that the cue had come, it began to take a feeling hold upon her. Both Hurstwood and Drouet noted the rising sentiment as she proceeded.

"I thought you had gone with Pearl," she said to her lover.

"I did go part of the way, but I left the party a mile down the road."

"You and Pearl had no disagreement?"

"No—yes; that is, we always have. Our social barometers always stand at 'cloudy' and 'overcast.' "

"And whose fault is that?" she said, easily.

"Not mine," he answered, pettishly. "I know I do all I can—I say all I can—but she—"

This was rather awkwardly put by Patton, but Carrie redeemed it with a grace which was inspiring.

"But she is your wife," she said, fixing her whole attention upon the stilled actor, and softening the quality of her voice until it was again low and musical. "Ray, my friend, courtship is the text from which the whole sermon of married life takes its theme. Do not let yours be discontented and unhappy."

She put her two little hands together and pressed them appealingly.

Hurstwood gazed with slightly parted lips. Drouet was fidgeting with satisfaction.

"To be my wife, yes," went on the actor in a manner which was weak by comparison, but which could not now spoil the tender atmosphere which Carrie had created and maintained. She did not seem to feel that he was wretched. She would have done nearly as well with a block of wood. The accessories she needed were within her own imagination. The acting of others could not affect them.

"And you repent already?" she said, slowly.

"I lost you," he said, seizing her little hand, "and I was at the mercy of any flirt who chose to give me an inviting look. It was your fault— you know it was—why did you leave me?"

Carrie turned slowly away, and seemed to be mastering some impulse in silence. Then she turned back.

"Ray," she said, "the greatest happiness I have ever felt has been the thought that all your affection was forever bestowed upon a virtuous woman, your equal in family, fortune, and accomplishments. What a revelation do you make to me now! What is it makes you continually war with your happiness?"

The last question was asked so simply that it came to the audience and the lover as a personal thing.

At last it came to the part where the lover exclaimed, "Be to me as you used to be."

Carrie answered, with affecting sweetness, "I cannot be that to you, but I can speak in the spirit of the Laura who is dead to you forever."

"Be it as you will," said Patton.

Hurstwood leaned forward. The whole audience was silent and intent.

"Let the woman you look upon be wise or vain," said Carrie, her eyes bent sadly upon the lover, who had sunk into a seat, "beautiful or homely, rich or poor, she has but one thing she can really give or refuse—her heart."

Drouet felt a scratch in his throat.

"Her beauty, her wit, her accomplishments, she may sell to you; but her love is the treasure without money and without price."

The manager suffered this as a personal appeal. It came to him as if they were alone, and he could hardly restrain the tears for sorrow over the hopeless, pathetic, and yet dainty and appealing woman whom he loved. Drouet also was beside himself. He was resolving that he would be to Carrie what he had never been before. He would marry her, by George! She was worth it.

"She asks only in return," said Carrie, scarcely hearing the small, scheduled reply of her lover, and putting herself even more in harmony with the plaintive melody now issuing from the orchestra, "that when you look upon her your eyes shall speak devotion; that when you address her your voice shall be gentle, loving, and kind; that you shall not despise her because she cannot understand all at once your vigorous thoughts and ambitious designs; for, when misfortune and evil have defeated your greatest purposes, her love remains to console you. You look to the trees," she continued, while Hurstwood restrained his feelings only by the grimmest repression, "for strength and grandeur; do not despise the flowers because their fragrance is all they have to give. Remember," she concluded, tenderly, "love is all a woman has to give," and she laid a strange, sweet accent on the all, "but it is the only thing which God permits us to carry beyond the grave."

The two men were in the most harrowed state of affection. They scarcely heard the few remaining words with which the scene concluded. They only saw their idol, moving about with appealing grace, continuing a power which to them was a revelation.

Hurstwood resolved a thousand things, Drouet as well. They joined equally in the burst of applause which called Carrie out. Drouet pounded his hands until they ached. Then he jumped up again and started out. As he went, Carrie came out, and, seeing an immense basket of flowers being hurried down the aisle toward her, she waited. They were Hurstwood's. She looked toward the manager's box for a moment, caught his eye, and smiled. He could have leaped out of the box to enfold her. He forgot the need of circumspectness which his married state enforced. He almost forgot that he had with him in the box those who knew him. By the Lord, he would have that lovely girl if it took his all. He would act at once. This should be the end of Drouet, and don't you forget it. He would not wait another day. The drummer should not have her.

He was so excited that he could not stay in the box. He went into the lobby, and then into the street, thinking. Drouet did not return. In a few minutes the last act was over, and he was crazy to have Carrie alone. He cursed the luck that could keep him smiling, bowing, shamming, when he wanted to tell her that he loved her, when he wanted to whisper to her alone. He groaned as he saw that his hopes were futile. He must even take her to supper, shamming. He finally went about and asked how she was getting along. The actors were all dressing, talking, hurrying about. Drouet was palavering himself with the looseness of excitement and passion. The manager mastered himself only by a great effort.

"We are going to supper, of course," he said, with a voice that was a mockery of his heart.

"Oh, yes," said Carrie, smiling.

The little actress was in fine feather. She was realising now what it was to be petted. For once she was the admired, the sought-for. The independence of success now made its first faint showing. With the tables turned, she was looking down, rather than up, to her lover. She did not fully realise that this was so, but there was something in condescension coming from her which was infinitely sweet. When she was ready they climbed into the waiting coach and drove down town; once, only, did she find an opportunity to express her feeling, and that was when the manager preceded Drouet in the coach and sat beside her. Before Drouet was fully in she had squeezed Hurstwood's hand in a gentle, impulsive manner. The manager was beside himself with affection. He could have sold his soul to be with her alone. "Ah," he thought, "the agony of it."

Drouet hung on, thinking he was all in all. The dinner was spoiled by his enthusiasm. Hurstwood went home feeling as if he should die if he did not find affectionate relief. He whispered "to-morrow" passionately to Carrie, and she understood. He walked away from the drummer and his prize at parting feeling as if he could slay him and not regret. Carrie also felt the misery of it.

"Good-night," he said, simulating an easy friendliness.

"Good-night," said the little actress, tenderly.

"The fool!" he said, now hating Drouet. "The idiot! I'll do him yet, and that quick! We'll see to-morrow."

"Well, if you aren't a wonder," Drouet was saying, complacently, squeezing Carrie's arm. "You are the dandiest little girl on earth."

Chapter XX

THE LURE OF THE SPIRIT: THE FLESH IN PURSUIT

Passion in a man of Hurstwood's nature takes a vigorous form. It is no musing, dreamy thing. There is none of the tendency to sing outside of my lady's window—to languish and repine in the face of difficulties. In the night he was long getting to sleep because of too much thinking, and in the morning he was early awake, seizing with alacrity upon the same dear subject and pursuing it with vigour. He was out of sorts physically, as well as disordered mentally, for did he not delight in a new manner in his Carrie, and was not Drouet in the way? Never was man more harassed than he by the thoughts of his love being held by the elated, flush-mannered drummer. He would have given anything, it seemed to him, to have the complication ended—to have Carrie acquiesce to an arrangement which would dispose of Drouet effectually and forever.

What to do. He dressed thinking. He moved about in the same chamber with his wife, unmindful of her presence.

At breakfast he found himself without an appetite. The meat to which he helped himself remained on his plate untouched. His coffee grew cold, while he scanned the paper indifferently. Here and there he read a little thing, but remembered nothing. Jessica had not yet come down. His wife sat at one end of the table revolving thoughts of her own in silence. A new servant had been recently installed and had forgot the napkins. On this account the silence was irritably broken by a reproof.

"I've told you about this before, Maggie," said Mrs. Hurstwood. "I'm not going to tell you again."

Hurstwood took a glance at his wife. She was frowning. Just now her manner irritated him excessively. Her next remark was addressed to him.

"Have you made up your mind, George, when you will take your vacation?"

It was customary for them to discuss the regular summer outing at this season of the year.

"Not yet," he said, "I'm very busy just now."

"Well, you'll want to make up your mind pretty soon, won't you, if we're going?" she returned.

"I guess we have a few days yet," he said.

"Hmff," she returned. "Don't wait until the season's over."

She stirred in aggravation as she said this.

"There you go again," he observed. "One would think I never did anything, the way you begin."

"Well, I want to know about it," she reiterated.

"You've got a few days yet," he insisted. "You'll not want to start before the races are over."

He was irritated to think that this should come up when he wished to have his thoughts for other purposes.

"Well, we may. Jessica doesn't want to stay until the end of the races."

"What did you want with a season ticket, then?"

"Uh!" she said, using the sound as an exclamation of disgust, "I'll not argue with you," and therewith arose to leave the table.

"Say," he said, rising, putting a note of determination in his voice which caused her to delay her departure, "what's the matter with you of late? Can't I talk with you any more?"

"Certainly, you can *talk* with me," she replied, laying emphasis on the word.

"Well, you wouldn't think so by the way you act. Now, you want to know when I'll be ready—not for a month yet. Maybe not then."

"We'll go without you."

"You will, eh?" he sneered.

"Yes, we will."

He was astonished at the woman's determination, but it only irritated him the more.

"Well, we'll see about that. It seems to me you're trying to run things with a pretty high hand of late. You talk as though you settled my affairs for me. Well, you don't. You don't regulate anything that's connected with me. If you want to go, go, but you won't hurry me by any such talk as that."

He was thoroughly aroused now. His dark eyes snapped, and he crunched his paper as he laid it down. Mrs. Hurstwood said nothing more. He was just finishing when she turned on her heel and went out into the hall and upstairs. He paused for a moment, as if hesitating, then sat down and drank a little coffee, and thereafter arose and went for his hat and gloves upon the main floor.

His wife had really not anticipated a row of this character. She had come down to the breakfast table feeling a little out of sorts with herself and revolving a scheme which she had in her mind. Jessica had called her attention to the fact that the races were not what they were supposed to be. The social opportunities were not what they had thought they would be this year. The beautiful girl found going every day a dull thing. There was an earlier exodus this year of people who were anybody to the watering places and Europe. In her own circle of acquaintances several young men in whom she was interested had gone to Waukesha. She began to feel that she would like to go too, and her mother agreed with her.

Accordingly, Mrs. Hurstwood decided to broach the subject. She was thinking this over when she came down to the table, but for some reason the atmosphere was wrong. She was not sure, after it was all over, just how the trouble had begun. She was determined now, however, that her husband was a brute, and that, under no circumstances, would she let this go by unsettled. She would have more lady-like treatment or she would know why.

For his part, the manager was loaded with the care of this new argument until he reached his office and started from there to meet Carrie. Then the other complications of love, desire, and opposition possessed him. His thoughts fled on before him upon eagles' wings. He could hardly wait until he should meet Carrie face to face. What was the night, after all, without her—what the day? She must and should be his.

For her part, Carrie had experienced a world of fancy and feeling since she had left him, the night before. She had listened to Drouet's enthusiastic maunderings with much regard for that part which concerned herself, with very little for that which affected his own gain. She kept him at such lengths as she could, because her thoughts were with her own triumph. She felt Hurstwood's passion as a delightful background to her own achievement, and she wondered what he would have to say. She was sorry for him, too, with that peculiar sorrow which finds something complimentary to itself in the misery of another. She was now experiencing the first shades of feeling of that subtle change which removes one out of the ranks of the suppliants into the lines of the dispensers of charity. She was, all in all, exceedingly happy.

On the morrow, however, there was nothing in the papers concerning the event, and, in view of the flow of common, everyday things about, it now lost a shade of the glow of the previous evening. Drouet himself was not talking so much *of* as *for* her. He felt instinctively that, for some reason or other, he needed reconstruction in her regard.

"I think," he said, as he spruced around their chambers the next morning, preparatory to going down town, "that I'll straighten out that little deal of mine this month and then we'll get married. I was talking with Mosher about that yesterday."

"No, you won't," said Carrie, who was coming to feel a certain faint power to jest with the drummer.

"Yes, I will," he exclaimed, more feelingly than usual, adding, with the tone of one who pleads, "Don't you believe what I've told you?"

Carrie laughed a little.

"Of course I do," she answered.

Drouet's assurance now misgave him. Shallow as was his mental observation, there was that in the things which had happened which made his little power of analysis useless. Carrie was still with him, but not helpless and pleading. There was a lilt in her voice which was new. She did not study him with eyes expressive of dependence. The drummer was feeling the shadow of something which was coming. It coloured his feelings and made him develop those little attentions and say those little words which were mere forefendations against danger.

Shortly afterward he departed, and Carrie prepared for her meeting with Hurstwood. She hurried at her toilet, which was soon made, and hastened down the stairs. At the corner she passed Drouet, but they did not see each other.

The drummer had forgotten some bills which he wished to turn into his house. He hastened up the stairs and burst into the room, but found only the chambermaid, who was cleaning up.

"Hello," he exclaimed, half to himself, "has Carrie gone?"

"Your wife? Yes, she went out just a few minutes ago."

"That's strange," thought Drouet. "She didn't say a word to me. I wonder where she went?"

He hastened about, rummaging in his valise for what he wanted, and finally pocketing it. Then he turned his attention to his fair neighbour, who was good-looking and kindly disposed towards him.

"What are you up to?" he said, smiling.

"Just cleaning," she replied, stopping and winding a dusting towel about her hand.

"Tired of it?"

"Not so very."

"Let me show you something," he said, affably, coming over and taking out of his pocket a little lithographed card which had been issued by a wholesale tobacco company. On this was printed a picture of a pretty girl, holding a striped parasol, the colours of which could be changed by means of a revolving disk in the back, which showed red, yellow, green, and blue through little interstices made in the ground occupied by the umbrella top.

"Isn't that clever?" he said, handing it to her and showing her how it worked. "You never saw anything like that before."

"Isn't it nice?" she answered.

"You can have it if you want it," he remarked.

"That's a pretty ring you have," he said, touching a commonplace setting which adorned the hand holding the card he had given her.

"Do you think so?"

"That's right," he answered, making use of a pretence at examination to secure her finger. "That's fine."

The ice being thus broken, he launched into further observation, pretending to forget that her fingers were still retained by his. She soon withdrew them, however, and retreated a few feet to rest against the window-sill.

"I didn't see you for a long time," she said, coquettishly, repulsing one of his exuberant approaches. "You must have been away."

"I was," said Drouet.

"Do you travel far?"

"Pretty far—yes."

"Do you like it?"

"Oh, not very well. You get tired of it after a while."

"I wish I could travel," said the girl, gazing idly out of the window.

"What has become of your friend, Mr. Hurstwood?" she suddenly asked, bethinking herself of the manager, who, from her own observation, seemed to contain promising material.

"He's here in town. What makes you ask about him?"

"Oh, nothing, only he hasn't been here since you got back."

"How did you come to know him?"

"Didn't I take up his name a dozen times in the last month?"

"Get out," said the drummer, lightly. "He hasn't called more than half a dozen times since we've been here."

"He hasn't, eh?" said the girl, smiling. "That's all you know about it."

Drouet took on a slightly more serious tone. He was uncertain as to whether she was joking or not.

"Tease," he said, "what makes you smile that way?"

"Oh, nothing."

"Have you seen him recently?"

"Not since you came back," she laughed.

"Before?"

"Certainly."

"How often?"

"Why, nearly every day."

She was a mischievous newsmonger, and was keenly wondering what the effect of her words would be.

"Who did he come to see?" asked the drummer, incredulously.

"Mrs. Drouet."

He looked rather foolish at this answer, and then attempted to correct himself so as not to appear a dupe.

"Well," he said, "what of it?"

"Nothing," replied the girl, her head cocked coquettishly on one side.

"He's an old friend," he went on, getting deeper into the mire.

He would have gone on further with his little flirtation, but the taste for it was temporarily removed. He was quite relieved when the girl's name was called from below.

"I've got to go," she said, moving away from him airily.

"I'll see you later," he said, with a pretence of disturbance at being interrupted.

When she was gone, he gave freer play to his feelings. His face, never easily controlled by him, expressed all the perplexity and disturbance which he felt. Could it be that Carrie had received so many visits and yet said nothing about them? Was Hurstwood lying? What did the chambermaid mean by it, anyway? He had thought there was something odd about Carrie's manner at the time. Why did she look so disturbed when he had asked her how many times Hurstwood had called? By George! he remembered now. There was something strange about the whole thing.

He sat down in a rocking-chair to think the better, drawing up one leg on his knee and frowning mightily. His mind ran on at a great rate.

And yet Carrie hadn't acted out of the ordinary. It couldn't be, by George, that she was deceiving him. She hadn't acted that way. Why, even last night she had been as friendly toward him as could be, and

Hurstwood too. Look how they acted! He could hardly believe they would try to deceive him.

His thoughts burst into words.

"She did act sort of funny at times. Here she had dressed and gone out this morning and never said a word."

He scratched his head and prepared to go down town. He was still frowning. As he came into the hall he encountered the girl, who was now looking after another chamber. She had on a white dusting cap, beneath which her chubby face shone good-naturedly. Drouet almost forgot his worry in the fact that she was smiling on him. He put his hand familiarly on her shoulder, as if only to greet her in passing.

"Got over being mad?" she said, still mischievously inclined.

"I'm not mad," he answered.

"I thought you were," she said, smiling.

"Quit your fooling about that," he said, in an offhand way. "Were you serious?"

"Certainly," she answered. Then, with an air of one who did not intentionally mean to create trouble, "He came lots of times. I thought you knew."

The game of deception was up with Drouet. He did not try to simulate indifference further.

"Did he spend the evenings here?" he asked.

"Sometimes. Sometimes they went out."

"In the evening?"

"Yes. You mustn't look so mad, though."

"I'm not," he said. "Did any one else see him?"

"Of course," said the girl, as if, after all, it were nothing in particular.

"How long ago was this?"

"Just before you came back."

The drummer pinched his lip nervously.

"Don't say anything, will you?" he asked, giving the girl's arm a gentle squeeze.

"Certainly not," she returned. "I wouldn't worry over it."

"All right," he said, passing on, seriously brooding for once, and yet not wholly unconscious of the fact that he was making a most excellent impression upon the chambermaid.

"I'll see her about that," he said to himself, passionately, feeling that he had been unduly wronged. "I'll find out, b'George, whether she'll act that way or not."

Chapter XXI

THE LURE OF THE SPIRIT: THE FLESH IN PURSUIT

When Carrie came Hurstwood had been waiting many minutes. His blood was warm; his nerves wrought up. He was anxious to see the woman who had stirred him so profoundly the night before.

"Here you are," he said, repressedly, feeling a spring in his limbs and an elation which was tragic in itself.

"Yes," said Carrie.

They walked on as if bound for some objective point, while Hurstwood drank in the radiance of her presence. The rustle of her pretty skirt was like music to him.

"Are you satisfied?" he asked, thinking of how well she did the night before.

"Are you?"

He tightened his fingers as he saw the smile she gave him.

"It was wonderful."

Carrie laughed ecstatically.

"That was one of the best things I've seen in a long time," he added.

He was dwelling on her attractiveness as he had felt it the evening before, and mingling it with the feeling her presence inspired now.

Carrie was dwelling in the atmosphere which this man created for her. Already she was enlivened and suffused with a glow. She felt his drawing toward her in every sound of his voice.

"Those were such nice flowers you sent me," she said, after a moment or two. "They were beautiful."

"Glad you liked them," he answered, simply.

He was thinking all the time that the subject of his desire was being delayed. He was anxious to turn the talk to his own feelings. All was ripe for it. His Carrie was beside him. He wanted to plunge in and expostulate with her, and yet he found himself fishing for words and feeling for a way.

"You got home all right," he said, gloomily, of a sudden, his tone modifying itself to one of self-commiseration.

"Yes," said Carrie, easily.

He looked at her steadily for a moment, slowing his pace and fixing her with his eye.

She felt the flood of feeling.

"How about me?" he asked.

This confused Carrie considerably, for she realised the flood-gates were open. She didn't know exactly what to answer.

"I don't know," she answered.

He took his lower lip between his teeth for a moment, and then let it go. He stopped by the walk side and kicked the grass with his toe. He searched her face with a tender, appealing glance.

"Won't you come away from him?" he asked, intensely.

"I don't know," returned Carrie, still illogically drifting and finding nothing at which to catch.

As a matter of fact, she was in a most hopeless quandary. Here was a man whom she thoroughly liked, who exercised an influence over her, sufficient almost to delude her into the belief that she was possessed of a lively passion for him. She was still the victim of his keen eyes, his suave manners, his fine clothes. She looked and saw before her a man who was most gracious and sympathetic, who leaned toward her with a feeling that was a delight to observe. She could not resist the glow of his temperament, the light of his eye. She could hardly keep from feeling what he felt.

And yet she was not without thoughts which were disturbing. What did he know? What had Drouet told him? Was she a wife in his eyes, or what? Would he marry her? Even while he talked, and she softened, and her eyes were lighted with a tender glow, she was asking herself if Drouet had told him they were not married. There was never anything at all convincing about what Drouet said.

And yet she was not grieved at Hurstwood's love. No strain of bitterness was in it for her, whatever he knew. He was evidently sincere. His passion was real and warm. There was power in what he said. What should she do? She went on thinking this, answering vaguely, languishing affectionately, and altogether drifting, until she was on a borderless sea of speculation.

"Why don't you come away?" he said, tenderly. "I will arrange for you whatever—"

"Oh, don't," said Carrie.

"Don't what?" he asked. "What do you mean?"

There was a look of confusion and pain in her face. She was wondering why that miserable thought must be brought in. She was struck as by a blade with the miserable provision which was outside the pale of marriage.

He himself realised that it was a wretched thing to have dragged in. He wanted to weigh the effects of it, and yet he could not see. He went beating on, flushed by her presence, clearly awakened, intensely enlisted in his plan.

"Won't you come?" he said, beginning over and with a more reverent feeling. "You know I can't do without you—you know it—it can't go on this way—can it?"

"I know," said Carrie.

"I wouldn't ask if I—I wouldn't argue with you if I could help it. Look at me, Carrie. Put yourself in my place. You don't want to stay away from me, do you?"

She shook her head as if in deep thought.

"Then why not settle the whole thing, once and for all?"

"I don't know," said Carrie.

"Don't know! Ah, Carrie, what makes you say that? Don't torment me. Be serious."

"I am," said Carrie, softly.

"You can't be, dearest, and say that. Not when you know how I love you. Look at last night."

His manner as he said this was the most quiet imaginable. His face and body retained utter composure. Only his eyes moved, and they flashed a subtle, dissolving fire. In them the whole intensity of the man's nature was distilling itself.

Carrie made no answer.

"How can you act this way, dearest?" he inquired, after a time. "You love me, don't you?"

He turned on her such a storm of feeling that she was over-whelmed. For the moment all doubts were cleared away.

"Yes," she answered, frankly and tenderly.

"Well, then you'll come, won't you—come to-night?"

Carrie shook her head in spite of her distress.

"I can't wait any longer," urged Hurstwood. "If that is too soon, come Saturday."

"When will we be married?" she asked, diffidently, forgetting in her difficult situation that she had hoped he took her to be Drouet's wife.

The manager started, hit as he was by a problem which was more difficult than hers. He gave no sign of the thoughts that flashed like messages to his mind.

"Any time you say," he said, with ease, refusing to discolour his present delight with this miserable problem.

"Saturday?" asked Carrie.

He nodded his head.

"Well, if you will marry me then," she said, "I'll go."

The manager looked at his lovely prize, so beautiful, so winsome, so difficult to be won, and made strange resolutions. His passion had gotten to that stage now where it was no longer coloured with reason. He did not trouble over little barriers of this sort in the face of so much loveliness. He would accept the situation with all its difficulties; he would not try to answer the objections which cold truth thrust upon him. He would promise anything, everything, and trust to fortune to disentangle him. He would make a try for Paradise, whatever might be the result. He would be happy, by the Lord, if it cost all honesty of statement, all abandonment of truth.

Carrie looked at him tenderly. She could have laid her head upon his shoulder, so delightful did it all seem.

"Well," she said, "I'll try and get ready then."

Hurstwood looked into her pretty face, crossed with little shadows of wonder and misgiving, and thought he had never seen anything more lovely.

"I'll see you again to-morrow," he said, joyously, "and we'll talk over the plans."

He walked on with her, elated beyond words, so delightful had been the result. He impressed a long story of joy and affection upon her, though there was but here and there a word. After a half-hour he began to realise that the meeting must come to an end, so exacting is the world.

"To-morrow," he said at parting, a gayety of manner adding wonderfully to his brave demeanour.

"Yes," said Carrie, tripping elatedly away.

There had been so much enthusiasm engendered that she was believing herself deeply in love. She sighed as she thought of her handsome adorer. Yes, she would get ready by Saturday. She would go, and they would be happy.

Chapter XXII

THE BLAZE OF THE TINDER: FLESH WARS WITH THE FLESH

The misfortune of the Hurstwood household was due to the fact that jealousy, having been born of love, did not perish with it. Mrs. Hurstwood retained this in such form that subsequent influences could transform it into hate. Hurstwood was still worthy, in a physical sense, of the affection his wife had once bestowed upon him, but in a social sense he fell short. With his regard died his power to be attentive to her, and this, to a woman, is much greater than outright crime toward another. Our self-love dictates our appreciation of the good or evil in another. In Mrs. Hurstwood it discoloured the very hue of her husband's indifferent nature. She saw design in deeds and phrases which sprung only from a faded appreciation of her presence.

As a consequence, she was resentful and suspicious. The jealousy that prompted her to observe every falling away from the little amenities of the married relation on his part served to give her notice of the airy grace with which he still took the world. She could see from the scrupulous care which he exercised in the matter of his personal appearance that his interest in life had abated not a jot. Every motion, every glance had something in it of the pleasure he felt in Carrie, of the zest this new pursuit of pleasure lent to his days. Mrs. Hurstwood felt something, sniffing change, as animals do danger, afar off.

This feeling was strengthened by actions of a direct and more potent nature on the part of Hurstwood. We have seen with what irritation he shirked those little duties which no longer contained any amusement or satisfaction for him, and the open snarls with which, more recently, he resented her irritating goads. These little rows were really precipitated by an atmosphere which was surcharged with dissension. That it would shower, with a sky so full of blackening thunder-clouds, would scarcely be thought worthy of comment. Thus, after leaving the breakfast table this morning, raging inwardly at his blank declaration of indifference at her plans, Mrs. Hurstwood encountered Jessica in her dressing-room, very leisurely arranging her hair. Hurstwood had already left the house.

"I wish you wouldn't be so late coming down to breakfast," she said, addressing Jessica, while making for her crochet basket. "Now here the things are quite cold, and you haven't eaten."

Her natural composure was sadly ruffled, and Jessica was doomed to feel the fag end of the storm.

"I'm not hungry," she answered.

"Then why don't you say so, and let the girl put away the things, instead of keeping her waiting all morning?"

"She doesn't mind," answered Jessica, coolly.

"Well, I do, if she doesn't," returned the mother, "and, anyhow, I don't like you to talk that way to me. You're too young to put on such an air with your mother."

"Oh, mamma, don't row," answered Jessica. "What's the matter this morning, anyway?"

"Nothing's the matter, and I'm not rowing. You mustn't think because I indulge you in some things that you can keep everybody waiting. I won't have it."

"I'm not keeping anybody waiting," returned Jessica, sharply, stirred out of a cynical indifference to a sharp defence. "I said I wasn't hungry. I don't want any breakfast."

"Mind how you address me, missy. I'll not have it. Hear me now; I'll not have it!"

Jessica heard this last while walking out of the room, with a toss of her head and a flick of her pretty skirts indicative of the independence and indifference she felt. She did not propose to be quarrelled with.

Such little arguments were all too frequent, the result of a growth of natures which were largely independent and selfish. George, Jr., manifested even greater touchiness and exaggeration in the matter of his individual rights, and attempted to make all feel that he was a man with a man's privileges—an assumption which, of all things, is most groundless and pointless in a youth of nineteen.

Hurstwood was a man of authority and some fine feeling, and it irritated him excessively to find himself surrounded more and more by a world upon which he had no hold, and of which he had a lessening understanding.

Now, when such little things, such as the proposed earlier start to Waukesha, came up, they made clear to him his position. He was being made to follow, was not leading. When, in addition, a sharp temper was manifested, and to the process of shouldering him out of his authority was added a rousing intellectual kick, such as a sneer or a cynical laugh, he was unable to keep his temper. He flew into hardly repressed passion, and wished himself clear of the whole household. It seemed a most irritating drag upon all his desires and opportunities.

For all this, he still retained the semblance of leadership and control, even though his wife was straining to revolt. Her display of temper and open assertion of opposition were based upon nothing more than the feeling that she could do it. She had no special evidence wherewith to justify herself—the knowledge of something which would give her both authority and excuse. The latter was all that was lacking, however, to give a solid foundation to what, in a way, seemed groundless discontent. The clear proof of one overt deed was the cold breath needed to convert the lowering clouds of suspicion into a rain of wrath.

An inkling of untoward deeds on the part of Hurstwood had come. Doctor Beale, the handsome resident physician of the neighbourhood, met Mrs. Hurstwood at her own doorstep some days after Hurstwood and Carrie had taken the drive west on Washington Boulevard. Dr. Beale, coming east on the same drive, had recognised Hurstwood, but not before he was quite past him. He was not so sure of Carrie—did not know whether it was Hurstwood's wife or daughter.

"You don't speak to your friends when you meet them out driving, do you?" he said, jocosely, to Mrs. Hurstwood.

"If I see them, I do. Where was I?"

"On Washington Boulevard," he answered, expecting her eye to light with immediate remembrance.

She shook her head.

"Yes, out near Hoyne Avenue. You were with your husband."

"I guess you're mistaken," she answered. Then, remembering her husband's part in the affair, she immediately fell a prey to a host of young suspicions, of which, however, she gave no sign.

"I know I saw your husband," he went on. "I wasn't so sure about you. Perhaps it was your daughter."

"Perhaps it was," said Mrs. Hurstwood, knowing full well that such was not the case, as Jessica had been her companion for weeks. She had recovered herself sufficiently to wish to know more of the details.

"Was it in the afternoon?" she asked, artfully, assuming an air of acquaintanceship with the matter.

"Yes, about two or three."

"It must have been Jessica," said Mrs. Hurstwood, not wishing to seem to attach any importance to the incident.

The physician had a thought or two of his own, but dismissed the matter as worthy of no further discussion on his part at least.

Mrs. Hurstwood gave this bit of information considerable thought during the next few hours, and even days. She took it for granted that the doctor had really seen her husband, and that he had been riding, most likely, with some other woman, after announcing himself as *busy* to her. As a consequence, she recalled, with rising feeling, how often he had refused to go to places with her, to share in little visits, or, indeed, take part in any of the social amenities which furnished the diversion of her existence. He had been seen at the theatre with people whom he called Moy's friends; now he was seen driving, and, most likely, would have an excuse for that. Perhaps there were others of whom she did not hear, or why should he be so busy, so indifferent, of late? In the last six weeks he had become strangely irritable—strangely satisfied to pick up and go out, whether things were right or wrong in the house. Why?

She recalled, with more subtle emotions, that he did not look at her now with any of the old light of satisfaction or approval in his eye. Evidently, along with other things, he was taking her to be getting old and uninteresting. He saw her wrinkles, perhaps. She was fading, while he was still preening himself in his elegance and youth. He was still an interested factor in the merry-makings of the world, while she—but she did not pursue the thought. She only found the whole situation bitter, and hated him for it thoroughly.

Nothing came of this incident at the time, for the truth is it did not seem conclusive enough to warrant any discussion. Only the atmosphere of distrust and ill-feeling was strengthened, precipitating every now and then little sprinklings of irritable conversation, enlivened by flashes of wrath. The matter of the Waukesha outing was merely a continuation of other things of the same nature.

The day after Carrie's appearance on the Avery stage, Mrs. Hurstwood visited the races with Jessica and a youth of her acquaintance, Mr. Bart Taylor, the son of the owner of a local house-furnishing establishment. They had driven out early, and, as it chanced, encountered several friends of Hurstwood, all Elks, and two of whom had attended the performance the evening before. A thousand chances the subject of the performance had never been brought up had Jessica not been so engaged by the attentions of her young companion, who usurped as much time as possible. This left Mrs. Hurstwood in the mood to extend the perfunctory greetings of some who knew her into short conversations, and the short conversations of friends into long ones. It was from one who meant but to greet her perfunctorily that this interesting intelligence came.

"I see," said this individual, who wore sporting clothes of the most attractive pattern, and had a field-glass strung over his shoulder, "that you did not get over to our little entertainment last evening."

"No?" said Mrs. Hurstwood, inquiringly, and wondering why he should be using the tone he did in noting the fact that she had not been to something she knew nothing about. It was on her lips to say, "What was it?" when he added, "I saw your husband."

Her wonder was at once replaced by the more subtle quality of suspicion.

"Yes," she said, cautiously, "was it pleasant? He did not tell me much about it."

"Very. Really one of the best private theatricals I ever attended. There was one actress who surprised us all."

"Indeed," said Mrs. Hurstwood.

"It's too bad you couldn't have been there, really. I was sorry to hear you weren't feeling well."

Feeling well! Mrs. Hurstwood could have echoed the words after him open-mouthed. As it was, she extricated herself from her mingled impulse to deny and question, and said, almost raspingly:

"Yes, it is too bad."

"Looks like there will be quite a crowd here to-day, doesn't it?" the acquaintance observed, drifting off upon another topic.

The manager's wife would have questioned farther, but she saw no opportunity. She was for the moment wholly at sea, anxious to think for herself, and wondering what new deception was this which caused him to give out that she was ill when she was not. Another case of her company not wanted, and excuses being made. She resolved to find out more.

"Were you at the performance last evening?" she asked of the next of Hurstwood's friends who greeted her, as she sat in her box.

"Yes. You didn't get around."

"No," she answered, "I was not feeling very well."

"So your husband told me," he answered. "Well, it was really very enjoyable. Turned out much better than I expected."

"Were there many there?"

"The house was full. It was quite an Elk night. I saw quite a number of your friends—Mrs. Harrison, Mrs. Barnes, Mrs. Collins."

"Quite a social gathering."

"Indeed it was. My wife enjoyed it very much."

Mrs. Hurstwood bit her lip.

"So," she thought, "that's the way he does. Tells my friends I am sick and cannot come."

She wondered what could induce him to go alone. There was something back of this. She rummaged her brain for a reason.

By evening, when Hurstwood reached home, she had brooded herself into a state of sullen desire for explanation and revenge. She wanted to know what this peculiar action of his imported. She was certain there was more behind it all than what she had heard, and evil curiosity mingled well with distrust and the remnants of her wrath of the morning. She, impending disaster itself, walked about with gathered shadow at the eyes and the rudimentary muscles of savagery fixing the hard lines of her mouth.

On the other hand, as we may well believe, the manager came home in the sunniest mood. His conversation and agreement with Carrie had raised his spirits until he was in the frame of mind of one who sings joyously. He was proud of himself, proud of his success, proud of Carrie. He could have been genial to all the world, and he bore no grudge against his wife. He meant to be pleasant, to forget her presence, to live in the atmosphere of youth and pleasure which had been restored to him.

So now, the house, to his mind, had a most pleasing and comfortable appearance. In the hall he found an evening paper, laid there by the maid and forgotten by Mrs. Hurstwood. In the dining-room the table was clean laid with linen and napery and shiny with glasses and decorated china. Through an open door he saw into the kitchen, where the fire was crackling in the stove and the evening meal already well under way. Out in the small back yard was George, Jr., frolicking with a young dog he had recently purchased, and in the parlour Jessica was playing at the piano, the sound of a merry waltz filling every nook and corner of the comfortable home. Every one, like himself, seemed to have regained his good spirits, to be in sympathy with youth and beauty, to be inclined to joy and merry-making. He felt as if he could say a good word all around himself, and took a most genial glance at the spread table and polished sideboard before going upstairs to read his paper in the comfortable arm-chair of the sitting-room which looked through the open windows into the street. When he entered there, however, he found his wife brushing her hair and musing to herself the while.

He came lightly in, thinking to smooth over any feeling that might still exist by a kindly word and a ready promise, but Mrs. Hurstwood said nothing. He seated himself in the large chair, stirred lightly in making himself comfortable, opened his paper, and began to read. In a few moments he was smiling merrily over a very comical account of a baseball game which had taken place between the Chicago and Detroit teams.

The while he was doing this Mrs. Hurstwood was observing him casually though the medium of the mirror which was before her. She noticed his pleasant and contented manner, his airy grace and smiling humour, and it merely aggravated her the more. She wondered how he could think to carry himself so in her presence after the cynicism, indifference, and neglect he had heretofore manifested and would continue to manifest so long as she would endure it. She thought how she should like to tell him—what stress and emphasis she would lend her assertions, how she could drive over this whole affair until satisfaction should be rendered her. Indeed, the shining sword of her wrath was but weakly suspended by a thread of thought.

In the meanwhile Hurstwood encountered a humorous item concerning a stranger who had arrived in the city and became entangled with a bunco-steerer.[1] It amused him immensely, and at last he stirred and chuckled to himself. He wished that he might enlist his wife's attention and read it to her.

"Ha, ha," he exclaimed softly, as if to himself, "that's funny."

Mrs. Hurstwood kept on arranging her hair, not so much as deigning a glance.

He stirred again and went on to another subject. At last he felt as if his good-humour must find some outlet. Julia was probably still out of humour over that affair of this morning, but that could easily be straightened. As a matter of fact, she was in the wrong, but he didn't care. She could go to Waukesha right away if she wanted to. The sooner the better. He would tell her that as soon as he got a chance, and the whole thing would blow over.

"Did you notice," he said, at last, breaking forth concerning another item which he had found, "that they have entered suit to compel the Illinois Central to get off the lake front, Julia?" he asked.

She could scarcely force herself to answer, but managed to say "No," sharply.

Hurstwood pricked up his ears. There was a note in her voice which vibrated keenly.

"It would be a good thing if they did," he went on, half to himself, half to her, though he felt that something was amiss in that quarter. He withdrew his attention to his paper very circumspectly, listening mentally for the little sounds which should show him what was on foot.

As a matter of fact, no man as clever as Hurstwood—as observant and sensitive to atmospheres of many sorts, particularly upon his own plane of thought—would have made the mistake which he did in regard to his wife, wrought up as she was, had he not been occupied mentally with a very different train of thought. Had not the influence of Carrie's regard for him, the elation which her promise aroused in him, lasted over, he would not have seen the house in so pleasant a mood. It was not extraordinarily bright and merry this

1. A confidence man who leads unwary country visitors into areas where they are robbed, either by force or by trickery.

evening. He was merely very much mistaken, and would have been much more fitted to cope with it had he come home in his normal state.

After he had studied his paper a few moments longer, he felt that he ought to modify matters in some way or other. Evidently his wife was not going to patch up peace at a word. So he said:

"Where did George get the dog he has there in the yard?"

"I don't know," she snapped.

He put his paper down on his knees and gazed idly out of the window. He did not propose to lose his temper, but merely to be persistent and agreeable, and by a few questions bring around a mild understanding of some sort.

"Why do you feel so bad about that affair of this morning?" he said, at last. "We needn't quarrel about that. You know you can go to Waukesha if you want to."

"So you can stay here and trifle around with some one else?" she exclaimed, turning to him a determined countenance upon which was drawn a sharp and wrathful sneer.

He stopped as if slapped in the face. In an instant his persuasive, conciliatory manner fled. He was on the defensive at a wink and puzzled for a word to reply.

"What do you mean?" he said at last, straightening himself and gazing at the cold, determined figure before him, who paid no attention, but went on arranging herself before the mirror.

"You know what I mean," she said, finally, as if there were a world of information which she held in reserve—which she did not need to tell.

"Well, I don't," he said, stubbornly, yet nervous and alert for what should come next. The finality of the woman's manner took away his feeling of superiority in battle.

She made no answer.

"Hmph!" he murmured, with a movement of his head to one side. It was the weakest thing he had ever done. It was totally unassured.

Mrs. Hurstwood noticed the lack of colour in it. She turned upon him, animal-like, able to strike an effectual second blow.

"I want the Waukesha money to-morrow morning," she said.

He looked at her in amazement. Never before had he seen such a cold, steely determination in her eye—such a cruel look of indifference. She seemed a thorough master of her mood—thoroughly confident and determined to wrest all control from him. He felt that all his resources could not defend him. He must attack.

"What do you mean?" he said, jumping up. "You want! I'd like to know what's got into you to-night."

"Nothing's got into me," she said, flaming. "I want that money. You can do your swaggering afterwards."

"Swaggering, eh! What! You'll get nothing from me. What do you mean by your insinuations, anyhow?"

"Where were you last night?" she answered. The words were hot as they came. "Who were you driving with on Washington Boulevard? Who were you with at the theatre when George saw you? Do you think I'm a fool to be duped by you? Do you think I'll sit at home here and take your 'too busys' and 'can't come,' while you parade around and make out that I'm unable to come? I want you to know that lordly airs have come to an end so far as I am concerned. You can't dictate to me nor my children. I'm through with you entirely."

"It's a lie," he said, driven to a corner and knowing no other excuse.

"Lie, eh!" she said, fiercely, but with returning reserve; "you may call it a lie if you want to, but I know."

"It's a lie, I tell you," he said, in a low, sharp voice. "You've been searching around for some cheap accusation for months, and now you think you have it. You think you'll spring something and get the upper hand. Well, I tell you, you can't. As long as I'm in this house I'm master of it, and you or any one else won't dictate to me—do you hear?"

He crept toward her with a light in his eye that was ominous. Something in the woman's cool, cynical, upper-handish manner, as if she were already master, caused him to feel for the moment as if he could strangle her.

She gazed at him—a pythoness in humour.

"I'm not dictating to you," she returned; "I'm telling you what I want."

The answer was so cool, so rich in bravado, that somehow it took the wind out of his sails. He could not attack her, he could not ask her for proofs. Somehow he felt evidence, law, the remembrance of all his property which she held in her name, to be shining in her glance. He was like a vessel, powerful and dangerous, but rolling and floundering without sail.

"And I'm telling you," he said in the end, slightly recovering himself, "what you'll not get."

"We'll see about it," she said. "I'll find out what my rights are. Perhaps you'll talk to a lawyer, if you won't to me."

It was a magnificent play, and had its effect. Hurstwood fell back beaten. He knew now that he had more than mere bluff to contend with. He felt that he was face to face with a dull proposition. What to say he hardly knew. All the merriment had gone out of the day. He was disturbed, wretched, resentful. What should he do?

"Do as you please," he said, at last. "I'll have nothing more to do with you," and out he strode.

Chapter XXIII

A SPIRIT IN TRAVAIL: ONE RUNG PUT BEHIND

When Carrie reached her own room she had already fallen a prey to those doubts and misgivings which are ever the result of a lack of decision. She could not persuade herself as to the advisability of her promise, or that now, having given her word, she ought to keep it. She went over the whole ground in Hurstwood's absence, and discovered little objections that had not occurred to her in the warmth of the manager's argument. She saw where she had put herself in a peculiar light, namely, that of agreeing to marry when she was already supposedly married. She remembered a few things Drouet had done, and now that it came to walking away from him without a word, she felt as if she were doing wrong. Now, she was comfortably situated, and to one who is more or less afraid of the world, this is an urgent matter, and one which puts up strange, uncanny arguments. "You do not know what will come. There are miserable things outside. People go a-begging. Women are wretched. You never can tell what will happen. Remember the time you were hungry. Stick to what you have."

Curiously, for all her leaning towards Hurstwood, he had not taken a firm hold on her understanding. She was listening, smiling, approving, and yet not finally agreeing. This was due to a lack of power on his part, a lack of that majesty of passion that sweeps the mind from its seat, fuses and melts all arguments and theories into a tangled mass, and destroys for the time being the reasoning power. This majesty of passion is possessed by nearly every man once in his life, but it is usually an attribute of youth and conduces to the first successful mating.

Hurstwood, being an older man, could scarcely be said to retain the fire of youth, though he did possess a passion warm and unreasoning. It was strong enough to induce the leaning toward him which, on Carrie's part, we have seen. She might have been said to be imagining herself in love, when she was not. Women frequently do this. It flows from the fact that in each exists a bias toward affection, a craving for the pleasure of being loved. The longing to be shielded, bettered, sympathised with, is one of the attributes of the sex. This, coupled with sentiment and a natural tendency to emotion, often makes refusing difficult. It persuades them that they are in love.

Once at home, she changed her clothes and straightened the rooms for herself. In the matter of the arrangement of the furniture she never took the house-maid's opinion. That young woman invariably put one of the rocking-chairs in the corner, and Carrie as regularly moved it out. To-day she hardly noticed that it was in the wrong place, so absorbed was she in her own thoughts. She worked about the room until Drouet put in appearance at five o'clock. The drummer was flushed and excited and full of determination to know all about her relations with Hurstwood. Nevertheless, after going over the subject in his mind the livelong day, he was rather weary of it and wished it over with. He did not foresee serious consequences of any sort, and yet he rather hesitated to begin. Carrie was sitting by the window when he came in, rocking and looking out.

"Well," she said innocently, weary of her own mental discussion and wondering at his haste and ill-concealed excitement, "what makes you hurry so?"

Drouet hesitated, now that he was in her presence, uncertain as to what course to pursue. He was no diplomat. He could neither read nor see.

"When did you get home?" he asked foolishly.

"Oh, an hour or so ago. What makes you ask that?"

"You weren't here," he said, "when I came back this morning, and I thought you had gone out."

"So I did," said Carrie simply. "I went for a walk."

Drouet looked at her wonderingly. For all his lack of dignity in such matters he did not know how to begin. He stared at her in the most flagrant manner until at last she said:

"What makes you stare at me so? What's the matter?"

"Nothing," he answered. "I was just thinking."

"Just thinking what?" she returned smilingly, puzzled by his attitude.

"Oh, nothing—nothing much."

"Well, then, what makes you look so?"

Drouet was standing by the dresser, gazing at her in a comic manner. He had laid off his hat and gloves and was now fidgeting with the little toilet pieces which were nearest him. He hesitated to believe that the pretty woman before him was involved in anything so unsatisfactory to himself. He was very much inclined to feel that it was all right, after all. Yet the knowledge imparted to him by the chambermaid was rankling in his mind. He wanted to plunge in with a straight remark of some sort, but he knew not what.

"Where did you go this morning?" he finally asked weakly.

"Why, I went for a walk," said Carrie.

"Sure you did?" he asked.

"Yes, what makes you ask?"

She was beginning to see now that he knew something. Instantly she drew herself into a more reserved position. Her cheeks blanched slightly.

"I thought maybe you didn't," he said, beating about the bush in the most useless manner.

Carrie gazed at him, and as she did so her ebbing courage halted. She saw that he himself was hesitating, and with a woman's intuition realised that there was no occasion for great alarm.

"What makes you talk like that?" she asked, wrinkling her pretty forehead. "You act so funny to-night."

"I feel funny," he answered.

They looked at one another for a moment, and then Drouet plunged desperately into his subject.

"What's this about you and Hurstwood?" he asked.

"Me and Hurstwood—what do you mean?"

"Didn't he come here a dozen times while I was away?"

"A dozen times," repeated Carrie, guiltily. "No, but what do you mean?"

"Somebody said that you went out riding with him and that he came here every night."

"No such thing," answered Carrie. "It isn't true. Who told you that?"

She was flushing scarlet to the roots of her hair, but Drouet did not catch the full hue of her face, owing to the modified light of the room. He was regaining much confidence as Carrie defended herself with denials.

"Well, some one," he said. "You're sure you didn't?"

"Certainly," said Carrie. "You know how often he came."

Drouet paused for a moment and thought.

"I know what you told me," he said finally.

He moved nervously about, while Carrie looked at him confusedly.

"Well, I know that I didn't tell you any such thing as that," said Carrie, recovering herself.

"If I were you," went on Drouet, ignoring her last remark, "I wouldn't have anything to do with him. He's a married man, you know."

"Who—who is?" said Carrie, stumbling at the word.

"Why, Hurstwood," said Drouet, noting the effect and feeling that he was delivering a telling blow.

"Hurstwood!" exclaimed Carrie, rising. Her face had changed several shades since this announcement was made. She looked within and without herself in a half-dazed way.

"Who told you this?" she asked, forgetting that her interest was out of order and exceedingly incriminating.

"Why, I know it. I've always known it," said Drouet.

Carrie was feeling about for a right thought. She was making a most miserable showing, and yet feelings were generating within her which were anything but crumbling cowardice.

"I thought I told you," he added.

"No, you didn't," she contradicted, suddenly recovering her voice. "You didn't do anything of the kind."

Drouet listened to her in astonishment. This was something new.

"I thought I did," he said.

Carrie looked around her very solemnly, and then went over to the window.

"You oughtn't to have had anything to do with him," said Drouet in an injured tone, "after all I've done for you."

"You," said Carrie, "you! What have you done for me?"

Her little brain had been surging with contradictory feelings—shame at exposure, shame at Hurstwood's perfidy, anger at Drouet's deception, the mockery he had made of her. Now one clear idea came into her head. He was at fault. There was no doubt about it. Why did he bring Hurstwood out—Hurstwood, a married man, and never say a word to her? Never mind now about Hurstwood's perfidy—why had he done this? Why hadn't he warned her? There he stood now, guilty of this miserable breach of confidence and talking about what he had done for her!

"Well, I like that," exclaimed Drouet, little realising the fire his remark had generated. "I think I've done a good deal."

"You have, eh?" she answered. "You've deceived me—that's what you've done. You've brought your friends out here under false pretences. You've made me out to be—Oh," and with this her voice broke and she pressed her two little hands together tragically.

"I don't see what that's got to do with it," said the drummer quaintly.

"No," she answered, recovering herself and shutting her teeth. "No, of course you don't see. There isn't anything you see. You couldn't have told me in the first place, could you? You had to make me out wrong until it was too late. Now you come sneaking around with your information and your talk about what you have done."

Drouet had never suspected this side of Carrie's nature. She was alive with feeling, her eyes snapping, her lips quivering, her whole body sensible of the injury she felt, and partaking of her wrath.

"Who's sneaking?" he asked, mildly conscious of error on his part, but certain that he was wronged.

"You are," stamped Carrie. "You're a horrid, conceited coward, that's what you are. If you had any sense of manhood in you, you wouldn't have thought of doing any such thing."

The drummer stared.

"I'm not a coward," he said. "What do you mean by going with other men, anyway?"

"Other men!" exclaimed Carrie. "Other men—you know better than that. I did go with Mr. Hurstwood, but whose fault was it?

Didn't you bring him here? You told him yourself that he should come out here and take me out. Now, after it's all over, you come and tell me that I oughtn't to go with him and that he's a married man."

She paused at the sound of the last two words and wrung her hands. The knowledge of Hurstwood's perfidy wounded her like a knife.

"Oh," she sobbed, repressing herself wonderfully and keeping her eyes dry. "Oh, oh!"

"Well, I didn't think you'd be running around with him when I was away," insisted Drouet.

"Didn't think!" said Carrie, now angered to the core by the man's peculiar attitude. "Of course not. You thought only of what would be to your satisfaction. You thought you'd make a toy of me—a plaything. Well, I'll show you that you won't. I'll have nothing more to do with you at all. You can take your old things and keep them," and unfastening a little pin he had given her, she flung it vigorously upon the floor and began to move about as if to gather up the things which belonged to her.

By this Drouet was not only irritated but fascinated the more. He looked at her in amazement, and finally said:

"I don't see where your wrath comes in. I've got the right of this thing. You oughtn't to have done anything that wasn't right after all I did for you."

"What have you done for me?" asked Carrie blazing, her head thrown back and her lips parted.

"I think I've done a good deal," said the drummer, looking around. "I've given you all the clothes you wanted, haven't I? I've taken you everywhere you wanted to go. You've had as much as I've had, and more too."

Carrie was not ungrateful, whatever else might be said of her. In so far as her mind could construe, she acknowledged benefits received. She hardly knew how to answer this, and yet her wrath was not placated. She felt that the drummer had injured her irreparably.

"Did I ask you to?" she returned.

"Well, I did it," said Drouet, "and you took it."

"You talk as though I had persuaded you," answered Carrie. "You stand there and throw up what you've done. I don't want your old things. I'll not have them. You take them to-night and do what you please with them. I'll not stay here another minute."

"That's nice!" he answered, becoming angered now at the sense of his own approaching loss. "Use everything and abuse me and then walk off. That's just like a woman. I take you when you haven't got anything, and then when some one else comes along, why I'm no good. I always thought it'd come out that way."

He felt really hurt as he thought of his treatment, and looked as if he saw no way of obtaining justice.

"It's not so," said Carrie, "and I'm not going with anybody else. You have been as miserable and inconsiderate as you can be. I hate you, I tell you, and I wouldn't live with you another minute. You're a big, insulting"—here she hesitated and used no word at all—"or you wouldn't talk that way."

She had secured her hat and jacket and slipped the latter on over her little evening dress. Some wisps of wavy hair had loosened from the bands at the side of her head and were straggling over her hot, red cheeks. She was angry, mortified, grief-stricken. Her large eyes were full of the anguish of tears, but her lids were not yet wet. She was distracted and uncertain, deciding and doing things without an aim or conclusion, and she had not the slightest conception of how the whole difficulty would end.

"Well, that's a fine finish," said Drouet. "Pack up and pull out, eh? You take the cake. I bet you were knocking around with Hurstwood or you wouldn't act like that. I don't want the old rooms. You needn't pull out for me. You can have them for all I care, but b'George, you haven't done me right."

"I'll not live with you," said Carrie. "I don't want to live with you. You've done nothing but brag around ever since you've been here."

"Aw, I haven't anything of the kind," he answered.

Carrie walked over to the door.

"Where are you going?" he said, stepping over and heading her off.

"Let me out," she said.

"Where are you going?" he repeated.

He was, above all, sympathetic, and the sight of Carrie wandering out, he knew not where, affected him, despite his grievance.

Carrie merely pulled at the door.

The strain of the situation was too much for her, however. She made one more vain effort and then burst into tears.

"Now, be reasonable, Cad," said Drouet gently. "What do you want to rush out for this way? You haven't any place to go. Why not stay here now and be quiet? I'll not bother you. I don't want to stay here any longer."

Carrie had gone sobbing from the door to the window. She was so overcome she could not speak.

"Be reasonable now," he said. "I don't want to hold you. You can go if you want to, but why don't you think it over? Lord knows, I don't want to stop you."

He received no answer. Carrie was quieting, however, under the influence of his plea.

"You stay here now, and I'll go," he added at last.

Carrie listened to this with mingled feelings. Her mind was shaken loose from the little mooring of logic that it had. She was stirred by this thought, angered by that—her own injustice, Hurstwood's, Drouet's, their respective qualities of kindness and favour, the threat of the world outside, in which she had failed once before, the impossibility of this state inside, where the chambers were no longer justly hers, the effect of the argument upon her nerves, all combined to make her a mass of jangling fibres—an anchorless, storm-beaten little craft which could do absolutely nothing but drift.

"Say," said Drouet, coming over to her after a few moments, with a new idea, and putting his hand upon her.

"Don't!" said Carrie, drawing away, but not removing her handkerchief from her eyes.

"Never mind about this quarrel now. Let it go. You stay here until the month's out, anyhow, and then you can tell better what you want to do. Eh?"

Carrie made no answer.

"You'd better do that," he said. "There's no use your packing up now. You can't go anywhere."

Still he got nothing for his words.

"If you'll do that, we'll call it off for the present and I'll get out."

Carrie lowered her handkerchief slightly and looked out of the window.

"Will you do that?" he asked.

Still no answer.

"Will you?" he repeated.

She only looked vaguely into the street.

"Aw! come on," he said, "tell me. Will you?"

"I don't know," said Carrie softly, forced to answer.

"Promise me you'll do that," he said, "and we'll quit talking about it. It'll be the best thing for you."

Carrie heard him, but she could not bring herself to answer reasonably. She felt that the man was gentle, and that his interest in her had not abated, and it made her suffer a pang of regret. She was in a most helpless plight.

As for Drouet, his attitude had been that of the jealous lover. Now his feelings were a mixture of anger at deception, sorrow at losing Carrie, misery at being defeated. He wanted his rights in some way or other, and yet his rights included the retaining of Carrie, the making her feel her error.

"Will you?" he urged.

"Well, I'll see," said Carrie.

This left the matter as open as before, but it was something. It looked as if the quarrel would blow over, if they could only get some way of talking to one another. Carrie was ashamed, and Drouet aggrieved. He pretended to take up the task of packing some things in a valise.

Now, as Carrie watched him out of the corner of her eye, certain sound thoughts came into her head. He had erred, true, but what had she done? He was kindly and good-natured for all his egotism. Throughout this argument he had said nothing very harsh. On the other hand, there was Hurstwood—a greater deceiver than he. He had pretended all this affection, all this passion, and he was lying to her all the while. Oh, the perfidy of men! And she had loved him. There could be nothing more in that quarter. She would see Hurstwood no more. She would write him and let him know what she thought. Thereupon what would she do? Here were these rooms. Here was Drouet, pleading for her to remain. Evidently things could go on here somewhat as before, if all were arranged. It would be better than the street, without a place to lay her head.

All this she thought of as Drouet rummaged the drawers for collars and laboured long and painstakingly at finding a shirt-stud. He was in no hurry to rush this matter. He felt an attraction to Carrie which would not down. He could not think that the thing would end by his walking out of the room. There must be some way round, some way to make her own up that he was right and she was wrong—to patch up a peace and shut out Hurstwood for ever. Mercy, how he turned at the man's shameless duplicity.

"Do you think," he said, after a few moments' silence, "that you'll try and get on the stage?"

He was wondering what she was intending.

"I don't know what I'll do yet," said Carrie.

"If you do, maybe I can help you. I've got a lot of friends in that line."

She made no answer to this.

"Don't go and try to knock around now without any money. Let me help you," he said. "It's no easy thing to go on your own hook here."

Carrie only rocked back and forth in her chair.

"I don't want you to go up against a hard game that way."

He bestirred himself about some other details and Carrie rocked on.

"Why don't you tell me all about this thing," he said, after a time, "and let's call it off? You don't really care for Hurstwood, do you?"

"Why do you want to start on that again?" said Carrie. "You were to blame."

"No, I wasn't," he answered.

"Yes, you were, too," said Carrie. "You shouldn't have ever told me such a story as that."

"But you didn't have much to do with him, did you?" went on

Drouet, anxious for his own peace of mind to get some direct denial from her.

"I won't talk about it," said Carrie, pained at the quizzical turn the peace arrangement had taken.

"What's the use of acting like that now, Cad?" insisted the drummer, stopping in his work and putting up a hand expressively. "You might let me know where I stand, at least."

"I won't," said Carrie, feeling no refuge but in anger. "Whatever has happened is your own fault."

"Then you do care for him?" said Drouet, stopping completely and experiencing a rush of feeling.

"Oh, stop!" said Carrie.

"Well, I'll not be made a fool of," exclaimed Drouet. "You may trifle around with him if you want to, but you can't lead me. You can tell me or not, just as you want to, but I won't fool any longer!"

He shoved the last few remaining things he had laid out into his valise and snapped it with a vengeance. Then he grabbed his coat, which he had laid off to work, picked up his gloves, and started out.

"You can go to the deuce as far as I am concerned," he said, as he reached the door. "I'm no sucker," and with that he opened it with a jerk and closed it equally vigorously.

Carrie listened at her window view, more astonished than anything else at this sudden rise of passion in the drummer. She could hardly believe her senses—so good-natured and tractable had he invariably been. It was not for her to see the wellspring of human passion. A real flame of love is a subtle thing. It burns as a will-o'-the-wisp, dancing onward to fairy lands of delight. It roars as a furnace. Too often jealousy is the quality upon which it feeds.

Chapter XXIV

ASHES OF TINDER: A FACE AT THE WINDOW

That night Hurstwood remained down town entirely, going to the Palmer House for a bed after his work was through.[1] He was in a fevered state of mind, owing to the blight his wife's action threatened to cast upon his entire future. While he was not sure how much significance might be attached to the threat she had made, he was sure that her attitude, if long continued, would cause him no end of trouble. She was determined, and had worsted him in a very important contest. How would it be from now on? He walked the floor of his little office, and later that of his room, putting one thing and another together to no avail.

Mrs. Hurstwood, on the contrary, had decided not to lose her

1. The Palmer House (at State and Monroe) and the Grand Pacific (at Clark and Jackson; see p. 163) were the principal Chicago hotels of the 1880s.

advantage by inaction. Now that she had practically cowed him, she would follow up her work with demands, the acknowledgment of which would make her word *law* in the future. He would have to pay her the money which she would now regularly demand or there would be trouble. It did not matter what he did. She really did not care whether he came home any more or not. The household would move along much more pleasantly without him, and she could do as she wished without consulting any one. Now she proposed to consult a lawyer and hire a detective. She would find out at once just what advantages she could gain.

Hurstwood walked the floor, mentally arranging the chief points of his situation. "She has that property in her name," he kept saying to himself. "What a fool trick that was. Curse it! What a fool move that was."

He also thought of his managerial position. "If she raises a row now I'll lose this thing. They won't have me around if my name gets in the papers. My friends, too!" He grew more angry as he thought of the talk any action on her part would create. How would the papers talk about it? Every man he knew would be wondering. He would have to explain and deny and make a general mark of himself. Then Moy would come and confer with him and there would be the devil to pay.

Many little wrinkles gathered between his eyes as he contemplated this, and his brow moistened. He saw no solution of anything—not a loophole left.

Through all this thoughts of Carrie flashed upon him, and the approaching affair of Saturday. Tangled as all his matters were, he did not worry over that. It was the one pleasing thing in this whole rout of trouble. He could arrange that satisfactorily, for Carrie would be glad to wait, if necessary. He would see how things turned out to-morrow, and then he would talk to her. They were going to meet as usual. He saw only her pretty face and neat figure and wondered why life was not arranged so that such joy as he found with her could be steadily maintained. How much more pleasant it would be. Then he would take up his wife's threat again, and the wrinkles and moisture would return.

In the morning he came over from the hotel and opened his mail, but there was was nothing in it outside the ordinary run. For some reason he felt as if something might come that way, and was relieved when all the envelopes had been scanned and nothing suspicious noticed. He began to feel the appetite that had been wanting before he had reached the office, and decided before going out to the park to meet Carrie to drop in at the Grand Pacific and have a pot of coffee and some rolls. While the danger had not lessened, it had not as yet materialised, and with him no news was good news. If he could only get plenty of time to think, perhaps something would turn up. Surely, surely, this thing would not drift along to catastrophe and he not find a way out.

His spirits fell, however, when, upon reaching the park, he waited and waited and Carrie did not come. He held his favourite post for an hour or more, then arose and began to walk about restlessly. Could something have happened out there to keep her away? Could she have been reached by his wife? Surely not. So little did he consider Drouet that it never once occurred to him to worry about his finding out. He grew restless as he ruminated, and then decided that perhaps it was nothing. She had not been able to get away this morning. That was why no letter notifying him had come. He would get one today. It would probably be on his desk when he got back. He would look for it at once.

After a time he gave up waiting and drearily headed for the Madison car. To add to his distress, the bright blue sky became overcast with little fleecy clouds which shut out the sun. The wind veered to the east, and by the time he reached his office it was threatening to drizzle all afternoon.

He went in and examined his letters, but there was nothing from Carrie. Fortunately, there was nothing from his wife either. He thanked his stars that he did not have to confront that proposition just now when he needed to think so much. He walked the floor again, pretending to be in an ordinary mood, but secretly troubled beyond the expression of words.

At one-thirty he went to Rector's for lunch, and when he returned a messenger was waiting for him. He looked at the little chap with a feeling of doubt.

"I'm to bring an answer," said the boy.

Hurstwood recognised his wife's writing. He tore it open and read without a show of feeling. It began in the most formal manner and was sharply and coldly worded throughout.

"I want you to send the money I asked for at once. I need it to carry out my plans. You can stay away if you want to. It doesn't matter in the least. I must have some money. So don't delay, but send it by the boy."

When he had finished it, he stood holding it in his hands. The audacity of the thing took his breath. It roused his ire also—the deepest element of revolt in him. His first impulse was to write but four words in reply—"Go to the devil!"—but he compromised by telling the boy that there would be no reply. Then he sat down in his chair and gazed without seeing, contemplating the result of his work. What would she do about that? The confounded wretch! Was she going to try to bulldoze him into submission? He would go up there and have it out with her, that's what he would do. She was carrying things with too high a hand. These were his first thoughts.

Later, however, his old discretion asserted itself. Something had to be done. A climax was near and she would not sit idle. He knew her well enough to know that when she had decided upon a plan she would follow it up. Possibly matters would go into a lawyer's hands at once.

"Damn her!" he said softly, with his teeth firmly set, "I'll make it hot for her if she causes me trouble. I'll make her change her tone if I have to use force to do it!"

He arose from his chair and went and looked out into the street. The long drizzle had begun. Pedestrians had turned up collars, and trousers at the bottom. Hands were hidden in the pockets of the umbrellaless; umbrellas were up. The street looked like a sea of round black cloth roofs, twisting, bobbing, moving. Trucks and vans were rattling in a noisy line and everywhere men were shielding themselves as best they could. He scarcely noticed the picture. He was forever confronting his wife, demanding of her to change her attitude toward him before he worked her bodily harm.

At four o'clock another note came, which simply said that if the money was not forthcoming that evening the matter would be laid before Fitzgerald and Moy on the morrow, and other steps would be taken to get it.

Hurstwood almost exclaimed out loud at the insistency of this thing. Yes, he would send her the money. He'd take it to her—he would go up there and have a talk with her, and that at once.

He put on his hat and looked around for his umbrella. He would have some arrangement of this thing.

He called a cab and was driven through the dreary rain to the North Side. On the way his temper cooled as he thought of the details of the case. What did she know? What had she done? Maybe she'd got hold of Carrie, who knows or—or Drouet. Perhaps she really had evidence, and was prepared to fell him as a man does another from secret ambush. She was shrewd. Why should she taunt him this way unless she had good grounds?

He began to wish that he had compromised in some way or other— that he had sent the money. Perhaps he could do it up here. He would go in and see, anyhow. He would have no row.

By the time he reached his own street he was keenly alive to the difficulties of his situation and wished over and over that some solution would offer itself, that he could see his way out. He alighted and went up the steps to the front door, but it was with a nervous palpitation of the heart. He pulled out his key and tried to insert it, but another key was on the inside. He shook at the knob, but the

door was locked. Then he rang the bell. No answer. He rang again—
this time harder. Still no answer. He jangled it fiercely several times
in succession, but without avail. Then he went below.

There was a door which opened under the steps into the kitchen,
protected by an iron grating, intended as a safeguard against bur-
glars. When he reached this he noticed that it also was bolted and
that the kitchen windows were down. What could it mean? He rang
the bell and then waited. Finally, seeing that no one was coming, he
turned and went back to his cab.

"I guess they've gone out," he said apologetically to the individual
who was hiding his red face in a loose tarpaulin rain-coat.

"I saw a young girl up in that winder," returned the cabby.

Hurstwood looked, but there was no face there now. He climbed
moodily into the cab, relieved and distressed.

So this was the game, was it? Shut him out and make him pay.
Well, by the Lord, that did beat all!

Chapter XXV

ASHES OF TINDER: THE LOOSING OF STAYS

When Hurstwood got back to his office again he was in a greater
quandary than ever. Lord, Lord, he thought, what had he got into?
How could things have taken such a violent turn, and so quickly?
He could hardly realise how it had all come about. It seemed a mon-
strous, unnatural, unwarranted condition which had suddenly
descended upon him without his let or hindrance.

Meanwhile he gave a thought now and then to Carrie. What could
be the trouble in that quarter? No letter had come, no word of any
kind, and yet here it was late in the evening and she had agreed to
meet him that morning. To-morrow they were to have met and gone
off—where? He saw that in the excitement of recent events he had
not formulated a plan upon that score. He was desperately in love,
and would have taken great chances to win her under ordinary circumstances, but now—now what? Supposing she had found out
something? Supposing she, too, wrote him and told him that she
knew all—that she would have nothing more to do with him? It
would be just like this to happen as things were going now. Meanwhile he had not sent the money.

He strolled up and down the polished floor of the resort, his hands
in his pockets, his brow wrinkled, his mouth set. He was getting some
vague comfort out of a good cigar, but it was no panacea for the ill
which affected him. Every once in a while he would clinch his fingers
and tap his foot—signs of the stirring mental process he was under-
going. His whole nature was vigorously and powerfully shaken up,

and he was finding what limits the mind has to endurance. He drank more brandy and soda than he had any evening in months. He was altogether a fine example of great mental perturbation.

For all his study nothing came of the evening except this—he sent the money. It was with great opposition, after two or three hours of the most urgent mental affirmation and denial, that at last he got an envelope, placed in it the requested amount, and slowly sealed it up.

Then he called Harry, the boy of all work around the place.

"You take this to this address," he said, handing him the envelope, "and give it to Mrs. Hurstwood."

"Yes, sir," said the boy.

"If she isn't there bring it back."

"Yes, sir."

"You've seen my wife?" he asked as a precautionary measure as the boy turned to go.

"Oh, yes, sir. I know her."

"All right, now. Hurry right back."

"Any answer?"

"I guess not."

The boy hastened away and the manager fell to his musings. Now he had done it. There was no use speculating over that. He was beaten for to-night and he might just as well make the best of it. But, oh, the wretchedness of being forced this way! He could see her meeting the boy at the door and smiling sardonically. She would take the envelope and know that she had triumphed. If he only had that letter back he wouldn't send it. He breathed heavily and wiped the moisture from his face.

For relief, he arose and joined in conversation with a few friends who were drinking. He tried to get the interest of things about him, but it was not to be. All the time his thoughts would run out to his home and see the scene being therein enacted. All the time he was wondering what she would say when the boy handed her the envelope.

In about an hour and three-quarters the boy returned. He had evidently delivered the package, for, as he came up, he made no sign of taking anything out of his pocket.

"Well?" said Hurstwood.

"I gave it to her."

"My wife?"

"Yes, sir."

"Any answer?"

"She said it was high time."

Hurstwood scowled fiercely.

There was no more to be done upon that score that night. He went on brooding over his situation until midnight, when he repaired again to the Palmer House. He wondered what the morning would bring forth, and slept anything but soundly upon it.

Next day he went again to the office and opened his mail, suspicious and hopeful of its contents. No word from Carrie. Nothing from his wife, which was pleasant.

The fact that he had sent the money and that she had received it worked to the ease of his mind, for, as the thought that he had done it receded, his chagrin at it grew less and his hope of peace more. He fancied, as he sat at his desk, that nothing would be done for a week or two. Meanwhile, he would have time to think.

This process of *thinking* began by a reversion to Carrie and the arrangement by which he was to get her away from Drouet. How about that now? His pain at her failure to meet or write him rapidly increased as he devoted himself to this subject. He decided to write her care of the West Side Post-office and ask for an explanation, as well as to have her meet him. The thought that this letter would probably not reach her until Monday chafed him exceedingly. He must get some speedier method—but how?

He thought upon it for a half-hour, not contemplating a messenger or a cab direct to the house, owing to the exposure of it, but finding that time was slipping away to no purpose, he wrote the letter and then began to think again.

The hours slipped by, and with them the possibility of the union he had contemplated. He had thought to be joyously aiding Carrie by now in the task of joining her interests to his, and here it was afternoon and nothing done. Three o'clock came, four, five, six, and no letter. The helpless manager paced the floor and grimly endured the gloom of defeat. He saw a busy Saturday ushered out, the Sabbath in, and nothing done. All day, the bar being closed, he brooded alone, shut out from home, from the excitement of his resort, from Carrie, and without the ability to alter his condition one iota. It was the worst Sunday he had spent in his life.

In Monday's second mail he encountered a very legal-looking letter which held his interest for some time. It bore the imprint of the law offices of McGregor, James and Hay, and with a very formal "Dear Sir," and "We beg to state," went on to inform him briefly that they had been retained by Mrs. Julia Hurstwood to adjust certain matters which related to her sustenance and property rights, and would he kindly call and see them about the matter at once.

He read it through carefully several times, and then merely shook his head. It seemed as if his family troubles were just beginning.

"Well!" he said after a time, quite audibly, "I don't know."

Then he folded it up and put it in his pocket.

To add to his misery there was no word from Carrie. He was quite certain now that she knew he was married and was angered at his perfidy. His loss seemed all the more bitter now that he needed her most. He thought he would go out and insist on seeing her if she did not send him word of some sort soon. He was really affected most miserably of all by this desertion. He had loved her earnestly enough, but now that the possibility of losing her stared him in the face she seemed much more attractive. He really pined for a word, and looked out upon her with his mind's eye in the most wistful manner. He did not propose to lose her, whatever she might think. Come what might, he would adjust this matter, and soon. He would go to her and tell her all his family complications. He would explain to her just where he stood and how much he needed her. Surely she couldn't go back on him now? It wasn't possible. He would plead until her anger would melt—until she would forgive him.

Suddenly he thought: "Supposing she isn't out there—suppose she has gone?"

He was forced to take his feet. It was too much to think of and sit still.

Nevertheless, his rousing availed him nothing.

On Tuesday it was the same way. He did manage to bring himself into the mood to go out to Carrie, but when he got in Ogden Place he thought he saw a man watching him and went away. He did not go within a block of the house.

One of the galling incidents of this visit was that he came back on a Randolph Street car, and without noticing arrived almost opposite the building of the concern with which his son was connected. This sent a pang through his heart. He had called on his boy there several times. Now the lad had not sent him a word. His absence did not seem to be noticed by either of his children. Well, well, fortune plays a man queer tricks. He got back to his office and joined in a conversation with friends. It was as if idle chatter deadened the sense of misery.

That night he dined at Rector's and returned at once to his office. In the bustle and show of the latter was his only relief. He troubled over many little details and talked perfunctorily to everybody. He stayed at his desk long after all others had gone, and only quitted it when the night watchman on his round pulled at the front door to see if it was safely locked.

On Wednesday, he received another polite note from McGregor, James and Hay. It read:

Dear Sir:
We beg to inform you that we are instructed to wait until to-morrow (Thursday) at one o'clock, before filing suit against you, on behalf of Mrs. Julia Hurstwood, for divorce and alimony. If

we do not hear from you before that time we shall consider that
you do not wish to compromise the matter in any way and act
accordingly.   Very truly yours, etc.

"Compromise!" exclaimed Hurstwood bitterly. "Compromise!"
Again he shook his head.

So here it was spread out clear before him, and now he knew what
to expect. If he didn't go and see them they would sue him promptly.
If he did, he would be offered terms that would make his blood boil.
He folded the letter and put it with the other one. Then he put on
his hat and went for a turn about the block.

Chapter XXVI

THE AMBASSADOR FALLEN: A SEARCH FOR THE GATE

Carrie, left alone by Drouet, listened to his retreating steps,
scarcely realising what had happened. She knew that he had stormed
out. It was some moments before she questioned whether he would
return, not now exactly, but ever. She looked around her upon the
rooms, out of which the evening light was dying, and wondered why
she did not feel quite the same towards them. She went over to the
dresser and struck a match, lighting the gas. Then she went back to
the rocker to think.

It was some time before she could collect her thoughts, but when
she did, this truth began to take on importance. She was quite alone.
Suppose Drouet did not come back? Suppose she should never hear
anything more of him? This fine arrangement of chambers would not
last long. She would have to quit them.

To her credit, be it said, she never once counted on Hurstwood.
She could only approach that subject with a pang of sorrow and
regret. For a truth, she was rather shocked and frightened by this
evidence of human depravity. He would have tricked her without
turning an eyelash. She would have been led into a newer and worse
situation. And yet she could not keep out the pictures of his looks
and manners. Only this one deed seemed strange and miserable. It
contrasted sharply with all she felt and knew concerning the man.

But she was alone. That was the greater thought just at present.
How about that? Would she go out to work again? Would she begin
to look around in the business district? The stage! Oh, yes. Drouet
had spoken about that. Was there any hope there? She moved to and
fro, in deep and varied thoughts, while the minutes slipped away and
night fell completely. She had had nothing to eat, and yet there she
sat, thinking it over.

She remembered that she was hungry and went to the little cup-

board in the rear room where were the remains of one of their break-
fasts. She looked at these things with certain misgivings. The
contemplation of food had more significance than usual.

While she was eating she began to wonder how much money she
had. It struck her as exceedingly important, and without ado she
went to look for her purse. It was on the dresser, and in it were seven
dollars in bills and some change. She quailed as she thought of the
insignificance of the amount and rejoiced because the rent was paid
until the end of the month. She began also to think what she would
have done if she had gone out into the street when she first started.
By the side of that situation, as she looked at it now, the present
seemed agreeable. She had a little time at least, and then, perhaps,
everything would come out all right, after all.

Drouet had gone, but what of it? He did not seem seriously angry.
He only acted as if he were huffy. He would come back—of course
he would. There was his cane in the corner. Here was one of his
collars. He had left his light overcoat in the wardrobe. She looked
about and tried to assure herself with the sight of a dozen such
details, but, alas, the secondary thought arrived. Supposing he did
come back. Then what?

Here was another proposition nearly, if not quite, as disturbing.
She would have to talk with and explain to him. He would want her
to admit that he was right. It would be impossible for her to live with
him.

On Friday Carrie remembered her appointment with Hurstwood,
and the passing of the hour when she should, by all right of promise,
have been in his company served to keep the calamity which had
befallen her exceedingly fresh and clear. In her nervousness and
stress of mind she felt it necessary to act, and consequently put on
a brown street dress, and at eleven o'clock started to visit the business portion once again. She must look for work.

The rain, which threatened at twelve and began at one, served
equally well to cause her to retrace her steps and remain within doors
as it did to reduce Hurstwood's spirits and give him a wretched day.

The morrow was Saturday, a half-holiday in many business quarters, and besides it was a balmy, radiant day, with the trees and grass
shining exceedingly green after the rain of the night before. When
she went out the sparrows were twittering merrily in joyous choruses.
She could not help feeling, as she looked across the lovely park, that
life was a joyous thing for those who did not need to worry, and she
wished over and over that something might interfere now to preserve
for her the comfortable state which she had occupied. She did not
want Drouet or his money when she thought of it, nor anything more
to do with Hurstwood, but only the content and ease of mind she

had experienced, for, after all, she had been happy—happier, at least, than she was now when confronted by the necessity of making her way alone.

When she arrived in the business part it was quite eleven o'clock, and the business had little longer to run. She did not realise this at first, being affected by some of the old distress which was a result of her earlier adventure into this strenuous and exacting quarter. She wandered about, assuring herself that she was making up her mind to look for something, and at the same time feeling that perhaps it was not necessary to be in such haste about it. The thing was difficult to encounter, and she had a few days. Besides, she was not sure that she was really face to face again with the bitter problem of self-sustenance. Anyhow, there was one change for the better. She knew that she had improved in appearance. Her manner had vastly changed. Her clothes were becoming, and men—well-dressed men, some of the kind who before had gazed at her indifferently from behind their polished railings and imposing office partitions—now gazed into her face with a soft light in their eyes. In a way, she felt the power and satisfaction of the thing, but it did not wholly reassure her. She looked for nothing save what might come legitimately and without the appearance of special favour. She wanted something, but no man should buy her by false protestations or favour. She proposed to earn her living honestly.

"This store closes at one on Saturdays," was a pleasing and satis-factory legend to see upon doors which she felt she ought to enter and inquire for work. It gave her an excuse, and after encountering quite a number of them, and noting that the clock registered 12.15, she decided that it would be no use to seek further to-day, so she got on a car and went to Lincoln Park. There was always something to see there—the flowers, the animals, the lake—and she flattered herself that on Monday she would be up betimes and searching. Besides, many things might happen between now and Monday.

Sunday passed with equal doubts, worries, assurances, and heaven knows what vagaries of mind and spirit. Every half-hour in the day the thought would come to her most sharply, like the tail of a swish-ing whip, that action—immediate action—was imperative. At other times she would look about her and assure herself that things were not so bad—that certainly she would come out safe and sound. At such times she would think of Drouet's advice about going on the stage, and saw some chance for herself in that quarter. She decided to take up that opportunity on the morrow.

Accordingly, she arose early Monday morning and dressed herself carefully. She did not know just how such applications were made, but she took it to be a matter which related more directly to the theatre buildings. All you had to do was to inquire of some one about

the theatre for the manager and ask for a position. If there was anything, you might get it, or, at least, he could tell you how.

She had had no experience with this class of individuals whatsoever, and did not know the salacity and humour of the theatrical
tribe. She only knew of the position which Mr. Hale occupied, but,
of all things, she did not wish to encounter that personage, on
account of her intimacy with his wife.

There was, however, at this time, one theatre, the Chicago Opera
House, which was considerably in the public eye, and its manager,
David A. Henderson, had a fair local reputation.[1] Carrie had seen
one or two elaborate performances there and had heard of several
others. She knew nothing of Henderson nor of the methods of applying, but she instinctively felt that this would be a likely place, and
accordingly strolled about in that neighbourhood. She came bravely
enough to the showy entrance way, with the polished and begilded
lobby, set with framed pictures out of the current attraction, leading
up to the quiet box-office, but she could get no further. A noted
comic opera comedian was holding forth that week, and the air of
distinction and prosperity overawed her. She could not imagine that
there would be anything in such a lofty sphere for her. She almost
trembled at the audacity which might have carried her on to a terrible
rebuff. She could find heart only to look at the pictures which were
showy and then walk out. It seemed to her as if she had made a
splendid escape and that it would be foolhardy to think of applying
in that quarter again.

This little experience settled her hunting for one day. She looked
around elsewhere, but it was from the outside. She got the location
of several playhouses fixed in her mind—notably the Grand Opera
House and McVickar's, both of which were leading in attractions—
and then came away. Her spirits were materially reduced, owing to
the newly restored sense of magnitude of the great interests and the
insignificance of her claims upon society, such as she understood
them to be.

That night she was visited by Mrs. Hale, whose chatter and pro-
tracted stay made it impossible to dwell upon her predicament or
the fortune of the day. Before retiring, however, she sat down to
think, and gave herself up to the most gloomy forebodings. Drouet
had not put in an appearance. She had had no word from any quarter, she had spent a dollar of her precious sum in procuring food and
paying car fare. It was evident that she would not endure long.
Besides, she had discovered no resource.

1. A major Chicago theater (at Washington and Clark), which was actually managed in the
1880s by David Henderson and which specialized in musical extravaganzas. It should be
noted that in the late nineteenth century "opera" signified light entertainment, often a
combination of vaudeville acts and chorus numbers. The operas of a Verdi or Wagner
were "grand opera."

In this situation her thoughts went out to her sister in Van Buren Street, whom she had not seen since the night of her flight, and to her home at Columbia City, which seemed now a part of something that could not be again. She looked for no refuge in that direction. Nothing but sorrow was brought her by thoughts of Hurstwood, which would return. That he could have chosen to dupe her in so ready a manner seemed a cruel thing.

Tuesday came, and with it appropriate indecision and speculation. She was in no mood, after her failure of the day before, to hasten forth upon her work-seeking errand, and yet she rebuked herself for what she considered her weakness the day before. Accordingly she started out to revisit the Chicago Opera House, but possessed scarcely enough courage to approach.

She did manage to inquire at the box-office, however.

"Manager of the company or the house?" asked the smartly dressed individual who took care of the tickets. He was favourably impressed by Carrie's looks.

"I don't know," said Carrie, taken back by the question.

"You couldn't see the manager of the house to-day, anyhow," volunteered the young man. "He's out of town."

He noted her puzzled look, and then added: "What is it you wish to see about?"

"I want to see about getting a position," she answered.

"You'd better see the manager of the company," he returned, "but he isn't here now."

"When will he be in?" asked Carrie, somewhat relieved by this information.

"Well, you might find him in between eleven and twelve. He's here after two o'clock."

Carrie thanked him and walked briskly out, while the young man gazed after her through one of the side windows of his gilded coop.

"Good-looking," he said to himself, and proceeded to visions of condescensions on her part which were exceedingly flattering to himself.

One of the principal comedy companies of the day was playing an engagement at the Grand Opera House. Here Carrie asked to see the manager of the company. She little knew the trivial authority of this individual, or that had there been a vacancy an actor would have been sent on from New York to fill it.

"His office is upstairs," said a man in the box-office.

Several persons were in the manager's office, two lounging near a window, another talking to an individual sitting at a roll-top desk—the manager. Carrie glanced nervously about, and began to fear that she should have to make her appeal before the assembled company, two of whom—the occupants of the window—were already observing her carefully.

"I can't do it," the manager was saying; "it's a rule of Mr. Frohman's never to allow visitors back of the stage.[2] No, no!"

Carrie timidly waited, standing. There were chairs, but no one motioned her to be seated. The individual to whom the manager had been talking went away quite crestfallen. That luminary gazed earnestly at some papers before him, as if they were of the greatest concern.

"Did you see that in the 'Herald' this morning about Nat Goodwin, Harris?"

"No," said the person addressed. "What was it?"

"Made quite a curtain address at Hooley's last night.[3] Better look it up."

Harris reached over to a table and began to look for the "Herald."

"What is it?" said the manager to Carrie, apparently noticing her for the first time. He thought he was going to be held up for free tickets.

Carrie summoned up all her courage, which was little at best. She realised that she was a novice, and felt as if a rebuff were certain. Of this she was so sure that she only wished now to pretend she had called for advice.

"Can you tell me how to go about getting on the stage?"

It was the best way after all to have gone about the matter. She was interesting, in a manner, to the occupant of the chair, and the simplicity of her request and attitude took his fancy. He smiled, as did the others in the room, who, however, made some slight effort to conceal their humour.

"I don't know," he answered, looking her brazenly over. "Have you ever had any experience upon the stage?"

"A little," answered Carrie. "I have taken part in amateur performances."

She thought she had to make some sort of showing in order to retain his interest.

"Never studied for the stage?" he said, putting on an air intended as much to impress his friends with his discretion as Carrie.

"No, sir."

"Well, I don't know," he answered, tipping lazily back in his chair while she stood before him. "What makes you want to get on the stage?"

2. Daniel Frohman's Lyceum Stock Company of New York frequently played at the Grand Opera House on Clark Street.
3. Hooley's (at Randolph and La Salle) ranked with McVicker's as a leading Chicago theater. Nat Goodwin, a famous comedian of the day (see also p. 217), usually played there when in Chicago.

She felt abashed at the man's daring, but could only smile in answer to his engaging smirk, and say:

"I need to make a living."

"Oh," he answered, rather taken by her trim appearance, and feeling as if he might scrape up an acquaintance with her. "That's a good reason, isn't it? Well, Chicago is not a good place for what you want to do. You ought to be in New York. There's more chance there. You could hardly expect to get started out here."

Carrie smiled genially, grateful that he should condescend to advise her even so much. He noticed the smile, and put a slightly different construction on it. He thought he saw an easy chance for a little flirtation.

"Sit down," he said, pulling a chair forward from the side of his desk and dropping his voice so that the two men in the room should not hear. Those two gave each other the suggestion of a wink.

"Well, I'll be going, Barney," said one, breaking away and so addressing the manager. "See you this afternoon."

"All right," said the manager.

The remaining individual took up a paper as if to read.

"Did you have any idea what sort of part you would like to get?" asked the manager softly.

"Oh, no," said Carrie. "I would take anything to begin with."

"I see," he said. "Do you live here in the city?"

"Yes, sir."

The manager smiled most blandly.

"Have you ever tried to get in as a chorus girl?" he asked, assuming a more confidential air.

Carrie began to feel that there was something exuberant and unnatural in his manner.

"No," she said.

"That's the way most girls begin," he went on, "who go on the stage. It's a good way to get experience."

He was turning on her a glance of the companionable and persuasive manner.

"I didn't know that," said Carrie.

"It's a difficult thing," he went on, "but there's always a chance, you know." Then, as if he suddenly remembered, he pulled out his watch and consulted it. "I've an appointment at two," he said, "and I've got to go to lunch now. Would you care to come and dine with me? We can talk it over there."

"Oh, no," said Carrie, the whole motive of the man flashing on her at once. "I have an engagement myself."

"That's too bad," he said, realising that he had been a little beforehand in his offer and that Carrie was about to go away. "Come in later. I may know of something."

"Thank you," she answered, with some trepidation, and went out.

"She was good-looking, wasn't she?" said the manager's companion, who had not caught all the details of the game he had played.

"Yes, in a way," said the other, sore to think the game had been lost. "She'd never make an actress, though. Just another chorus girl—that's all."

This little experience nearly destroyed her ambition to call upon the manager at the Chicago Opera House, but she decided to do so after a time. He was of a more sedate turn of mind. He said at once that there was no opening of any sort, and seemed to consider her search foolish.

"Chicago is no place to get a start," he said. "You ought to be in New York."

Still she persisted, and went to McVickar's, where she could not find any one. "The Old Homestead" was running there,[1] but the person to whom she was referred was not to be found.

These little expeditions took up her time until quite four o'clock, when she was weary enough to go home. She felt as if she ought to continue and inquire elsewhere, but the results so far were too dispiriting. She took the car and arrived at Ogden Place in three-quarters of an hour, but decided to ride on to the West Side branch of the Post-office, where she was accustomed to receive Hurstwood's letters. There was one there now, written Saturday, which she tore open and read with mingled feelings. There was so much warmth in it and such tense complaint at her having failed to meet him, and her subsequent silence, that she rather pitied the man. That he loved her was evident enough. That he had wished and dared to do so, married as he was, was the evil. She felt as if the thing deserved an answer, and consequently decided that she would write and let him know that she knew of his married state and was justly incensed at his deception. She would tell him that it was all over between them.

At her room, the wording of this missive occupied her for some time, for she fell to the task at once. It was most difficult.

"You do not need to have me explain why I did not meet you," she wrote in part. "How could you deceive me so? You cannot expect me to have anything more to do with you. I wouldn't under any circumstances. Oh, how could you act so?" she added in a burst of feeling. "You have caused me more misery than you can think. I hope you will get over your infatuation for me. We must not meet any more. Good-bye."

She took the letter the next morning, and at the corner dropped it reluctantly into the letter-box, still uncertain as to whether she should do so or not. Then she took the car and went down town.

---

4. *The Old Homestead*, by Denman Thompson, was a folksy comedy of rural life that was popular throughout the 1880s and 1890s.

This was the dull season with the department stores, but she was listened to with more consideration than was usually accorded to young women applicants, owing to her neat and attractive appearance. She was asked the same old questions with which she was already familiar.

"What can you do? Have you ever worked in a retail store before? Are you experienced?"

At The Fair, See and Company's, and all the great stores it was much the same.[5] It was the dull season, she might come in a little later, possibly they would like to have her.

When she arrived at the house at the end of the day, weary and disheartened, she discovered that Drouet had been there. His umbrella and light overcoat were gone. She thought she missed other things, but could not be sure. Everything had not been taken.

So his going was crystallising into staying. What was she to do now? Evidently she would be facing the world in the same old way within a day or two. Her clothes would get poor. She put her two hands together in her customary expressive way and pressed her fingers. Large tears gathered in her eyes and broke hot across her cheeks. She was alone, very much alone.

Drouet really had called, but it was with a very different mind from that which Carrie had imagined. He expected to find her, to justify his return by claiming that he came to get the remaining portion of his wardrobe, and before he got away again to patch up a peace.

Accordingly, when he arrived, he was disappointed to find Carrie out. He trifled about, hoping that she was somewhere in the neighbourhood and would soon return. He constantly listened, expecting to hear her foot on the stair.

When he did so, it was his intention to make believe that he had just come in and was disturbed at being caught. Then he would explain his need of his clothes and find out how things stood.

Wait as he did, however, Carrie did not come. From pottering around among the drawers, in momentary expectation of her arrival, he changed to looking out of the window, and from that to resting himself in the rocking-chair. Still no Carrie. He began to grow restless and lit a cigar. After that he walked the floor. Then he looked out of the window and saw clouds gathering. He remembered an appointment at three. He began to think that it would be useless to wait, and got hold of his umbrella and light coat, intending to take these things, any way. It would scare her, he hoped. To-morrow he would come back for the others. He would find out how things stood.

As he started to go he felt truly sorry that he had missed her. There was a little picture of her on the wall, showing her arrayed in the little jacket he had first bought her—her face a little more wistful than he had seen it lately. He was really touched by it, and looked into the eyes of it with a rather rare feeling for him.

"You didn't do me right, Cad," he said, as if he were addressing her in the flesh.

Then he went to the door, took a good look around, and went out.

Chapter XXVII

WHEN WATERS ENGULF US WE REACH FOR A STAR

It was when he returned from his disturbed stroll about the streets, after receiving the decisive note from McGregor, James and Hay, that Hurstwood found the letter Carrie had written him that morning. He thrilled intensely as he noted the handwriting, and rapidly tore it open.

"Then," he thought, "she loves me or she would not have written to me at all."

He was slightly depressed at the tenor of the note for the first few minutes, but soon recovered. "She wouldn't write at all if she didn't care for me."

This was his one resource against the depression which held him. He could extract little from the wording of the letter, but the spirit he thought he knew.

There was really something exceedingly human—if not pathetic— in his being thus relieved by a clearly worded reproof. He who had for so long remained satisfied with himself now looked outside of himself for comfort—and to such a source. The mystic cords of affection! How they bind us all.

The colour came to his cheeks. For the moment he forgot the letter from McGregor, James and Hay. If he could only have Carrie, per-haps he could get out of the whole entanglement—perhaps it would not matter. He wouldn't care what his wife did with herself if only he might not lose Carrie. He stood up and walked about, dreaming his delightful dream of a life continued with this lovely possessor of his heart.

It was not long, however, before the old worry was back for con-sideration, and with it what weariness! He thought of the morrow and the suit. He had done nothing, and here was the afternoon slip-ping away. It was now a quarter of four. At five the attorneys would have gone home. He still had the morrow until noon. Even as he thought, the last fifteen minutes passed away and it was five. Then he abandoned the thought of seeing them any more that day and turned to Carrie.

It is to be observed that the man did not justify himself to himself. He was not troubling about that. His whole thought was the possibility of persuading Carrie. Nothing was wrong in that. He loved her dearly. Their mutual happiness depended upon it. Would that Drouet were only away!

While he was thinking thus elatedly, he remembered that he wanted some clean linen in the morning.

This he purchased, together with a half-dozen ties, and went to the Palmer House. As he entered he thought he saw Drouet ascending the stairs with a key. Surely not Drouet! Then he thought, perhaps they had changed their abode temporarily. He went straight up to the desk.

"Is Mr. Drouet stopping here?" he asked of the clerk.

"I think he is," said the latter, consulting his private registry list. "Yes."

"Is that so?" exclaimed Hurstwood, otherwise concealing his astonishment. "Alone?" he added.

"Yes," said the clerk.

Hurstwood turned away and set his lips so as best to express and conceal his feelings.

"How's that?" he thought. "They've had a row."

He hastened to his room with rising spirits and changed his linen. As he did so, he made up his mind that if Carrie was alone, or if she had gone to another place, it behooved him to find out. He decided to call at once.

"I know what I'll do," he thought. "I'll go to the door and ask if Mr. Drouet is at home. That will bring out whether he is there or not and where Carrie is."

He was almost moved to some muscular display as he thought of it. He decided to go immediately after supper.

On coming down from his room at six, he looked carefully about to see if Drouet was present and then went out to lunch. He could scarcely eat, however, he was so anxious to be about his errand. Before starting he thought it well to discover where Drouet would be, and returned to his hotel.

"Has Mr. Drouet gone out?" he asked of the clerk.

"No," answered the latter, "he's in his room. Do you wish to send up a card?"

"No, I'll call around later," answered Hurstwood, and strolled out.

He took a Madison car and went direct to Ogden Place, this time walking boldly up to the door. The chambermaid answered his knock.

"Is Mr. Drouet in?" said Hurstwood blandly.

"He is out of the city," said the girl, who had heard Carrie tell this to Mrs. Hale.

"Is Mrs. Drouet in?"

"No, she has gone to the theatre."

"Is that so?" said Hurstwood, considerably taken back; then, as if burdened with something important, "You don't know to which theatre?"

The girl really had no idea where she had gone, but not liking Hurstwood, and wishing to cause him trouble, answered: "Yes, Hooley's."

"Thank you," returned the manager, and tipping his hat slightly, went away.

"I'll look in at Hooley's," thought he, but as a matter of fact he did not. Before he had reached the central portion of the city he thought the whole matter over and decided it would be useless. As much as he longed to see Carrie, he knew she would be with some one and did not wish to intrude with his plea there. A little later he might do so—in the morning. Only in the morning he had the lawyer question before him.

This little pilgrimage threw quite a wet blanket upon his rising spirits. He was soon down again to his old worry, and reached the resort anxious to find relief. Quite a company of gentlemen were making the place lively with their conversation. A group of Cook County politicians were conferring about a round cherry-wood table in the rear portion of the room. Several young merry-makers were chattering at the bar before making a belated visit to the theatre. A shabbily-genteel individual, with a red nose and an old high hat, was sipping a quiet glass of ale alone at one end of the bar. Hurstwood nodded to the politicians and went into his office.

About ten o'clock a friend of his, Mr. Frank L. Taintor, a local sport and racing man, dropped in, and seeing Hurstwood alone in his office came to the door.

"Hello, George!" he exclaimed.

"How are you, Frank?" said Hurstwood, somewhat relieved by the sight of him. "Sit down," and he motioned him to one of the chairs in the little room.

"What's the matter, George?" asked Taintor. "You look a little glum. Haven't lost at the track, have you?"

"I'm not feeling very well to-night. I had a slight cold the other day."

"Take whiskey, George," said Taintor. "You ought to know that."

Hurstwood smiled.

While they were still conferring there, several other of Hurstwood's friends entered, and not long after eleven, the theatres being out, some actors began to drop in—among them some notabilities.

Then began one of those pointless social conversations so common in America resorts where the would-be *gilded* attempt to rub off gilt from those who have it in abundance. If Hurstwood had one leaning, it was toward notabilities. He considered that, if anywhere, he belonged among them. He was too proud to toady, too keen not to strictly observe the plane he occupied when there were those present who did not appreciate him, but, in situations like the present, where he could shine as a gentleman and be received without equivocation as a friend and equal among men of known ability, he was most delighted. It was on such occasions, if ever, that he would "take something." When the social flavour was strong enough he would even unbend to the extent of drinking glass for glass with his associates, punctiliously observing his turn to pay as if he were an outsider like the others. If he ever approached intoxication—or rather that ruddy warmth and comfortableness which precedes the more sloven state—it was when individuals such as these were gathered about him, when he was one of a circle of chatting celebrities. To-night, disturbed as was his state, he was rather relieved to find company, and now that notabilities were gathered, he laid aside his troubles for the nonce, and joined in right heartily.

It was not long before the imbibing began to tell. Stories began to crop up—those ever-enduring, droll stories which form the major portion of the conversation among American men under such circumstances.

Twelve o'clock arrived, the hour for closing, and with it the company took leave. Hurstwood shook hands with them most cordially. He was very roseate physically. He had arrived at that state where his mind, though clear, was, nevertheless, warm in its fancies. He felt as if his troubles were not very serious. Going into his office, he began to turn over certain accounts, awaiting the departure of the bartenders and the cashier, who soon left.

It was the manager's duty, as well as his custom, after all were gone to see that everything was safely closed up for the night. As a rule, no money except the cash taken in after banking hours was kept about the place, and that was locked in the safe by the cashier, who, with the owners, was joint keeper of the secret combination, but, nevertheless, Hurstwood nightly took the precaution to try the cash drawers and the safe in order to see that they were tightly closed. Then he would lock his own little office and set the proper light burning near the safe, after which he would take his departure.

Never in his experience had he found anything out of order, but to-night, after shutting down his desk, he came out and tried the safe. His way was to give a sharp pull. This time the door responded. He was slightly surprised at that, and looking in found the money cases as left for the day, apparently unprotected. His first thought was, of course, to inspect the drawers and shut the door.

"I'll speak to Mayhew about this to-morrow," he thought.

The latter had certainly imagined upon going out a half-hour before that he had turned the knob on the door so as to spring the lock. He had never failed to do so before. But to-night Mayhew had other thoughts. He had been revolving the problem of a business of his own.

"I'll look in here," thought the manager, pulling out the money drawers. He did not know why he wished to look in there. It was quite a superfluous action, which another time might not have happened at all.

As he did so, a layer of bills, in parcels of a thousand, such as banks issue, caught his eye. He could not tell how much they represented, but paused to view them. Then he pulled out the second of the cash drawers. In that were the receipts of the day.

"I didn't know Fitzgerald and Moy ever left any money this way," his mind said to itself. "They must have forgotten it."

He looked at the other drawer and paused again.

"Count them," said a voice in his ear.

He put his hand into the first of the boxes and lifted the stack, letting the separate parcels fall. They were bills of fifty and one hundred dollars done in packages of a thousand. He thought he counted ten such.

"Why don't I shut the safe?" his mind said to itself, lingering. "What makes me pause here?"

For answer there came the strangest words:

"Did you ever have ten thousand dollars in ready money?"

Lo, the manager remembered that he had never had so much. All his property had been slowly accumulated, and now his wife owned that. He was worth more than forty thousand, all told—but she would get that.

He puzzled as he thought of these things, then pushed in the drawers and closed the door, pausing with his hand upon the knob, which might so easily lock it all beyond temptation. Still he paused. Finally he went to the windows and pulled down the curtains. Then he tried the door, which he had previously locked. What was this thing, making him suspicious? Why did he wish to move about so quietly. He came back to the end of the counter as if to rest his arm and think. Then he went and unlocked his little office door and turned on the light. He also opened his desk, sitting down before it, only to think strange thoughts.

"The safe is open," said a voice. "There is just the least little crack in it. The lock has not been sprung."

The manager floundered among a jumble of thoughts. Now all the entanglement of the day came back. Also the thought that here was a solution. That money would do it. If he had that and Carrie. He rose up and stood stock-still, looking at the floor.

"What about it?" his mind asked, and for answer he put his hand slowly up and scratched his head.

The manager was no fool to be led blindly away by such an errant proposition as this, but his situation was peculiar. Wine was in his veins. It had crept up into his head and given him a warm view of the situation. It also coloured the possibilities of ten thousand for him. He could see great opportunities with that. He could get Carrie. Oh, yes, he could! He could get rid of his wife. That letter, too, was waiting discussion to-morrow morning. He would not need to answer that. He went back to the safe and put his hand on the knob. Then he pulled the door open and took the drawer with the money quite out.

With it once out and before him, it seemed a foolish thing to think about leaving it. Certainly it would. Why, he could live quietly with Carrie for years.

Lord! what was that? For the first time he was tense, as if a stern hand had been laid upon his shoulder. He looked fearfully around. Not a soul was present. Not a sound. Some one was shuffling by on the sidewalk. He took the box and the money and put it back in the safe. Then he partly closed the door again.

To those who have never wavered in conscience, the predicament of the individual whose mind is less strongly constituted and who trembles in the balance between duty and desire is scarcely appreciable, unless graphically portrayed. Those who have never heard that solemn voice of the ghostly clock which ticks with awful distinctness, "thou shalt," "thou shalt not," "thou shalt," "thou shalt not," are in no position to judge. Not alone in sensitive, highly organised natures is such a mental conflict possible. The dullest specimen of humanity, when drawn by desire toward evil, is recalled by a sense of right, which is proportionate in power and strength to his evil tendency. We must remember that it may not be a knowledge of right, for no knowledge of right is predicated of the animal's instinctive recoil at evil. Men are still led by instinct before they are regulated by knowledge. It is instinct which recalls the criminal—it is instinct (where highly organised reasoning is absent) which gives the criminal his feeling of danger, his fear of wrong.

At every first adventure, then, into some untried evil, the mind wavers. The clock of thought ticks out its wish and its denial. To those who have never experienced such a mental dilemma, the following will appeal on the simple ground of revelation.

When Hurstwood put the money back, his nature again resumed its ease and daring. No one had observed him. He was quite alone. No one could tell what he wished to do. He could work this thing out for himself.

The imbibation of the evening had not yet worn off. Moist as was his brow, tremble as did his hand once after the nameless fright, he was still flushed with the fumes of liquor. He scarcely noticed that the time was passing. He went over his situation once again, his eye always seeing the money in a lump, his mind always seeing what it would do. He strolled into his little room, then to the door, then to the safe again. He put his hand on the knob and opened it. There was the money! Surely no harm could come from looking at it!

He took out the drawer again and lifted the bills. They were so smooth, so compact, so portable. How little they made, after all. He decided he would take them. Yes, he would. He would put them in his pocket. Then he looked at that and saw they would not go there. His hand satchel! To be sure, his hand satchel. They would go in that—all of it would. No one would think anything of it either. He went into the little office and took it from the shelf in the corner. Now he set it upon his desk and went out toward the safe. For some reason he did not want to fill it out in the big room.

First he brought the bills and then the loose receipts of the day. He would take it all. He put the empty drawers back and pushed the iron door almost to, then stood beside it meditating.

The wavering of a mind under such circumstances is an almost inexplicable thing, and yet it is absolutely true. Hurstwood could not bring himself to act definitely. He wanted to think about it—to ponder over it, to decide whether it were best. He was drawn by such a keen desire for Carrie, driven by such a state of turmoil in his own affairs that he thought constantly it would be best, and yet he wavered. He did not know what evil might result from it to him— how soon he might come to grief. The true ethics of the situation never once occurred to him, and never would have, under any circumstances.

After he had all the money in the hand bag, a revulsion of feeling seized him. He would not do it—no! Think of what a scandal it would make. The police! They would be after him. He would have to fly, and where? Oh, the terror of being a fugitive from justice! He took out the two boxes and put all the money back. In his excitement he forgot what he was doing, and put the sums in the wrong boxes. As he pushed the door to, he thought he remembered doing it wrong and opened the door again. There were the two boxes mixed.

He took them out and straightened the matter, but now the terror had gone. Why be afraid?

While the money was in his hand the lock clicked. It had sprung! Did he do it? He grabbed at the knob and pulled vigorously. It had closed. Heavens! he was in for it now, sure enough.

The moment he realised that the safe was locked for a surety, the sweat burst out upon his brow and he trembled violently. He looked about him and decided instantly. There was no delaying now.

"Supposing I do lay it on the top," he said, "and go away, they'll know who took it. I'm the last to close up. Besides, other things will happen."

At once he became the man of action.

"I must get out of this," he thought.

He hurried into his little room, took down his light overcoat and hat, locked his desk, and grabbed the satchel. Then he turned out all but one light and opened the door. He tried to put on his old assured air, but it was almost gone. He was repenting rapidly.

"I wish I hadn't done that," he said. "That was a mistake."

He walked steadily down the street, greeting a night watchman whom he knew who was trying doors. He must get out of the city, and that quickly.

"I wonder how the trains run?" he thought.

Instantly he pulled out his watch and looked. It was nearly half-past one.

At the first drug store he stopped, seeing a long-distance telephone booth inside. It was a famous drug store, and contained one of the first private telephone booths ever erected.[1]

"I want to use your 'phone a minute," he said to the night clerk.

The latter nodded.

"Give me 1643," he called to Central, after looking up the Michigan Central depot number. Soon he got the ticket agent.

"How do the trains leave here for Detroit?" he asked.

The man explained the hours.

"No more to-night?"

"Nothing with a sleeper. Yes, there is, too," he added. "There is a mail train out of here at three o'clock."

"All right," said Hurstwood. "What time does that get to Detroit?"

He was thinking if he could only get there and cross the river into Canada, he could take his time about getting to Montreal. He was relieved to learn that it would reach there by noon.

"Mayhew won't open the safe till nine," he thought. "They can't get on my track before noon."

Then he thought of Carrie. With what speed must he get her, if he got her at all. She would have to come along. He jumped into the nearest cab standing by.

"To Ogden Place," he said sharply. "I'll give you a dollar more if you make good time."

The cabby beat his horse into a sort of imitation gallop, which was fairly fast, however. On the way Hurstwood thought what to do.

---

1. Bessie L. Pierce, in her *History of Chicago*, notes several well-known downtown drugstores in the 1880s and early 1890s. Dreiser may have been referring to the Sargeant Drug Store, on Wabash, a few blocks from Fitzgerald and Moy's at Adams and Clark. The telephone was widely used in business establishments by the late 1880s, but private phones or phones for public use in stores were still a rarity.

Reaching the number, he hurried up the steps and did not spare the bell in waking the servant.

"Is Mrs. Drouet in?" he asked.

"Yes," said the astonished girl.

"Tell her to dress and come to the door at once. Her husband is in the hospital, injured, and wants to see her."

The servant girl hurried upstairs, convinced by the man's strained and emphatic manner.

"What!" said Carrie, lighting the gas and searching for her clothes.

"Mr. Drouet is hurt and in the hospital. He wants to see you. The cab's downstairs."

Carrie dressed very rapidly, and soon appeared below, forgetting everything save the necessities.

"Drouet is hurt," said Hurstwood quickly. "He wants to see you. Come quickly."

Carrie was so bewildered that she swallowed the whole story.

"Get in," said Hurstwood, helping her and jumping after.

The cabby began to turn the horse around.

"Michigan Central depot," he said, standing up and speaking so low that Carrie could not hear, "as fast as you can go."

Chapter XXVIII

A PILGRIM, AN OUTLAW: THE SPIRIT DETAINED

The cab had not travelled a short block before Carrie, settling herself and thoroughly waking in the night atmosphere, asked:

"What's the matter with him? Is he hurt badly?"

"It isn't anything very serious," Hurstwood said solemnly. He was very much disturbed over his own situation, and now that he had Carrie with him, he only wanted to get safely out of reach of the law. Therefore he was in no mood for anything save such words as would further his plans distinctly.

Carrie did not forget that there was something to be settled between her and Hurstwood, but the thought was ignored in her agitation. The one thing was to finish this strange pilgrimage.

"Where is he?"

"Way out on the South Side," said Hurstwood. "We'll have to take the train. It's the quickest way."

Carrie said nothing, and the horse gambolled on. The weirdness of the city by night held her attention. She looked at the long receding rows of lamps and studied the dark, silent houses.

"How did he hurt himself?" she asked—meaning what was the nature of his injuries. Hurstwood understood. He hated to lie any more than necessary, and yet he wanted no protests until he was out of danger.

"I don't know exactly," he said. "They just called me up to go and get you and bring you out. They said there wasn't any need for alarm, but that I shouldn't fail to bring you."

The man's serious manner convinced Carrie, and she became silent, wondering.

Hurstwood examined his watch and urged the man to hurry. For one in so delicate a position he was exceedingly cool. He could only think of how needful it was to make the train and get quietly away. Carrie seemed quite tractable, and he congratulated himself.

In due time they reached the depot, and after helping her out he handed the man a five-dollar bill and hurried on.

"You wait here," he said to Carrie, when they reached the waiting-room, "while I get the tickets."

"Have I much time to catch that train for Detroit?" he asked of the agent.

"Four minutes," said the latter.

He paid for two tickets as circumspectly as possible.

"Is it far?" said Carrie, as he hurried back.

"Not very," he said. "We must get right in."

He pushed her before him at the gate, stood between her and the ticket man while the latter punched their tickets, so that she could not see, and then hurried after.

There was a long line of express and passenger cars and one or two common day coaches. As the train had only recently been made up and few passengers were expected, there were only one or two brakemen waiting. They entered the rear day coach and sat down. Almost immediately, "All aboard," resounded faintly from the outside, and the train started.

Carrie began to think it was a little bit curious—this going to a depot—but said nothing. The whole incident was so out of the natural that she did not attach too much weight to anything she imagined.

"How have you been?" asked Hurstwood gently, for he now breathed easier.

"Very well," said Carrie, who was so disturbed that she could not bring a proper attitude to bear in the matter. She was still nervous to reach Drouet and see what could be the matter. Hurstwood contemplated her and felt this. He was not disturbed that it should be so. He did not trouble because she was moved sympathetically in the matter. It was one of the qualities in her which pleased him exceedingly. He was only thinking how he should explain. Even this was not the most serious thing in his mind, however. His own deed and present flight were the great shadows which weighed upon him.

"What a fool I was to do that," he said over and over. "What a mistake!"

In his sober senses, he could scarcely realise that the thing had been done. He could not begin to feel that he was a fugitive from justice. He had often read of such things, and had thought they must be terrible, but now that the thing was upon him, he only sat and looked into the past. The future was a thing which concerned the Canadian line. He wanted to reach that. As for the rest, he surveyed his actions for the evening, and counted them parts of a great mistake.

"Still," he said, "what could I have done?"

Then he would decide to make the best of it, and would begin to do so by starting the whole inquiry over again. It was a fruitless, harassing round, and left him in a queer mood to deal with the proposition he had in the presence of Carrie.

The train clacked through the yards along the lake front, and ran rather slowly to Twenty-fourth Street. Brakes and signals were visible without. The engine gave short calls with its whistle, and frequently the bell rang. Several brakemen came through, bearing lanterns. They were locking the vestibules and putting the cars in order for a long run.

Presently it began to gain speed, and Carrie saw the silent streets flashing by in rapid succession. The engine also began its whistle-calls of four parts, with which it signalled danger to important crossings.

"Is it very far?" asked Carrie.

"Not so very," said Hurstwood. He could hardly repress a smile at her simplicity. He wanted to explain and conciliate her, but he also wanted to be well out of Chicago.

In the lapse of another half-hour it became apparent to Carrie that it was quite a run to wherever he was taking her, anyhow.

"Is it in Chicago?" she asked nervously. They were now far beyond the city limits, and the train was scudding across the Indiana line at a great rate.

"No," he said, "not where we are going."

There was something in the way he said this which aroused her in an instant.

Her pretty brow began to contract.

"We are going to see Charlie, aren't we?" she asked.

He felt that the time was up. An explanation might as well come now as later. Therefore, he shook his head in the most gentle negative.

"What?" said Carrie. She was nonplussed at the possibility of the errand being different from what she had thought.

He only looked at her in the most kindly and mollifying way.

"Well, where are you taking me, then?" she asked, her voice showing the quality of fright.

"I'll tell you, Carrie, if you'll be quiet. I want you to come along with me to another city."

"Oh," said Carrie, her voice rising into a weak cry. "Let me off. I don't want to go with you."

She was quite appalled at the man's audacity. This was something which had never for a moment entered her head. Her one thought now was to get off and away. If only the flying train could be stopped, the terrible trick would be amended.

She arose and tried to push out into the aisle—anywhere. She knew she had to do something. Hurstwood laid a gentle hand on her.

"Sit still, Carrie," he said. "Sit still. It won't do you any good to get up here. Listen to me and I'll tell you what I'll do. Wait a moment."

She was pushing at his knees, but he only pulled her back. No one saw this little altercation, for very few persons were in the car, and they were attempting to doze.

"I won't," said Carrie, who was, nevertheless, complying against her will. "Let me go," she said. "How dare you?" and large tears began to gather in her eyes.

Hurstwood was now fully aroused to the immediate difficulty, and ceased to think of his own situation. He must do something with this girl, or she would cause him trouble. He tried the art of persuasion with all his powers aroused.

"Look here now, Carrie," he said, "you mustn't act this way. I didn't mean to hurt your feelings. I don't want to do anything to make you feel bad."

"Oh," sobbed Carrie, "oh, oh—oo—o!"

"There, there," he said, "you mustn't cry. Won't you listen to me? Listen to me a minute, and I'll tell you why I came to do this thing. I couldn't help it. I assure you I couldn't. Won't you listen?"

Her sobs disturbed him so that he was quite sure she did not hear a word he said.

"Won't you listen?" he asked.

"No, I won't," said Carrie, flashing up. "I want you to take me out of this, or I'll tell the conductor. I won't go with you. It's a shame," and again sobs of fright cut off her desire for expression.

Hurstwood listened with some astonishment. He felt that she had just cause for feeling as she did, and yet he wished that he could straighten this thing out quickly. Shortly the conductor would come through for the tickets. He wanted no noise, no trouble of any kind. Before everything he must make her quiet.

"You couldn't get out until the train stops again," said Hurstwood. "It won't be very long until we reach another station. You can get out then if you want to. I won't stop you. All I want you to do is to listen a moment. You'll let me tell you, won't you?"

Carrie seemed not to listen. She only turned her head toward the window, where outside all was black. The train was speeding with steady grace across the fields and through patches of wood. The long whistles came with sad, musical effect as the lonely woodland crossings were approached.

Now the conductor entered the car and took up the one or two fares that had been added at Chicago. He approached Hurstwood, who handed out the tickets. Poised as she was to act, Carrie made no move. She did not look about.

When the conductor had gone again Hurstwood felt relieved.

"You're angry at me because I deceived you," he said. "I didn't mean to, Carrie. As I live I didn't. I couldn't help it. I couldn't stay away from you after the first time I saw you."

He was ignoring the last deception as something that might go by the board. He wanted to convince her that his wife could no longer be a factor in their relationship. The money he had stolen he tried to shut out of his mind.

"Don't talk to me," said Carrie, "I hate you. I want you to go away from me. I am going to get out at the very next station."

She was in a tremble of excitement and opposition as she spoke.

"All right," he said, "but you'll hear me out, won't you? After all you have said about loving me, you might hear me. I don't want to do you any harm. I'll give you the money to go back with when you go. I merely want to tell you, Carrie. You can't stop me from loving you, whatever you may think."

He looked at her tenderly, but received no reply.

"You think I have deceived you badly, but I haven't. I didn't do it willingly. I'm through with my wife. She hasn't any claims on me. I'll never see her any more. That's why I'm here to-night. That's why I came and got you."

"You said Charlie was hurt," said Carrie, savagely. "You deceived me. You've been deceiving me all the time, and now you want to force me to run away with you."

She was so excited that she got up and tried to get by him again. He let her, and she took another seat. Then he followed.

"Don't run away from me, Carrie," he said gently. "Let me explain. If you will only hear me out you will see where I stand. I tell you my wife is nothing to me. She hasn't been anything for years or I wouldn't have ever come near you. I'm going to get a divorce just as soon as I can. I'll never see her again. I'm done with all that. You're the only person I want. If I can have you I won't ever think of another woman again."

Carrie heard all this in a very ruffled state. It sounded sincere enough, however, despite all he had done. There was a tenseness in Hurstwood's voice and manner which could but have some effect.

She did not want anything to do with him. He was married, he had deceived her once, and now again, and she thought him terrible. Still there is something in such daring and power which is fascinating to a woman, especially if she can be made to feel that it is all prompted by love of her.

The progress of the train was having a great deal to do with the solution of this difficult situation. The speeding wheels and disappearing country put Chicago farther and farther behind. Carrie could feel that she was being borne a long distance off—that the engine was making an almost through run to some distant city. She felt at times as if she could cry out and make such a row that some one would come to her aid; at other times it seemed an almost useless thing—so far was she from any aid, no matter what she did. All the while Hurstwood was endeavouring to formulate his plea in such a way that it would strike home and bring her into sympathy with him.

"I was simply put where I didn't know what else to do."

Carrie deigned no suggestion of hearing this.

"When I saw you wouldn't come unless I could marry you, I decided to put everything else behind me and get you to come away with me. I'm going off now to another city. I want to go to Montreal for a while, and then anywhere you want to. We'll go and live in New York, if you say."

"I'll not have anything to do with you," said Carrie. "I want to get off this train. Where are we going?"

"To Detroit," said Hurstwood.

"Oh!" said Carrie, in a burst of anguish. So distant and definite a point seemed to increase the difficulty.

"Won't you come along with me?" he said, as if there was great danger that she would not. "You won't need to do anything but travel with me. I'll not trouble you in any way. You can see Montreal and New York, and then if you don't want to stay you can go back. It will be better than trying to go back to-night."

The first gleam of fairness shone in this proposition for Carrie. It seemed a plausible thing to do, much as she feared his opposition if she tried to carry it out. Montreal and New York! Even now she was speeding toward those great, strange lands, and could see them if she liked. She thought, but made no sign.

Hurstwood thought he saw a shade of compliance in this. He redoubled his ardour.

"Think," he said, "what I've given up. I can't go back to Chicago any more. I've got to stay away and live alone now, if you don't come with me. You won't go back on me entirely, will you, Carrie?"

"I don't want you to talk to me," she answered forcibly.

Hurstwood kept silent for a while.

Carrie felt the train to be slowing down. It was the moment to act if she was to act at all. She stirred uneasily.

"Don't think of going, Carrie," he said. "If you ever cared for me at all, come along and let's start right. I'll do whatever you say. I'll marry you, or I'll let you go back. Give yourself time to think it over. I wouldn't have wanted you to come if I hadn't loved you. I tell you, Carrie, before God, I can't live without you. I won't!"

There was the tensity of fierceness in the man's plea which appealed deeply to her sympathies. It was a dissolving fire which was actuating him now. He was loving her too intensely to think of giving her up in this, his hour of distress. He clutched her hand nervously and pressed it with all the force of an appeal.

The train was now all but stopped. It was running by some cars on a side track. Everything outside was dark and dreary. A few sprinkles on the window began to indicate that it was raining. Carrie hung in a quandary, balancing between decision and helplessness. Now the train stopped, and she was listening to his plea. The engine backed a few feet and all was still.

She wavered, totally unable to make a move. Minute after minute slipped by and still she hesitated, he pleading.

"Will you let me come back if I want to?" she asked, as if she now had the upper hand and her companion was utterly subdued.

"Of course," he answered, "you know I will."

Carrie only listened as one who has granted a temporary amnesty. She began to feel as if the matter were in her hands entirely.

The train was again in rapid motion. Hurstwood changed the subject.

"Aren't you very tired?" he said.

"No," she answered.

"Won't you let me get you a berth in the sleeper?"

She shook her head, though for all her distress and his trickery she was beginning to notice what she had always felt—his thoughtfulness.

"Oh, yes," he said, "you will feel so much better."

She shook her head.

"Let me fix my coat for you, anyway," and he arose and arranged his light coat in a comfortable position to receive her head.

"There," he said tenderly, "now see if you can't rest a little." He could have kissed her for her compliance. He took his seat beside her and thought a moment.

"I believe we're in for a heavy rain," he said.

"So it looks," said Carrie, whose nerves were quieting under the sound of the rain drops, driven by a gusty wind, as the train swept on frantically through the shadow to a newer world.

The fact that he had in a measure mollified Carrie was a source of satisfaction to Hurstwood, but it furnished only the most temporary relief. Now that her opposition was out of the way, he had all of his time to devote to the consideration of his own error.

His condition was bitter in the extreme, for he did not want the miserable sum he had stolen. He did not want to be a thief. That sum or any other could never compensate for the state which he had thus foolishly doffed. It could not give him back his host of friends, his name, his house and family, nor Carrie, as he had meant to have her. He was shut out from Chicago—from his easy, comfortable state. He had robbed himself of his dignity, his merry meetings, his pleasant evenings. And for what? The more he thought of it the more unbearable it became. He began to think that he would try and restore himself to his old state. He would return the miserable thievings of the night and explain. Perhaps Moy would understand. Perhaps they would forgive him and let him come back.

By noontime the train rolled into Detroit and he began to feel exceedingly nervous. The police must be on his track by now. They had probably notified all the police of the big cities, and detectives would be watching for him. He remembered instances in which defaulters had been captured. Consequently, he breathed heavily and paled somewhat. His hands felt as if they must have something to do. He simulated interest in several scenes without which he did not feel. He repeatedly beat his foot upon the floor.

Carrie noticed his agitation, but said nothing. She had no idea what it meant or that it was important.

He wondered now why he had not asked whether this train went on through to Montreal or some Canadian point. Perhaps he could have saved time. He jumped up and sought the conductor.

"Does any part of this train go to Montreal?" he asked.

"Yes, the next sleeper back does."

He would have asked more, but it did not seem wise, so he decided to inquire at the depot.

The train rolled into the yards, clanging and puffing.

"I think we had better go right on through to Montreal," he said to Carrie. "I'll see what the connections are when we get off."

He was exceedingly nervous, but did his best to put on a calm exterior. Carrie only looked at him with large, troubled eyes. She was drifting mentally, unable to say to herself what to do.

The train stopped and Hurstwood led the way out. He looked warily around him, pretending to look after Carrie. Seeing nothing that indicated studied observation, he made his way to the ticket office.

"The next train for Montreal leaves when?" he asked.

"In twenty minutes," said the man.

He bought two tickets and Pullman berths. Then he hastened back to Carrie.

"We go right out again," he said, scarcely noticing that Carrie looked tired and weary.

"I wish I was out of all this," she exclaimed gloomily.

"You'll feel better when we reach Montreal," he said.

"I haven't an earthly thing with me," said Carrie; "not even a hand-kerchief."

"You can buy all you want as soon as you get there, dearest," he explained. "You can call in a dressmaker."

Now the crier called the train ready and they got on. Hurstwood breathed a sigh of relief as it started. There was a short run to the river, and there they were ferried over,[1] They had barely pulled the train off the ferry-boat when he settled back with a sigh.

"It won't be so very long now," he said, remembering her in his relief. "We get there the first thing in the morning."

Carrie scarcely deigned to reply.

"I'll see if there is a dining-car," he added. "I'm hungry."

Chapter XXIX

THE SOLACE OF TRAVEL: THE BOATS OF THE SEA

To the untravelled, territory other than their own familiar heath is invariably fascinating. Next to love, it is the one thing which solaces and delights. Things new are too important to be neglected, and mind, which is a mere reflection of sensory impressions, succumbs to the flood of objects. Thus lovers are forgotten, sorrows laid aside, death hidden from view. There is a world of accumulated feeling back of the trite dramatic expression—"I am going away."

As Carrie looked out upon the flying scenery she almost forgot that she had been tricked into this long journey against her will and that she was without the necessary apparel for travelling. She quite forgot Hurstwood's presence at times, and looked away to homely farmhouses and cosey cottages in villages with wondering eyes. It was an interesting world to her. Her life had just begun. She did not feel herself defeated at all. Neither was she blasted in hope. The great city held much. Possibly she would come out of bondage into freedom—who knows? Perhaps she would be happy. These thoughts raised her above the level of erring. She was saved in that she was hopeful.

The following morning the train pulled safely into Montreal and they stepped down, Hurstwood glad to be out of danger, Carrie

---

1. Carrie and Hurstwood are crossing the Detroit River to Windsor, Ontario.

wondering at the novel atmosphere of the northern city. Long before, Hurstwood had been here, and now he remembered the name of the hotel at which he had stopped. As they came out of the main entrance of the depot he heard it called anew by a busman.

"We'll go right up and get rooms," he said.

At the clerk's office Hurstwood swung the register about while the clerk came forward. He was thinking what name he would put down. With the latter before him he found no time for hesitation. A name he had seen out of the car window came swiftly to him. It was pleasing enough. With an easy hand he wrote, "G. W. Murdock and wife." It was the largest concession to necessity he felt like making. His initials he could not spare.

When they were shown their room Carrie saw at once that he had secured her a lovely chamber.

"You have a bath there," said he. "Now you can clean up when you are ready."

Carrie went over and looked out the window, while Hurstwood looked at himself in the glass. He felt dusty and unclean. He had no trunk, no change of linen, not even a hair-brush.

"I'll ring for soap and towels," he said, "and send you up a hair-brush. Then you can bathe and get ready for breakfast. I'll go for a shave and come back and get you, and then we'll go out and look for some clothes for you."

He smiled good-naturedly as he said this.

"All right," said Carrie.

She sat down in one of the rocking-chairs, while Hurstwood waited for the boy, who soon knocked.

"Soap, towels, and a pitcher of ice-water."

"Yes, sir."

"I'll go now," he said to Carrie, coming toward her and holding out his hands, but she did not move to take them.

"You're not mad at me, are you?" he asked softly.

"Oh, no!" she answered, rather indifferently.

"Don't you care for me at all?"

She made no answer, but looked steadily toward the window.

"Don't you think you could love me a little?" he pleaded, taking one of her hands, which she endeavoured to draw away. "You once said you did."

"What made you deceive me so?" asked Carrie.

"I couldn't help it," he said, "I wanted you too much."

"You didn't have any right to want me," she answered, striking cleanly home.

"Oh, well, Carrie," he answered, "here I am. It's too late now. Won't you try and care for me a little?"

He looked rather worsted in thought as he stood before her.

She shook her head negatively.

"Let me start all over again. Be my wife from today on."

Carrie rose up as if to step away, he holding her hand. Now he slipped his arm about her and she struggled, but in vain. He held her quite close. Instantly there flamed up in his body the all-compelling desire. His affection took an ardent form.

"Let me go," said Carrie, who was folded close to him.

"Won't you love me?" he said. "Won't you be mine from now on?"

Carrie had never been ill-disposed toward him. Only a moment before she had been listening with some complacency, remembering her old affection for him. He was so handsome, so daring!

Now, however, this feeling had changed to one of opposition, which rose feebly. It mastered her for a moment, and then, held close as she was, began to wane. Something else in her spoke. This man, to whose bosom she was being pressed, was strong; he was passionate, he loved her, and she was alone. If she did not turn to him—accept of his love—where else might she go? Her resistance half dissolved in the flood of his strong feeling.

She found him lifting her head and looking into her eyes. What magnetism there was she could never know. His many sins, however, were for the moment all forgotten.

He pressed her closer and kissed her, and she felt that further opposition was useless.

"Will you marry me?" she asked, forgetting *how*.

"This very day," he said, with all delight.

Now the hall-boy pounded on the door and he released his hold upon her regretfully.

"You get ready now, will you," he said, "at once?"

"Yes," she answered.

"I'll be back in three-quarters of an hour."

Carrie, flushed and excited, moved away as he admitted the boy.

Below stairs, he halted in the lobby to look for a barber shop. For the moment, he was in fine feather. His recent victory over Carrie seemed to atone for much he had endured during the last few days. Life seemed worth fighting for. This eastward flight from all things customary and attached seemed as if it might have happiness in store. The storm showed a rainbow at the end of which might be a pot of gold.

He was about to cross to a little red-and-white striped bar which was fastened up beside a door when a voice greeted him familiarly. Instantly his heart sank.

"Why, hello, George, old man!" said the voice. "What are you doing down here?"

Hurstwood was already confronted, and recognised his friend Kenny, the stock-broker.

"Just attending to a little private matter," he answered, his mind working like a key-board of a telephone station. This man evidently did not know—he had not read the papers.

"Well, it seems strange to see you way up here," said Mr. Kenny genially. "Stopping here?"

"Yes," said Hurstwood uneasily, thinking of his handwriting on the register.

"Going to be in town long?"

"No, only a day or so."

"Is that so? Had your breakfast?"

"Yes," said Hurstwood, lying blandly. "I'm just going for a shave."

"Won't you come have a drink?"

"Not until afterwards," said the ex-manager. "I'll see you later. Are you stopping here?"

"Yes," said Mr. Kenny, and then, turning the word again, added: "How are things out in Chicago?"

"About the same as usual," said Hurstwood, smiling genially.

"Wife with you?"

"No."

"Well, I must see more of you to-day. I'm just going in here for breakfast. Come in when you're through."

"I will," said Hurstwood, moving away. The whole conversation was a trial to him. It seemed to add complications with every word. This man called up a thousand memories. He represented everything he had left. Chicago, his wife, the elegant resort—all these were in his greeting and inquiries. And here he was in this same hotel expecting to confer with him, unquestionably waiting to have a good time with him. All at once the Chicago papers would arrive. The local papers would have accounts in them this very day. He forgot his triumph with Carrie in the possibility of soon being known for what he was, in this man's eyes, a safe-breaker. He could have groaned as he went into the barber shop. He decided to escape and seek a more secluded hotel.

Accordingly, when he came out he was glad to see the lobby clear, and hastened toward the stairs. He would get Carrie and go out by the ladies' entrance. They would have breakfast in some more inconspicuous place.

Across the lobby, however, another individual was surveying him. He was of a commonplace Irish type, small of stature, cheaply dressed, and with a head that seemed a smaller edition of some huge ward politician's. This individual had been evidently talking with the clerk, but now he surveyed the ex-manager keenly.

Hurstwood felt the long-range examination and recognised the type. Instinctively he felt that the man was a detective—that he was being watched. He hurried across, pretending not to notice, but in his mind was a world of thoughts. What would happen now? What could these people do? He began to trouble concerning the extradition laws. He did not understand them absolutely. Perhaps he could be arrested. Oh, if Carrie should find out! Montreal was too warm for him. He began to long to be out of it.

Carrie had bathed and was waiting when he arrived. She looked refreshed—more delightful than ever, but reserved. Since he had gone she had resumed somewhat of her cold attitude towards him. Love was not blazing in her heart. He felt it, and his troubles seemed increased. He could not take her in his arms; he did not even try. Something about her forbade it. In part his opinion was the result of his own experiences and reflections below stairs.

"You're ready, are you?" he said kindly.

"Yes," she answered.

"We'll go out for breakfast. This place down here doesn't appeal to me very much."

"All right," said Carrie.

They went out, and at the corner the commonplace Irish individual was standing, eyeing him. Hurstwood could scarcely refrain from showing that he knew of this chap's presence. The insolence in the fellow's eye was galling. Still they passed, and he explained to Carrie concerning the city. Another restaurant was not long in showing itself, and here they entered.

"What a queer town this is," said Carrie, who marvelled at it solely because it was not like Chicago.

"It isn't as lively as Chicago," said Hurstwood. "Don't you like it?"

"No," said Carrie, whose feelings were already localised in the great Western city.

"Well, it isn't as interesting," said Hurstwood.

"What's here?" asked Carrie, wondering at his choosing to visit this town.

"Nothing much," returned Hurstwood. "It's quite a resort. There's some pretty scenery about here."

Carrie listened, but with a feeling of unrest. There was much about her situation which destroyed the possibility of appreciation.

"We won't stay here long," said Hurstwood, who was now really glad to note her dissatisfaction. "You pick out your clothes as soon as breakfast is over and we'll run down to New York soon. You'll like that. It's a lot more like a city than any place outside Chicago."

He was really planning to slip out and away. He would see what these detectives would do—what move his employers at Chicago would make—then he would slip away—down to New York, where it was easy to hide. He knew enough about that city to know that its mysteries and possibilities of mystification were infinite.

The more he thought, however, the more wretched his situation became. He saw that getting here did not exactly clear up the ground. The firm would probably employ detectives to watch him—Pinkerton men or agents of Mooney and Boland.[1] They might arrest him the moment he tried to leave Canada. So he might be compelled to remain here months, and in what a state!

Back at the hotel Hurstwood was anxious and yet fearful to see the morning papers. He wanted to know how far the news of his criminal deed had spread. So he told Carrie he would be up in a few moments, and went to secure and scan the dailies. No familiar or suspicious faces were about, and yet he did not like reading in the lobby, so he sought the main parlour on the floor above and, seated by a window there, looked them over. Very little was given to his crime, but it was there, several "sticks" in all, among all the riffraff of telegraphed murders, accidents, marriages, and other news. He wished, half sadly, that he could undo it all. Every moment of his time in this far-off abode of safety but added to his feeling that he had made a great mistake. There could have been an easier way out if he had only known.

He left the papers before going to the room, thinking thus to keep them out of the hands of Carrie.

"Well, how are you feeling?" he asked of her. She was engaged in looking out of the window.

"Oh, all right," she answered.

He came over, and was about to begin a conversation with her, when a knock came at their door.

"Maybe it's one of my parcels," said Carrie.

Hurstwood opened the door, outside of which stood the individual whom he had so thoroughly suspected.

"You're Mr. Hurstwood, are you?" said the latter, with a volume of affected shrewdness and assurance.

"Yes," said Hurstwood calmly. He knew the type so thoroughly that some of his old familiar indifference to it returned. Such men as these were of the lowest stratum welcomed at the resort. He stepped out and closed the door.

"Well, you know what I am here for, don't you?" said the man confidentially.

"I can guess," said Hurstwood softly.

"Well, do you intend to try and keep the money?"

"That's my affair," said Hurstwood grimly.

"You can't do it, you know," said the detective, eyeing him coolly.

"Look here, my man," said Hurstwood authoritatively, "you don't understand anything about this case, and I can't explain to you.

1. Pinkerton's National Detective Agency was then the most famous in the country. The Mooney and Boland Detective Agency had offices in Chicago, New York, and other large cities.

Whatever I intend to do I'll do without advice from the outside. You'll have to excuse me."

"Well, now, there's no use of your talking that way," said the man, "when you're in the hands of the police. We can make a lot of trouble for you if we want to. You're not registered right in this house, you haven't got your wife with you, and the newspapers don't know you're here yet. You might as well be reasonable."

"What do you want to know?" asked Hurstwood.

"Whether you're going to send back that money or not."

Hurstwood paused and studied the floor.

"There's no use explaining to you about this," he said at last. "There's no use of your asking me. I'm no fool, you know. I know just what you can do and what you can't. You can create a lot of trouble if you want to. I know that all right, but it won't help you to get the money. Now, I've made up my mind what to do. I've already written Fitzgerald and Moy, so there's nothing I can say. You wait until you hear more from them."

All the time he had been talking he had been moving away from the door, down the corridor, out of the hearing of Carrie. They were now near the end where the corridor opened into the large general parlour.

"You won't give it up?" said the man.

The words irritated Hurstwood greatly. Hot blood poured into his brain. Many thoughts formulated themselves. He was no thief. He didn't want the money. If he could only explain to Fitzgerald and Moy, maybe it would be all right again.

"See here," he said, "there's no use my talking about this at all. I respect your power all right, but I'll have to deal with the people who know."

"Well, you can't get out of Canada with it," said the man.

"I don't want to get out," said Hurstwood. "When I get ready there'll be nothing to stop me for."

He turned back, and the detective watched him closely. It seemed an intolerable thing. Still he went on and into the room.

"Who was it?" asked Carrie.

"A friend of mine from Chicago."

The whole of this conversation was such a shock that, coming as it did after all the other worry of the past week, it sufficed to induce a deep gloom and moral revulsion in Hurstwood. What hurt him most was the fact that he was being pursued as a thief. He began to see the nature of that social injustice which sees but one side—often but a single point in a long tragedy. All the newspapers noted but one thing, his taking the money. How and wherefore were but indifferently dealt with. All the complications which led up to it were unknown. He was accused without being understood.

Sitting in his room with Carrie the same day, he decided to send the money back. He would write Fitzgerald and Moy, explain all, and then send it by express. Maybe they would forgive him. Perhaps they would ask him back. He would make good the false statement he had made about writing them. Then he would leave this peculiar town.

For an hour he thought over this plausible statement of the tangle. He wanted to tell them about his wife, but couldn't. He finally narrowed it down to an assertion that he was light-headed from entertaining friends, had found the safe open, and having gone so far as to take the money out, had accidentally closed it. This act he regretted very much. He was sorry he had put them to so much trouble. He would undo what he could by sending the money back—the major portion of it. The remainder he would pay up as soon as he could. Was there any possibility of his being restored? This he only hinted at.

The troubled state of the man's mind may be judged by the very construction of this letter. For the nonce he forgot what a painful thing it would be to resume his old place, even if it were given him. He forgot that he had severed himself from the past as by a sword, and that if he did manage to in some way reunite himself with it, the jagged line of separation and reunion would always show. He was always forgetting something—his wife, Carrie, his need of money, present situation, or something—and so did not reason clearly. Nevertheless, he sent the letter, waiting a reply before sending the money.

Meanwhile, he accepted his present situation with Carrie, getting what joy out of it he could.

Out came the sun by noon, and poured a golden flood through their open windows. Sparrows were twittering. There were laughter and song in the air. Hurstwood could not keep his eyes from Carrie. She seemed the one ray of sunshine in all his trouble. Oh, if she would only love him wholly—only throw her arms around him in the blissful spirit in which he had seen her in the little park in Chicago—how happy he would be! It would repay him; it would show him that he had not lost all. He would not care.

"Carrie," he said, getting up once and coming over to her, "are you going to stay with me from now on?"

She looked at him quizzically, but melted with sympathy as the value of the look upon his face forced itself upon her. It was love now, keen and strong—love enhanced by difficulty and worry. She could not help smiling.

"Let me be everything to you from now on," he said. "Don't make me worry any more. I'll be true to you. We'll go to New York and get a nice flat. I'll go into business again, and we'll be happy. Won't you be mine?"

Carrie listened quite solemnly. There was no great passion in her, but the drift of things and this man's proximity created a semblance of affection. She felt rather sorry for him—a sorrow born of what had only recently been a great admiration. True love she had never felt for him. She would have known as much if she could have analysed her feelings, but this thing which she now felt aroused by his great feeling broke down the barriers between them.

"You'll stay with me, won't you?" he asked.

"Yes," she said, nodding her head.

He gathered her to himself, imprinting kisses upon her lips and checks.

"You must marry me, though," she said.

"I'll get a license to-day," he answered.

"How?" she asked.

"Under a new name," he answered. "I'll take a new name and live a new life. From now on I'm Murdock."

"Oh, don't take that name," said Carrie.

"Why not?" he said.

"I don't like it."

"Well, what shall I take?" he asked.

"Oh, anything, only don't take that."

He thought a while, still keeping his arms about her, and then said:

"How would Wheeler do?"

"That's all right," said Carrie.

"Well, then, Wheeler," he said. "I'll get the license this afternoon."

They were married by a Baptist minister, the first divine they found convenient.

At last the Chicago firm answered. It was by Mr. Moy's dictation. He was astonished that Hurstwood had done this; very sorry that it had come about as it had. If the money were returned, they would not trouble to prosecute him, as they really bore him no ill-will. As for his returning, or their restoring him to his former position, they had not quite decided what the effect of it would be. They would think it over and correspond with him later, possibly, after a little time, and so on.

The sum and substance of it was that there was no hope, and they wanted the money with the least trouble possible. Hurstwood read his doom. He decided to pay $9,500 to the agent whom they said they would send, keeping $1,300 for his own use. He telegraphed his acquiescence, explained to the representative who called at the hotel the same day, took a certificate of payment, and told Carrie to pack her trunk. He was slightly depressed over this newest move at the time he began to make it, but eventually restored himself. He feared that even yet he might be seized and taken back, so he tried to conceal his movements, but it was scarcely possible. He ordered Carrie's trunk sent to the depot, where he had it sent by express to New York. No one seemed to be observing him, but he left at night. He was greatly agitated lest at the first station across the border or at the depot in New York there should be waiting for him an officer of the law.

Carrie, ignorant of his theft and his fears, enjoyed the entry into the latter city in the morning. The round green hills sentinelling the broad, expansive bosom of the Hudson held her attention by their beauty as the train followed the line of the stream. She had heard of the Hudson River, the great city of New York, and now she looked out, filling her mind with the wonder of it.

As the train turned east at Spuyten Duyvil and followed the east bank of the Harlem River, Hurstwood nervously called her attention to the fact that they were on the edge of the city. After her experience with Chicago, she expected long lines of cars—a great highway of tracks—and noted the difference. The sight of a few boats in the Harlem and more in the East River tickled her young heart. It was the first sign of the great sea. Next came a plain street with five-story brick flats, and then the train plunged into the tunnel.

"Grand Central Station!" called the trainman, as, after a few minutes of darkness and smoke, daylight reappeared. Hurstwood arose and gathered up his small grip. He was screwed up to the highest tension. With Carrie he waited at the door and then dismounted. No one approached him, but he glanced furtively to and fro as he made for the street entrance. So excited was he that he forgot all about Carrie, who fell behind, wondering at his self-absorption. As he passed through the depot proper the strain reached its climax and began to wane. All at once he was on the sidewalk, and none but cabmen hailed him. He heaved a great breath and turned, remembering Carrie.

"I thought you were going to run off and leave me," she said.

"I was trying to remember which car takes us to the Gilsey,"[2] he answered.

Carrie hardly heard him, so interested was she in the busy scene.

"How large is New York?" she asked.

" 'Oh, a million or more," said Hurstwood.[3]

He looked around and hailed a cab, but he did so in a changed way.

2. The Gilsey, at Broadway and Twenty-ninth, was a fashionable and expensive hotel.
3. The official census of 1890 for New York City was a million and a half.

For the first time in years the thought that he must count these little expenses flashed through his mind. It was a disagreeable thing.

He decided he would lose no time living in hotels but would rent a flat. Accordingly he told Carrie, and she agreed.

"We'll look to-day, if you want to," she said.

Suddenly he thought of his experience in Montreal. At the more important hotels he would be certain to meet Chicagoans whom he knew. He stood up and spoke to the driver.

"Take me to the Belford,"[4] he said, knowing it to be less frequented by those whom he knew. Then he sat down.

"Where is the residence part?" asked Carrie, who did not take the tall five-story walls on either hand to be the abodes of families.

"Everywhere," said Hurstwood, who knew the city fairly well. "There are no lawns in New York. All these are houses."

"Well, then, I don't like it," said Carrie, who was coming to have a few opinions of her own.

Chapter XXX

THE KINGDOM OF GREATNESS: THE PILGRIM ADREAM

Whatever a man like Hurstwood could be in Chicago, it is very evident that he would be but an inconspicuous drop in an ocean like New York. In Chicago, whose population still ranged about 500,000, millionaires were not numerous. The rich had not become so conspicuously rich as to drown all moderate incomes in obscurity. The attention of the inhabitants was not so distracted by local celebrities in the dramatic, artistic, social, and religious fields as to shut the well-positioned man from view. In Chicago the two roads to distinction were politics and trade. In New York the roads were any one of a half-hundred, and each had been diligently pursued by hundreds, so that celebrities were numerous. The sea was already full of whales. A common fish must needs disappear wholly from view remain unseen. In other words, Hurstwood was nothing.

There is a more subtle result of such a situation as this, which, though not always taken into account, produces the tragedies of the world. The great create an atmosphere which reacts badly upon the small. This atmosphere is easily and quickly felt. Walk among the magnificent residences, the splendid equipages, the gilded shops, restaurants, resorts of all kinds; scent the flowers, the silks, the wines; drink of the laughter springing from the soul of luxurious content, of the glances which gleam like light from defiant spears; feel the quality of the smiles which cut like glistening swords and of

4. A fictitious name.

strides born of place, and you shall know of what is the atmosphere
of the high and mighty. Little use to argue that of such is not the
kingdom of greatness, but so long as the world is attracted by this
and the human heart views this as the one desirable realm which it
must attain, so long, to that heart, will this remain the realm of
greatness. So long, also, will the atmosphere of this realm work its
desperate results in the soul of man. It is like a chemical reagent.
One day of it, like one drop of the other, will so affect and discolour
the views, the aims, the desire of the mind, that it will thereafter
remain forever dyed. A day of it to the untried mind is like opium to
the untried body. A craving is set up which, if gratified, shall eternally
result in dreams and death. Aye! dreams unfulfilled—gnawing, luring, idle phantoms which beckon and lead, beckon and lead, until
death and dissolution dissolve their power and restore us blind to
nature's heart.

A man of Hurstwood's age and temperament is not subject to the
illusions and burning desires of youth, but neither has he the
strength of hope which gushes as a fountain in the heart of youth.
Such an atmosphere could not incite in him the cravings of a boy of
eighteen, but in so far as they were excited, the lack of hope made
them proportionately bitter. He could not fail to notice the signs of
affluence and luxury on every hand. He had been to New York before
and knew the resources of its folly. In part it was an awesome place
to him, for here gathered all that he most respected on this earth—
wealth, place, and fame. The majority of the celebrities with whom
he had tipped glasses in his day as manager hailed from this self-
centred and populous spot. The most inviting stories of pleasure and
luxury had been told of places and individuals here. He knew it to
be true that unconsciously he was brushing elbows with fortune the
livelong day; that a hundred or five hundred thousand gave no one
the privilege of living more than comfortably in so wealthy a place.
Fashion and pomp required more ample sums, so that the poor man
was nowhere. All this he realised, now quite sharply, as he faced the
city, cut off from his friends, despoiled of his modest fortune, and
even his name, and forced to begin the battle for place and comfort
all over again. He was not old, but he was not so dull but that he
could feel he soon would be. Of a sudden, then, this show of fine
clothes, place, and power took on peculiar significance. It was
emphasised by contrast with his own distressing state.

And it was distressing. He soon found that freedom from fear of
arrest was not the *sine qua non* of his existence. That danger dissolved, the next necessity became the grievous thing. The paltry sum
of thirteen hundred and some odd dollars set against the need of
rent, clothing, food, and pleasure for years to come was a spectacle
little calculated to induce peace of mind in one who had been accus-

tomed to spend five times that sum in the course of a year. He thought upon the subject rather actively the first few days he was in New York, and decided that he must act quickly. As a consequence, he consulted the business opportunities advertised in the morning papers and began investigations on his own account.

That was not before he had become settled, however. Carrie and he went looking for a flat, as arranged, and found one in Seventy-eighth Street near Amsterdam Avenue. It was a five-story building, and their flat was on the third floor. Owing to the fact that the street was not yet built up solidly, it was possible to see east to the green tops of the trees in Central Park and west to the broad waters of the Hudson, a glimpse of which was to be had out of the west windows. For the privilege of six rooms and a bath, running in a straight line, they were compelled to pay thirty-five dollars a month—an average, and yet exorbitant, rent for a home at the time.[1] Carrie noticed the difference between the size of the rooms here and in Chicago and mentioned it.

"You'll not find anything better, dear," said Hurstwood, "unless you go into one of the old-fashioned houses, and then you won't have any of these conveniences."

Carrie picked out the new abode because of its newness and bright wood-work. It was one of the very new ones supplied with steam heat, which was a great advantage. The stationary range, hot and cold water, dumb-waiter, speaking tubes, and call-bell for the janitor pleased her very much. She had enough of the instincts of a house-wife to take great satisfaction in these things.

Hurstwood made arrangement with one of the instalment houses whereby they furnished the flat complete and accepted fifty dollars down and ten dollars a month. He then had a little plate, bearing the name G. W. Wheeler, made, which he placed on his letter-box in the hall. It sounded exceedingly odd to Carrie to be called Mrs. Wheeler by the janitor, but in time she became used to it and looked upon the name as her own.

These house details settled, Hurstwood visited some of the adver-tised opportunities to purchase an interest in some flourishing down-town bar. After the palatial resort in Adams Street, he could not stomach the commonplace saloons which he found advertised. He lost a number of days looking up these and finding them disagree-able. He did, however, gain considerable knowledge by talking, for he discovered the influence of Tammany Hall and the value of stand-ing in with the police. The most profitable and flourishing places he found to be those which conducted anything but a legitimate busi-

---

1. The upper West Side was still comparatively sparsely populated in the 1890s because the subway system, which was to provide cheap rapid transit to the downtown area, was yet to be built. Carrie and Hurstwood's apartment is a so-called railway flat.

ness, such as that controlled by Fitzgerald and Moy. Elegant back rooms and private drinking booths on the second floor were usually adjuncts of very profitable places. He saw by portly keepers, whose shirt fronts shone with large diamonds, and whose clothes were properly cut, that the liquor business here, as elsewhere, yielded the same golden profit.

At last he found an individual who had a resort in Warren Street, which seemed an excellent venture.[2] It was fairly well-appearing and susceptible of improvement. The owner claimed the business to be excellent, and it certainly looked so.

"We deal with a very good class of people," he told Hurstwood. "Merchants, salesmen, and professionals. It's a well-dressed class. No bums. We don't allow 'em in the place."

Hurstwood listened to the cash-register ring, and watched the trade for a while.

"It's profitable enough for two, is it?" he asked.

"You can see for yourself if you're any judge of the liquor trade," said the owner. "This is only one of the two places I have. The other is down in Nassau Street. I can't tend to them both alone. If I had some one who knew the business thoroughly I wouldn't mind sharing with him in this one and letting him manage it."

"I've had experience enough," said Hurstwood blandly, but he felt a little diffident about referring to Fitzgerald and Moy.

"Well, you can suit yourself, Mr. Wheeler," said the proprietor.

He only offered a third interest in the stock, fixtures, and goodwill, and this in return for a thousand dollars and managerial ability on the part of the one who should come in. There was no property involved, because the owner of the saloon merely rented from an estate.

The offer was genuine enough, but it was a question with Hurstwood whether a third interest in that locality could be made to yield one hundred and fifty dollars a month, which he figured he must have in order to meet the ordinary family expenses and be comfortable. It was not the time, however, after many failures to find what he wanted, to hesitate. It looked as though a third would pay a hundred a month now. By judicious management and improvement, it might be made to pay more. Accordingly he agreed to enter into partnership, and made over his thousand dollars, preparing to enter the next day.

His first inclination was to be elated, and he confided to Carrie that he thought he had made an excellent arrangement. Time, however, introduced food for reflection. He found his partner to be very

---

2. Warren near Hudson (see p. 235), on the lower West Side, was in the wholesale food and merchandise section of the city. It was a considerable distance from the hotel and theater center above Fourteenth Street.

disagreeable. Frequently he was the worse for liquor, which made him surly. This was the last thing which Hurstwood was used to in business. Besides, the business varied. It was nothing like the class of patronage which he had enjoyed in Chicago. He found that it would take a long time to make friends. These people hurried in and out without seeking the pleasures of friendship. It was no gathering or lounging place. Whole days and weeks passed without one such hearty greeting as he had been wont to enjoy every day in Chicago.

For another thing, Hurstwood missed the celebrities—those well-dressed, *élite* individuals who lend grace to the average bars and bring news from far-off and exclusive circles. He did not see one such in a month. Evenings, when still at his post, he would occasionally read in the evening papers incidents concerning celebrities whom he knew—whom he had drunk a glass with many a time. They would visit a bar like Fitzgerald and Moy's in Chicago, or the Hoffman House, uptown,[3] but he knew that he would never see them down here.

Again, the business did not pay as well as he thought. It increased a little, but he found he would have to watch his household expenses, which was humiliating.

In the very beginning it was a delight to go home late at night, as he did, and find Carrie. He managed to run up and take dinner with her between six and seven, and to remain home until nine o'clock in the morning, but the novelty of this waned after a time, and he began to feel the drag of his duties.

The first month had scarcely passed before Carrie said in a very natural way: "I think I'll go down this week and buy a dress."

"What kind?" said Hurstwood.

"Oh, something for street wear."

"All right," he answered, smiling, although he noted mentally that it would be more agreeable to his finances if she didn't. Nothing was said about it the next day, but the following morning he asked:

"Have you done anything about your dress?"

"Not yet," said Carrie.

He paused a few moments, as if in thought, and then said:

"Would you mind putting it off a few days?"

"No," replied Carrie, who did not catch the drift of his remarks. She had never thought of him in connection with money troubles before. "Why?"

"Well, I'll tell you," said Hurstwood. "This investment of mine is taking a lot of money just now. I expect to get it all back shortly, but just at present I am running close."

---

3. The Hoffman House, an old hotel on Broadway and Twenty-fifth, had a famous bar.

"Oh!" answered Carrie. "Why, certainly, dear. Why didn't you tell me before?"

"It wasn't necessary," said Hurstwood.

For all her acquiescence, there was something about the way Hurstwood spoke which reminded Carrie of Drouet and his little deal which he was always about to put through. It was only the thought of a second, but it was a beginning. It was something new in her thinking of Hurstwood.

Other things followed from time to time, little things of the same sort, which in their cumulative effect were eventually equal to a full revelation. Carrie was not dull by any means. Two persons cannot long dwell together without coming to an understanding of one another. The mental difficulties of an individual reveal themselves whether he voluntarily confesses them or not. Trouble gets in the air and contributes gloom, which speaks for itself. Hurstwood dressed as nicely as usual, but they were the same clothes he had in Canada. Carrie noticed that he did not install a large wardrobe, though his own was anything but large. She noticed, also, that he did not suggest many amusements, said nothing about the food, seemed concerned about his business. This was not the easy Hurstwood of Chicago—not the liberal, opulent Hurstwood she had known. The change was too obvious to escape detection.

In time she began to feel that a change had come about, and that she was not in his confidence. He was evidently secretive and kept his own counsel. She found herself asking him questions about little things. This is a disagreeable state to a woman. Great love makes it seem reasonable, sometimes plausible, but never satisfactory. Where great love is not, a more definite and less satisfactory conclusion is reached.

As for Hurstwood, he was making a great fight against the difficulties of a changed condition. He was too shrewd not to realise the tremendous mistake he had made, and appreciate that he had done well in getting where he was, and yet he could not help contrasting his present state with his former, hour after hour, and day after day.

Besides, he had the disagreeable fear of meeting old-time friends, ever since one such encounter which he made shortly after his arrival in the city. It was in Broadway that he saw a man approaching him whom he knew. There was no time for simulating non-recognition. The exchange of glances had been too sharp, the knowledge of each other too apparent. So the friend, a buyer for one of the Chicago wholesale houses, felt, perforce, the necessity of stopping.

"How are you?" he said, extending his hand with an evident mixture of feeling and a lack of plausible interest.

"Very well," said Hurstwood, equally embarrassed. "How is it with you?"

"All right; I'm down here doing a little buying. Are you located here now?"

"Yes," said Hurstwood, "I have a place down in Warren Street."

"Is that so?" said the friend. "Glad to hear it. I'll come down and see you."

"Do," said Hurstwood.

"So long," said the other, smiling affably and going on.

"He never asked for my number," thought Hurstwood; "he wouldn't think of coming." He wiped his forehead, which had grown damp, and hoped sincerely he would meet no one else.

These things told upon his good-nature, such as it was. His one hope was that things would change for the better in a money way. He had Carrie. His furniture was being paid for. He was maintaining his position. As for Carrie, the amusements he could give her would have to do for the present. He could probably keep up his pretensions sufficiently long without exposure to make good, and then all would be well. He failed therein to take account of the frailties of human nature—the difficulties of matrimonial life. Carrie was young. With him and with her varying mental states were common. At any moment the extremes of feeling might be anti-polarised at the dinner table. This often happens in the best regulated families. Little things brought out on such occasions need great love to obliterate them afterward. Where that is not, both parties count two and two and make a problem after a while.

Chapter XXXI

A PET OF GOOD FORTUNE: BROADWAY FLAUNTS ITS JOYS

The effect of the city and his own situation on Hurstwood was paralleled in the case of Carrie, who accepted the things fortune provided with the most genial good-nature. New York, despite her first expression of disapproval, soon interested her exceedingly. Its clear atmosphere, more populous thoroughfares, and peculiar indifference struck her forcibly. She had never seen such a little flat as hers, and yet it soon enlisted her affection. The new furniture made an excellent showing, the sideboard which Hurstwood himself arranged gleamed brightly. The furniture for each room was appropriate, and in the so-called parlour, or front room, was installed a piano, because Carrie said she would like to learn to play. She kept a servant and developed rapidly in household tactics and information. For the first time in her life she felt settled, and somewhat justified in the eyes of society as she conceived of it. Her thoughts were merry and innocent enough. For a long while she concerned herself over the arrangement of New York flats, and wondered at ten families living in one building and all remaining strange and indifferent to each other. She also marvelled at the whistles of the hundreds of vessels in the harbour—the long, low cries of the Sound steamers and ferry-boats when fog was on. The mere fact that these things spoke from the sea made them wonderful. She looked much at what she could see of the Hudson from her west windows and of the great city building up rapidly on either hand. It was much to ponder over, and sufficed to entertain her for more than a year without becoming stale.

For another thing, Hurstwood was exceedingly interesting in his affection for her. Troubled as he was, he never exposed his difficulties to her. He carried himself with the same self-important air, took his new state with easy familiarity, and rejoiced in Carrie's proclivities and successes. Each evening he arrived promptly to dinner, and found the little dining-room a most inviting spectacle. In a way, the smallness of the room added to its luxury. It looked full and replete. The white-covered table was arrayed with pretty dishes and lighted with a four-armed candelabra, each light of which was topped with a red shade. Between Carrie and the girl the steaks and chops came out all right, and canned goods did the rest for a while. Carrie studied the art of making biscuit, and soon reached the stage where she could show a plate of light, palatable morsels for her labour.

In this manner the second, third, and fourth months passed. Winter came, and with it a feeling that indoors was best, so that the attending of theatres was not much talked of. Hurstwood made great efforts to meet all expenditures without a show of feeling one way or the other. He pretended that he was reinvesting his money in strengthening the business for greater ends in the future. He contented himself with a very moderate allowance of personal apparel, and rarely suggested anything for Carrie. Thus the first winter passed.

In the second year, the business which Hurstwood managed did increase somewhat. He got out of it regularly the $150 per month which he had anticipated. Unfortunately, by this time Carrie had reached certain conclusions, and he had scraped up a few acquaintances.

Being of a passive and receptive rather than an active and aggressive nature, Carrie accepted the situation. Her state seemed satisfactory enough. Once in a while they would go to a theatre together, occasionally in season to the beaches and different points about the city, but they picked up no acquaintances. Hurstwood naturally abandoned his show of fine manners with her and modified his attitude to one of easy familiarity. There were no misunderstandings, no apparent differences of opinion. In fact, without money or visiting friends, he led a life which could neither arouse jealousy nor comment. Carrie rather sympathised with his efforts and thought nothing upon her lack of entertainment such as she had enjoyed in Chicago. New York as a corporate entity and her flat temporarily seemed sufficient.

However, as Hurstwood's business increased, he, as stated, began to pick up acquaintances. He also began to allow himself more clothes. He convinced himself that his home life was very precious to him, but allowed that he could occasionally stay away from dinner. The first time he did this he sent a message saying that he would be detained. Carrie ate alone, and wished that it might not happen again. The second time, also, he sent word, but at the last moment. The third time he forgot entirely and explained afterwards. These events were months apart, each.

"Where were you, George?" asked Carrie, after the first absence.

"Tied up at the office," he said genially. "There were some accounts I had to straighten."

"I'm sorry you couldn't get home," she said kindly. "I was fixing to have such a nice dinner."

The second time he gave a similar excuse, but the third time the feeling about it in Carrie's mind was a little bit out of the ordinary.

"I couldn't get home," he said, when he came in later in the evening, "I was so busy."

"Couldn't you have sent me word?" asked Carrie.

"I meant to," he said, "but you know I forgot it until it was too late to do any good."

"And I had such a good dinner!" said Carrie.

Now, it so happened that from his observations of Carrie he began to imagine that she was of the thoroughly domestic type of mind. He really thought, after a year, that her chief expression in life was finding its natural channel in household duties. Notwithstanding the fact that he had observed her act in Chicago, and that during the past year he had only seen her limited in her relations to her flat and him by conditions which he made, and that she had not gained any friends or associates, he drew this peculiar conclusion. With it came a feeling of satisfaction in having a wife who could thus be content, and this satisfaction worked its natural result. That is, since he imagined he saw her satisfied, he felt called upon to give only that which contributed to such satisfaction. He supplied the furniture, the decorations, the food, and the necessary clothing. Thoughts of entertaining her, leading her out into the shine and show of life, grew less and less. He felt attracted to the outer world, but did not think she would care to go along. Once he went to the theatre alone. Another time he joined a couple of his new friends at an evening game of poker. Since his money-feathers were beginning to grow again he felt like sprucing about. All this, however, in a much less imposing way than had been his wont in Chicago. He avoided the gay places where he would be apt to meet those who had known him.

Now, Carrie began to feel this in various sensory ways. She was not the kind to be seriously disturbed by his actions. Not loving him greatly, she could not be jealous in a disturbing way. In fact, she was not jealous at all. Hurstwood was pleased with her placid manner, when he should have duly considered it. When he did not come home it did not seem anything like a terrible thing to her. She gave him credit for having the usual allurements of men—people to talk to, places to stop, friends to consult with. She was perfectly willing that he should enjoy himself in his way, but she did not care to be neglected herself. Her state still seemed fairly reasonable, however. All she did observe was that Hurstwood was somewhat different.

Some time in the second year of their residence in Seventy-eighth Street the flat across the hall from Carrie became vacant, and into it moved a very handsome young woman and her husband, with both of whom Carrie afterwards became acquainted. This was brought about solely by the arrangement of the flats, which were united in one place, as it were, by the dumb-waiter. This useful elevator, by which fuel, groceries, and the like were sent up from the basement, and garbage and waste sent down, was used by both residents on one floor; that is, a small door opened into it from each flat.

If the occupants of both flats answered to the whistle of the janitor at the same time, they would stand face to face when they opened the dumb-waiter doors. One morning, when Carrie went to remove her paper, the newcomer, a handsome brunette of perhaps twenty-three years of age, was there for a like purpose. She was in a night-robe and dressing-gown, with her hair very much tousled, but she looked so pretty and good-natured that Carrie instantly conceived a liking for her. The newcomer did no more than smile shamefacedly, but it was sufficient. Carrie felt that she would like to know her, and a similar feeling stirred in the mind of the other, who admired Carrie's innocent face.

"That's a real pretty woman who has moved in next door," said Carrie to Hurstwood at the breakfast table.

"Who are they?" asked Hurstwood.

"I don't know," said Carrie. "The name on the bell is Vance. Some one over there plays beautifully. I guess it must be she."

"Well, you never can tell what sort of people you're living next to in this town, can you?" said Hurstwood, expressing the customary New York opinion about neighbours.

"Just think," said Carrie, "I have been in this house with nine other families for over a year and I don't know a soul. These people have been here over a month, and I haven't seen any one before this morning."

"It's just as well," said Hurstwood. "You never know who you're going to get in with. Some of these people are pretty bad company."

"I expect so," said Carrie, agreeably.

The conversation turned to other things, and Carrie thought no more upon the subject until a day or two later, when, going out to market, she encountered Mrs. Vance coming in. The latter recognised her and nodded, for which Carrie returned a smile. This settled the probability of acquaintanceship. If there had been no faint recognition on this occasion, there would have been no future association.

Carrie saw no more of Mrs. Vance for several weeks, but she heard her play through the thin walls which divided the front rooms of the flats, and was pleased by the merry selection of pieces and the brilliance of their rendition. She could play only moderately herself, and such variety as Mrs. Vance exercised bordered, for Carrie, upon the verge of great art. Everything she had seen and heard thus far—the merest scraps and shadows—indicated that these people were, in a measure, refined and in comfortable circumstances. So Carrie was ready for any extension of the friendship which might follow.

One day Carrie's bell rang and the servant, who was in the kitchen, pressed the button which caused the front door of the general entrance on the ground floor to be electrically unlatched. When Carrie waited at her own door on the third floor to see who it might be coming up to call on her, Mrs. Vance appeared.

"I hope you'll excuse me," she said. "I went out a while ago and forgot my outside key, so I thought I'd ring your bell."

This was a common trick of other residents of the building, whenever they had forgotten their outside keys. They did not apologise for it, however.

"Certainly," said Carrie. "I'm glad you did. I do the same thing sometimes."

"Isn't it just delightful weather?" said Mrs. Vance, pausing for a moment.

Thus, after a few more preliminaries, this visiting acquaintance was well launched, and in the young Mrs. Vance Carrie found an agreeable companion.

On several occasions Carrie visited her and was visited. Both flats were good to look upon, though that of the Vances tended somewhat more to the luxurious.

"I want you to come over this evening and meet my husband," said Mrs. Vance, not long after their intimacy began. "He wants to meet you. You play cards, don't you?"

"A little," said Carrie.

"Well, we'll have a game of cards. If your husband comes home bring him over."

"He's not coming to dinner to-night," said Carrie.

"Well, when he does come we'll call him in."

Carrie acquiesced, and that evening met the portly Vance, an individual a few years younger than Hurstwood, and who owed his seemingly comfortable matrimonial state much more to his money than to his good looks. He thought well of Carrie upon the first glance and laid himself out to be genial, teaching her a new game of cards and talking to her about New York and its pleasures. Mrs. Vance played some upon the piano, and at last Hurstwood came.

"I am very glad to meet you," he said to Mrs. Vance when Carrie introduced him, showing much of the old grace which had captivated Carrie.

"Did you think your wife had run away?" said Mr. Vance, extending his hand upon introduction.

"I didn't know but what she might have found a better husband," said Hurstwood.

He now turned his attention to Mrs. Vance, and in a flash Carrie saw again what she for some time had sub-consciously missed in Hurstwood—the adroitness and flattery of which he was capable. She also saw that she was not well dressed—not nearly as well dressed—as Mrs. Vance. These were not vague ideas any longer. Her situation was cleared up for her. She felt that her life was becoming stale, and therein she felt cause for gloom. The old helpful, urging melancholy was restored. The desirous Carrie was whispered to concerning her possibilities.

There were no immediate results to this awakening, for Carrie had little power of initiative; but, nevertheless, she seemed ever capable of getting herself into the tide of change where she would be easily borne along. Hurstwood noticed nothing. He had been unconscious of the marked contrasts which Carrie had observed. He did not even detect the shade of melancholy which settled in her eyes. Worst of all, she now began to feel the loneliness of the flat and seek the company of Mrs. Vance, who liked her exceedingly.

"Let's go to the matinée this afternoon," said Mrs. Vance, who had stepped across into Carrie's flat one morning, still arrayed in a soft pink dressing-gown, which she had donned upon rising. Hurstwood and Vance had gone their separate ways nearly an hour before.

"All right," said Carrie, noticing the air of the petted and well-groomed woman in Mrs. Vance's general appearance. She looked as though she was dearly loved and her every wish gratified. "What shall we see?"

"Oh, I do want to see Nat Goodwin," said Mrs. Vance. "I do think he is the jolliest actor. The papers say this is such a good play."

"What time will we have to start?" asked Carrie.

"Let's go at one and walk down Broadway from Thirty-fourth Street," said Mrs. Vance. "It's such an interesting walk. He's at the Madison Square."

"I'll be glad to go," said Carrie. "How much will we have to pay for seats?"

"Not more than a dollar," said Mrs. Vance.

The latter departed, and at one o'clock reappeared, stunningly arrayed in a dark-blue walking dress, with a nobby hat to match. Carrie had gotten herself up charmingly enough, but this woman pained her by contrast. She seemed to have so many dainty little things which Carrie had not. There were trinkets of gold, an elegant green leather purse set with her initials, a fancy handkerchief, exceedingly rich in design, and the like. Carrie felt that she needed more and better clothes to compare with this woman, and that any one looking at the two would pick Mrs. Vance for her raiment alone. It was a trying, though rather unjust thought, for Carrie had now developed an equally pleasing figure, and had grown in comeliness until she was a thoroughly attractive type of her colour of beauty. There was some difference in the clothing of the two, both of quality and age, but this difference was not especially noticeable. It served, however, to augment Carrie's dissatisfaction with her state.

The walk down Broadway then as now, was one of the remarkable features of the city.[1] There gathered, before the matinée and afterwards, not only all the pretty women who love a showy parade, but the men who love to gaze upon and admire them. It was a very imposing procession of pretty faces and fine clothes. Women appeared in their very best hats, shoes, and gloves, and walked arm in arm on their way to the fine shops or theatres strung along from Fourteenth to Thirty-fourth streets. Equally the men paraded with the very latest they could afford. A tailor might have secured hints on suit measurements, a shoemaker on proper lasts and colours, a hatter on hats. It was literally true that if a lover of fine clothes secured a new suit, it was sure to have its first airing on Broadway. So true and well understood was this fact, that several years later a popular song,

1. During the 1890s, the principal hotels, restaurants, and theaters of New York, as well as many of its major stores, were on Broadway between Union Square (Fourteenth Street) and Greeley Square (Thirty-fourth Street). The center of city life was Madison Square (dominated by the imposing Madison Square Garden auditorium and restaurant), at the intersection of Broadway, Fifth Avenue, and Twenty-third to Twenty-sixth Streets. This center was beginning to be challenged, however, by the new hotels and restaurants adjacent to the Plaza (near the entrance to Central Park at Fifth Avenue and Fifty-ninth Street) and by the extension of the theater district to Forty-second Street.

detailing this and other facts concerning the afternoon parade on
matinée days, and entitled "What Right Has He on Broadway?"[2] was
published, and had quite a vogue about the music-halls of the city.

In all her stay in the city, Carrie had never heard of this showy
parade; had never even been on Broadway when it was taking place.
On the other hand, it was a familiar thing to Mrs. Vance, who not
only knew of it as an entity, but had often been in it, going purposely
to see and be seen, to create a stir with her beauty and dispel any
tendency to fall short in dressiness by contrasting herself with the
beauty and fashion of the town.

Carrie stepped along easily enough after they got out of the car at
Thirty-fourth Street, but soon fixed her eyes upon the lovely company
which swarmed by and with them as they proceeded. She noticed
suddenly that Mrs. Vance's manner had rather stiffened under the
gaze of handsome men and elegantly dressed ladies, whose glances
were not modified by any rules of propriety. To stare seemed the
proper and natural thing. Carrie found herself stared at and ogled.
Men in flawless top-coats, high hats, and silver-headed walking
sticks elbowed near and looked too often into conscious eyes. Ladies
rustled by in dresses of stiff cloth, shedding affected smiles and perfume. Carrie noticed among them the sprinkling of goodness and
the heavy percentage of vice. The rouged and powdered cheeks and
lips, the scented hair, the large, misty, and languorous eye, were
common enough. With a start she awoke to find that she was in
fashion's crowd, on parade in a show place—and such a show place!
Jewellers' windows gleamed along the path with remarkable fre-
quency. Florist shops, furriers, haberdashers, confectioners—all followed in rapid succession. The street was full of coaches. Pompous
doormen in immense coats, shiny brass belts and buttons, waited in
front of expensive salesrooms. Coachmen in tan boots, white tights,
and blue jackets waited obsequiously for the mistresses of carriages
who were shopping inside. The whole street bore the flavour of riches
and show, and Carrie felt that she was not of it. She could not, for
the life of her, assume the attitude and smartness of Mrs. Vance,
who, in her beauty, was all assurance. She could only imagine that
it must be evident to many that she was the less handsomely dressed
of the two. It cut her to the quick, and she resolved that she would
not come here again until she looked better. At the same time she
longed to feel the delight of parading here as an equal. Ah, then she
would be happy!

2. "What Right Has He on Broadway," a song by Harry Dillon and Nat Mann on the need
to be fashionably dressed on Broadway, was published in 1895.

Chapter XXXII

THE FEAST OF BELSHAZZAR: A SEER TO TRANSLATE[1]

Such feelings as were generated in Carrie by this walk put her in an exceedingly receptive mood for the pathos which followed in the play. The actor whom they had gone to see had achieved his popularity by presenting a mellow type of comedy, in which sufficient sorrow was introduced to lend contrast and relief to humour. For Carrie, as we well know, the stage had a great attraction. She had never forgotten her one histrionic achievement in Chicago. It dwelt in her mind and occupied her consciousness during many long afternoons in which her rocking-chair and her latest novel contributed the only pleasures of her state. Never could she witness a play without having her own ability vividly brought to consciousness. Some scenes made her long to be a part of them—to give expression to the feelings which she, in the place of the character represented, would feel. Almost invariably she would carry the vivid imaginations away with her and brood over them the next day alone. She lived as much in these things as in the realities which made up her daily life.

It was not often that she came to the play stirred to her heart's core by actualities. To-day a low song of longing had been set singing in her heart by the finery, the merriment, the beauty she had seen. Oh, these women who had passed her by, hundreds and hundreds strong, who were they? Whence came the rich, elegant dresses, the astonishingly coloured buttons, the knick-knacks of silver and gold? Where were these lovely creatures housed? Amid what elegancies of carved furniture, decorated walls, elaborate tapestries did they move? Where were their rich apartments, loaded with all that money could provide? In what stables champed these sleek, nervous horses and rested the gorgeous carriages? Where lounged the richly groomed footmen? Oh, the mansions, the lights, the perfume, the loaded boudoirs and tables! New York must be filled with such bowers, or the beautiful, insolent, supercilious creatures could not be. Some hothouses held them. It ached her to know that she was not one of them—that, alas, she had dreamed a dream and it had not come true. She wondered at her own solitude these two years past—her indifference to the fact that she had never achieved what she had expected.

The play was one of those drawing-room concoctions in which charmingly overdressed ladies and gentlemen suffer the pangs of love and jealousy amid gilded surroundings. Such bon-mots are ever

---

1. A reference to the Biblical account, in the Book of Daniel, in which mysterious writing that appears on a wall during a feast given by Balshazzar, the king of Babylon, is correctly interpreted by the prophet Daniel to foretell the death of Balshazzar and the fall of Babylon.

enticing to those who have all their days longed for such material surroundings and have never had them gratified. They have the charm of showing suffering under ideal conditions. Who would not grieve upon a gilded chair? Who would not suffer amid perfumed tapestries, cushioned furniture, and liveried servants? Grief under such circumstances becomes an enticing thing. Carrie longed to be of it. She wanted to take her sufferings, whatever they were, in such a world, or failing that, at least to simulate them under such charming conditions upon the stage. So affected was her mind by what she had seen, that the play now seemed an extraordinarily beautiful thing. She was soon lost in the world it represented, and wished that she might never return. Between the acts she studied the galaxy of matinée attendants in front rows and boxes, and conceived a new idea of the possibilities of New York. She was sure she had not seen it all—that the city was one whirl of pleasure and delight.

Going out, the same Broadway taught her a sharper lesson. The scene she had witnessed coming down was now augmented and at its height. Such a crush of finery and folly she had never seen. It clinched her convictions concerning her state. She had not lived, could not lay claim to having lived, until something of this had come into her own life. Women were spending money like water; she could see that in every elegant shop she passed. Flowers, candy, jewelry, seemed the principal things in which the elegant dames were interested. And she—she had scarcely enough pin money to indulge in such outings as this a few times a month.

That night the pretty little flat seemed a commonplace thing. It was not what the rest of the world was enjoying. She saw the servant working at dinner with an indifferent eye. In her mind were running scenes of the play. Particularly she remembered one beautiful actress—the sweetheart who had been wooed and won. The grace of this woman had won Carrie's heart. Her dresses had been all that art could suggest, her sufferings had been so real. The anguish which she had portrayed Carrie could feel. It was done as she was sure she could do it. There were places in which she could even do better. Hence she repeated the lines to herself. Oh, if she could only have such a part, how broad would be her life! She, too, could act appealingly.

When Hurstwood came, Carrie was moody. She was sitting, rocking and thinking, and did not care to have her enticing imaginations broken in upon; so she said little or nothing.

"What's the matter, Carrie?" said Hurstwood after a time, noticing her quiet, almost moody state.

"Nothing," said Carrie. "I don't feel very well to-night."

"Not sick, are you?" he asked, approaching very close.

"Oh, no," she said, almost pettishly, "I just don't feel very good."

"That's too bad," he said, stepping away and adjusting his vest after his slight bending over. "I was thinking we might go to a show to-night."

"I don't want to go," said Carrie, annoyed that her fine visions should have thus been broken into and driven out of her mind. "I've been to the matinée this afternoon."

"Oh, you have?" said Hurstwood. "What was it?"

"A Gold Mine."[2]

"How was it?"

"Pretty good," said Carrie.

"And you don't want to go again to-night?"

"I don't think I do," she said.

Nevertheless, wakened out of her melancholia and called to the dinner table, she changed her mind. A little food in the stomach does wonders. She went again, and in so doing temporarily recovered her equanimity. The great awakening blow had, however, been delivered. As often as she might recover from these discontented thoughts now, they would occur again. Time and repetition—ah, the wonder of it! The dropping water and the solid stone—how utterly it yields at last!

Not long after this matinée experience—perhaps a month—Mrs. Vance invited Carrie to an evening at the theatre with them. She heard Carrie say that Hurstwood was not coming home to dinner.

"Why don't you come with us? Don't get dinner for yourself. We're going down to Sherry's for dinner and then over to the Lyceum.[3] Come along with us."

"I think I will," answered Carrie.

She began to dress at three o'clock for her departure at half-past five for the noted dining-room which was then crowding Delmonico's for position in society. In this dressing Carrie showed the influence of her association with the dashing Mrs. Vance. She had constantly had her attention called by the latter to novelties in everything which pertains to a woman's apparel.

"Are you going to get such and such a hat?" or, "Have you seen the new gloves with the oval pearl buttons?" were but sample phrases out of a large selection.

"The next time you get a pair of shoes, dearie," said Mrs. Vance, "get button, with thick soles and patent-leather tips. They're all the rage this fall."

"I will," said Carrie.

2. *A Gold Mine* (1889), by Brander Matthews and George H. Jessop, was a popular Nat Goodwin vehicle for several years.

3. In the mid-1890s Louis Sherry's (at Fifth Avenue and Thirty-seventh) began to rival Delmonico's (at Fifth Avenue and Twenty-sixth) as the city's most fashionable restaurant. The Lyceum Theatre, at Fourth Avenue and Thirty-fourth, specialized in drawing room comedy, such as Belasco and De Mille's *Lord Chumley* (1888). See p. 223.

"Oh, dear, have you seen the new shirtwaists at Altman's? They have some of the loveliest patterns. I saw one there that I know would look stunning on you. I said so when I saw it."

Carrie listened to these things with considerable interest, for they were suggested with more of friendliness than is usually common between pretty women. Mrs. Vance liked Carrie's stable good-nature so well that she really took pleasure in suggesting to her the latest things.

"Why don't you get yourself one of those nice serge skirts they're selling at Lord & Taylor's?"[4] she said one day. "They're the circular style, and they're going to be worn from now on. A dark blue one would look so nice on you."

Carrie listened with eager ears. These things never came up between her and Hurstwood. Nevertheless, she began to suggest one thing and another, which Hurstwood agreed to without any expression of opinion. He noticed the new tendency on Carrie's part, and finally, hearing much of Mrs. Vance and her delightful ways, suspected whence the change came. He was not inclined to offer the slightest objection so soon, but he felt that Carrie's wants were expanding. This did not appeal to him exactly, but he cared for her in his own way, and so the thing stood. Still, there was something in the details of the transactions which caused Carrie to feel that her requests were not a delight to him. He did not enthuse over the purchases. This led her to believe that neglect was creeping in, and so another small wedge was entered.

Nevertheless, one of the results of Mrs. Vance's suggestions was the fact that on this occasion Carrie was dressed somewhat to her own satisfaction. She had on her best, but there was comfort in the thought that if she must confine herself to a *best*, it was neat and fitting. She looked the well-groomed woman of twenty-one, and Mrs. Vance praised her, which brought colour to her plump cheeks and a noticeable brightness into her large eyes. It was threatening rain, and Mr. Vance, at his wife's request, had called a coach.

"Your husband isn't coming?" suggested Mr. Vance, as he met Carrie in his little parlour.

"No, he said he wouldn't be home for dinner."

"Better leave a little note for him, telling him where we are. He might turn up."

"I will," said Carrie, who had not thought of it before.

"Tell him we'll be at Sherry's until eight o'clock. He knows, though, I guess."

Carrie crossed the hall with rustling skirts, and scrawled the note, gloves on. When she returned a newcomer was in the Vance flat.

4. Altman's (on Sixth Avenue) and Lord & Taylor's (on Broadway) were well-known and expensive New York clothing stores.

"Mrs. Wheeler, let me introduce Mr. Ames, a cousin of mine," said Mrs. Vance. "He's going along with us, aren't you, Bob?"

"I'm very glad to meet you," said Ames, bowing politely to Carrie.

The latter caught in a glance the dimensions of a very stalwart figure. She also noticed that he was smooth-shaven, good looking, and young, but nothing more.

"Mr. Ames is just down in New York for a few days," put in Vance, "and we're trying to show him around a little."

"Oh, are you?" said Carrie, taking another glance at the newcomer.

"Yes, I am just on here from Indianapolis for a week or so," said young Ames, seating himself on the edge of a chair to wait while Mrs. Vance completed the last touches of her toilet.

"I guess you find New York quite a thing to see, don't you?" said Carrie, venturing something to avoid a possible deadly silence.

"It is rather large to get around in a week," answered Ames, pleasantly.

He was an exceedingly genial soul, this young man, and wholly free of affectation. It seemed to Carrie he was as yet only overcoming the last traces of the bashfulness of youth. He did not seem apt at conversation, but he had the merit of being well dressed and wholly courageous. Carrie felt as if it were not going to be hard to talk to him.

"Well, I guess we're ready now. The coach is outside."

"Come on, people," said Mrs. Vance, coming in smiling. "Bob, you'll have to look after Mrs. Wheeler."

"I'll try to," said Bob smiling, and edging closer to Carrie. "You won't need much watching, will you?" he volunteered, in a sort of ingratiating and help-me-out kind of way.

"Not very, I hope," said Carrie.

They descended the stairs, Mrs. Vance offering suggestions, and climbed into the open coach.

"All right," said Vance, slamming the coach door, and the conveyance rolled away.

"What is it we're going to see?" asked Ames.

"Sothern," said Vance, "in 'Lord Chumley.' "[5]

"Oh, he is so good!" said Mrs. Vance. "He's just the funniest man."

"I notice the papers praise it," said Ames.

"I haven't any doubt," put in Vance, "but we'll all enjoy it very much."

Ames had taken a seat beside Carrie, and accordingly he felt it his bounden duty to pay her some attention. He was interested to find her so young a wife, and so pretty, though it was only a respectful interest. There was nothing of the dashing lady's man about him. He

5. Lord Chumley was one of E. H. Sothern's most popular roles, though he later became a successful Shakespearean actor.

had respect for the married state, and thought only of some pretty marriageable girls in Indianapolis.

"Are you a born New Yorker?" asked Ames of Carrie.

"Oh, no; I've only been here for two years."

"Oh, well, you've had time to see a great deal of it, anyhow."

"I don't seem to have," answered Carrie. "It's about as strange to me as when I first came here."

"You're not from the West, are you?"

"Yes. I'm from Wisconsin," she answered.

"Well, it does seem as if most people in this town haven't been here so very long. I hear of lots of Indiana people in my line who are here."

"What is your line?" asked Carrie.

"I'm connected with an electrical company," said the youth.

Carrie followed up this desultory conversation with occasional interruptions from the Vances. Several times it became general and partially humorous, and in that manner the restaurant was reached.

Carrie had noticed the appearance of gayety and pleasure-seeking in the streets which they were following. Coaches were numerous, pedestrians many, and in Fifty-ninth Street the street cars were crowded. At Fifty-ninth Street and Fifth Avenue a blaze of lights from several new hotels which bordered the Plaza Square gave a suggestion of sumptuous hotel life.[6] Fifth Avenue, the home of the wealthy, was noticeably crowded with carriages, and gentlemen in evening dress. At Sherry's an imposing doorman opened the coach door and helped them out. Young Ames held Carrie's elbow as he helped her up the steps. They entered the lobby already swarming with patrons, and then, after divesting themselves of their wraps, went into a sumptuous dining-room.

In all Carrie's experience she had never seen anything like this. In the whole time she had been in New York Hurstwood's modified state had not permitted his bringing her to such a place. There was an almost indescribable atmosphere about it which convinced the new-comer that this was the proper thing. Here was the place where the matter of expense limited the patrons to the moneyed or pleasure-loving class. Carrie had read of it often in the "Morning" and "Evening World." She had seen notices of dances, parties, balls, and suppers at Sherry's. The Misses So-and-so would give a party on Wednesday evening at Sherry's. Young Mr. So-and-so would entertain a party of friends at a private luncheon on the sixteenth, at Sherry's. The common run of conventional, perfunctory notices of the doings of society, which she could scarcely refrain from scanning each day, had given her a distinct idea of the gorgeousness and luxury

6. The Plaza (1890), the New Netherlands (1892), and the Savoy (1892) made Plaza Square an uptown hotel center in the 1890s.

desirable

of this wonderful temple of gastronomy. Now, at last, she was really in it. She had come up the imposing steps, guarded by the large and portly doorman. She had seen the lobby, guarded by another large and portly gentleman, and been waited upon by uniformed youths who took care of canes, overcoats, and the like. Here was the splendid dining-chamber, all decorated and aglow, where the wealthy ate. Ah, how fortunate was Mrs. Vance; young, beautiful, and well off— at least, sufficiently so to come here in a coach. What a wonderful thing it was to be rich.

Vance led the way through lanes of shining tables, at which were seated parties of two, three, four, five, or six. The air of assurance and dignity about it all was exceedingly noticeable to the novitiate. Incandescent lights, the reflection of their glow in polished glasses, and the shine of gilt upon the walls, combined into one tone of light which it requires minutes of complacent observation to separate and take particular note of. The white shirt fronts of the gentlemen, the bright costumes of the ladies, diamonds, jewels, fine feathers—all were exceedingly noticeable.

Carrie walked with an air equal to that of Mrs. Vance, and accepted the seat which the head waiter provided for her. She was keenly aware of all the little things that were done—the little genuflections and attentions of the waiters and head waiter which Americans pay for. The air with which the latter pulled out each chair, and the wave of the hand with which he motioned them to be seated, were worth several dollars in themselves.

Once seated, there began that exhibition of showy, wasteful, and unwholesome gastronomy as practised by wealthy Americans, which is the wonder and astonishment of true culture and dignity the world over. The large bill of fare held an array of dishes sufficient to feed an army, sidelined with prices which made reasonable expenditure a ridiculous impossibility—an order of soup at fifty cents or a dollar, with a dozen kinds to choose from; oysters in forty styles and at sixty cents the half-dozen; entrées, fish, and meats at prices which would house one over night in an average hotel. One dollar fifty and two dollars seemed to be the most common figures upon this most tastefully printed bill of fare.

Carrie noticed this, and in scanning it the price of spring chicken carried her back to that other bill of fare and far different occasion when, for the first time, she sat with Drouet in a good restaurant in Chicago. It was only momentary—a sad note as out of an old song— and then it was gone. But in that flash was seen the other Carrie— poor, hungry, drifting at her wits' ends, and all Chicago a cold and closed world, from which she only wandered because she could not find work.

On the walls were designs in colour, square spots of robin's-egg blue, set in ornate frames of gilt, whose corners were elaborate mouldings of fruit and flowers, with fat cupids hovering in angelic comfort. On the ceilings were coloured traceries with more gilt, leading to a centre where spread a cluster of lights—incandescent globes mingled with glittering prisms and stucco tendrils of gilt. The floor was of a reddish hue, waxed and polished, and in every direction were mirrors—tall, brilliant, bevel-edged mirrors—reflecting and re-reflecting forms, faces, and candelabra a score and a hundred times.

The tables were not so remarkable in themselves, and yet the imprint of Sherry upon the napery, the name of Tiffany upon the silverware, the name of Haviland upon the china, and over all the glow of the small, red-shaded candelabra and the reflected tints of the walls on garments and faces, made them seem remarkable. Each waiter added an air of exclusiveness and elegance by the manner in which he bowed, scraped, touched, and trifled with things. The exclusively personal attention which he devoted to each one, standing half bent, ear to one side, elbows akimbo, saying: "Soup—green turtle, yes. One portion, yes. Oysters—certainly—half-dozen—yes. Asparagus. Olives—yes."

It would be the same with each one, only Vance essayed to order for all, inviting counsel and suggestions. Carrie studied the company with open eyes. So this was high life in New York. It was so that the rich spent their days and evenings. Her poor little mind could not rise above applying each scene to all society. Every fine lady must be in the crowd on Broadway in the afternoon, in the theatre at the matinée, in the coaches and dining-halls at night. It must be glow and shine everywhere, with coaches waiting, and footmen attending, and she was out of it all. In two long years she had never even been in such a place as this.

Vance was in his element here, as Hurstwood would have been in former days. He ordered freely of soup, oysters, roast meats, and side dishes, and had several bottles of wine brought, which were set down beside the table in a wicker basket.

Ames was looking away rather abstractedly at the crowd and showed an interesting profile to Carrie. His forehead was high, his nose rather large and strong, his chin moderately pleasing. He had a good, wide, well-shaped mouth, and his dark-brown hair was parted slightly on one side. He seemed to have the least touch of boyishness to Carrie, and yet he was a man full grown.

"Do you know," he said, turning back to Carrie, after his reflection, "I sometimes think it is a shame for people to spend so much money this way."

Carrie looked at him a moment with the faintest touch of surprise at his seriousness. He seemed to be thinking about something over which she had never pondered.

"Do you?" she answered, interestedly.

"Yes," he said, "they pay so much more than these things are worth. They put on so much show."

"I don't know why people shouldn't spend when they have it," said Mrs. Vance.

"It doesn't do any harm," said Vance, who was still studying the bill of fare, though he had ordered.

Ames was looking away again, and Carrie was again looking at his forehead. To her he seemed to be thinking about strange things. As he studied the crowd his eye was mild.   —unusual

"Look at that woman's dress over there," he said, again turning to Carrie, and nodding in a direction.

"Where?" said Carrie, following his eyes.

"Over there in the corner—way over. Do you see that brooch?"

"Isn't it large?" said Carrie.

"One of the largest clusters of jewels I have ever seen," said Ames.

"It is, isn't it?" said Carrie. She felt as if she would like to be agreeable to this young man, and also there came with it, or perhaps preceded it, the slightest shade of a feeling that he was better educated than she was—that his mind was better. He seemed to look it, and the saving grace in Carrie was that she could understand that people could be wiser. She had seen a number of people in her life who reminded her of what she had vaguely come to think of as scholars. This strong young man beside her, with his clear, natural look, seemed to get a hold of things which she did not quite understand, but approved of. It was fine to be so, as a man, she thought.

The conversation changed to a book that was having its vogue at the time—"Moulding a Maiden," by Albert Ross.[7] Mrs. Vance had read it. Vance had seen it discussed in some of the papers.

"A man can make quite a strike writing a book," said Vance. "I notice this fellow Ross is very much talked about." He was looking at Carrie as he spoke.

"I hadn't heard of him," said Carrie, honestly.

"Oh, I have," said Mrs. Vance. "He's written lots of things. This last story is pretty good."

"He doesn't amount to much," said Ames.

Carrie turned her eyes toward him as to an oracle.

"His stuff is nearly as bad as 'Dora Thorne,' " concluded Ames.

Carrie felt this as a personal reproof. She read "Dora Thorne," or had a great deal in the past. It seemed only fair to her, but she supposed that people thought it very fine. Now this clear-eyed, fine-headed youth, who looked something like a student to her, made fun

7. Albert Ross was the pseudonym of Linn Boyd Porter. *Moulding a Maiden* (1891) sold over a half-million copies within three years of publication. Like Bertha Clay's *Dora Thorne* (see p. 74), it is a melodramatic, sentimental romance.

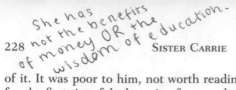
She has not the benefits of money OR the wisdom of education.

of it. It was poor to him, not worth reading. She looked down, and for the first time felt the pain of not understanding.

Yet there was nothing sarcastic or supercilious in the way Ames spoke. He had very little of that in him. Carrie felt that it was just kindly thought of a high order—the right thing to think, and wondered what else was right, according to him. He seemed to notice that she listened and rather sympathised with him, and from now on he talked mostly to her.

As the waiter bowed and scraped about, felt the dishes to see if they were hot enough, brought spoons and forks, and did all those little attentive things calculated to impress the luxury of the situation upon the diner, Ames also leaned slightly to one side and told her of Indianapolis in an intelligent way. He really had a very bright mind, which was finding its chief development in electrical knowledge. His sympathies for other forms of information, however, and for types of people, were quick and warm. The red glow on his head gave it a sandy tinge and put a bright glint in his eye. Carrie noticed all these things as he leaned toward her and felt exceedingly young. This man was far ahead of her. He seemed wiser than Hurstwood, saner and brighter than Drouet. He seemed innocent and clean, and she thought that he was exceedingly pleasant. She noticed, also, that his interest in her was a far-off one. She was not in his life, nor any of the things that touched his life, and yet now, as he spoke of these things, they appealed to her.

"I shouldn't care to be rich," he told her, as the dinner proceeded and the supply of food warmed up his sympathies; "not rich enough to spend my money this way."

"Oh, wouldn't you?" said Carrie, the, to her, new attitude forcing itself distinctly upon her for the first time.

"No," he said. "What good would it do? A man doesn't need this sort of thing to be happy."

Carrie thought of this doubtfully; but, coming from him, it had weight with her.

"He probably could be happy," she thought to herself, "all alone. He's so strong."

Mr. and Mrs. Vance kept up a running fire of interruptions, and these impressive things by Ames came at odd moments. They were sufficient, however, for the atmosphere that went with this youth impressed itself upon Carrie without words. There was something in him, or the world he moved in, which appealed to her. He reminded her of scenes she had seen on the stage—the sorrows and sacrifices that always went with she knew not what. He had taken away some of the bitterness of the contrast between this life and her life, and all by a certain calm indifference which concerned only him.

As they went out, he took her arm and helped her into the coach, and then they were off again, and so to the show.

During the acts Carrie found herself listening to him very attentively. He mentioned things in the play which she most approved of—things which swayed her deeply.

"Don't you think it rather fine to be an actor?" she asked once.

"Yes, I do," he said, "to be a good one. I think the theatre a great thing."

Just this little approval set Carrie's heart bounding. Ah, if she could only be an actress—a good one! This man was wise—he knew—and he approved of it. If she were a fine actress, such men as he would approve of her. She felt that he was good to speak as he had, although it did not concern her at all. She did not know why she felt this way.

At the close of the show it suddenly developed that he was not going back with them.

"Oh, aren't you?" said Carrie, with an unwarrantable feeling.

"Oh, no," he said; "I'm stopping right around here in Thirty-third Street."

Carrie could not say anything else, but somehow this development shocked her. She had been regretting the wane of a pleasant evening, but she had thought there was a half-hour more. Oh, the half-hours, the minutes of the world; what miseries and griefs are crowded into them!

She said good-bye with feigned indifference. What matter could it make? Still, the coach seemed lorn.

When she went into her own flat she had this to think about. She did not know whether she would ever see this man any more. What difference could it make—what difference could it make?

Hurstwood had returned, and was already in bed. His clothes were scattered loosely about. Carrie came to the door and saw him, then retreated. She did not want to go in yet a while. She wanted to think. It was disagreeable to her.

Back in the dining-room she sat in her chair and rocked. Her little hands were folded tightly as she thought. Through a fog of longing and conflicting desires she was beginning to see. Oh, ye legions of hope and pity—of sorrow and pain! She was rocking, and beginning to see.

Chapter XXXIII

WITHOUT THE WALLED CITY: THE SLOPE OF THE YEARS

The immediate result of this was nothing. Results from such things are usually long in growing. Morning brings a change of feeling. The existent condition invariably pleads for itself. It is only at odd moments that we get glimpses of the misery of things. The heart understands when it is confronted with contrasts. Take them away and the ache subsides.

Carrie went on, leading much this same life for six months thereafter or more. She did not see Ames any more. He called once upon the Vances, but she only heard about it through the young wife. Then he went West, and there was a gradual subsidence of whatever personal attraction had existed. The mental effect of the thing had not gone, however, and never would entirely. She had an ideal to contrast men by—particularly men close to her.

During all this time—a period rapidly approaching three years— Hurstwood had been moving along in an even path. There was no apparent slope downward, and distinctly none upward, so far as the casual observer might have seen. But psychologically there was a change, which was marked enough to suggest the future very distinctly indeed. This was in the mere matter of the halt his career had received when he departed from Chicago. A man's fortune or material progress is very much the same as his bodily growth. Either he is growing stronger, healthier, wiser, as the youth approaching manhood, or he is growing weaker, older, less incisive mentally, as the man approaching old age. There are no other states. Frequently there is a period between the cessation of youthful accretion and the setting in, in the case of the middle-aged man, of the tendency toward decay when the two processes are almost perfectly balanced and there is little doing in either direction. Given time enough, however, the balance becomes a sagging to the grave side. Slowly at first, then with a modest momentum, and at last the graveward process is in the full swing. So it is frequently with man's fortune. If its process of accretion is never halted, if the balancing stage is never reached, there will be no toppling. Rich men are, frequently, in these days, saved from this dissolution of their fortune by their ability to hire younger brains. These younger brains look upon the interests of the fortune as their own, and so steady and direct its progress. If each individual were left absolutely to the care of his own interests, and were given time enough in which to grow exceedingly old, his fortune would pass as his strength and will. He and his would be utterly dissolved and scattered unto the four winds of the heavens.

But now see wherein the parallel changes. A fortune, like a man, is an organism which draws to itself other minds and other strength than that inherent in the founder. Beside the young minds drawn to it by salaries, it becomes allied with young forces, which make for its existence even when the strength and wisdom of the founder are fading. It may be conserved by the growth of a community or of a state. It may be involved in providing something for which there is a growing demand. This removes it at once beyond the special care of the founder. It needs not so much foresight now as direction. The man wanes, the need continues or grows, and the fortune, fallen into whose hands it may, continues. Hence, some men never recognise the turning in the tide of their abilities. It is only in chance cases, where a fortune or a state of success is wrested from them, that the lack of ability to do as they did formerly becomes apparent. Hurstwood, set down under new conditions, was in a position to see that he was no longer young. If he did not, it was due wholly to the fact that his state was so well balanced that an absolute change for the worse did not show.

Not trained to reason or introspect himself, he could not analyse the change that was taking place in his mind, and hence his body, but he felt the depression of it. Constant comparison between his old state and his new showed a balance for the worse, which pro- duced a constant state of gloom or, at least, depression. Now, it has been shown experimentally that a constantly subdued frame of mind produces certain poisons in the blood, called katastates, just as virtuous feelings of pleasure and delight produce helpful chemicals called anastates. The poisons generated by remorse inveigh against the system, and eventually produce marked physical deterioration. To these Hurstwood was subject.[1]

In the course of time it told upon his temper. His eye no longer possessed that buoyant, searching shrewdness which had characterised it in Adams Street. His step was not as sharp and firm. He was given to thinking, thinking, thinking. The new friends he made were not celebrities. They were of a cheaper, a slightly more sensual and cruder, grade. He could not possibly take the pleasure in this company that he had in that of those fine frequenters of the Chicago resort. He was left to brood.

Slowly, exceedingly slowly, his desire to greet, conciliate, and make at home these people who visited the Warren Street place passed from him. More and more slowly the significance of the realm he had left began to be clear. It did not seem so wonderful to be in it when he was in it. It had seemed very easy for any one to get up there and have ample raiment and money to spend, but now that he was out of it, how far off it became. He began to see as one sees a city with a wall about it. Men were posted at the gates. You could

1. Anastates and katastates were terms in common usage among physiologists in the 1890s. Anastates were stored energy substances in the metabolic process; katastates were the waste products of energy use. Dreiser derived his specialized (and generally unaccepted) concept of these substances from Elmer Gates, an eccentric scientist about whom he was attempting to write an article in early 1900. See Ellen Moers, *Two Dreisers* (New York: Viking, 1969), 160–69.

not get in. Those inside did not care to come out to see who you were. They were so merry inside there that all those outside were forgotten, and he was on the outside.

Each day he could read in the evening papers of the doings within this walled city. In the notices of passengers for Europe he read the names of eminent frequenters of his old resort. In the theatrical column appeared, from time to time, announcements of the latest successes of men he had known. He knew that they were at their old gayeties. Pullmans were hauling them to and fro about the land, papers were greeting them with interesting mentions, the elegant lobbies of hotels and the glow of polished dining-rooms were keeping them close within the walled city. Men whom he had known, men whom he had tipped glasses with—rich men, and he was forgotten! Who was Mr. Wheeler? What was the Warren Street resort? Bah!

If one thinks that such thoughts do not come to so common a type of mind—that such feelings require a higher mental development—I would urge for their consideration the fact that it is the higher mental development that does away with such thoughts. It is the higher mental development which induces philosophy and that fortitude which refuses to dwell upon such things—refuses to be made to suffer by their consideration. The common type of mind is exceedingly keen on all matters which relate to its physical welfare—exceedingly keen. It is the unintellectual miser who sweats blood at the loss of a hundred dollars. It is the Epictetus[2] who smiles when the last vestige of physical welfare is removed.

The time came, in the third year, when this thinking began to produce results in the Warren Street place. The tide of patronage dropped a little below what it had been at its best since he had been there. This irritated and worried him.

There came a night when he confessed to Carrie that the business was not doing as well this month as it had the month before. This was in lieu of certain suggestions she had made concerning little things she wanted to buy. She had not failed to notice that he did not seem to consult her about buying clothes for himself. For the first time, it struck her as a ruse, or that he said it so that she would not think of asking for things. Her reply was mild enough, but her thoughts were rebellious. He was not looking after her at all. She was depending for her enjoyment upon the Vances.

And now the latter announced that they were going away. It was approaching spring, and they were going North.

"Oh, yes," said Mrs. Vance to Carrie, "we think we might as well give up the flat and store our things. We'll be gone for the summer,

2. Epictetus (ca. 60–120) was a Greek Stoic philosopher who emphasized indifference to worldly goods.

and it would be a useless expense. I think we'll settle a little farther down town when we come back."

Carrie heard this with genuine sorrow. She had enjoyed Mrs. Vance's companionship so much. There was no one else in the house whom she knew. Again she would be all alone.

Hurstwood's gloom over the slight decrease in profits and the departure of the Vances came together. So Carrie had loneliness and this mood of her husband to enjoy at the same time. It was a grievous thing. She became restless and dissatisfied, not exactly, as she thought, with Hurstwood, but with life. What was it? A very dull round indeed. What did she have? Nothing but this narrow, little flat. The Vances could travel, they could do the things worth doing, and here she was. For what was she made, anyhow? More thought followed, and then tears—tears seemed justified, and the only relief in the world.

For another period this state continued, the twain leading a rather monotonous life, and then there was a slight change for the worse. One evening, Hurstwood, after thinking about a way to modify Carrie's desire for clothes and the general strain upon his ability to provide, said:

"I don't think I'll ever be able to do much with Shaughnessy."

"What's the matter?" said Carrie.

"Oh, he's a slow, greedy 'mick'! He won't agree to anything to improve the place, and it won't ever pay without it."

"Can't you make him?" said Carrie.

"No; I've tried. The only thing I can see, if I want to improve, is to get hold of a place of my own."

"Why don't you?" said Carrie.

"Well, all I have is tied up in there just now. If I had a chance to save a while I think I could open a place that would give us plenty of money."

"Can't we save?" said Carrie.

"We might try it," he suggested. "I've been thinking that if we'd take a smaller flat down town and live economically for a year, I would have enough, with what I have invested, to open a good place. Then we could arrange to live as you want to."

"It would suit me all right," said Carrie, who, nevertheless, felt badly to think it had come to this. Talk of a smaller flat sounded like poverty.

"There are lots of nice little flats down around Sixth Avenue, below Fourteenth Street. We might get one down there."

"I'll look at them if you say so," said Carrie.

"I think I could break away from this fellow inside of a year," said Hurstwood. "Nothing will ever come of this arrangement as it's going on now."

"I'll look around," said Carrie, observing that the proposed change seemed to be a serious thing with him.

The upshot of this was that the change was eventually effected; not without great gloom on the part of Carrie. It really affected her more seriously than anything that had yet happened. She began to look upon Hurstwood wholly as a man, and not as a lover or husband. She felt thoroughly bound to him as a wife, and that her lot was cast with his, whatever it might be; but she began to see that he was gloomy and taciturn, not a young, strong, and buoyant man. He looked a little bit old to her about the eyes and mouth now, and there were other things which placed him in his true rank, so far as her estimation was concerned. She began to feel that she had made a mistake. Incidentally, she also began to recall the fact that he had practically forced her to flee with him.

The new flat was located in Thirteenth Street, a half block west of Sixth Avenue, and contained only four rooms.[3] The new neighbourhood did not appeal to Carrie as much. There were no trees here, no west view of the river. The street was solidly built up. There were twelve families here, respectable enough, but nothing like the Vances. Richer people required more space.

Being left alone in this little place, Carrie did without a girl. She made it charming enough, but could not make it delight her. Hurstwood was not inwardly pleased to think that they should have to modify their state, but he argued that he could do nothing. He must put the best face on it, and let it go at that.

He tried to show Carrie that there was no cause for financial alarm, but only congratulation over the chance he would have at the end of the year by taking her rather more frequently to the theatre and by providing a liberal table. This was for the time only. He was getting in the frame of mind where he wanted principally to be alone and to be allowed to think. The disease of brooding was beginning to claim him as a victim. Only the newspapers and his own thoughts were worth while. The delight of love had again slipped away. It was a case of live, now, making the best you can out of a very commonplace station in life.

The road downward has but few landings and level places. The very state of his mind, superinduced by his condition, caused the breach to widen between him and his partner. At last that individual began to wish that Hurstwood was out of it. It so happened, however, that a real estate deal on the part of the owner of the land arranged things even more effectually than ill-will could have schemed.

"Did you see that?" said Shaughnessy one morning to Hurstwood,

---

3. When Dreiser visited New York in 1894, he found Emma Dreiser and L. A. Hopkins (the prototypes of Carrie and Hurstwood) living on Fifteenth Street near Sixth Avenue. See p. 383.

pointing to the real estate column in a copy of the "Herald," which he held.

"No, what is it?" said Hurstwood, looking down the items of news.

"The man who owns this ground has sold it."

"You don't say so?" said Hurstwood.

He looked, and there was the notice. Mr. August Viele had yesterday registered the transfer of the lot, 25 × 75 feet, at the corner of Warren and Hudson streets, to J. F. Slawson for the sum of $57,000.

"Our lease expires when?" asked Hurstwood, thinking. "Next February, isn't it?"

"That's right," said Shaughnessy.

"It doesn't say what the new man's going to do with it," remarked Hurstwood, looking back to the paper.

"We'll hear, I guess, soon enough," said Shaughnessy.

Sure enough, it did develop. Mr. Slawson owned the property adjoining, and was going to put up a modern office building. The present one was to be torn down. It would take probably a year and a half to complete the other one.

All these things developed by degrees, and Hurstwood began to ponder over what would become of the saloon. One day he spoke about it to his partner.

"Do you think it would be worth while to open up somewhere else in the neighbourhood?"

"What would be the use?" said Shaughnessy. "We couldn't get another corner around here."

"It wouldn't pay anywhere else, do you think?"

"I wouldn't try it," said the other.

The approaching change now took on a most serious aspect to Hurstwood. Dissolution meant the loss of his thousand dollars, and he could not save another thousand in the time. He understood that Shaughnessy was merely tired of the arrangement, and would probably lease the new corner, when completed, alone. He began to worry about the necessity of a new connection and to see impending serious financial straits unless something turned up. This left him in no mood to enjoy his flat or Carrie, and consequently the depression invaded that quarter.

Meanwhile, he took such time as he could to look about, but opportunities were not numerous. More, he had not the same impressive personality which he had when he first came to New York. Bad thoughts had put a shade into his eyes which did not impress others favourably. Neither had he thirteen hundred dollars in hand to talk with. About a month later, finding that he had not made any progress, Shaughnessy reported definitely that Slawson would not extend the lease.

"I guess this thing's got to come to an end," he said, affecting an air of concern.

"Well, if it has, it has," answered Hurstwood, grimly. He would not give the other a key to his opinions, whatever they were. He should not have the satisfaction.

A day or two later he saw that he must say something to Carrie.

"You know," he said, "I think I'm going to get the worst of my deal down there."

"How is that?" asked Carrie in astonishment.

"Well, the man who owns the ground has sold it, and the new owner won't release it to us. The business may come to an end."

"Can't you start somewhere else?"

"There doesn't seem to be any place. Shaughnessy doesn't want to."

"Do you lose what you put in?"

"Yes," said Hurstwood, whose face was a study.

"Oh, isn't that too bad?" said Carrie.

"It's a trick," said Hurstwood. "That's all. They'll start another place there all right."

Carrie looked at him, and gathered from his whole demeanour what it meant. It was serious, very serious.

"Do you think you can get something else?" she ventured, timidly.

Hurstwood thought a while. It was all up with the bluff about money and investment. She could see now that he was "broke."

"I don't know," he said solemnly; "I can try."

Chapter XXXIV

THE GRIND OF THE MILLSTONES: A SAMPLE OF CHAFF

Carrie pondered over this situation as consistently as Hurstwood, once she got the facts adjusted in her mind. It took several days for her to fully realise that the approach of the dissolution of her husband's business meant commonplace struggle and privation. Her mind went back to her early venture in Chicago, the Hansons and their flat, and her heart revolted. That was terrible! Everything about poverty was terrible. She wished she knew a way out. Her recent experiences with the Vances had wholly unfitted her to view her own state with complacence. The glamour of the high life of the city had, in the few experiences afforded her by the former, seized her completely. She had been taught how to dress and where to go without having ample means to do either. Now, these things—ever-present realities as they were—filled her eyes and mind. The more circumscribed became her state, the more entrancing seemed this other. And now poverty threatened to seize her entirely and to remove this other world far upward like a heaven to which any Lazarus might extend, appealingly, his hands.

So, too, the ideal brought into her life by Ames remained. He had gone, but here was his word that riches were not everything; that there was a great deal more in the world than she knew; that the stage was good, and the literature she read poor. He was a strong man and clean—how much stronger and better than Hurstwood and Drouet she only half formulated to herself, but the difference was painful. It was something to which she voluntarily closed her eyes.

During the last three months of the Warren Street connection, Hurstwood took parts of days off and hunted, tracking the business advertisements. It was a more or less depressing business, wholly because of the thought that he must soon get something or he would begin to live on the few hundred dollars he was saving, and then he would have nothing to invest—he would have to hire out as a clerk.

Everything he discovered in his line advertised as an opportunity, was either too expensive or too wretched for him. Besides, winter was coming, the papers were announcing hardships, and there was a general feeling of hard times in the air, or, at least, he thought so. In his worry, other people's worries became apparent. No item about a firm failing, a family starving, or a man dying upon the streets, supposedly of starvation, but arrested his eye as he scanned the morning papers. Once the "World" came out with a flaring announcement about "80,000 people out of employment in New York this winter," which struck as a knife at his heart.[1]

"Eighty thousand!" he thought. "What an awful thing that is."

This was new reasoning for Hurstwood. In the old days the world had seemed to be getting along well enough. He had been wont to see similar things in the "Daily News," in Chicago, but they did not hold his attention. Now, these things were like grey clouds hovering along the horizon of a clear day. They threatened to cover and obscure his life with chilly greyness. He tried to shake them off, to forget and brace up. Sometimes he said to himself, mentally:

"What's the use worrying? I'm not out yet. I've got six weeks more. Even if worst comes to worst, I've got enough to live on for six months."

Curiously, as he troubled over his future, his thoughts occasionally reverted to his wife and family. He had avoided such thoughts for the first three years as much as possible. He hated her, and he could get along without her. Let her go. He would do well enough. Now, however, when he was not doing well enough, he began to wonder what she was doing, how his children were getting along. He could see them living as nicely as ever, occupying the comfortable house and using his property.

1. The financial panic of 1893 caused a severe depression and much unemployment during the winter of 1893–94. (Hurstwood loses his Warren Street saloon in February 1894; see The Chronology of *Sister Carrie*, pp. 605–06).

"By George! it's a shame they should have it all," he vaguely thought to himself on several occasions. "I didn't do anything."

As he looked back now and analysed the situation which led up to his taking the money, he began mildly to justify himself. What had he done—what in the world—that should bar him out this way and heap such difficulties upon him? It seemed only yesterday to him since he was comfortable and well-to-do. But now it was all wrested from him.

"She didn't deserve what she got out of me, that is sure. I didn't do so much, if everybody could just know."

There was no thought that the facts ought to be advertised. It was only a mental justification he was seeking from himself—something that would enable him to bear his state as a righteous man.

One afternoon, five weeks before the Warren Street place closed up, he left the saloon to visit three or four places he saw advertised in the "Herald." One was down in Gold Street, and he visited that, but did not enter. It was such a cheap looking place he felt that he could not abide it. Another was on the Bowery, which he knew contained many showy resorts. It was near Grand Street, and turned out to be very handsomely fitted up. He talked around about investments for fully three-quarters of an hour with the proprietor, who maintained that his health was poor, and that was the reason he wished a partner.

"Well, now, just how much money would it take to buy a half interest here?" said Hurstwood, who saw seven hundred dollars as his limit.

"Three thousand," said the man.

Hurstwood's jaw fell.

"Cash?" he said.

"Cash."

He tried to put on an air of deliberation, as one who might really buy; but his eyes showed gloom. He wound up by saying he would think it over, and came away. The man he had been talking to sensed his condition in a vague way.

"I don't think he wants to buy," he said to himself. "He doesn't talk right."

The afternoon was as grey as lead and cold. It was blowing up a disagreeable winter wind. He visited a place far up on the east side, near Sixty-ninth Street, and it was five o'clock, and growing dim, when he reached there. A portly German kept this place.

"How about this ad. of yours?" asked Hurstwood, who rather objected to the looks of the place.

"Oh, dat iss all over," said the German. "I vill not sell now."

"Oh, is that so?"

"Yes; dere is nothing to dat. It iss all over."

"Very well," said Hurstwood, turning around.

The German paid no more attention to him, and it made him angry.

"The crazy ass!" he said to himself. "What does he want to advertise for?"

Wholly depressed, he started for Thirteenth Street. The flat had only a light in the kitchen, where Carrie was working. He struck a match and, lighting the gas, sat down in the dining-room without even greeting her. She came to the door and looked in.

"It's you, is it?" she said, and went back.

"Yes," he said, without even looking up from the evening paper he had bought.

Carrie saw things were wrong with him. He was not so handsome when gloomy. The lines at the sides of the eyes were deepened. Naturally dark of skin, gloom made him look slightly sinister. He was quite a disagreeable figure.

Carrie set the table and brought in the meal.

"Dinner's ready," she said, passing him for something.

He did not answer, reading on.

She came in and sat down at her place, feeling exceedingly wretched.

"Won't you eat now?" she asked.

He folded his paper and drew near, silence holding for a time, except for the "Pass me's."

"It's been gloomy to-day, hasn't it?" ventured Carrie, after a time.

"Yes," he said.

He only picked at his food.

"Are you still sure to close up?" said Carrie, venturing to take up the subject which they had discussed often enough.

"Of course we are," he said, with the slightest modification of sharpness.

This retort angered Carrie. She had had a dreary day of it herself.

"You needn't talk like that," she said.

"Oh!" he exclaimed, pushing back from the table, as if to say more, but letting it go at that. Then he picked up his paper. Carrie left her seat, containing herself with difficulty. He saw she was hurt.

"Don't go 'way," he said, as she started back into the kitchen. "Eat your dinner."

She passed, not answering.

He looked at the paper a few moments, and then rose up and put on his coat.

"I'm going down town, Carrie," he said, coming out. "I'm out of sorts to-night."

She did not answer.

"Don't be angry," he said. "It will be all right to-morrow."

He looked at her, but she paid no attention to him, working at her dishes.

"Good-bye!" he said finally, and went out.

This was the first strong result of the situation between them, but with the nearing of the last day of business the gloom became almost a permanent thing. Hurstwood could not conceal his feelings about the matter. Carrie could not help wondering where she was drifting. It got so that they talked even less than usual, and yet it was not Hurstwood who felt any objection to Carrie. It was Carrie who shied away from him. This he noticed. It aroused an objection to her becoming indifferent to him. He made the possibility of friendly intercourse almost a giant task, and then noticed with discontent that Carrie added to it by her manner and made it more impossible.

At last the final day came. When it actually arrived, Hurstwood, who had got his mind into such a state where a thunder-clap and raging storm would have seemed highly appropriate, was rather relieved to find that it was a plain, ordinary day. The sun shone, the temperature was pleasant. He felt, as he came to the breakfast table, that it wasn't so terrible, after all.

"Well," he said to Carrie, "to-day's my last day on earth."

Carrie smiled in answer to his humour.

Hurstwood glanced over his paper rather gayly. He seemed to have lost a load.

"I'll go down for a little while," he said after breakfast, "and then I'll look around. To-morrow I'll spend the whole day looking about. I think I can get something, now this thing's off my hands."

He went out smiling and visited the place. Shaughnessy was there. They had made all arrangements to share according to their interests. When, however, he had been there several hours, gone out three more, and returned, his elation had departed. As much as he had objected to the place, now that it was no longer to exist, he felt sorry. He wished that things were different.

Shaughnessy was coolly business-like.

"Well," he said at five o'clock, "we might as well count the change and divide."

They did so. The fixtures had already been sold and the sum divided.

"Good-night," said Hurstwood at the final moment, in a last effort to be genial.

"So long," said Shaughnessy, scarcely deigning a notice.

Thus the Warren Street arrangement was permanently concluded.

Carrie had prepared a good dinner at the flat, but after his ride up, Hurstwood was in a solemn and reflective mood.

"Well?" said Carrie, inquisitively.

"I'm out of that," he answered, taking off his coat.

As she looked at him, she wondered what his financial state was now. They ate and talked a little.

"Will you have enough to buy in anywhere else?" asked Carrie.

"No," he said. "I'll have to get something else and save up."

"It would be nice if you could get some place," said Carrie, prompted by anxiety and hope.

"I guess I will," he said reflectively.

For some days thereafter he put on his overcoat regularly in the morning and sallied forth. On these ventures he first consoled himself with the thought that with the seven hundred dollars he had he could still make some advantageous arrangement. He thought about going to some brewery, which, as he knew, frequently controlled saloons which they leased, and get them to help him. Then he remembered that he would have to pay out several hundred any way for fixtures and that he would have nothing left for his monthly expenses. It was costing him nearly eighty dollars a month to live.

"No," he said, in his sanest moments, "I can't do it. I'll get something else and save up."

This getting-something proposition complicated itself the moment he began to think of what it was he wanted to do. Manage a place? Where should he get such a position? The papers contained no requests for managers. Such positions, he knew well enough, were either secured by long years of service or were bought with a half or third interest. Into a place important enough to need such a manager he had not money enough to buy.

Nevertheless, he started out. His clothes were very good and his appearance still excellent, but it involved the trouble of deluding. People, looking at him, imagined instantly that a man of his age, stout and well dressed, must be well off. He appeared a comfortable owner of something, a man from whom the common run of mortals could well expect gratuities. Being now forty three years of age, and comfortably built, walking was not easy. He had not been used to exercise for many years. His legs tired, his shoulders ached, and his feet pained him at the close of the day, even when he took street cars in almost every direction. The mere getting up and down, if long continued, produced this result.

The fact that people took him to be better off than he was, he well understood. It was so painfully clear to him that it retarded his search. Not that he wished to be less well-appearing, but that he was ashamed to belie his appearance by incongruous appeals. So he hesitated, wondering what to do.

He thought of the hotels, but instantly he remembered that he had had no experience as a clerk, and, what was more important, no acquaintances or friends in that line to whom he could go. He did know some hotel owners in several cities, including New York, but they knew of his dealings with Fitzgerald and Moy. He could not apply to them. He thought of other lines suggested by large buildings or businesses which he knew of—wholesale groceries, hardware, insurance concerns, and the like—but he had had no experience.

How to go about getting anything was a bitter thought. Would he have to go personally and ask; wait outside an office door, and, then, distinguished and affluent looking, announce that he was looking for something to do? He strained painfully at the thought. No, he could not do that.

He really strolled about, thinking, and then, the weather being cold, stepped into a hotel. He knew hotels well enough to know that any decent looking individual was welcome to a chair in the lobby. This was in the Broadway Central which was then one of the most important hotels in the city.[2] Taking a chair here was a painful thing to him. To think he should come to this! He had heard loungers about hotels called chair-warmers. He had called them that himself in his day. But here he was, despite the possibility of meeting some one who knew him, shielding himself from cold and the weariness of the streets in a hotel lobby.

"I can't do this way," he said to himself. "There's no use of my starting out mornings without first thinking up some place to go. I'll think of some places and then look them up."

It occurred to him that the positions of bartenders were sometimes open, but he put this out of his mind. Bartender—he, the ex-manager!

It grew awfully dull sitting in the hotel lobby, and so at four he went home. He tried to put on a business air as he went in, but it was a feeble imitation. The rocking-chair in the dining-room was comfortable. He sank into it gladly, with several papers he had bought, and began to read.

As she was going through the room to begin preparing dinner, Carrie said:

"The man was here for the rent to-day."

"Oh, was he?" said Hurstwood.

The least wrinkle crept into his brow as he remembered that this was February 2d, the time the man always called. He fished down in his pocket for his purse, getting the first taste of paying out when nothing is coming in. He looked at the fat, green roll as a sick man looks at the one possible saving cure. Then he counted off twenty-eight dollars.

"Here you are," he said to Carrie, when she came through again.

He buried himself in his papers and read. Oh, the rest of it—the relief from walking and thinking! What Lethean waters were these

2. One of the largest hotels in the city, the Broadway Central was at Broadway and Bond, a few blocks west of Houston Street.

floods of telegraphed intelligence! He forgot his troubles, in part. Here was a young, handsome woman, if you might believe the newspaper drawing, suing a rich, fat, candy-making husband in Brooklyn for divorce. Here was another item detailing the wrecking of a vessel in ice and snow off Prince's Bay[3] on Staten Island. A long, bright column told of the doings in the theatrical world—the plays produced, the actors appearing, the managers making announcements. Fannie Davenport was just opening at the Fifth Avenue. Daly was producing "King Lear."[4] He read of the early departure for the season of a party composed of the Vanderbilts and their friends for Florida. An interesting shooting affray was on in the mountains of Kentucky. So he read, read, read, rocking in the warm room near the radiator and waiting for dinner to be served.

Chapter XXXV

THE PASSING OF EFFORT: THE VISAGE OF CARE

The next morning he looked over the papers and waded through a long list of advertisements, making a few notes. Then he turned to the male-help-wanted column, but with disagreeable feelings. The day was before him—a long day in which to discover something— and this was how he must begin to discover. He scanned the long column, which mostly concerned bakers, bushelmen, cooks, compositors, drivers, and the like, finding two things only which arrested his eye. One was a cashier wanted in a wholesale furniture house, and the other a salesman for a whiskey house. He had never thought of the latter. At once he decided to look that up.

The firm in question was Alsbery & Co., whiskey brokers.[1]

He was admitted almost at once to the manager on his appearance.

"Good-morning, sir," said the latter, thinking at first that he was encountering one of his out-of-town customers.

"Good-morning," said Hurstwood. "You advertised, I believe, for a salesman?"

"Oh," said the man, showing plainly the enlightenment which had come to him. "Yes. Yes, I did."

"I thought I'd drop in," said Hurstwood, with dignity. "I've had some experience in that line myself."

"Oh, have you?" said the man. "What experience have you had?"

"Well, I've managed several liquor houses in my time. Recently I owned a third-interest in a saloon at Warren and Hudson streets."

"I see," said the man.

3. An error for Princess Bay.
4. Fanny (not Fannie) Davenport was a major tragic actress of the 1890s; Daly's Theatre (at Broadway and Twenty-eighth) was known for its Shakespeare revivals.
1. A fictitious name.

Hurstwood ceased, waiting for some suggestion.

"We did want a salesman," said the man. "I don't know as it's anything you'd care to take hold of, though."

"I see," said Hurstwood. "Well, I'm in no position to choose, at present. If it were open, I should be glad to get it."

The man did not take kindly at all to his "No position to choose." He wanted some one who wasn't thinking of a choice or something better. Especially not an old man. He wanted some one young, active, and glad to work actively for a moderate sum. Hurstwood did not please him at all. He had more of an air than his employers.

"Well," he said in answer, "we'd be glad to consider your application. We shan't decide for a few days yet. Suppose you send us your references."

"I will," said Hurstwood.

He nodded good-morning and came away. At the corner he looked at the furniture company's address, and saw that it was in West Twenty-third Street. Accordingly, he went up there. The place was not large enough, however. It looked moderate, the men in it idle and small salaried. He walked by, glancing in, and then decided not to go in there.

"They want a girl, probably, at ten a week," he said.

At one o'clock he thought of eating, and went to a restaurant in Madison Square. There he pondered over places which he might look up. He was tired. It was blowing up grey again. Across the way, through Madison Square Park, stood the great hotels, looking down upon a busy scene.[2] He decided to go over to the lobby of one and sit a while. It was warm in there and bright. He had seen no one he knew at the Broadway Central. In all likelihood he would encounter no one here. Finding a seat on one of the red plush divans close to the great windows which look out on Broadway's busy rout, he sat musing. His state did not seem so bad in here. Sitting still and looking out, he could take some slight consolation in the few hundred dollars he had in his purse. He could forget, in a measure, the weariness of the street and his tiresome searches. Still, it was only escape from a severe to a less severe state. He was still gloomy and disheartened. There, minutes seemed to go very slowly. An hour was a long, long time in passing. It was filled for him with observations and mental comments concerning the actual guests of the hotel, who passed in and out, and those more prosperous pedestrians whose good fortune showed in their clothes and spirits as they passed along Broadway, outside. It was nearly the first time since he had arrived in the city that his leisure afforded him ample opportunity to con-

---

2. The major hotels at Madison Square were the Fifth Avenue Hotel and the Hoffman House.

template this spectacle. Now, being, perforce, idle himself, he wondered at the activity of others. How gay were the youths he saw, how pretty the women. Such fine clothes they all wore. They were so intent upon getting somewhere. He saw coquettish glances cast by magnificent girls. Ah, the money it required to train with such—how well he knew! How long it had been since he had had the opportunity to do so!

The clock outside registered four. It was a little early, but he thought he would go back to the flat.

This going back to the flat was coupled with the thought that Carrie would think he was sitting around too much if he came home early. He hoped he wouldn't have to, but the day hung heavily on his hands. Over there he was on his own ground. He could sit in his rocking-chair and read. This busy, distracting, suggestive scene was shut out. He could read his papers. Accordingly, he went home. Carrie was reading, quite alone. It was rather dark in the flat, shut in as it was.

"You'll hurt your eyes," he said when he saw her.

After taking off his coat, he felt it incumbent upon him to make some little report of his day.

"I've been talking with a wholesale liquor company," he said. "I may go out on the road."

"Wouldn't that be nice!" said Carrie.

"It wouldn't be such a bad thing," he answered.

Always from the man at the corner now he bought two papers—the "Evening World" and "Evening Sun." So now he merely picked his papers up, as he came by, without stopping.

He drew up his chair near the radiator and lighted the gas. Then it was as the evening before. His difficulties vanished in the items he so well loved to read.

The next day was even worse than the one before, because now he could not think of where to go. Nothing he saw in the papers he studied—till ten o'clock—appealed to him. He felt that he ought to go out, and yet he sickened at the thought. Where to, where to?

"You mustn't forget to leave me my money for this week," said Carrie, quietly.

They had an arrangement by which he placed twelve dollars a week in her hands, out of which to pay current expenses. He heaved a little sigh as she said this, and drew out his purse. Again he felt the dread of the thing. Here he was taking off, taking off, and nothing coming in.

"Lord!" he said, in his own thoughts, "this can't go on."

To Carrie he said nothing whatsoever. She could feel that her request disturbed him. To pay her would soon become a distressing thing.

"Yet, what have I got to do with it?" she thought. "Oh, why should I be made to worry?"

Hurstwood went out and made for Broadway. He wanted to think up some place. Before long, though, he reached the Grand Hotel at Thirty-first Street. He knew of its comfortable lobby. He was cold after his twenty blocks' walk.

"I'll go in their barber shop and get a shave," he thought.

Thus he justified himself in sitting down in here after his tonsorial treatment.

Again, time hanging heavily on his hands, he went home early, and this continued for several days, each day the need to hunt paining him, and each day disgust, depression, shamefacedness driving him into lobby idleness.

At last three days came in which a storm prevailed, and he did not go out at all. The snow began to fall late one afternoon. It was a regular flurry of large, soft, white flakes. In the morning it was still coming down with a high wind, and the papers announced a blizzard.[3] From out the front windows one could see a deep, soft bedding.

"I guess I'll not try to go out to-day," he said to Carrie at breakfast. "It's going to be awful bad, so the papers say."

"The man hasn't brought my coal, either," said Carrie, who ordered by the bushel.

"I'll go over and see about it," said Hurstwood. This was the first time he had ever suggested doing an errand, but, somehow, the wish to sit about the house prompted it as a sort of compensation for the privilege.

All day and all night it snowed, and the city began to suffer from a general blockade of traffic. Great attention was given to the details of the storm by the newspapers, which played up the distress of the poor in large type.

Hurstwood sat and read by his radiator in the corner. He did not try to think about his need of work. This storm being so terrific, and tying up all things, robbed him of the need. He made himself wholly comfortable and toasted his feet.

Carrie observed his ease with some misgiving. For all the fury of the storm she doubted his comfort. He took his situation too philosophically.

Hurstwood, however, read on and on. He did not pay much attention to Carrie. She fulfilled her household duties and said little to disturb him.

The next day it was still snowing, and the next, bitter cold. Hurstwood took the alarm of the paper and sat still. Now he volunteered

3. New York was severely affected by a heavy snowstorm in late February 1894.

to do a few other little things. One was to go to the butcher, another to the grocery. He really thought nothing of these little services in connection with their true significance. He felt as if he were not wholly useless—indeed, in such a stress of weather, quite worth while about the house.

On the fourth day, however, it cleared, and he read that the storm was over. Now, however, he idled, thinking how sloppy the streets would be.

It was noon before he finally abandoned his papers and got under way. Owing to the slightly warmer temperature the streets were bad. He went across Fourteenth Street on the car and got a transfer south on Broadway. One little advertisement he had, relating to a saloon down in Pearl Street. When he reached the Broadway Central, however, he changed his mind.[4]

"What's the use?" he thought, looking out upon the slop and snow. "I couldn't buy into it. It's a thousand to one nothing comes of it. I guess I'll get off," and off he got. In the lobby he took a seat and waited again, wondering what he could do.

While he was idly pondering, satisfied to be inside, a well-dressed man passed up the lobby, stopped, looked sharply, as if not sure of his memory, and then approached. Hurstwood recognised Cargill, the owner of the large stables in Chicago of the same name, whom he had last seen at Avery Hall, the night Carrie appeared there. The remembrance of how this individual brought up his wife to shake hands on that occasion was also on the instant clear.

Hurstwood was greatly abashed. His eyes expressed the difficulty he felt.

"Why, it's Hurstwood!" said Cargill, remembering now, and sorry that he had not recognised him quickly enough in the beginning to have avoided this meeting.

"Yes," said Hurstwood. "How are you?"

"Very well," said Cargill, troubled for something to talk about. "Stopping here?"

"No," said Hurstwood, "just keeping an appointment."

"I knew you had left Chicago. I was wondering what had become of you."

"Oh, I'm here now," answered Hurstwood, anxious to get away.

"Doing well, I suppose?"

"Excellent."

"Glad to hear it."

They looked at one another, rather embarrassed.

4. Pearl Street is south of Canal, off Broadway. Hurstwood would pass the Broadway Central (at Bond) before reaching Pearl. During the 1890s New York had four kinds of public street transportation: horse cars (rapidly disappearing), cable cars, trolley cars, and elevated railroads.

"Well, I have an engagement with a friend upstairs. I'll leave you. So long."

Hurstwood nodded his head.

"Damn it all," he murmured, turning toward the door. "I knew that would happen."

He walked several blocks up the street. His watch only registered 1.30. He tried to think of some place to go or something to do. The day was so bad he wanted only to be inside. Finally his feet began to feel wet and cold, and he boarded a car. This took him to Fifty-ninth Street, which was as good as anywhere else. Landed here, he turned to walk back along Seventh Avenue, but the slush was too much. The misery of lounging about with nowhere to go became intolerable. He felt as if he were catching cold.

Stopping at a corner, he waited for a car south bound. This was no day to be out; he would go home.

Carrie was surprised to see him at a quarter of three.

"It's a miserable day out," was all he said. Then he took off his coat and changed his shoes.

That night he felt a cold coming on and took quinine. He was feverish until morning, and sat about the next day while Carrie waited on him. He was a helpless creature in sickness, not very handsome in a dull-coloured bath gown and his hair uncombed. He looked haggard about the eyes and quite old. Carrie noticed this, and it did not appeal to her. She wanted to be good-natured and sympathetic, but something about the man held her aloof.

Toward evening he looked so badly in the weak light that she suggested he go to bed.

"You'd better sleep alone," she said, "you'll feel better. I'll open your bed for you now."

"All right," he said.

As she did all these things, she was in a most despondent state.

"What a life! What a life!" was her one thought.

Once during the day, when he sat near the radiator, hunched up and reading, she passed through, and seeing him, wrinkled her brows. In the front room, where it was not so warm, she sat by the window and cried. This was the life cut out for her, was it? To live cooped up in a small flat with some one who was out of work, idle, and indifferent to her. She was merely a servant to him now, nothing more.

This crying made her eyes red, and when, in preparing his bed, she lighted the gas, and, having prepared it, called him in, he noticed the fact.

"What's the matter with you?" he asked, looking into her face. His voice was hoarse and his unkempt head only added to its grewsome quality.

"Nothing," said Carrie, weakly.

"You've been crying," he said.

"I haven't either," she answered.

It was not for love of him, that he knew.

"You needn't cry," he said, getting into bed. "Things will come out all right."

In a day or two he was up again, but rough weather holding, he stayed in. The Italian newsdealer now delivered the morning papers, and these he read assiduously. A few times after that he ventured out, but meeting another of his old-time friends, he began to feel uneasy sitting about hotel corridors.

Every day he came home early, and at last made no pretence of going anywhere. Winter was no time to look for anything.

Naturally, being about the house, he noticed the way Carrie did things. She was far from perfect in household methods and economy, and her little deviations on this score first caught his eye. Not, however, before her regular demand for her allowance became a grievous thing. Sitting around as he did, the weeks seemed to pass very quickly. Every Tuesday Carrie asked for her money.

"Do you think we live as cheaply as we might?" he asked one Tuesday morning.

"I do the best I can," said Carrie.

Nothing was added to this at the moment, but the next day he said:

"Do you ever go to the Gansevoort Market over here?"

"I didn't know there was such a market," said Carrie.

"They say you can get things lots cheaper there."[5]

Carrie was very indifferent to the suggestion. These were things which she did not like at all.

"How much do you pay for a pound of meat?" he asked one day.

"Oh, there are different prices," said Carrie. "Sirloin steak is twenty-two cents."

"That's steep, isn't it?" he answered.

So he asked about other things, until finally, with the passing days, it seemed to become a mania with him. He learned the prices and remembered them.

His errand-running capacity also improved. It began in a small way, of course. Carrie, going to get her hat one morning, was stopped by him.

"Where are you going, Carrie?" he asked.

"Over to the baker's," she answered.

"I'd just as leave go for you," he said.

5. The Gansevoort, a large public market, was at Bloomfield and Thirteenth, a short walk from Carrie and Hurstwood's flat.

She acquiesced, and he went. Each afternoon he would go to the corner for the papers.

"Is there anything you want?" he would say.

By degrees she began to use him. Doing this, however, she lost the weekly payment of twelve dollars.

"You want to pay me to-day," she said one Tuesday, about this time.

"How much?" he asked.

She understood well enough what it meant.

"Well, about five dollars," she answered. "I owe the coal man."

The same day he said:

"I think this Italian up here on the corner sells coal at twenty-five cents a bushel. I'll trade with him."

Carrie heard this with indifference.

"All right," she said.

Then it came to be:

"George, I must have some coal to-day," or, "You must get some meat of some kind for dinner."

He would find out what she needed and order.

Accompanying this plan came skimpiness.

"I only got a half-pound of steak," he said, coming in one afternoon with his papers. "We never seem to eat very much."

These miserable details ate the heart out of Carrie. They blackened her days and grieved her soul. Oh, how this man had changed! All day and all day, here he sat, reading his papers. The world seemed to have no attraction. Once in a while he would go out, in fine weather, it might be four or five hours, between eleven and four. She could do nothing but view him with gnawing contempt.

It was apathy with Hurstwood, resulting from his inability to see his way out. Each month drew from his small store. Now, he had only five hundred dollars left, and this he hugged, half feeling as if he could stave off absolute necessity for an indefinite period. Sitting around the house, he decided to wear some old clothes he had. This came first with the bad days. Only once he apologised in the very beginning:

"It's so bad to-day, I'll just wear these around."

Eventually these became the permanent thing.

Also, he had been wont to pay fifteen cents for a shave, and a tip of ten cents. In his first distress, he cut down the tip to five, then to nothing. Later, he tried a ten-cent barber shop, and, finding that the shave was satisfactory, patronised regularly. Later still, he put off shaving to every other day, then to every third, and so on, until once a week became the rule. On Saturday he was a sight to see.

Of course, as his own self-respect vanished, it perished for him in Carrie. She could not understand what had gotten into the man. He had some money, he had a decent suit remaining, he was not bad looking when dressed up. She did not forget her own difficult struggle in Chicago, but she did not forget either that she had never ceased trying. He never tried. He did not even consult the ads. in the papers any more.

Finally, a distinct impression escaped from her.

"What makes you put so much butter on the steak?" he asked her one evening, standing around in the kitchen.

"To make it good, of course," she answered.

"Butter is awful dear these days," he suggested.

"You wouldn't mind it if you were working," she answered.

He shut up after this, and went in to his paper, but the retort rankled in his mind. It was the first cutting remark that had come from her.

That same evening, Carrie, after reading, went off to the front room to bed. This was unusual. When Hurstwood decided to go, he retired, as usual, without a light. It was then that he discovered Carrie's absence.

"That's funny," he said; "maybe she's sitting up."

He gave the matter no more thought, but slept. In the morning she was not beside him. Strange to say, this passed without comment.

Night approaching, and a slightly more conversational feeling prevailing, Carrie said:

"I think I'll sleep alone to-night. I have a headache."

"All right," said Hurstwood.

The third night she went to her front bed without apologies.

This was a grim blow to Hurstwood, but he never mentioned it.

"All right," he said to himself, with an irrepressible frown, "let her sleep alone."

Chapter XXXVI

A GRIM RETROGRESSION: THE PHANTOM OF CHANCE

The Vances, who had been back in the city ever since Christmas, had not forgotten Carrie; but they, or rather Mrs. Vance, had never called on her, for the very simple reason that Carrie had never sent her address. True to her nature, she corresponded with Mrs. Vance as long as she still lived in Seventy-eighth Street, but when she was compelled to move into Thirteenth, her fear that the latter would take it as an indication of reduced circumstances caused her to study some way of avoiding the necessity of giving her address. Not finding any convenient method, she sorrowfully resigned the privilege of writing to her friend entirely. The latter wondered at this strange silence, thought Carrie must have left the city, and in the end gave her up as lost. So she was thoroughly surprised to encounter her in Fourteenth Street, where she had gone shopping. Carrie was there for the same purpose.

"Why, Mrs. Wheeler," said Mrs. Vance, looking Carrie over in a glance, "where have you been? Why haven't you been to see me? I've been wondering all this time what had become of you. Really, I——"

"I'm so glad to see you," said Carrie, pleased and yet nonplussed. Of all times, this was the worst to encounter Mrs. Vance. "Why, I'm living down town here. I've been intending to come and see you. Where are you living now?"

"In Fifty-eighth Street," said Mrs. Vance, "just off Seventh Avenue—218. Why don't you come and see me?"

"I will," said Carrie. "Really, I've been wanting to come. I know I ought to. It's a shame. But you know——"

"What's your number?" said Mrs. Vance.

"Thirteenth Street," said Carrie, reluctantly. "112 West."

"Oh," said Mrs. Vance, "that's right near here, isn't it?"

"Yes," said Carrie. "You must come down and see me some time."

"Well, you're a fine one," said Mrs. Vance, laughing, the while noting that Carrie's appearance had modified somewhat. "The address, too," she added to herself. "They must be hard up."

Still she liked Carrie well enough to take her in tow.

"Come with me in here a minute," she exclaimed, turning into a store.

When Carrie returned home, there was Hurstwood, reading as usual. He seemed to take his condition with the utmost nonchalance. His beard was at least four days old.

"Oh," thought Carrie, "if she were to come here and see him?"

She shook her head in absolute misery. It looked as if her situation was becoming unbearable.

Driven to desperation, she asked at dinner:

"Did you ever hear any more from that wholesale house?"

"No," he said. "They don't want an inexperienced man."

Carrie dropped the subject, feeling unable to say more.

"I met Mrs. Vance this afternoon," she said, after a time.

"Did, eh?" he answered.

"They're back in New York now," Carrie went on. "She did look so nice."

"Well, she can afford it as long as he puts up for it," returned Hurstwood. "He's got a soft job."

Hurstwood was looking into the paper. He could not see the look of infinite weariness and discontent Carrie gave him.

"She said she thought she'd call here some day."

"She's been long getting round to it, hasn't she?" said Hurstwood, with a kind of sarcasm.

The woman didn't appeal to him from her spending side.

"Oh, I don't know," said Carrie, angered by the man's attitude. "Perhaps I didn't want her to come."

"She's too gay," said Hurstwood, significantly. "No one can keep up with her pace unless they've got a lot of money."

"Mr. Vance doesn't seem to find it very hard."

"He may not now," answered Hurstwood, doggedly, well understanding the inference; "but his life isn't done yet. You can't tell what'll happen. He may get down like anybody else."

There was something quite knavish in the man's attitude. His eye seemed to be cocked with a twinkle upon the fortunate, expecting their defeat. His own state seemed a thing apart—not considered.

This thing was the remains of his old-time cocksureness and independence. Sitting in his flat, and reading of the doings of other people, sometimes this independent, undefeated mood came upon him. Forgetting the weariness of the streets and the degradation of search, he would sometimes prick up his ears. It was as if he said:

"I can do something. I'm not down yet. There's a lot of things coming to me if I want to go after them."

It was in this mood that he would occasionally dress up, go for a shave, and, putting on his gloves, sally forth quite actively. Not with any definite aim. It was more a barometric condition. He felt just right for being outside and doing something.

On such occasions, his money went also. He knew of several poker rooms down town. A few acquaintances he had in downtown resorts and about the City Hall. It was a change to see them and exchange a few friendly commonplaces.

He had once been accustomed to hold a pretty fair hand at poker. Many a friendly game had netted him a hundred dollars or more at the time when that sum was merely sauce to the dish of the game— not the all in all. Now, he thought of playing.

"I might win a couple of hundred. I'm not out of practice."

It is but fair to say that this thought had occurred to him several times before he acted upon it.

The poker room which he first invaded was over a saloon in West Street, near one of the ferries. He had been there before. Several games were going. These he watched for a time and noticed that the pots were quite large for the ante involved.

"Deal me a hand," he said at the beginning of a new shuffle. He pulled up a chair and studied his cards. Those playing made that quiet study of him which is so unapparent, and yet invariably so searching.

Poor fortune was with him at first. He received a mixed collection without progression or pairs. The pot was opened.

"I pass," he said.

On the strength of this, he was content to lose his ante. The deals did fairly by him in the long run, causing him to come away with a few dollars to the good.

The next afternoon he was back again, seeking amusement and profit. This time he followed up three of a kind to his doom. There was a better hand across the table, held by a pugnacious Irish youth, who was a political hanger-on of the Tammany district in which they were located. Hurstwood was surprised at the persistence of this individual, whose bets came with a *sangfroid* which, if a bluff, was excellent art. Hurstwood began to doubt, but kept, or thought to keep, at least, the cool demeanour with which, in olden times, he deceived those psychic students of the gaming table, who seem to read thoughts and moods, rather than exterior evidences, however subtle. He could not down the cowardly thought that this man had something better and would stay to the end, drawing his last dollar into the pot, should he choose to go so far. Still, he hoped to win much—his hand was excellent. Why not raise it five more?

"I raise you three," said the youth.

"Make it five," said Hurstwood, pushing out his chips.

"Come again," said the youth, pushing out a small pile of reds.

"Let me have some more chips," said Hurstwood to the keeper in charge, taking out a bill.

A cynical grin lit up the face of his youthful opponent. When the chips were laid out, Hurstwood met the raise.

"Five again," said the youth.[1]

Hurstwood's brow was wet. He was deep in now—very deep for him. Sixty dollars of his good money was up. He was ordinarily no coward, but the thought of losing so much weakened him. Finally he gave way. He would not trust to this fine hand any longer.

"I call," he said.

"A full house!" said the youth, spreading out his cards.

Hurstwood's hand dropped.

"I thought I had you," he said, weakly.

The youth raked in his chips, and Hurstwood came away, not without first stopping to count his remaining cash on the stair.

"Three hundred and forty dollars," he said.

With this loss and ordinary expenses, so much had already gone. Back in the flat, he decided he would play no more.

Remembering Mrs. Vance's promise to call, Carrie made one other mild protest. It was concerning Hurstwood's appearance. This very day, coming home, he changed his clothes to the old togs he sat around in.

---

1. Here and on p. 258 Dreiser appears to be unaware of the rule in poker that it is not possible to raise an opponent who has met or called your raise. He must raise you back in order for you to raise again.

"What makes you always put on those old clothes?" asked Carrie.

"What's the use wearing my good ones around here?" he asked.

"Well, I should think you'd feel better." Then she added: "Some one might call."

"Who?" he said.

"Well, Mrs. Vance," said Carrie.

"She needn't see me," he answered, sullenly.

This lack of pride and interest made Carrie almost hate him.

"Oh," she thought, "there he sits. 'She needn't see me.' I should think he would be ashamed of himself."

The real bitterness of this thing was added when Mrs. Vance did call. It was on one of her shopping rounds. Making her way up the commonplace hall, she knocked at Carrie's door. To her subsequent and agonising distress, Carrie was out. Hurstwood opened the door, half thinking that the knock was Carrie's. For once, he was taken honestly aback. The lost voice of youth and pride spoke in him.

"Why," he said, actually stammering, "how do you do?"

"How do you do?" said Mrs. Vance, who could scarcely believe her eyes. His great confusion she instantly perceived. He did not know whether to invite her in or not.

"Is your wife at home?" she inquired.

"No," he said, "Carrie's out; but won't you step in? She'll be back shortly."

"No-o," said Mrs. Vance, realising the change of it all. "I'm really very much in a hurry. I thought I'd just run up and look in, but I couldn't stay. Just tell your wife she must come and see me."

"I will," said Hurstwood, standing back, and feeling intense relief at her going. He was so ashamed that he folded his hands weakly, as he sat in the chair afterwards, and thought.

Carrie, coming in from another direction, thought she saw Mrs. Vance going away. She strained her eyes, but could not make sure.

"Was anybody here just now?" she asked of Hurstwood.

"Yes," he said guiltily; "Mrs. Vance."

"Did she see you?" she asked, expressing her full despair.

This cut Hurstwood like a whip, and made him sullen.

"If she had eyes, she did. I opened the door."

"Oh," said Carrie, closing one hand tightly out of sheer nervousness. "What did she have to say?"

"Nothing," he answered. "She couldn't stay."

"And you looking like that!" said Carrie, throwing aside a long reserve.

"What of it?" he said, angering. "I didn't know she was coming, did I?"

"You knew she might," said Carrie. "I told you she said she was coming. I've asked you a dozen times to wear your other clothes. Oh, I think this is just terrible."

"Oh, let up," he answered. "What difference does it make? You couldn't associate with her, anyway. They've got too much money."

"Who said I wanted to?" said Carrie, fiercely.

"Well, you act like it, rowing around over my looks. You'd think I'd committed——"

Carrie interrupted:

"It's true," she said. "I couldn't if I wanted to, but whose fault is it? You're very free to sit and talk about who I could associate with. Why don't you get out and look for work?"

This was a thunderbolt in camp.

"What's it to you?" he said, rising, almost fiercely. "I pay the rent, don't I? I furnish the——"

"Yes, you pay the rent," said Carrie. "You talk as if there was nothing else in the world but a flat to sit around in. You haven't done a thing for three months except sit around and interfere here. I'd like to know what you married me for?"

"I didn't marry you," he said, in a snarling tone.

"I'd like to know what you did, then, in Montreal?" she answered.

"Well, I didn't marry you," he answered. "You can get that out of your head. You talk as though you didn't know."

Carrie looked at him a moment, her eyes distending. She had believed it was all legal and binding enough.

"What did you lie to me for, then?" she asked, fiercely. "What did you force me to run away with you for?"

Her voice became almost a sob.

"Force!" he said, with curled lip. "A lot of forcing I did."

"Oh!" said Carrie, breaking under the strain, and turning. "Oh, oh!" and she hurried into the front room.

Hurstwood was now hot and waked up. It was a great shaking up for him, both mental and moral. He wiped his brow as he looked around, and then went for his clothes and dressed. Not a sound came from Carrie; she ceased sobbing when she heard him dressing. She thought, at first, with the faintest alarm, of being left without money—not of losing him, though he might be going away permanently. She heard him open the top of the wardrobe and take out his hat. Then the dining-room door closed, and she knew he had gone.

After a few moments of silence, she stood up, dry-eyed, and looked out the window. Hurstwood was just strolling up the street, from the flat, toward Sixth Avenue.

The latter made progress along Thirteenth and across Fourteenth Street to Union Square.

"Look for work!" he said to himself. "Look for work! She tells me to get out and look for work."

He tried to shield himself from his own mental accusation, which told him that she was right.

"What a cursed thing that Mrs. Vance's call was, anyhow," he thought. "Stood right there, and looked me over. I know what she was thinking."

He remembered the few times he had seen her in Seventy-eighth Street. She was always a swell-looker, and he had tried to put on the air of being worthy of such as she, in front of her. Now, to think she had caught him looking this way. He wrinkled his forehead in his distress.

"The devil!" he said a dozen times in an hour.

It was a quarter after four when he left the house. Carrie was in tears. There would be no dinner that night.

"What the deuce," he said, swaggering mentally to hide his own shame from himself. "I'm not so bad. I'm not down yet."

He looked around the square, and seeing the several large hotels, decided to go to one for dinner. He would get his papers and make himself comfortable there.

He ascended into the fine parlour of the Morton House, then one of the best New York hotels, and, finding a cushioned seat, read. It did not trouble him much that his decreasing sum of money did not allow of such extravagance. Like the morphine fiend, he was becoming addicted to his ease. Anything to relieve his mental distress, to satisfy his craving for comfort. He must do it. No thoughts for the morrow—he could not stand to think of it any more than he could of any other calamity. Like the certainty of death, he tried to shut the certainty of soon being without a dollar completely out of his mind, and he came very near doing it.

Well-dressed guests moving to and fro over the thick carpets carried him back to the old days. A young lady, a guest of the house, playing a piano in an alcove pleased him. He sat there reading.

His dinner cost him $1.50. By eight o'clock he was through, and then, seeing guests leaving and the crowd of pleasure-seekers thickening outside, wondered where he should go. Not home. Carrie would be up. No, he would not go back there this evening. He would stay out and knock around as a man who was independent—not broke—well might. He bought a cigar, and went outside on the corner where other individuals were lounging—brokers, racing people, thespians—his own flesh and blood. As he stood there, he thought of the old evenings in Chicago, and how he used to dispose of them. Many's the game he had had. This took him to poker.

"I didn't do that thing right the other day," he thought, referring to his loss of sixty dollars. "I shouldn't have weakened. I could have bluffed that fellow down. I wasn't in form, that's what ailed me."

Then he studied the possibilities of the game as it had been played, and began to figure how he might have won, in several instances, by bluffing a little harder.

"I'm old enough to play poker and do something with it. I'll try my hand to-night."

Visions of a big stake floated before him. Supposing he did win a couple of hundred, wouldn't he be in it? Lots of sports he knew made their living at this game, and a good living, too.

"They always had as much as I had," he thought.

So off he went to a poker room in the neighbourhood, feeling much as he had in the old days. In this period of self-forgetfulness, aroused first by the shock of argument and perfected by a dinner in the hotel, with cocktails and cigars, he was as nearly like the old Hurstwood as he would ever be again. It was not the old Hurstwood—only a man arguing with a divided conscience and lured by a phantom.

This poker room was much like the other one, only it was a back room in a better drinking resort. Hurstwood watched a while, and then, seeing an interesting game, joined in. As before, it went easy for a while, he winning a few times and cheering up, losing a few pots and growing more interested and determined on that account. At last the fascinating game took a strong hold on him. He enjoyed its risks and ventured, on a trifling hand, to bluff the company and secure a fair stake. To his self-satisfaction intense and strong, he did it.

In the height of this feeling he began to think his luck was with him. No one else had done so well. Now came another moderate hand, and again he tried to open the jack-pot on it. There were others there who were almost reading his heart, so close was their observation.

"I have three of a kind," said one of the players to himself. "I'll just stay with the fellow to the finish."

The result was that bidding began.

"I raise you ten."

"Good."

"Ten more."

"Good."

"Ten again."

"Right you are."

It got to where Hurstwood had seventy-five dollars up. The other man really became serious. Perhaps this individual (Hurstwood) really did have a stiff hand.

"I call," he said.

Hurstwood showed his hand. He was done. The bitter fact that he had lost seventy-five dollars made him desperate.

"Let's have another pot," he said, grimly.

"All right," said the man.

Some of the other players quit, but observant loungers took their places. Time passed, and it came to twelve o'clock. Hurstwood held on, neither winning nor losing much. Then he grew weary, and on a last hand lost twenty more. He was sick at heart.

At a quarter after one in the morning he came out of the place. The chill, bare streets seemed a mockery of his state. He walked slowly west, little thinking of his row with Carrie. He ascended the stairs and went into his room as if there had been no trouble. It was his loss that occupied his mind. Sitting down on the bedside he counted his money. There was now but a hundred and ninety dollars and some change. He put it up and began to undress.

"I wonder what's getting into me, anyhow?" he said.

In the morning Carrie scarcely spoke, and he felt as if he must go out again. He had treated her badly, but he could not afford to make up. Now desperation seized him, and for a day or two, going out thus, he lived like a gentleman—or what he conceived to be a gentleman—which took money. For his escapades he was soon poorer in mind and body, to say nothing of his purse, which had lost thirty by the process. Then he came down to cold, bitter sense again.

"The rent man comes to-day," said Carrie, greeting him thus indifferently three mornings later.

"He does?"

"Yes; this is the second," answered Carrie.

Hurstwood frowned. Then in despair he got out his purse.

"It seems an awful lot to pay for rent," he said.

He was nearing his last hundred dollars.

Chapter XXXVII

THE SPIRIT AWAKENS: NEW SEARCH FOR THE GATE

It would be useless to explain how in due time the last fifty dollars was in sight. The seven hundred, by his process of handling, had only carried them into June. Before the final hundred mark was reached he began to indicate that a calamity was approaching.

"I don't know," he said one day, taking a trivial expenditure for meat as a text, "it seems to take an awful lot for us to live."

"It doesn't seem to me," said Carrie, "that we spend very much."

"My money is nearly gone," he said, "and I hardly know where it's gone to."

"All that seven hundred dollars?" asked Carrie.

"All but a hundred."

He looked so disconsolate that it scared her. She began to see that she herself had been drifting. She had felt it all the time.

"Well, George," she exclaimed, "why don't you get out and look for something? You could find something."

"I have looked," he said. "You can't make people give you a place."

She gazed weakly at him and said: "Well, what do you think you will do? A hundred dollars won't last long."

"I don't know," he said. "I can't do any more than look."

Carrie became frightened over this announcement. She thought desperately upon the subject. Frequently she had considered the stage as a door through which she might enter that gilded state which she had so much craved. Now, as in Chicago, it came as a last resource in distress. Something must be done if he did not get work soon. Perhaps she would have to go out and battle again alone.

She began to wonder how one would go about getting a place. Her experience in Chicago proved that she had not tried the right way. There must be people who would listen to and try you—men who would give you an opportunity.

They were talking at the breakfast table, a morning or two later, when she brought up the dramatic subject by saying that she saw that Sarah Bernhardt was coming to this country.[1] Hurstwood had seen it, too.

"How do people get on the stage, George?" she finally asked, innocently.

"I don't know," he said. "There must be dramatic agents."

Carrie was sipping coffee, and did not look up.

"Regular people who get you a place?"

"Yes, I think so," he answered.

Suddenly the air with which she asked attracted his attention.

"You're not still thinking about being an actress, are you?" he asked.

"No," she answered, "I was just wondering."

Without being clear, there was something in the thought which he objected to. He did not believe any more, after three years of observation, that Carrie would ever do anything great in that line. She seemed too simple, too yielding. His idea of the art was that it involved something more pompous. If she tried to get on the stage she would fall into the hands of some cheap manager and become like the rest of them. He had a good idea of what he meant by *them*. Carrie was pretty. She would get along all right, but where would he be?

"I'd get that idea out of my head, if I were you. It's a lot more difficult than you think."

1. The great French actress made frequent tours of America.

Carrie felt this to contain, in some way, an aspersion upon her ability.

"You said I did real well in Chicago," she rejoined.

"You did," he answered, seeing that he was arousing opposition, "but Chicago isn't New York, by a big jump."

Carrie did not answer this at all. It hurt her.

"The stage," he went on, "is all right if you can be one of the big guns, but there's nothing to the rest of it. It takes a long while to get up."

"Oh, I don't know," said Carrie, slightly aroused.

In a flash, he thought he foresaw the result of this thing. Now, when the worst of his situation was approaching, she would get on the stage in some cheap way and forsake him. Strangely, he had not conceived well of her mental ability. That was because he did not understand the nature of emotional greatness. He had never learned that a person might be emotionally—instead of intellectually—great. Avery Hall was too far away for him to look back and sharply remember. He had lived with this woman too long.

"Well, I do," he answered. "If I were you I wouldn't think of it. It's not much of a profession for a woman."

"It's better than going hungry," said Carrie. "If you don't want me to do that, why don't you get work yourself?"

There was no answer ready for this. He had got used to the suggestion.

"Oh, let up," he answered.

The result of this was that she secretly resolved to try. It didn't matter about him. She was not going to be dragged into poverty and something worse to suit him. She could act. She could get something and then work up. What would he say then? She pictured herself already appearing in some fine performance on Broadway; of going every evening to her dressing-room and making up. Then she would come out at eleven o'clock and see the carriages ranged about, waiting for the people. It did not matter whether she was the star or not. If she were only once in, getting a decent salary, wearing the kind of clothes she liked, having the money to do with, going here and there as she pleased, how delightful it would all be. Her mind ran over this picture all the day long. Hurstwood's dreary state made its beauty become more and more vivid.

Curiously this idea soon took hold of Hurstwood. His vanishing sum suggested that he would need sustenance. Why could not Carrie assist him a little until he could get something?

He came in one day with something of this idea in his mind.

"I met John B. Drake to-day," he said. "He's going to open a hotel here in the fall. He says that he can make a place for me then."

"Who is he?" asked Carrie.

"He's the man that runs the Grand Pacific in Chicago."

"Oh," said Carrie.

"I'd get about fourteen hundred a year out of that."

"That would be good, wouldn't it?" she said, sympathetically.

"If I can only get over this summer," he added, "I think I'll be all right. I'm hearing from some of my friends again."

Carrie swallowed this story in all its pristine beauty. She sincerely wished he could get through the summer. He looked so hopeless.

"How much money have you left?"

"Only fifty dollars."

"Oh, mercy," she exclaimed, "what will we do? It's only twenty days until the rent will be due again."

Hurstwood rested his head on his hands and looked blankly at the floor.

"Maybe you could get something in the stage line?" he blandly suggested.

"Maybe I could," said Carrie, glad that some one approved of the idea.

"I'll lay my hand to whatever I can get," he said, now that he saw her brighten up. "I can get something."

She cleaned up the things one morning after he had gone, dressed as neatly as her wardrobe permitted, and set out for Broadway. She did not know that thoroughfare very well. To her it was a wonderful conglomeration of everything great and mighty. The theatres were there—these agencies must be somewhere about.

She decided to stop in at the Madison Square Theatre and ask how to find the theatrical agents. This seemed the sensible way. Accordingly, when she reached that theatre she applied to the clerk at the box office.

"Eh?" he said, looking out. "Dramatic agents? I don't know. You'll find them in the 'Clipper,' though. They all advertise in that."

"Is that a paper?" said Carrie.

"Yes," said the clerk, marvelling at such ignorance of a common fact. "You can get it at the news-stands," he added politely, seeing how pretty the inquirer was.[2]

Carrie proceeded to get the "Clipper," and tried to find the agents by looking over it as she stood beside the stand. This could not be done so easily. Thirteenth Street was a number of blocks off, but she went back, carrying the precious paper and regretting the waste of time.

Hurstwood was already there, sitting in his place.

"Where were you?" he asked.

"I've been trying to find some dramatic agents."

2. The *New York Clipper* was one of the two professional theater newspapers published in New York during the 1890s.

He felt a little diffident about asking concerning her success. The paper she began to scan attracted his attention.

"What have you got there?" he asked.

"The 'Clipper.' The man said I'd find their addresses in here."

"Have you been all the way over to Broadway to find that out? I could have told you."

"Why didn't you?" she asked, without looking up.

"You never asked me," he returned.

She went hunting aimlessly through the crowded columns. Her mind was distracted by this man's indifference. The difficulty of the situation she was facing was only added to by all he did. Self-commiseration brewed in her heart. Tears trembled along her eyelids but did not fall. Hurstwood noticed something.

"Let me look."

To recover herself she went into the front room while he searched. Presently she returned. He had a pencil, and was writing upon an envelope.

"Here're three," he said.

Carrie took it and found that one was Mrs. Bermudez, another Marcus Jenks, a third Percy Weil. She paused only a moment, and then moved toward the door.

"I might as well go right away," she said, without looking back.

Hurstwood saw her depart with some faint stirrings of shame, which were the expression of a manhood rapidly becoming stultified. He sat a while, and then it became too much. He got up and put on his hat.

"I guess I'll go out," he said to himself, and went, strolling nowhere in particular, but feeling somehow that he must go.

Carrie's first call was upon Mrs. Bermudez, whose address was quite the nearest. It was an old-fashioned residence turned into offices. Mrs. Bermudez's offices consisted of what formerly had been a back chamber and a hall bedroom, marked "Private."

As Carrie entered she noticed several persons lounging about—men, who said nothing and did nothing.

While she was waiting to be noticed, the door of the hall bedroom opened and from it issued two very mannish-looking women, very tightly dressed, and wearing white collars and cuffs. After them came a portly lady of about forty-five, light-haired, sharp-eyed, and evidently good-natured. At least she was smiling.

"Now, don't forget about that," said one of the mannish women.

"I won't," said the portly woman. "Let's see," she added, "where are you the first week in February?"

"Pittsburg," said the woman.

"I'll write you there."

"All right," said the other, and the two passed out.

Instantly the portly lady's face became exceedingly sober and shrewd. She turned about and fixed on Carrie a very searching eye.

"Well," she said, "young woman, what can I do for you?"

"Are you Mrs. Bermudez?"

"Yes."

"Well," said Carrie, hesitating how to begin, "do you get places for persons upon the stage?"

"Yes."

"Could you get me one?"

"Have you ever had any experience?"

"A very little," said Carrie.

"Whom did you play with?"

"Oh, with no one," said Carrie. "It was just a show gotten——"

"Oh, I see," said the woman, interrupting her. "No, I don't know of anything now."

Carrie's countenance fell.

"You want to get some New York experience," concluded the affable Mrs. Bermudez. "We'll take your name, though."

Carrie stood looking while the lady retired to her office.

"What is your address?" inquired a young lady behind the counter, taking up the curtailed conversation.

"Mrs. George Wheeler," said Carrie, moving over to where she was writing. The woman wrote her address in full and then allowed her to depart at her leisure.

She encountered a very similar experience in the office of Mr. Jenks, only he varied it by saying at the close: "If you could play at some local house, or had a programme with your name on it, I might do something."

In the third place the individual asked:

"What sort of work do you want to do?"

"What do you mean?" said Carrie.

"Well, do you want to get in a comedy or on the vaudeville stage or in the chorus?"

"Oh, I'd like to get a part in a play," said Carrie.

"Well," said the man, "it'll cost you something to do that."

"How much?" said Carrie, who, ridiculous as it may seem, had not thought of this before.

"Well, that's for you to say," he answered shrewdly.

Carrie looked at him curiously. She hardly knew how to continue the inquiry.

"Could you get me a part if I paid?"

"If we didn't you'd get your money back."

"Oh," she said.

The agent saw he was dealing with an inexperienced soul, and continued accordingly.

"You'd want to deposit fifty dollars, anyway. No agent would trouble about you for less than that."

Carrie saw a light.

"Thank you," she said. "I'll think about it."

She started to go, and then bethought herself.

"How soon would I get a place?" she asked.

"Well, that's hard to say," said the man. "You might get one in a week, or it might be a month. You'd get the first thing that we thought you could do."

"I see," said Carrie, and then, half-smiling to be agreeable, she walked out.

The agent studied a moment, and then said to himself:

"It's funny how anxious these women are to get on the stage."

Carrie found ample food for reflection in the fifty-dollar proposition. "Maybe they'd take my money and not give me anything," she thought. She had some jewelry—a diamond ring and pin and several other pieces. She could get fifty dollars for those if she went to a pawnbroker.

Hurstwood was home before her. He had not thought she would be so long seeking.

"Well?" he said, not venturing to ask what news.

"I didn't find out anything to-day," said Carrie, taking off her gloves. "They all want money to get you a place."

"How much?" asked Hurstwood.

"Fifty dollars."

"They don't want anything, do they?"

"Oh, they're like everybody else. You can't tell whether they'd ever get you anything after you did pay them."

"Well, I wouldn't put up fifty on that basis," said Hurstwood, as if he were deciding, money in hand.

"I don't know," said Carrie. "I think I'll try some of the managers."

Hurstwood heard this, dead to the horror of it. He rocked a little to and fro, and chewed at his finger. It seemed all very natural in such extreme states. He would do better later on.

Chapter XXXVIII

IN ELF LAND DISPORTING: THE GRIM WORLD WITHOUT

When Carrie renewed her search, as she did the next day, going to the Casino, she found that in the opera chorus, as in other fields, employment is difficult to secure.[1] Girls who can stand in a line and look pretty are as numerous as labourers who can swing a pick. She

---

1. Carrie follows a rather roundabout route in her job-hunting. The Casino was at Broadway and Thirty-ninth, Daly's at Broadway and Twenty-ninth, the Empire at Broadway and Forty-first, and the Lyceum at Fourth Avenue and Twenty-third.

found there was no discrimination between one and the other of applicants, save as regards a conventional standard of prettiness and form. Their own opinion or knowledge of their ability went for nothing.

"Where shall I find Mr. Gray?" she asked of a sulky doorman at the stage entrance of the Casino.

"You can't see him now; he's busy."

"Do you know when I can see him?"

"Got an appointment with him?"

"No."

"Well, you'll have to call at his office."

"Oh, dear!" exclaimed Carrie. "Where is his office?"

He gave her the number.

She knew there was no need of calling there now. He would not be in. Nothing remained but to employ the intermediate hours in search.

The dismal story of ventures in other places is quickly told. Mr. Daly saw no one save by appointment. Carrie waited an hour in a dingy office, quite in spite of obstacles, to learn this fact of the placid, indifferent Mr. Dorney.[2]

"You will have to write and ask him to see you."

So she went away.

At the Empire Theatre she found a hive of peculiarly listless and indifferent individuals. Everything ornately upholstered, everything carefully finished, everything remarkably reserved.

At the Lyceum she entered one of those secluded, under-stairway closets, berugged and bepanneled, which causes one to feel the greatness of all positions of authority. Here was reserve itself done into a box-office clerk, a doorman, and an assistant, glorying in their fine positions.

"Ah, be very humble now—very humble indeed. Tell us what it is you require. Tell it quickly, nervously, and without a vestige of self-respect. If no trouble to us in any way, we may see what we can do."

This was the atmosphere of the Lyceum—the attitude, for that matter, of every managerial office in the city. These little proprietors of businesses are lords indeed on their own ground.

Carrie came away wearily, somewhat more abashed for her pains.

Hurstwood heard the details of the weary and unavailing search that evening.

"I didn't get to see any one," said Carrie. "I just walked, and walked, and waited around."

Hurstwood only looked at her.

2. Richard Dorney was Augustin Daly's business manager.

"I suppose you have to have some friends before you can get in," she added, disconsolately.

Hurstwood saw the difficulty of this thing, and yet it did not seem so terrible. Carrie was tired and dispirited, but now she could rest. Viewing the world from his rocking-chair, its bitterness did not seem to approach so rapidly. To-morrow was another day.

To-morrow came, and the next, and the next.

Carrie saw the manager at the Casino once.

"Come around," he said, "the first of next week. I may make some changes then."

He was a large and corpulent individual, surfeited with good clothes and good eating, who judged women as another would horseflesh. Carrie was pretty and graceful. She might be put in even if she did not have any experience. One of the proprietors had suggested that the chorus was a little weak on looks.

The first of next week was some days off yet. The first of the month was drawing near. Carrie began to worry as she had never worried before.

"Do you really look for anything when you go out?" she asked Hurstwood one morning as a climax to some painful thoughts of her own.

"Of course I do," he said pettishly, troubling only a little over the disgrace of the insinuation.

"I'd take anything," she said, "for the present. It will soon be the first of the month again."

She looked the picture of despair.

Hurstwood quit reading his paper and changed his clothes.

"He would look for something," he thought. "He would go and see if some brewery couldn't get him in somewhere. Yes, he would take a position as bartender, if he could get it."

It was the same sort of pilgrimage he had made before. One or two slight rebuffs, and the bravado disappeared.

"No use," he thought, "I might as well go on back home."

Now that his money was so low, he began to observe his clothes and feel that even his best ones were beginning to look commonplace. This was a bitter thought.

Carrie came in after he did.

"I went to see some of the variety managers," she said, aimlessly. "You have to have an act. They don't want anybody that hasn't."

"I saw some of the brewery people to-day," said Hurstwood. "One man told me he'd try to make a place for me in two or three weeks."

In the face of so much distress on Carrie's part, he had to make some showing, and it was thus he did so. It was lassitude's apology to energy.

Monday Carrie went again to the Casino.[3]

"Did I tell you to come around to-day?" said the manager, looking her over as she stood before him.

"You said the first of the week," said Carrie, greatly abashed.

"Ever had any experience?" he asked again, almost severely.

Carrie owned to ignorance.

He looked her over again as he stirred among some papers. He was secretly pleased with this pretty, disturbed-looking young woman. "Come around to the theatre to-morrow morning."

Carrie's heart bounded to her throat.

"I will," she said with difficulty. She could see he wanted her, and turned to go.

"Would he really put her to work? Oh, blessed fortune, could it be?"

Already the hard rumble of the city through the open windows became pleasant.

A sharp voice answered her mental interrogation, driving away all immediate fears on that score.

"Be sure you're there promptly," the manager said roughly. "You'll be dropped if you're not."

Carrie hastened away. She did not quarrel now with Hurstwood's idleness. She had a place—she had a place! This sang in her ears.

In her delight she was almost anxious to tell Hurstwood. But, as she walked homeward, and her survey of the facts of the case became larger, she began to think of the anomaly of her finding work in several weeks and his lounging in idleness for a number of months.

"Why don't he get something?" she openly said to herself. "If I can he surely ought to. It wasn't very hard for me."

She forgot her youth and her beauty. The handicap of age she did not, in her enthusiasm, perceive.

Thus, ever, the voice of success.

Still, she could not keep her secret. She tried to be calm and indifferent, but it was a palpable sham.

"Well?" he said, seeing her relieved face.

"I have a place."

"You have?" he said, breathing a better breath.

"Yes."

"What sort of a place is it?" he asked, feeling in his veins as if now he might get something good also.

"In the chorus," she answered.

"Is it the Casino show you told me about?"

"Yes," she answered. "I begin rehearsing tomorrow."

3. One of the largest theaters in New York, the Casino specialized in musicals. Lillian Russell was one of its perennial attractions during the 1890s.

There was more explanation volunteered by Carrie, because she was happy. At last Hurstwood said:

"Do you know how much you'll get?"

"No, I didn't want to ask," said Carrie. "I guess they pay twelve or fourteen dollars a week."

"About that, I guess," said Hurstwood.

There was a good dinner in the flat that evening, owing to the mere lifting of the terrible strain. Hurstwood went out for a shave, and returned with a fair-sized sirloin steak.

"Now, to-morrow," he thought, "I'll look around myself," and with renewed hope he lifted his eyes from the ground.

On the morrow Carrie reported promptly and was given a place in the line. She saw a large, empty, shadowy play-house, still redolent of the perfumes and blazonry of the night, and notable for its rich, oriental appearance. The wonder of it awed and delighted her. Blessed be its wondrous reality. How hard she would try to be worthy of it. It was above the common mass, above idleness, above want, above insignificance. People came to it in finery and carriages to see. It was ever a center of light and mirth. And here she was of it. Oh, if she could only remain, how happy would be her days!

"What is your name?" said the manager, who was conducting the drill.

"Madenda," she replied, instantly mindful of the name Drouet had selected in Chicago. "Carrie Madenda."

"Well, now, Miss Madenda," he said, very affably, as Carrie thought, "you go over there."

Then he called to a young woman who was already of the company:

"Miss Clark, you pair with Miss Madenda."

This young lady stepped forward, so that Carrie saw where to go, and the rehearsal began.

Carrie soon found that while this drilling had some slight resemblance to the rehearsals as conducted at Avery Hall, the attitude of the manager was much more pronounced. She had marvelled at the insistence and superior airs of Mr. Millice, but the individual conducting here had the same insistence, coupled with almost brutal roughness. As the drilling proceeded, he seemed to wax exceedingly wroth over trifles, and to increase his lung power in proportion. It was very evident that he had a great contempt for any assumption of dignity or innocence on the part of these young women.

"Clark," he would call—meaning, of course, Miss Clark—"why don't you catch step there?"

"By fours, right! Right, I said, right! For heaven's sake, get on to yourself! Right!" and in saying this he would lift the last sounds into a vehement roar.

"Maitland! Maitland!" he called once.

A nervous, comely-dressed little girl stepped out. Carrie trembled for her out of the fulness of her own sympathies and fear.

"Yes, sir," said Miss Maitland.

"Is there anything the matter with your ears?"

"No, sir."

"Do you know what 'column left' means?"

"Yes, sir."

"Well, what are you stumbling around the right for? Want to break up the line?"

"I was just—"

"Never mind what you were just. Keep your ears open."

Carrie pitied, and trembled for her turn.

Yet another suffered the pain of personal rebuke.

"Hold on a minute," cried the manager, throwing up his hands, as if in despair. His demeanour was fierce.

"Elvers," he shouted, "what have you got in your mouth?"

"Nothing," said Miss Elvers, while some smiled and stood nervously by.

"Well, are you talking?"

"No, sir."

"Well, keep your mouth still then. Now, all together again."

At last Carrie's turn came. It was because of her extreme anxiety to do all that was required that brought on trouble.

She heard some one called.

"Mason," said the voice. "Miss Mason."

She looked around to see who it could be. A girl behind shoved her a little, but she did not understand.

"You, you!" said the manager. "Can't you hear?"

"Oh," said Carrie, collapsing, and blushing fiercely.

"Isn't your name Mason?" asked the manager.

"No, sir," said Carrie, "it's Madenda."

"Well, what's the matter with your feet? Can't you dance?"

"Yes, sir," said Carrie, who had long since learned this art.

"Why don't you do it then? Don't go shuffling along as if you were dead. I've got to have people with life in them."

Carrie's cheek burned with a crimson heat. Her lips trembled a little.

"Yes, sir," she said.

It was this constant urging, coupled with irascibility and energy, for three long hours. Carrie came away worn enough in body, but too excited in mind to notice it. She meant to go home and practise her evolutions as prescribed. She would not err in any way, if she could help it.

When she reached the flat Hurstwood was not there. For a wonder

he was out looking for work, as she supposed. She took only a mouthful to eat and then practised on, sustained by visions of freedom from
financial distress—"The sound of glory ringing in her ears."[4]

When Hurstwood returned he was not so elated as when he went
away, and now she was obliged to drop practice and get dinner. Here
was an early irritation. She would have her work and this. Was she
going to act and keep house?

"I'll not do it," she said, "after I get started. He can take his meals
out."

Each day thereafter brought its cares. She found it was not such
a wonderful thing to be in the chorus, and she also learned that her
salary would be twelve dollars a week. After a few days she had her
first sight of those high and mighties—the leading ladies and gentlemen. She saw that they were privileged and deferred to. She was
nothing—absolutely nothing at all.

At home was Hurstwood, daily giving her cause for thought. He
seemed to get nothing to do, and yet he made bold to inquire how
she was getting along. The regularity with which he did this smacked
of some one who was waiting to live upon her labour. Now that she
had a visible means of support, this irritated her. He seemed to be
depending upon her little twelve dollars.

"How are you getting along?" he would blandly inquire.

"Oh, all right," she would reply.

"Find it easy?"

"It will be all right when I get used to it."

His paper would then engross his thoughts.

"I got some lard," he would add, as an afterthought. "I thought
maybe you might want to make some biscuit."

The calm suggestion of the man astonished her a little, especially
in the light of recent developments. Her dawning independence gave
her more courage to observe, and she felt as if she wanted to say
things. Still she could not talk to him as she had to Drouet. There
was something in the man's manner of which she had always stood
in awe. He seemed to have some invisible strength in reserve.

One day, after her first week's rehearsal, what she expected came
openly to the surface.

"We'll have to be rather saving," he said, laying down some meat
he had purchased. "You won't get any money for a week or so yet."

"No," said Carrie, who was stirring a pan at the stove.

"I've only got the rent and thirteen dollars more," he added.

"That's it," she said to herself. "I'm to use my money now."

Instantly she remembered that she had hoped to buy a few things
for herself. She needed clothes. Her hat was not nice.

4. Apparently a quotation from a poem or song. Quotation marks are in the holograph text
as well as in the 1900 edition.

"What will twelve dollars do towards keeping up this flat?" she thought. "I can't do it. Why doesn't he get something to do?"

The important night of the first real performance came. She did not suggest to Hurstwood that he come and see. He did not think of going. It would only be money wasted. She had such a small part.

The advertisements were already in the papers; the posters upon the bill-boards. The leading lady and many members were cited. Carrie was nothing.

As in Chicago, she was seized with stage fright as the very first entrance of the ballet approached, but later she recovered. The apparent and painful insignificance of the part took fear away from her. She felt that she was so obscure it did not matter. Fortunately, she did not have to wear tights. A group of twelve were assigned pretty golden-hued skirts which came only to a line about an inch above the knee. Carrie happened to be one of the twelve.

In standing about the stage, marching, and occasionally lifting up her voice in the general chorus, she had a chance to observe the audience and to see the inauguration of a great hit. There was plenty of applause, but she could not help noting how poorly some of the women of alleged ability did.

"I could do better than that," Carrie ventured to herself, in several instances. To do her justice, she was right.

After it was over she dressed quickly, and as the manager had scolded some others and passed her, she imagined she must have proved satisfactory. She wanted to get out quickly, because she knew but few, and the stars were gossiping. Outside were carriages and some correct youths in attractive clothing, waiting. Carrie saw that she was scanned closely. The flutter of an eyelash would have brought her a companion. That she did not give.

One experienced youth volunteered, anyhow.

"Not going home alone, are you?" he said.

Carrie merely hastened her steps and took the Sixth Avenue car. Her head was so full of the wonder of it that she had time for nothing else.

"Did you hear any more from the brewery?" she asked at the end of the week, hoping by the question to stir him on to action.

"No," he answered, "they're not quite ready yet. I think something will come of that, though."

She said nothing more then, objecting to giving up her own money, and yet feeling that such would have to be the case. Hurstwood felt the crisis, and artfully decided to appeal to Carrie. He had long since realised how good-natured she was, how much she would stand. There was some little shame in him at the thought of doing so, but he justified himself with the thought that he really would get something. Rent day gave him his opportunity.

"Well," he said, as he counted it out, "that's about the last of my money. I'll have to get something pretty soon."

Carrie looked at him askance, half-suspicious of an appeal.

"If I could only hold out a little longer I think I could get something. Drake is sure to open a hotel here in September."

"Is he?" said Carrie, thinking of the short month that still remained until that time.

"Would you mind helping me out until then?" he said appealingly. "I think I'll be all right after that time."

"No," said Carrie, feeling sadly handicapped by fate.

"We can get along if we economise. I'll pay you back all right."

"Oh, I'll help you," said Carrie, feeling quite hard-hearted at thus forcing him to humbly appeal, and yet her desire for the benefit of her earnings wrung a faint protest from her.

"Why don't you take anything, George, temporarily?" she said. "What difference does it make? Maybe, after a while, you'll get something better."

"I will take anything," he said, relieved, and wincing under reproof. "I'd just as leave dig on the streets. Nobody knows me here."

"Oh, you needn't do that," said Carrie, hurt by the pity of it. "But there must be other things."

"I'll get something!" he said, assuming determination.

Then he went back to his paper.

Chapter XXXIX

OF LIGHTS AND OF SHADOWS: THE PARTING OF WORLDS

What Hurstwood got as the result of the determination was more self-assurance that each particular day was not the day. At the same time, Carrie passed through thirty days of mental distress.

Her need of clothes—to say nothing of her desire for ornaments—grew rapidly as the fact developed that for all her work she was not to have them. The sympathy she felt for Hurstwood, at the time he asked her to tide him over, vanished with these newer urgings of decency. He was not always renewing his request, but this love of good appearance was. It insisted, and Carrie wished to satisfy it, wished more and more that Hurstwood was not in the way.

Hurstwood reasoned, when he neared the last ten dollars, that he had better keep a little pocket change and not become wholly dependent for car-fare, shaves, and the like; so when this sum was still in his hand he announced himself as penniless.

"I'm clear out," he said to Carrie one afternoon. "I paid for some coal this morning, and that took all but ten or fifteen cents."

"I've got some money there in my purse."

Hurstwood went to get it, starting for a can of tomatoes. Carrie scarcely noticed that this was the beginning of the new order. He took out fifteen cents and bought the can with it. Thereafter it was dribs and drabs of this sort, until one morning Carrie suddenly remembered that she would not be back until close to dinner time.

"We're all out of flour," she said; "you'd better get some this afternoon. We haven't any meat, either. How would it do if we had liver and bacon?"

"Suits me," said Hurstwood.

"Better get a half or three-quarters of a pound of that."

"Half'll be enough," volunteered Hurstwood.

She opened her purse and laid down a half dollar. He pretended not to notice it.

Hurstwood bought the flour—which all grocers sold in 3½-pound packages—for thirteen cents and paid fifteen cents for a half-pound of liver and bacon. He left the packages, together with the balance of thirty-two cents, upon the kitchen table, where Carrie found it.[1] It did not escape her that the change was accurate. There was something sad in realising that, after all, all that he wanted of her was something to eat. She felt as if hard thoughts were unjust. Maybe he would get something yet. He had no vices.

That very evening, however, on going into the theatre, one of the chorus girls passed her all newly arrayed in a pretty mottled tweed suit, which took Carrie's eye. The young woman wore a fine bunch of violets and seemed in high spirits. She smiled at Carrie good-naturedly as she passed, showing pretty, even teeth, and Carrie smiled back.

"She can afford to dress well," thought Carrie, "and so could I, if I could only keep my money. I haven't a decent tie of any kind to wear."

She put out her foot and looked at her shoe reflectively.

"I'll get a pair of shoes Saturday, anyhow; I don't care what happens."

One of the sweetest and most sympathetic little chorus girls in the company made friends with her because in Carrie she found nothing to frighten her away. She was a gay little Manon,[2] unwitting of society's fierce conception of morality, but, nevertheless, good to her neighbour and charitable. Little license was allowed the chorus in the matter of conversation, but, nevertheless, some was indulged in.

"It's warm to-night, isn't it?" said this girl, arrayed in pink fleshings and an imitation golden helmet. She also carried a shining shield.

"Yes; it is," said Carrie, pleased that some one should talk to her.

1. Dreiser's arithmetic seems awry here. Hurstwood has spent twenty-eight cents and should therefore return only twenty-two cents from the half-dollar.
2. Abbé Prévost's novel Manon Lescaut (1731) and the operas based on it by Massenet and Puccini had popularized the character of Manon as an unsophisticated country girl who leads an immoral life in Paris.

"I'm almost roasting," said the girl.

Carrie looked into her pretty face, with its large blue eyes, and saw little beads of moisture.

"There's more marching in this opera than ever I did before," added the girl.

"Have you been in others?" asked Carrie, surprised at her experience.

"Lots of them," said the girl; "haven't you?"

"This is my first experience."

"Oh, is it? I thought I saw you the time they ran 'The Queen's Mate' here."[3]

"No," said Carrie, shaking her head; "not me."

This conversation was interrupted by the blare of the orchestra and the sputtering of the calcium lights in the wings as the line was called to form for a new entrance. No further opportunity for conversation occurred, but the next evening, when they were getting ready for the stage, this girl appeared anew at her side.

"They say this show is going on the road next month."

"Is it?" said Carrie.

"Yes; do you think you'll go?"

"I don't know; I guess so, if they'll take me."

"Oh, they'll take you. I wouldn't go. They won't give you any more, and it will cost you everything you make to live. I never leave New York. There are too many shows going on here."

"Can you always get in another show?"

"I always have. There's one going on up at the Broadway this month. I'm going to try and get in that if this one really goes."

Carrie heard this with aroused intelligence. Evidently it wasn't so very difficult to get on. Maybe she also could get a place if this show went away.

"Do they all pay about the same?" she asked.

"Yes. Sometimes you get a little more. This show doesn't pay very much."

"I get twelve," said Carrie.

"Do you?" said the girl. "They pay me fifteen, and you do more work than I do. I wouldn't stand it if I were you. They're just giving you less because they think you don't know. You ought to be making fifteen."

"Well, I'm not," said Carrie.

"Well, you'll get more at the next place if you want it," went on the girl, who admired Carrie very much. "You do fine, and the manager knows it."

To say the truth, Carrie did unconsciously move about with an air

3. A musical comedy by Henry Paulton, which was first performed in 1888 and which frequently starred Lillian Russell.

pleasing and somewhat distinctive. It was due wholly to her natural manner and total lack of self-consciousness.

"Do you suppose I could get more up at the Broadway?"[4]

"Of course you can," answered the girl. "You come with me when I go. I'll do the talking."

Carrie heard this, flushing with thankfulness. She liked this little gaslight soldier. She seemed so experienced and self-reliant in her tinsel helmet and military accoutrements.

"My future must be assured if I can always get work this way," thought Carrie.

Still, in the morning, when her household duties would infringe upon her and Hurstwood sat there, a perfect load to contemplate, her fate seemed dismal and unrelieved. It did not take so very much to feed them under Hurstwood's close-measured buying, and there would possibly be enough for rent, but it left nothing else. Carrie bought the shoes and some other things, which complicated the rent problem very seriously. Suddenly, a week from the fatal day, Carrie realised that they were going to run short.

"I don't believe," she exclaimed, looking into her purse at breakfast, "that I'll have enough to pay the rent."

"How much have you?" inquired Hurstwood.

"Well, I've got twenty-two dollars, but there's everything to be paid for this week yet, and if I use all I get Saturday to pay this, there won't be any left for next week. Do you think your hotel man will open his hotel this month?"

"I think so," returned Hurstwood. "He said he would."

After a while, Hurstwood said:

"Don't worry about it. Maybe the grocer will wait. He can do that. We've traded there long enough to make him trust us for a week or two."

"Do you think he will?" she asked.

"I think so."

On this account, Hurstwood, this very day, looked grocer Oeslogge clearly in the eye as he ordered a pound of coffee, and said:

"Do you mind carrying my account until the end of every week?"

"No, no, Mr. Wheeler," said Mr. Oeslogge. "Dat iss all right."

Hurstwood, still tactful in distress, added nothing to this. It seemed an easy thing. He looked out of the door, and then gathered up his coffee when ready and came away. The game of a desperate man had begun.

Rent was paid, and now came the grocer. Hurstwood managed by paying out of his own ten and collecting from Carrie at the end of

---

4. The Broadway (at Broadway and Forty-first) was a large house that, like the Casino, specialized in musicals. It was famous for its comedians, particularly De Wolfe Hopper and Francis Wilson.

the week. Then he delayed a day next time settling with the grocer, and so soon had his ten back, with Oeslogge getting his pay on this Thursday or Friday for last Saturday's bill.

This entanglement made Carrie anxious for a change of some sort. Hurstwood did not seem to realise that she had a right to anything. He schemed to make what she earned cover all expenses, but seemed not to trouble over adding anything himself.

"He talks about worrying," thought Carrie. "If he worried enough he couldn't sit there and wait for me. He'd get something to do. No man could go seven months without finding something if he tried."

The sight of him always around in his untidy clothes and gloomy appearance drove Carrie to seek relief in other places. Twice a week there were matinées, and then Hurstwood ate a cold snack, which he prepared himself. Two other days there were rehearsals beginning at ten in the morning and lasting usually until one. Now, to this Carrie added a few visits to one or two chorus girls, including the blue-eyed soldier of the golden helmet. She did it because it was pleasant and a relief from dulness of the home over which her husband brooded.

The blue-eyed soldier's name was Osborne—Lola Osborne. Her room was in Nineteenth Street near Fourth Avenue, a block now given up wholly to office buildings. Here she had a comfortable back room, looking over a collection of back yards in which grew a number of shade trees pleasant to see.

"Isn't your home in New York?" she asked of Lola one day.

"Yes; but I can't get along with my people. They always want me to do what they want. Do you live here?"

"Yes," said Carrie.

"With your family?"

Carrie was ashamed to say that she was married. She had talked so much about getting more salary and confessed to so much anxiety about her future, that now, when the direct question of fact was waiting, she could not tell this girl.

"With some relatives," she answered.

Miss Osborne took it for granted that, like herself, Carrie's time was her own. She invariably asked her to stay, proposing little outings and other things of that sort until Carrie began neglecting her dinner hours. Hurstwood noticed it, but felt in no position to quarrel with her. Several times she came so late as scarcely to have an hour in which to patch up a meal and start for the theatre.

"Do you rehearse in the afternoons?" Hurstwood once asked, concealing almost completely the cynical protest and regret which prompted it.

"No; I was looking around for another place," said Carrie.

As a matter of fact she was, but only in such a way as furnished the least straw of an excuse. Miss Osborne and she had gone to the office of the manager who was to produce the new opera at the Broadway and returned straight to the former's room, where they had been since three o'clock.

Carrie felt this question to be an infringement on her liberty. She did not take into account how much liberty she was securing. Only the last step, the newest freedom, must not be questioned.

Hurstwood saw it all clearly enough. He was shrewd after his kind, and yet there was enough decency in the man to stop him from making an effectual protest. In his almost inexplicable apathy he was content to droop supinely while Carrie drifted out of his life, just as he was willing supinely to see opportunity pass beyond his control. He could not help clinging and protesting in a mild, irritating, and ineffectual way, however—a way that simply widened the breach by slow degrees.

A further enlargement of this chasm between them came when the manager, looking between the wings upon the brightly lighted stage where the chorus was going through some of its glittering evolutions, said to the master of the ballet:

"Who is that fourth girl there on the right—the one coming round at the end now?"

"Oh," said the ballet-master, "that's Miss Madenda."

"She's good looking. Why don't you let her head that line?"

"I will," said the man.

"Just do that. She'll look better there than the woman you've got."

"All right. I will do that," said the master.

The next evening Carrie was called out, much as if for an error.

"You lead your company to-night," said the master.

"Yes, sir," said Carrie.

"Put snap into it," he added. "We must have snap."

"Yes, sir," replied Carrie.

Astonished at this change, she thought that the heretofore leader must be ill; but when she saw her in the line, with a distinct expression of something unfavourable in her eye, she began to think that perhaps it was merit.

She had a chic way of tossing her head to one side, and holding her arms as if for action—not listlessly. In front of the line this showed up even more effectually.

"That girl knows how to carry herself," said the manager, another evening. He began to think that he should like to talk with her. If he hadn't made it a rule to have nothing to do with the members of the chorus, he would have approached her most unbendingly.

"Put that girl at the head of the white column," he suggested to the man in charge of the ballet.

This white column consisted of some twenty girls, all in snow-white flannel trimmed with silver and blue. Its leader was most stunningly arrayed in the same colours, elaborated, however, with epaulets and a belt of silver, with a short sword dangling at one side. Carrie was fitted for this costume, and a few days later appeared, proud of her new laurels. She was especially gratified to find that her salary was now eighteen instead of twelve.

Hurstwood heard nothing about this.

"I'll not give him the rest of my money," said Carrie. "I do enough. I am going to get me something to wear."

As a matter of fact, during this second month she had been buying for herself as recklessly as she dared, regardless of the consequences. There were impending more complications rent day, and more extension of the credit system in the neighbourhood. Now, however, she proposed to do better by herself.

Her first move was to buy a shirt waist, and in studying these she found how little her money would buy—how much, if she could only use all. She forgot that if she were alone she would have to pay for a room and board, and imagined that every cent of her eighteen could be spent for clothes and things that she liked.

At last she picked upon something, which not only used up all her surplus above twelve, but invaded that sum. She knew she was going too far, but her feminine love of finery prevailed. The next day Hurstwood said:

"We owe the grocer five dollars and forty cents this week."

"Do we?" said Carrie, frowning a little.

She looked in her purse to leave it.

"I've only got eight dollars and twenty cents altogether."

"We owe the milkman sixty cents," added Hurstwood.

"Yes, and there's the coal man," said Carrie.

Hurstwood said nothing. He had seen the new things she was buying; the way she was neglecting household duties; the readiness with which she was slipping out afternoons and staying. He felt that something was going to happen. All at once she spoke:

"I don't know," she said; "I can't do it all. I don't earn enough."

This was a direct challenge. Hurstwood had to take it up. He tried to be calm.

"I don't want you to do it all," he said. "I only want a little help until I can get something to do."

"Oh, yes," answered Carrie. "That's always the way. It takes more than I can earn to pay for things. I don't see what I'm going to do."

"Well, I've tried to get something," he exclaimed. "What do you want me to do?"

"You couldn't have tried so very hard," said Carrie. "I got something."

"Well, I did," he said, angered almost to harsh words. "You needn't throw up your success to me. All I asked was a little help until I could get something. I'm not down yet. I'll come up all right."

He tried to speak steadily, but his voice trembled a little.

Carrie's anger melted on the instant. She felt ashamed.

"Well," she said, "here's the money," and emptied it out on the table. "I haven't got quite enough to pay it all. If they can wait until Saturday, though, I'll have some more."

"You keep it," said Hurstwood, sadly. "I only want enough to pay the grocer."

She put it back, and proceeded to get dinner early and in good time. Her little bravado made her feel as if she ought to make amends.

In a little while their old thoughts returned to both.

"She's making more than she says," thought Hurstwood. "She says she's making twelve, but that wouldn't buy all those things. I don't care. Let her keep her money. I'll get something again one of these days. Then she can go to the deuce."

He only said this in his anger, but it prefigured a possible course of action and attitude well enough.

"I don't care," thought Carrie. "He ought to be told to get out and do something. It isn't right that I should support him."

In these days Carrie was introduced to several youths, friends of Miss Osborne, who were of the kind most aptly described as gay and festive. They called once to get Miss Osborne for an afternoon drive. Carrie was with her at the time.

"Come and go along," said Lola.

"No, I can't," said Carrie.

"Oh, yes, come and go. What have you got to do?"

"I have to be home by five," said Carrie.

"What for?"

"Oh, dinner."

"They'll take us to dinner," said Lola.

"Oh, no," said Carrie. "I won't go. I can't."

"Oh, do come. They're awful nice boys. We'll get you back in time. We're only going for a drive in Central Park."

Carrie thought a while, and at last yielded.

"Now, I must be back by half-past four," she said.

The information went in one ear of Lola and out the other.

After Drouet and Hurstwood, there was the least touch of cynicism in her attitude toward young men—especially of the gay and frivolous sort. She felt a little older than they. Some of their pretty compliments seemed silly. Still, she was young in heart and body and youth appealed to her.

"Oh, we'll be right back, Miss Madenda," said one of the chaps, bowing. "You wouldn't think we'd keep you over time, now, would you?"

"Well, I don't know," said Carrie, smiling.

They were off for a drive—she, looking about and noticing fine clothing, the young men voicing those silly pleasantries and weak quips which pass for humour in coy circles. Carrie saw the great park parade of carriages, beginning at the Fifty-ninth Street entrance and winding past the Museum of Art to the exit at One Hundred and Tenth Street and Seventh Avenue. Her eye was once more taken by the show of wealth—the elaborate costumes, elegant harnesses, spirited horses, and, above all, the beauty. Once more the plague of poverty galled her, but now she forgot in a measure her own troubles so far as to forget Hurstwood. He waited until four, five, and even six. It was getting dark when he got up out of his chair.

"I guess she isn't coming home," he said, grimly.

"That's the way," he thought. "She's getting a start now. I'm out of it."

Carrie had really discovered her neglect, but only at a quarter after five, and the open carriage was now far up Seventh Avenue, near the Harlem River.

"What time is it?" she inquired. "I must be getting back."

"A quarter after five," said her companion, consulting an elegant, open-faced watch.

"Oh, dear me!" exclaimed Carrie. Then she settled back with a sigh. "There's no use crying over spilt milk," she said. "It's too late."

"Of course it is," said the youth, who saw visions of a fine dinner now, and such invigorating talk as would result in a reunion after the show. He was greatly taken with Carrie. "We'll drive down to Delmonico's now and have something there, won't we, Orrin?"

"To be sure," replied Orrin, gaily.

Carrie thought of Hurstwood. Never before had she neglected dinner without an excuse.

They drove back, and at 6.15 sat down to dine. It was the Sherry incident over again, the remembrance of which came painfully back to Carrie. She remembered Mrs. Vance, who had never called again after Hurstwood's reception, and Ames.

At this figure her mind halted. It was a strong, clean vision. He liked better books than she read, better people than she associated with. His ideals burned in her heart.

"It's fine to be a good actress," came distinctly back.

What sort of an actress was she?

"What are you thinking about, Miss Madenda?" inquired her merry companion. "Come, now, let's see if I can guess."

"Oh, no," said Carrie. "Don't try."

She shook it off and ate. She forgot, in part, and was merry. When it came to the after-theatre proposition, however, she shook her head.

"No," she said, "I can't. I have a previous engagement."

"Oh, now, Miss Madenda," pleaded the youth.

"No," said Carrie, "I can't. You've been so kind, but you'll have to excuse me."

The youth looked exceedingly crestfallen.

"Cheer up, old man," whispered his companion. "We'll go around, anyhow. She may change her mind."

Chapter XL

A PUBLIC DISSENSION: A FINAL APPEAL

There was no after-theatre lark, however, so far as Carrie was concerned. She made her way homeward, thinking about her absence. Hurstwood was asleep, but roused up to look as she passed through to her own bed.

"Is that you?" he said.

"Yes," she answered.

The next morning at breakfast she felt like apologising.

"I couldn't get home last evening," she said.

"Ah, Carrie," he answered, "what's the use saying that? I don't care. You needn't tell me that, though."

"I couldn't," said Carrie, her colour rising. Then, seeing that he looked as if he said "I know," she exclaimed: "Oh, all right. I don't care."

From now on, her indifference to the flat was even greater. There seemed no common ground on which they could talk to one another. She let herself be asked for expenses. It became so with him that he hated to do it. He preferred standing off the butcher and baker. He ran up a grocery bill of sixteen dollars with Oeslogge, laying in a supply of staple articles, so that they would not have to buy any of those things for some time to come. Then he changed his grocery. It was the same with the butcher and several others. Carrie never heard anything of this directly from him. He asked for such as he could expect, drifting farther and farther into a situation which could have but one ending.

In this fashion, September went by.

"Isn't Mr. Drake going to open his hotel?" Carrie asked several times.

"Yes. He won't do it before October, though, now."

Carrie became disgusted. "Such a man," she said to herself frequently. More and more she visited. She put most of her spare money in clothes, which, after all, was not an astonishing amount. At last the opera she was with announced its departure within four weeks.

"Last two weeks of the Great Comic Opera success—The——," etc.,
was upon all billboards and in the newspapers, before she acted.

"I'm not going out on the road," said Miss Osborne.

Carrie went with her to apply to another manager.

"Ever had any experience?" was one of his questions.

"I'm with the company at the Casino now."

"Oh, you are?" he said.

The end of this was another engagement at twenty per week.

Carrie was delighted. She began to feel that she had a place in the
world. People recognised ability.

So changed was her state that the home atmosphere became intolerable. It was all poverty and trouble there, or seemed to be, because
it was a load to bear. It became a place to keep away from. Still she
slept there, and did a fair amount of work, keeping it in order. It was
a sitting place for Hurstwood. He sat and rocked, rocked and read,
enveloped in the gloom of his own fate. October went by, and
November. It was the dead of winter almost before he knew it, and
there he sat.

Carrie was doing better, that he knew. Her clothes were improved
now, even fine. He saw her coming and going, sometimes picturing
to himself her rise. Little eating had thinned him somewhat. He had
no appetite. His clothes, too, were a poor man's clothes. Talk about
getting something had become even too threadbare and ridiculous
for him. So he folded his hands and waited—for what, he could not
anticipate.

At last, however, troubles became too thick. The hounding of creditors, the indifference of Carrie, the silence of the flat, and presence
of winter, all joined to produce a climax. It was effected by the arrival
of Oeslogge, personally, when Carrie was there.

"I call about my bill," said Mr. Oeslogge.

Carrie was only faintly surprised.

"How much is it?" she asked.

"Sixteen dollars," he replied.

"Oh, that much?" said Carrie. "Is this right?" she asked, turning
to Hurstwood.

"Yes," he said.

"Well, I never heard anything about it."

She looked as if she thought he had been contracting some need-
less expense.

"Well, we had it all right," he answered. Then he went to the door.
"I can't pay you anything on that to-day," he said, mildly.

"Well, when can you?" said the grocer.

"Not before Saturday, anyhow," said Hurstwood.

"Huh!" returned the grocer. "This is fine. I must have that. I need
the money."

Carrie was standing farther back in the room, hearing it all. She was greatly distressed. It was so bad and commonplace. Hurstwood was annoyed also.

"Well," he said, "there's no use talking about it now. If you'll come in Saturday, I'll pay you something on it."

The grocery man went away.

"How are we going to pay it?" asked Carrie, astonished by the bill. "I can't do it."

"Well, you don't have to," he said. "He can't get what he can't get. He'll have to wait."

"I don't see how we ran up such a bill as that," said Carrie.

"Well, we ate it," said Hurstwood.

"It's funny," she replied, still doubting.

"What's the use of your standing there and talking like that, now?" he asked. "Do you think I've had it alone? You talk as if I'd taken something."

"Well, it's too much, anyhow," said Carrie. "I oughtn't to be made to pay for it. I've got more than I can pay for now."

"All right," replied Hurstwood, sitting down in silence. He was sick of the grind of this thing.

Carrie went out, and there he sat, determining to do something.

There had been appearing in the papers about this time rumours and notices of an approaching strike on the trolley lines in Brooklyn. There was general dissatisfaction as to the hours of labour required and the wages paid. As usual—and for some inexplicable reason— the men chose the winter for the forcing of the hand of their employers and the settlement of their difficulties.

Hurstwood had been reading of this thing, and wondering concerning the huge tie-up which would follow. A day or two before this trouble with Carrie, it came. On a cold afternoon, when everything was grey and it threatened to snow, the papers announced that the men had been called out on all the lines.

Being so utterly idle, and his mind filled with the numerous predictions which had been made concerning the scarcity of labour this winter and the panicky state of the financial market, Hurstwood read this with interest. He noted the claims of the striking motormen and conductors, who said that they had been wont to receive two dollars a day in times past, but that for a year or more "trippers" had been introduced, which cut down their chance of livelihood one-half, and increased their hours of servitude from ten to twelve, and even fourteen. These "trippers" were men put on during the busy and *rush* hours, to take a car out for one trip. The compensation paid for such a trip was only twenty-five cents. When the rush or busy hours were over, they were laid off. Worst of all, no man might know when he was going to get a car. He must come to the barns in the morning

and wait around in fair and foul weather until such time as he was
needed. Two trips were an average reward for so much waiting—a
little over three hours' work for fifty cents. The work of waiting was
not counted.

The men complained that this system was extending, and that the
time was not far off when but a few out of 7,000 employees would
have regular two-dollar-a-day work at all. They demanded that the
system be abolished, and that ten hours be considered a day's work,
barring unavoidable delays, with $2.25 pay. They demanded imme-
diate acceptance of these terms, which the various trolley companies
refused.[1]

Hurstwood at first sympathised with the demands of these men—
indeed, it is a question whether he did not always sympathise with
them to the end, belie him as his actions might. Reading nearly all
the news, he was attracted first by the scareheads with which the
trouble was noted in the "World." He read it fully—the names of the
seven companies involved, the number of men.

"They're foolish to strike in this sort of weather," he thought to
himself. "Let 'em win if they can, though."

The next day there was even a larger notice of it. "Brooklynites
Walk," said the "World." "Knights of Labour Tie up the Trolley Lines
Across the Bridge." "About Seven Thousand Men Out."

Hurstwood read this, formulating to himself his own idea of what
would be the outcome. He was a great believer in the strength of
corporations.

"They can't win," he said, concerning the men. "They haven't any
money. The police will protect the companies. They've got to. The
public has to have its cars."

He didn't sympathise with the corporations, but strength was with
them. So was property and public utility.

"Those fellows can't win," he thought.

Among other things, he noticed a circular issued by one of the
companies, which read:

ATLANTIC AVENUE RAILROAD
SPECIAL NOTICE
The motormen and conductors and other employees of this
company having abruptly left its service, an opportunity is now

1. The Brooklyn street car strike of 1895 began on January 14. The strikers were demanding,
as Dreiser reports, $2.25 for a ten-hour day. The strike lasted almost a month, and was
marked by much violence. Dreiser based his account of the strike on his own experiences
as a reporter during a Toledo trolley strike of March 1894 (see pp. 413–20) and on reports
of the Brooklyn strike in the New York newspapers of January 1895. Both the newspaper
headlines that Hurstwood reads (p. 285) and the "Special Notice" on pp. 285–86 appear
verbatim in the New York World of 15 Jan. 1895: 1–2, and many of the details of the strike
that follow in chapter XLI are from the World of 15 and 16 Jan. 1895. (Dreiser was a
space-rate reporter for the World during the winter of 1894–95.)

given to all loyal men who have struck against their will to be reinstated, providing they will make their applications by twelve o'clock noon on Wednesday, January 16th. Such men will be given employment (with guaranteed protection) in the order in which such applications are received, and runs and positions assigned them accordingly. Otherwise, they will be considered discharged, and every vacancy will be filled by a new man as soon as his services can be secured.

(Signed)
Benjamin Norton,
PRESIDENT

He also noted among the want ads. one which read:

WANTED—50 skilled motormen, accustomed to Westinghouse system, to run U.S. mail cars only in the City of Brooklyn; protection guaranteed.

He noted particularly in each the "protection guaranteed." It signified to him the unassailable power of the companies.

"They've got the militia on their side," he thought. "There isn't anything those men can do."

While this was still in his mind, the incident with Oeslogge and Carrie occurred. There had been a good deal to irritate him, but this seemed much the worst. Never before had she accused him of stealing—or very near that. She doubted the naturalness of so large a bill. And he had worked so hard to make expenses seem light. He had been "doing" butcher and baker in order not to call on her. He had eaten very little—almost nothing.

"Damn it all!" he said. "I can get something. I'm not down yet."

He thought that he really must do something now. It was too cheap to sit around after such an insinuation as this. Why, after a little, he would be standing anything.

He got up and looked out the window into the chilly street. It came gradually into his mind, as he stood there, to go to Brooklyn.

"Why not?" his mind said. "Any one can get work over there. You'll get two a day."

"How about accidents?" said a voice. "You might get hurt."

"Oh, there won't be much of that," he answered. "They've called out the police. Any one who wants to run a car will be protected all right."

"You don't know how to run a car," rejoined the voice.

"I won't apply as a motorman," he answered. "I can ring up fares all right."

"They'll want motormen mostly."

"They'll take anybody; that I know."

For several hours he argued pro and con with this mental counsellor, feeling no need to act at once in a matter so sure of profit.

In the morning he put on his best clothes, which were poor
enough, and began stirring about, putting some bread and meat into
a page of a newspaper. Carrie watched him, interested in this new
move.

"Where are you going?" she asked.

"Over to Brooklyn," he answered. Then, seeing her still inquisitive,
he added: "I think I can get on over there."

"On the trolley lines?" said Carrie, astonished.

"Yes," he rejoined.

"Aren't you afraid?" she asked.

"What of?" he answered. "The police are protecting them."

"The paper said four men were hurt yesterday."

"Yes," he returned; "but you can't go by what the papers say. They'll
run the cars all right."

He looked rather determined now, in a desolate sort of way, and
Carrie felt very sorry. Something of the old Hurstwood was here—
the least shadow of what was once shrewd and pleasant strength.
Outside, it was cloudy and blowing a few flakes of snow.

"What a day to go over there," thought Carrie.

Now he left before she did, which was a remarkable thing, and
tramped eastward to Fourteenth Street and Sixth Avenue, where he
took the car. He had read that scores of applicants were applying at
the office of the Brooklyn City Railroad building and were being
received. He made his way there by horse-car and ferry—a dark,
silent man—to the offices in question. It was a long way, for no cars
were running, and the day was cold; but he trudged along grimly.
Once in Brooklyn, he could clearly see and feel that a strike was on.
People showed it in their manner. Along the routes of certain tracks
not a car was running. About certain corners and nearby saloons
small groups of men were lounging. Several spring wagons passed
him, equipped with plain wooden chairs, and labelled "Flatbush" or
"Prospect Park. Fare, Ten Cents." He noticed cold and even gloomy
faces. Labour was having its little war.

When he came near the office in question, he saw a few men
standing about, and some policemen. On the far corners were other
men—whom he took to be strikers—watching. All the houses were
small and wooden, the streets poorly paved. After New York, Brooklyn looked actually poor and hard-up.

He made his way into the heart of the small group, eyed by
policemen and the men already there. One of the officers addressed
him.

"What are you looking for?"

"I want to see if I can get a place."

"The offices are up those steps," said the bluecoat. His face was a very neutral thing to contemplate. In his heart of hearts, he sympathised with the strikers and hated this "scab." In his heart of hearts, also, he felt the dignity and use of the police force, which commanded order. Of its true social significance, he never once dreamed. His was not the mind for that. The two feelings blended in him—neutralised one another and him. He would have fought for this man as determinedly as for himself, and yet only so far as commanded. Strip him of his uniform, and he would have soon picked his side.

Hurstwood ascended a dusty flight of steps and entered a small, dust-coloured office, in which were a railing, a long desk, and several clerks.

"Well, sir?" said a middle-aged man, looking up at him from the long desk.

"Do you want to hire any men?" inquired Hurstwood.

"What are you—a motorman?"

"No; I'm not anything," said Hurstwood.

He was not at all abashed by his position. He knew these people needed men. If one didn't take him, another would. This man could take him or leave him, just as he chose.

"Well, we prefer experienced men, of course," said the man. He paused, while Hurstwood smiled indifferently. Then he added: "Still, I guess you can learn. What is your name?"

"Wheeler," said Hurstwood.

The man wrote an order on a small card. "Take that to our barns," he said, "and give it to the foreman. He'll show you what to do."

Hurstwood went down and out. He walked straight away in the direction indicated, while the policemen looked after.

"There's another wants to try it," said Officer Kiely to Officer Macey.

"I have my mind he'll get his fill," returned the latter, quietly.

They had been in strikes before.

Chapter XLI

THE STRIKE

The barn at which Hurstwood applied was exceedingly short-handed, and was being operated practically by three men as directors. There were a lot of green hands around—queer, hungry-looking men, who looked as if want had driven them to desperate means. They tried to be lively and willing, but there was an air of hang-dog diffidence about the place.

Hurstwood went back through the barns and out into a large,

enclosed lot, where were a series of tracks and loops. A half-dozen cars were there, manned by instructors, each with a pupil at the lever. More pupils were waiting at one of the rear doors of the barn.

In silence Hurstwood viewed this scene, and waited. His companions took his eye for a while, though they did not interest him much more than the cars. They were an uncomfortable-looking gang, however. One or two were very thin and lean. Several were quite stout. Several others were rawboned and sallow, as if they had been beaten upon by all sorts of rough weather.

"Did you see by the paper they are going to call out the militia?" Hurstwood heard one of them remark.

"Oh, they'll do that," returned the other. "They always do."

"Think we're liable to have much trouble?" said another, whom Hurstwood did not see.

"Not very."

"That Scotchman that went out on the last car," put in a voice, "told me that they hit him in the ear with a cinder."

A small, nervous laugh accompanied this.

"One of those fellows on the Fifth Avenue line must have had a hell of a time, according to the papers," drawled another. "They broke his car windows and pulled him off into the street 'fore the police could stop 'em."

"Yes; but there are more police around to-day," was added by another.

Hurstwood hearkened without much mental comment. These talkers seemed scared to him. Their gabbling was feverish—things said to quiet their own minds. He looked out into the yard and waited.

Two of the men got around quite near him, but behind his back. They were rather social, and he listened to what they said.

"Are you a railroad man?" said one.

"Me? No. I've always worked in a paper factory."

"I had a job in Newark until last October," returned the other, with reciprocal feeling.

There were some words which passed too low to hear. Then the conversation became strong again.

"I don't blame these fellers for striking," said one. "They've got the right of it, all right, but I had to get something to do."

"Same here," said the other. "If I had any job in Newark I wouldn't be over here takin' chances like these."

"It's hell these days, ain't it?" said the man. "A poor man ain't nowhere. You could starve, by God, right in the streets, and there ain't most no one would help you."

"Right you are," said the other. "The job I had I lost 'cause they shut down. They run all summer and lay up a big stock, and then shut down."

Hurstwood paid some little attention to this. Somehow, he felt a little superior to these two—a little better off. To him these were ignorant and commonplace, poor sheep in a driver's hand.

"Poor devils," he thought, speaking out of the thoughts and feelings of a bygone period of success.

"Next," said one of the instructors.

"You're next," said a neighbour, touching him.

He went out and climbed on the platform. The instructor took it for granted that no preliminaries were needed.

"You see this handle," he said, reaching up to an electric cut-off, which was fastened to the roof. "This throws the current off or on. If you want to reverse the car you turn it over here. If you want to send it forward, you put it over here. If you want to cut off the power, you keep it in the middle."

Hurstwood smiled at the simple information.

"Now, this handle here regulates your speed. To here," he said, pointing with his finger, "gives you about four miles an hour. This is eight. When it's full on, you make about fourteen miles an hour."

Hurstwood watched him calmly. He had seen motormen work before. He knew just about how they did it, and was sure he could do as well, with a very little practice.

The instructor explained a few more details, and then said:

"Now, we'll back her up."

Hurstwood stood placidly by, while the car rolled back into the yard.

"One thing you want to be careful about and that is to start easy. Give one degree time to act before you start another. The one fault of most men is that they always want to throw her wide open. That's bad. It's dangerous, too. Wears out the motor. You don't want to do that."

"I see," said Hurstwood.

He waited and waited, while the man talked on.

"Now you take it," he said, finally.

The cx-manager laid hand to the lever and pushed it gently, as he thought. It worked much easier than he imagined, however, with the result that the car jerked quickly forward, throwing him back against the door. He straightened up sheepishly, while the instructor stopped the car with the brake.

"You want to be careful about that," was all he said.

Hurstwood found, however, that handling a brake and regulating speed were not so instantly mastered as he had imagined. Once or twice he would have ploughed through the rear fence if it had not been for the hand and word of his companion. The latter was rather patient with him, but he never smiled.

"You've got to get the knack of working both arms at once," he said. "It takes a little practice."

One o'clock came while he was still on the car practising, and he began to feel hungry. The day set in snowing, and he was cold. He grew weary of running to and fro on the short track.

They ran the car to the end and both got off. Hurstwood went into the barn and sought a car step, pulling out his paper-wrapped lunch from his pocket. There was no water and the bread was dry, but he enjoyed it. There was no ceremony about dining. He swallowed and looked about, contemplating the dull, homely labour of the thing. It was disagreeable—miserably disagreeable—in all its phases. Not because it was bitter, but because it was hard. It would be hard to any one, he thought.

After eating, he stood about as before, waiting until his turn came.

The intention was to give him an afternoon of practice, but the greater part of the time was spent in waiting about.

At last evening came, and with it hunger and a debate with himself as to how he should spend the night. It was half-past five. He must soon eat. If he tried to go home, it would take him two hours and a half of cold walking and riding. Besides, he had orders to report at seven the next morning, and going home would necessitate his rising at an unholy and disagreeable hour. He had only something like a dollar and fifteen cents of Carrie's money, with which he had intended to pay the two weeks' coal bill before the present idea struck him.

"They must have some place around here," he thought. "Where does that fellow from Newark stay?"

Finally he decided to ask. There was a young fellow standing near one of the doors in the cold, waiting a last turn. He was a mere boy in years—twenty one about—but with a body lank and long, because of privation. A little good living would have made this youth plump and swaggering.

"How do they arrange this, if a man hasn't any money?" inquired Hurstwood, discreetly.

The fellow turned a keen, watchful face on the inquirer.

"You mean eat?" he replied.

"Yes, and sleep. I can't go back to New York tonight."

"The foreman 'll fix that if you ask him, I guess. He did me."

"That so?"

"Yes. I just told him I didn't have anything. Gee, I couldn't go home. I live way over in Hoboken."

Hurstwood only cleared his throat by way of acknowledgment.

"They've got a place upstairs here, I understand. I don't know what sort of a thing it is. Purty tough, I guess. He gave me a meal ticket this noon. I know that wasn't much."

Hurstwood smiled grimly, and the boy laughed.

"It ain't no fun, is it?" he inquired, wishing vainly for a cheery reply.

"Not much," answered Hurstwood.

"I'd tackle him now," volunteered the youth. "He may go 'way."

Hurstwood did so.

"Isn't there some place I can stay around here tonight?" he inquired. "If I have to go back to New York, I'm afraid I won't—"

"There're some cots upstairs," interrupted the man, "if you want one of them."

"That'll do," he assented.

He meant to ask for a meal ticket, but the seemingly proper moment never came, and he decided to pay himself that night.

"I'll ask him in the morning."

He ate in a cheap restaurant in the vicinity, and, being cold and lonely, went straight off to seek the loft in question. The company was not attempting to run cars after nightfall. It was so advised by the police.

The room seemed to have been a lounging place for night workers. There were some nine cots in the place, two or three wooden chairs, a soap box, and a small, round-bellied stove, in which a fire was blazing. Early as he was, another man was there before him. The latter was sitting beside the stove warming his hands.

Hurstwood approached and held out his own toward the fire. He was sick of the bareness and privation of all things connected with his venture, but was steeling himself to hold out. He fancied he could for a while.

"Cold, isn't it?" said the early guest.

"Rather."

A long silence.

"Not much of a place to sleep in, is it?" said the man.

"Better than nothing," replied Hurstwood.

Another silence.

"I believe I'll turn in," said the man.

Rising, he went to one of the cots and stretched himself, removing only his shoes, and pulling the one blanket and dirty old comforter over him in a sort of bundle. The sight disgusted Hurstwood, but he did not dwell on it, choosing to gaze into the stove and think of something else. Presently he decided to retire, and picked a cot, also removing his shoes.

While he was doing so, the youth who had advised him to come here entered, and, seeing Hurstwood, tried to be genial.

"Better'n nothin'," he observed, looking around.

Hurstwood did not take this to himself. He thought it to be an expression of individual satisfaction, and so did not answer. The youth imagined he was out of sorts, and set to whistling softly. Seeing another man asleep, he quit that and lapsed into silence.

Hurstwood made the best of a bad lot by keeping on his clothes and pushing away the dirty covering from his head, but at last he dozed in sheer weariness. The covering became more and more comfortable, its character was forgotten, and he pulled it about his neck and slept.

In the morning he was aroused out of a pleasant dream by several men stirring about in the cold, cheerless room. He had been back in Chicago in fancy, in his own comfortable home. Jessica had been arranging to go somewhere, and he had been talking with her about it. This was so clear in his mind, that he was startled now by the contrast of this room. He raised his head, and the cold, bitter reality jarred him into wakefulness.

"Guess I'd better get up," he said.

There was no water on this floor. He put on his shoes in the cold and stood up, shaking himself in his stiffness. His clothes felt disagreeable, his hair bad.

"Hell!" he muttered, as he put on his hat.

Downstairs things were stirring again.

He found a hydrant, with a trough which had once been used for horses, but there was no towel here, and his handkerchief was soiled from yesterday. He contented himself with wetting his eyes with the ice-cold water. Then he sought the foreman, who was already on the ground.

"Had your breakfast yet?" inquired that worthy.

"No," said Hurstwood.

"Better get it, then; your car won't be ready for a little while."

Hurstwood hesitated.

"Could you let me have a meal ticket?" he asked, with an effort.

"Here you are," said the man, handing him one.

He breakfasted as poorly as the night before on some fried steak and bad coffee. Then he went back.

"Here," said the foreman, motioning him, when he came in. "You take this car out in a few minutes."

Hurstwood climbed up on the platform in the gloomy barn and waited for a signal. He was nervous, and yet the thing was a relief. Anything was better than the barn.

On this the fourth day of the strike, the situation had taken a turn for the worse. The strikers, following the counsel of their leaders and the newspapers, had struggled peaceably enough. There had been no great violence done. Cars had been stopped, it is true, and the men argued with. Some crews had been won over and led away, some windows broken, some jeering and yelling done; but in no more than five or six instances had men been seriously injured. These by crowds whose acts the leaders disclaimed.

Idleness, however, and the sight of the company, backed by the police, triumphing, angered the men. They saw that each day more cars were going on, each day more declarations were being made by the company officials that the effective opposition of the strikers was broken. This put desperate thoughts in the minds of the men. Peaceful methods meant, they saw, that the companies would soon run all their cars and those who had complained would be forgotten. There was nothing so helpful to the companies as peaceful methods.

All at once they blazed forth, and for a week there was storm and stress. Cars were assailed, men attacked, policemen struggled with, tracks torn up, and shots fired, until at last street fights and mob movements became frequent, and the city was invested with militia.

Hurstwood knew nothing of the change of temper.

"Run your car out," called the foreman, waving a vigorous hand at him. A green conductor jumped up behind and rang the bell twice as a signal to start. Hurstwood turned the lever and ran the car out through the door into the street in front of the barn. Here two brawny policemen got up beside him on the platform—one on either hand.

At the sound of a gong near the barn door, two bells were given by the conductor and Hurstwood opened his lever.

The two policemen looked about them calmly.

" 'Tis cold, all right, this morning," said the one on the left, who possessed a rich brogue.

"I had enough of it yesterday," said the other. "I wouldn't want a steady job of this."

"Nor I."

Neither paid the slightest attention to Hurstwood, who stood facing the cold wind, which was chilling him completely, and thinking of his orders.

"Keep a steady gait," the foreman had said. "Don't stop for any one who doesn't look like a real passenger. Whatever you do, don't stop for a crowd."

The two officers kept silent for a few moments.

"The last man must have gone through all right," said the officer on the left. "I don't see his car anywhere."

"Who's on there?" asked the second officer, referring, of course, to its complement of policemen.

"Schaeffer and Ryan."

There was another silence, in which the car ran smoothly along. There were not so many houses along this part of the way. Hurstwood did not see many people either. The situation was not wholly disagreeable to him. If he were not so cold, he thought he would do well enough.

He was brought out of this feeling by the sudden appearance of a curve ahead, which he had not expected. He shut off the current and did an energetic turn at the brake, but not in time to avoid an unnaturally quick turn. It shook him up and made him feel like making some apologetic remarks, but he refrained.

"You want to look out for them things," said the officer on the left, condescendingly.

"That's right," agreed Hurstwood, shamefacedly.

"There's lots of them on this line," said the officer on the right.

Around the corner a more populated way appeared. One or two pedestrians were in view ahead. A boy coming out of a gate with a tin milk bucket gave Hurstwood his first objectionable greeting.

"Scab!" he yelled. "Scab!"

Hurstwood heard it, but tried to make no comment, even to himself. He knew he would get that, and much more of the same sort, probably.

At a corner farther up a man stood by the track and signalled the car to stop.

"Never mind him," said one of the officers. "He's up to some game."

Hurstwood obeyed. At the corner he saw the wisdom of it. No sooner did the man perceive the intention to ignore him, than he shook his fist.

"Ah, you bloody coward!" he yelled.

Some half dozen men, standing on the corner, flung taunts and jeers after the speeding car.

Hurstwood winced the least bit. The real thing was slightly worse than the thoughts of it had been.

Now came in sight, three or four blocks farther on, a heap of something on the track.

"They've been at work, here, all right," said one of the policemen.

"We'll have an argument, maybe," said the other.

Hurstwood ran the car close and stopped. He had not done so wholly, however, before a crowd gathered about. It was composed of ex-motormen and conductors in part, with a sprinkling of friends and sympathisers.

"Come off the car, pardner," said one of the men in a voice meant to be conciliatory. "You don't want to take the bread out of another man's mouth, do you?"

Hurstwood held to his brake and lever, pale and very uncertain what to do.

"Stand back," yelled one of the officers, leaning over the platform railing. "Clear out of this, now. Give the man a chance to do his work."

"Listen, pardner," said the leader, ignoring the policeman and addressing Hurstwood. "We're all working men, like yourself. If you were a regular motorman, and had been treated as we've been, you wouldn't want any one to come in and take your place, would you? You wouldn't want any one to do you out of your chance to get your rights, would you?"

"Shut her off! shut her off!" urged the other of the policemen, roughly. "Get out of this, now," and he jumped the railing and landed before the crowd and began shoving. Instantly the other officer was down beside him.

"Stand back, now," they yelled. "Get out of this. What the hell do you mean? Out, now."

It was like a small swarm of bees.

"Don't shove me," said one of the strikers, determinedly. "I'm not doing anything."

"Get out of this!" cried the officer, swinging his club. "I'll give ye a bat on the sconce. Back, now."

"What the hell!" cried another of the strikers, pushing the other way, adding at the same time some lusty oaths.

Crack came an officer's club on his forehead. He blinked his eyes blindly a few times, wabbled on his legs, threw up his hands, and staggered back. In return, a swift fist landed on the officer's neck.

Infuriated by this, the latter plunged left and right, laying about madly with his club. He was ably assisted by his brother of the blue, who poured ponderous oaths upon the troubled waters. No severe damage was done, owing to the agility of the strikers in keeping out of reach. They stood about the sidewalk now and jeered.

"Where is the conductor?" yelled one of the officers, getting his eye on that individual, who had come nervously forward to stand by Hurstwood. The latter had stood gazing upon the scene with more astonishment than fear.

"Why don't you come down here and get these stones off the track?" inquired the officer. "What you standing there for? Do you want to stay here all day? Get down."

Hurstwood breathed heavily in excitement and jumped down with the nervous conductor as if he had been called.

"Hurry up, now," said the other policeman.

Cold as it was, these officers were hot and mad. Hurstwood worked with the conductor, lifting stone after stone and warming himself by the work.

"Ah, you scab, you!" yelled the crowd. "You coward! Steal a man's job, will you? Rob the poor, will you, you thief? We'll get you yet, now. Wait."

Not all of this was delivered by one man. It came from here and there, incorporated with much more of the same sort and curses.

"Work, you blackguards," yelled a voice. "Do the dirty work. You're the suckers that keep the poor people down!"

"May God starve ye yet," yelled an old Irish woman, who now threw open a nearby window and stuck out her head.

"Yes, and you," she added, catching the eye of one of the policemen. "You bloody, murtherin' thafe! Crack my own son over the head, will you, you hard-hearted, murtherin' divil? Ah, ye——"

But the officer turned a deaf ear.

"Go to the devil, you old hag," he half muttered as he stared round upon the scattered company.

Now the stones were off, and Hurstwood took his place again amid a continued chorus of epithets. Both officers got up beside him and the conductor rang the bell, when, bang! bang! through window and door came rocks and stones. One narrowly grazed Hurstwood's head. Another shattered the window behind.

"Throw open your lever," yelled one of the officers, grabbing at the handle himself.

Hurstwood complied and the car shot away, followed by a rattle of stones and a rain of curses.

"That —— —— —— hit me in the neck,"[1] said one of the officers. "I gave him a good crack for it, though."

"I think I must have left spots on some of them," said the other.

"I know that big guy that called us a —— —— —— ——," said the first. "I'll get him yet for that."

"I thought we were in for it sure, once there," said the second.

Hurstwood, warmed and excited, gazed steadily ahead. It was an astonishing experience for him. He had read of these things, but the reality seemed something altogether new. He was no coward in spirit. The fact that he had suffered this much now rather operated to arouse a stolid determination to stick it out. He did not recur in thought to New York or the flat. This one trip seemed a consuming thing.

They now ran into the business heart of Brooklyn uninterrupted. People gazed at the broken windows of the car and at Hurstwood in his plain clothes. Voices called "scab" now and then, as well as other epithets, but no crowd attacked the car. At the downtown end of the line, one of the officers went to call up his station and report the trouble.

1. Here and below Dreiser also used dashes in the holograph of *Sister Carrie*.

"There's a gang out there," he said, "laying for us yet. Better send some one over there and clean them out."

The car ran back more quietly—hooted, watched, flung at, but not attacked. Hurstwood breathed freely when he saw the barns.

"Well," he observed to himself, "I came out of that all right."

The car was turned in and he was allowed to loaf a while, but later he was again called. This time a new team of officers was aboard. Slightly more confident, he sped the car along the commonplace streets and felt somewhat less fearful. On one side, however, he suffered intensely. The day was raw, with a sprinkling of snow and a gusty wind, made all the more intolerable by the speed of the car. His clothing was not intended for this sort of work. He shivered, stamped his feet, and beat his arms as he had seen other motormen do in the past, but said nothing. The novelty and danger of the situation modified in a way his disgust and distress at being compelled to be here, but not enough to prevent him from feeling grim and sour. This was a dog's life, he thought. It was a tough thing to have to come to.

The one thought that strengthened him was the insult offered by Carrie. He was not down so low as to take all that, he thought. He could do something—this, even—for a while. It would get better. He would save a little.

A boy threw a clod of mud while he was thus reflecting and hit him upon the arm. It hurt sharply and angered him more than he had been any time since morning.

"The little cur!" he muttered.

"Hurt you?" asked one of the policemen.

"No," he answered.

At one of the corners, where the car slowed up because of a turn, an ex-motorman, standing on the sidewalk, called to him:

"Won't you come out, pardner, and be a man? Remember we're fighting for decent day's wages, that's all. We've got families to support." The man seemed most peaceably inclined.

Hurtwood pretended not to see him. He kept his eyes straight on before and opened the lever wide. The voice had something appealing in it.

All morning this went on and long into the afternoon. He made three such trips. The dinner he had was no stay for such work and the cold was telling on him. At each end of the line he stopped to thaw out, but he could have groaned at the anguish of it. One of the barnmen, out of pity, loaned him a heavy cap and a pair of sheepskin gloves, and for once he was extremely thankful.

On the second trip of the afternoon he ran into a crowd about half way along the line, that had blocked the car's progress with an old telegraph pole.

"Get that thing off the track," shouted the two policemen.

"Yah, yah, yah!" yelled the crowd. "Get it off yourself."

The two policemen got down and Hurstwood started to follow.

"You stay there," one called. "Some one will run away with your car."

Amid the babel of voices, Hurstwood heard one close beside him.

"Come down, pardner, and be a man. Don't fight the poor. Leave that to the corporations."

He saw the same fellow who had called to him from the corner. Now, as before, he pretended not to hear him.

"Come down," the man repeated gently. "You don't want to fight poor men. Don't fight at all." It was a most philosophic and jesuitical motorman.

A third policeman joined the other two from somewhere and some one ran to telephone for more officers. Hurstwood gazed about, determined but fearful.

A man grabbed him by the coat.

"Come off of that," he exclaimed, jerking at him and trying to pull him over the railing.

"Let go," said Hurstwood, savagely.

"I'll show you—you scab!" cried a young Irishman, jumping up on the car and aiming a blow at Hurstwood. The latter ducked and caught it on the shoulder instead of the jaw.

"Away from here," shouted an officer, hastening to the rescue, and adding, of course, the usual oaths.

Hurstwood recovered himself, pale and trembling. It was becoming serious with him now. People were looking up and jeering at him. One girl was making faces.

He began to waver in his resolution, when a patrol wagon rolled up and more officers dismounted. Now the track was quickly cleared and the release effected.

"Let her go now, quick," said the officer, and again he was off.

The end came with a real mob, which met the car on its return trip a mile or two from the barns. It was an exceedingly poor-looking neighbourhood. He wanted to run fast through it, but again the track was blocked. He saw men carrying something out to it when he was yet a half-dozen blocks away.

"There they are again!" exclaimed one policeman.

"I'll give them something this time," said the second officer, whose patience was becoming worn. Hurstwood suffered a qualm of body as the car rolled up. As before, the crowd began hooting, but now, rather than come near, they threw things. One or two windows were smashed and Hurstwood dodged a stone.

Both policemen ran out toward the crowd, but the latter replied by running toward the car. A woman—a mere girl in appearance—

was among these, bearing a rough stick. She was exceedingly wrathful and struck at Hurstwood, who dodged. Thereupon, her companions, duly encouraged, jumped on the car and pulled Hurstwood over. He had hardly time to speak or shout before he fell.

"Let go of me," he said, falling on his side.

"Ah, you sucker," he heard some one say. Kicks and blows rained on him. He seemed to be suffocating. Then two men seemed to be dragging him off and he wrestled for freedom.

"Let up," said a voice, "you're all right. Stand up."

He was let loose and recovered himself. Now he recognised two officers. He felt as if he would faint from exhaustion. Something was wet on his chin. He put up his hand and felt, then looked. It was red.

"They cut me," he said, foolishly, fishing for his handkerchief.

"Now, now," said one of the officers. "It's only a scratch."

His senses became cleared now and he looked around. He was standing in a little store, where they left him for the moment. Outside, he could see, as he stood wiping his chin, the car and the excited crowd. A patrol wagon was there, and another.

He walked over and looked out. It was an ambulance, backing in.

He saw some energetic charging by the police and arrests being made.

"Come on, now, if you want to take your car," said an officer, opening the door and looking in.

He walked out, feeling rather uncertain of himself. He was very cold and frightened.

"Where's the conductor?" he asked.

"Oh, he's not here now," said the policeman.

Hurstwood went toward the car and stepped nervously on. As he did so there was a pistol shot. Something stung his shoulder.

"Who fired that?" he heard an officer exclaim. "By God! who did that?" Both left him, running toward a certain building. He paused a moment and then got down.

"George!" exclaimed Hurstwood, weakly, "this is too much for me."

He walked nervously to the corner and hurried down a side street.

"Whew!" he said, drawing in his breath.

A half block away, a small girl gazed at him.

"You'd better sneak," she called.

He walked homeward in a blinding snowstorm, reaching the ferry by dusk. The cabins were filled with comfortable souls, who studied him curiously. His head was still in such a whirl that he felt confused. All the wonder of the twinkling lights of the river in a white storm passed for nothing. He trudged doggedly on until he reached the flat. There he entered and found the room warm. Carrie was gone. A couple of evening papers were lying on the table where she left them. He lit the gas and sat down. Then he got up and stripped to examine his shoulder. It was a mere scratch. He washed his hands and face, still in a brown study, apparently, and combed his hair. Then he looked for something to eat, and finally, his hunger gone, sat down in his comfortable rocking-chair. It was a wonderful relief.

He put his hand to his chin, forgetting, for the moment, the papers.

"Well," he said, after a time, his nature recovering itself, "That's a pretty tough game over there."

Then he turned and saw the papers. With half a sigh he picked up the "World."

"Strike Spreading in Brooklyn," he read. "Rioting Breaks Out in all Parts of the City."

He adjusted his paper very comfortably and continued. It was the one thing he read with absorbing interest.

Chapter XLII

A TOUCH OF SPRING: THE EMPTY SHELL

Those who look upon Hurstwood's Brooklyn venture as an error of judgment will none the less realise the negative influence on him of the fact that he had tried and failed. Carrie got a wrong idea of it. He said so little that she imagined he had encountered nothing worse than the ordinary roughness—quitting so soon in the face of this seemed trifling. He did not want to work.

She was now one of a group of oriental beauties who, in the second act of the comic opera, were paraded by the vizier before the new potentate as the treasures of his harem. There was no word assigned to any of them, but on the evening when Hurstwood was housing himself in the loft of the street-car barn, the leading comedian and star, feeling exceedingly facetious, said in a profound voice, which created a ripple of laughter:

"Well, who are you?"

It merely happened to be Carrie who was courtesying before him. It might as well have been any of the others, so far as he was concerned. He expected no answer and a dull one would have been reproved. But Carrie, whose experience and belief in herself gave her daring, courtesied sweetly again and answered:

"I am yours truly."

It was a trivial thing to say, and yet something in the way she did it caught the audience, which laughed heartily at the mock-fierce potentate towering before the young woman. The comedian also liked it, hearing the laughter.

"I thought your name was Smith," he returned, endeavouring to get the last laugh.

Carrie almost trembled for her daring after she had said this. All members of the company had been warned that to interpolate lines or "business" meant a fine or worse. She did not know what to think.

As she was standing in her proper position in the wings, awaiting another entry, the great comedian made his exit past her and paused in recognition.

"You can just leave that in hereafter," he remarked, seeing how intelligent she appeared. "Don't add any more, though."

"Thank you," said Carrie, humbly. When he went on she found herself trembling violently.

"Well, you're in luck," remarked another member of the chorus. "There isn't another one of us has got a line."

There was no gainsaying the value of this. Everybody in the company realised that she had got a start. Carrie hugged herself when next evening the lines got the same applause. She went home rejoicing, knowing that soon something must come of it. It was Hurstwood who, by his presence, caused her merry thoughts to flee and replaced them with sharp longings for an end of distress.

The next day she asked him about his venture.

"They're not trying to run any cars except with police. They don't want anybody just now—not before next week."

Next week came, but Carrie saw no change. Hurstwood seemed more apathetic than ever. He saw her off mornings to rehearsals and the like with the utmost calm. He read and read. Several times he found himself staring at an item, but thinking of something else. The first of these lapses that he sharply noticed concerned a hilarious party he had once attended at a driving club, of which he had been a member. He sat, gazing downward, and gradually thought he heard the old voices and the clink of glasses.

"You're a dandy, Hurstwood," his friend Walker said. He was standing again well dressed, smiling, good-natured, the recipient of encores for a good story.

All at once he looked up. The room was so still it seemed ghostlike. He heard the clock ticking audibly and half suspected that he had been dozing. The paper was so straight in his hands, however, and the items he had been reading so directly before him, that he rid himself of the doze idea. Still, it seemed peculiar. When it occurred a second time, however, it did not seem quite so strange.

Butcher and grocery man, baker and coal man—not the group with whom he was then dealing, but those who had trusted him to the limit—called. He met them all blandly, becoming deft in excuse. At last he became bold, pretended to be out, or waved them off.

"They can't get blood out of a turnip," he said. "If I had it I'd pay them."

Carrie's little soldier friend, Miss Osborne, seeing her succeeding, had become a sort of satellite. Little Osborne could never of herself amount to anything. She seemed to realise it in a sort of pussy-like way and instinctively concluded to cling with her soft little claws to Carrie.

"Oh, you'll get up," she kept telling Carrie with admiration. "You're so good."

Timid as Carrie was, she was strong in capability. The reliance of others made her feel as if she must, and when she must she dared. Experience of the world and of necessity was in her favour. No longer the lightest word of a man made her head dizzy. She had learned that men could change and fail. Flattery in its most palpable form had lost its force with her. It required superiority—kindly superiority—to move her—the superiority of a genius like Ames.

"I don't like the actors in our company," she told Lola one day. "They're all so stuck on themselves."

"Don't you think Mr. Barclay's pretty nice?" inquired Lola, who had received a condescending smile or two from that quarter.

"Oh, he's nice enough," answered Carrie; "but he isn't sincere. He assumes such an air."

Lola felt for her first hold upon Carrie in the following manner:

"Are you paying room-rent where you are?"

"Certainly," answered Carrie. "Why?"

"I know where I could get the loveliest room and bath, cheap. It's too big for me, but it would be just right for two, and the rent is only six dollars a week for both."

"Where?" said Carrie.

"In Seventeenth Street."

"Well, I don't know as I'd care to change," said Carrie, who was already turning over the three-dollar rate in her mind. She was thinking if she had only herself to support this would leave her seventeen for herself.

Nothing came of this until after the Brooklyn adventure of Hurstwood's and her success with the speaking part. Then she began to feel as if she must be free. She thought of leaving Hurstwood and thus making him act for himself, but he had developed such peculiar traits she feared he might resist any effort to throw him off. He might hunt her out at the show and hound her in that way. She did not wholly believe that he would, but he might. This, she knew, would be an embarrassing thing if he made himself conspicuous in any way. It troubled her greatly.

Things were precipitated by the offer of a better part. One of the actresses playing the part of a modest sweetheart gave notice of leaving and Carrie was selected.

"How much are you going to get?" asked Miss Osborne, on hearing the good news.

"I didn't ask him," said Carrie.

"Well, find out. Goodness, you'll never get anything if you don't ask. Tell them you must have forty dollars, anyhow."

"Oh, no," said Carrie.

"Certainly!" exclaimed Lola. "Ask 'em, anyway."

Carrie succumbed to this prompting, waiting, however, until the manager gave her notice of what clothing she must have to fit the part.

"How much do I get?" she inquired.

"Thirty-five dollars," he replied.

Carrie was too much astonished and delighted to think of mentioning forty. She was nearly beside herself, and almost hugged Lola, who clung to her at the news.

"It isn't as much as you ought to get," said the latter, "especially when you've got to buy clothes."

Carrie remembered this with a start. Where to get the money? She had none laid up for such an emergency. Rent day was drawing near.

"I'll not do it," she said, remembering her necessity. "I don't use the flat. I'm not going to give up my money this time. I'll move."

Fitting into this came another appeal from Miss Osborne, more urgent than ever.

"Come live with me, won't you?" she pleaded. "We can have the loveliest room. It won't cost you hardly anything that way."

"I'd like to," said Carrie, frankly.

"Oh, do," said Lola. "We'll have such a good time."

Carrie thought a while.

"I believe I will," she said, and then added: "I'll have to see first, though."

With the idea thus grounded, rent day approaching, and clothes calling for instant purchase, she soon found excuse in Hurstwood's lassitude. He said less and drooped more than ever.

As rent day approached, an idea grew in him. It was fostered by the demands of creditors and the impossibility of holding up many more. Twenty-eight dollars was too much for rent. "It's hard on her," he thought. "We could get a cheaper place."

Stirred with this idea, he spoke at the breakfast table.

"Don't you think we pay too much rent here?" he asked.

"Indeed I do," said Carrie, not catching his drift.

"I should think we could get a smaller place," he suggested. "We don't need four rooms."

Her countenance, had he been scrutinising her, would have exhibited the disturbance she felt at this evidence of his determination to stay by her. He saw nothing remarkable in asking her to come down lower.

"Oh, I don't know," she answered, growing wary.

"There must be places around here where we could get a couple of rooms, which would do just as well."

Her heart revolted. "Never!" she thought. Who would furnish the money to move? To think of being in two rooms with him! She resolved to spend her money for clothes quickly, before something terrible happened. That very day she did it. Having done so, there was but one other thing to do.

"Lola," she said, visiting her friend, "I think I'll come."

"Oh, jolly!" cried the latter.

"Can we get it right away?" she asked, meaning the room.

"Certainly," cried Lola.

They went to look at it. Carrie had saved ten dollars from her expenditures—enough for this and her board beside. Her enlarged salary would not begin for ten days yet—would not reach her for seventeen. She paid half of the six dollars with her friend.

"Now, I've just enough to get on to the end of the week," she confided.

"Oh, I've got some," said Lola. "I've got twenty-five dollars, if you need it."

"No," said Carrie. "I guess I'll get along."

They decided to move Friday, which was two days away. Now that the thing was settled, Carrie's heart misgave her. She felt very much like a criminal in the matter. Each day looking at Hurstwood, she had realised that, along with the disagreeableness of his attitude, there was something pathetic.

She looked at him the same evening she had made up her mind to go, and now he seemed not so shiftless and worthless, but run down and beaten upon by chance. His eyes were not keen, his face marked, his hands flabby. She thought his hair had a touch of grey. All unconscious of his doom, he rocked and read his paper, while she glanced at him.

Knowing that the end was so near, she became rather solicitous.

"Will you go over and get some canned peaches?" she asked Hurstwood, laying down a two-dollar bill.

"Certainly," he said, looking in wonder at the money.

"See if you can get some nice asparagus," she added. "I'll cook it for dinner."

Hurstwood rose and took the money, slipping on his overcoat and getting his hat. Carrie noticed that both of these articles of apparel were old and poor looking in appearance. It was plain enough before, but now it came home with peculiar force. Perhaps he couldn't help it, after all. He had done well in Chicago. She remembered his fine appearance the days he had met her in the park. Then he was so sprightly, so clean. Had it been all his fault?

He came back and laid the change down with the food.

"You'd better keep it," she observed. "We'll need other things."

"No," he said, with a sort of pride; "you keep it."

"Oh, go on and keep it," she replied, rather unnerved. "There'll be other things."

He wondered at this, not knowing the pathetic figure he had become in her eyes. She restrained herself with difficulty from showing a quaver in her voice.

To say truly, this would have been Carrie's attitude in any case. She had looked back at times upon her parting from Drouet and had regretted that she had served him so badly. She hoped she would never meet him again, but she was ashamed of her conduct. Not that she had any choice in the final separation. She had gone willingly to seek him, with sympathy in her heart, when Hurstwood had reported him ill. There was something cruel somewhere, and not being able to track it mentally to its logical lair, she concluded with feeling that he would never understand what Hurstwood had done and would see hard-hearted decision in her deed; hence her shame. Not that she cared for him. She did not want to make any one who had been good to her feel badly.

She did not realise what she was doing by allowing these feelings to possess her. Hurstwood, noticing the kindness, conceived better of her. "Carrie's good-natured, anyhow," he thought.

Going to Miss Osborne's that afternoon, she found that little lady packing and singing.

"Why don't you come over with me to-day?" she asked.

"Oh, I can't," said Carrie. "I'll be there Friday. Would you mind lending me the twenty-five dollars you spoke of?"

"Why, no," said Lola, going for her purse.

"I want to get some other things," said Carrie.

"Oh, that's all right," answered the little girl, good-naturedly, glad to be of service.

It had been days since Hurstwood had done more than go to the grocery or to the news-stand. Now the weariness of indoors was upon him—had been for two days—but chill, grey weather had held him back. Friday broke fair and warm. It was one of those lovely harbingers of spring, given as a sign in dreary winter that earth is not forsaken of warmth and beauty. The blue heaven, holding its one golden orb, poured down a crystal wash of warm light. It was plain, from the voice of the sparrows, that all was halcyon outside. Carrie raised the front windows, and felt the south wind blowing.

"It's lovely out to-day," she remarked.

"Is it?" said Hurstwood.

After breakfast, he immediately got his other clothes.

"Will you be back for lunch?" asked Carrie, nervously.

"No," he said.

He went out into the streets and tramped north, along Seventh Avenue, idly fixing upon the Harlem River as an objective point. He had seen some ships up there, the time he had called upon the brewers. He wondered how the territory thereabouts was growing.

Passing Fifty-ninth Street, he took the west side of Central Park, which he followed to Seventy-eighth Street. Then he remembered the neighbourhood and turned over to look at the mass of buildings erected. It was very much improved. The great open spaces were filling up. Coming back, he kept to the Park until 110th Street, and then turned into Seventh Avenue again, reaching the pretty river by one o'clock.

There it ran winding before his gaze, shining brightly in the clear light, between the undulating banks on the right and the tall, tree-covered heights on the left. The spring-like atmosphere woke him to a sense of its loveliness, and for a few moments he stood looking at it, folding his hands behind his back. Then he turned and followed it toward the east side, idly seeking the ships he had seen. It was four o'clock before the waning day, with its suggestion of a cooler evening, caused him to return. He was hungry and would enjoy eating in the warm room.

When he reached the flat by half-past five, it was still dark. He knew that Carrie was not there, not only because there was no light showing through the transom, but because the evening papers were stuck between the outside knob and the door. He opened with his key and went in. Everything was still dark. Lighting the gas, he sat down, preparing to wait a little while. Even if Carrie did come now, dinner would be late. He read until six, then got up to fix something for himself.

As he did so, he noticed that the room seemed a little queer. What was it? He looked around, as if he missed something, and then saw an envelope near where he had been sitting. It spoke for itself, almost without further action on his part.

Reaching over, he took it, a sort of chill settling upon him even while he reached. The crackle of the envelope in his hands was loud. Green paper money lay soft within the note.

"Dear George," he read, crunching the money in one hand. "I'm going away. I'm not coming back any more. It's no use trying to keep up the flat; I can't do it. I wouldn't mind helping you, if I could, but I can't support us both, and pay the rent. I need what little I make to pay for my clothes. I'm leaving twenty dollars. It's all I have just now. You can do whatever you like with the furniture. I won't want it.—Carrie."

He dropped the note and looked quietly round. Now he knew what he missed. It was the little ornamental clock, which was hers. It had gone from the mantel-piece. He went into the front room, his bedroom, the parlour, lighting the gas as he went. From the chiffonier had gone the knick-knacks of silver and plate. From the table-top, the lace coverings. He opened the wardrobe—no clothes of hers. He opened the drawers—nothing of hers. Her trunk was gone from its accustomed place. Back in his own room hung his old clothes, just as he had left them. Nothing else was gone.

He stepped onto the parlour and stood for a few moments looking vacantly at the floor. The silence grew oppressive. The little flat seemed wonderfully deserted. He wholly forgot that he was hungry, that it was only dinner-time. It seemed later in the night.

Suddenly, he found that the money was still in his hands. There were twenty dollars in all, as she had said. Now he walked back, leaving the lights ablaze, and feeling as if the flat were empty.

"I'll get out of this," he said to himself.

Then the sheer loneliness of his situation rushed upon him in full.

"Left me!" he muttered, and repeated, "left me!"

The place that had been so comfortable, where he had spent so many days of warmth, was now a memory. Something colder and chillier confronted him. He sank down in his chair, resting his chin in his hand—mere sensation, without thought, holding him.

Then something like a bereaved affection and self-pity swept over him.

"She needn't have gone away," he said. "I'd have got something."

He sat a long while without rocking, and added quite clearly, out loud:

"I tried, didn't I?"

At midnight he was still rocking, staring at the floor.

Chapter XLIII

THE WORLD TURNS FLATTERER: AN EYE IN THE DARK

Installed in her comfortable room, Carrie wondered how Hurstwood had taken her departure. She arranged a few things hastily and then left for the theatre, half expecting to encounter him at the door. Not finding him, her dread lifted, and she felt more kindly toward him. She quite forgot him until about to come out, after the show, when the chance of his being there frightened her. As day after day passed and she heard nothing at all, the thought of being bothered by him passed. In a little while she was, except for occasional thoughts, wholly free of the gloom with which her life had been weighed in the flat.

It is curious to note how quickly a profession absorbs one. Carrie became wise in theatrical lore, hearing the gossip of little Lola. She learned what the theatrical papers were, which ones published items about actresses and the like. She began to read the newspaper notices, not only of the opera in which she had so small a part, but of others. Gradually the desire for notice took hold of her. She longed to be renowned like others, and read with avidity all the complimentary or critical comments made concerning others high in her profession. The showy world in which her interest lay completely absorbed her.

It was about this time that the newspapers and magazines were beginning to pay that illustrative attention to the beauties of the stage which has since become fervid. The newspapers, and particularly the Sunday newspapers, indulged in large decorative-theatrical pages, in which the faces and forms of well-known theatrical celebrities appeared, enclosed with artistic scrolls. The magazines also—or at least one or two of the newer ones—published occasional portraits of pretty stars, and now and again photos of scenes from various plays. Carrie watched these with growing interest. When would a scene from her opera appear? When would some paper think her photo worth while?[1]

The Sunday before taking her new part she scanned the theatrical pages for some little notice. It would have accorded with her expectations if nothing had been said, but there in the squibs, tailing off several more substantial items, was a wee notice. Carrie read it with a tingling body:

> The part of Katisha, the country maid, in "The Wives of Abdul" at the Broadway, heretofore played by Inez Carew, will be hereafter filled by Carrie Madenda, one of the cleverest members of the chorus.[2]

Carrie hugged herself with delight. Oh, wasn't it just fine! At last! The first, the long-hoped for, the delightful notice! And they called her clever. She could hardly restrain herself from laughing loudly. Had Lola seen it?

"They've got a notice here of the part I'm going to play tomorrow night," said Carrie to her friend.

"Oh, jolly! Have they?" cried Lola, running to her. "That's all right," she said, looking. "You'll get more now, if you do well. I had my picture in the 'World' once."

"Did you?" asked Carrie.

"Did I? Well, I should say," returned the little girl. "They had a frame around it."

Carrie laughed.

1. A newly developed cheap photoengraving process in the early 1890s had made such newspaper and magazine illustrations possible.
2. *The Wives of Abdul* is a fictitious name. It accurately reflects, however, the tendency during the 1890s to use an Arabian Nights setting for musical comedies in order to exploit the possibilities for scanty costuming and for jokes about harems. *Aladdin, Jr.*, for example, played at the Broadway in April 1895.

"They've never published my picture."

"But they will," said Lola. "You'll see. You do better than most that get theirs in now."

Carrie felt deeply grateful for this. She almost loved Lola for the sympathy and praise she extended. It was so helpful to her—so almost necessary.

Fulfilling her part capably brought another notice in the papers that she was doing her work acceptably. This pleased her immensely. She began to think the world was taking note of her.

The first week she got her thirty-five dollars, it seemed an enormous sum. Paying only three dollars for room rent seemed ridiculous. After giving Lola her twenty-five, she still had seven dollars left. With four left over from previous earnings, she had eleven. Five of this went to pay the regular installment on the clothes she had to buy. The next week she was even in greater feather. Now, only three dollars need be paid for room rent and five on her clothes. The rest she had for food and her own whims.

"You'd better save a little for summer," cautioned Lola. "We'll probably close in May."

"I intend to," said Carrie.

The regular entrance of thirty-five dollars a week to one who has endured scant allowances for several years is a demoralising thing. Carrie found her purse bursting with good green bills of comfortable denominations. Having no one dependent upon her, she began to buy pretty clothes and pleasing trinkets, to eat well, and to ornament her room. Friends were not long in gathering about. She met a few young men who belonged to Lola's staff. The members of the opera company made her acquaintance without the formality of introduction. One of these discovered a fancy for her. On several occasions he strolled home with her.

"Let's stop in and have a rarebit," he suggested one midnight.

"Very well," said Carrie.

In the rosy restaurant, filled with the merry lovers of late hours, she found herself criticising this man. He was too stilted, too self-opinionated. He did not talk of anything that lifted her above the common run of clothes and material success. When it was all over, he smiled most graciously.

"Got to go straight home, have you?" he said.

"Yes," she answered, with an air of quiet understanding.

"She's not so inexperienced as she looks," he thought, and thereafter his respect and ardour were increased.

She could not help sharing in Lola's love for a good time. There were days when they went carriage riding, nights when after the show they dined, afternoons when they strolled along Broadway, tastefully dressed. She was getting in the metropolitan whirl of pleasure.

At last her picture appeared in one of the weeklies. She had not known of it, and it took her breath. "Miss Carrie Madenda," it was labelled. "One of the favourites of 'The Wives of Abdul' company." At Lola's advice she had had some pictures taken by Sarony.[3] They had got one there. She thought of going down and buying a few copies of the paper, but remembered that there was no one she knew well enough to send them to. Only Lola, apparently, in all the world was interested.

The metropolis is a cold place socially, and Carrie soon found that a little money brought her nothing. The world of wealth and distinction was quite as far away as ever. She could feel that there was no warm, sympathetic friendship back of the easy merriment with which many approached her. All seemed to be seeking their own amusement, regardless of the possible sad consequence to others. So much for the lessons of Hurstwood and Drouet.

In April she learned that the opera would probably last until the middle or the end of May, according to the size of the audiences. Next season it would go on the road. She wondered if she would be with it. As usual, Miss Osborne, owing to her moderate salary, was for securing a home engagement.

"They're putting on a summer play at the Casino," she announced, after figuratively putting her ear to the ground. "Let's try and get in that."

"I'm willing," said Carrie.

They tried in time and were apprised of the proper date to apply again. That was May 16th. Meanwhile their own show closed May 5th.

"Those that want to go with the show next season," said the manager, "will have to sign this week."

"Don't you sign," advised Lola. "I wouldn't go."

"I know," said Carrie, "but maybe I can't get anything else."

"Well, I won't," said the little girl, who had a resource in her admirers. "I went once and I didn't have anything at the end of the season."

Carrie thought this over. She had never been on the road.

"We can get along," added Lola. "I always have."

Carrie did not sign.

The manager who was putting on the summer skit at the Casino had never heard of Carrie, but the several notices she had received, her published picture, and the programme bearing her name had some little weight with him. He gave her a silent part at thirty dollars a week.[4]

---

3. Napoleon Sarony was the leading theatrical photographer of the day.
4. The Casino was one of the few New York theaters to play throughout the summer, since it had a roof garden and featured light entertainment. In *A Book About Myself* (New York: 1922), 445, Dreiser recalled "its choruses of girls, the Mecca of the night-loving Johnnies."

"Didn't I tell you?" said Lola. "It doesn't do you any good to go away from New York. They forget all about you if you do."

Now, because Carrie was pretty, the gentlemen who made up the advance illustrations of shows about to appear for the Sunday papers selected Carrie's photo along with others to illustrate the announcement. Because she was very pretty, they gave it excellent space and drew scrolls about it. Carrie was delighted. Still, the management did not seem to have seen anything of it. At least, no more attention was paid to her than before. At the same time there seemed very little in her part. It consisted of standing around in all sorts of scenes, a silent little Quakeress. The author of the skit had fancied that a great deal could be made of such a part, given to the right actress, but now, since it had been doled out to Carrie, he would as leave have had it cut out.

"Don't kick, old man," remarked the manager. "If it don't go the first week we will cut it out."

Carrie had no warning of this halcyon intention. She practised her part ruefully, feeling that she was effectually shelved. At the dress rehearsal she was disconsolate.

"That isn't so bad," said the author, the manager noting the curious effect which Carrie's blues had upon the part. "Tell her to frown a little more when Sparks dances."

Carrie did not know it, but there was the least show of wrinkles between her eyes and her mouth was puckered quaintly.

"Frown a little more, Miss Madenda," said the stage manager.

Carrie instantly brightened up, thinking he had meant it as a rebuke.

"No; frown," he said. "Frown as you did before."

Carrie looked at him in astonishment.

"I mean it," he said. "Frown hard when Mr. Sparks dances. I want to see how it looks."

It was easy enough to do. Carrie scowled. The effect was something so quaint and droll it caught even the manager.

"That *is* good," he said. "If she'll do that all through, I think it will take."

Going over to Carrie, he said:

"Suppose you try frowning all through. Do it hard. Look mad. It'll make the part really funny."

On the opening night it looked to Carrie as if there were nothing to her part, after all. The happy, sweltering audience did not seem to see her in the first act. She frowned and frowned, but to no effect. Eyes were riveted upon the more elaborate efforts of the stars.

In the second act, the crowd, wearied by a dull conversation, roved with its eyes about the stage and sighted her. There she was, gray-suited, sweet-faced, demure, but scowling. At first the general idea was that she was temporarily irritated, that the look was genuine and not fun at all. As she went on frowning, looking now at one principal and now at the other, the audience began to smile. The portly gentlemen in the front rows began to feel that she was a delicious little morsel. It was the kind of frown they would have loved to force away with kisses. All the gentlemen yearned toward her. She was capital.

At last, the chief comedian, singing in the centre of the stage, noticed a giggle where it was not expected. Then another and another. When the place came for loud applause it was only moderate. What could be the trouble? He realised that something was up.

All at once, after an exit, he caught sight of Carrie. She was frowning alone on the stage and the audience was giggling and laughing.

"By George, I won't stand that!" thought the thespian. "I'm not going to have my work cut up by some one else. Either she quits that when I do my turn or I quit."

"Why, that's all right," said the manager, when the kick came. "That's what she's supposed to do. You needn't pay any attention to that."

"But she ruins my work."

"No, she don't," returned the former, soothingly. "It's only a little fun on the side."

"It is, eh?" exclaimed the big comedian. "She killed my hand all right. I'm not going to stand that."

"Well, wait until after the show. Wait until tomorrow. We'll see what we can do."

The next act, however, settled what was to be done. Carrie was the chief feature of the play. The audience, the more it studied her, the more it indicated its delight. Every other feature paled beside the quaint, teasing, delightful atmosphere which Carrie contributed while on the stage. Manager and company realised she had made a hit.

The critics of the daily papers completed her triumph. There were long notices in praise of the quality of the burlesque, touched with recurrent references to Carrie. The contagious mirth of the thing was repeatedly emphasised.

"Miss Madenda presents one of the most delightful bits of character work ever seen on the Casino stage," observed the sage critic of the "Sun." "It is a bit of quiet, unassuming drollery which warms like good wine. Evidently the part was not intended to take precedence, as Miss Madenda is not often on the stage, but the audience, with the characteristic perversity of such bodies, selected for itself. The little Quakeress was marked for a favourite the moment she appeared, and thereafter easily held attention and applause. The vagaries of fortune are indeed curious."

The critic of the "Evening World," seeking as usual to establish a catch phrase which should "go" with the town, wound up by advising: "If you wish to be merry, see Carrie frown."

The result was miraculous so far as Carrie's fortune was concerned. Even during the morning she received a congratulatory message from the manager.

"You seem to have taken the town by storm," he wrote. "This is delightful. I am as glad for your sake as for my own."

The author also sent word.

That evening when she entered the theatre the manager had a most pleasant greeting for her.

"Mr. Stevens," he said, referring to the author, "is preparing a little song, which he would like you to sing next week."

"Oh, I can't sing," returned Carrie.

"It isn't anything difficult. 'It's something that is very simple,' he says, 'and would suit you exactly.' "

"Of course, I wouldn't mind trying," said Carrie, archly.

"Would you mind coming to the box-office a few moments before you dress?" observed the manager, in addition. "There's a little matter I want to speak to you about."

"Certainly," replied Carrie.

In that latter place the manager produced a paper.

"Now, of course," he said, "we want to be fair with you in the matter of salary. Your contract here only calls for thirty dollars a week for the next three months. How would it do to make it, say, one hundred and fifty a week and extend it for twelve months?"

"Oh, very well," said Carrie, scarcely believing her ears.

"Supposing, then, you just sign this."

Carrie looked and beheld a new contract made out like the other one, with the exception of the new figures of salary and time. With a hand trembling from excitement she affixed her name.

"One hundred and fifty a week!" she murmured, when she was again alone. She found, after all—as what millionaire has not?—that there was no realising, in consciousness, the meaning of large sums. It was only a shimmering, glittering phrase in which lay a world of possibilities.

Down in a third-rate Bleecker Street hotel,[5] the brooding Hurstwood read the dramatic item covering Carrie's success, without at first realising who was meant. Then suddenly it came to him and he read the whole thing over again.

"That's her, all right, I guess," he said.

Then he looked about upon a dingy, moth-eaten hotel lobby.

"I guess she's struck it," he thought, a picture of the old shiny,

5. Bleecker Street runs off the Bowery and through Greenwich Village.

plush-covered world coming back, with its lights, its ornaments, its carriages, and flowers. Ah, she was in the walled city now! Its splendid gates had opened, admitting her from a cold, dreary outside. She seemed a creature afar off—like every other celebrity he had known.

"Well, let her have it," he said. "I won't bother her."

It was the grim resolution of a bent, bedraggled, but unbroken pride.

Chapter XLIV

AND THIS IS NOT ELF LAND: WHAT GOLD WILL NOT BUY

When Carrie got back on the stage, she found that over night her dressing-room had been changed.

"You are to use this room, Miss Madenda," said one of the stage lackeys.

No longer any need of climbing several flights of steps to a small coop shared with another. Instead, a comparatively large and commodious chamber with conveniences not enjoyed by the small fry overhead. She breathed deeply and with delight. Her sensations were more physical than mental. In fact, she was scarcely thinking at all. Heart and body were having their say.

Gradually the deference and congratulation gave her a mental appreciation of her state. She was no longer ordered, but requested, and that politely. The other members of the cast looked at her enviously as she came out arrayed in her simple habit, which she wore all through the play. All those who had supposedly been her equals and superiors now smiled the smile of sociability, as much as to say: "How friendly we have always been." Only the star comedian whose part had been so deeply injured stalked by himself. Figuratively, he could not kiss the hand that smote him.

Doing her simple part, Carrie gradually realised the meaning of the applause which was for her, and it was sweet. She felt mildly guilty of something—perhaps unworthiness. When her associates addressed her in the wings she only smiled weakly. The pride and daring of place were not for her. It never once crossed her mind to be reserved or haughty—to be other than she had been. After the performances she rode to her room with Lola, in a carriage provided.

Then came a week in which the first fruits of success were offered to her lips—bowl after bowl. It did not matter that her splendid salary had not begun. The world seemed satisfied with the promise. She began to get letters and cards. A Mr. Withers—whom she did not know from Adam—having learned by some hook or crook where she resided, bowed himself politely in.

"You will excuse me for intruding," he said; "but have you been thinking of changing your apartments?"

"I hadn't thought of it," returned Carrie.

"Well, I am connected with the Wellington—the new hotel on Broadway.[1] You have probably seen notices of it in the papers." Carrie recognised the name as standing for one of the newest and most imposing hostelries. She had heard it spoken of as having a splendid restaurant.

"Just so," went on Mr. Withers, accepting her acknowledgment of familiarity. "We have some very elegant rooms at present which we would like to have you look at, if you have not made up your mind where you intend to reside for the summer. Our apartments are perfect in every detail—hot and cold water, private baths, special hall service for every floor, elevators and all that. You know what our restaurant is."

Carrie looked at him quietly. She was wondering whether he took her to be a millionaire.

"What are your rates?" she inquired.

"Well, now, that is what I came to talk with you privately about. Our regular rates are anywhere from three to fifty dollars a day."

"Mercy!" interrupted Carrie. "I couldn't pay any such rate as that."

"I know how you feel about it," exclaimed Mr. Withers, halting. "But just let me explain. I said those are our regular rates. Like every other hotel we make special ones, however. Possibly you have not thought about it, but your name is worth something to us."

"Oh!" ejaculated Carrie, seeing at a glance.

"Of course. Every hotel depends upon the repute of its patrons. A well-known actress like yourself," and he bowed politely, while Carrie flushed, "draws attention to the hotel, and—although you may not believe it—patrons."

"Oh, yes," returned Carrie, vacantly, trying to arrange this curious proposition in her mind.

"Now," continued Mr. Withers, swaying his derby hat softly and beating one of his polished shoes upon the floor, "I want to arrange, if possible, to have you come and stop at the Wellington. You need not trouble about terms. In fact, we need hardly discuss them. Anything will do for the summer—a mere figure—anything that you think you could afford to pay."

Carrie was about to interrupt, but he gave her no chance.

"You can come to-day or to-morrow—the earlier the better—and we will give you your choice of nice, light, outside rooms—the very best we have."

"You're very kind," said Carrie, touched by the agent's extreme affability. "I should like to come very much. I would want to pay what is right, however. I shouldn't want to——"

---

1. The Wellington was not new at that time (the summer of 1895), though it was one of the better Broadway hotels.

"You need not trouble about that at all," interrupted Mr. Withers. "We can arrange that to your entire satisfaction at any time. If three dollars a day is satisfactory to you, it will be so to us. All you have to do is to pay that sum to the clerk at the end of the week or month, just as you wish, and he will give you a receipt for what the rooms would cost if charged for at our regular rates."

The speaker paused.

"Suppose you come and look at the rooms," he added.

"I'd be glad to," said Carrie, "but I have a rehearsal this morning."

"I did not mean at once," he returned. "Any time will do. Would this afternoon be inconvenient?"

"Not at all," said Carrie.

Suddenly she remembered Lola, who was out at the time.

"I have a room mate," she added, "who will have to go wherever I do. I forgot about that."

"Oh, very well," said Mr. Withers, blandly. "It is for you to say whom you want with you. As I say, all that can be arranged to suit yourself."

He bowed and backed toward the door.

"At four, then, we may expect you?"

"Yes," said Carrie.

"I will be there to show you," and so Mr. Withers withdrew.

After rehearsal Carrie informed Lola.

"Did they really?" exclaimed the latter, thinking of the Wellington as a group of managers. "Isn't that fine? Oh, jolly! It's so swell. That's where we dined that night we went with those two Cushing boys. Don't you know?"

"I remember," said Carrie.

"Oh, it's as fine as it can be."

"We'd better be going up there," observed Carrie, later in the afternoon.

The rooms which Mr. Withers displayed to Carrie and Lola were three and bath—a suite on the parlour floor. They were done in chocolate and dark red, with rugs and hangings to match. Three windows looked down into busy Broadway on the east, three into a side street which crossed there. There were two lovely bedrooms, set with brass and white enamel beds, white, ribbon-trimmed chairs and chiffoniers to match. In the third room, or parlour, was a piano, a heavy piano lamp, with a shade of gorgeous pattern, a library table, several huge easy rockers, some dado book shelves,[2] and a gilt curio case, filled with oddities. Pictures were upon the walls, soft Turkish pillows upon the divan, footstools of brown plush upon the floor. Such accommodations would ordinarily cost a hundred dollars a week.

2. Dado shelves consist of horizontal boards fitted into grooved vertical boards.

"Oh, lovely!" exclaimed Lola, walking about.

"It is comfortable," said Carrie, who was lifting a lace curtain and looking down into crowded Broadway.

The bath was a handsome affair, done in white enamel, with a large, blue-bordered stone tub and nickel trimmings. It was bright and commodious, with a bevelled mirror set in the wall at one end and incandescent lights arranged in three places.

"Do you find these satisfactory?" observed Mr. Withers.

"Oh, very," answered Carrie.

"Well, then, any time you find it convenient to move in, they are ready. The boy will bring you the keys at the door."

Carrie noted the elegantly carpeted and decorated hall, the marbelled lobby, and showy waiting-room. It was such a place as she had often dreamed of occupying.

"I guess we'd better move right away, don't you think so?" she observed to Lola, thinking of the commonplace chamber in Seventeenth Street.

"Oh, by all means," said the latter.

The next day her trunks left for the new abode.

Dressing, after the matinée on Wednesday, a knock came at her dressing-room door.

Carrie looked at the card handed by the boy and suffered a shock of surprise.

"Tell her I'll be right out," she said softly. Then, looking at the card, added: "Mrs. Vance."

"Why, you little sinner," the latter exclaimed, as she saw Carrie coming toward her across the now vacant stage. "How in the world did this happen?"

Carrie laughed merrily. There was no trace of embarrassment in her friend's manner. You would have thought that the long separation had come about accidentally.

"I don't know," returned Carrie, warming, in spite of her first troubled feelings, toward this handsome, good-natured young matron.

"Well, you know, I saw your picture in the Sunday paper, but your name threw me off. I thought it must be you or somebody that looked just like you, and I said: 'Well, now, I will go right down there and see.' I was never more surprised in my life. How are you, anyway?"

"Oh, very well," returned Carrie. "How have you been?"

"Fine. But aren't you a success! Dear, oh! All the papers talking about you. I should think you would be just too proud to breathe. I was almost afraid to come back here this afternoon."

"Oh, nonsense," said Carrie, blushing. "You know I'd be glad to see you."

"Well, anyhow, here you are. Can't you come up and take dinner with me now? Where are you stopping?"

"At the Wellington," said Carrie, who permitted herself a touch of pride in the acknowledgment.

"Oh, are you?" exclaimed the other, upon whom the name was not without its proper effect.

Tactfully, Mrs. Vance avoided the subject of Hurstwood, of whom she could not help thinking. No doubt Carrie had left him. That much she surmised.

"Oh, I don't think I can," said Carrie, "to-night. I have so little time. I must be back here by 7.30. Won't you come and dine with me?"

"I'd be delighted, but I can't to-night," said Mrs. Vance, studying Carrie's fine appearance. The latter's good fortune made her seem more than ever worthy and delightful in the other's eyes. "I promised faithfully to be home at six." Glancing at the small gold watch pinned to her bosom, she added: "I must be going, too. Tell me when you're coming up, if at all."

"Why, any time you like," said Carrie.

"Well, to-morrow then. I'm living at the Chelsea now."[3]

"Moved again?" exclaimed Carrie, laughing.

"Yes. You know I can't stay six months in one place. I just have to move. Remember now—half-past five."

"I won't forget," said Carrie, casting a glance at her as she went away. Then it came to her that she was as good as this woman now— perhaps better. Something in the other's solicitude and interest made her feel as if she were the one to condescend.

Now, as on each preceding day, letters were handed her by the doorman at the Casino. This was a feature which had rapidly developed since Monday. What they contained she well knew. *Mash notes* were old affairs in their mildest form. She remembered having received her first one far back in Columbia City. Since then, as a chorus girl, she had received others—gentlemen who prayed for an engagement. They were common sport between her and Lola, who received some also. They both frequently made light of them.

Now, however, they came thick and fast. Gentlemen with fortunes did not hesitate to note, as an addition to their own amiable collection of virtues, that they had their horses and carriages. Thus one:

I have a million in my own right. I could give you every luxury. There isn't anything you could ask for that you couldn't have. I say this, not because I want to speak of my money, but because I love you and wish to gratify your every desire. It is love that prompts me to write. Will you not give me one half-hour in which to plead my cause?

3. The Chelsea, on West Twenty-third Street, was a fashionable apartment building.

Such of these letters as came while Carrie was still in the Seventeenth Street place were read with more interest—though never
delight—than those which arrived after she was installed in her
luxurious quarters at the Wellington. Even there her vanity—or that
self-appreciation which, in its more rabid form, is called vanity—was
not sufficiently cloyed to make these things wearisome. Adulation,
being new in any form, pleased her. Only she was sufficiently wise
to distinguish between her old condition and her new one. She had
not had fame or money before. Now they had come. She had not
had adulation and affectionate propositions before. Now they had
come. Wherefore? She smiled to think that men should suddenly
find her so much more attractive. In the least way it incited her to
coolness and indifference.

"Do look here," she remarked to Lola. "See what this man says: 'If
you will only deign to grant me one half-hour,' " she repeated, with
an imitation of languor. "The idea. Aren't men silly?"

"He must have lots of money, the way he talks," observed Lola.

"That's what they all say," said Carrie, innocently.

"Why don't you see him," suggested Lola, "and hear what he has
to say?"

"Indeed I won't," said Carrie. "I know what he'd say. I don't want
to meet anybody that way."

Lola looked at her with big, merry eyes.

"He couldn't hurt you," she returned. "You might have some fun
with him."

Carrie shook her head.

"You're awfully queer," returned the little, blue-eyed soldier.

Thus crowded fortune. For this whole week, though her large salary had not yet arrived, it was as if the world understood and trusted
her. Without money—or the requisite sum, at least—she enjoyed
the luxuries which money could buy. For her the doors of fine places
seemed to open quite without the asking. These palatial chambers,
how marvellously they came to her. The elegant apartments of Mrs.
Vance in the Chelsea—these were hers. Men sent flowers, love
notes, offers of fortune. And still her dreams ran riot. The one hundred and fifty! the one hundred and fifty! What a door to an Aladdin's
cave it seemed to be. Each day, her head almost turned by developments, her fancies of what her fortune must be, with ample
money, grew and multiplied. She conceived of delights which were
not—saw lights of joy that never were on land or sea. Then, at last,
after a world of anticipation, came her first installment of one hundred and fifty dollars.

It was paid to her in greenbacks—three twenties, six tens, and six
fives. Thus collected it made a very convenient roll. It was accompanied by a smile and a salutation from the cashier who paid it.

"Ah, yes," said the latter, when she applied; "Miss Madenda—one hundred and fifty dollars. Quite a success the show seems to have made."

"Yes, indeed," returned Carrie.

Right after came one of the insignificant members of the company, and she heard the changed tone of address.

"How much?" said the same cashier, sharply. One, such as she had only recently been, was waiting for her modest salary. It took her back to the few weeks in which she had collected—or rather had received almost with the air of a domestic, four-fifty per week from a lordly foreman in a shoe factory—a man who, in distributing the envelopes, had the manner of a prince doling out favours to a servile group of petitioners. She knew that out in Chicago this very day the same factory chamber was full of poor homely-clad girls working in long lines at clattering machines; that at noon they would eat a miserable lunch in a half-hour; that Saturday they would gather, as they had when she was one of them, and accept the small pay for work a hundred times harder than she was now doing. Oh, it was so easy now! The world was so rosy and bright. She felt so thrilled that she must needs walk back to the hotel to think, wondering what she should do.

It does not take money long to make plain its impotence, providing the desires are in the realm of affection. With her one hundred and fifty in hand, Carrie could think of nothing particularly to do. In itself, as a tangible, apparent thing which she could touch and look upon, it was a diverting thing for a few days, but this soon passed. Her hotel bill did not require its use. Her clothes had for some time been wholly satisfactory. Another day or two and she would receive another hundred and fifty. It began to appear as if this were not so startlingly necessary to maintain her present state. If she wanted to do anything better or move higher she must have more—a great deal more.

Now a critic called to get up one of those tinsel interviews which shine with clever observations, show up the wit of critics, display the folly of celebrities, and divert the public. He liked Carrie, and said so, publicly—adding, however, that she was merely pretty, good-natured, and lucky. This cut like a knife. The "Herald," getting up an entertainment for the benefit of its free ice fund, did her the honour to beg her to appear along with celebrities for nothing. She was visited by a young author, who had a play which he thought she could produce. Alas, she could not judge. It hurt her to think it. Then she found she must put her money in the bank for safety, and so moving, finally reached the place where it struck her that the door to life's perfect enjoyment was not open.

Gradually she began to think it was because it was summer. Nothing was going on much save such entertainments as the one in which she was star. Fifth Avenue was boarded up where the rich had deserted their mansions. Madison Avenue was little better. Broadway was full of loafing thespians in search of next season engagements. The whole city was quiet and her nights were taken up with her work. Hence the feeling that there was little to do.

"I don't know," she said to Lola one day, sitting at one of the windows which looked down into Broadway, "I get lonely; don't you?"

"No," said Lola, "not very often. You won't go anywhere. That's what's the matter with you."

"Where can I go?"

"Why, there're lots of places," returned Lola, who was thinking of her own lightsome tourneys with the gay youths. "You won't go with anybody."

"I don't want to go with these people who write to me. I know what kind they are."

"You oughtn't to be lonely," said Lola, thinking of Carrie's success. "There're lots would give their ears to be in your shoes."

Carrie looked out again at the passing crowd.

"I don't know," she said.

Unconsciously her idle hands were beginning to weary.

Chapter XLV

CURIOUS SHIFTS OF THE POOR[1]

The gloomy Hurstwood, sitting in his cheap hotel, where he had taken refuge with seventy dollars—the price of his furniture—between him and nothing, saw a hot summer out and a cool fall in, reading. He was not wholly indifferent to the fact that his money was slipping away. As fifty cents after fifty cents were paid out for a day's lodging he became uneasy, and finally took a cheaper room—thirty-five cents a day—to make his money last longer. Frequently he saw notices of Carrie. Her picture was in the "World" once or twice, and an old "Herald" he found in a chair informed him that she had recently appeared with some others at a benefit for something or other. He read these things with mingled feelings. Each one seemed to put her farther and farther away into a realm which became more imposing as it receded from him. On the bill-boards, too, he saw a pretty poster, showing her as the Quaker Maid, demure and dainty. More than once he stopped and looked at these, gazing at the pretty face in a sullen sort of way. His clothes were shabby, and he presented a marked contrast to all that she now seemed to be.

1. The title of Dreiser's November 1899 article in *Demorest's Magazine*. See pp. 403–12.

Somehow, so long as he knew she was at the Casino, though he had never any intention of going near her, there was a subconscious comfort for him—he was not quite alone. The show seemed such a fixture that, after a month or two, he began to take it for granted that it was still running. In September it went on the road and he did not notice it. When all but twenty dollars of his money was gone, he moved to a fifteen-cent lodging-house in the Bowery, where there was a bare lounging-room filled with tables and benches as well as some chairs. Here his preference was to close his eyes and dream of other days, a habit which grew upon him. It was not sleep at first, but a mental hearkening back to scenes and incidents in his Chicago life. As the present became darker, the past grew brighter, and all that concerned it stood in relief.

He was unconscious of just how much this habit had hold of him until one day he found his lips repeating an old answer he had made to one of his friends. They were in Fitzgerald and Moy's. It was as if he stood in the door of his elegant little office, comfortably dressed, talking to Sagar Morrison about the value of South Chicago real estate in which the latter was about to invest.

"How would you like to come in on that with me?" he heard Morrison say.

"Not me," he answered, just as he had years before. "I have my hands full now."

The movement of his lips aroused him. He wondered whether he had really spoken. The next time he noticed anything of the sort he did talk.

"Why don't you jump, you bloody fool?" he was saying. "Jump!"

It was a funny English story he was telling to a company of actors. Even as his voice recalled him, he was smiling. A crusty old codger, sitting near by, seemed disturbed; at least, he stared in a most pointed way. Hurstwood straightened up. The humour of the memory fled in an instant and he felt ashamed. For relief, he left his chair and strolled out into the streets.

One day, looking down the ad. columns of the "Evening World," he saw where a new play was at the Casino. Instantly, he came to a mental halt. Carrie had gone! He remembered seeing a poster of her only yesterday, but no doubt it was one left uncovered by the new signs. Curiously, this fact shook him up. He had almost to admit that somehow he was depending upon her being in the city. Now she was gone. He wondered how this important fact had skipped him. Goodness knows when she would be back now. Impelled by a nervous fear, he rose and went into the dingy hall, where he counted his remaining money, unseen. There were but ten dollars in all.

He wondered how all these other lodging-house people around him got along. They didn't seem to do anything. Perhaps they begged—unquestionably they did. Many was the dime he had given to such as they in his day. He had seen other men asking for money on the streets. Maybe he could get some that way. There was horror in this thought.

Sitting in the lodging-house room, he came to his last fifty cents. He had saved and counted until his health was affected. His stoutness had gone. With it, even the semblance of a fit in his clothes. Now he decided he must do something, and, walking about, saw another day go by, bringing him down to his last twenty cents—not enough to eat for the morrow.

Summoning all his courage, he crossed to Broadway and up to the Broadway Central hotel. Within a block he halted, undecided. A big, heavy-faced porter was standing at one of the side entrances, looking out. Hurstwood purposed to appeal to him. Walking straight up, he was upon him before he could turn away.

"My friend," he said, recognising even in his plight the man's inferiority, "is there anything about this hotel that I could get to do?"

The porter stared at him the while he continued to talk.

"I'm out of work and out of money and I've got to get something— it doesn't matter what. I don't care to talk about what I've been, but if you'd tell me how to get something to do, I'd be much obliged to you. It wouldn't matter if it only lasted a few days just now. I've got to have something."

The porter still gazed, trying to look indifferent. Then, seeing that Hurstwood was about to go on, he said:

"I've nothing to do with it. You'll have to ask inside."

Curiously, this stirred Hurstwood to further effort.

"I thought you might tell me."

The fellow shook his head irritably.

Inside went the ex-manager and straight to an office off the clerk's desk. One of the managers of the hotel happened to be there. Hurstwood looked him straight in the eye.

"Could you give me something to do for a few days?" he said. "I'm in a position where I have to get something at once."

The comfortable manager looked at him, as much as to say: "Well, I should judge so."

"I came here," explained Hurstwood, nervously, "because I've been a manager myself in my day. I've had bad luck in a way, but I'm not here to tell you that. I want something to do, if only for a week."

The man imagined he saw a feverish gleam in the applicant's eye.

"What hotel did you manage?" he inquired.

"It wasn't a hotel," said Hurstwood. "I was manager of Fitzgerald and Moy's place in Chicago for fifteen years."

"Is that so?" said the hotel man. "How did you come to get out of that?"

The figure of Hurstwood was rather surprising in contrast to the fact.

"Well, by foolishness of my own. It isn't anything to talk about now. You could find out if you wanted to. I'm 'broke' now and, if you will believe me, I haven't eaten anything to-day."

The hotel man was slightly interested in this story. He could hardly tell what to do with such a figure, and yet Hurstwood's earnestness made him wish to do something.

"Call Olsen," he said, turning to the clerk.

In reply to a bell and a disappearing hall-boy, Olsen, the head porter, appeared.

"Olsen," said the manager, "is there anything downstairs you could find for this man to do? I'd like to give him something."

"I don't know, sir," said Olsen. "We have about all the help we need. I think I could find something, sir, though, if you like."

"Do. Take him to the kitchen and tell Wilson to give him something to eat."

"All right, sir," said Olsen.

Hurstwood followed. Out of the manager's sight, the head porter's manner changed.

"I don't know what the devil there is to do," he observed.

Hurstwood said nothing. To him the big trunk hustler was a subject for private contempt.

"You're to give this man something to eat," he observed to the cook.

The latter looked Hurstwood over, and seeing something keen and intellectual in his eyes, said:

"Well, sit down over there."

Thus was Hurstwood installed in the Broadway Central, but not for long. He was in no shape or mood to do the scrub work that exists about the foundation of every hotel. Nothing better offering, he was set to aid the fireman, to work about the basement, to do anything and everything that might offer. Porters, cooks, firemen, clerks—all were over him. Moreover his appearance did not please these individuals—his temper was too lonely—and they made it disagreeable for him.

With the stolidity and indifference of despair, however, he endured it all, sleeping in an attic at the roof of the house, eating what the cook gave him, accepting a few dollars a week, which he tried to save. His constitution was in no shape to endure.

One day the following February he was sent on an errand to a large coal company's office. It had been snowing and thawing and the streets were sloppy. He soaked his shoes in his progress and came back feeling dull and weary. All the next day he felt unusually depressed and sat about as much as possible, to the irritation of those who admired energy in others.

In the afternoon some boxes were to be moved to make room for new culinary supplies. He was ordered to handle a truck. Encountering a big box, he could not lift it.

"What's the matter there?" said the head porter. "Can't you handle it?"

He was straining hard to lift it, but now he quit.

"No," he said, weakly.

The man looked at him and saw that he was deathly pale.

"Not sick, are you?" he asked.

"I think I am," returned Hurstwood.

"Well, you'd better go sit down, then."

This he did, but soon grew rapidly worse. It seemed all he could do to crawl to his room, where he remained for a day.

"That man Wheeler's sick," reported one of the lackeys to the night clerk.

"What's the matter with him?"

"I don't know. He's got a high fever."

The hotel physician looked at him.

"Better send him to Bellevue," he recommended. "He's got pneumonia."[2]

Accordingly, he was carted away.

In three weeks the worst was over, but it was nearly the first of May before his strength permitted him to be turned out. Then he was discharged.

No more weakly looking object ever strolled out into the spring sunshine than the once hale, lusty manager. All his corpulency had fled. His face was thin and pale, his hands white, his body flabby. Clothes and all, he weighed but one hundred and thirty-five pounds. Some old garments had been given him—a cheap brown coat and misfit pair of trousers. Also some change and advice. He was told to apply to the charities.

Again he resorted to the Bowery lodging-house, brooding over where to look. From this it was but a step to beggary.

"What can a man do?" he said. "I can't starve."

His first application was in sunny Second Avenue. A well-dressed man came leisurely strolling toward him out of Stuyvesant Park. Hurstwood nerved himself and sidled near.

"Would you mind giving me ten cents?" he said, directly. "I'm in a position where I must ask someone."

The man scarcely looked at him, but fished in his vest pocket and took out a dime.

"There you are," he said.

---

2. The largest charity hospital in New York, on First Avenue and Twenty-Sixth.

"Much obliged," said Hurstwood, softly, but the other paid no more attention to him.

Satisfied with his success and yet ashamed of his situation, he decided that he would only ask for twenty-five cents more, since that would be sufficient. He strolled about sizing up people, but it was long before just the right face and situation arrived. When he asked, he was refused. Shocked by this result, he took an hour to recover and then asked again. This time a nickel was given him. By the most watchful effort he did get twenty cents more, but it was painful.

The next day he resorted to the same effort, experiencing a variety of rebuffs and one or two generous receptions. At last it crossed his mind that there was a science of faces, and that a man could pick the liberal countenance if he tried.

It was no pleasure to him, however, this stopping of passers-by. He saw one man taken up for it and now troubled lest he should be arrested. Nevertheless, he went on, vaguely anticipating that indefinite something which is always better.

It was with a sense of satisfaction, then, that he saw announced one morning the return of the Casino Company, "with Miss Carrie Madenda." He had thought of her often enough in days past. How successful she was—how much money she must have! Even now, however, it took a severe run of ill-luck to decide him to appeal to her. He was truly hungry before he said:

"I'll ask her. She won't refuse me a few dollars."

Accordingly, he headed for the Casino one afternoon, passing it several times in an effort to locate the stage entrance. Then he sat in Bryant Park, a block away, waiting. "She can't refuse to help me a little," he kept saying to himself.

Beginning with half-past six, he hovered like a shadow about the Thirty-ninth Street entrance, pretending always to be a hurrying pedestrian and yet fearful lest he should miss his object. He was slightly nervous, too, now that the eventful hour had arrived, but being weak and hungry, his ability to suffer was modified. At last he saw that the actors were beginning to arrive, and his nervous tension increased, until it seemed as if he could not stand much more.

Once he thought he saw Carrie coming and moved forward, only to see that he was mistaken.

"She can't be long, now," he said to himself, half fearing to encounter her and equally depressed at the thought that she might have gone in by another way. His stomach was so empty that it ached.

Individual after individual passed him, nearly all well dressed, almost all indifferent. He saw coaches rolling by, gentlemen passing with ladies—the evening's merriment was beginning in this region of theatres and hotels.

Suddenly a coach rolled up and the driver jumped down to open
the door. Before Hurstwood could act, two ladies flounced across
the broad walk and disappeared in the stage door. He thought he
saw Carrie, but it was so unexpected, so elegant and far away, he
could hardly tell. He waited a while longer, growing feverish with
want, and then seeing that the stage door no longer opened, and that
a merry audience was arriving, he concluded it must have been Carrie and turned away.

"Lord," he said, hastening out of the street into which the more
fortunate were pouring, "I've got to get something."

At that hour, when Broadway is wont to assume its most interesting aspect, a peculiar individual invariably took his stand at the corner of Twenty-sixth Street and Broadway—a spot which is also
intersected by Fifth Avenue.[3] This was the hour when the theatres
were just beginning to receive their patrons. Fire signs announcing
the night's amusements blazed on every hand.[4] Cabs and carriages,
their lamps gleaming like yellow eyes, pattered by. Couples and parties of three and four freely mingled in the common crowd, which
poured by in a thick stream, laughing and jesting. On Fifth Avenue
were loungers—a few wealthy strollers, a gentleman in evening dress
with his lady on his arm, some clubmen passing from one smoking-
room to another. Across the way the great hotels showed a hundred
gleaming windows, their cafés and billiard-rooms filled with a comfortable, well-dressed, and pleasure-loving throng. All about was the
night, pulsating with the thoughts of pleasure and exhilaration—the
curious enthusiasm of a great city bent upon finding joy in a thousand different ways.[5]

3. That is, at one of the corners of Madison Square Park, in the heart of the theater district.
4. Outdoor electric advertising ("fire signs") was first used in New York in 1891. By the mid-
   1890s such advertising ran the length of Broadway, making it the "Great White Way."
5. Dreiser's pictorial sense of this and other characteristic New York scenes was probably
   influenced by the illustrator W. L. Sonntag, Jr., with whom he became friends in 1895.
   Sonntag died in 1898, and in 1901 Dreiser recalled him in "The Color of Today," *Harper's
   Weekly* 45 (December 14, 1901): 1272–73. He remembered in particular an occasion
   when he and Sonntag were walking on Broadway:

   The street, as usual, was crowded. On every hand blazed the fire signs. The yellow light
   was beautifully reflected in the wet sidewalks and gray cobblestones shiny with water.
        When we reached Greeley Square, that brilliant and almost sputtering spectacle of light
   and merriment, S——took me by the arm.
        "Come over here," he said. "I want you to look at it from here."
        He took me to a point where by the intersection of the lines of the converging streets,
   one could not only see Greeley Square, but a large part of Herald Square, with its huge
   theatrical sign of fire and its measure of store lights and lamps of vehicles. It was, of
   course, an inspiring scene. The broad, converging walks were alive with people. A perfect
   jam of vehicles marked the spot where the horse and cable cars intersected. Overhead was
   the elevated station, its lights augmented every few minutes by long trains of brightly
   lighted cars filled with truly metropolitan crowds.
        "Do you see the quality of that? Look at the blend of the lights and shadows in there
   under the L."
        I looked and gazed in silent admiration.
        "See, right here before us—that pool of water there—do you get that? Now, that isn't

This unique individual was no less than an ex-soldier turned religionist, who, having suffered the whips and privations of our peculiar social system, had concluded that his duty to the God which he conceived lay in aiding his fellow-man. The form of aid which he chose to administer was entirely original with himself. It consisted of securing a bed for all such homeless wayfarers as should apply to him at this particular spot, though he had scarcely the wherewithal to provide a comfortable habitation for himself.

Taking his place amid this lightsome atmosphere, he would stand, his stocky figure cloaked in a great cape overcoat, his head protected by a broad slouch hat, awaiting the applicants who had in various ways learned the nature of his charity. For a while he would stand alone, gazing like any idler upon an ever-fascinating scene. On the evening in question, a policeman passing saluted him as "captain," in a friendly way. An urchin who had frequently seen him before, stopped to gaze. All others took him for nothing out of the ordinary, save in the matter of dress, and conceived of him as a stranger whistling and idling for his own amusement.

As the first half-hour waned, certain characters appeared. Here and there in the passing crowds one might see, now and then, a loiterer edging interestedly near. A slouchy figure crossed the opposite corner and glanced furtively in his direction. Another came down Fifth Avenue to the corner of Twenty-sixth Street, took a general survey, and hobbled off again. Two or three noticeable Bowery types edged along the Fifth Avenue side of Madison Square, but did not venture over. The soldier, in his cape over-coat, walked a short line of ten feet at his corner, to and fro, indifferently whistling.

As nine o'clock approached, some of the hubbub of the earlier hour passed. The atmosphere of the hotels was not so youthful. The air, too, was colder. On every hand curious figures were moving— watchers and peepers, without an imaginary circle, which they seemed afraid to enter—a dozen in all. Presently, with the arrival of a keener sense of cold, one figure came forward. It crossed Broadway from out the shadow of Twenty-sixth Street, and, in a halting, circuitous way, arrived close to the waiting figure. There was something

---

silver colored, as it's usually represented. It's a prism. Don't you see the hundred points of light?"

I acknowledged the variety of color, which I had scarcely observed before.

"You may think one would skip that in viewing a great scene, but the artist mustn't. He must get that all, whether you notice it or not. It gives feeling, even when you don't see it."

I acknowledged the value of this ideal.

"It's a great spectacle," he said. "It's got more flesh and blood in it than people usually think for."

"Why don't you paint it?" I asked.

He turned on me as if he had been waiting for the suggestion.

"That's something I want to tell you," he said. "I am. I've sketched it a half-dozen times already. I haven't got it yet. But I'm going to."

shamefaced or diffident about the movement, as if the intention were to conceal any idea of stopping until the very last moment. Then suddenly, close to the soldier, came the halt.

The captain looked in recognition, but there was no especial greeting. The newcomer nodded slightly and murmured something like one who waits for gifts. The other simply motioned toward the edge of the walk.

"Stand over there," he said.

By this the spell was broken. Even while the soldier resumed his short, solemn walk, other figures shuffled forward. They did not so much as greet the leader, but joined the one, sniffling and hitching and scraping their feet.

"Cold, ain't it?"

"I'm glad winter's over."

"Looks as though it might rain."

The motley company had increased to ten. One or two knew each other and conversed. Others stood off a few feet, not wishing to be in the crowd and yet not counted out. They were peevish, crusty, silent, eying nothing in particular and moving their feet.

There would have been talking soon, but the soldier gave them no chance. Counting sufficient to begin, he came forward.

"Beds, eh, all of you?"

There was a general shuffle and murmur of approval.

"Well, line up here. I'll see what I can do. I haven't a cent myself."

They fell into a sort of broken, ragged line. One might see, now, some of the chief characteristics by contrast. There was a wooden leg in the line. Hats were all drooping, a group that would ill become a second-hand Hester Street basement collection.[6] Trousers were all warped and frayed at the bottom and coats worn and faded. In the glare of the store lights, some of the faces looked dry and chalky; others were red with blotches and puffed in the cheeks and under the eyes; one or two were rawboned and reminded one of railroad hands. A few spectators came near, drawn by the seemingly conferring group, then more and more, and quickly there was a pushing, gaping crowd. Some one in the line began to talk.

"Silence!" exclaimed the captain. "Now, then, gentlemen, these men are without beds. They have to have some place to sleep tonight. They can't lie out in the streets. I need twelve cents to put one of them to bed. Who will give it to me?"

No reply.

"Well, we'll have to wait here, boys, until some one does. Twelve cents isn't so very much for one man."

6. A cheap shopping street in the Jewish section of the lower East Side.

"Here's fifteen," exclaimed a young man, peering forward with strained eyes. "It's all I can afford."

"All right. Now I have fifteen. Step out of the line," and seizing one by the shoulder, the captain marched him off a little way and stood him up alone.

Coming back, he resumed his place and began again.

"I have three cents left. These men must be put to bed somehow. There are"—counting—"one, two, three, four, five, six, seven, eight, nine, ten, eleven, twelve men. Nine cents more will put the next man to bed; give him a good, comfortable bed for the night. I go right along and look after that myself. Who will give me nine cents?"

One of the watchers, this time a middle-aged man, handed him a five-cent piece.

"Now, I have eight cents. Four more will give this man a bed. Come, gentlemen. We are going very slow this evening. You all have good beds. How about these?"

"Here you are," remarked a bystander, putting a coin into his hand.

"That," said the captain, looking at the coin, "pays for two beds for two men and gives me five on the next one. Who will give me seven cents more?"

"I will," said a voice.

Coming down Sixth Avenue this evening, Hurstwood chanced to cross east through Twenty-sixth Street toward Third Avenue. He was wholly disconsolate in spirit, hungry to what he deemed an almost mortal extent, weary, and defeated. How should he get at Carrie now? It would be eleven before the show was over. If she came in a coach, she would go away in one. He would need to interrupt under most trying circumstances. Worst of all, he was hungry and weary, and at best a whole day must intervene, for he had not heart to try again to-night. He had no food and no bed.

When he neared Broadway, he noticed the captain's gathering of wanderers, but thinking it to be the result of a street preacher or some patent medicine fakir, was about to pass on. However, in crossing the street toward Madison Square Park, he noticed the line of men whose beds were already secured, stretching out from the main body of the crowd. In the glare of the neighbouring electric light he recognised a type of his own kind—the figures whom he saw about the streets and in the lodging-houses, drifting in mind and body like himself. He wondered what it could be and turned back.

There was the captain curtly pleading as before. He heard with astonishment and a sense of relief the oft-repeated words: "These men must have a bed." Before him was the line of unfortunates whose beds were yet to be had, and seeing a newcomer quietly edge up and take a position at the end of the line, he decided to do likewise. What use to contend? He was weary to-night. It was a simple way out of one difficulty, at least. To-morrow, maybe, he would do better.

Back of him, where some of those were whose beds were safe, a relaxed air was apparent. The strain of uncertainty being removed, he heard them talking with moderate freedom and some leaning toward sociability. Politics, religion, the state of the government, some newspaper sensations, and the more notorious facts the world over, found mouthpieces and auditors there. Cracked and husky voices pronounced forcibly upon odd matters. Vague and rambling observations were made in reply.

There were squints, and leers, and some dull, ox-like stares from those who were too dull or too weary to converse.

Standing tells. Hurstwood became more weary waiting. He thought he should drop soon and shifted restlessly from one foot to the other. At last his turn came. The man ahead had been paid for and gone to the blessed line of success. He was now first, and already the captain was talking for him.

"Twelve cents, gentlemen—twelve cents puts this man to bed. He wouldn't stand here in the cold if he had any place to go." Hurstwood swallowed something that rose to his throat. Hunger and weakness had made a coward of him.

"Here you are," said a stranger, handing money to the captain.

Now the latter put a kindly hand on the ex-manager's shoulder.

"Line up over there," he said.

Once there, Hurstwood breathed easier. He felt as if the world were not quite so bad with such a good man in it. Others seemed to feel like himself about this.

"Captain's a great feller, ain't he?" said the man ahead—a little, woe-begone, helpless-looking sort of individual, who looked as though he had ever been the sport and care of fortune.

"Yes," said Hurstwood, indifferently.

"Huh! there's a lot back there yet," said a man farther up, leaning out and looking back at the applicants for whom the captain was pleading.

"Yes. Must be over a hundred to-night," said another.

"Look at the guy in the cab," observed a third.

A cab had stopped. Some gentleman in evening dress reached out a bill to the captain, who took it with simple thanks and turned away to his line. There was a general craning of necks as the jewel in the white shirt front sparkled and the cab moved off. Even the crowd gaped in awe.

"That fixes up nine men for the night," said the captain, counting out as many of the line near him. "Line up over there. Now, then, there are only seven. I need twelve cents."

Money came slowly. In the course of time the crowd thinned out to a meagre handful. Fifth Avenue, save for an occasional cab or foot passenger, was bare. Broadway was thinly peopled with pedestrians. Only now and then a stranger passing noticed the small group, handed out a coin, and went away, unheeding.

The captain remained stolid and determined. He talked on, very slowly, uttering the fewest words and with a certain assurance, as though he could not fail.

"Come; I can't stay out here all night. These men are getting tired and cold. Some one give me four cents."

There came a time when he said nothing at all. Money was handed him, and for each twelve cents he singled out a man and put him in the other line. Then he walked up and down as before, looking at the ground.

The theatres let out. Fire signs disappeared. A clock struck eleven. Another half-hour and he was down to the last two men.

"Come, now," he exclaimed to several curious observers; "eighteen cents will fix us all up for the night. Eighteen cents. I have six. Somebody give me the money. Remember, I have to go over to Brooklyn yet to-night. Before that I have to take these men down and put them to bed. Eighteen cents."

No one responded. He walked to and fro, looking down for several minutes, occasionally saying softly: "Eighteen cents." It seemed as if this paltry sum would delay the desired culmination longer than all the rest had. Hurstwood, buoyed up slightly by the long line of which he was a part, refrained with an effort from groaning, he was so weak.

At last a lady in opera cape and rustling skirts came down Fifth Avenue, accompanied by her escort. Hurstwood gazed wearily, reminded by her both of Carrie in her new world and of the time when he had escorted his own wife in like manner.

While he was gazing, she turned and, looking at the remarkable company, sent her escort over. He came, holding a bill in his fingers, all elegant and graceful.

"Here you are," he said.

"Thanks," said the captain, turning to the two remaining applicants. "Now we have some for to-morrow night," he added.

Therewith he lined up the last two and proceeded to the head, counting as he went.

"One hundred and thirty-seven," he announced. "Now, boys, line up. Right dress there. We won't be much longer about this. Steady, now."

He placed himself at the head and called out "Forward." Hurstwood moved with the line. Across Fifth Avenue, through Madison Square by the winding paths, east on Twenty-third Street, and down Third Avenue wound the long, serpentine company. Midnight pedestrians and loiterers stopped and stared as the company passed. Chatting policemen, at various corners, stared indifferently or nodded to the leader, whom they had seen before. On Third Avenue they marched, a seemingly weary way, to Eighth Street, where there was a lodging-house,[7] closed, apparently, for the night. They were expected, however.

Outside in the gloom they stood, while the leader parleyed within. Then doors swung open and they were invited in with a "Steady, now."

Some one was at the head showing rooms, so that there was no delay for keys. Toiling up the creaky stairs, Hurstwood looked back and saw the captain, watching; the last one of the line being included in his broad solicitude. Then he gathered his cloak about him and strolled out into the night.

"I can't stand much of this," said Hurstwood, whose legs ached him painfully, as he sat down upon the miserable bunk in the small, lightless chamber allotted to him. "I've got to eat, or I'll die."

Chapter XLVI

STIRRING TROUBLED WATERS

Playing in New York one evening on this her return, Carrie was putting the finishing touches to her toilet before leaving for the night, when a commotion near the stage door caught her ear. It included a familiar voice.

"Never mind, now. I want to see Miss Madenda."

"You'll have to send in your card."

"Oh, come off! Here."

A half-dollar was passed over, and now a knock came at her dressing-room door.

Carrie opened it.

"Well, well!" said Drouet. "I do swear! Why, how are you? I knew that was you the moment I saw you."

Carrie fell back a pace, expecting a most embarrassing conversation.

"Aren't you going to shake hands with me? Well, you're a dandy! That's all right, shake hands."

Carrie put out her hand, smiling, if for nothing more than the man's exuberant good-nature. Though older, he was but slightly changed. The same fine clothes, the same stocky body, the same rosy countenance.

"That fellow at the door there didn't want to let me in, until I paid

7. On the northeast edge of the Bowery area.

him. I knew it was you, all right. Say, you've got a great show. You do your part fine. I knew you would. I just happened to be passing tonight and thought I'd drop in for a few minutes. I saw your name on the programme, but I didn't remember it until you came on the stage. Then it struck me all at once. Say, you could have knocked me down with a feather. That's the same name you used out there in Chicago, isn't it?"

"Yes," answered Carrie, mildly, overwhelmed by the man's assurance.

"I knew it was, the moment I saw you. Well, how have you been, anyhow?"

"Oh, very well," said Carrie, lingering in her dressing-room. She was rather dazed by the assault. "How have you been?"

"Me? Oh, fine. I'm here now."

"Is that so?" said Carrie.

"Yes. I've been here for six months. I've got charge of a branch here."

"How nice!"

"Well, when did you go on the stage, anyhow?" inquired Drouet.

"About three years ago," said Carrie.

"You don't say so! Well, sir, this is the first I've heard of it. I knew you would, though. I always said you could act—didn't I?"

Carrie smiled.

"Yes, you did," she said.

"Well, you do look great," he said. "I never saw anybody improve so. You're taller, aren't you?"

"Me? Oh, a little, maybe."

He gazed at her dress, then at her hair, where a becoming hat was set jauntily, then into her eyes, which she took all occasion to avert. Evidently he expected to restore their old friendship at once and without modification.

"Well," he said, seeing her gather up her purse, handkerchief, and the like, preparatory to departing, "I want you to come out to dinner with me; won't you? I've got a friend out here."

"Oh, I can't," said Carrie. "Not to-night. I have an early engagement to-morrow."

"Aw, let the engagement go. Come on. I can get rid of him. I want to have a good talk with you."

"No, no," said Carrie; "I can't. You mustn't ask me any more. I don't care for a late dinner."

"Well, come on and have a talk, then, anyhow."

"Not to-night," she said, shaking her head. "We'll have a talk some other time."

As a result of this, she noticed a shade of thought pass over his face, as if he were beginning to realise that things were changed. Good-nature dictated something better than this for one who had always liked her.

"You come around to the hotel to-morrow," she said, as sort of penance for error. "You can take dinner with me."

"All right," said Drouet, brightening. "Where are you stopping?"

"At the Waldorf," she answered, mentioning the fashionable hostelry then but newly erected.

"What time?"

"Well, come at three," said Carrie, pleasantly.

The next day Drouet called, but it was with no especial delight that Carrie remembered her appointment. However, seeing him, handsome as ever, after his kind, and most genially disposed, her doubts as to whether the dinner would be disagreeable were swept away. He talked as volubly as ever.

"They put on a lot of lugs here, don't they?" was his first remark.

"Yes; they do," said Carrie.

Genial egotist that he was, he went at once into a detailed account of his own career.

"I'm going to have a business of my own pretty soon," he observed in one place. "I can get backing for two hundred thousand dollars."

Carrie listened most good-naturedly.

"Say," he said, suddenly; "where is Hurstwood now?"

Carrie flushed a little.

"He's here in New York, I guess," she said. "I haven't seen him for some time."

Drouet mused for a moment. He had not been sure until now that the ex-manager was not an influential figure in the background. He imagined not; but this assurance relieved him. It must be that Carrie had got rid of him—as well she ought, he thought.

"A man always makes a mistake when he does anything like that," he observed.

"Like what?" said Carrie, unwitting of what was coming.

"Oh, you know," and Drouet waved her intelligence, as it were, with his hand.

"No, I don't," she answered. "What do you mean?"

"Why that affair in Chicago—the time he left."

"I don't know what you are talking about," said Carrie. Could it be he would refer so rudely to Hurstwood's flight with her?

"Oho!" said Drouet, incredulously. "You knew he took ten thousand dollars with him when he left, didn't you?"

"What!" said Carrie. "You don't mean to say he stole money, do you?"

"Why," said Drouet, puzzled at her tone, "you knew that, didn't you?"

"Why, no," said Carrie. "Of course I didn't."

"Well, that's funny," said Drouet. "He did, you know. It was in all the papers."

"How much did you say he took?" said Carrie.

"Ten thousand dollars. I heard he sent most of it back afterwards, though."

Carrie looked vacantly at the richly carpeted floor. A new light was shining upon all the years since her enforced flight. She remembered now a hundred things that indicated as much. She also imagined that he took it on her account. Instead of hatred springing up there was a kind of sorrow generated. Poor fellow! What a thing to have had hanging over his head all the time.

At dinner Drouet, warmed up by eating and drinking and softened in mood, fancied he was winning Carrie to her old-time good-natured regard for him. He began to imagine it would not be so difficult to enter into her life again, high as she was. Ah, what a prize! he thought. How beautiful, how elegant, how famous! In her theatrical and Waldorf setting, Carrie was to him the all-desirable.

"Do you remember how nervous you were that night at the Avery?" he asked.

Carrie smiled to think of it.

"I never saw anybody do better than you did then, Cad," he added ruefully, as he leaned an elbow on the table; "I thought you and I were going to get along fine those days."

"You mustn't talk that way," said Carrie, bringing in the least touch of coldness.

"Won't you let me tell you——"

"No," she answered, rising. "Besides, it's time I was getting ready for the theatre. I'll have to leave you. Come, now."

"Oh, stay a minute," pleaded Drouet. "You've got plenty of time."

"No," said Carrie, gently.

Reluctantly Drouet gave up the bright table and followed. He saw her to the elevator and, standing there, said:

"When do I see you again?"

"Oh, some time, possibly," said Carrie. "I'll be here all summer. Good-night!"

The elevator door was open.

"Good-night!" said Drouet, as she rustled in.

Then he strolled sadly down the hall, all his old longing revived, because she was now so far off. He thought himself hardly dealt with. Carrie, however, had other thoughts.

That night it was that she passed Hurstwood, waiting at the Casino, without observing him.

The next night, walking to the theatre, she encountered him face to face. He was waiting, more gaunt than ever, determined to see her, if he had to send in word. At first she did not recognise the shabby, baggy figure. He frightened her, edging so close, a seemingly hungry stranger.

"Carrie," he half whispered, "can I have a few words with you?"

She turned and recognised him on the instant. If there ever had lurked any feeling in her heart against him, it deserted her now. Still, she remembered what Drouet said about his having stolen the money.

"Why, George," she said; "what's the matter with you?"

"I've been sick," he answered. "I've just got out of the hospital. For God's sake, let me have a little money, will you?"

"Of course," said Carrie, her lip trembling in a strong effort to maintain her composure. "But what's the matter with you, anyhow?"

She was opening her purse, and now pulled out all the bills in it—a five and two twos.

"I've been sick, I told you," he said, peevishly, almost resenting her excessive pity. It came hard to him to receive it from such a source.

"Here," she said. "It's all I have with me."

"All right," he answered, softly. "I'll give it back to you some day."

Carrie looked at him, while pedestrians stared at her. She felt the strain of publicity. So did Hurstwood.

"Why don't you tell me what's the matter with you?" she asked, hardly knowing what to do. "Where are you living?"

"Oh, I've got a room down in the Bowery," he answered. "There's no use trying to tell you here. I'm all right now."

He seemed in a way to resent her kindly inquiries—so much better had fate dealt with her.

"Better go on in," he said. "I'm much obliged, but I won't bother you any more."

She tried to answer, but he turned away and shuffled off toward the east.

For days this apparition was a drag on her soul before it began to wear partially away. Drouet called again, but now he was not even seen by her. His attentions seemed out of place.

"I'm out," was her reply to the boy.

So peculiar, indeed, was her lonely, self-withdrawing temper, that she was becoming an interesting figure in the public eye—she was so quiet and reserved.

Not long after the management decided to transfer the show to London. A second summer season did not seem to promise well here.

"How would you like to try subduing London?" asked her manager, one afternoon.

"It might be just the other way," said Carrie.

"I think we'll go in June," he answered.

In the hurry of departure, Hurstwood was forgotten. Both he and Drouet were left to discover that she was gone. The latter called once, and exclaimed at the news. Then he stood in the lobby, chewing the ends of his moustache. At last he reached a conclusion—the old days had gone for good.

"She isn't so much," he said; but in his heart of hearts he did not believe this.

Hurstwood shifted by curious means through a long summer and fall. A small job as janitor of a dance hall helped him for a month. Begging, sometimes going hungry, sometimes sleeping in the park, carried him over more days. Resorting to those peculiar charities, several of which, in the press of hungry search, he accidentally stumbled upon, did the rest. Toward the dead of winter, Carrie came back, appearing on Broadway in a new play; but he was not aware of it. For weeks he wandered about the city, begging, while the fire sign, announcing her engagement, blazed nightly upon the crowded street of amusements. Drouet saw it, but did not venture in.

About this time Ames returned to New York.[1] He had made a little success in the West, and now opened a laboratory in Wooster Street. Of course, he encountered Carrie through Mrs. Vance; but there was nothing responsive between them. He thought she was still united to Hurstwood, until otherwise informed. Not knowing the facts then, he did not profess to understand, and refrained from comment.

With Mrs. Vance, he saw the new play, and expressed himself accordingly.

"She ought not to be in comedy," he said. "I think she could do better than that."

One afternoon they met at the Vances' accidentally, and began a very friendly conversation. She could hardly tell why the one-time keen interest in him was no longer with her. Unquestionably, it was because at that time he had represented something which she did not have; but this she did not understand. Success had given her the momentary feeling that she was now blessed with much of which he would approve. As a matter of fact, her little newspaper fame was nothing at all to him. He thought she could have done better, by far.

"You didn't go into comedy-drama, after all?" he said, remembering her interest in that form of art.[2]

"No," she answered; "I haven't, so far."

He looked at her in such a peculiar way that she realised she had failed. It moved her to add: "I want to, though."

1. From this point to the end of the chapter, Dreiser severely revised and cut his initial version of Carrie's final encounters with Ames. See p. 423 and, for an omitted passage, pp. 367–69, below.
2. "Comedy-drama" (as becomes apparent on pp. 341–42) was a term for any serious play not a tragedy.

"I should think you would," he said. "You have the sort of disposition that would do well in comedy-drama."

It surprised her that he should speak of disposition. Was she, then, so clearly in his mind?

"Why?" she asked.

"Well," he said, "I should judge you were rather sympathetic in your nature."

Carrie smiled and coloured slightly. He was so innocently frank with her that she drew nearer in friendship. The old call of the ideal was sounding.

"I don't know," she answered, pleased, nevertheless, beyond all concealment.

"I saw your play," he remarked. "It's very good."

"I'm glad you liked it."

"Very good, indeed," he said, "for a comedy."

This is all that was said at the time, owing to an interruption, but later they met again. He was sitting in a corner after dinner, staring at the floor, when Carrie came up with another of the guests. Hard work had given his face the look of one who is weary. It was not for Carrie to know the thing in it which appealed to her.

"All alone?" she said.

"I was listening to the music."

"I'll be back in a moment," said her companion, who saw nothing in the inventor.

Now he looked up in her face, for she was standing a moment, while he sat.

"Isn't that a pathetic strain?" he inquired, listening.

"Oh, very," she returned, also catching it, now that her attention was called.

"Sit down," he added, offering her the chair beside him.

They listened a few moments in silence, touched by the same feeling, only hers reached her through the heart. Music still charmed her as in the old days.

"I don't know what it is about music," she started to say, moved by the inexplicable longings which surged within her; "but it always makes me feel as if I wanted something—I——"

"Yes," he replied; "I know how you feel."

Suddenly he turned to considering the peculiarity of her disposition, expressing her feelings so frankly.

"You ought not to be melancholy," he said.

He thought a while, and then went off into a seemingly alien observation which, however, accorded with their feelings.

"The world is full of desirable situations, but, unfortunately, we can occupy but one at a time. It doesn't do us any good to wring our hands over the far-off things."

The music ceased and he arose, taking a standing position before her, as if to rest himself.

"Why don't you get into some good, strong comedy-drama?" he said. He was looking directly at her now, studying her face. Her large, sympathetic eyes and pain-touched mouth appealed to him as proofs of his judgment.

"Perhaps I shall," she returned.

"That's your field," he added.

"Do you think so?"

"Yes," he said, "I do. I don't suppose you're aware of it, but there is something about your eyes and mouth which fits you for that sort of work."

Carrie thrilled to be taken so seriously. For the moment, loneliness deserted her. Here was praise which was keen and analytical.

"It's in your eyes and mouth," he went on abstractedly. "I remember thinking, the first time I saw you, that there was something peculiar about your mouth. I thought you were about to cry."

"How odd," said Carrie, warm with delight. This was what her heart craved.

"Then I noticed that that was your natural look, and to-night I saw it again. There's a shadow about your eyes, too, which gives your face much this same character. It's in the depth of them, I think."

Carrie looked straight into his face, wholly aroused.

"You probably are not aware of it," he added.

She looked away, pleased that he should speak thus, longing to be equal to this feeling written upon her countenance. It unlocked the door to a new desire.

She had cause to ponder over this until they met again—several weeks or more. It showed her she was drifting away from the old ideal which had filled her in the dressing-rooms of the Avery stage and thereafter, for a long time. Why had she lost it?

"I know why you should be a success," he said, another time, "if you had a more dramatic part. I've studied it out——"

"What is it?" said Carrie.

"Well," he said, as one pleased with a puzzle, "the expression in your face is one that comes out in different things. You get the same thing in a pathetic song, or any picture which moves you deeply. It's a thing the world likes to see, because it's a natural expression of its longing."

Carrie gazed without exactly getting the import of what he meant.

"The world is always struggling to express itself," he went on. "Most people are not capable of voicing their feelings. They depend upon others. That is what genius is for. One man expresses their desires for them in music; another one in poetry; another one in a play. Sometimes nature does it in a face—it makes the face representative of all desire. That's what has happened in your case."

He looked at her with so much of the import of the thing in his eyes that she caught it. At least, she got the idea that her look was something which represented the world's longing. She took it to heart as a creditable thing, until he added:

"That puts a burden of duty on you. It so happens that you have this thing. It is no credit to you—that is, I mean, you might not have had it. You paid nothing to get it. But now that you have it, you must do something with it."

"What?" asked Carrie.

"I should say, turn to the dramatic field. You have so much sympathy and such a melodious voice. Make them valuable to others. It will make your powers endure."

Carrie did not understand this last. All the rest showed her that her comedy success was little or nothing.

"What do you mean?" she asked.

"Why, just this. You have this quality in your eyes and mouth and in your nature. You can lose it, you know. If you turn away from it and live to satisfy yourself alone, it will go fast enough. The look will leave your eyes. Your mouth will change. Your power to act will disappear. You may think they won't, but they will. Nature takes care of that."

He was so interested in forwarding all good causes that he sometimes became enthusiastic, giving vent to these preachments. Something in Carrie appealed to him. He wanted to stir her up.

"I know," she said, absently, feeling slightly guilty of neglect.

"If I were you," he said, "I'd change."

The effect of this was like roiling helpless waters. Carrie troubled over it in her rocking-chair for days.

"I don't believe I'll stay in comedy so very much longer," she eventually remarked to Lola.

"Oh, why not?" said the latter.

"I think," she said, "I can do better in a serious play."

"What put that idea in your head?"

"Oh, nothing," she answered; "I've always thought so."

Still, she did nothing—grieving. It was a long way to this better thing—or seemed so—and comfort was about her; hence the inactivity and longing.

Chapter XLVII

THE WAY OF THE BEATEN: A HARP IN THE WIND

In the city, at that time, there were a number of charities similar in nature to that of the captain's, which Hurstwood now patronised in a like unfortunate way. One was a convent mission-house of the Sisters of Mercy in Fifteenth Street—a row of red brick family dwellings, before the door of which hung a plain wooden contribution box, on which was painted the statement that every noon a meal was given free to all those who might apply and ask for aid. This simple announcement was modest in the extreme, covering, as it did, charity so broad. Institutions and charities are so large and so numerous in New York that such things as this are not often noticed by the more comfortably situated. But to one whose mind is upon the matter, they grow exceedingly under inspection. Unless one were looking up this matter in particular, he could have stood at Sixth Avenue and Fifteenth Street for days around the noon hour and never have noticed that out of the vast crowd that surged along that busy thoroughfare there turned out, every few seconds, some weather-beaten, heavy-footed specimen of humanity, gaunt in countenance and dilapidated in the matter of clothes. The fact is none the less true, however, and the colder the day the more apparent it became. Space and a lack of culinary room in the mission-house, compelled an arrangement which permitted of only twenty-five or thirty eating at one time, so that a line had to be formed outside and an orderly entrance effected. This caused a daily spectacle which, however, had become so common by repetition during a number of years that now nothing was thought of it. The men waited patiently, like cattle, in the coldest weather—waited for several hours before they could be admitted. No questions were asked and no service rendered. They ate and went away again, some of them returning regularly day after day the winter through.

A big, motherly looking woman invariably stood guard at the door during the entire operation and counted the admissible number. The men moved up in solemn order. There was no haste and no eagerness displayed. It was almost a dumb procession. In the bitterest weather this line was to be found here. Under an icy wind there was a prodigious slapping of hands and a dancing of feet. Fingers and the features of the face looked as if severely nipped by the cold. A study of these men in broad light proved them to be nearly all of a type. They belonged to the class that sit on the park benches during the endurable days and sleep upon them during the summer nights. They frequent the Bowery and those down-at-the-heels East Side streets where poor clothes and shrunken features are not singled out as curious. They are the men who are in the lodging-house sitting-rooms during bleak and bitter weather and who swarm about the cheaper shelters which only open at six in a number of the lower East Side streets. Miserable food, ill-timed and greedily eaten, had played havoc with bone and muscle. They were all pale, flabby, sunken-eyed, hollow-chested, with eyes that glinted and shone and lips that were a sickly red by contrast. Their hair was but half attended to, their ears anæmic in hue, and their shoes broken in leather and run down at heel and toe. They were of the class which simply floats and drifts, every wave of people washing up one, as breakers do driftwood upon a stormy shore.

For nearly a quarter of a century, in another section of the city, Fleischmann, the baker, had given a loaf of bread to any one who would come for it to the side door of his restaurant at the corner of Broadway and Tenth Street, at midnight.[1] Every night during twenty years about three hundred men had formed in line and at the appointed time marched past the doorway, picked their loaf from a great box placed just outside, and vanished again into the night. From the beginning to the present time there had been little change in the character or number of these men. There were two or three figures that had grown familiar to those who had seen this little procession pass year after year. Two of them had missed scarcely a night in fifteen years. There were about forty, more or less, regular callers. The remainder of the line was formed of strangers. In times of panic and unusual hardships there were seldom more than three hundred. In times of prosperity, when little is heard of the unemployed, there were seldom less. The same number, winter and summer, in storm or calm, in good times and bad, held this melancholy midnight rendezvous at Fleischmann's bread box.

At both of these two charities, during the severe winter which was now on, Hurstwood was a frequent visitor. On one occasion it was peculiarly cold, and finding no comfort in begging about the streets, he waited until noon before seeking this free offering to the poor. Already, at eleven o'clock of this morning, several such as he had shambled forward out of Sixth Avenue, their thin clothes flapping and fluttering in the wind. They leaned against the iron railing which protects the walls of the Ninth Regiment Armory, which fronts upon that section of Fifteenth Street, having come early in order to be first in. Having an hour to wait, they at first lingered at a respectful distance; but others coming up, they moved closer in order to protect their right of precedence. To this collection Hurstwood came up from the west out of Seventh Avenue and stopped close to the door, nearer than all the others. Those who had been waiting before him, but farther away, now drew near, and by a certain stolidity of demeanour, no words being spoken, indicated that they were first.

Seeing the opposition to his action, he looked sullenly along the line, then moved out, taking his place at the foot. When order had been restored, the animal feeling of opposition relaxed.

1. Fleischmann's Vienna Model Bakery was a famous Broadway cafe-restaurant in the 1890s. A number of writers before Dreiser had depicted its bread line in their fiction.

"Must be pretty near noon," ventured one.

"It is," said another. "I've been waiting nearly an hour."

"Gee, but it's cold!"

They peered eagerly at the door, where all must enter. A grocery man drove up and carried in several baskets of eatables. This started some words upon grocery men and the cost of food in general.

"I see meat's gone up," said one.

"If there wuz war, it would help this country a lot."

The line was growing rapidly. Already there were fifty or more, and those at the head, by their demeanour, evidently congratulated themselves upon not having so long to wait as those at the foot. There was much jerking of heads, and looking down the line.

"It don't matter how near you get to the front, so long as you're in the first twenty-five," commented one of the first twenty-five. "You all go in together."

"Humph!" ejaculated Hurstwood, who had been so sturdily displaced.

"This here Single Tax is the thing," said another. "There ain't going to be no order till it comes."[2]

For the most part there was silence; gaunt men shuffling, glancing, and beating their arms.

At last the door opened and the motherly-looking sister appeared. She only looked an order. Slowly the line moved up and, one by one, passed in, until twenty-five were counted. Then she interposed a stout arm, and the line halted, with six men on the steps. Of these the ex-manager was one. Waiting thus, some talked, some ejaculated concerning the misery of it; some brooded, as did Hurstwood. At last he was admitted, and, having eaten, came away, almost angered because of his pains in getting it.

At eleven o'clock of another evening, perhaps two weeks later, he was at the midnight offering of a loaf—waiting patiently. It had been an unfortunate day with him, but now he took his fate with a touch of philosophy. If he could secure no supper, or was hungry late in the evening, here was a place he could come. A few minutes before twelve, a great box of bread was pushed out, and exactly on the hour a portly, round-faced German took position by it, calling "Ready." The whole line at once moved forward, each taking his loaf in turn and going his separate way. On this occasion, the ex-manager ate his as he went, plodding the dark streets in silence to his bed.

By January he had about concluded that the game was up with him. Life had always seemed a precious thing, but now constant

2. Henry George's radical single tax movement had a wide following in the 1880s and 1890s. George had almost won the mayoralty of New York in 1886 and he was to run again in November 1897.

want and weakened vitality had made the charms of earth rather dull and inconspicuous. Several times, when fortune pressed most harshly, he thought he would end his troubles; but with a change of weather, or the arrival of a quarter or a dime, his mood would change, and he would wait. Each day he would find some old paper lying about and look into it, to see if there was any trace of Carrie, but all summer and fall he had looked in vain. Then he noticed that his eyes were beginning to hurt him, and this ailment rapidly increased until, in the dark chambers of the lodgings he frequented, he did not attempt to read. Bad and irregular eating was weakening every function of his body. The one recourse left him was to doze when a place offered and he could get the money to occupy it.

He was beginning to find, in his wretched clothing and meagre state of body, that people took him for a chronic type of bum and beggar. Police hustled him along, restaurant and lodging-house keepers turned him out promptly the moment he had his due; pedestrians waved him off. He found it more and more difficult to get anything from anybody.

At last he admitted to himself that the game was up. It was after a long series of appeals to pedestrians, in which he had been refused and refused—every one hastening from contact.

"Give me a little something, will you, mister?" he said to the last one. "For God's sake, do; I'm starving."

"Aw, get out," said the man, who happened to be a common type himself. "You're no good. I'll give you nawthin'."

Hurstwood put his hands, red from cold, down in his pockets. Tears came into his eyes.

"That's right," he said; "I'm no good now. I was all right. I had money. I'm going to quit this," and, with death in his heart, he started down toward the Bowery. People had turned on the gas before and died; why shouldn't he? He remembered a lodging-house where there were little, close rooms, with gas-jets in them, almost pre-arranged, he thought, for what he wanted to do, which rented for fifteen cents. Then he remembered that he had no fifteen cents.

On the way he met a comfortable-looking gentleman, coming, clean-shaven, out of a fine barber shop.

"Would you mind giving me a little something?" he asked this man boldly.

The gentleman looked him over and fished for a dime. Nothing but quarters were in his pocket.

"Here," he said, handing him one, to be rid of him. "Be off, now."

Hurstwood moved on, wondering. The sight of the large, bright coin pleased him a little. He remembered that he was hungry and that he could get a bed for ten cents. With this, the idea of death passed, for the time being, out of his mind. It was only when he could get nothing but insults that death seemed worth while.

One day, in the middle of the winter, the sharpest spell of the season set in. It broke grey and cold in the first day, and on the second snowed. Poor luck pursuing him, he had secured but ten cents by nightfall, and this he had spent for food. At evening he found himself at the Boulevard and Sixty-seventh Street,[3] where he finally turned his face Bowery-ward. Especially fatigued because of the wandering propensity which had seized him in the morning, he now half dragged his wet feet, shuffling the soles upon the sidewalk. An old, thin coat was turned up about his red ears—his cracked derby hat was pulled down until it turned them outward. His hands were in his pockets.

"I'll just go down Broadway," he said to himself.

When he reached Forty-second Street, the fire signs were already blazing brightly. Crowds were hastening to dine. Through bright windows, at every corner, might be seen gay companies in luxuriant restaurants. There were coaches and crowded cable cars.

In his weary and hungry state, he should never have come here. The contrast was too sharp. Even he was recalled keenly to better things.

"What's the use?" he thought. "It's all up with me. I'll quit this."

People turned to look after him, so uncouth was his shambling figure. Several officers followed him with their eyes, to see that he did not beg of anybody.

Once he paused in an aimless, incoherent sort of way and looked through the windows of an imposing restaurant, before which blazed a fire sign, and through the large, plate windows of which could be seen the red and gold decorations, the palms, the white napery, and shining glassware, and, above all, the comfortable crowd. Weak as his mind had become, his hunger was sharp enough to show the importance of this. He stopped stock still, his frayed trousers soaking in the slush, and peered foolishly in.

"Eat," he mumbled. "That's right, eat. Nobody else wants any."

Then his voice dropped even lower, and his mind half lost the fancy it had.

"It's mighty cold," he said. "Awful cold."

At Broadway and Thirty-ninth Street was blazing, in incandescent fire, Carrie's name. "Carrie Madenda," it read, "and the Casino Company." All the wet, snowy sidewalk was bright with this radiated fire. It was so bright that it attracted Hurstwood's gaze. He looked up, and then at a large, gilt-framed posterboard, on which was a fine lithograph of Carrie, life-size.

3. In the 1890s upper Broadway above Fifty-ninth Street was called the Boulevard.

Hurstwood gazed at it a moment, snuffling and hunching one shoulder, as if something were scratching him. He was so run down, however, that his mind was not exactly clear.

"That's you," he said at last, addressing her. "Wasn't good enough for you, was I? Huh!"

He lingered, trying to think logically. This was no longer possible with him.

"She's got it," he said, incoherently, thinking of money. "Let her give me some."

He started around to the side door. Then he forgot what he was going for and paused, pushing his hands deeper to warm the wrists. Suddenly it returned. The stage door! That was it.

He approached that entrance and went in.

"Well?" said the attendant, staring at him. Seeing him pause, he went over and shoved him. "Get out of here," he said.

"I want to see Miss Madenda," he said.

"You do, eh?" the other said, almost tickled at the spectacle. "Get out of here," and he shoved him again. Hurstwood had no strength to resist.

"I want to see Miss Madenda," he tried to explain, even as he was being hustled away. "I'm all right. I——"

The man gave him a last push and closed the door. As he did so, Hurstwood slipped and fell in the snow. It hurt him, and some vague sense of shame returned. He began to cry and swear foolishly.

"God damned dog!" he said. "Damned old cur," wiping the slush from his worthless coat. "I—I hired such people as you once."

Now a fierce feeling against Carrie welled up—just one fierce, angry thought before the whole thing slipped out of his mind.

"She owes me something to eat," he said. "She owes it to me."

Hopelessly he turned back into Broadway again and slopped onward and away, begging, crying, losing track of his thoughts, one after another, as a mind decayed and disjointed is wont to do.

It was truly a wintry evening, a few days later, when his one distinct mental decision was reached. Already, at four o'clock, the sombre hue of night was thickening the air. A heavy snow was falling—a fine picking, whipping snow, borne forward by a swift wind in long, thin lines. The streets were bedded with it—six inches of cold, soft carpet, churned to a dirty brown by the crush of teams and the feet of men. Along Broadway men picked their way in ulsters and umbrellas. Along the Bowery, men slouched through it with collars and hats pulled over their ears. In the former thoroughfare business men and travellers were making for comfortable hotels. In the latter, crowds on cold errands shifted past dingy stores, in the deep recesses of which lights were already gleaming. There were early lights in the cable cars, whose usual clatter was reduced by the mantle about the wheels. The whole city was muffled by this fast-thickening mantle.[4]

In her comfortable chambers at the Waldorf,[5] Carrie was reading at this time "Pére Goriot,"[6] which Ames had recommended to her. It was so strong, and Ames's mere recommendation had so aroused her interest, that she caught nearly the full sympathetic significance of it. For the first time, it was being borne in upon her how silly and worthless had been her earlier reading, as a whole. Becoming wearied, however, she yawned and came to the window, looking out upon the old winding procession of carriages rolling up Fifth Avenue.

"Isn't it bad?" she observed to Lola.

"Terrible!" said that little lady, joining her. "I hope it snows enough to go sleigh riding."

"Oh, dear," said Carrie, with whom the sufferings of Father Goriot were still keen. "That's all you think of. Aren't you sorry for the people who haven't anything to-night?"

"Of course I am," said Lola; "but what can I do? I haven't anything."

Carrie smiled.

"You wouldn't care, if you had," she returned.

"I would, too," said Lola. "But people never gave me anything when I was hard up."

"Isn't it just awful?" said Carrie, studying the winter's storm.

"Look at that man over there," laughed Lola, who had caught sight of some one falling down. "How sheepish men look when they fall, don't they?"

"We'll have to take a coach to-night," answered Carrie, absently.

In the lobby of the Imperial,[7] Mr. Charles Drouet was just arriving, shaking the snow from a very handsome ulster. Bad weather had driven him home early and stirred his desire for those pleasures which shut out the snow and gloom of life. A good dinner, the company of a young woman, and an evening at the theatre were the chief things for him.

"Why, hello, Harry!" he said, addressing a lounger in one of the comfortable lobby chairs. "How are you?"

"Oh, about six and six," said the other.

"Rotten weather, isn't it?"

---

4. Ellen Moers has suggested that Dreiser's depiction of this and other winter scenes in *Sister Carrie* was influenced by Alfred Stieglitz's pioneer photographs of New York in winter. See "The Blizzard," in her *Two Dreisers* (New York: Viking, 1969), pp. 3–14.
5. The Waldorf Hotel, at Fifth Avenue and Thirty-third, opened in early 1893.
6. Honoré de Balzac's *Le Père Goriot* (1834), a novel in which an ambitious young man from the provinces discovers in Paris the ruthless nature of life.
7. The Imperial Hotel, at Broadway and Thirty-second, was popular with successful businessmen.

"Well, I should say," said the other. "I've been just sitting here thinking where I'd go to-night."

"Come along with me," said Drouet. "I can introduce you to something dead swell."

"Who is it?" said the other.

"Oh, a couple of girls over here in Fortieth Street. We could have a dandy time. I was just looking for you."

"Supposing we get 'em and take 'em out to dinner?"

"Sure," said Drouet. "Wait'll I go upstairs and change my clothes."

"Well, I'll be in the barber shop," said the other. "I want to get a shave."

"All right," said Drouet, creaking off in his good shoes toward the elevator. The old butterfly was as light on the wing as ever.

On an incoming vestibuled Pullman, speeding at forty miles an hour through the snow of the evening, were three others, all related.

"First call for dinner in the dining-car," a Pullman servitor was announcing, as he hastened through the aisle in snow-white apron and jacket.

"I don't believe I want to play any more," said the youngest, a black-haired beauty, turned supercilious by fortune, as she pushed a euchre hand away from her.

"Shall we go into dinner?" inquired her husband, who was all that fine raiment can make.

"Oh, not yet," she answered. "I don't want to play any more, though."

"Jessica," said her mother, who was also a study in what good clothing can do for age, "push that pin down in your tie—it's coming up."

Jessica obeyed, incidentally touching at her lovely hair and looking at a little jewel-faced watch. Her husband studied her, for beauty, even cold, is fascinating from one point of view.

"Well, we won't have much more of this weather," he said. "It only takes two weeks to get to Rome."

Mrs. Hurstwood nestled comfortably in her corner and smiled. It was so nice to be the mother-in-law of a rich young man—one whose financial state had borne her personal inspection.

"Do you suppose the boat will sail promptly?" asked Jessica, "if it keeps up like this?"

"Oh, yes," answered her husband. "This won't make any difference."

Passing down the aisle came a very fair-haired banker's son, also of Chicago, who had long eyed this supercilious beauty. Even now he did not hesitate to glance at her, and she was conscious of it. With a specially conjured show of indifference, she turned her pretty face wholly away. It was not wifely modesty at all. By so much was her pride satisfied.

At this moment Hurstwood stood before a dirty four-story building in a side street quite near the Bowery, whose one-time coat of buff had been changed by soot and rain. He mingled with a crowd of men—a crowd which had been, and was still, gathering by degrees.

It began with the approach of two or three, who hung about the closed wooden doors and beat their feet to keep them warm. They had on faded derby hats with dents in them. Their misfit coats were heavy with melted snow and turned up at the collars. Their trousers were mere bags, frayed at the bottom and wobbling over big, soppy shoes, torn at the sides and worn almost to shreds. They made no effort to go in, but shifted ruefully about, digging their hands deep in their pockets and leering at the crowd and the increasing lamps. With the minutes, increased the number. Three were old men with grizzled beards and sunken eyes, men who were comparatively young but shrunken by diseases, men who were middle-aged. None were fat. There was a face in the thick of the collection which was as white as drained veal. There was another red as brick. Some came with thin, rounded shoulders, others with wooden legs, still others with frames so lean that clothes only flapped about them. There were great ears, swollen noses, thick lips, and, above all, red, blood-shot eyes. Not a normal, healthy face in the whole mass; not a straight figure; not a straightforward, steady glance.

In the drive of the wind and sleet they pushed in on one another. There were wrists, unprotected by coat or pocket, which were red with cold. There were ears, half coverd by every conceivable semblance of a hat, which still looked stiff and bitten. In the snow they shifted, now one foot, now another, almost rocking in unison.

With the growth of the crowd about the door came a murmur. It was not conversation, but a running comment directed at any one in general. It contained oaths and slang phrases.

"By damn, I wish they'd hurry up."

"Look at the copper watchin'."

"Maybe it ain't winter, nuther!"

"I wisht I was in Sing Sing."[8]

Now a sharper lash of wind cut down and they huddled closer. It was an edging, shifting, pushing throng. There was no anger, no pleading, no threatening words. It was all sullen endurance, unlightened by either wit or good fellowship.

A carriage went jingling by with some reclining figure in it. One of the men nearest the door saw it.

---

8. A New York state prison, at Ossining in Westchester County.

"Look at the bloke ridin'."

"He ain't so cold."

"Eh, eh, eh!" yelled another, the carriage having long since passed out of hearing.

Little by little the night crept on. Along the walk a crowd turned out on its way home. Men and shop-girls went by with quick steps. The cross-town cars began to be crowded. The gas lamps were blazing, and every window bloomed ruddy with a steady flame. Still the crowd hung about the door, unwavering.

"Ain't they ever goin' to open up?" queried a hoarse voice, suggestively.

This seemed to renew the general interest in the closed door, and many gazed in that direction. They looked at it as dumb brutes look, as dogs paw and whine and study the knob. They shifted and blinked and muttered, now a curse, now a comment. Still they waited and still the snow whirled and cut them with biting flakes. On the old hats and peaked shoulders it was piling. It gathered in little heaps and curves and no one brushed it off. In the centre of the crowd the warmth and steam melted it, and water trickled off hat rims and down noses, which the owners could not reach to scratch. On the outer rim the piles remained unmelted. Hurstwood, who could not get in the centre, stood with head lowered to the weather and bent his form.

A light appeared through the transom overhead. It sent a thrill of possibility through the watchers. There was a murmur of recognition. At last the bars grated inside and the crowd pricked up its ears. Footsteps shuffled within and it murmured again. Some one called: "Slow up there, now," and then the door opened. It was push and jam for a minute, with grim, beast silence to prove its quality, and then it melted inward, like logs floating, and disappeared. There were wet hats and wet shoulders, a cold, shrunken, disgruntled mass, pouring in between bleak walls. It was just six o'clock and there was supper in every hurrying pedestrian's face. And yet no supper was provided here—nothing but beds.

Hurstwood laid down his fifteen cents and crept off with weary steps to his allotted room. It was a dingy affair—wooden, dusty, hard. A small gas-jet furnished sufficient light for so rueful a corner.

"Hm!" he said, clearing his throat and locking the door.

Now he began leisurely to take off his clothes, but stopped first with his coat, and tucked it along the crack under the door. His vest he arranged in the same place. His old wet, cracked hat he laid softly upon the table. Then he pulled off his shoes and lay down.

It seemed as if he thought a while, for now he arose and turned the gas out, standing calmly in the blackness, hidden from view.

After a few moments, in which he reviewed nothing, but merely hesitated, he turned the gas on again, but applied no match. Even then he stood there, hidden wholly in that kindness which is night, while the uprising fumes filled the room. When the odour reached his nostrils, he quit his attitude and fumbled for the bed.

"What's the use?" he said, weakly, as he stretched himself to rest.

And now Carrie had attained that which in the beginning seemed life's object, or, at least, such fraction of it as human beings ever attain of their original desires. She could look about on her gowns and carriage, her furniture and bank account. Friends there were, as the world takes it—those who would bow and smile in acknowledgment of her success. For these she had once craved. Applause there was, and publicity—once far off, essential things, but now grown trivial and indifferent. Beauty also—her type of loveliness—and yet she was lonely. In her rocking-chair she sat, when not otherwise engaged—singing and dreaming.

Thus in life there is ever the intellectual and the emotional nature—the mind that reasons, and the mind that feels. Of one come the men of action—generals and statesmen; of the other, the poets and dreamers—artists all.

As harps in the wind, the latter respond to every breath of fancy, voicing in their moods all the ebb and flow of the ideal.

Man has not yet comprehended the dreamer any more than he has the ideal. For him the laws and morals of the world are unduly severe. Ever hearkening to the sound of beauty, straining for the flash of its distant wings, he watches to follow, wearying his feet in travelling. So watched Carrie, so followed, rocking and singing.

And it must be remembered that reason had little part in this. Chicago dawning, she saw the city offering more of loveliness than she had ever known, and instinctively, by force of her moods alone, clung to it. In fine raiment and elegant surroundings, men seemed to be contented. Hence, she drew near these things. Chicago, New York; Drouet, Hurstwood; the world of fashion and the world of stage—these were but incidents. Not them, but that which they represented, she longed for. Time proved the representation false.

Oh, the tangle of human life! How dimly as yet we see. Here was Carrie, in the beginning poor, unsophisticated, emotional; responding with desire to everything most lovely in life, yet finding herself turned as by a wall. Laws to say: "Be allured, if you will, by everything lovely, but draw not nigh unless by righteousness." Convention to say: "You shall not better your situation save by honest labour." If honest labour be unremunerative and difficult to endure; if it be the long, long road which never reaches beauty, but wearies the feet and the heart; if the drag to follow beauty be such that one abandons the admired way, taking rather the despised path leading to her dreams quickly, who shall cast the first stone? Not evil, but longing for that which is better, more often directs the steps of the erring. Not evil, but goodness more often allures the feeling mind unused to reason.

Amid the tinsel and shine of her state walked Carrie, unhappy. As when Drouet took her, she had thought: "Now am I lifted into that which is best"; as when Hurstwood seemingly offered her the better way: "Now am I happy." But since the world goes its way past all who will not partake of its folly, she now found herself alone. Her purse was open to him whose need was greatest. In her walks on Broadway, she no longer thought of the elegance of the creatures who passed her. Had they more of that peace and beauty which glimmered afar off, then were they to be envied.

Drouet abandoned his claim and was seen no more. Of Hurstwood's death she was not even aware. A slow, black boat setting out from the pier at Twenty-seventh Street upon its weekly errand bore, with many others, his nameless body to the Potter's Field.[9]

Thus passed all that was of interest concerning these twain in their relation to her. Their influence upon her life is explicable alone by the nature of her longings. Time was when both represented for her all that was most potent in earthly success. They were the personal representatives of a state most blessed to attain—the titled ambassadors of comfort and peace, aglow with their credentials. It is but natural that when the world which they represented no longer allured her, its ambassadors should be discredited. Even had Hurstwood returned in his original beauty and glory, he could not now have allured her. She had learned that in his world, as in her own present state, was not happiness.

Sitting alone, she was now an illustration of the devious ways by which one who feels, rather than reasons, may be led in the pursuit of beauty. Though often disillusioned, she was still waiting for that halcyon day when she should be led forth among dreams become real. Ames had pointed out a farther step, but on and on beyond that, if accomplished, would lie others for her. It was forever to be the pursuit of that radiance of delight which tints the distant hilltops of the world.

Oh, Carrie, Carrie! Oh, blind strivings of the human heart! Onward, onward, it saith, and where beauty leads, there it follows. Whether it be the tinkle of a lone sheep bell o'er some quiet landscape, or the glimmer of beauty in sylvan places, or the show of soul in some passing eye, the heart knows and makes answer, following. It is when the feet weary and hope seems vain that the heartaches

---

9. New York's Potter's Field in the 1890s was on Hart's Island, in Long Island Sound.

and the longings arise. Know, then, that for you is neither surfeit nor content. In your rocking-chair, by your window dreaming, shall you long, alone. In your rocking-chair, by your window, shall you dream such happiness as you may never feel.

THE END

APPENDIX

Passages Cut by Dreiser and Arthur Henry in the Typescript Version of *Sister Carrie*

For each cut passage that follows, page and line numbers that indicate where the passage occurs in this edition are followed by the phrase that precedes the passage. The page number following the passage is that of its location in the Pennsylvania Edition. Where an entire cut passage is not here reprinted, omissions are indicated by ellipses.

The material in the Appendix is from *Sister Carrie*, The Pennsylvania Edition, ed. John C. Berkey et al. (Philadelphia: U of Pennsylvania P, 1981). Reprinted by permission of the University of Pennsylvania Press.

19:20 Don't come here."

In another factory she was leered upon by a most sensual-faced individual who endeavored to turn the natural questions of the inquiry into a personal interview, asking all sorts of embarrassing questions and endeavoring to satisfy himself evidently that she was of loose enough morals to suit his purpose. In that case she had been relieved enough to get away and found the busy, indifferent streets to be again a soothing refuge. (27)

37:33 "I'll tell her," said Minnie.

Meanwhile Carrie was in the door below, looking at the lights in the stores about, the people passing, and the street cars jingling merrily past toward the heart of the city or out toward the suburbs,—directions which to her were interesting mysteries. She enjoyed looking at the boys playing tag about the street, and the young girls who went by in companies laughing and talking. Once in awhile she would see a young girl particularly well-dressed or particularly pretty, or both, which excited her envy and enhanced her longing for nice clothes. Once in awhile a dapper young fellow in his best suit would stride lightly past, bound, she was sure, to call upon some young lady. There were other youths, not so well-dressed, who came in pairs or groups, ogling her, pushing one another and cutting up in such a way as to attract attention. These she gave an assumed look of coldness, or turned her gaze away entirely, which did not, however, seem to faze the young gentlemen in question. They would laugh, whistle, perhaps shout a little and look back still hopeful, but without daring

to attempt more intimate overtures—the kind of young men whose
faint hearts are concealed behind a show of boisterous enthusiasm.
Once in awhile a figure in the distance would look as if it might be
that of Drouet and then she would straighten up and become tense
in the nerves until, with a nearer approach, her whole flutter and
strain would collapse in the face of certain outlines which would
prove that the scent was false. (51)

47:11 beasts alone.

That is but the religious expression of a material and spiritual truth
that has guided the evolution of the race. If not, then what led and
schooled the race before it thought logically—before it came into the
wisdom to lead itself? (64)

47:14 overtures of Drouet.

Evil was not in him. On the contrary there was kindliness, non-
understanding, strong physical desire, vainglory, a great admiration
for the sex, laughter, even tears, but at these no woman trembles.
The moth, the pig, the clown, the butterfly, the actor, the business
man and the sensualist mingled in combination. He was an enlivening spectacle of them all. (64)

58:3 city's hypnotic influence.

the subject of the mesmeric operations of super-intelligible forces.
We have heard of the strange power of Niagara, the contemplation
of whose rushing flood leads to thoughts of dissolution. We have
heard of the influence of the hypnotic ball, a scientific fact. Man is
too intimate with the drag of unexplainable, invisible forces to doubt
longer that the human mind is colored, moved, swept on by things
which neither resound nor speak. The waters of the sea are not the
only things which the moon sways. All that the individual imagines
in contemplating a dazzling, alluring, or disturbing spectacle is created more by the spectacle than the mind observing it. These strange,
insensible inflowings which alternate, reform, dissolve, are, we are
beginning to see, foreshadowing the solution of Shakespeare's mystic
line, "There are more things in heaven and earth, Horatio, than are
dreamt of in your philosophy." We are, after all, more passive than
active, more mirrors than engines, and the origin of human action
has neither yet been measured nor calculated. (78)

72:3 o'er its own

In considering Carrie's mental state, the culmination of reasoning
which held her at anchorage in so strange a harbor, we must fail of

a just appreciation if we do not give due weight to those subtle influences, not human, which environ and appeal to the young imagination when it drifts. Trite though it may seem, it is well to remember that in life, after all, we are most wholly controlled by desire. The things that appeal to desire are not always visible objects. Let us not confuse this with selfishness. It is more virtuous than that. Desire is the variable wind which blows now zephyrlike, now shrill, filling our sails for some far-off port, flapping them idly upon the high seas in sunny weather, scudding us now here, now there, before its terrific breath, speeding us anon to accomplishment; as often rending our sails and leaving us battered and dismantled, a picturesque wreck in some forgotten harbor. Selfishness is the twin-screw motive power of the human steamer. It drives unchangingly, unpoetically on. Its one danger is that of miscalculation. Personalities such as Carrie's would come under the former category. The art by which her rather confused consciousness of right and duty might be overcome is not easily perceived.

In the progress of all such minds environment is a subtle, persuasive control. It works hand in hand with desire. For instance, by certain conditions which her intellect was scarcely able to control, she was pushed into a situation where for the first time she could see a strikingly different way of living from her own. Fine clothes, rich foods, superior residence, a conspicuously apparent assumption of position in others,—these she saw. She was not more clever in observing this than any shop girl. No matter how dull is the perception in other things, in such matters all women are clear. It is scarcely remarkable also, in view of the struggle for these things which is everywhere apparent, that she should suppose them to be best. If the sight of them aroused a desire in her bosom, is it strange?

It must next be considered that if desire be rife in the mind and no channel of satisfaction is provided; if there be ambition, however weak, and it is not schooled in lovely principle and precept—if no way be shown, be sure it will learn a way of the world. Need it be said that the lesson of the latter is not always uplifting. We know that the common run of mortals *struggle* to be happy. Is not that comment sufficient?

Lastly, let all men remember that in the main, the world's virtue has never been tested. Wherefore was he good—the heavens rained goodness on the soil that nourished him. Where severe tests have been made, there have been some lamentable failures. Too often we move along ignoring the fact, of our own advantages in every criticism we make concerning others. We do this because we are ignorant of the subtleties of life. Be sure that the vileness which you attribute to some object is a mirage. It is a sky illumination of your own lack of understanding—the confusion of your own soul.

In the light of these truths, it is well to admit the possibility of persuasion and control other than by men. Did Drouet persuade her entirely? Ah, the magnitude attributed to simple Drouet! The leading strings were with neither of them. (97–98)

79:33 AMBASSADOR'S PLEA

If there was one quality which might be predicated more than another of Hurstwood at this time it was circumspectness, which the state of his home life and the tenure of his position depended upon. While there was in him no feeling of affection which could bind him to his wife and children, there was, as has been pointed out, a certain vanity in the good showing which his home life made. He was respected. His family was on speaking terms with his immediate neighbors, several of whom had considerable money. When he rode down town in the cars of a morning, he had the satisfaction of brushing elbows with numerous plethoric-pursed merchants and of answering solicitations concerning his wife and children which were made in that perfunctory manner common to Americans of the money-making variety. These things seemed to give him standing and as such they were worth while.

At the same time, there were moral guy ropes of a more subtle character. His wife was of a cold, self-satisfied disposition which he did not quite comprehend. For a truth he had never really understood the woman. Passion and self-advantage were mixed attributes of the courtship which had terminated in their marriage. When the former had been satisfied, they drifted along together bound by those mutual interests which married people feel. There was no reason for dissatisfaction since they had enough to live on and were saving money. Both saw something ahead and their relations were for many years cordial if not enthusiastic.

In these latter days, however, the dispositions and habits of each had intensified owing to the fact that they were very much separated during the hours of the day and evening. Mrs. Hurstwood centered more and more of her interest in her children, particularly her daughter. Hurstwood depended more and more upon the artificial gaiety of the resort over which he presided for his individual amusement. The children were not sufficiently refined in feeling or interesting in motive to draw the twain together. This common object—the success of the children—how many homes have owed their stability to it. (111–12)

85:12 used to cover.

Let me not be quarreled with for predicating these psychologic truths of these two individuals. The great forces of nature must not be arrogated by the intellectual alone. Refinement is nothing more than the perception and understanding of these things, and whoso understands and feels that these things are true is refined. But the forces themselves may be perceived by the wise, working in the commonest moulds. The forces which regulate the pig are subtle, strange and wonderful, and require refinement of thought in the observer to understand. The forces which regulate two individuals of the character of Carrie and Hurstwood are as strange and as subtle as described. We have been writing our novels and our philosophies without sufficiently emphasizing them—we have been neglecting to set forth what all men must know and feel about these things before a true and natural life may be led. We must understand that not we, but the things of which we are the evidence, are the realities. That it is not true of beauty alone that

> ". . . it speaketh through the landscape
> And it speaketh through the sky."

but that

> "All its realms are earth and heaven
> Good and evil, thou and I." (118–19)

92:3 appealing to her.

It affected her much as the magnificence of God affects the mind of the Christian when he reads of His wondrous state and finds at the end an appeal to him to come and make it perfect. (129)

94:15 results accordingly.

That worthy, on the contrary, had formulated no plan of action, though he listened, almost unreservedly, to his desires. He was in fine feather now that his suit had prospered so well. There was no question but that Carrie's fascination for him was genuine. He felt deeply attached to her and only awaited their next meeting to prosper his relationship. He was lured exceedingly by the joy he felt in her presence. The thought of her affectionate glance was sufficient to send pleasing thrills throughout his body. He awaited his next opportunity to see her with impatience. In short, for the time being he walked in a lighter atmosphere and saw all things through a more rosy medium. It might have been said of him, under these circumstances, that he was truly in love.

What his intentions were we may readily guess from our knowledge of men. Many individuals are so constituted that their only thought is to obtain pleasure and shun responsibility. They would like, butterfly-like, to wing forever in a summer garden, flitting from flower to flower, and sipping honey for their sole delight. They have no feeling that any result which might flow from their action should concern them. They have no conception of the necessity of a well-organized society wherein all shall accept a certain quota of responsibility and all realize a reasonable amount of happiness. They think only of themselves because they have not yet been taught to think of society. For them pain and necessity are the great taskmasters. Laws are but the fences which circumscribe the sphere of their operations. When, after error, pain falls as a lash, they do not comprehend that their suffering is due to misbehavior. Many such an individual is so lashed by necessity and law that he falls fainting to the ground, dies hungry in the gutter or rotting in the jail and it never once flash across his mind that he has been lashed only in so far as he has persisted in attempting to trespass the boundaries which necessity sets. A prisoner of fate, held enchained for his own delight, he does not know that the walls are tall, that the sentinels of life are forever pacing, musket in hand. He cannot perceive that all joy is within and not without. He must be for scaling the bounds of society, for overpowering the sentinel. When we hear the cries of the individual strung up by the thumbs, when we hear the ominous shot which marks the end of another victim who has thought to break loose, we may be sure that in another instance life has been misunderstood—we may be sure that society has been struggled against until death alone would stop the individual from contention and evil. (132–33)

98:3   Drouet left again.

Her heart was wholly with her handsome manager who seemed so sincere, so considerate, so much more tactful than the drummer.

When a young girl finds herself in such a tangled and anomalous position, she either develops commensurate resources of tact and daring or she fails utterly. In the case of Carrie, the sight of wealth and the merry life of the city had awakened in her a desire to reach something higher and to live better. The vacillation and indifference of Drouet made it perfectly plain to her that the door of escape was closed in that quarter. The dress and manner of Hurstwood deluded her as to the height and luxury of his position. She imagined that his attraction to her could only mean that entrance for her in a higher world which she craved. So now when he promised a plan of some sort, her mind rested itself. (138)

102:18   could there express.

An essay might be written to illuminate this one point in a passion which is neither young nor idyllic. The man of the world of experience, who considers many points of his affection, who imagines he has all the ends of his passion, who can lead, master and destroy, is still drawn and controlled by these very thoughts. He is the moth who knows all about his own feelings, all about the attraction of the flame, but who cannot bring himself to even wish to keep away. So much for the human conception of the natural forces which work in them. (144)

112:38   while it lasted.

Dramatic art is most peculiar in this respect, that it inspires thoughts of emulation in the most hopeless of its observers and arouses a feeling of equal ability. This is due no doubt to the fact that it is at once the most natural as well as the most understandable of the graces. It presents that which its observers daily live and feel. It scarcely occurs to the inexperienced onlooker that it must be difficult to be natural—to do as we see each and all others doing about us. They see, mirrored upon the stage, scenes which they would like to witness, situations in which they would rejoice to be placed, passions which they would be happy to feel. The simulation of merriment and grief, laughter and tears, affection and hate are so real, that the art of the thing itself is lost. The observer sees what, with the flight of years, will be presented to him outside—everyday human nature and events, heightened and crowded together for his temporary delectation. These things, while they attract, deceive. They allure the languorously inclined, the luxuriants of all classes, promising ease and that shift and play of feeling which is the hope of all.

Carrie could scarcely be numbered among the latter. Rather, she would have been classed among the elect of the field by reason of her sensitive, receptive nature, her barometric feelings and almost hopeless lack of logic. Her impressionable feelings were the actor's own—her lack of initiative and decision were also characteristic of the tribe. In short, she could feel without reasoning therefrom, and this has ever been the true state of the thespians, since dramatic representation began. (158)

142:2   FLESH IN PURSUIT

To understand the power of Hurstwood's affection one must understand the man of the world. He was no longer young. He was no longer youthful in spirit, but he carried in his memory some old fancies which were of the day of his love time. His observation was keen, his affections lively. His love of the light of youth intense.

In Carrie he saw the embodiment of old experiences and old dreams. There was in her fresh cheeks something of the old garden of spring. He had loved—yes, long ago, and once in awhile there

came a sense of the round moon that hung in a serene heaven of a
May night, of odours that were sweet because wafted to nostrils
young and sensitive, of rare feelings which came because love had
loosened his mind and strengthened the springs of perception. In
short he had been in love, and what feelings of that old time came
back, cut as a knife and stung as a whip, for he feared—and oh, how
keenly the man of exuberant passions ever fears—that the like might
never come again.

And now, lo, it was come. In a fading, an almost desolate garden
here, was sprung up a new flower. Eyes of soft radiance. Form of
graceful, attractive lines, cheeks soft and colorful, hair that was
pleasant to look upon—a lightsome step, a youthful fancy, a radiant
fire of feeling as he had so recently seen. Here was something which
was new, something which took him back. (203)

144:17   come to-night?"

"I don't know whether I can or not," she answered, troubled by
the old thought and her present situation. She was not one to whom
change was agreeable. She had not the shifting and daring of an
adventuress. She was too uncertain of herself, too much afraid of
the world. This man, while she liked him, possessed qualities which
awed her. She felt safer with the easy Drouet, to whom she was used.
She had got the hang of that simple-souled individual's personality.
She saw shades of its weakness wherever she was strong. Moreover,
she was fixed in a comfortable apartment, where she could at least
house herself and speculate. How would it be somewhere else? She
seemed called upon to loosen her moorings, uncertain and unsatis-
fying as they were, and drift somewhere else. She was being called
to come and could scarcely make answer. . . . (207)

170:10   about the block.

The trouble with his present situation was that there were too
many ends to consider. Whichever way he might move, he would
not gain anything. It was all so sudden that he had not yet recovered
from the dazing effect of it—from a curious desire he had to study
it out. This last was due to a more or less speculative turn of mind.
He had never been given to instantaneous decisions.

With the last proposition to contemplate he hastened not a little.
He could not bring himself to go to this firm's office. He could not
agree to talk with them about this matter which seemed such a personal thing. He had a crude feeling about something turning up—
the hope of it—certain as he was that it would not. He even thought
of his wife's compromising the thing after a talk with him, and then
he remembered his visit in the rain. His whole, strong, passionate

nature rebelled at being forced, and he was too much the lover of power to play the part of the suppliant.

"I ought to go over there," he brought himself once to admit, and later, "I ought to get a lawyer."

"What good would that do?" said another voice in his mind. "They'll sue tomorrow, lawyer or no lawyer, if you don't see them. What are you going to do about that?"

"I don't know what I'm going to do," he admitted to himself secretly, and then started to consider other parts of the situation, which would, by a circuitous method, lead around to the same conclusion not ten minutes later. (243–44)

185:38 Why be afraid?

Could he not get away? What would be the use of remaining? He would never get such a chance again. He emptied the good money into the satchel. There was something fascinating about the soft green stack—the loose silver and gold. He felt sure now that he could not leave that. No, no. He would do it. He would lock the safe before he had time to change his mind.

He went over and restored the empty boxes. Then he pushed the door to for somewhere near the sixth time. He wavered, thinking, putting his hand to his brow. (270–71)

193:44 a newer world.

. . . "Don't you think you can ever forgive me, Carrie?" he said, "for deceiving you this way?"

"No," she answered, without looking at him, "I can't."

"Even if I make every amend in my power?"

She did not answer.

"Can't you see," he said, ignoring her silence, "that I wouldn't have done as I did if I didn't love you. I wouldn't want you with me if I didn't care for you."

He stopped, but she only looked out upon the moving panorama of rural life.

"If you will only believe in me again," he went on, "I'll lead a life that you can be proud of. I'll go into business of some kind," he said, "and we'll live in a nice home."

Carrie thought of this but did not wish to do so. Hurstwood waited a few moments, studying the profile of her face, which was turned away.

"Don't you care for me at all?" he asked.

She was comparing this picture of the future with that which lay behind. Here was offered her a chance for a decent life in another city. She would be away from all past associations, she would be in a new world. Hurstwood was not an evil individual. As yet he had worked her no harm. He had deceived her, but he was not attempting to brutally force her to do something which she seriously objected to. So far he had given her liberty to act for herself. He had promised to let her return, to give her money to do so if she wished. Also he wished to do the only thing possible, get a divorce and marry her. It was a pleasing thing to see him so attentive, so anxious. He was offering everything except her absence from him, and that was because he loved her too much to let her go away. More, he opened a kindly door out of many troubles, and that was something. She could not well forget that she had nowhere else to go . . . . (284–85)

194:16   come back.

Wild as this imagining was, it seemed plausible enough in the face of the wilder actualities in which he had figured. It could not be worse than this future which lay before him—dark, friendless, exiled. He had no profession. Managing was nothing which could be had for the asking. He would have to explain his experience, and how could he do that without telling what he had done? The money he had taken he did not want to use. He ought to send it back. Then he remembered how ridiculous it would have seemed the day before if anyone had told him that today he would be worrying about money. The horrible truth that he, anyone, everyone could be where they needed money and could not get it flashed upon him with a sickening panoramic effect. He felt that his position was most difficult. He would have to look about at once and get started. Ah, and how. And oh, worst of all, it would need to be done in a strange city and among strange people. He would not have his friends. Nostalgy began to affect his vitals. That dread yearning for the fixed, the stable, the accustomed, which seizes those who reflect an atmosphere in their blood, began to make its way in him. He longed for Chicago, for his old ways and pleasant places. He wanted to go back and remain there, let the cost be what it would. . . . (287–88)

214:14   somewhat different.

When, however, after a year, the novelty of her surroundings wore off and the flat had become a very pleasant but no longer remarkable thing; after the city as a geographic and corporate entity had ceased to allure her and she began to wonder concerning its details; after she had noticed Hurstwood's changed state and had assured herself that he was doing the very best under given conditions, then came the slight change in his money affairs, and the operation of the opinion which he had formed concerning her house-wifely instincts.

"Dearest," he said on a number of occasions now, "I don't think

I'll be up to dinner this evening," or, "Dearest, I shall be working late tonight."

"All right," said Carrie very pleasantly, taking the excuse as natural and turning to her novel for resource against ennui. Heretofore he had taken her much about the city, but now she noticed that she occasionally asked him. Often she thought that it was because they had seen most all of the general details and he was weary of them or averse to walking. At any rate, she asked him. This thing went on until at last, in addition, she began to see that she was getting along with only such clothes as she seemed really to need. She went out so little that what she had lasted her a long while and Hurstwood, schooled in saving by his year of adversity, said nothing. Still he forgot the lessons of adversity when it came to himself, and by contrast with his new blossoming, she began to see that she was, comparatively, rather poorly dressed. This was the proper lever to move her mind. It awoke her to keener observations and consequent decisions. (317)

283:25   not anticipate.

Mental apathy of this sort is a marvelous thing. He was a fit case for scientific investigation. A splendid paper might be prepared on the operation of certain preconceived notions which he had concerning dignity in the matter of his downfall. We know that certain forms of life, used to certain conditions, die quickly when exposed. The common canary, hardy enough when captured, loses, after a few years of confinement in a gilded cage, its power to shift for itself. The house-dog, held until middle age in comfort, will die of starvation if turned out into the woods to hunt alone. The house-dog, turned out a puppy, becomes a wolf, or so much like one that the difference is one of appearance only. So man, held until middle age in peace and plenty, forgets the art of shifting and doing. The skill and wit of the mind is atrophied. He appears to be something and lo, the poor brain argues that it must live up to that something, else it is disgraced. Courage to belie its feelings is not there. It must sit and wonder, waiting for the thing which it can do. It can scarcely change itself sufficiently to do as the thing requires.

This was Hurstwood. The butcher knocked at his door, and he made excuses. The grocer called also. More excuses. He would return to his chair after one of these disagreeable and sharp encounters thinking that he must get some money from Carrie. When she gave him only what he constantly asked for, he would think of putting off the butcher. The absent trouble was always the easiest to deal with. (407)

301:23 wants to work.

During his absence, brief as it was—only from ten o'clock of one morning to seven o'clock of the next evening, she had felt intensely relieved. With him there passed out of the flat a great shadow. In its place came hopes for the future—hopes of freedom from annoyance and money-drain. She had got a taste of what it is to grow weary of the idler. Now, after a gleam of pleasant energy, he returned. Her heart sank at the sight.

It was not because hard-heartedness was a characteristic of her nature. It was weariness and an ache for change. When she saw him in bed that night, she knew that it imported failure. Coming on top of a further improvement in her own situation which must now be detailed, and as a destroyer of her hope that he had really roused himself, it was a shock. She could only shake her head in despair.

"Oh, me!" she sighed.

The improvement referred to concerned some attention her work had attracted. (430)

305:25 something pathetic.

The winter was cold, his clothes were poor, he had no money. Moreover he looked less robust than formerly, as if confinement had bleached him.

Carrie had experienced too much of the bitterness of search and poverty, not to sympathize keenly with one about to be cast out upon his own resources. She remembered the time when she walked the streets of Chicago—and only recently when she searched here. Where would he go? Without money he must starve. (435)

339:36 done better, by far.

. . . At table the tendency was to talk lightly of things in general, there being other guests, besides Carrie and Ames, but the latter was too much of an original thinker to have much regard for convention. The fact is, he was prone to forget the little niceties of attention unless constantly reminded. Now Carrie seemed the most pleasing character present. She extended to him that sympathy and attention which he needed to show his mind at its best. At its best it was speculative and idealistic—far above anything which she had as yet conceived, and yet, curiously, he could talk to her. She made him feel as if she understood, and he unconsciously strove to make himself plain. Thus the bond between them was drawn closer than they knew.

"I've been reading the books you suggested," she said in one place, when the conversation was between them alone.

He turned his serious eyes upon her, and a happy sense of having fulfilled a duty answered in her own, until he said:—

"What were they?"

His having forgotten stole away some of the charm for her.

" 'Saracinesca,' " she answered. " 'The Great Man from the Provinces.' 'The Mayor of Casterbridge.' "

"Oh, yes," he interrupted. "How do you like Balzac?"

"Oh, he's delightful to me. I liked 'The Mayor of Casterbridge,' though, as well as any," she answered.

"I should imagine you would," he said, submitting one of those keen observations which was the result of his comprehension of her nature.

"Why?" she asked.

"Well," he said, "you are rather gloomy in your disposition, and all of Hardy's novels have that in them."

"I?" asked Carrie.

"Not exactly gloomy," he added. "There's another word—melancholia, sad. I should judge you were rather lonely in your disposition."

For answer Carrie only looked.

"Let's see," put in Mrs. Vance, "didn't Hardy write 'Tess of the D'Urbervilles,' or something like that?"

"Yes," said Ames.

"Well, I couldn't see so much in that. It's too sad."

Carrie turned her eyes on Ames for a reply.

"No one who didn't feel the pathetic side of life would," he retorted.

"There!" thought Carrie triumphantly.

"Oh, I don't know," replied Mrs. Vance, rather shocked at the blunt reply. "I think I feel something of it."

"Not so very much," laughed Ames.

This served to ward off interference for awhile.

"I think you would enjoy 'Père Goriot,' " he said, turning to Carrie, "if you haven't read it. That's one of Balzac's."

"I haven't," said Carrie.

"Well, you get it." He was thinking to start her off on a course of reading which would improve her. Anyone so susceptible to improvement should be aided. Her mind seemed free and quick enough to grasp most anything. "Read all of Balzac's. They will do you good."

Carrie expressed something about the sadness of the failure of Lucien de Rubemfré in "The Great Man from the Provinces."

"Yes," he answered, "if a man doesn't make knowledge his object, he's very likely to fail. He didn't fail in anything but love and fortune, and that isn't everything. Balzac makes too much of those things. He wasn't any poorer in mind when he left Paris than when he came to it. In fact he was richer, if he had only thought so. Failure in love isn't so much."

"Oh, don't you think so?" asked Carrie, wistfully.

"No. It's the man who fails in his mind who fails completely. Some people get the idea that their happiness lies in wealth and position. Balzac thought so, I believe. Many people do. They look about and wring their hands over every passing vision of joy. They forget that if they had that, they couldn't have something else. The world is full of desirable situations, but unfortunately we can only occupy one at a time. Most people occupy one and neglect it too long for the others."

Carrie looked at him, closely, but he did not see her. He seemed to be stating her case. Had not she done that very thing, and often?

"Your happiness is within yourself wholly if you will only believe it," he went on. "When I was quite young I felt as if I were ill-used because other boys were dressed better than I was, were more sprightly with the girls than I, and I grieved and grieved, but now I'm over that. I have found out that everyone is more or less dissatisfied. No one has exactly what his heart wishes."

"Not anybody?" she asked.

"No," he said.

Carrie looked wistfully away.

"It comes down to this," he went on. "If you have powers, cultivate them. The work of doing it will bring you as much satisfaction as you will ever get. The huzzas of the public don't mean anything. That's the aftermath—you've been paid and satisfied if you are not selfish and greedy long before that reaches you."

"Oh, I don't know," said Carrie, thinking of her own short struggle, and feeling as if her whole life had been one of turmoil, for which her present state was no reward.

Suddenly he seemed to have reached the state of her mind without talking.

"You ought not to be gloomy, however," he said, looking at her— "as young as you are."

"I'm not," she replied, "exactly. I don't know what it is. I don't seem to be doing what I want to do. I thought once I was; but now I—"

Their eyes had met, and for the first time Ames felt the shock of sympathy, keen and strong. (481–83)

BACKGROUNDS AND SOURCES I

CARRIE, HURSTWOOD, DROUET, THE CITY, AND THE STRIKE

Carrie*

Dreiser based the central incident of *Sister Carrie*—Hurstwood's theft and his "abduction" of Carrie—on the experience of one of his sisters, Emma Dreiser. In early 1886 L. A. Hopkins, a clerk in a Chicago saloon, stole approximately $3,500 from his employers and fled with Emma to New York. Dreiser was then fourteen and was living with his mother in the small town of Warsaw, Indiana. He heard of Emma's escapade at that time and also when he moved to Chicago in mid-1887, but it was probably not until the early 1890s that he learned of it fully from his brother Paul and from Emma herself.

There are a number of major as well as minor differences between contemporary newspaper accounts of the theft and Dreiser's fictional version of it in *Sister Carrie*. These differences stemmed both from Dreiser's sources of information—Emma in particular no doubt wished to portray herself as favorably as possible—and from his reshaping of what he knew about the incident. The most important differences involve the social status of Hopkins and the nature of the elopement. Hurstwood is a manager who lives on the upper-middle-class North Side; Hopkins, a "trusted clerk," has a home on the less fashionable West Side. And Hopkins and Emma appear to have carefully planned the theft and the flight, unlike the "accident" and "abduction" themes that characterize these events in the novel.

At one point in the history of Dreiser's critical reputation it was conventional to accuse him of merely "copying from life" because of his close use of documentary sources. But Dreiser's fictional version of the Hopkins affair reveals that he transformed a tawdry and occasionally comic event into a narrative of depth and complexity by his introduction of such new elements as Hurstwood's social distinction, Carrie's "innocence," and the accidental closing of the safe.

---

* Editorial omissions within selections are indicated by asterisks. All notes are my own unless otherwise indicated. For published letters, I have followed the text of the letter as published. For unpublished letters, I have made minor editorial emendations.

Emma Dreiser as a young woman. From a photograph in the W. A. Swanberg Papers, Rare Book and Manuscript Library, University of Pennsylvania Library. Reproduced by permission of the Trustees of the University of Pennsylvania.

CHICAGO MAIL

He Cleaned Out the Safe†

One of Chapin & Gore's Clerks Disappears with $3,500 and Some Jewelry

At 6 o'clock last evening Mr. L. A. Hopkins, a trusted employe at the main house of Chapin & Gore,[1] closed up the safes and vault, and disappeared. When the house was opened this morning it was discovered that about $3,500, and jewelry worth about $200, had also disappeared. Hopkins left his home on West Madison street yesterday morning and has not been seen there since. He was today traced to a depot, where he boarded a train at 9 o'clock last evening. He has been in the employ of the firm since 1872 and had the implicit confidence of his employers. He is about 40 years of age and has a wife and a charming daughter of 18, who are almost prostrated with grief. He was a rather fine appearing man and bore such a strong resemblance to president Cleveland that at the store he had been nicknamed "Grove." It is hardly possible that he can escape. It is the opinion at the store that his mind must have been affected, for the amount of money he took cannot, in itself, explain his act, with all of its inevitable consequences.

CHICAGO TRIBUNE

Clerk and Cash‡

Both Missed by Chapin & Gore About the Same Time— $3,500 Booty

Chapin & Gore are out $3,500, or nearly so, and it is more than suggested that a hitherto-trusted employe is richer by that amount. It has been the duty of the shipping clerk, L. A. Hopkins, to be in attendance at the firm's warehouse on Monroe street every alternate

---

† *Chicago Mail* 15 Feb. 1886: 1.
1. In later years Dreiser mistakenly stated that Hopkins's employers were Hannah and Hogg, the owners of several well-known Chicago saloons. (Hurstwood's saloon is called Hannah and Hogg's in the manuscript of *Sister Carrie*.) Although Hannah and Hogg did not own a "resort" on Adams Street (the location of Fitzgerald and Moy's), their saloons (principally in downtown Chicago) were much more pretentious than those of Chapin and Gore, which were on the South Side. Dreiser's error was repeated by biographers and critics until corrected by George Steinbrecker in his "Inaccurate Accounts of *Sister Carrie*," *American Literature* 23 (January 1952): 490–93.
‡ *Chicago Tribune* 16 Feb. 1886: 8.

Sunday to close up the place and set things to right generally after the departure of the other employes. When the head bookkeeper reached the office this morning and opened the vault he discovered a good deal of confusion amongst the books and papers stored there and the absence of any vestige of United States currency. As there ought to have been close on to the before mentioned amount there, the bookkeeper went on a rapid tour of investigation amongst the clerks and found the desk of Mr. Hopkins vacant. The ex-shipping clerk is a man of 40, and married, and a message sent to his late house, No. 740 West Monroe Street, elicited information to the effect that he had not been seen there since Sunday.

It is the custom of the firm to receive cash deposits from sporting men, giving in exchange deposit certificates similar to those issued by banks. About $1,750 worth of these deposits were issued Saturday, and the cash placed in the safe along with a little less than $2,000 that was already there. The total constituted the booty secured by the thief.

A feature of the case that strengthens the tenet of the firm that Hopkins is the marauder is the fact that he was seen Sunday afternoon counting over the receipts of the cigar-stand amounting to $100, that had just been turned over to him, and that this sum, which consisted entirely of small bills and silver, has also disappeared. A representative of the firm expressed to a TRIBUNE reporter a belief that Hopkins had carefully planned the deed beforehand and timed his theft so as to catch the 6 o'clock Michigan Central express for Canada, where he would arrive about as soon as it was discovered. Hopkins was paid a salary of $2,400 a year, and, it was said, had hitherto served his employers faithfully and proven himself in every respect an honest and efficient servant. He was not known to be addicted to any vice, except perhaps a little fondness for draw-poker. The case has been placed in the hands of detectives.

CHICAGO MAIL

A Woman in the Case†

Chapin & Gore's Embezzling Employe Said to Have Left with a Fair Companion

When L. A. Hopkins, Chapin & Gore's trusted employe, and $3,500 of the firm's money disappeared together yesterday morning, it appears they had still another companion. It is now said a pretty

† *Chicago Mail* 16 Feb. 1886: 1.

West Side woman is also missing, and as Hopkins had called on her very frequently previous to his departure the detectives are trying to show that she went with him. The Employes in Chapin & Gore's place now remember that Hopkins was called to the telephone twice on Saturday, a somewhat unusual thing, and that on one occasion a female voice said: "This woman is bothering me. Come right away." The words were spoken by a Mrs. Nelson, of 344 South Morgan street, a sister of the woman whom the detectives think has decamped with Hopkins. Mrs. Nelson says her sister is not with Hopkins. She is a respectable lady, and is married to a man named Frazier.[1]

"My sister Emma, or, as some called her, Minnie,[2] has been living with me for the past week, as she was sick," said Mrs. Nelson, "but when I heard of the trouble and the talk that Hopkins had run away with my sister I sent her away."

"She is not at home, then!"

"No, sir, she is not. I have two telegrams from her and she is all right. This thing will break her husband's heart when he hears of it."

"Do you know Hopkins?" asked the reporter.

"Yes, he has been here occasionally."

"He was here Saturday evening!"

"No, sir, he was not. He has not been here since last Thursday night, and I telephoned to him Saturday not to dare come into my house again. Hopkins is all right, though. I don't know where he is. I only know he is on a big drunk, but he is in good hands, and when he gets sober he will be back again. The money is all right, too, unless he has been robbed or something has happened to him. I would not be surprised to see him on duty at Chapin & Gore's tomorrow morning, in fact. I know he will be there if he is sobered up."

Mrs. Nelson also told the reporter that her sister Minnie never had anything to do with Hopkins, and that she knew Hopkins had a wife and daughter living on West Madison street. The neighbors say a hack called at the Nelson house yesterday afternoon and took a lady's trunk away. A further investigation proved that the trunk was taken to the American Express company's office and was transferred by a driver named Hopkins. The detectives will endeavor to trace the trunk today. Hopkins is supposed to have jumped the town last Sunday night. The total amount of money missing is $3,500 and $200 worth of jewelry. Hopkins is 40 years old and has a wife and 18-year-

---

1. "Mrs. Nelson" is probably Theresa Dreiser, another of Dreiser's five sisters, who was then living in Chicago and who was herself involved with a wealthy, middle-aged lover. Theresa was undoubtedly, attempting to avoid disclosing both Emma's name and her whereabouts; hence the "Mrs. Frazier" in this account and the "Mamie Tracey Treigh" on February 17.
2. Emma, whose full name was Emma Wilhelmina, was indeed often called Minnie, which suggests that Dreiser may have derived the name Carrie as a diminutive parallel to Minnie. Carrie's sister, it should also be recalled, is named Minnie Hanson.

old daughter living at 776 West Madison street. The home is beautifully furnished, and has about it the air of a very pleasant home.

CHICAGO MAIL

A Dashing Blonde†

*Embezzler Hopkins Had a Fair Companion When He Skipped
for Canada*

THE CROOKED CLERK PROVED FALSE TO HIS MARRIAGE VOWS,
AND MADE HIS HOME MISERABLE

It is now certain that a woman was with L. A. Hopkins, Chapin &
Gore's cashier, when he disappeared Sunday night. Her name is
Mamie Tracey Treigh, a young married woman who has not been
living with her husband for the last year.[1] She is described as a dashing blonde, with an abundance of auburn hair and good features.
She has been living, up to last Friday, with Mrs. Millie Nelson, at
344 North Morgan street, near Blue Island avenue, and it is here
where Hopkins passed most of his time. During the whole winter, it
is said, he has not spent five days out of a month with his wife and
pretty daughter at his home at 747 West Madison street.

A reporter for THE MAIL called on Mrs. Hopkins, but, as she is
affected with heart disease and is almost prostrated by the conduct
of her husband, she refused to be seen. Her daughter Mamie, however, a refined girl of 18, was induced to say something.

"I must admit," she said, "that papa was not home very often.
About a woman being in the case, of course I know nothing, as I was
not made a confidant."

It was further learned that Hopkins and his wife frequently quarreled about Mamie Treigh, and that lively scenes occurred in the
Hopkins household, the Treigh woman being the subject of the dispute.

Mrs. Hopkins wished to file a bill for separate maintenance. To
prove her husband's unfaithfulness she placed one of Pinkerton's
detectives on his track. He was followed from the store to 344 South
Morgan street last Thursday evening. When Mrs. Hopkins was
informed by the detectives of the whereabouts of her unfaithful husband, she, with several friends and a policeman, went to Mrs. Nelson's house at 1 o'clock Friday morning. They did not enter boldly,

---

† *Chicago Mail* 17 Feb. 1886: 1.
1. The "husband" is probably the "aged architect" who was living with Emma in 1884 when
   Dreiser spent a summer in Chicago. See p. 381.

but cautiously approached the building in the darkness. Gaining the porch, the front window was noiselessly raised. Mrs. Hopkins dropped into the front parlor and discovered her husband and his paramour in the room together. She watched the sleeping couple for a moment, and then called him by name. He was awake in a moment, and upon beholding his wife's white face at the window, he exclaimed:

"My God! ma (he sometimes called her ma), is that you!"

He jumped from the bed, and, rushing to the window, he prayed to his wife to forgive him. The moment the Treigh woman heard Hopkins call to his wife she ran into the back parlor where Mrs. Nelson was sleeping.

The policeman wanted to arrest Hopkins and the woman at that time, but his wife only wished to procure evidence of his infidelity, and would not consent to it. The guilty couple were left together, and Mrs. Hopkins, the detective, and other witnesses returned to their homes.[2] Friday afternoon the Treigh woman received a letter from Hopkins, and soon after she left the house. It is believed they met that afternoon and arranged the plan to leave the city together Sunday night.

Up to 9 o'clock no remittance from the runaway had been received. If the draft was sent, as the telegram of yesterday said, it should arrive here some time today.

CHICAGO TRIBUNE

Hopkins Is Sorry,
And Will Send Back the Money and Jewelry
He Stole From Chapin & Gore†

A dispatch dated Montreal and signed "Hopkins" was received by Chapin & Gore yesterday to the effect that most of the money stolen from their safe Sunday night would be returned shortly by New York draft, and that certain "jewelry" would follow by express. The jewelry referred to consisted of a gold watch and chain and a diamond ring and stud, which belonged to employes of the firm and had been placed in the vault for safe-keeping. "We are playing it for genuine," said a representative of the firm to a TRIBUNE reporter yesterday, who asked whether the telegram was considered as a sign of repentance

---

2. Since Dreiser never mentioned this incident in any later recollection, he was probably unaware of it. It nevertheless anticipates a number of situations in his fiction in which detectives are used to discover an illicit romance.

† *Chicago Tribune* 17 Feb. 1886: 8.

or a subterfuge engineered by the thief to procure a relaxation of anticipated pursuit. "We suppose here that Hopkins, seeing the mess he had got himself into, grew desperate, almost insane, in fact, and planned his scheme of robbery and flight while laboring under a fit of despair brought on by the contemplation of his difficulties; that probably after a ride of thirty-six hours on a railroad-train he realized the position in which he stood, and resolved to make restitution and retrieve himself so far as lay in his power."

Great satisfaction was expressed by the erring clerk's fellow employes, amongst whom he had been extremely popular, at the receipt of the telegram and much speculation was indulged in as to whether, should he return, his old position would be given back to him. With regard to this the members of the firm were reticent, but it is not thought likely they will be hard with him. The stories as to Hopkins' relationships with a notorious West Side woman were corroborated, but it is denied that she accompanied him in his flight.

THEODORE DREISER

[Sisters and Suitors]†

Early in 1914 Dreiser began a four-volume autobiography that he intended to call "A History of Myself." During the following five years he completed two of these volumes, *Dawn* and *Newspaper Days*. (The third and fourth books; "Literary Apprenticeship" and "Literary Experiences," were never written.) He soon realized that *Dawn* dealt too openly with his family's private life for publication while most of his sisters and brothers were still alive. He therefore put the manuscript aside and published instead, in 1922, the second volume of his autobiography. (At his publisher's insistence, the work was called *A Book About Myself*, though Dreiser restored its title to *Newspaper Days* in 1931.) *Dawn* itself did not appear until 1931. Even at this late date, Dreiser felt that he should disguise the names of his sisters. In order of age he called them Eleanor (Mame), Janet (Emma), Ruth (Theresa), Amy (Sylvia), and Trina (Claire).

In his autobiographies Dreiser often mixed narrative accounts of his sisters' experiences with observations about sexual morality—a combination that had already received fictional expression in *Sister Carrie* and *Jennie Gerhardt*.

But as bad if not worse, were the heart romances of each of the several daughters to be taken into account. For my own confused part, between selling newspapers and running errands for the cara-

† From Theodore Dreiser, *Dawn* (New York: 1931), 172–74, 233–34.

mel man downstairs, I was nevertheless dimly aware of a certain
emotional activity in connection with my sisters and their suitors;[1]
the manufacturer who admired my sister Ruth appearing to take her
out driving of an afternoon or evening; the aristocratic Harahan stopping at one of the principal hotels and inviting Eleanor, Ruth and a
friend of theirs to dinner; Janet and Amy and even Trina, as young
as she was, finding youths or men who, attracted by their looks, were
anxious to occupy their time. I might attempt to disentangle what
was unquestionably a knot or network of emotions and interests, all
relating to the particular love life of each, but I would fail for lack
of any real knowledge of the underlying subtleties and beauties—as,
of course, beauties and subtleties there were.

I have described, for instance, how Eleanor came to Chicago and
met Harahan, but not, I think, how he in turn introduced her and
Ruth to the wealthy manufacturer who came to Evansville to visit
Ruth. From all appearances, his courtship of Ruth, or at least his
friendship for her, was sanctioned by my mother. Whether this was
wise or unwise, I cannot say. He was much older albeit a widower
and wealthy. My one idea of it is that as usual my mother was at
once strangely nebulous and optimistic. She had no ability to advise
shrewdly in a situation of this kind, had she thought it important to
advise. Being dubious of life and its various manifestations, I think
she thought it as well to let her daughters face their own problems—
a viewpoint with which I find myself in agreement. Life is to be
learned from life, and in no other way. That Ruth was obviously
intrigued by this man I came to know when I chanced to enter the
apartment one day when all of the others were out and discovered
her in his arms. By what arrangement, if any, he chanced to be there,
I do not know. No doubt, she had calculated on the house being
empty. At any rate, she requested me afterward to say nothing about
it, and while I was shocked or moved in a strange way, I did as she
wished. It seemed to me that my sister, being so much older, should
be able to regulate her own life.

Similarly, Janet, who had been chided for her conduct this long
while, had on coming to Chicago taken up with an able and well-to-
do, though somewhat aged, architect, and was now living with him
in a hotel on South Halstead Street. I recall her giving Ed and myself
a meal ticket issued by a semi-public restaurant attached to this hotel
and afterwards being invited to her rooms in the absence of the liege
lord. I was filled with wonder at her clothes, furniture and the like,
which seemed to contrast more than favorably with our own. Her
boudoir dressing-table, for instance, was piled with bright silver toilet
articles and a closet into which I peered was plentifully supplied with

1. The time is the summer of 1884; Dreiser was thirteen, and most of the Dreiser family was
temporarily in Chicago.

clothes. Janet herself looked prosperous and cheerful. I remember going back through the grey, foggy streets of Chicago, looking at the huge sign-boards of the shows then playing: "Humpty Dumpty," "Eight Bells"—and thinking how fine it all was.

Moral problems such as the lives of my several sisters presented to me had no great weight. And have not now—any more than do those of other men's sisters or daughters. It is the way of life, however much socially it may be denied, concealed, or disguised. At times, assuming I heard someone else discussing them moralistically—my father, say—I was inclined to experience a depression or reduction in pride which was purely osmatic—a process of emotional absorption—no more. Had I not heard someone else criticizing, I would not have been so moved. And yet, at times, and because of this, I had the notion that they were not doing right; that men (this must have been gathered from my father's many preachments) were using them as mere playthings; but most of the time I had a feeling that they were their own masters, or might be if they would. Also that perhaps they enjoyed being playthings. Why not? And through it all ran the feeling that good, bad, or indifferent as individuals or things might be, life was a splendid surge, a rich sensation, and that it was fine to be alive. And in so far as my sister Janet was concerned, my final feeling was that she was prosperous and individual and perhaps as well off as some others, if not more so.

But to return to my sister Eleanor.[2] Being in love and waiting to be taken over completely by Harahan, she was leading a trying, and yet to her, I assume, invaluable life. In later years I heard all about the love woes of this period: the eagerness of letters, the despair of not receiving them, the agony of suspecting other flirtations, and so on and so forth. Until at last she had found herself desperately in love with this man, as she once told me, she had been moderately entertained by the admirations and attentions of first one man and then another. But mere flirtations these—not complete sex relations. She had not been sufficiently interested. The thought that comes to me now, though, is that by reason of criticism on the part of others—taboos and the like—and however generally evaded or ignored—we do not prefer to contemplate these youthful sex variations, either in real life or in literature. And yet, how common! You may measure the thinness of literature and of moral dogma and religious control by your own observations and experiences. Look back over your own life and see!

* * *

2. Dreiser had used Mame (Eleanor) as one of the principal sources for his portrayal of Jennie Gerhardt.

But then, that very winter, following close on these social discrepancies, came news of my sister Janet's marriage in Chicago.[3] I recall being very much impressed, for after all of the most riotous condemnation of her I had heard from my father, if not my mother, here was (as my parents seemed to see it) this much desired thing, marriage, and that to a man who if "no great shakes" socially in our world was nevertheless of some little position elsewhere, in New York City, no less; a New York politician, as I heard him called, a deputy or second deputy somebody in the New York Street Cleaning Department, who also, as time was to prove, was of some small political influence, and hence means. That is, he was connected with Tammany Hall—one of its ward or district lieutenants—and as such up to his arm-pits, as I, if no other, learned later, in the shameful political conniving and legerdemain that was a part of all politics and jobholding in New York City in the 1890's.

But what appeared to be conveyed at this time was that he was still comparatively young—forty or so—and had means, for subsequently there were rumors of a charming apartment in 15th Street in New York, also jewels, furs, and exciting trips to Saratoga and other places, and finally the birth of a boy, and later a girl, both well-favored physically as time was to prove, and in their subsequent years as successful and conventional as the average person, no more and no less so.

But in regard to all this, I recall meditating a little at the time. For after all, the tirades I have spoken of were of so recent a day. And I had been so reduced by them, emotionally and physically. And more, considering all that had been said, I had been strongly of the opinion that no respectable man anywhere would have either Janet or Amy. And yet here was Janet already taken over by one, and that one, presumably at least, respectable. For was he not an officeholder in the great city of New York, and more, as a letter in regard to all this stated, a Catholic? This latter fact appeared to relieve if not impress my mother, and as I well knew would pass as pure gold with my father. For what more than that could be desired in a man? Honesty was excellent enough, but even the lack of that forgiven if one remained a true Catholic! I saw the fact sticking out of all my father's arguments. Weakness of character? A commonplace mind? Trudging dumbness? Were not nearly all Catholics like that? But faith in the Church! Ah, how excellent! What more could be desired?

And true enough, when my father heard of this very sudden and all too dimly outlined marriage, complete silence as to Janet's past. So she was married at last! High time! And to a Catholic! Well, she

3. The time is early 1886, soon after the elopement of Emma and Hopkins. The Dreiser family was then living in Warsaw.

was lucky! So harum-scarum a girl scarcely deserved so much. Had anyone witnessed the marriage? Was there any proof? There appeared to be, since both Ruth and Eleanor vouched for it. They had witnessed the marriage in some outlandish Saint Something-or-other Church in Chicago. Very good, let bygones be bygones! And in so far as Janet and her father were concerned, they were. In short, the typical happy ending. Or, as we say in these days: "Swell!"

THEODORE DREISER

[Emma's Elopement]†

My sister's husband having something to do with this narrative, I will touch upon his history as well as that of my sister. In her youth E—— was one of the most attractive of the girls in our family.¹ She never had any intellectual or artistic interests of any kind; if she ever read a book I never heard of it. But as for geniality, sympathy, industry, fairmindedness and an unchanging and self-sacrificing devotion to her children, I have never known any one who could rival her. With no adequate intellectual training, save such as is provided by the impossible theories and teachings of the Catholic Church, she was but thinly capacitated to make her way in the world.

At eighteen or nineteen she had run away and gone to Chicago, where she had eventually met H——, who had apparently fallen violently in love with her. He was fifteen years older than she and moderately well versed in the affairs of this world. At the time she met him he was the rather successful manager of a wholesale drug company, reasonably well-placed socially, married and the father of two or three children, the latter all but grown to maturity. They eloped, going direct to New York.

This was a great shock to my mother, who managed to conceal it from my father although it was a three-days' wonder in the journalistic or scandal world of Chicago. Nothing more was heard of her for several years, when a dangerous illness overtook my mother in Warsaw and E——came hurrying back for a few days' visit. This was followed by another silence, which was ended by the last illness and death of my mother in Chicago, and she again appeared, a distrait and hysteric soul. I never knew any one to yield more completely to her emotions than she did on this occasion; she was almost fantastic

† From Theodore Dreiser, *A Book About Myself* (New York: 1922), 438–39.
1. In *A Book About Myself* Dreiser used initials for the names of his sisters as well as for a few other figures. E——is Emma; H——is Hopkins. Emma visited her mother in Warsaw in 1886 and attended her funeral in Chicago in 1890. Dreiser spoke to his brother Paul in St. Louis in 1893.

in her grief. During all this time she had been living in New York, and she and her husband were supposed to be well off. Later, talking to Paul in St. Louis, I gathered that H——, while not so successful since he had gone East, was not a bad sort and that he had managed to connect himself with politics in some way, and that they were living comfortably in Fifteenth Street. But when I arrived there I found that they were by no means comfortable.[2] The Tammany administration, under which a year or two before he had held an inspectorship of some kind, had been ended by the investigations of the Lexow Committee, and he was now without work of any kind. Also, instead of having proved a faithful and loving husband, he had long since wearied of his wife and strayed elsewhere. Now, having fallen from his success, he was tractable. Until the arrival of my brother Paul, who for reasons of sympathy had agreed to share the expenses here during the summer season, he had induced E——to rent rooms, but for this summer this had been given up. With the aid of my brother and some occasional work H——still did they were fairly comfortable. My sister if not quite happy was still the devoted slave of her children and a most pathetically dependent housewife. Whatever fires or vanities of her youth had compelled her to her meteoric career, she had now settled down and was content to live for her children. Her youth was over, love gone. And yet she managed to convey an atmosphere of cheer and hopefulness.[3]

2. Dreiser was visiting New York (for the first time) in the early summer of 1894.
3. In the manuscript versions of both *Dawn* and *Newspaper Days* Dreiser described more openly and fully the New York experiences of Emma and Hopkins than he did in the published books. The runaway couple had at first supported themselves by renting rooms for prostitution. By the time Dreiser moved to New York in late 1894, Hopkins had lost his job in the street-cleaning department and was no longer supporting his family. Emma was now anxious to be separated from Hopkins and appealed to Dreiser for aid. Sometime during the winter of 1894–95, Dreiser pretended that he had to return to Pittsburgh. He then had a friend mail a letter from that city in which Dreiser asked Emma to come live with him. She thereupon seemingly left for Pittsburgh, though in reality she moved to another New York apartment, leaving Hopkins for good.

Hurstwood

Dreiser drew upon a number of sources for his concept and portrait of Hurstwood's decline. Among these were his discovery, while a newspaperman, of the vagaries of human nature; his awareness of Hopkins's collapse; and his fear that he himself, out of work in a "huge and cruel" New York, might suffer the same fate as a Clark or a Hopkins.

THEODORE DREISER

[Downfall in the City]†

I remember one man in particular, Clark I think his name was, who arrived on the scene just about this time and who fascinated me. He was so able and sure of touch mentally and from an editorial point of view, and yet financially and in every material way he was such a failure. He came from Kansas City or Omaha while I was on the *Republic* and had worked in many, many places before that.[1] He was a stocky, dark, clerkly figure, with something of the manager or owner or leader about him, a most shrewd and capable-looking person. And when he first came to the *Republic* he seemed destined to rise rapidly and never to want for anything, so much self-control and force did he appear to have. He was a hard worker, quiet, unostentatious, and once I had gained his confidence, he gradually revealed a tale of past position and comfort which, verified as it was by Wandell and Williams, was startling when contrasted with his present position. Although he was not much over forty he had been editor or managing editor of several important papers in the West but had lost them through some primary disaster which had caused him to take to drink—his wife's unfaithfulness, I believe—and his inability in recent years to stay sober for more than three months at a stretch.

† From Theodore Dreiser, *A Book About Myself* (New York: 1922), 223–25, 461–62, 463–64.

1. Dreiser was a reporter for the *St. Louis Republic* from April 1893, to February 1894. Wandell and Williams were *Republic* editors. Dick and Peter were staff artists on the *St. Louis Globe-Democrat*, the newspaper for which Dreiser had worked before moving over to the *Republic*.

In some other city he had been an important factor in politics. Here he was, still clean and spruce apparently (when I first saw him, at any rate), going about his work with a great deal of energy, writing the most satisfactory newspaper stories; and then, once two or three months of such labor had gone by, disappearing. When I inquired of Williams and Wandell as to his whereabouts the former stared at me with his one eye and smiled, then lifted his fingers in the shape of a glass to his mouth. Wandell merely remarked: "Drink, I think. He may show up and he may not. He had a few weeks' wages when he left."

I did not hear anything more of him for some weeks, when suddenly one day, in that wretched section of St. Louis beloved of Dick and Peter as a source of literary material, I was halted by a figure which I assumed to be one of the lowest of the low. A short, matted, dirty black beard concealed a face that bore no resemblance to Clark. A hat that looked as though it might have been lifted out of an ash-barrel was pulled slouchily and defiantly over long uncombed black hair. His face was filthy, as were his clothes and shoes, slimy even. An old brown coat (how come by, I wonder?) was marked by a green-ish slime across the back and shoulders, slime that could only have come from a gutter.

"Don't you know me, Dreiser?" he queried in a deep, rasping voice, a voice so rusty that it sounded as though it had not been used for years "—Clark, Clark of the *Republic*. You know me—" and then when I stared in amazement he added shrewdly: "I've been sick and in a hospital. You haven't a dollar about you, have you? I have to rest a little and get myself in shape again before I can go to work."

"Well, of all things!" I exclaimed in amazement, and then: "I'll be damned!" I could not help laughing: he looked so queer, impossible almost. A stage tramp could scarcely have done better, I gave him the dollar. "What in the world are you doing—drinking?" and then, overawed by the memory of his past efficiency and force I could not go on. It was too astonishing.

"Yes, I've been drinking," he admitted, a little defiantly, I thought, "but I've been sick too, just getting out now. I got pneumonia there in the summer and couldn't work. I'll be all right after a while. What's news at the *Republic*?"

"Nothing."

He mumbled something about having played in bad luck, that he would soon be all right again, then ambled up the wretched rickety street and disappeared.

I bustled out of that vicinity as fast as I could. I was so startled and upset by this that I hurried back to the lobby of the Southern Hotel (my favorite cure for all despondent days), where all was brisk, comfortable, gay. Here I purchased a newspaper and sat down in a rocking-chair. Here at least was no sign of poverty or want. In order to be rid of that sense of failure and degradation which had crept over me I took a drink or two myself. That any one as capable as Clark could fall so low in so short a time was quite beyond me. The still strongly puritan and moralistic streak in me was shocked beyond measure, and for days I could do little but contrast the figure of the man I had seen about the *Republic* office with that I had met in that street of degraded gin-mills and tumbledown tenements. Could people really vary so greatly and in so short a time? What must be the nature of their minds if they could do that? Was mine like that? Would it become so? For days thereafter I was wandering about in spirit with this man from gin-mill to gin-mill and lodging-house to lodging-house, seeing him drink at scummy bars and lying down at night on a straw pallet in some wretched hole.

*   *   *

My sister, on seeing me again, was delighted.[2] I did not know then, and perhaps if I had I should not have been so pleased, that I was looked upon by her as the possible way out of a very difficult and trying crisis which she and her two children were then facing. For H——, from being a one-time fairly resourceful and successful and aggressive man, had slipped into a most disconcerting attitude of weakness and all but indifference before the onslaughts of the great city.

My brother Paul, being away, saw no reason why he should be called upon to help them, since H——was as physically able as himself. Aside from renting their rooms there was apparently no other source of income here, at least none which H——troubled to provide. He appeared to be done for, played out. Like so many who have fought a fair battle and then lost, he had wearied of the game and was drifting. And my sister, like so many of the children of ordinary families the world over, had received no practical education or training and knew nothing other than housework, that profitless trade. In consequence, within a very short time after my arrival, I found myself faced by one of two alternatives: that of retiring and leaving her to shift as best she might (a step which, in view of what followed, would have been wiser but which my unreasoning sympathy would not permit me to do), or of assisting her with what means I had. But this would be merely postponing the day of reckoning for all of them and bringing a great deal of trouble upon myself. For, finding me

2. Dreiser resigned from the *Pittsburgh Dispatch* in the late fall of 1894 and came to New York with the hope of getting a job with a New York paper. He had little success and suffered considerable poverty and depression until his brother Paul, a songwriter and entertainer, helped found the magazine *Ev'ry Month* in the spring of 1895 and made Dreiser the editor.

willing to pay for my room and board here, and in addition to advance certain sums which had nothing to do with my obligations, H—felt that he could now drift a little while longer and so did, accepting through his wife such doles as I was willing to make. My sister, fumbling, impractical soul, flowing like water into any crevice of opportunity, accepted this sacrifice on my part.

* * *

Rather dourly and speculatively, therefore, after I had visited four or five of these offices with exactly the same result in each instance, I went finally to City Hall Park, which fronted the majority of them— the *Sun*, the *Tribune*, the *Times*, the *World*, the *Press*—and stared at their great buildings. About me was swirling the throng which has always made that region so interesting, the vast mass that bubbles upward from the financial district and the regions south of it and crosses the plaza to Brooklyn Bridge and the elevated roads (the subways had not come yet). About me on the benches of the park was, even in this gray, chill December weather, that large company of bums, loafers, tramps, idlers, the flotsam and jetsam of the great city's whirl and strife to be seen there today. I presume I looked at them and then considered myself and these great offices, and it was then that the idea of *Hurstwood* was born. The city seemed so huge and cruel. I recalled gay Broadway of the preceding summer, and the baking, isolated, exclusive atmosphere of Fifth Avenue, all boarded up. And now I was here and it was winter, with this great newspaper world to be conquered, and I did not see how it was to be done. At four in the afternoon I dubiously turned my steps north-ward along the great, bustling, solidly commercial Broadway to Fif-teenth Street, walking all the way and staring into the shops. Those who recall *Sister Carrie*'s wanderings may find a taste of it here. In Union Square, before Tiffany's, I stared at an immense Christmas throng. Then in the darkness I wandered across to my sister's apart-ment, and in the warmth and light there set me down thinking what to do.

Drouet

There appears to be no specific source for the character of Drouet. Dreiser introduces him to the reader as a type—the "masher"—and it is perhaps as a type that Dreiser first conceived of his character. This view of the origin of Drouet is supported by Dreiser's use in chapter 1 of George Ade's description of the masher type. Ade's mock fables, which he had begun writing in 1897, were immensely successful and were widely reprinted. His "Fable of the Two Mandolin Players and the Willing Performer" appeared initially in the *Chicago Record* on October 7, 1899, and was republished later that month in Ade's *Fables in Slang*. Dreiser, who had begun *Sister Carrie* in September, revised in manuscript his initial characterization of Drouet and incorporated into it a number of sentences taken verbatim from Ade's description of the Willing Performer. Several reviewers noted the similarity, and Dreiser rewrote the passage for his 1907 edition of *Sister Carrie*—the only change he ever made in the published version of the novel. (See pp. 3–4 above for the original passage and for the 1907 revision.)

GEORGE ADE

The Fable of the Two Mandolin Players and the Willing Performer†

A very attractive Debutante knew two young Men who called on her every Thursday Evening, and brought their Mandolins along.

They were Conventional Young Men, of the Kind that you see wearing Spring Overcoats in the Clothing Advertisements. One was named Fred, and the other was Eustace.

The Mothers of the Neighborhood often remarked, "What Perfect Manners Fred and Eustace have!" Merely as an aside it may be added that Fred and Eustace were more Popular with the Mothers than they were with the Younger Set, although no one could say a Word against either of them. Only it was rumored in Keen Society that they didn't Belong. The Fact that they went Calling in a Crowd, and

† *Fables in Slang* (Chicago: 1900), 181–94.

took their Mandolins along, may give the Acute Reader some Idea
of the Life that Fred and Eustace held out to the Young Women of
their Acquaintance.

The Debutante's name was Myrtle. Her Parents were very Watchful, and did not encourage her to receive Callers, except such as were
known to be Exemplary Young Men. Fred and Eustace were a few
of those who escaped the Black List. Myrtle always appeared to be
glad to see them, and they regarded her as a Darned Swell Girl.

Fred's Cousin came from St. Paul on a Visit; and one Day, in the
Street, he saw Myrtle, and noticed that Fred tipped his Hat, and
gave her a Stage Smile.

"Oh, Queen of Sheba!" exclaimed the Cousin from St. Paul, whose
name was Gus, as he stood stock still, and watched Myrtle's Revers-
ible Plaid disappear around a Corner. "She's a Bird. Do you know
her well?"

"I know her Quite Well," replied Fred, coldly. "She is a Charming
Girl."

"She is all of that. You're a great Describer. And now what Night
are you going to take me around to Call on her?"

Fred very naturally Hemmed and Hawed. It must be remembered
that Myrtle was a member of an Excellent Family, and had been
schooled in the Proprieties, and it was not to be supposed that she
would crave the Society of slangy old Gus, who had an abounding
Nerve, and furthermore was as Fresh as the Mountain Air.

He was the Kind of Fellow who would see a Girl twice, and then,
upon meeting her the Third Time, he would go up and straighten
her Cravat for her, and call her by her First Name.

Put him into a Strange Company—en route to a Picnic—and by
the time the Baskets were unpacked he would have a Blonde all to
himself, and she would have traded her Fan for his College Pin.

If a Fair-Looker on the Street happened to glance at him Hard he
would run up and seize her by the Hand, and convince her that they
had Met. And he always Got Away with it, too.

In a Department Store, while waiting for the Cash Boy to come
back with the Change, he would find out the Girl's Name, her Favorite Flower, and where a Letter would reach her.

Upon entering a Parlor Car at St. Paul he would select a Chair
next to the Most Promising One in Sight, and ask her if she cared
to have the Shade lowered.

Before the Train cleared the Yards he would have the Porter bringing a Foot-Stool for the Lady.

At Hastings he would be asking her if she wanted Something to
Read.

At Red Wing he would be telling her that she resembled Maxine

Elliott,[1] and showing her his Watch, left to him by his Grandfather, a Prominent Virginian.

At La Crosse he would be reading the Menu Card to her, and telling her how different it is when you have Some One to join you in a Bite.

At Milwaukee he would go out and buy a Bouquet for her, and when they rode into Chicago they would be looking out of the same Window, and he would be arranging for her Baggage with the Transfer Man. After that they would be Old Friends.

Now, Fred and Eustace had been at School with Gus, and they had seen his Work, and they were not disposed to Introduce him into One of the most Exclusive Homes in the City.

They had known Myrtle for many Years; but they did not dare to Address her by her First Name, and they were Positive that if Gus attempted any of his usual Tactics with her she would be Offended; and, naturally enough they would be Blamed for bringing him to the House.

But Gus insisted. He said he had seen Myrtle, and she Suited him from the Ground up, and he proposed to have Friendly Doings with her. At last they told him they would take him if he promised to Behave. Fred warned him that Myrtle would frown down any attempt to be Familiar on Short Acquaintance, and Eustace said that as long as he had known Myrtle he had never Presumed to be Free and Forward with her. He had simply played the Mandolin. That was as Far Along as he had ever got.

Gus told them not to Worry about him. All he asked was a Start. He said he was a Willing Performer, but as yet he never had been Disqualified for Crowding. Fred and Eustace took this to mean that he would not Overplay his Attentions, so they escorted him to the House.

As soon as he had been Presented, Gus showed her where to sit on the Sofa, then he placed himself about Six Inches away and began to Buzz, looking her straight in the Eye. He said that when he first saw her he Mistook her for Miss Prentice, who was said to be the Most Beautiful Girl in St. Paul, only, when he came closer, he saw that it couldn't be Miss Prentice, because Miss Prentice didn't have such Lovely Hair. Then he asked her the Month of her Birth and told her Fortune, thereby coming nearer to Holding her Hand within Eight Minutes than Eustace had come in a Lifetime.

"Play something, Boys," he ordered, just as if he had paid them Money to come along and make Music for him.

They unlimbered their Mandolins and began to play a Sousa

---

1. A famous theatrical beauty of the 1890s.

March. He asked Myrtle if she had seen the New Moon. She replied that she had not, so they went Outside.

When Fred and Eustace finished the first Piece, Gus appeared at the open Window, and asked them to play "The Georgia Camp-Meeting," which had always been one of his Favorites.

So they played that, and when they had Concluded there came a Voice from the Outer Darkness, and it was the Voice of Myrtle. She said: "I'll tell you what to Play; play the Intermezzo."

Fred and Eustace exchanged Glances. They began to Perceive that they had been backed into a Siding. With a few Potted Palms in front of them, and two Cards from the Union, they would have been just the same as a Hired Orchestra.

But they played the Intermezzo and felt Peevish. Then they went to the Window and looked out. Gus and Myrtle were sitting in the Hammock, which had quite a Pitch toward the Center. Gus had braced himself by Holding to the back of the Hammock. He did not have his Arm around Myrtle, but he had it Extended in a Line parallel with her Back. What he had done wouldn't Justify a Girl in saying, "Sir!" but it started a Real Scandal with Fred and Eustace. They saw that the only Way to Get Even with her was to go Home without saying "Good Night." So they slipped out the Side Door, shivering with Indignation.

After that, for several Weeks, Gus kept Myrtle so Busy that she had no Time to think of considering other Candidates. He sent Books to her Mother, and allowed the Old Gentleman to take Chips away from him at Poker.

They were Married in the Autumn, and Father-in-Law took Gus into the Firm, saying that he had needed a good Pusher for a Long Time.

At the Wedding the two Mandolin Players were permitted to act as Ushers.

MORAL: *To get a fair Trial of Speed, use a Pace-Maker.*

The City

Dreiser first saw a major American city in the summer of 1884 when he and his family lived in Chicago for several months. From 1887 to 1892 (except for one year as a student at Indiana University), he held a series of miscellaneous jobs in Chicago, some of which (laundry driver, bill collector, and real estate agent) took him to all sections and among all classes of the city. He began his career as a reporter in Chicago in mid-1892 but soon moved on to St. Louis, where he spent a year and a half. After an additional nine months in Pittsburgh, he moved to New York in late 1894 and was still living there when he began *Sister Carrie* in the fall of 1899.

Dreiser recorded his reaction to the city in his autobiographies, in various articles of the 1890s, and in *Sister Carrie* as well as in other novels. To Dreiser the city was always a magical land in which all the power and wealth available to man was displayed. A few men, favored by fortune in strength and in natural ability, gained these rewards, though the majority lived empty and futile lives. The worlds of luxury and poverty, of beauty and degradation, were thus, in Dreiser's view, both complementary and inseparable. Neither the poor nor the rich could exist without the other, and neither could achieve the happiness conventionally attributed to honest labor or great wealth. Like a romantic poet responding to an object in nature, Dreiser found that the city was a compelling "objective correlative" of his response to experience. But Dreiser was a novelist, not a poet, and he therefore spoke primarily through plot rather than through image. The plots of the rise of Carrie and the fall of Hurstwood within the worlds of Chicago and New York are Dreiser's metaphoric expression of the "mystery and terror and wonder" he found in all life.

THEODORE DREISER

[Chicago]†

How shall one hymn, let alone suggest, a city as great as this in spirit? Possibly it had six or seven hundred thousand population at this

† From Theodore Dreiser, *Dawn* (New York: 1931), 159–60, 297–98.

time.[1] To it, and at the rate of perhaps fifty thousand or more a year, were hurrying all of the life-hungry natives of a hundred thousand farming areas, of small cities and towns, in America and elsewhere. The American of this time, native, for the most part, of endless backwoods communities, was a naive creature, coming with all the notions which political charlatans of the most uninformed character had poured into his ears. He was gauche, green, ignorant. But how ambitious and courageous! (Think of our family!) Such bumptiousness! Such assurance! Such a mixture of illusions concerning God, the characteristics of the human animal, and himself! He was distinctly one thing the while he was every imagining himself another.

Would that I might sense it all again! Would that I were able to suggest in prose the throb and urge and sting of my first days in Chicago! A veritable miracle of pleasing sensations and fascinating scenes. The spirit of Chicago flowed into me and made me ecstatic. Its personality was different from anything I had ever known; it was compound of hope and joy in existence, intense hope and intense joy. Cities, like individuals, can flare up with a great flare of hope. They have that miracle, personality, which as in the case of the individual is always so fascinating and so arresting.

* * *

I washed my face and brushed my clothes, then knelt down by the window—because I could hang farther out by doing so—and looked out.[2] East and west, for miles, as it seemed to me, was a double row of gas lamps already flaring in the dusk, and behind them the lighted faces of shops and, as they seemed to me, very brightly lighted, glowing in fact. And again, there were those Madison Street horsecars, yellow in color, jingling to and fro, their horses' feet plop-plopping as they came and went, and just as they had when I sold papers here four years before. And the scores and scores of pedestrians walking in the rain, some with umbrellas, some not, some hurrying, some not. New land, new life, was what my heart was singing! Inside the street cars, like toy men and women, were the acclimated Chicagoans, those who had been here long before I came, no doubt. Beautiful! Like a scene in a play: an Aladdin view in the Arabian nights. Cars, people, lights, shops! The odor and flavor of the city, the vastness of its reaches, seemed to speak or sing or tinkle like a living, breathing thing. It came to me again with inexpressible variety and richness, as if to say: "I am the soul of a million people! I am their joys, their prides, their loves, their appetites, their hungers, their sorrows! I am their good clothes and their poor ones, their light, their

1. The summer of 1884.
2. The time is the summer of 1887. Dreiser had just arrived in Chicago and was to begin looking for work the following day.

food, their lusts, their industries, their enthusiasms, their dreams! In me are all the pulses and wonders and tastes and loves of life itself! I am life! This is paradise! This is the mirage of the heart and brain and blood of which people dream. I am the pulsing urge of the universe! You are a part of me, I of you! All that life or hope is or can be or do, this I am, and it is here before you! Take of it! Live, live, satisfy your heart! Strive to be what you wish to be now while you are young and of it! Reflect its fire, its tang, its color, its greatness! Be, be, wonderful or strong or great, if you will but be!"

THEODORE DREISER

[New York]†

[New York] was not a handsome city. As I look back on it now, there was much that was gross and soggy and even repulsive about it.[1] It had too many hard and treeless avenues and cross streets, bare of anything save stone walls and stone or cobble pavements and wretched iron lamp-posts. There were regions that were painfully crowded with poverty, dirt, despair. The buildings were too uniformly low, compact, squeezed. Outside the exclusive residence and commercial areas there was no sense of length or space.

But having seen Broadway and this barren section of Fifth Avenue, I could not think of it in a hostile way, the magnetism of large bodies over small ones holding me. Its barrenness did not now appall me, nor its lack of beauty irritate. There was something else here, a quality of life and zest and security and ease for some, cheek by jowl with poverty and longing and sacrifice, which gives to life everywhere its keenest most pathetic edge. Here was none of that eager clattering snap so characteristic of many of our Western cities, which, while it arrests at first, eventually palls. No city that I had ever seen had exactly what this had. As a boy, of course, I had invested Chicago with immense color and force, and it was there, ignorant, American, semi-conscious, seeking, inspiring. But New York was entirely different. It had the feeling of gross and blissful and parading self-indulgence. It was as if self-indulgence whispered to you that here was its true home; as if, for the most part, it was here secure. Life here was harder perhaps, for some more aware, more cynical and ruthless and brazen and shameless, and yet more alluring for these very reasons. Wherever one turned one felt a consciousness of ease and gluttony, indifference to ideals, however low or high, and cou-

---

† From Theodore Dreiser, *A Book About Myself* (New York: 1922), 451–42, 480–81.
1. Dreiser was visiting New York as a guest of his brother Paul in the early summer of 1894.

pled with a sense of power that had found itself and was not easily
to be dislodged, of virtue that has little idealism and is willing to yield
for a price. Here, as one could feel, were huge dreams and lusts and
vanities being gratified hourly. I wanted to know the worst and the
best of it.

* * *

Nowhere before had I seen such a lavish show of wealth, or, such
bitter poverty. In my reporting rounds[2] I soon came upon the East
Side; the Bowery, with its endless line of degraded and impossible
lodging-houses, a perfect whorl of bums and failures; the Brooklyn
waterfront, part of it terrible in its degradation; and then by way of
contrast again the great hotels, the mansions along Fifth Avenue,
the smart shops and clubs and churches. When I went into Wall
Street, the Tenderloin, the Fifth Avenue district, the East and West
sides, I seemed everywhere to sense either a terrifying desire for lust
or pleasure or wealth, accompanied by a heartlessness which was
freezing to the soul, or a dogged resignation to deprivation and misery. Never had I seen so many down-and-out men—in the parks,
along the Bowery and in the lodging-houses which lined that pathetic
street. They slept over gratings anywhere from which came a little
warm air, or in doorways or cellar-ways. At a half dozen points in
different parts of the city I came upon those strange charities which
supply a free meal to a man lodging for the night, providing that he
came at a given hour and waited long enough.

And never anywhere had I seen so much show and luxury. Nearly
all of the houses along upper Fifth Avenue and its side streets
boasted their liveried footmen. Wall Street was a sea of financial
trickery and legerdemain, a realm so crowded with sharklike geniuses
of finance that one's poor little arithmetic intelligence was entirely
discounted and made ridiculous. How was a sniveling scribbler to
make his way in such a world? Nothing but chance and luck, as I
saw it, could further the average man or lift him out of his rut, and
since when had it been proved that I was a favorite of fortune? A
crushing sense of incompetence and general inefficiency seemed to
settle upon me, and I could not shake it off. Whenever I went out
on an assignment—and I was always being sent upon those trivial,
shoe-wearing affairs—I carried with me this sense of my unimpor-
tance.

---

2. During the winter of 1894–95, Dreiser worked as a space-rate reporter for the *New York
World*.

THEODORE DREISER

Reflections†

To those who are infatuated with the thought of living in a city and of enjoying the so called delights of metropolitan life, the recent strikes in the sweater shops of New York may furnish a little food for reflection.[1] Usually the thought of miles of streets, lined with glimmering lamps; of great, brilliant thoroughfares, thronged with hurrying pedestrians and lined with glittering shop windows; of rumbling vehicles rolling to and fro in noisy counter procession, fascinates and hypnotizes the mind, so that reason fades to an all-possessing desire to rush forward and join with the countless throng. Usually, to the mass of humans, the vision of a great metropolis, throbbing with ceaseless life, pulsating after the fashion of a great heart and extending its influence by means of tracks to all parts of the world, is one of the most inspiring and impressive visions imaginable. To go to the city is the changeless desire of the mind. To join in the great, hurrying throng; to see the endless lights, the great shops and stores, the towering structures and palatial mansions, becomes a desire which the mind can scarcely resist. Mansions and palaces, libraries, museums, the many theatres and resorts of wealth and pleasure all attract, just as a great cataract attracts. There is a magnetism in nature that gives more to the many, and this you will see in the constant augmentation of population in the great cities, the constant rushing of wealth to those who have wealth, the great hurrying of all waters to where there are endless waters and of stars to where there are myriads of stars already gathered, until the heavens are white with them. It is a magnetism which no one understands, which philosophers call the law of segregation, and which simply means that there is something in nature to make the many wish to be where the many are.[2] From that law there is no escape and both men and planets obey it. It makes towns, cities, nations and worlds, and does nothing perhaps, except show what mites we are in the stream and current of nature.

This desire to attend and be part of the great current of city life is

† *Ev'ry Month* 3 (October 1896): 6–7.

1. *Ev'ry Month* began to appear in October 1895. Dreiser's contribution to each issue included an introductory column called "Reflections" and signed "The Prophet." A "sweater" or "sweat" shop was a factory in which many workers were crowded together in a small area, often a room or two in an East Side tenement.
2. The philosopher is Herbert Spencer, whose *First Principles* Dreiser had read in 1894 while a Pittsburgh reporter. To Spencer the natural law of segregation operated in social life beneficially because it brought men into the complex world of the city and therefore played a role in the universal evolutionary progress from homogeneity to heterogeneity. Dreiser, however, stressed the irresistible power of this "law" and the whirlpool of flux in nature and society that it represented.

one that seldom bases itself upon well mastered reasons. It is simply a desire, and as such, seldom begs for explanation. Men do not ask themselves whether once in the great city its wonders will profit them any. They do not stop to consider whether the great flood will catch them up and whirl them on helpless and unheeded. They never consider that the life, and dash and fire of metropolitan life is based on something and not a mere exotic sprung from nothing and living on air. They seldom reflect that all here is a mere picture of wondrous, living detail, but as cold and helpless as any vision, and as far from their grasp as the gems of a wintry sky. If they did it would appall them and make them cautious of the magnetic charm that draws them on, for they would perhaps come to realize that men may starve at the base of cold, ornate columns of marble, the cost of which would support them and many like them for the remainder of their earthly days. All is not gold that glitters, nor will anything that delights your fancy give you food. Certainly the city glitters, but it is not always your gold.

Perceive first, that what delights you is only the outer semblance, the bloom of the plant. These streets and boulevards, these splendid mansions and gorgeous hotels, these vast structures about which thousands surge and toward which luxurious carriages roll, are the fair flowers of a rugged stalk. Not of color and softness and rare odor are the masses upon which as a stalk these bloom; not for fresh air and sunshine are they. Down in the dark earth are the roots, drawing life and strength and sending them coursing up the veins; and down in alleys and byways, in the shop and small dark chambers are the roots of this luxurious high life, starving and toiling the long year through, that carriages may roll and great palaces stand brilliant with ornaments. These endless streets which only present their fascinating surface are the living semblance of the hands and hearts that lie unseen within them. They are the gay covering which conceals the sorrow and want, the ceaseless toil upon which all this is built. They hide the hands and hearts, the groups of ill-clad workers, the chambers stifling with the fumes of midnight oil consumed over ceaseless tasks, the pallets of the poor and sick, the bare tables of the hopeless slaves who work for bread. Endless are these rows of shadowy chambers, countless the miseries which these great walls hide. If they could be swept away, or dissolved, and only the individuals left in view, there would be a new story to tell. Like a sinful Magdalen the city decks herself gayly, fascinating all by her garments of scarlet and silk, awing by her jewels and perfumes, when in truth there lies hid beneath these a torn and miserable heart, and a soiled and unhappy conscience that will not be still but is forever moaning and crying "for shame."

The striking tailors, coat makers, pressers, bushelmen, they are of this vast substrata on which the city stands; a part of the roots that are down in the ground, delving, that the vast flower-like institutions may bloom over head. They belong to that part of the city which is never seen and seldom heard. Strange tales could be told of their miseries, strange pictures drawn of their haunts and habitations, but that is not for here nor now. When they issued their queer circular it was published as a curiosity because it told a strange and peculiar story, and to those who are fascinated by dreams of the great metropolis it may prove a lesson. All is not gold that glitters. Neither is the city a place of luxurious abode despite the brilliancy of its surging streets. Here is the circular:

EXTRA.

TO THE PRESSERS:

Brethren—The last hour of need, misery and hunger has come. We are now on the lowest step of the ladder of human life. We can do nothing more than starve. Take pity on your wives. Are not your children for whom you have struggled so hard with your sweat and blood, dear to you? Do you think you have a right to live? Do you think you ought to get pay for your work? We only strive for a miserable piece of bread.

Signed,   COAT PRESSERS UNION, NO. 17.

There is surely no need for comment here, certainly no call for explanation. They are down there in narrow rooms working away again. The great thoroughfares are just as bright as ever. Thousands are lounging idly in cafes, thousands thronging the places of amusements, thousands rolling in gaily caparisoned equipages, and so it will continue. Some imagine this condition can be done away with but it cannot. As well imagine that men can be made equal in brain, intelligence and perception, by law. As well imagine that this law of segregation which brings thousands together can be reversed, or that men can be made to desire complete isolation and solitude. Oppression can be avoided, that is true, but the vine must have roots else how are its leaves to grow high into the world of sunlight and air. Some must enact the role of leaves, others the role of roots, and as no one has the making of his brain in embryo he must take the result as it comes.

For those who are inclined to believe that the above is mere rhetorical sentiment, unwarranted by any facts, the fruit, as it were, of a morbid imagination, let an incident in point suffice. It would seem as though one who enters a stranger into a city, enters as into the gorgeous storehouse of that eastern king whose jewels were heaped in glittering masses, and upon which he was left chained and helpless, to stare and starve. Endless jewels can this city show; treasures

so vast as to seem improbable; glories so numerous that in their very
number they rob each other of their individual charm; pleasure so
elaborate and costly as to pall upon the pursuing imagination; yet,
amid all, men starve. It strikes one as the acme of the paradoxical,
but nevertheless court records do not lie. Of one such case the
papers have spoken only recently and the singular description is here
presented as evidence. It says:

"A wretched, dwarfed specimen of masculine humanity picked up
by the police late Monday night was brought into Jefferson Market
Court yesterday charged with vagrancy. The creature had been seen
lurking in back alleyways in the neighborhood of Minetta street, and
persons whose curiosity had been aroused noticed that he spent his
time rummaging in garbage cans under back stoops. Those who
observed more closely declare that the man was devouring parts of
the refuse. The man ate this because he was starving. Policeman
McCarthy, of the Mercer Street Station, approached the wild-eyed,
busy-haired and shrunken outcast, whose clothes fell from him in
rags, and he slunk away like a hunted animal. He had not gone far
when he staggered and fell against a lamppost and cut his head. He
then started to crawl into a hallway. The policeman found him and
took him to the station house. The man, who was about 4 feet 3
inches high, was dreadfully emaciated. His hair was 18 inches long.
His beard had been uncut and untrained for so long that little of his
face could be seen. He wore no shirt, and was clad in a ragged coat
and a pair of tattered trousers. A pair of soles which had once
belonged to shoes were tied to his feet. At the station house he
devoured soup and bread with an eagerness which showed his pitiable condition. When led before Magistrate Cornell yesterday he was
still so weak he could scarcely stand. He is a native of the West
Indies, and gave the name of William Wilson. He could not obtain
work nor aid and was obliged to go to the garbage cans in trying to
stave off starvation. Wilson was committed to the workhouse."

Thus runs the dry description of one creature. Thus could be written the story of many another. And between this one and that top-
most type, whose clothes are costly and delicate of texture; whose
linen is ever immaculate; whose chambers are soft with comforts
and ever resplendent in detail; how many graduations are there? How
many of the half hungry? the half weary? the half clothed? the half
happy, are there? How many who endure severe privations uncom-
plaining, and how many who endure moderate wants with a trusting
heart? Ah! this is a wonderfully conglomerate world, filled with a
million grades, and still a million, and the one cares not for the wants
of another. There are shades of suffering innumerable as the countless tints of a roseate sky; grades of poverty as various as the hues of

a changeful sea. No type so faint but what there is one fainter still, and none so marked but that another more impressive rises. Indeed, they are as the sands of the desert, as the stars of the trackless night, and he who enters among them does so as one who ventures his frail craft amid the massive ships of a crowded sea, the idle rocking of which may insure his watery doom. But this is trite, perhaps; very wearisome, no doubt; very much like the threshing of straw upon a forsaken field.

THE PROPHET

THEODORE DREISER

Curious Shifts of the Poor†

Strange Ways of Relieving Desperate Poverty.—Last Resources of New York's Pitiful Mendicants.

After editing Ev'ry Month for two years, Dreiser became a free-lance magazine writer in late 1897. For over three years he ground out hack articles for the popular magazines. Little of this writing is of permanent interest. "Curious Shifts of the Poor," however, is an exception, for when Dreiser wrote the closing chapters of Sister Carrie in the spring of 1900, he adapted its striking Bowery vignettes to his fictional form. He entitled chapter 45 "Curious Shifts of the Poor," and within it and several following chapters he introduced (in modified form) each of his Bowery scenes. But each now has Hurstwood as its "dynamic emotional center" (in F. O. Matthiessen's phrase) and each therefore contributes to the finely controlled movement of Hurstwood's fall.

At the hour when Broadway assumes its most interesting aspect, a peculiar individual takes his stand at the corner of Twenty-sixth street.[1] It is the hour when the theatres are just beginning to receive their patrons. Five signs, announcing the night's amusements, blaze on every hand. Cabs and carriages, their lamps gleaming like yellow eyes, patter by. Couples and parties of three and four are freely mingled in the common crowd which passes by in a thick stream, laughing and jesting. On Fifth avenue are loungers, a few wealthy strollers, a gentleman in evening dress with a lady at his side, some clubmen, passing from one smoking room to another. Across the way the great hotels, the Hoffman House and the Fifth Avenue, show a hundred gleaming windows, their cafés and billiard rooms filled with a

---

† Demorest's 36 (November 1899): 22–26.
1. Cf. pp. 328–34. Dreiser wrote yet another account of the Captain in "A Touch of Human Brotherhood," Success 5 (March 1902): 140–41, 176.

pleasure-loving throng. All about, the night has a feeling of pleasure and exhilaration, the curious enthusiasm of a great city, bent upon finding joy in a thousand different ways.

In the midst of this lightsome atmosphere a short, stocky-built soldier, in a great cape-overcoat and soft felt hat, takes his stand at the corner. For a while he is alone, gazing like any idler upon an ever-fascinating scene. A policeman passes, saluting him as Captain, in a friendly way. An urchin, who has seen him there before, stops and gazes. To all others he is nothing out of the ordinary save in dress, a stranger, whistling for his own amusement.

As the first half hour wanes, certain characters appear. Here and there in the passing crowd one may see now and then a loiterer, edging interestedly near. A slouchy figure crosses the opposite corner and glances furtively in his direction. Another comes down Fifth avenue to the corner of Twenty-sixth street, takes a general survey and hobbles off again. Two or three noticeable Bowery types edge along the Fifth avenue side of Madison Square, but do not venture over. The soldier in his cape-overcoat walks a line of ten feet at his corner, to and fro, whistling.

As nine o'clock approaches, some of the hub-bub of the earlier hour passes. On Broadway the crowd is neither so thick nor so gay. There are fewer cabs passing. The atmosphere of the hotels is not so youthful. The air, too, is colder. On every hand move curious figures, watchers and peepers without an imaginary circle, which they are afraid to enter—dozens in all. Presently, with the arrival of a keener sense of cold, one figure comes forward. It crosses Broadway from out the shadow of Twenty-sixth street, and, in a halting, circuitous way, arrives close to the waiting figure. There is something shamefaced, a diffident air about the movement, as if the intention were to conceal any idea of stopping until the very last moment. Then, suddenly, close to the soldier comes the halt. The Captain looks in recognition, but there is no especial greeting. The newcomer nods slightly, and murmurs something, like one who waits for gifts. The other simply motions toward the edge of the walk.

"Stand over there."

The spell is broken. Even while the soldier resumes his short, solemn walk, other figures shuffle forward. They do not so much as greet the leader, but join the one, shuffling and hitching and scraping their feet.

"Cold, isn't it?"

"I don't like winter."

"Looks as though it might snow."

The motley company has increased to ten. One or two know each other and converse. Others stand off a few feet, not wishing to be in the crowd, and yet not counted out. They are peevish, crusty, silent, eying nothing in particular, and moving their feet. The soldier, counting sufficient to begin, comes forward.

"Beds, eh, all of you?"

There is a general shuffle and murmur of approval.

"Well line up here. I'll see what I can do. I haven't a cent myself."

They fall into a sort of broken, ragged line. One sees now some of the chief characteristics by contrast. There is a wooden leg in the line. Hats are all drooping, a collection that would ill become a second-hand Hester street basement collection. Trousers are all warped and frayed at the bottom, and coats worn and faded. In the glare of the street lights, some of the faces look dry and chalky. Others are red with blotches, and puffed in the cheeks and under the eyes. One or two are raw-boned and remind one of railroad hands. A few spectators come near, drawn by the seemingly conferring group, then more and more, and quickly there is a pushing, gaping crowd. Someone in the line begins to talk.

"Silence!" exclaims the Captain. "Now, then, gentlemen, these men are without beds. They have got to have some place to sleep to-night. They can't lie out in the street. I need twelve cents to put one to bed. Who will give it to me?"

No reply.

"Well, we'll have to wait here, boys, until someone does. Twelve cents isn't so very much for one man."

"Here is fifteen," exclaims a young man, who is peering forward with strained eyes. "It's all I can afford."

"All right; now I have fifteen. Step out of the line," and seizing the one at the end of the line nearest him by the shoulder, the Captain marches him off a little way and stands him up alone.

Coming back, he resumes his place before the little line and begins again.

"I have three cents here. These men must be put to bed somehow. There are," counting, "one, two, three, four, five, six, seven, eight, nine, ten, eleven, twelve men. Nine cents more will put the next man to bed, give him a good, comfortable bed for the night. I go right along and look after that myself. Who will give me nine cents?"

One of the watchers, this time a middle-aged man, hands in a five-cent piece.

"Good. Now I have eight cents. Four more will give this man a bed. Come, gentlemen, we are going very slow this evening. You will have good beds. How about these?"

"Here you are," remarked a bystander, putting a coin into his hand.

"That," says the Captain, looking at the coin, "pays for two beds for two men and leaves five for the next one. Who will give seven cents more?"

On the one hand the little line of those whose beds are secure is growing, but on the other the bedless waxes long. Silently the queer drift of poverty washes in, and they take their places at the foot of the line unnoticed. Ever and anon the Captain counts and announces the number remaining. Its growth neither dismays nor interests him. He does not even speak of it. His concern is wholly over the next, and the securing of twelve cents. Strangers, gazing out of mere curiosity, find their sympathies enlisted, and pay into the hands of the Captain dimes and quarters, as he states in a short, brusque, unaffected way, the predicament of the men.

In the line of men whose beds are secure, a relaxed air is apparent. The strain of uncertainty being removed, there is moderate good feeling, and some leaning toward sociability. Those nearest one another begin to talk. Politics, religion, the state of the government, some newspaper sensations, and the more notorious facts of the world find mouth-pieces and auditors here. Vague and rambling are the discussions. Cracked and husky voices pronounce forcibly on odd things. There are squints and leers and dull ox-like stares from those who are too dull or too weary to converse.

Standing tells. In the course of time the earliest arrivals become weary and uneasy. There is a constant shifting from one foot to the other, a leaning out and looking back to see how many more must be provided for before the company can march away. Comments are made and crude wishes for the urging forward of things.

"Huh! There's a lot back there yet."

"Yes, must be over a hundred to-night."

"Look at the guy in the cab."

"Captain's a great fellow, isn't he?"

A cab has stopped. Some gentleman in evening dress reaches out a bill to the Captain, who takes it with simple thanks, and turns away to his line. There is a general craning of necks as the jewel in the broad white shirt-front sparkles and the cab moves off. Even the crowd gapes in awe.

"That fixes up nine men for the night," says the Captain, counting out as many of the line near him. Line up over there. Now, then, there are only seven. I need twelve cents."

Money comes slow. In the course of time the crowd thins out to a meagre handful. Fifth avenue, save for an occasional cab or foot-passenger, is bare. Broadway is thinly peopled with pedestrians. Only now and then a stranger passing notices the small group, hands out a coin and goes away, unheeding.

The Captain is stolid and determined. He talks on, very slowly, uttering the fewest words, and with a certain assurance, as though he could not fail.

"Come, I can't stay out here all night. These men are getting tired and cold. Someone give me four cents."

There comes a time when he says nothing at all. Money is handed him, and for each twelve cents he singles out a man and puts him in the other line. Then he walks up and down as before, looking at the ground.

The theatres let out. Fire signs disappear. A clock strikes eleven. Another half hour, and he is down to the last two men.

A lady in opera cape and rustling silk skirt comes down Fifth avenue, supported by her escort. The latter glances at the line and comes over. There is a bill in his fingers.

"Here you are," he says.

"Thanks," says the Captain. "Now we have some for to-morrow night."

The last two are lined up. The soldier walks along, studying his line and counting.

"One hundred and thirty-seven," he exclaims, when he reaches the head.

"Now, boys, line up there. Steady now, we'll be off in a minute."

He places himself at the head and calls out, "Forward, march!" and away they go.

Across Fifth avenue, through Madison Square, by the winding path, east on Twenty-third street, and down Third avenue trudges the long, serpentine company.

Below Tenth street is a lodging house, and here the queer, ragamuffin line brings up, while the Captain enters in to arrange. In a few minutes the deal is consummated, and the line marches slowly in, each being provided with a key as the Captain looks on. When the last one has disappeared up the dingy stairway, he comes out, muffles his great coat closer in the cold air, pulls down his slouch brim, and tramps, a solitary figure, into the night.

Such is the Captain's idea of his duty to his fellow man. He is a strange man, with a strange bias. Utter confidence in Providence, perfectly sure that he deals direct with God, he takes this means of fulfilling his own destiny.

Outside the door of what was once a row of red brick family dwellings, in Fifteenth street, but what is now a mission or convent house of the Sisters of Mercy, hangs a plain wooden contribution box, on which is painted the statement that every noon a meal is given free to all those who apply and ask for aid.[2] This simple announcement is modest in the extreme, covering, as it does, a charity so broad. Unless one were looking up this matter in particular, he could stand at Sixth avenue and Fifteenth street for days, around the noon hour, and never notice that, out of the vast crowd that surges along that

2. Cf. pp. 343–44

busy thoroughfare, there turned out, every few seconds, some
weather-beaten, heavy-footed specimen of humanity, gaunt in countenance, and dilapidated in the matter of clothes. The fact is true,
however, and the colder the day the more apparent it becomes. Space
and lack of culinary room compels an arrangement which permits of
only twenty-five or thirty eating at one time, so that a line has to be
formed outside, and an orderly entrance effected.

One such line formed on a January day last year. It was peculiarly
cold. Already, at eleven in the morning, several shambled forward
out of Sixth avenue, their thin clothes flapping and fluttering in the
wind, and leaned up against the iron fence. One came up from the
west out of Seventh avenue and stopped close to the door, nearer
than all the others. Those who had been waiting before him, but
farther away, now drew near, and by a certain stolidity of demeanor,
no words being spoken, indicated that they were first. The newcomer
looked sullenly along the line and then moved out, taking his place
at the foot. When order had been restored, the animal feeling of
opposition relaxed.

"Must be pretty near noon," ventured one.

"It is," said another; "I've been waitin' nearly an hour."

"Gee, but it's cold."

The line was growing rapidly. Those at the head evidently congratulated themselves upon not having long to wait. There was much
jerking of heads and looking down the line.

"It don't matter much how near you get to the front, so long as
you're in the first twenty-five. You all go in together," commented
one of the first twenty-five.

"This here Single Tax is the thing. There ain't goin' to be no order
till it comes," said another, discussing that broader topic.

At last the door opened and the motherly Sister looked out. Slowly
the line moved up, and one by one thirty men passed in. Then she
interposed a stout arm and the line halted with six men on the steps.
In this position they waited. After a while one of the earliest to go
in came out, and then another. Every time one came out the line
moved up. And this continued until two o'clock, when the last hungry dependent crossed the threshold, and the door was closed.

It was a winter evening.[3] Already, at four o'clock, the sombre hue
of night was thickening the air. A heavy snow was falling—a fine,
picking, whipping snow, borne forward by a swift wind in long, thin
lines. The street was bedded with it, six inches of cold, soft carpet,

---

3. Cf. pp. 351–53. When Dreiser republished this vignette in *The Color of a Great City*
(1923), he called it "The Men in the Storm." Both the later title and the sketch itself recall
Stephen Crane's "The Men in the Storm," first published in 1894 and reprinted in the
Philistine in 1897.

churned brown by the crush of teams and the feet of men. Along the
Bowery, men slouched through it with collars up and hats pulled
over their ears.

Before a dirty four-story building gathered a crowd of men. It
began with the approach of two or three, who hung about the closed
wooden doors, and beat their feet to keep them warm. They made
no effort to go in, but shifted ruefully about, digging their hands
deep in their pockets, and leering at the crowd and the increasing
lamps. There were old men with grizzled beards and sunken eyes;
men who were comparatively young, but shrunken by disease; men
who were middle-aged.

With the growth of the crowd about the door came a murmur. It
was not conversation, but a running comment directed at anyone in
general. It contained oaths and slang phrases.

"I wisht they'd hurry up."

"Look at the copper watchin'."

"Maybe it ain't winter, nuther."

"I wisht I was with Otis."

Now a sharper lash of wind cut down, and they huddled closer.
There was no anger, no threatening words. It was all sullen endurance, unlightened by either wit or good fellowship.

A carriage went jingling by with some reclining figure in it. One
of the members nearest the door saw it.

"Look at the bloke ridin'."

"He ain't so cold."

"Eh! Eh! Eh!" yelled another, the carriage having long since passed
out of hearing.

Little by little the night crept on. Along the walk a crowd turned
out on its way home. Still the men hung around the door, unwavering.

"Ain't they ever goin' to open up?" queried a hoarse voice suggestively.

This seemed to renew general interest in the closed door, and
many gazed in that direction. They looked at it as dumb brutes look,
as dogs paw and whine and study the knob. They shifted and blinked
and muttered, now a curse, now a comment. Still they waited, and
still the snow whirled and cut them.

A glimmer appeared through the transom overhead, where someone was lighting the gas. It sent a thrill of possibility through the
watcher. On the old hats and peaked shoulders snow was piling. It
gathered in little heaps and curves, and no one brushed it off. In the
center of the crowd the warmth and steam melted it, and water trickled off hat-rims and down noses which the owners could not reach
to scratch. On the outer rim the piles remained unmelted. Those

who could not get in the center lowered their heads to the weather and bent their forms.

At last the bars grated inside and the crowd pricked up its ears. There was someone who called, "Slow up there now!" and then the door opened. It was push and jam for a minute, with grim, beast silence to prove its quality, and then the crowd lessened. It melted inward like logs floating, and disappeared. There were wet hats and shoulders, a cold, shrunken, disgruntled mass, pouring in between bleak walls. It was just six o'clock, and there was supper in every hurrying pedestrian's face.

"Do you sell anything to eat here?" questioned one of the grizzled old carpet-slippers who opened the door.

"No; nothin' but beds."

The waiting throng had been housed.

For nearly a quarter of a century Fleischman, the caterer, has given a loaf of bread to anyone who will come for it to the rear door of his restaurant, on the corner of Broadway and Ninth street, at midnight.[4] Every night, during twenty-three years, about three hundred men have formed in line, and at the appointed time, marched past the doorway, picked their loaf from a great box placed just outside, and vanished again into the night. From the beginning to the present time there has been little change in the character or number of these men. There are two or three figures that have grown familiar to those who have seen this little procession pass year after year. Two of them have missed scarcely a night in fifteen years. There are about forty, more or less, regular callers. The remainder of the line is formed of strangers every night.

The line is not allowed to form before eleven o'clock. At this hour, perhaps a single figure shambles around the corner and halts on the edge of the sidewalk. Other figures appear and fall in behind. They come almost entirely one at a time. Haste is seldom manifest in their approach. Figures appear from every direction, limping slowly, slouching stupidly, or standing with assumed or real indifference, until the end of the line is reached, when they take their places and wait.

Most of those in the line are over thirty. There is seldom one under twenty. A low murmur of conversation is heard, but for the most part the men stand in stupid, unbroken silence. Here and there are two or three talkative ones, and if you pass close enough you will hear every topic of the times discussed or referred to, except those which are supposed to interest the poor. Wretchedness, poverty, hunger and distress are never mentioned. The possibilities of a match

4. Cf. pp. 343–44, 345.

between prize-ring favorites, the day's evidence in the latest murder trial, the chance of war in Africa, the latest improvements in automobiles, the prosperity or depression of some other portion of the world, or the mistakes of the Government, from Washington to the campaign in Manila. These, or others like them, are the topics of whatever conversation is held. It is for the most part a rambling, disconnected conversation.

"Wait until Dreyfus gets out of prison," said one to his little black-eyed neighbor one night, "and you'll see them guys fallin' on his neck."

"Maybe they will and maybe they won't," the other muttered. "You needn't think, just because you see dagoes selling violets on Broadway, that the spring is here."

The passing of a Broadway car awakens a vague idea of progress, and some one remarks: "They'll have them things running by liquid air before we know it."

"I've driv mule cars by here myself," replies another.

A few moments before twelve a great box of bread is pushed outside the door, and exactly on the hour a portly round-faced German takes his position by it, and calls "Ready." The whole line at once, like a well-drilled company of regulars, moves swiftly, in good marching time diagonally across the sidewalk to the inner edge and pushes, with only the noise of tramping feet, past the box. Each man reaches for a loaf, and, breaking line, wanders off by himself. Most of them do not even glance at their bread, but put it indifferently under their coats or in their pockets.

In the great sea of men here are these little eddies of driftwood, a hundred nightly in Madison Square, 300 outside a bakery at midnight, crowds without the lodging-houses in stormy weather, and all this day after day. These are the poor in body and in spirit. The lack of houses and lands and fine clothing is nothing. Many have these and are equally wretched. The cause of misery lies elsewhere. The attitude of pity which the world thinks proper to hold toward poverty is misplaced—a result of the failure to see and to realize. Poverty of worldly goods is not in itself pitiful. A sickly body, an ignorant mind, a narrow spirit, brutal impulses and perverted appetites are the pitiful things. The adding of material riches to one thus afflicted would not remove him out of the pitiful. On the other hand, there are so-called poor people in every community among its ornaments. There is no pity for them, but rather love and honor. They are rich in wisdom and influence.

The individuals composing this driftwood are no more miserable than others. Most of them would be far more uncomfortable if compelled to lead respectable lives. They cannot be benefited by money. There may be a class of poor for whom a little money judiciously expended would result in good, but these are the lifeless flotsam and jetsam of society without vitality to ever revive. Few among them would survive a month if they should come suddenly into the possession of a fortune.

Their parade before us should not appeal to our pity, but should awaken us to what we are—for society is no better than its poorest type. They expose what is present, though better concealed, everywhere. They are the few skeletons of the sunlight—types of these with which society's closets are full. Civilization, in spite of its rapid progress, is still in profound ignorance of the things essential to a healthy, happy and prosperous life. Ignorance and error are everywhere manifest in the miseries and sufferings of men. Wealth may create an illusion, or modify a ghastly appearance of ignorance and error, but it cannot change the effect. The result is as real in the mansions of Fifth avenue as in the midnight throng outside a baker's door.

The livid-faced dyspeptic who rides from his club to his apartment and pauses on the way to hand his dollar to the Captain should awaken the same pity as the shivering applicant for a free bed whom his dollar aids—pity for the ignorance and error that cause the distress of the world.

The Strike

After leaving the *St. Louis Republic* in early March 1894, Dreiser spent over a month traveling from one midwestern city to another looking for a job as a reporter. In Toledo he called at the offices of the *Toledo Blade*, one of whose editors was Arthur Henry, a young man with literary aspirations. The two men took an instant liking to each other, but Henry could offer only a temporary job reporting a local streetcar strike that had begun a few days earlier, on March 21. Dreiser's two reports appeared on the twenty-fourth, but the strike was settled on the twenty-seventh and Dreiser soon moved on to another city.

When Dreiser decided to include a trolley strike in *Sister Carrie*, he of course drew upon his Toledo experiences. However, there had also been a widely reported streetcar strike in Brooklyn in January and February of 1895, during which the state militia had been called out and many men were injured. In *Sister Carrie* Dreiser used details from both strikes, combining his recollection of a day on a Toledo car with his awareness of the much more violent conditions of the Brooklyn strike.

THEODORE DREISER

[A Street-Car Strike]†

"Well," [Arthur Henry said,] "I'll tell you about it. There's a street-car strike on and I could use a man who had nerve enough to ride around on the cars the company is attempting to run and report how things are. But I'll tell you frankly: it's dangerous. You may be shot or hit with a brick."

I indicated my willingness to undertake this and he looked at me in a mock serious and yet approving way. He took me on and I went about the city on one car-line and another, studying the strange streets, expecting and fearing every moment that a brick might be shied at me through the window or that a gang of irate workingmen would board the car and beat me up. But nothing happened, not a single threatening workman anywhere; I so reported and was told to

† From *A Book About Myself* (New York: 1922), 372–73.

write it up and make as much of the "story" as possible. Without knowing anything of the merits of the case, my sympathies were all with the workingmen. I had seen enough of strikes, and of poverty, and of the quarrels between the money-lords and the poor, to be all on one side. As was the custom in all newspaper offices with which I ever had anything to do, where labor and capital were concerned I was told to be neutral and not antagonize either side. I wrote my "story" and it was published in the first edition.

THEODORE DREISER

The Strike To-day†

Robisons Are Wrestling with Their Trolleys.

*David Robison, Jr., Jim and the Second Son
Are Running the Cars Around the Belt.*

Night Police Force Is on Duty with the Day.

*Nothing Worse Has Occurred Than the Havoc Caused by
Rotten Eggs and Mud Balls—Four Cars Are in Operation.*

With the night police force out on duty with the day service men, and crowds lining the various streets along which the Toledo Electric Street Railroad cars travel, the strike assumed pretentious proportions to-day.

The company's transfer office at Madison and Summit streets, was crowded by "scab" applicants for positions, though a great crowd of idle strikers lingered outside and talked over the situation, having at the same time an eye to business, should any develop. Along the line the Robison family and managers conducted the cars with a few wayworn emigrants who had sorrowfully drifted in, and miserably assisted the company in holding its own. There was a slump in the egg market, also, owing to certain precocious merchants who had reveled in an enormous sale of eggs at a moderate profit, and accordingly brought down the price. The stale variety were at a premium, however, and brought as high as 11 cents along Canton avenue near the barns. In fact, several huge chalk signs were exposed conveying the information that desirable quantities were on hand.

At other points, mud and chunks of dry clay were used. Several solid pieces were donated to C. R. Herbert, the able Robison manager. His tile has been caved in and decorated. The strikers were

† *Toledo Blade* 24 March 1894: 1, 6.

sarcastic. They developed a facetiousness that added great scornful weight to their every remark when addressed to the temporary employes, who are filling their rightful places.

"No negotiations have been opened between the Robisons and the men," said President Mahon, of the International union, to The Blade to-day. "The men are out, and are offering no interference in running cars. We are law-abiding citizens, and have acted as such ever since the trouble began.

"We certainly all recognize the authority of the law, and shall abide by it. The restraining order of Judge Lemmon we recognize and honor. Any violation of that order will certainly not be countenanced by the union. Still we have rights as peaceable citizens, and are not to be bluffed out of them.

"We are willing and ready at any time to submit the matter to a local arbitration committee or to the state board. We believe that our cause is just, and we will endeavor to secure our rights."

The statement in the injunction that President Mahon came here of his own free will to incite the men and stir up dissension is vigorously denied by the employes. By a unanimous vote of the union President Mahon was summoned to Toledo.

M. F. Bittner, of 1003 Summit street, to-day sent three boxes of cigars to the committee for distribution among the men who are out. George Tait, the well-known Adams street baker, sent four baskets of lunch to the "boys" watching at the Canton avenue barns this morning. The baskets were called for and offers made to refill them.

Free cots have also been furnished the men stationed there. The women, too, are distributing popcorn for the men to eat while on their watch.

Several business men have made proffers of money to the men, but this has been refused at present for the reason that the men are yet in good shape. The boys of the Consolidated lines, however, will on Monday contribute $3 each to the support of the striking men.

Although trouble in connection with the strike is not considered imminent, Chief Raltz has prepared for any emergency that may spring up. The entire night squad is on duty, and ready for detail. Ten were dispatched in the patrol wagon from the central station at 10 o'clock this morning to drive away the mob at the corner of Summit and Adams streets. Eight men are constantly on duty at the Canton avenue barns, and the men on their beats are instructed to be vigilantly on the outlook for outbreaks from thoughtless spectators.

At 3:30 yesterday afternoon Detective Manley arrested Edward J. Scott for the alleged grounding of wires. Deputy Ernsthausen left

his home at 6:30 to issue bail bond for $200, and Scott was released.
This morning the case against him was continued to March 28th.

Of the four cars that sallied so bravely forth and trailed over the
route at breakneck speed regardless of passengers or profits, No. 19
was one. C. R. Herbert, the husky and able manager, stood on the
front platform of this with the door open behind him, guaranteeing
a mode of defensive shelter, should such be necessary. On the rear
platform, minding the trolley bar, stood Allen J. Andrews, one of the
"scab" conductors, who held his place and his job per the order of
his employer in front. The car began its pilgrimage around at 8:30
a.m. and was still going in the same direction at 12:30 noon, little
the worse except for shied eggs and heaped up anathemas. During
the entire forenoon few persons entered the car or sought to part
with a nickel for the sake of such excitement as the thing offered. A
few venturesome citizens, however, did try it along with several officials. There was a charming looking lady of about 28, who had all
the perquisites about her of a dashing widow, who climbed on at
Monroe street, and rode a few delicious blocks. Later there came a
very fat gentleman who puffed and smiled, and said he would "be
blessed if them strikers could scare him." However, his anxious attitude told a different story, for he watched the passing territory with
almost an eagle eye, so fearful was he of a well directed brick or a
handsome egg, generously donated from without. A Catholic priest
happened along on Michigan avenue near Adams, and hailed the car
with a gold-headed cane. He, too, ensconced himself comfortably in
the rear portion of the car, and looked boldly out. However, to a
Blade representative he admitted that a berth under the seat would
be an excellent haven in case of a brick storm or a soft egg simoon.

As the morning proceeded and nothing of import happened, Mr.
Herbert and Mr. Andrews grew less apprehensive, and looked about.
They even went so far as to jest with passengers and make inquiries
as to the strength of feeling among the watching strikers without.
About 10 a.m. as Mr. Herbert was so discussing, passing along Canton avenue, an artful and sagacious citizen greeted him with the first
missile of the day. It was an egg, and lingered in large gobs about
the brim of his black slouch hat.

The sight of the egg remaining seems to have been an inspiration
to others for the car had not gone two more blocks before another
bystander shied a chunk of mud and took Mr. Herbert square upon
the crown of his hat. It hurt, and he said so—to himself. He danced
around a moment, expressed himself as much disgusted and then
endeavored to make the best of it. In this he had some assistance,
for Mr. Andrews was hit not long after by a similar chunk of mud,

and left to feel his wound in much wrath. There were discouraging incidents, however, without number. People were inclined to yell "scab" and "don't you want to earn a dollar" along Summit street. Every conductor of a passing car and motorman took the opportunity as a good one and called out some stinging greeting, that was bitter enough to make most any one wince. They often went further, however, and cast corn or beans at their object. In addition the crews of cars ahead, belonging to other lines, often slowed up and fairly crawled along, making the Robison car to travel slow and thus receive the benefit of whatever jeering and hooting might be going on around.

Number 19 fared well. Of course Conductor Andrews was nervous and unsophisticated, and of course Motorman Herbert was consequently irritable and out of humor. Once Conductor Andrews forgot to watch the trolley bar and then twice and so on, into many times, when Motorman Herbert got warm under the collar. It was on Monroe street the trolley bar jumped the wire, while conductor Andrews was inside collecting the darling widow's fare.

"I say," wailed out Motorman Herbert, "gol darn the goldarned luck! Are you going to watch that trolley bar?"

"Scab!" yelled some one from without, "want a dollar?"

In the excitement of the moment Conductor Andrews dropped his change on the floor, and retired to readjust the trolley. The darling widow opened her eyes wide in astonishment and said, "My, oh!"

Motorman Herbert simply looked back and said "Damn," turning time to speed the car on its way once more.

After 10 a.m. there was trouble with the register. Some one had trifled with its affections, apparently. It didn't work. Up to that hour 23 fares had been registered, but there it stopped short. Worst of all, Conductor Andrews did not notice it. Whenever any one climbed on, he collected and rang up. The bell rang as usual, but indicated nothing. Finally a passenger called:

"What's ailing your register?"

"Nothing."

"It doesn't ring up."

"Don't, hey? The bell rings."

"Well, try it for yourself. It hasn't moved the last five fares."

On the strength of this, Andrews tried it and found that a count was not made, which left his fares collected at his own able discretion in accounting for.

So it went all morning, one misery after another piling up until life on the line seemed nothing but discouragements multiplied. All idea of time was abandoned. Trips were made just as fast as possible, the idea being simply to keep the cars moving. Cars 29, 31, and 37 were also operated but with no more grace or satisfaction than came to the lot of 19.

At a little after 10 o'clock Robison Car No. 11 crashed around the corner of Adams and Summit streets and into the side of a Consolidated car moving north. The corner was instantly swarming with people, shouting and jeering at the clumsy work of a "scab." The motorman, dripping with rotten eggs, the shells of which stuck to his clothes and hung from his hair, abandoned his dilapidated car and disappeared from sight. The crowd undertook to release the imprisoned Consolidated car. Twenty strong arms lifted No. 11 from the track and laid it in the Adams street gutter. By this time, three thousand people had gathered along Summit and Adams, and crowded around the corner. They ran over the abandoned car, sounded the gongs and hooted at its filthy condition.

Chief Raltz appeared and attempted to clear the streets. He managed to clear a few inches, when the patrol wagon, with seven stalwart bluecoats, dashed upon the scene. Then there was a scattering, and a lone woman with a baby carriage was the only person within an area of 200 feet.

David Robison, Jr., pale and covered with dust, his hat pulled sidewise over his eyes and his pants rolled up, appeared. He turned to his forsaken property and looked it over. He mounted the motorman's platform, and the crowd yelled "Scab!" from a distance. Chief Raltz called the police and attempted to place the car on the tracks. David Robison tugged and pushed and lifted with them. He did not say anything. He looked tired, and his delicate hands did not seem formidable. The crowd laughed and Mr. Robison and the policemen still tugged and lifted. The car was finally rolled into position and Mr. Robison held the trolley in while his superintendent manipulated the motor, running No. 11 back to the barns.

The car was returned to the barn at 10:30, and was received with cheers by the bystanders.

"You'd better get some oats and coax the car out again!" yelled one.

"How many fares did you ring up?" cried another.

"There was no swing crew today; so Uncle David put away his car for dinner," was the explanation given by one of the men for abandoning the car.

The bombardment of mud balls began at 8:30 when "Jim" Robison mounted the platform of a belt line car and drove it out of the barn. "Dick" Momy, whom the boys say has been "fired" three times off the Robison car, held the trolley rope behind. A shower of mud balls and a little guying by the men standing near was all the objection raised to the movement of the cars. No violence was attempted by any of the street car employes and a large part of the jeering was done by sympathizers of the men. The first car was followed by a second with Superintendent Herbert as motorman. A stranger held the trolley rope behind. The third car carried Superintendent Adler as conductor and Will Robison at the motor, and the fourth a pick-up named Dick Snitchiker at the motor and David Robison, Jr., while two strangers operated the trolley on the third and fourth cars.

As the last car disappeared in a cloud of dust the men settled back to watch the next movement of the Robisons. Nothing was done until an hour later. The cars sped on down town and a crowd collected at the corner of Woodruff and Canton avenues to see the first car as it completed its circuit around the belt.

On its arrival it was met with jeering and a volley of mud balls by the boys. There were very few street car men at this place at all. The crowd remained and as each car came around the belt the yelling continued.

At 9:30 o'clock James Robison took the sixth car out of the barn. On the platform with him were a stranger and Patrolman Olmns, while Transfer Agent Wagner operated the trolley rope. The men looked on the movement of this car and suffered in silence. Scarcely a word was spoken. The firm countenances of the men were fierce for a moment. There was a severe mental struggle and then the faces assumed the same determined air. The feelings must be restrained; there must be no violence; the law must be obeyed.

At 10 o'clock the patrol wagon from the Lagrange street substation dashed up to the barns.

A squad of police under Sergeant Ed. Kimes alighted to assist the force by Sergeant Robison, already on duty. As everything was quiet at the barns three of the men were detailed to watch the crowd at the corner of Canton and Woodruff avenues.

No Union Men
Need Apply to the Robison Company for Work.

There was much discretion used at the transfer office of the Robison company at Summit and Madison streets, where train crews were being hired. Union men were not wanted. They could not secure a place for love or money. Applicants were closely questioned as to their affiliations on this score, and their labor sentiments generally. Non-resident laborers were wanted, experience not being necessary.

T. H. Dreiser, of the Wood County Herald, applied at the office about noon and requested of the recruiting manager in charge nothing less than a job. That individual leaned back in his chair and surveyed the applicant leisurely, after which he condescended to remark:

"Where you from?"

"St. Louis."

"Want a place, eh?"

"Yes, sir."

"Ever run a car?"

"Endless numbers of them."

"Union man?"

"Yes."

"We don't want you."

"But I don't belong to the union here."

"That doesn't make any difference. You're a union man. Your ideas run that way. We don't want you. I couldn't hire you anyhow. The company wouldn't allow it."

"Would you take me if I wasn't a union man?"

"Oh, perhaps. If you looked all right we might. It's too late now, though. We don't want you."

BACKGROUNDS AND SOURCES II

COMPOSITION, PUBLICATION, AND LEGEND

Composition

Dreiser's accounts of the composition of *Sister Carrie* shed light on several distinctive characteristics of the novel. His recollections that he began the book with only a title in mind and that he wrote its conclusion after a nature vigil belie his early reputation as merely a note-taking, documentary novelist. Moreover, his lack of a definite initial plan is perhaps a source of the discrepancy between his somewhat moralistic tone toward Carrie early in the novel and his later more sympathetic attitude toward her failings.

Also of interest are the three points in the novel involving Hurstwood at which Dreiser remembered that he had difficulty: Hurstwood's early relationship with Carrie, his theft, and his decline. Dreiser's difficulties in the first two instances resulted primarily from his need to go beyond his sources. The cheap adultery and planned robbery and elopement of Emma Dreiser and Hopkins were no longer relevant to his themes as the novel took shape under his pen. Thus, the rather complex plotting of this portion of the novel—Hurstwood tricking Carrie both about his marriage and about Drouet's accident, and the "chance" robbery—probably reflects Dreiser's calling upon a hitherto unused and therefore slow-working fictional ingenuity in order to give narrative expression to his "new" themes of the relative innocence of Hurstwood and Carrie. As far as Dreiser's third difficulty is concerned, he was perhaps remembering, in 1930, his intense personal involvement with Hurstwood's decline as a delay in composition. He does not mention stopping at this point in any of his earlier accounts of the writing of the novel.

At the close of his handwritten draft of *Sister Carrie*, Dreiser wrote "The End. Thursday, March 29—1900." But even as this draft was being typed, Dreiser became dissatisfied with two aspects of its final chapters—the intimation in the penultimate chapter that Carrie and Ames are to be romantically involved, and the conclusion of the work with the death of Hurstwood. He therefore rewrote a large portion of Carrie's final encounter with Ames to remove any suggestion of a relationship between them. And he cut from the final chapter two paragraphs on Carrie (the paragraphs beginning "Oh, blind strivings of the human heart") and expanded them during his Palisades vigil (see pp. 428, below) into a full-scale epilogue on Carrie. (For a thorough analysis of the two conclusions of *Sister Carrie*, see Stephen C. Brennan, "The Two Endings of *Sister Carrie*," *Studies in American Fiction* 16 (Spring 1988): 13–26.) The typescript of *Sister Carrie*, with its revised conclusion, was then severely cut by Dreiser and Arthur Henry (see A Note on the Text, p. xi, above).

424

THEODORE DREISER

To H. L. Mencken†

165 West 10th [Street
New York, N.Y.]
May 13, 1916

Dear H. L. M.:

I feel that you need a serious talking to or with about this whole business but since you are not here I will make a few remarks[.] *Sister Carrie* was written in the fall, winter and spring of 1899–1900. I never saw or heard of *McTeague* or Norris until after the novel had been written and turned in to Harper and Brothers who promptly rejected it with a sharp slap.[1] Then I took it to Doubleday, Page & Co. and left it, curiously, in the hands of Frank Doubleday, who was sitting in the office usually occupied by Walter H. Page. I was as green as grass about such matters, totally unsophisticated and I remember his looking at me with a kind of condescending, examining smirk. At that I like Doubleday. He is such a big husky incoherent clown.

The week after I took *Sister Carrie* to Harper's, Rose White, a sister of Mrs. Dreiser[,] came to visit us. We were then living at 102nd St. & Central Park West. She was reading a book called *McTeague* and liked it. Rose, who was [a] peach in her way intellectually and otherwise, persuaded me to read it. It made a great hit with me and I talked of nothing else for months. It was the first real American book

† From *The Letters of Theodore Dreiser*, ed. Robert H. Elias, vol. 1 (Philadelphia: U of Pennsylvania P, 1959), 210–14. Reprinted by permission of The University of Pennsylvania Press. Hereafter referred to as *Letters*. I have retained here and elsewhere some of Elias's notes; these are indicated by an R. H. E. in brackets.

1. The opinion from Harper's, rendered May 2, 1900, stated, according to a copy in Dreiser's hand:

"This is a superior piece of reportial realism—of highclass newspaper work, such as might have been done by George Ade. It contains many elements of strength—it is graphic, the local color is excellent, the portrayal of a certain below-the-surface life in the Chicago of twenty years ago faithful to fact. There are chapters that reveal a very keen insight into this phase of life and incidents that disclose a sympathetic appreciation of the motives of the characters of the story. But when this has been said there remains the feeling that the author has not risen to the standard necessary for the efficient handling of the theme. His touch is neither firm enough nor sufficiently delicate to depict without offense to the reader the continued illicit relations of the heroine. The long succession of chapters dealing with this important feature of the story begin to weary very quickly. Their very realism weakens and hinders the development of the plot. The final scenes in New York are stronger and better—But I cannot conceive of the book arousing the interest or inviting the attention, after the opening chapters, of the feminine readers who control the destinies of so many novels.

"The style is uneven. At times singularly good (and generally so,) it is disfigured by such colloquialisms as 'suspicioned,' 'pulled off on schedule time,' 'staved off,' 'it's up to you,' etc." [R. H. E.]

I had ever read—and I had read quite a number by W. D. Howells and others.

As a matter of fact my reading up to this time had been the standard American school reading of the time—Dickens, Scott, Thackeray, E. P. Roe (Yes, E. P. Roe)[,] George Ebers, Lew Wallace, Washington Irving, Kingsley, etc., etc., etc., etc. At fourteen years of age I was dippy over Washington Irving, *Twice-Told Tales* and *Water Babies* and used to lie under our trees by the hour and read them. I thought *The Alhambra* was a perfect creation and I still have a lingering affection for it.

I went into newspaper work—(*Chicago Globe*, June 1—1891)[2] and from that time dates my real contact with life—murders, arson, rape, sodomy, bribery, corruption[,] trickery and false witness in every conceivable form. The cards were put down so fast before me for a while that I was a little stunned. Finally I got used to the game and rather liked it.

Incidentally in Pittsburgh—1894—I discovered Herbert Spencer and Huxley and Tyndall. They shifted my point of view tremendously, confirmed my worst suspicions and destroyed the last remaining traces of Catholicism which I now detest as a political organization or otherwise. At the same time I discovered Honoré de Balzac—quite by accident—found one book on him and then got down *The Great Man from the Provinces* and began to read it.

Need I tell you that it was a knockout. It was. I was quite beside myself and read three others without stopping. Then somehow I ceased and began reading George Eliot and Lord Lytton and seemed to get along very well. Incidentally I made a study of Henry Fielding, who seemed and still does, amazing[.] *Joseph Andrews* and *Tom Jones* have been favorites of mine for years.

Yet as late as 1897 and 1898 I never had the slightest idea that I would ever be a novelist. My bent, if you will believe it, was plays and had I been let alone I would have worked out in that form. As it was I then reencountered in New York a young fellow whom I had met in Toledo, Ohio, four years before. Arthur Henry[.] At that time, 1894, he [was] city editor of the *Toledo Blade*, newly married and very anxious to write. Somehow he had taken a fancy to me and now he hung about me all the time. He was tremendously well read, a genial critic and an able man. I think I told you something about him here. He was then advance agent for "Herrmann the Great" but tremendously interested in the novel as a form and in short stories[.] He went on the road then, but a year later when I had married, came back and camped in my apartment. It was he who persuaded me to

2. 1892 is the correct year. [R. H. E.]

write my first short story. This is literally true. He nagged until I did, saying he saw short stories in me. I wrote one finally, sitting in the same room with him in a house on the Maumee River, at Maumee, Ohio, outside Toledo. This was in the summer of 1898[.][3] And after every paragraph I blushed for my folly—it seemed so asinine[.] He insisted on my going on—that it was good—and I thought he was kidding me, that it was rotten, but that he wanted to let me down easy. Finally HE took [it], had it typewritten and sent it to *Ainslee's*. They sent me a check for $75. Thus I began[.]

The above is exact and sacredly true[.]

Later he began to ding-dong about a novel. I must write a novel, I must write a novel. By then I had written four short stories or five, and sold them all[:]

1. "Of the Shining Slave Makers"
2. "The Door of the Butcher Rogaum"
3. "The World and the Bubble"
4. "Nigger Jeff"
5. "When the Old Century Was New."

He had a novel in mind—*A Princess of Arcady* (Doubleday[,] Page—1900—same year as *Carrie*)[.] He wanted to write it but he needed me, he confessed, to help him. Finally—September 1899 I took a piece of yellow paper and to please him wrote down a title at random—*Sister Carrie*—and began. From September to Oct. 15th or thereabouts I wrote steadily to where Carrie met Hurstwood[.] Then I quit, disgusted[.] I thought it was rotten. I neglected it for two months, when under pressure from him again I began because curiously he had quit and couldn't go on. (Isn't that strange[?]) Then I started and laughed at myself for being a fool. Jan. 25th or thereabouts I quit again, just before Hurstwood steals the money, because I couldn't think how to have him do it. Two months more of idleness. I was through with the book apparently[.] Actually I never expected to finish it[.]

About March 1 he got after me again and under pressure I returned to it. This time I nearly stopped because of various irritating circumstances—money principally—but since he was there to watch I pressed on and finally got it done. I took an intense interest in the last few [chapters] much more so than in anything which had gone before. After it was done considerable cutting was suggested by Henry and this was done. I think all of 40,000 words came out. Anyhow there is the history[.]

* * *

Th. D.

3. 1899 is the correct date. [R. H. E.]

DOROTHY DUDLEY

[The Composition of *Sister Carrie*]†

I asked Dreiser if really it were true that the name came first and the characters and theme afterwards. "Yes, actually! My mind was a blank except for the name. I had no idea who or what she was to be. I have often thought there was something mystic about it, as if I were being used, like a medium." Curiously I remember hearing Masters speak of his *Spoon River* in the same way: "Sometimes I think I didn't write it. It passed through me, I was only the medium for it." So the two first imageries of the two Americans most native and subversive to their period were conceived mysteriously, out of the unknown, if we take their word for it. Though labeled realism, they bear in truth the footprints of the inevitable, the signature of Nature.

With Dreiser, the identity of Sister Carrie coming alone from her small country town to Chicago, to sink or swim in that "sea of life," and the identity of the other lives as they were linked with hers and unlinked—these, he said, followed as if out of a dream, whole and alive. He began at once to weave them into their story in October, 1899. He worked with ease until some time in December. Then something interfered, he doesn't know what, but he had to quit for a while. He and Henry were at work separately now, although they still advised and consulted.

* * *

Something blocked the way. He says of these months, December and January: "I had to quit, it seemed to me the thing was a failure, a total frost. . . . I think I experienced a defeat in the face of Hurstwood's defeat as to Carrie. I took it up again once or twice but had to quit. I tried writing stories; thought I had better go back to articles. . . . I had reached the place where Hurstwood robs the safe. I didn't know where I was going; I had lost the thread. . . . Then in February, Arthur Henry, off flirting with some girl, came back and read it. He thought there was nothing wrong with it, told me I must go on. . . . I managed to solve the problem and for a while it went pretty good, until I came to the question of Hurstwood's decline, which took me back to the World days. Then I had to stop again. Somehow I felt unworthy to write all that. It seemed too big, too baffling, don't you know? . . . But after a month I managed to get the thread, and finished it up in May. . . . Henry read it and said 'Don't change a word.'

† From *Dreiser and the Land of the Free* (1932; New York: Beechhurst Press, 1946), 160–62.

But I spent some weeks revising it; he helped me. In May or June 1900 I sent it to Harper's. I knew one of the editors. They refused it. Then I took it down to Doubleday's. In November it was out."

  I quote this as he told it to me in July 1930.

NEW YORK HERALD

"Sister Carrie": Theodore Dreiser†

Speaking of this new novel, its author said to the present reviewer:— "There is one odd circumstance about the book. When I finished it I felt that it was not done. It was a continuous strip of life to me that seemed to be driven onward by those logical forces that had impelled the book to motion. The narrative, I felt, was finished, but not completed. The problem in my mind was not to round it out with literary grace, but to lead the story to a point, an elevation where it could be left and yet continue into the future. The story had to stop, and yet I wanted in the final picture to suggest the continuation of Carrie's fate along the lines of established truths.

  "The note, the exact impression that I sought, evaded me. The drain of sustained imagination was beginning to tell. Finally, with note book and pencil I made a trip to the Palisades, hoping that the change of scene would bring out just what I was trying to express.

  "Finding a broad, overhanging, shelf, I stretched out flat on my back and allowed my thoughts to wander—gave them a sort of open air holiday.

  "Two hours passed in a delicious mental drifting. Then suddenly came the inspiration of its own accord. I reached for my note book and pencil and wrote. And when I left the Palisades 'Sister Carrie' was completed."

† *New York Herald* 7 July 1907: 2.

Publication

Dreiser's controversy with Doubleday, Page and Company over the publication of *Sister Carrie* is one of the most frequently noted events in American literary history. Yet very little verifiable information was available about this event until the last several decades. The following collection of letters constitutes a documentary account of the publication of *Sister Carrie*.

Dreiser offered the novel to Doubleday, Page in early May 1900. He apparently chose this firm because Harper's, an old, established publisher, had just rejected the novel. Doubleday, Page was a new and therefore presumably more adventurous firm. Another reason for choosing Doubleday, Page was that it published the work of Frank Norris, and indeed had Norris on its staff as a reader. Norris had had his first four novels published by Doubleday and McClure. But when this firm dissolved in late 1899 and Frank N. Doubleday formed a new company with Walter H. Page, Norris decided to go along with the new firm. It is not surprising that Dreiser, who had read and admired Norris's *McTeague* while *Sister Carrie* was being considered by Harper's (see p. 424), should send his novel to Doubleday, Page after its refusal by Harper's.

The cast in the drama which developed over the publication of the novel thus involved Page, Doubleday, and Henry Lanier (a Doubleday editor) on one side; Dreiser and Arthur Henry on the other; and Norris somewhere in the middle. Of these figures, Norris, Doubleday, and Henry undoubtedly played the most significant roles. It was Norris's initial enthusiasm that led Doubleday, Page to accept the book, despite the absence of Doubleday himself; it was Doubleday's attitude on his return which prompted the firm to attempt to reject the novel; and it was Henry's insistence that Dreiser should stand upon his legal rights (see his letters of July 19 and 26) which seems to have modified Dreiser's early willingness to permit another publisher to issue the book. Indeed, Henry is the pivotal figure in the entire controversy. Since Dreiser was in Missouri visiting his wife's family when the dispute arose, Henry became his principal source of information both about the dispute and about means of resolving it. Henry's views therefore colored and conditioned Dreiser's, and the publication of the book by Doubleday, Page after the firm attempted to reject it can be attributed largely to Henry's anger and insistence.

FRANK NORRIS

To Theodore Dreiser†

[New York] May 28 1900

My Dear Mr. Dreiser:

My report of *Sister Carrie* has gone astray and I cannot now put my hands on it.

But I remember that I said, and it gives me pleasure to repeat it, that it was the best novel I have read in M.S. since I had been reading for the firm, and that it pleased me as well as *any* novel I have read in any form, published or otherwise.

I have passed it up to Mr. Lanier[1] to read who is now about half way through it, from him it will go to Mr. Page, and when *he* is through with it, the three of us will have a pow-wow on it and come to a decision.

You may rest assured I shall do all in my power to see that the decision is for publication. I shall rush it through as fast as may be and possibly you will hear from me by the end of this week.

Till then with every wish for your good success, I am

Very Sincerely Yrs.
Frank Norris

FRANK NORRIS

To Theodore Dreiser‡

[New York] June 8th [1900]

My Dear Mr. Dreiser:

Will you come down to see me at my rooms in the Angelsea. 60 Washington Square South. Saturday tomorrow night, about 8:30. Don't fail if you possibly can help it.[1]

Very Sincerely Yrs
Norris

If you cant come let me know

---

† From *Collected Letters: Frank Norris*, ed. Jesse S. Crisler (San Francisco: The Book Club of California, 1986), 113. Reprinted by permission of the Book Club of California.
1. Henry Lanier, the son of the poet Sidney Lanier, was a senior editor of Doubleday, Page.
‡ From *Collected Letters: Frank Norris*, ed. Jesse S. Crisler (San Francisco: The Book Club of California, 1986), 116. Reprinted by permission of the Book Club of California.
1. Norris, as is clear from Page's letter of June 9, undoubtedly wanted to tell Dreiser personally of the firm's decision to publish *Sister Carrie*.

WALTER H. PAGE

To Theodore Dreiser†

[New York] June 9, 1900

Dear Sir:

As, we hope, Mr. Norris has informed you, we are much pleased with your novel. If you will be kind enough to call here on Monday—preferably later than two o'clock, we shall be glad to talk it over with you.[1]

With congratulations on so good a piece of work, we are very Sincerely Yours,

Doubleday, Page & Co
by Walter H. Page

Theodore Dreiser Esq.

ARTHUR HENRY

To Theodore Dreiser.‡

New York, July 14, 1900

Dear Teddy:

Yesterday, I had a hot time up at Doubleday & Page's. In talking with Norris, he suggested that I see Lanier,[1] and ask him when he was going to publish your book, as they ought to be getting about it. I asked Lanier, and he said that he didn't know—that he had only been back a little while, and hadn't got around to it yet. Norris also suggested that I speak to Lanier about changing the names from those of real people to fictitious ones. Lanier wants all of them changed. He don't want Frohman or Daly, or the real names of newspapers or any of those things. The fact is, that Lanier is a good deal of a cad. He knows nothing at all of real life—his nature is very shallow, and he is exceedingly conceited. We had a warm argument on the subject. He said that all those things seemed to him like a

† In the Theodore Dreiser Papers, Rare Book and Manuscript Library, University of Pennsylvania. This letter and other letters to Dreiser by Page, Arthur Henry, and S. A. Everitt in this section are used by permission of the Trustees of the University of Pennsylvania.
1. It was probably at this meeting that an informal agreement to publish *Sister Carrie* was made. A formal agreement was not signed at this time, perhaps because Doubleday was in England.
‡ In the Dreiser Papers, University of Pennsylvania Library.
1. Throughout his correspondence with Dreiser, Henry spelled *Lanier* as *Lenier*. I have silently corrected this error.

straining after realism. I told him that any one who could get such an impression from that book must, in the nature of things, be mistaken, because I knew for a certainty that there had been no straining for realism; and that, on the other hand, were the names of Frohman and Daly, and the newspapers to be changed, that here would be an actual straining, and that, in my opinion, were you to do it, you would stultify yourself.

I presume that the name of Hanna & Hogg will have to be changed because of the crime you have enacted there.[2] For my part, I can see no reason for changing any other thing in the book, and several against it. They also want the name of the book changed. They do not like "Sister Carrie." They think it ought to have a more imposing and pretentious name. This may be true, if you can get a good one.[3]

I was up to Norris's the other night, on his invitation; Mrs. Norris had just read your story, and we there discussed among ourselves the idea of giving the theatrical managers fictitious names. Mrs. Norris didn't think that it was at all necessary, and Norris himself thinks that it is immaterial, one way or the other. In talking over the matter, he said to me that he didn't think you ought to stand in the way of such changes if the matter were made a serious issue. I told Norris that I thought you were the man who had the right to take a stand in the matter. However, this is all for you to decide, and Norris has asked me to write to you and find out what you will do about it. Lanier intimated to me that he would be opposed to publishing the book unless these changes were made. I don't believe, however, that he could prevent that. If the book is to be got out this fall, they will have to begin to set it up before long; and if I were you I would get this matter settled at once. Get the MSS. in shape and see that they go at it.

*   *   *

Yours,
Hen.

<hr />

2. See p. 375, n. 1.
3. Dreiser eventually did agree to substitute some fictional names for actual ones, though in a number of instances he refused to do so. (See the letters of Doubleday and Dreiser on pp. 447–49.) In the contract that Dreiser signed on August 20 (or shortly thereafter), the novel is called "The Flesh and the Spirit" (in an unknown hand) and "or Sister Carrie" (in Dreiser's hand). Frank Doubleday's letter of September 4 indicates that the firm finally accepted *Sister Carrie* as the title. One further late change was the addition of chapter titles. These were added, in pencil, by Dreiser and Henry after Dreiser's return from Missouri. They were probably added at the insistence of Doubleday, Page, for in later years Dreiser occasionally expressed a desire to have them removed. But his use of the 1900 plates throughout his lifetime made this omission difficult, and they remained.

FRANK NORRIS

To Arthur Henry†

[New York] July 18th [1900]

My Dear Arthur Henry:

I have just had a talk with Mr. Page about Dreiser, and it seems that he—Page—has written a long *personal* letter to Dreiser, in which there is much more than a "turning down" of Sister Carrie.[1]

He thinks—and so do I—that it should go to Dreiser at once so I would not hold it up as we talked of doing last night.

Page—and all of us—Mr. Doubleday too—are immensely interested in Dreiser and have every faith that he will go far. Page said today that even if we waited till T. D. got back it would yet be time for MacMillan or some other firm to get out Sister Carrie as a fall book.

Mr. Page has some suggestions to make to T. D. and is very anxious to have a talk with him as soon as he gets back.

Very Sincerely Yrs.
Norris

ARTHUR HENRY

To Theodore Dreiser‡

The enclosed letter from Norris just came.[1]

[New York] July 19, 1900

Dear Teddie:

It has dazed me. I am amazed and enraged. Doubleday has turned down your story. He did it all by himself and to the intense surprise of Norris and Lanier.

I don't exactly know the real attitude of Page in the matter but I do know that he is not to be taken seriously. I think that he is more

† From *Collected Letters: Frank Norris*, ed. Jesse S. Crisler (San Francisco: The Book Club of California, 1986), 119–20. Reprinted by permission of the Book Club of California.
1. Norris's letter of July 18, Page's of July 19, and Henry's of July 19 all stem from the same cause—Frank Doubleday's rejection of the novel. In their correspondence Page and Norris attempted to disguise Doubleday's role but Norris spoke openly to Henry about it. Norris, who had had the publication of his own *McTeague* delayed a year because of its subject matter, was in a difficult position. His sympathy for Dreiser had to be reconciled with his loyalty to a firm that was subsidizing his career while he was working on *The Octopus*.
‡ In the Dreiser Papers, University of Pennsylvania Library.
1. Norris's letter of July 18.

suave than honest. Doubleday simply read the story by accident. Norris praised it so highly and talked so much about how great it was that he read it and took a violent dislike to it.

I called on Norris last Tuesday evening and he met me with a long face. He blurted out the news as if he were stunned by it.

"Doubleday," he said, "thinks the story immoral and badly written. He don't make any of the objections to it that might be made—he simply don't think the story *ought* to be published by anybody first of all because it is immoral."

Norris suggested that I hold the letter the firm was going to send you, until he and I had got you an offer from Macmillan's and at first I listened to this idea favorably but as soon as I had left him that night and thought the matter out I was convinced that you ought to know about it at once.[2] It suddenly occurred to me that Doubleday and Page could be held to their first agreement if you wished to do so. I went to see Norris the next day and told him that I did not believe the firm could legally turn the book down at this stage of the game. He said that was probably true and asked me to talk with Doubleday.

I saw Doubleday and had a long talk with him—too long to detail in a letter. He told me just what Norris said he had told him. He said that Page had told him there had been no contract signed but that you had been led to believe that the firm would publish the book. I told him that the story had been accepted by a letter and that certain terms had been offered you which you had accepted.

Doubleday finally admitted that if the firm had agreed to publish the book it would have to do so if you forced them to, but he thought that would be a serious mistake as he would publish it only if so forced to and would make no effort to sell it as the more it sold the worse he would feel about it.

Now here are the cold facts. I took the trouble to get them and I tell them to you because I don't believe they will be absolutely sincere in any letter they may write.

I think this is an outrage pure and simple and am dumbfounded by it.

If Doubleday thought his house had made a mistake, he should have swallowed it and not have sought to crawl out by threatening the success of your book. He objects to the morality of your novel and in defense of his notions of virtue commits an injustice by a cowardly proceeding.

Write to me at once. The book is still at Doubleday & Page's. If you want it taken to Macmillan's telegraph me. If you want to make Doubleday keep his agreement with you, you had better come on.

2. Page's letter of July 19 was to be sent to Dreiser's New York address, from where Henry would presumably forward it to Dreiser in Missouri.

Don't let this distress you, old man, too much. The story will make
all its objectors look small when it gets to the public.

Hen.

The letter from Doubleday and Page has not come. I will forward it
as soon as it does.

WALTER H. PAGE

To Theodore Dreiser†

[New York, July 19, 1900]

Dear Mr. Dreiser:

I told you that we would publish *Sister Carrie*; but, since you went
away, we have had an opportunity, which had not presented itself
before, thoroughly to discuss the book; and the more we have discussed it, I am sorry to report to you, the more uncertain do we all
feel about it. The feeling has grown upon us that, excellent as your
workmanship is, the choice of your characters has been unfortunate.
I think I told you that, personally, this kind of people did not interest
me, and we find it hard to believe they will interest the great majority
of readers. We all feel, too, that the mention of real names and places
is a mistake, because it destroys the illusion and reduces the story,
as it seems to us, more nearly to the level of a mere narrative.

I do not mean, however, to repeat these criticisms to your weariness, which you recall I made on the day we talked it over; but I
write to say that we do fear that they are more vital than they may
have seemed in my conversational presentation of them—so vital, in
fact, that, to be frank, we prefer not to publish the book, and we
should like to be released from my agreement with you. If you have
suffered any injury, we stand ready, of course, to make amends.

And we wish you to be assured that we regard the vivid workmanship of the book as exceedingly attractive. We should be very glad to
have you on our publishing list, and we should like to indulge the
hope of having you in the near future. We believe heartily in you and
in the work that you will do; and we regret exceedingly that we feel
this difference with you about this particular book.

If you were to ask my advice, I should without hesitation say that
Sister Carrie is not the best kind of book for a young author to make
his first book. Whether you ever agree with my own feeling about it
(which, I confess, has changed a good deal since I saw you), a book

† *Letters* 1: 55–56.

about a different kind of material would be a better first book—even if this should be published afterwards.

I hope to see you as soon as convenient after you come back; for I have another subject that I should like to talk over with you—viz.—our new magazine.

Very sincerely yours,
Walter H. Page

THEODORE DREISER

To Arthur Henry†

Montgomery City, Missouri
July [23], 1900

My Dear Hen:—

Your letter has not disturbed me at all—at least no more so than if the intelligence concerned another person. I had a forewarning of this, as I shall detail later, about a week ago. Your letter came yesterday noon, and at five P.M. it was followed by Page's. As you suggested his is the height or insincerity. He now magnifies some remarks of his concerning the book of which I told you the day we visited Martin and finds the work vitally defective. The letter I mail to you herewith, wishing you to keep it however, as it frankly acknowledges the agreement and recognizes a possible injury to me.

I also enclose my letter to Mr. Page in reply which explains more explicitly the attitude I shall take. I think we had best be calm. I can return soon enough to New York, if necessary. This move surprising as it is, makes me feel that Doubleday is sincere. He has every reason to see merit in novels submitted, since out of them he derives his income. If he objects so strongly as to break his agreement—well, he must have ample reasons. They must be vital to him or he would not attempt this.

Nevertheless, I am inclined, for rather important reasons, to hold Doubleday and Page to their agreement. They have caused me and my friends to preach abroad my success until no one who knows me does not know of my book and their original attitude toward it. Not an editor in New York but is aware of its approaching issue. The knowledge of its being turned down in so summary a fashion will do harm, I have no doubt and that is not fair. I am sure they have not contemplated this phase of the situation and would not willingly injure me beyond the need of saving themselves.

† *Letters* 1: 51–54.

Only today I received a note of congratulation from Mr. Parker, the editor of the *Atlantic*. A newspaperman of Baltimore, an ex St. Louis associate of mine, has heard of it through Davenport of the *Journal* and written to congratulate me. It is known to all the boys in St. Louis and Pittsburgh, and to a very wide circle of clannish relatives here, all looking to purchase it. Miss Fanton has been as active as she has ever been enthusiastic and I have the element she has awakened to explain to, should the book fail to appear. Gates became so enthusiastic over the plot as I explained it to him, that he asked me to allow him to arrange for me to deliver a lecture on the purpose of the novel before the Players Club in New York, this fall.

For this reason I hesitate and it is not my purpose, temporarily at least, to accept the manuscript in return. Should it arrive here by express, I shall have it returned, unsigned for, C.O.D. Will notify them that they must hold it until the matter has been adjudicated that is until we have had an opportunity to discuss the matter personally. Meanwhile, if supposedly without my knowledge you and Norris choose to submit it elsewhere—say Macmillan's—well and good. I cannot object to what I in nowise know. Should Macmillan's take it, of course Doubleday & Page could pass. I would have the situation in such shape that it would do me no harm.

I see no need to telegraph you or to make especial haste. They are responsible for the manuscript and I have the original in storage. I can argue with them quietly and believe much can be done. If possible, you get the loan of the ms. & try Macmillan's, while I argue. They put themselves in a queer position by so strange a move and cast but poor credit upon their three readers—Norris, Lanier and Page. Are these gentlemen's opinions worth nothing then, when Mr. Doubleday objects[?]

If when better known and successful I should choose to make known this correspondence, every scrap of which I have, even to letters of commendation from others, the house of Doubleday would not shine so very brightly. I prefer to believe that the matter can be smoothed over, and that they will in view of my forthcoming book, (which, if I can raise the money I shall write this winter) publish *Sister Carrie* and preserve my credit. It will pay them to treat me fair. I shall not leave room for queries in my next. Those who have feelings may prepare to have them shaken. It shall be out of my heart truly.

There is a tenth sense stirring in the minds of men or I should not be able to add this curious experience for your consideration. Sometime about last Monday or Tuesday I found myself thinking that there was something in the wind which boded ill to me—something which I must know and could if I would. It was distinctly in my mind that it concerned my novel and once I deliberately said—"they may have turned it down." The proposition seemed so ridiculous that I put it aside, but always it came back.

"Go to a fortune teller" was a phrase repeatedly whispered in my ear. "She will tell you something." I went so far as to ask the negroes working for us here where a seeress lived, but neglected to seek the "Old Mammy" pointed out. I was not without faith however that something had happened, and that I would soon hear.

Friday your letter came, indicating Lanier's dissent. Instantly I knew what was coming. My letter to you must have borne the feeling if not the words. Friday night, for some reason, the thing culminated in a deep gloom for which I could give no reason. It held me tightly and I dropped everything to muse. I suffered a physical derangement of the nervous system[,] went to bed to roll until nearly morning. Then it seemed to pass and since then I have been in a steadily increasing contented frame of mind.

Don't think for a moment that my hours are discolored by your intelligence. I am exactly as I was before, plus this new knowledge. No little delay such as this could distress me. I am much of a fatalist as you know, and consider my career secure. Not that, after all, it is essential that I should have a career, but that these things which I feel are needed by society and will work for its improvement—the greater happiness of man. I wish, of course, that already my work was so perfect that such objections and delays as this could not occur—that my days were removed from the miserable consideration of a livelihood. I could work just as hard and with equal effect. Fortune need not forever feel that she must use the whip on me.

Well, say nothing to Jug,[1] and keep the matter secret from everyone until we see what the end is going to be. Perhaps it will come out all right. If, as I say, you can get the loan of the manuscript and submit it to Macmillan's for quick consideration do so. Let it not be understood that I countenance any such move, at least for the present. If you wish, after reading my letter to Page, to go forward to Doubleday and emphasize my situation as there detailed, I think it would have weight.

I am thoroughly pleased by your excitement on my behalf. It reflects my distress when things go wrong with you. Surely there were never better friends than we. If words were anything I think I would tell you how I feel, but it is of no use. You know. You are to me my other self a very excellent Dreiser minus some of my defects, & plus many laughable errors which I would not have. If I could not be what I am I would be you.

Always
Teddie

---

1. Mrs. Dreiser (Sara Osborne White). [R. H. E.]

N.B. Concerning the enclosed letter to Mr. Page, I want you to have it typewritten and to allow my signature to stand at the bottom typewritten, only underneath write in ink these little initials TD. It will give it directness. Let Montgomery City stand at the top and the date also, July 23rd.[2] If satisfactory to you, mail. If not, write.

THEODORE DREISER

To Walter H. Page†

Montgomery City, Missouri
July 23, 1900

My Dear Mr. Page:

To say that I am astonished by the intelligence which your letter of the 19th conveys, is but putting it mildly. I have, however, given the situation very serious consideration, and find that the question of release will not need an answer from me, until another phase of the situation has been looked into. This I herewith present.

Outside of the matter of preserving your own interest, I am loath to believe that the firm of Doubleday & Page would countenance an injury to me. It is not within the pale of literary dealings of any sort. I have all along taken the very flattering commendation of the book from yourself, Mr. Lanier and Mr. Norris in good faith. The letters expressing this warm approval have been, as you might well surmise, documents of value to me. On the strength of them, my closest friends have naturally rejoiced with me, and, in the certainty which they contributed, have preached my success abroad. There is not an editor in New York or Boston but has in one way and another heard very flatteringly of my work. From Mr. Parker, of the *Atlantic*, I have but this morning received a note of congratulation expressing pleasure in my connection with so good a house. Prof. Gates, of Washington, hearing of the nature of my story, sometime since requested permission to arrange for a lecture to be delivered by me before the Players Club of New York upon a phase of literature suggested by the story. He was very thoroughly interested, and has the project still clearly in mind. Others, of equal importance, have, out of friendship or other animating causes, seen fit to spread news of the matter in such a way that I would be looked upon as an object of curious interest if the work now failed to appear. Thus our mutual friend Mr. Morgan Robertson, the first to hear of the enthusiastic reception

2. See Dreiser's July 23 letter to Page.
† *Letters* 1: 56–59.

given the manuscript by your house, has spread the word as to the novel, myself and the supposed date of issue, until now I should be ashamed to face the literary coterie and the many others he has interested, with a story of rejection.

From your own experience, you must know that a matter of this sort would go very far in two months. The repute in which your firm is held, the warm and rather extra-ordinary reception accorded my effort by your readers—the number and enthusiasm of those interested in me—all could but combine to engender a state, the destruction of which must necessarily put me in an untoward and very unsatisfactory predicament. I ask you frankly to put yourself in my position and consider what you would do.

Mine is not a case similar to one who would ordinarily bring you his first production. Some years of labor in the magazine field, and previous to that a short experience in the newspaper world has tended very materially to enlarge my acquaintance and I may say, create an interest which has recently been accentuated by this latest intelligence. I have received a number of letters and have been beholden to acknowledge the good word. A family relationship of rather far-reaching extent, all informed as to my present prospects makes your proposition a very sensitive matter. I am now called upon to explain away a very justifiable hope—to acknowledge a peculiar defeat and say that the original good opinion was not warranted.

Aside from all this, the nature of which you must readily appreciate, I am satisfied that the attitude taken by your firm, if persisted in, will work me material injury. I depend upon the judgment of the magazine editors, as regards my shorter contributions for a livelihood. How much this judgment is affected, even in the larger instances, by current report and a record of success, I have ample cause to know. Let it be said that this much-praised manuscript, from which so much was anticipated, was thus summarily turned down, and I shall answer with what? More arduous labor? A need of greater determination to overcome an obstacle deliberately cast in my path!

Before bringing up the question of rejection I believe you will need to give this situation thorough consideration. For my part I do not choose to pass upon your attitude until you have had ample time to weigh the factors involved. A keen and honorable conception of justice and duty is I believe the pre-requisite of every great publishing firm. It is no less, I am convinced, a palladium with yours than with others. To that conception I bring these facts. You are disagreed as to the qualities of a story important enough to incite disagreement. Some of you, I know are enthusiastically for it. Others, uncertain or violently opposed. This is something to ponder over.

[In the next place, yours are a distinguished firm publishing a number of books each year, to whom one volume more or less is not all-important. It can neither injure you seriously nor bring you permanent success.][1] If disagreed as to a novel's quality, yet called by a weight of justice to fulfill an agreement, the great commonplace public might well be appealed to without dissension. If the book is worthy it will be honored with the public's approval and our mutual profit. If unworthy you have suffered a small loss, well compensated for in wisdom acquired and obligations fulfilled.

With this statement I am willing to rest the matter, leaving for another day my reply to your eventual decision. As it stands, I cannot credit you with having reached one until you have digested all the facts. You may however have this for a suggestion and a light. The public feeds upon nothing which is not helpful to it. Its selection of what some deem poison is I am sure wiser than the chemistry of the objectors. Of what it finds it will take only the best, leaving the chaff and the evil to blow away. [See to it that you have faith in the public—your greater arbiter. By so much as you accord with it, you will not fail.][2]

Very respectfully
Theodore Dreiser

ARTHUR HENRY

To Theodore Dreiser†

[New York] Received
July 26, 1900

Dear Teddie:

Hold Doubleday and Page to their agreement. I have talked with Norris several times and I am convinced that this is the best thing for you to do. They admit that they are bound to publish it, if you say so, and Norris agrees with me that if they do so Doubleday will soon get over his kick and that it will be a great seller. Norris, who attends to the newspapers, critics etc., will strain every nerve for the book and I know that he will be glad if the house publishes the book after all. I have firmly maintained with them all, that you could not afford to let them go back now as the fact that they had accepted the book had been too widely published and you have made your

---

1. The bracketed sentences were crossed out in Dreiser's filed draft or copy. What served to introduce this paragraph in the letter he sent cannot be ascertained. [R. H. E.]
2. This conclusion in brackets was struck out in Dreiser's copy. Probably no other was substituted in the letter sent to Page. [R. H. E.]
† In the Dreiser Papers, University of Pennsylvania Library.

winter plans on the strength of it. All you need to do now is to quietly and firmly request them to keep their agreement with you.

You can't afford to take any other position as it would be too late now to get it out this year with any other house. Doubleday is all wrong and he will himself see it sooner or later.

Let me hear from you before you answer Page's letter. Write soon or telegraph as I can think of nothing else until this is settled.

Hen.

ARTHUR HENRY

To Theodore Dreiser‡

[New York] Received July 31, 1900
Hen. never gives any date.

Dear Teddie:

We arrived at exactly the same conclusion. Your letter[1] to D.P. & Co. suits me to a hair. I will not take the MSS from them even as a loan for fear they would think we might weaken. And then too it would give them the chance for an argument that they do not have now with the book still in their possession. You had a better clue to go by with Page's letter before you than I had. I now understand, after reading it, why they delayed so long in writing it. Norris, when he told me Doubleday had turned the story down, thought the letter had already been sent to you. Evidently I was sounded first to see how the proceeding would be taken. They assured to me that all they had to do was to send you back the book with apologies. It was not until after my talk with Doubleday that the letter was mailed you. If they had written one before they must have torn it up and written a second one. Doubleday assured to me that they were really under no obligation to take the book. I told him almost identically what you had written, except of course about Gates and the editor of the Atlantic, and I also assured him that to all purposes the agreement between you and his house was as good as a contract. He finally admitted this and they hope now to coax you off. I believe that Doubleday is sincere, but he is mistaken and the public will prove him so and you surely should not suffer for his narrowness.

The only reason for haste is the fact that if it is to appear this fall it should be in the hands of the printer. It would be a mistake to

‡ In the Dreiser Papers, University of Pennsylvania Library.
1. Of July 23.

have it delayed in appearing and so lose some of the effects of the advertizing it has had.

* * *

Hen.

WALTER H. PAGE

To Theodore Dreiser†

[New York, August 2, 1900]

Dear Mr. Dreiser:

Your letter came a few days ago, and we have all read it and very carefully considered it; and we thank you for writing so frankly.

The matter stands thus, as you know: We agreed to publish your book (although there was left open the very serious matter of leaving out the names of real people, as you wrote them.)

Then, after fuller consideration, we became very doubtful of two points—first, the financial return from the novel; and second, the desirability, for your own good as well as ours, of publishing it, on account of your choice of material. We therefore asked you if you were willing to release us.

Your kindly letter not unnaturally expressed surprise—and, to a degree, also, disappointment; but you do not say specifically whether you will release us or not.

If, as we understand your plans, you will be in New York in a little while, we suggest that you give us your answer to our request to be released when you return. We shall be glad to see you as soon as you arrive.

Let us say in the meantime that we thoroughly understand your disappointment. But we are sure that you very greatly exaggerate the practical results of such a change of plan. You have told your friends. But they would quickly adapt themselves to a change of plan whereby your next book would be published first. Indeed such changes of plan—much more violent changes in fact—take place every day. Mr. James Lane Allen, for example, finished a novel a year ago. It was announced; it was, we think, even put in his publisher's catalogue. All his friends and all the literary world knew about it. But a change of plan was made and another novel which he has written since then has now appeared. The question is whether it really be best to change

† *Letters* 1: 59–60.

the plan, not what you may imagine others will think. (After all, other people, even our friends, think much less of our work than we imagine they do!)

Our wish to be released by you is quite as much for your own literary future as for our good; we think we can say even more for your benefit than for ours. If we are to be your publishers, as we hope to be, we are anxious that the development of your literary career should be made in the most natural and advantageous way. But we are sure that the publication of *Sister Carrie* as your first book would be a mistake. It would identify you in the minds of the public with the use of this sort of material; and we think it would require years and a long list of other different books by you to remove the impression. You will do better, in our judgment, both from a literary and a financial point of view, by publishing a novel on a different subject as your first book.

In giving this advice, and in asking you to release us, we are (we wish you to make sure) serving your best interests—both financial and literary.

While we believe very strongly in you and have high hopes of your future work, let us repeat that we do not believe that any considerable financial success can be achieved with *Sister Carrie*.

We beg pardon for writing so long a letter; but even in a long letter, we can hardly hope to cover the whole matter as satisfactorily as we could discuss it in conversation. We hope to see you (and we shall be glad to see you) as soon as you come home. We believe that you will regard the matter as we do; but, however you regard it we shall have the satisfaction of a full, frank, and friendly talk.

We wish to talk with you, too, about the possibility of work for the magazine that we are getting ready to publish—the *World's Work*.

> Very sincerely yours,
> Walter H. Page

THEODORE DREISER

To Walter H. Page†

> Montgomery City, [Missouri]
> August 6, 1900

My Dear Mr. Page:—

I have considered your reply (to the presentation of my views in this matter of your request for release from publishing my novel as

† *Letters* 1: 61–63.

agreed) and I have concluded to ask you to publish it as originally planned. Abrupt as this may seem I have given it two days of earnest thought and have, I believe, weighed all the particulars involved. I appreciate your kindness in consulting the advancement of my literary career as well as your own commercial interests, and would like to feel that the development of my literary life depended, as you say, upon a "natural and advantageous way" involving the elimination of *Sister Carrie*, but I cannot. I do not have much faith in the orderly progression of publication as regards novels. A great book will destroy conditions, unfavorable or indifferent, whether these be due to previous failures or hostile prejudice aroused by previous error. Even if this book should fail, I can either write another important enough in its nature to make its own conditions and be approved of for itself alone, or I can write something unimportant and fail, as the author of a triviality deserves to fail. Therefore I have no fear on this score.

As to the choice of material—I am willing to abide by your first spontaneous judgment of that. If the public will only make the same general error I shall be highly gratified. Whatever betides on that basis there will be room for contention, which a second novel may well endeavor to dissipate.

Neither can I agree with you that I exaggerate the practical results set forth in my last letter. You forget that I am no James Lane Allen nor have I so solid a reputation, capable of withstanding these rude literary shocks. I am placed where in a measurable degree the orderly development of my literary career depends upon the early publication of *Sister Carrie*, and therefore I have so decided.

Your change of opinion has not modified my own regarding the volume, sensible as I am of its just imperfection. I have faith to believe that no true picture of life is without its justification in the eyes of the public. I feel and I know that what I have seen and what I have heard of the rudenesses and bitternesses of life are in the eyes and the ears of all men justifiable—that the world is greedy for details of how men rise and fall. In the presence of a story which deals with the firm insistence of law, the elements of chance and sub-conscious direction, men will not, I have heart to feel, stand unanimously indifferent. There may be those who cannot perceive, or who reading, conceive wrongly, but the clearer intellects upon whose judgment after all depends the success of every important volume will see and approve.

In this faith I venture to move against all your objections and to beg you to proceed to the fulfillment of the original plan. I will ask you to publish the volume as quickly as possible and to that end will genially arbitrate all minor considerations. The book should firstly be a fall book, reaching the market with all of those for which you are now craving a fair field. In the face of this I beg of you to lay aside all hostility and submit the matter to the world outside. I assure you I shall not doubt your energy nor interest where the commercial features are concerned, nor shall I be able to feel that there has been anything but an honest & justifiable discussion equably overcome. I shall be happy to bring all future efforts to your table for consideration and I share with you whatever modicum of success my efforts may achieve, just as I am sure that you would be willing to share with me.

I would leave this matter until my return to New York if it were not that my opinion as here given is conclusive and that fall publication if consummated as planned, demands immediate action.

I beg you to believe that in all this discussion I have born only the kindliest feelings toward you and your house. I have assured myself of your sincerity & good wishes and now only wish to know that you accept my assurances in good faith. My one desire has been to view the situation as broadly as possible and to maintain kindly feelings and honest relationship. I hope that always in the future I may be able to avail myself of your personal judgment and good feeling toward me and that I may live to win your complete approval and friendship.

Very Respectfully,
Theodore Dreiser

ARTHUR HENRY

To Theodore Dreiser†

[August 1900?]

Dear Ted

I am convinced that D & P will publish your book but I am sure you must keep after them or it will be delayed too long to come out this winter. I can do nothing more as I think all they are working for now is delay in the hope that you will have your next novel done by spring and they can bring that out first. Since it is delay they are after your absence makes it easy for them to obtain it. I think you should come on here without delay and push this thing through at once. Leave Jug for a few weeks and come on here with me. You will surely come to grief if you stay there.

*   *   *

Hen

† In the Dreiser Papers, University of Pennsylvania Library.

WALTER H. PAGE

To Theodore Dreiser†

[New York] August 15, 1900

Dear Mr. Dreiser:

It has occurred to us that since we prefer not to publish "Sister Carrie" you might be willing for us to try to secure you a publisher. Would you release us from publishing it, if we get for you an acceptance of the book for publication this fall from any one of the following publishers—

    Appleton
    Macmillan
    Dodd, Mead & Co.
    Stokes
    Lippincott?

If we publish it, we shall have to insist on your making the changes of names in the MS. There are too many of them to leave for the proof—especially when every change might require a run-over—& thus almost (if not quite) double the cost of composition.

Very truly yours,
Walter H. Page

Theodore Dreiser Esq.

F. N. DOUBLEDAY

To Theodore Dreiser‡

[New York, September 4, 1900]

Dear Sir:—

We have been carefully over your manuscript, and wish to make the following suggestions, which we think are absolutely essential; namely, that the original title of the book shall be kept—*Sister Carrie*—and all the names of real persons should be changed. We have marked these in the manuscript, and understood that you had already taken them out. You will notice among these Francis Wilson, Charles Frohman, Schlesinger & Meyer, the Waldorf, the Morton House, Mr. Daly's office, etc. It is absolutely imperative that no real name should appear in the book.

† In the Dreiser Papers, University of Pennsylvania Library.
‡ *Letters* 1: 63–64.

We call attention to the fact that New York's parade of fashion from 14th Street to 34th Street on Broadway is a misnomer. We have taken out profanity which we regarded as imperative. You will notice that we have marked several passages in the manuscript with a question mark. These we think could be changed to advantage, and we trust you will agree with us and do this.

We return the manuscript to you herewith, as we do not wish to come to the necessity of making the changes in type.

Very truly yours,
F. N. Doubleday

THEODORE DREISER

To F. N. Doubleday†

[New York, N.Y.
after September 4, 1900]

My Dear Mr. Doubleday:—

I return herewith my novel partly revised according to your wishes. The names of Francis Wilson, Charles Frohman, Schlesinger and Meyer, the Waldorf, the Morton House[,] the Broadway[,] and so on have been removed. Also I have found occasion to agree with you in most of the passages indicated and to strike out those lines which seem to you too suggestive. In several instances there have been question marks opposite names which are wholly fictitious. These of course need not be disturbed.

As for the name of Sherry I have substituted Delmonico throughout the book. Your question mark is opposite that also as something to be removed but I cannot agree with you. Like Daly and Wallack, it is already too common in literature. Richard Harding Davis and Paul Leicester Ford have used these so frequently that I cannot be accused of going beyond the pale of literary usage in this matter. Daly, Wallack's, and Delmonico's must stand.

In one place you mark my mention of E. P. Roe's *The Opening of a Chestnut Burr* as something to be changed. In another place you leave Balzac's *Père Goriot* unquestioned. Why is this? Mr. Roe is dead? His novel was well known. May a writer not mention a standard piece of American fiction or a well known American author. Is the preference given to foreigners? As a publisher of Mr. Kipling's works you should have excoriated his mention of Besant and Stevenson, both contemporaries and living at the time he mentioned

† *Letters* 1: 64–65.

them. Mr. Ford and Mr. Davis err in the same seemingly to you objectionable manner and their novels are scarcely to [be] reckoned as failures.[1]

I have noted your statement—"We have taken out profanity which we regarded as imperative." If you mean you have already stricken it from the pages, I do not see where. If you mean that *all* you have questioned must be changed I will have to disagree with you. Since when has the expression "Lord Lord," become profane. Wherein is "Damn," "By the Lord," and "By God."[2]

THEODORE DREISER

To Frank Norris†

[New York, December 1900]

My dear Mr. Norris:

Owing as I do so very much to your earliest and most unqualified approval of this story in manuscript form it is my determination to inscribe a copy to you whether you will or no. That it reaches either you or the public "under covers" so soon is due entirely to you. Therefore refuse not a corner of the family table to the offspring you so generously fostered. Neither attempt to deny in the future that your sins do find you out. With the most grateful remembrances I am

Sincerely Yours
Dreiser

---

1. As a matter of fact, the names Charles Frohman, The Waldorf Hotel, the Morton House Hotel, the Broadway Theatre, and Sherry's restaurant appear in the novel, as do Delmonico's restaurant, Augustin Daly, and Daly's Theatre. Dreiser did eliminate Wallack's Theatre and Roe's novel as well as the actor Francis Wilson and Schlesinger and Mayer (not Meyer), a Chicago store.
2. Dreiser's copy ends here. [R. H. E.]
† Inscribed in Frank Norris's copy of *Sister Carrie* (New York: Doubleday, Page & Co., 1900), in the Bancroft Library, University of California, Berkeley. Published by permission of the Trustees of the University of Pennsylvania and the Bancroft Library.

FRANK NORRIS

To Theodore Dreiser‡

My Dear Dreiser.:

My work piled up so thick all through the first weeks of this month that until now I have had no opportunity of thanking you for *Carrie*. I have read most of her again, and must thank you for that pleasure too. It is a *true* book in all senses of the word. The review in the Com. Ad. was rather noncommittal but it certainly was lengthy and took the story seriously. I am looking forward to news of your next now.

* * *

Very Sincerely Yrs
Frank Norris

Roselle [New Jersey] Tuesday
Jan, 28
1901

‡ From *Collected Letters: Frank Norris*, ed. Jesse S. Crisler (San Francisco: The Book Club of California, 1986), 144. Reprinted by permission of the Book Club of California.

Legend

Sister Carrie was published on November 8, 1900. Although attacked by many critics, it nevertheless was widely noted and received a number of lengthy reviews. Moreover, William Heinemann of London published a condensed version in 1901 that was praised by English reviewers. But the book sold poorly in America, and Dreiser—who was already suffering from the effects of a disastrous marriage went into a major decline, from which he did not recover until late 1903. By 1905, however, Dreiser had begun a new and successful career as an editor of popular magazines. Although he was no longer writing fiction, his faith in the worth of Sister Carrie led him to buy the plates of the novel and to have it reissued by B. W. Dodge in 1907. The novel has been in print since that time.

Soon after the publication of Sister Carrie by Doubleday, Page, Dreiser began to discuss openly in interviews, letters, and conversation his version of the suppression of the novel. His account emphasized three points: the role of Mrs. Doubleday in the attempt by the firm to avoid publication; the failure of Doubleday, Page to properly distribute the book; and the heroic part played by Frank Norris. Mrs. Doubleday's name does not appear in any of the extant correspondence of 1900. Dreiser claimed, however, that he learned of her opposition to the book from Norris (though he perhaps heard of it from Arthur Henry, who had learned of it from Norris), from Heinemann, and from Thomas McKee, a former lawyer for Doubleday, Page who was a part-owner of the Broadway Magazine while Dreiser was its editor in 1905. McKee also reported to Dreiser the decision of the firm to discourage sales of the novel.

Dreiser returned to fiction in 1911 with Jennie Gerhardt, and by 1915—after three additional novels—was a major literary figure. The suppression of his novel The "Genius" in 1916 revived the story of the suppression of Sister Carrie. Both events were widely publicized by a group of radical critics as examples of the destructive force of American puritanism. H. L. Mencken recounted the earlier suppression fully in his A Book of Prefaces (1917), as did Frank Harris in Contemporary Portraits (1919) and Burton Rascoe in Theodore Dreiser (1925). In the early 1930s the story received full mythic expression in Dreiser's introduction to the Modern Library edition of Sister Carrie (1932) and in Dorothy Dudley's Forgotten Frontiers: Dreiser and the Land of the Free (1932). Dudley in particular transformed the publication of Sister Carrie by Doubleday, Page into a battle between the forces of Philistinism and Freedom.

451

The myth of the suppression of *Sister Carrie* has, like most myths, a twofold reality. As fact, it is often inaccurate or unverifiable. Dreiser, for example, neglected to recall that the firm did not sign a contract for publication until after it had expressed its opposition to the book. Whatever Doubleday's sentiments, he honored the word of his partner and editor, a fact that Dreiser failed to acknowledge. Moreover, Dreiser soon began to omit any mention of Henry's role in the affair and to obscure Norris's ambivalent position. By 1903 Dreiser had fallen out with Henry, but the legend required a hero—and Norris—who had died in 1902 at a tragically youthful age—was elevated to that role. In addition, as is clear from records and correspondence now in the Dreiser Collection of the University of Pennsylvania Library, the first edition of *Sister Carrie* was not burned or consigned to a moldy cellar. About half of its first printing of a thousand copies was sold, despite Doubleday's lack of aggressiveness. Finally, the pivotal role of Mrs. Doubleday—the dragon of the myth—cannot be determined. Her participation may have occurred or it may have been trade gossip of late 1900 that was later transformed into fact in the minds of such figures as Heinemann and McKee. Doubleday himself is generally acknowledged to have been a man of integrity, and his 1931 letter to Franklin Walker is firm on Mrs. Doubleday's lack of involvement.

But whatever its insubstantiality in fact, the legend of the suppression of *Sister Carrie* has an independent reality and significance in American cultural history. Like the myth of Sherwood Anderson walking out of his office to begin a career as a writer, it represented to the young writers of the 1920s and 1930s the irreconcilable division in American life between the values of a business civilization and those of the artist. To the generation of the 1920s, Dreiser was the symbol of the suppressed artist, Anderson of the artist seeking freedom. The facts of the publication of *Sister Carrie* are therefore one kind of truth, the myth of its suppression is another.

ST. LOUIS POST-DISPATCH

Author of *Sister Carrie*†

Theodore Dreiser, a former St. Louisan, who has newly gained fame as a novelist, was in the city last week on his way to Montgomery City, Mo., to visit the relatives of his wife, whom he married in that city.[1]

Mr. Dreiser was employed in newspaper work in St. Louis from 1891 to 1894. He went East and engaged in magazine work, publishing many short stories.

† *St. Louis Post-Dispatch* 26 Jan. 1902: 4.
1. Dreiser had been attempting for over a year to complete *Jennie Gerhardt* and was on the verge of a nervous collapse. I have left unnoted a number of minor errors in this interview.

It is his first novel, "Sister Carrie," which has brought him into prominence. The British literary reviews, in particular, give it high praise, ranking it with "The Octopus," by Frank Norris, at the top of the list of novels for the last year.

It is interesting to note that Frank Norris, as senior reader for a publishing firm, first saw the merit of "Sister Carrie," and recommended its acceptance.

To the Post-Dispatch Mr. Dreiser told the history of his novel, which is extraordinary in some features.

The novel was written in six months, from October, 1899, to March 1900. It was rejected by one publishing firm because it was not considered an all-around interesting story.

He took the manuscript to Doubleday, Page & Co. April 1, 1900, where Frank Norris, author of "The Octopus," in his capacity as senior reader, read it. He sent for Mr. Dreiser and congratulated him.

Mr. Norris passed it on to Mr. Lanier, one of the members of the firm who read it and thought it was a good story. He, in turn, handed it to Mr. Page, and that gentleman said he considered it the best book brought into the house that year.

When Mr. Doubleday, the senior partner, returned from Europe, he heard so much about the manuscript that he took it home. Mrs. Doubleday read "Sister Carrie" and took a violent dislike to it. Mr. Doubleday read it and agreed with her. Before Mr. Doubleday had come home a contract had been drawn up and signed by which the work was to be published in the fall, and upon this Mr. Dreiser stood.

A friendly member of the firm sent a number of copies to newspapers and critical journals. They attracted much attention.

The newspapers, in fact, hailed Dreiser as the producer of a masterpiece of naturalism, and the critical journals acquiesced. "Sister Carrie" became famous.

"A copy of the book," said Mr. Dreiser. "was sent to Mr. William Heinemann, a London publisher. That gentleman read it and entered into a contract with me and brought out the novel in England. It appeared in London in May, 1901."

At this point Mr. Dreiser's triumph really began. There was a unanimous critical uprising in favor of "Sister Carrie." The Spectator called it "a work of the utmost power, exact as life itself." The Academy passed upon it as the first important novel out of America.

The Atheneum, England's leading critical journal, used the phrase, "great, with all the greatness of the country which gave it birth," and declared that it introduced a new method of telling a story.

Other critical journals, such as the Times, the Literary World, the Chronicle and the Mail, devoted space to analyzing and declaring the power of this American novel.

This created a boom for the book in England, where it began to sell at once.

The American firm of J. F. Taylor & Co., hearing of its success abroad, sought the author and entered into a contract whereby the book was transferred to that firm, by which it is to be released the coming spring.

"Sister Carrie" has been attacked, in America (not in England), upon the score of morality. Concerning these attacks Mr. Dreiser said:

"In 'Sister Carrie' all the phases of life touched upon are handled truthfully. I have not tried to gloss over any evil any more than I have stopped to dwell upon it. Life is too short; its phases are too numerous.

"What I desired to do was to show two little human beings, or more, laying in and out among the giant legs of circumstance.

"Personally I see nothing immoral in discussing with a clean purpose any phase of life. I have never been able to understand the objection to considering every phase of life from a philosophic standpoint.

"If life is to be made better or more interesting, its conditions must be understood. No situation can be solved, no improvement can be effected, no evil remedied, unless the conditions which surround it are appreciated."

Mr. Dreiser is well remembered by St. Louis newspaper men and other citizens. He is still a young man.

S. A. EVERITT

To Theodore Dreiser†

February 9, 1905

Theodore Dreiser, Esq.
339 Mott Avenue,
Borough of the Bronx,
New York City.

Dear Sir:

By referring to our records, we find that the first edition of "Sister Carrie" was 1,000 copies. When the transfer to J. F. Taylor & Company was made, we delivered them 100 bound copies and 250 folded

† In the Dreiser Papers, University of Pennsylvania Library.

copies, which would indicate that there were sold and given away as editorial copies about 650 copies.[1]

Very truly yours,
Doubleday, Page & Co.
SAE[2]

THEODORE DREISER

To Fremont Older†

118 West 11th Street
New York, [N.Y.]
November 27, 1923

Dear Mr. Older.[1]

I feel like beginning " 'tis a sad story, mates." I finished *Sister Carrie* in the spring of 1900. It was written at 6 West 102nd Street, N.Y., by the way. I was a free-lancing magazine contributor at the time and was over-persuaded by a young literary friend of mine who was convinced that I could write a novel even when I knew that I couldn't. Once done, however, after many pains and aches, I took it to Harper and Brothers, who promptly rejected it. Then I took it to Doubleday, Page & Co. At that time Doubleday had newly parted from McClure and had employed Frank Norris as a reader of manuscripts. It was Norris who first read the book. He sent for me and told me quite enthusiastically that he thought it was a fine book, and that he was satisfied that Doubleday would be glad to publish it, but that more time for a final decision would be required. Subsequent to this, because he wanted to go on record in the matter, I presume, he wrote me a warm and very kindly letter praising the book, while I still have.

About a week or ten days later I had a letter from Walter H. Page, the late ambassador, who asked me to call. And when I came he congratulated me on the character of the work and announced that

1. In 1901 Dreiser had contracted to publish *Jennie Gerhardt* with J. F. Taylor and Company. This firm also agreed to reissue *Sister Carrie* upon the completion of *Jennie Gerhardt* and had bought the plates and unsold copies from Doubleday, Page for this purpose. Dreiser, who in 1905 was himself thinking of buying the plates from Taylor, had written Doubleday, Page about the sale of their edition. If at the most 150 review copies were distributed, approximately 500 copies were sold by Doubleday—a figure confirmed by royalty statements in the Dreiser Collection.
2. Samuel A. Everitt, a member of the Doubleday firm.
† *Letters* 2: 417–21.
1. Fremont Older, a San Francisco newspaperman, had written Dreiser to inquire about the suppression of *Sister Carrie*.

it was to be accepted for publication, and that he would send me a contract which I was to sign. Also, because he appeared to like the work very much, he announced that no pains would be spared to launch the book properly, and that,—(the glorious American press agent spirit of the day, I presume)—he was thinking of giving me a dinner, to which various literary people would be invited in order to attract attention to the work and to me. Being very young, very green, and very impressionable, this brought about very ponderous notions as to my own importance which might just as well have been allowed to rest, particularly in the light of what followed.

For this so stirred me that I decided to be about the work of another novel,—to join the one a year group, which seemed to be what was expected of me. And to this end I scraped together a little cash and retired to the country. Frank Doubleday, the head of the house, was in England at the time. In my absense he returned and hearing, as I was afterwards informed, that the book was much thought of, decided to read it or, at least, have it read for himself. Accordingly as Norris, and later William Heinemann of London, informed me, he took the book home and gave it to his wife. Being of a conventional and victorian turn, I believe—(I have always been told so)—she took a violent dislike to the book and proceeded to discourage her husband as to its publication. He in turn sent for me, and asked me to release him from the contract which had already been signed. His statement to me was that he did not like the book and would not publish it.

My personal wish was to take the book under my arm and walk out, of course. But before his letter had arrived I had been reached by Frank Norris as well as some other individual then connected with the house, a second reader, I believe, both of whom, for some strange reason urged me not to take the book away but to stand on the contract[2]—of all silly things—and insist that the house publish it. Norris's argument was that once the book was published and distributed to the critics the burst of approval which was sure to follow would cause Doubleday to change his mind and decide to push the book. He even took me in to Walter Page, who announced after some discussion that he thought this course might not be inadvisable. He appeared somewhat uncertain, but since Norris was so interested, he thought it might be all right.

And for this reason, and no other, I decided to do as Norris said, feeling, however, as I did at the time, that my position was wrong— ridiculous. It was true that the summer had been allowed to go by and the date of issue was comparatively near at hand, but still I might

2. This "second reader" is probably Arthur Henry, who was connected with Doubleday, Page only in the sense that the firm was about to publish his novel *A Princess of Arcady*.

have easily gotten the book published elsewhere if I had not been so silly as to do this. And Doubleday finding that I wished to stand by the contract, announced very savagely one day that he would publish the book but that was all that he would do. I returned to Norris, who said in substance,—"Never mind. He'll publish it. And when it comes out I'll see that all the worth-while critics are reached with it. Then, when he sees what happens he'll change. It's only his wife anyhow, and Page likes it."

When the book came out Norris did exactly as he said. He must have written many letters himself for I received many letters commenting on the work and the resulting newspaper comment was considerable. However, as Mr. Thomas McKee, who was then the legal counsel for Doubleday afterwards told me, Doubleday came to him and wanted to know how he could be made safe against a law suit in case he suppressed the book—refused to distribute or sell any copies. And McKee advised him that he could not be made safe— that I had rights under the contract which could be enforced by me if I were so minded.[3] Nevertheless, as he told me, Doubleday stored all of the 1,000 copies printed—minus three hundred distributed by Norris—in the basement of his Union Square plant, and there they remained, except for a number abstracted, until 1905, when I, having obtained work as an editor, finally decided to buy the plates and all bound copies. In the meantime, I had carried the bound book from publisher to publisher hoping to find someone who would take it over without cost to them, but I could not find anyone. In turn Appleton's, Stokes, Scribner's, Dodd, Mead, A. S. Barnes, and others promptly rejected it. In after years I heard many curious details as to the internal commotion this particular work caused in all the houses.

But here is an interesting bit for your private ear. At the time of my last conversation with Frank Doubleday I referred to the fact that not only Norris but Mr. Page were heartily for the book, and that Mr. Page had told me that not only would he be pleased to publish the book but that he proposed to make quite a stir about it,—in fact that he had suggested getting up a dinner for me. This seemed to irritate Doubleday not a little, and walking into the next room where Page was sitting at the time at his desk, and asking me to follow him, he said: "Page, did you say to Mr. Dreiser that you really like this

3. According to Thomas H.McKee (letters to present editor, 23 March 1949 and 12 Oct. 1956), he had suggested that Doubleday offer Dreiser the plates to buy peace. When Dreiser had refused, McKee had informed the publishers that "publish" meant the duty to manufacture the book, offer it for sale publicly, and deliver it when asked for. Doubleday, who disapproved of the book on his own, quite apart from what his wife may have thought, did decline to spend money on advertising because he declined to go against popular taste and what he construed to be an adverse critical tide. [R. H. E.]

book very much and that you intended to make a stir about it and give him a dinner?" And Mr. Page calmly looked me in the eye and replied, "I never said anything of the kind."

He was a man of about forty-five years of age, I should have said, at that time. I was just twenty-nine and not a little over-awed by editors and publishers in general. In consequence, although I resented this not a little, I merely got up and walked out. It seemed astounding to me that a man of his position would do such a thing. At the same time, I gathered from his manner and facial expression at the time that he stood not a little in awe of Doubleday. Also that finding Doubleday violently opposed to the book, he did not think it worth while to quarrel with him on this score. It was easier to dispense with me in the above manner.

Afterward—in 1901—Norris, personally, sent the book to Heinemann in London. And he published it. And it was much talked of there. Later Heinemann came to the United States and looked me up and gave me a dinner. At that dinner he told me how only the night before he and Mrs. Doubleday had actually quarreled over the book, principally because he made it plain that he considered her opinion of no great import. He stated that for some reason she appeared to be very bitter in regard to it all. Adverse critical comment, I believe.

In 1907, having by then laid aside sufficient cash for the purpose, I bought a third interest in the B. W. Dodge Company, then being organized, and, as a member of the firm, took the liberty of reissuing the book from the old plates. It sold about ten thousand copies. The next year a ten thousand edition was printed by Grosset and Dunlap, and sold at fifty cents a copy. In 1910, having finished *Jennie Gerhardt*, I took the book to Harper's, and that firm asked to be allowed to reissue *Sister Carrie* as a companion volume to *Jennie Gerhardt*, and at that time it sold some seven thousand copies more—at $1.50 per copy. Since then it has sold continuously, the average annual sale being something over a thousand copies.

To this I set my hand and seal.

Theodore Dreiser

F. N. DOUBLEDAY

To Franklin Walker†

Garden City, N.Y.
May 4, 1931

Franklin D. Walker, Esq.
State Teachers College
San Diego, California

My dear Mr. Walker:[1]
    I have read your letter of April 16th with care and attention.
    Personally, I had little or nothing to do with matters concerning "McTEAGUE," but I know that Mrs. Doubleday was not in the habit of passing on such matters for the publishing concern. Some one who has it in for me is always starting this story anew. Mrs. Doubleday died twelve years ago and the subject is very painful, and I wish it might be dropped. I am positive that she had nothing to do with any changes which may have been made and about which I know nothing.
    The same thing is true of "SISTER CARRIE." I don't think that Mrs. Doubleday ever saw the book; at all events, I know that she expressed no opinion which affected the treatment of it by the publishing house.

Very truly yours,
F. N. Doubleday

THEODORE DREISER

The Early Adventures of *Sister Carrie*‡

I am frequently asked for the story of the trials and tribulations attendant upon the publication of my first novel—*Sister Carrie*. The interest of the story to me at this time lies in the picture it presents of the moral taboos of that day as reflected by publishing conditions

† From *The Letters of Frank Norris*, ed. Franklin D. Walker (San Francisco: The Book Club of California, 1956). Reprinted by permission of The Book Club of California.
1. Walker, who was preparing a biography of Frank Norris, had written to Doubleday asking about the role of Mrs. Doubleday in the bowdlerization of a passage in the second issue of *McTeague* and in the suppression of *Sister Carrie*.
‡ *The Colophon*, part 5 (January 1931), and Preface, *Sister Carrie* (Modern Library Edition: 1932).

that made possible such an experience as mine in connection with *Sister Carrie*.

When I first turned to writing it was mainly articles for magazines that occupied my attention. But having no such "happy" stories to tell as those that filled the pages of the popular magazines of the day, I met with little success. My own reactions to life were so diametrically opposed to the fiction of that time. I then turned to a novel, beginning its first pages in the autumn of 1899 and finishing it in May, 1900. But even with the novel finished, I found little encouragement. I took it first to Henry Mills Alden, editor of *Harper's Magazine*, who read the manuscript and, while expressing approval, at the same time doubted whether any publisher would take it. The American mass mind of that day, as he knew, was highly suspicious of any truthful interpretation of life. However, he turned it over to Harper & Brothers, who kept it three weeks and then informed me that they could not publish it.

I next submitted it to Doubleday Page, where Frank Norris occupied the position of reader. He recommended it most enthusiastically to his employers, and it seemed that my book was really to be published, for a few weeks later I signed a contract with Doubleday Page and the book was printed.

In the meantime (as I was told by Frank Norris himself, and later by William Heinemann, the publisher, of London), Mrs. Frank Doubleday read the manuscript and was horrified by its frankness. She was a social worker and active in moral reform, and because of her strong dislike for the book and insistence that it be withdrawn from publication, Doubleday Page decided not to put it in circulation. However, Frank Norris remained firm in his belief that the book should come before the American public, and persuaded me to insist on the publishers carrying out the contract. Their legal adviser—one Thomas McKee, who afterwards personally narrated to me his share in all this—was called in, and he advised the firm that it was legally obliged to go on with the publication, it having signed a contract to do so, but that this did not necessarily include *selling*; in short, the books, after publication, might be thrown into the cellar! I believe this advice was followed to the letter, because no copies were ever sold. But Frank Norris, as he himself told me, did manage to send out some copies to book reviewers, probably a hundred of them.

After some five years, I induced J. F. Taylor & Company, rare book dealers, to undertake the publication of *Sister Carrie* providing I would precede it with a new novel. My intention was to furnish them with *Jennie Gerhardt*, but my health being poor I could not complete it. In the meantime the plates of *Sister Carrie* and some bound and unbound copies had been purchased by them for five hundred dollars or thereabouts. Later, having turned to editorial work, I laid up sufficient to repurchase the plates and copies and thereafter—until the reissue of the work by B. W. Dodge Company—that same remained in my possession, and still do.

In 1901 *Sister Carrie* was published by Heinemann in London and gained considerable publicity. Acting on this, I took the manuscript (in 1907, when I was editor of the Butterick publications) to the then newly formed publishing house of B. W. Dodge Company, who brought the book out in that year. In 1908 Grosset & Dunlap published *Sister Carrie*, using the same plates, but even at that day the outraged protests far outnumbered the plaudits. Later, in 1911, it was reissued by Harper & Brothers, who had just published *Jennie Gerhardt*. Still later after John Lane had thrown me out on account of *The "Genius"*, it was taken over by Boni & Liveright and published. That was in 1917. And there its harried and varied wanderings ended.

DOROTHY DUDLEY

[The "Suppression" Controversy]†

Now the novel becomes a hinge on which hangs an incident like luck in an Homeric legend. In the publishing company of Doubleday, Page & Co. there worked as proof-reader and adviser, when he was not off bass-fishing with his blonde, the one man to whom *Sister Carrie* would be like sudden rain, like frogs in March, a matter for elation. The man was Frank Norris, a young San Franciscan, already heroic as a novelist.

* * *

So between a dynamic personality, Dreiser, and a quivering personality, Norris, there blazed for a minute the fire-brand truth, luxury, art, whatever you prefer to call it—that element from which over and over again people fly. Truth like love is a luxury. We don't want luxury. Today we fly from it in an aeroplane. But this new fraction of it, *Sister Carrie*, got this time by luck a running start. "It must be published," Norris said. Lanier read it and hated it, and agreed that they must publish it. For him, he explains, a man loving old mellow things, it was hateful. "It had no background": the characters were

---

† From *Dreiser and the Land of the Free* (1932: New York: Beechhurst Press, 1946), 166, 169–70, 171–73, 180–84. Dudley's book, is more a polemic against American puritanism than a biography of Dreiser. But she did have the advantage of extensive conversations with Dreiser, and though her study is filled with errors, and is overwritten, it is still a valuable source work.

treated as of equal importance with the most cultivated delightful men and women: whereas "people are not of equal significance" in his opinion. Nevertheless it was powerful, unavoidable. Norris was right, it had to be published. Then Walter Hines Page read it, later ambassador to England, at this time partner of Frank Doubleday in the stead of S. S. McClure who had by now gravitated back to his magazine. He agreed with the younger men that it was a book to publish, "a natural," he called it. A contract was drawn up and signed by the author and these two gentelemen. *Sister Carrie* was on the way to the printing press.

* * *

The legend goes, and Mr. Lanier partly corroborates it, that at this moment Mr. and Mrs. Frank Doubleday, who had been traveling in Europe, returned to New York; and Mr. Doubleday, the senior partner, arriving at his offices in 25th Street, among other matters was confronted with this initial novel of an unknown Hoosier. Since it was Saturday he took it to his home in Oyster Bay, a suburb of Murray Hill and Washington Square, to read it over this week-end. And then . . . and then, according to fable, again enters the villain, Propriety—this time, if you have not guessed it, in the refined and engaging dress of Mrs. Frank Doubleday. And here since no one can or will recollect this particular week-end, there is nothing to do but to imagine the scene. First, however, it is possible to identify the enemy—according to her friends, an almost perfect woman, wife, mother, church member, hostess, in this well-fed, well-bred apex of New York in 1900. Mr. Charles P. Everitt, who with his brother Sam worked also at Doubleday, Page & Co., gave me a dilated picture: "She was beautiful, she was a lovely woman, she was stately. In fact, not long before he died, I met Walter Hines Page on the street, and I said to him, 'Walter, I don't believe there ever was such a woman as Mrs. Frank Doubleday.' And he said to me with tears in his eyes: 'Charlie, I have never known the equal of Mrs. Frank Doubleday.' "

Wrapt in such an aura, I imagine her now entering the study where Mr. Frank Doubleday was busy reading and possibly enjoying *Sister Carrie*.

* * *

In those days the more valiant New York matrons were occupied among their good works with purity leagues for the suppression of vice, for the lapsed and lost, for the social evil. Indeed at about this time they were making a pleasant sanitary prison where wayward girls too tender in years for the jail might be agreeably locked up— the Florence Crittendon Home. And here was Doubleday, Page about to publish a book about vulgar people, a Chicago drummer and a factory girl from the country, which apparently recommended prostitution as a way of life in little tan jackets with large pearl buttons. At least as she read Mrs. Doubleday could find no hint of condemnation. She looked into it again. Now there was a change of names, a new seducer, a saloon-manager if you please, and yet described as a handsome, well-dressed dependable citizen! It must have been she was mortified as she went from lewd facet to facet lighted by her orthodox mind.

* * *

So in this story everything is told just as it happened, with now the pathos of a bar-room ballad, now a ruthlessness of intellect. And why the editor's wife did not cry or even feel a pain around her heart to think that men are made for ends like this, is hard to know. Or why she did not feel that a precious record of the grim life on top of which she ate and slept and dressed and had her being, was in her hands, is hard to say. On Monday morning her husband took the proof sheets back to his office with instructions that the contract be broken. So do those without feeling and without much intelligence decree that life shall not be heightened or purified by understanding. Is it for fear that then it will leave them behind? At this particular period in this country of banks, Bibles and candy, the decree of such unofficial censors held singular sway.

There is an inclination, perhaps unconscious, among the men connected in that day with this publishing company to belittle the importance of Mrs. Doubleday in the suppression of a now historic book, which the firm itself can hardly repudiate. It is as if to protect her name from taint of prudery, now become unfashionable. The pellucid Mr. Lanier, for one, is not sure that she ever read the book: "It was Frank," he said, "who made the trouble. He hated it enough without other influence, called it 'indecent,' and begged us at once to break the contract. If we went ahead with it, although he couldn't stop us, he warned us he would do all in his power to ruin the sale." At the same time he volunteered that the publisher's wife was one of those deceptively beautiful characters who loved to dominate in the name of virtue. Mr. C. P. Everitt, however, remembers the affair more in accordance with the legend.

He remembers a dinner at the house of Mrs. Doubleday, "A most distinguished gathering," where she had said: "Frank, I would rather get down and scrub floors than have you publish that book." But he added protectively: "Don't say I said she was referring to *Sister Carrie*. I got into trouble once telling that. As a matter of fact she may have been referring to Tom Dickson's *Leopard's Spots*, a libel on the Negro race. In fact I think she was. She felt just as strong against race prejudice as against the social evil—she was a woman of very high principles." . . . These high-principled American matrons! How naïvely ignorant they have been in their pursuit of good works! And how their men have deferred to them, hoping thereby to concoct some sort of social stability in a hit-or-miss land! What fine institutions they have gathered money to build up, to house the victims of their bloodless code! And what bright human hopes they have helped to tear down! . . . "But did they publish *Leopard's Spots*?" I ventured to ask—"Oh, yes, it went into the hundred thousand class: we made a pile of money out of it."—"And did she get down and scrub floors?"—"No."—"Then don't you think it must have been *Sister Carrie* she was speaking of?"—No, my reasoning was specious. He was not prepared to indict his glamorous hostess for a deed which since that time has become an embarrassment to the "fine and reputable house of Doubleday."

Yet I believe the myth has legs to stand on—a symbol of the way Americans have always entrusted to women the matter of art along with the matter of society, as unworthy of their important lives. It was the story told Dreiser in a letter from Frank Norris cursing the company for planning to withdraw the book: "In her absurd opinion it was 'vulgar and immoral.'" And some years later Thomas H. McKee, lawyer for Doubleday, gossiping over the affair with Dreiser, spoke of Mrs. Doubleday as the original censor, and wondered why with so good a cause against his publishers he had not brought suit: expecting it, he had at once prepared a defense. In 1903 William Heinemann too, the English publisher of *Sister Carrie*, had confided to him: "I fear my admiration for your book has cost me the friendship, not only of Mrs. Doubleday, but of Doubleday himself." At another dinner party—Page and Norris were present—she asked him how he could have published so "vulgar and disgraceful" a book: his answer had been that he was "a distinguished privilege" to have done so, which the husband had taken as insulting to his wife.

Whether husband or wife or both were to blame, the undisputed fact is that not long after the fatal week-end Dreiser had a letter from his publishers asking them to come in for a talk. Mr. Lanier remembers "acutely the unhappy fifteen minutes" spent in this talk. He and Page had felt that with Doubleday against it, publication would be unfair to Dreiser, that the book was too good to be smothered in that way. He was prepared, he said, to explain to the young writer how deeply he admired his novel, "a fine piece of work," and how he wanted to do all in his power to help him sell it successfully elsewhere. And he is quite sure he could have succeeded. He hoped to make him see how little it would mean to merely print and catalogue: how easy it was for a publisher to kill a book just by hinting to his salesman not to push it, just by failing to advertise it. A heart-rending picture, but he was given no chance to paint it. He had calculated without the usually agreeable author of a first book. Dreiser, the terribly social savage after wistful years of neglect at the hands of society would not listen; had no use for Lanier's urbanities. He had been swimming against surf in the open sea long enough. This time he had his hands on the edge of the boat of acknowledgment. Whether they liked it or not he was going to climb in. "Crushed and tragically pathetic," Lanier remembers him, doggedly he repeated they had made a contract with him; they would have to go ahead; that was the end of the matter. And the tall, loose-jointed dreamer, less loose and dreamy than usual, gave his intense ultimatum and walked out of the office. That day the enemy in him must have taken a leap ahead, and have grown to almost full size, if not yet to full efficiency.

The office of Doubleday, Page & Company was now hard put to it. How to placate young Hoosier and older Episcopalian, the rugged new artist and the shrewd middle-aged merchant, who was not going to promote a questionable book unless (like *The Leopard's Spots*) he was convinced it would sell a hundred thousand copies. Mr. Lanier with his civilized impartiality is quick to admit that then their business chief would have felt it his "artistic" duty to waive morals and promote *Sister Carrie*. But the literary partners could not honestly assure him of this degree of popularity. McKee, their lawyer, was called in; nothing to do but fulfill the contract, he told them; anything else might be disastrous to a new ambitious firm. So on November 8, 1900, *Sister Carrie* had her humble debut—an edition of 1000 or so copies in what later reviewers agreed to call a "dull, cheap, red binding, with the name in small, dull, black lettering"; an assassin's edition in a country where books have to look expensive in order to be well thought of.

Then again the story of the disposition of these copies varies. It would be my instinct to believe the version repeated again and again in almost the same words in the reviews of the later Dodge and Harper editions, which must have been taken from these publishers' advertisements and from hearsay—that is, Dreiser's own version. According to him, and he had it from Frank Norris, the book was never marketed at all, but thrown into the cellar where anyone who felt like reading a "dirty book" helped himself. Norris, bitterly disappointed, salvaged as many copies as he could, and sent them to various book editors, and even after that continued dispensing them. Grant Richards, an English publisher, in a letter to Dreiser tells of Norris giving him a copy of *Sister Carrie* in 1901 with the hope that he would publish it in England. And then the legend divides again. Some say that after a while the remaining volumes of the disgraced *Carrie* were burned in the furnace of that cellar, and some that they merely lay there under the dust of years and that if one wrote enclosing a money-order for the amount, the book could be had. Mr. Lanier inclines toward the latter version, but probably a less dramatic account of the affair will in the end be held as fact.

In 1929 Mr. Vrest Orton published a bibliography of Dreiser's work, in which he gives a spirited account of his pains over several years to unearth the facts of this incident through the Doubleday office. At length Mr. S. A. Everitt answered that they had no records except the record of date, but that as he remembered, "the edition of from 1000 to 2000 copies was sold to the trade in the regular way, the same as any other novel published at the time. . . ." With this to encourage him he now wrote to Mr. Doubleday himself for a transcript of the sales-records, who doubted that they were "available," but would see what he could do; he did not believe that any copies had ever been "destroyed, burned, or remaindered." A day or so later a letter came from his secretary which for Mr. Orton contained "the whole story in a nutshell" as revealed by the analysis card: "The first edition consisted of 1008 copies, of which 129 were sent out for review, 465 were sold, and the balance of 423 copies was turned over to J. F. Taylor & Company," a remainder house now out of business. Yet an analysis card presented thirty years after the event is less convincing than a human memory recorded at the moment of it, and is as easy to fabricate.[1] To support Dreiser's and Lanier's memory is the sensitive attitude today of the firm, as of people ridiculed beyond composure for a literary and commercial error. Two things are sure—their sense of propriety had its way for a time, and as certainly Dreiser has had his revenge, but it was to be a distant and expensive one.

---

1. The analysis card is now in the Dreiser Papers of the University of Pennsylvania Library and is substantially as Orton reported it.

CRITICISM

THEODORE DREISER

True Art Speaks Plainly†

The sum and substance of literary as well as social morality may be expressed in three words—tell the truth. It matters not how the tongues of the critics may wag, or the voices of a partially developed and highly conventionalized society may complain, the business of the author, as well as of other workers upon this earth, is to say what he knows to be true, and, having said as much, to abide the result with patience.

Truth is what is; and the seeing of what is, the realization of truth. To express what we see honestly and without subterfuge: this is morality as well as art.

What the so-called judges of the truth or morality are really inveighing against most of the time is not the discussion of mere sexual lewdness, for no work with that as a basis could possibly succeed, but the disturbing and destroying of their own little theories concerning life, which in some cases may be nothing more than a quiet acceptance of things as they are without any regard to the well-being of the future. Life for them is made up of a variety of interesting but immutable forms and any attempt either to picture any of the wretched results of modern social conditions or to assail the critical defenders of the same is naturally looked upon with contempt or aversion.

It is true that the rallying cry of the critics against so-called immoral literature is that the mental virtue of the reader must be preserved; but this has become a house of refuge to which every form of social injustice hurries for protection. The influence of intellectual ignorance and physical and moral greed upon personal virtue produces the chief tragedies of the age, and yet the objection to the discussion of the sex question is so great as to almost prevent the handling of the theme entirely.

Immoral! Immoral! Under this cloak hide the vices of wealth as well as the vast unspoken blackness of poverty and ignorance; and between them must walk the little novelist, choosing neither truth nor beauty, but some half-conceived phase of life that bears no honest relationship to either the whole of nature or to man.

The impossibility of any such theory of literature having weight

† From *Booklover's Magazine* 1 (February 1903): 129. Omitted passages in the essays are indicated by asterisks.

with the true artist must be apparent to every clear reasoning mind. Life is not made up of any one phase or condition of being, nor can man's interest possibly be so confined.

The extent of all reality is the realm of the author's pen, and a true picture of life, honestly and reverentially set down, is both moral and artistic whether it offends the conventions or not.

OTIS NOTMAN

Mr. Dreiser†

"The mere living of your daily life," says Theodore Dreiser, "is drastic drama. To-day there may be some disease lurking in your veins that will end your life to-morrow. You may have a firm grasp on the opportunity that in a moment more will slip through your fingers. The banquet of tonight may crumble to the crust of the morning. Life is a tragedy."

"But isn't that a rather tragic view to take?" I asked. "Hasn't each man something in himself that makes life worth living? If, as you say, you want to write more than anything else, isn't that power or ability to write something that would make life worth while under all circumstances?"

"No, not under all circumstances, because you can't use ability except under certain favorable conditions. The very power of which you speak may, thwarted, only serve to make a man more miserable. I have had my share of the difficulties and discouragements that fall to the lot of most men. I know something of the handicap of ill health and the necessary diffusion of energy. A man with something imperative to say and no time or strength for the saying of it is as unfortunate as he is unhappy. I look into my own life and I realize that each human life is a similar tragedy. The infinite suffering and deprivation of great masses of men and women upon whom existence has been thrust unasked appalls me. My greatest desire is to devote every hour of my conscious existence to depicting phases of life as I see and understand them."

"What are you trying to show in what you write? Do you point out a moral?" I inquired.

"I simply want to tell about life as it is. Every human life is intensely interesting. If the human being has ideals, the struggle and the attempt to realize those ideals, the going back on his own trail, the failure, the success, the reason for the individual failure, the

† From "Talks with Four Novelists," *New York Times Saturday Review of Books* 15 June 1907: 393.

individual success—all these things are interesting, interesting even where there are no ideals, where there is only the personal desire to survive, the fight to win, the stretching out of the fingers to grasp—these are the things I want to write about—life as it is, the facts as they exist, the game as it is played! I said I was pointing out no moral. Well, I am not, unless this is a moral—that all humanity must stand together and war against and overcome the forces of nature. I think a time is coming when personal gain will rarely be sought at the expense of some one else."

"Where among people is there the greatest readiness to stand by one another, among the rich or the poor?" I asked.

"Among the poor. They are by far the most generous. They are never too crowded to take in another person, although there may be already three or four to share the same room. Their food they will always share, even though there is not enough to go around."

"Are you writing something else?" I inquired.

"I have another book partly finished, but I don't know when I shall get it done. I have not the time to work on it, much as I want to."

"Have you been satisfied with the reception of 'Sister Carrie'?"

"Well, the critics have not really understood what I was trying to do. Here is a book that is close to life. It is intended not as a piece of literary craftsmanship, but as a picture of conditions done as simply and effectively as the English language will permit. To sit up and criticise me for saying 'vest', instead of waistcoat, to talk about my splitting the infinitive and using vulgar commonplaces here and there, when the tragedy of a man's life is being displayed, is silly. More, it is ridiculous. It makes me feel that American criticism is the joke which English literary authorities maintain it to be. But the circulation is beginning to boom. When it gets to the people they will understand, because it is a story of real life, of their lives."

THEODORE DREISER

To John Howard Lawson†

New York City, October 10th, 1928.

My dear Lawson:

It does seem to me that you are getting much nearer the drama as well as the spirit of the book. And after a fashion I like the idea of the bum or down-and-out as suggesting what I emphasized—the

† From *Masses and Mainstream* 8 (December 1955): 21–22. Dreiser was advising the playwright John Howard Lawson about a projected dramatic version of *Sister Carrie*.

need of presenting clearly the drama of Hurstwood's decay. But I think you will not get this straight, or be able to present it to the best advantage, until you ask yourself, as I asked myself a long time ago, what was it exactly that brought about Hurstwood's decline? What psychic thing in himself? For most certainly it could not have been just the commonplace knocks and errors out of which most people take their rise. It is not enough to say that he is not a strong man, or that he lacked a first class brain. Granted. And it is obvious from the book. But there is something more. A distillation not only of his lack of strength and his mediocre brain, but of the day and the city and the circumstances of which, at say forty-odd, he found himself a part. And this is of a twofold character. First—a sense of folly or mistake in him because of his having taken the money of his employers and so having lost not only their friendship and confidence but the, for him, almost necessary milieu of Chicago—its significance as the center of his home, children, friends, connections—what you will. Next the ultimate folly of his hypnosis in regard to Carrie. For as the book shows her charm betrayed him. He erred, as he later saw it, in taking her, because she drifted from him—went her own mental way—did not sustain him. These two things, once he was out of Chicago and so away from all he had known and prized, concentrated to form a deep and cancerous sense of mistake which ate into his energy and force. It was no doubt finally the worm at the heart of his life. And without the power to destroy it he was doomed. And it is that *conviction* which is the thing that is stalking him and that is necessary to symbolize in some way. . . .

* * *

THEODORE DREISER

JULIAN MARKELS

Dreiser and the Plotting of Inarticulate Experience†

If one thinks that such thoughts do not come to so common a type of mind—that such feelings require a higher mental development— I would urge for their consideration the fact that it is the higher mental development that does away with such thoughts. It is the higher mental development which induces philosophy and that fortitude which refuses to dwell upon such things—refuses to be made to suffer by their consideration. The common type of mind is exceedingly keen on all matters which relate to its physical welfare—exceedingly keen. It is the unintellectual miser who sweats

† From *The Massachusetts Review* 2 (Spring 1961): 431–40. Reprinted by permission of *The Massachusetts Review*.

blood at the loss of a hundred dollars. It is the Epictetus who smiles
when the last vestige of physical welfare is removed.

Sister Carrie

By now the cataloguing of Dreiser's limitations has settled into a
rather dry routine: his turgid and graceless style, which led F. R.
Leavis to observe that Dreiser writes as if he hasn't a native language;
his limited insight into the psychology of his characters; his wearisome attention to detail; and his editorial pretentiousness and
inconsistency, in which he often seems bent on making metaphysical
mountains out of mechanistic molehills. Such characteristics are not
mere superfluous gimcrackery but part of Dreiser's substance, inseparable from his fictional method and from the conception of human
experience that he attempts to shape in his fiction. Yet to pigeonhole
Dreiser in this way is to obscure the fact that not all of his substance
is composed of such defects. Equally the product of his method and
conception, when he is at his best, is a powerful sense of the mystery
underlying human experience, of the fathomless processes which
hold our lives in suspension, of the deep sources of pain and desire
with which our human condition confronts us—in short, of what
Dreiser himself called the wonder of life. Even if he is not a Balzac
or a Dickens or a Dostoevsky, the whole of Dreiser's substance is
frequently rich and moving and powerful. It is time finally to
acknowledge him as our own and go on from there—to explore his
quality and unravel his meaning for us. If we cannot afford to ignore
his limitations, neither can we afford to let him lie bound in that
literary dungeon to which he has been consigned for some years by
the neoliberal Zeuses of contemporary criticism.

The greatest obstacle in the way of such an enterprise is not that
Dreiser writes as if he hasn't a native language, but that as critics we
are unprepared to pass beyond that fact. We are disconcerted to read
a statement like Saul Bellow's in his review of F. O. Matthiessen's
book on Dreiser: "But it is very odd that no one has thought to ask
just what the 'bad writing' of a powerful novelist signifies." Such a
remark suggests that in some significant way we are estranged from
the novel as a literary form, that to recover Dreiser we must recover
the suppleness of certain critical faculties which have been until
recently the victims of atrophy.

The first, if indirect step, in such a recovery is to confront the fact
that Dreiser's artistic purposes made no strenuous demands upon
his style, which after all may be true of a novelist though not of a
poet. Dreiser could on occasion produce a kind of "good writing," so
that his characteristic style is the result not only of ineptness but of
a choice of relevant means for communicating what he had to. At
scattered moments in his writing there is a compactness and fluency

which usually passes unnoticed. There is, for example this paragraph from *An American Tragedy*:

> The impact of this remark, a reflection of the exact truth, was not necessary to cause Clyde to gaze attentively, and even eagerly. For apart from her local position and means and taste in dress and manners, Sondra was of the exact order and spirit that most intrigued him—a somewhat refined (and because of means and position showered upon her) less savage, although scarcely less self-centered, Hortense Briggs. She was, in her small, intense way, a seeking Aphrodite, eager to prove to any who were sufficiently attractive the destroying power of her charm, while at the same time retaining her own personality and individuality free of any entangling alliance or compromise. However, for varying reasons which she could not quite explain to herself, Clyde appealed to her. He might not be anything socially or financially, but he was interesting to her.

Eliminate the flatulent next-to-last sentence, change the parenthetical into a subordinate clause, and you have in this passage a piece of smooth and deliberate prose such as might have been written by an imitator of Henry James. Just as it stands the passage has a liveliness and precision which, if more prevalent, would make Dreiser's style less vulnerable to attack. But such writing is not frequent and hence not memorable in Dreiser; and indeed, he writes in this way only when, as in the present instance, he is taking time out to summarize previously recounted information. When his eye is on his main business his ear goes flat, and he characteristically writes the thick prose by which we remember him.

The source of his power and his meaning for us lies elsewhere, then, and I think it is in his method of arranging the episodes of his plots in order to dramatize with perfect coherence that absence of foreordained purpose in the universe, and its corollary, the hegemony of chance, of which he speaks to awkwardly in his "philosophical" writings. Not consistently but in long and powerful sequences, Dreiser's plot construction results in a fully credible image of human experience as an amoral process; it implies the possibility of human purpose and dignity arising out of a necessary immersion in this process; and hence Dreiser's method excludes the deterministic pathos of the conventional naturalistic novel, which conceives of human experience as the closing of a trap rather than the unfolding of a process. Frequently in Dreiser's novels the moment-to-moment action gives us no reason to desire or expect either good or bad fortune for the characters, no reason to feel hopeful, fearful, sad, or angry on their behalf. We are convinced instead that for them whatever is, is right; and we are moved by the mystery of their experience being so coherently purposeless and yet possibly resulting for them in an enlargement of being. When we see Carrie Meeber respond to her experience directly in fear and desire, without imposing upon it any moral categories or expectations, when we see her enlarge her wordly status and her human identity by her unquestioning submission to the "whatever is" of her experience, then we know why Dreiser attributes to Carrie the quality of "emotional greatness." When we see Hurstwood and Clyde Griffiths ruined by an equally emotional and unquestioning submission, then perhaps we know in a glimmer what Dreiser must have meant by the mystery and terror and wonder of life.

Such knowledge arises from a rhythm in the sequence of Dreiser's episodes rather than from anything that can be communicated by a graceful style. It is the rhythm of inarticulate human experience, undifferentiated and hence by definition without style. Matthiessen suggested rightly that Dreiser's sea imagery, his symbol of the rocking chair, and his own fondness for a rocking chair, all point to "a physical basis for the rhythm of his thoughts." But where the imagery and symbols are only its symptoms, the "physical basis" itself is established by Dreiser's method of construction, which is his true source of strength. It is also the source of his weakness, as I will indicate later, in that his method of construction disables Dreiser from portraying the emergence in human experience of moral consciousness and its corollary, literary style.

I

In the opening sequence of *Sister Carrie,* in which Carrie arrives in Chicago wholly inarticulate, Dreiser employs his method with powerful effect and absolute credibility. The design of the novel's first eight chapters makes perfectly logical and coherent Carrie's silent drifting toward her own good, and at the same time the irrelevance of any moral categories by which she might judge or be judged. On the trip from her country home to make her way in the city, Carrie meets Drouet, whose gaudiness of dress and ostentatious *savoir-faire* impress her simply because they are new in her experience. Then the drabness of her life in the city, with its round of hunting, holding, and losing rough factory jobs which pay no more than her board in the dreary apartment of her listless sister and surly brother-in-law Hanson, makes the elegance of Drouet seem all the more attractive. When she has lost her job and is ready to go home in despair, she meets Drouet, who offers to provide the clothes and luxuries which she had come to the city to acquire. After much vacillation, she accepts his offer; and after he has taken her to dinner and to see *The Mikado,* a play that arouses in her "vain imaginings about place and power, about far-off lands and magnificent people," she becomes his mistress.

This material is not highly arresting. It seems an obvious occasion for the method of documentary determinism, in which Carrie is overwhelmed by the sheer weight of accumulated details exhibiting the drab restrictiveness of her environment and the bright expansiveness of Drouet's. But while Dreiser in fact presents an enormous amount of documentary detail, he does not simply pile it up to create an environmental "force" which explains Carrie's fall; and Matthiessen certainly was wrong when he suggested that Dreiser's characteristic method of construction is "Balzac's direct way of presenting solid slabs of continuous experience." The experience presented is indeed continuous, but its distinctive quality is that it is not presented in solid slabs that might make us aware of a shaping environment. Instead Dreiser breaks up and alternates in a precisely elaborated pattern the two main groups of details, so that the larger dialectic of the whole sequence is mirrored and repeated a hundred times in the minute episodes of the unfolding action. Though a Jamesian concern with the conscious life is alien to Dreiser, he works with a similar intensity of focus upon "manners" as the primary stuff of experience. And this makes Carrie's negotiation with her environment seem not so much a helpless response to overwhelming forces as a necessary immersion in a fundamental process.

In Chapter One, Carrie meets Drouet on the train, and is impressed with the vivacity, opulence, and assured contentment that he exhibits. At the end of the chapter Carrie, greeted at the Chicago station by her grim sister, immediately becomes aware of the sharp contrast between the "cold reality" represented by Minnie, and the "world of light and merriment" represented by Drouet. In Chapter Two, Dreiser documents Minnie's cold reality: her taciturn husband, who works in the stockyards and makes monthly payments on two parcels of real estate; and her threadbare third-floor apartment, with its general atmosphere of "a settled opposition to anything save a conservative round of toil." Carrie responds to this atmosphere by writing Drouet that she cannot receive him at her sister's. Thus the first two chapters establish the two poles of Carrie's world and of her range of awareness, the field of her experience at this early stage. And they initiate that process of shuttling back and forth from one pole to another which is to lead finally to an enlargement of identity accompanied by a rise in worldly status.

Chapter Three, which concerns Carrie's search for a job, is a microcosm of the entire method. In ten pages Dreiser reports nine separate encounters with prospective employers, not to mention time off for lunch. In her first, second, fourth, sixth and eighth attempts, Carrie is met with cold rebuffs which plunge her into hopelessness.

In her third, fifth and seventh encounters she is given a friendly reception which raises her spirits, but no job; and in her ninth and last try she gets a job in a shoe factory at $4.50 a week. The whole design is typified in the episode where Carrie acts on the advice of a friendly employment manager that she look for work in a department store. She becomes almost exuberant as she walks through the store and sees the elegant lady shoppers and the lovely clothes she might buy if she gets the job. Then she meets the gruffest employment manager in her experience so far, who not only refuses her a job but virtually chases her out of the store. But such incidents are immediately erased from her memory once she lands a job, and finally she comes home elated, remembering Drouet, certain that she will be happy in Chicago.

Chapter Four shows the step-by-step undermining of this elation. It begins with Carrie's fantasies of opulence as she sits in her rocking chair and spends her money in her mind many times over. Then the Hansons refuse to go to the theater with her to celebrate her success; and when she stands in the doorway to soak up the exciting life of the city as a substitute for going to the theater, her brother-in-law manifests cold disapproval. Her distress is complete when on her first day of work she is exposed to the stiff boredom of her job and the callowness of the young men who work with her.

Then Dreiser reverses direction again, leaving Carrie at the bottom and taking us to the "top," to witness a conversation between Drouet and Hurstwood in the "truly swell saloon" of Fitzgerald and Moy's. Here he expands and fills in with detail our image of Drouet's world, just when that world seems more inaccessible than ever to Carrie. In Chapter Six, Dreiser returns to Carrie, who is thoroughly disappointed in her job and in mounting friction with Hanson as she stands again in the doorway. She gets sick and loses her job, and on the fourth day of looking for work she runs into Drouet, who takes her to lunch in a fine restaurant, recognizes her distress, and gives her twenty dollars for clothes. In Chapter Seven, Carrie's worry about accepting the money is gradually purged—by her continued failure to find work, by further manifestations of Hanson's antagonism, and by Drouet's increasing generosity. The chapter ends with her moving into a place of her own, paid for by Drouet. And Chapter Eight, the last in the sequence, ends with her going to the theater at last, and with her seduction. Then Dreiser begins the pattern all over again, with a chapter about Hurstwood, the upper pole of the second major sequence.

Instead of piling up his material in solid slabs, then, Dreiser separates and stretches it out in minute gradations, and then shuttles Carrie back and forth. Hanson's cold disapproval of her aspirations is a single fact of the story; but Dreiser exhibits it on three distinct occasions, and each time after Carrie has had a success which gives rise to those aspirations. And her exposure to Hanson is usually followed by her exposure to Drouet. Her two main possibilities are presented to her mind serially and alternately instead of in simultaneous pairs, and the alternations are so swift that she has time to respond only in feeling but not in judgment to one set of circumstances before it is succeeded by its opposite. In view of her limited experience at this early stage, it is entirely credible that she should be aware at each moment only of what that moment brings. Nothing in her life has equipped her to stand apart from each moment and locate it in some larger system of expectations or judgments. Her consciousness of her identity does not precede, but arises out of, the ebb and flow of her experience. And this makes us feel that only by submitting to this ebb and flow, only by being loyal and responsive to each of her facts as it presents itself in turn, may Carrie attain her identity.

The sign of her emotional depth and of the wonder of life is that Carrie does attain her identity through such a seemingly aimless process. She arrives in Chicago a mere undifferentiated blob of feelings, just barely articulate. But her passage through the dialectic of desire and frustration does in fact enlarge her scope and refine her powers of discrimination. By responding only with her feelings she comes to perceive what James's heroines were spared any need to learn: that wealth is valuable not merely for itself, but as equipment for a free life in which one might engage the world in its full variety and complexity. To be sure, Drouet is no man to be chosen by a sophisticated woman. But his generosity and his buoyant appetite for living offer unmistakably richer possibilities than the Hansons' conservative round of toil or the young factory workers' crude fun. Drouet offers Carrie a way out of the spiritual death in which her environment does indeed threaten to trap her, an avenue leading toward the center of life. And when we see Carrie installed as Drouet's mistress, we are aware in her of a new presence, the weight of an actual person. She has learned to dress and move her body gracefully. She is acquiring the habit of speaking several sentences consecutively. She has begun to discriminate the tones of the world around her. As the process continues and her immersion is renewed, she learns to perceive Drouet's limitations and outgrows him too.[1] Her progress from Drouet to Hurstwood to Ames is marked by a continuing enlargement of identity and inner-direction. She is transformed from an amorphous into a differentiated human being.

1. Claude M. Simpson, who has studied the original manuscript of *Sister Carrie* from which Dreiser made cuts for the published version, tells me that Dreiser deleted a number of short passages describing Carrie in the process of outgrowing Drouet, and that these were arranged largely in the manner I have described. I am indebted to Professor Simpson for many valuable suggestions concerning *Sister Carrie*, and for his article, "*Sister Carrie* Reconsidered," *Southwest Review*, XLIV (Winter, 1959), 44–53.

The impression created by the plot that life is an amoral process is reinforced by Dreiser's descriptions of his characters. Even those more articulate than Carrie, like Drouet, are not permitted any long-range motives which might imply a significant degree of moral awareness. Drouet gives Carrie twenty dollars out of an immediate generosity, not as part of a deliberate plan to seduce her. Like Carrie, he takes each moment as it comes:

> Now, in regard to his pursuit of women, he meant them no harm, because he did not conceive the relation which he hoped to hold with them as being harmful. He loved to make advances to women, to have them succumb to his charms, not because he was a cold-blooded, dark, scheming villain, but because his inborn desire urged him to that as a chief delight. He was vain, he was boastful, he was as deluded by fine clothes as any silly-headed girl. A truly deep-dyed villain could have hornswaggled him as readily as he could have flattered a pretty shop girl. His fine success as a salesman lay in his geniality and the thoroughly reputable standing of his house. He bobbed about among men, a veritable bundle of enthusiasm—no power worthy the name of intellect, no thoughts worthy the adjective noble, no feeling long continued in one strain. . . . In short, he was as good as his intellect conceived.

He *bobbed about*, without needing or wanting to chart his course, but merely riding the waves of his "chief delight." Dreiser assigns Drouet not a dramatic persona capable of exerting influence, but rather *a gestalt*, a circumscribed field of activity which impinges upon the field of Carrie's passivity. He is simply *there* as one element in the total process which the plot unfolds. And the other characters are similarly adjusted and absorbed into the medium of the plot. They do not make the story, the story manifests them.

* * *

ELLEN MOERS

The Finesse of Dreiser†

We are reading Dreiser again. Without benefit of editorial fanfare or critical hoopla, a revival is upon us, solidified by that blessed invention of the fifties, the quality paperback book, with its attraction for

† From *American Scholar* 33 (Winter 1963–64): 109–14. Copyright © 1963 by Ellen Moers. Reprinted by permission of Curtis Brown, Ltd.

the young, the poor, the serious, the curious, the follower of fashion—for, in short, the reader. There are seventeen Dreiser volumes now in paper, including seven different imprints of *Sister Carrie*. (For the record, which has its interest as a signpost to taste, there are also seven Ambassadors, fourteen Red Badges of Courage, ten Moby Dicks, fifteen Scarlet Letters, twelve Huckleberry Finns.)

Young people have good reason to be reading Dreiser, as they obviously are, beyond the fact of his quality. He forms a bridge between the self-consciously inarticulate poets and novelists of their generation (the devotees of what Robert Brustein has called the Cult of Unthink) and the humanitarians of the last century, for whom the inability to articulate was in itself tragic, even disgusting. It is as the novelist of the inarticulate hero that Dreiser comes again upon the literary scene.

"One thing that you are to be praised for is that you have always been low," Edgar Lee Masters wrote Dreiser; "you have always loved low company, as Hawthorne and Emerson did and Whitman and before them as Goethe did. This passion conduces to honesty." But how is Dreiser in fact *low*? What is the social milieu of his novels? It is not low, certainly, in the Marxist sense, which seems relevant only because Dreiser's final political stand was with the Communist Party. Dreiser never wrote a proletarian novel: his favorite characters are an actress, a saloonkeeper, a traveling salesman, an art-collecting financial manipulator, a street preacher, a painter, a mistress, a bellboy. The fringe figures, wasters and spoilers and enjoyers, were for Dreiser, as for his master Balzac, the irresistible subject.

Dreiser's characters are low in the sense of being stupid. Carrie and Jennie and Clyde would probably rank well below the norm in any verbal intelligence test. Neither sentimentality nor disgust mars Dreiser's handling of inarticulate people—although both these patronizing attitudes repeatedly disfigured the "naturalist" tradition to which he is supposed to belong. That Dreiser loved his helpless, unconscious people has often been said, but he did so with the very special love of a sibling, carrying with it acceptance, identification, shame, detachment and an honesty related to the contempt that is bred by familiarity. In the most literal sense, as his letters and autobiographical writings show clearly, Dreiser wrote as a brother. This is the central fact about his work, far more important than the clichés thrown at him in the 1930's and '40's: that he was a peasant, a linguistic immigrant, a naturalist, a People's realist, an American and so on.

One of Dreiser's sisters ran off with a married saloon-manager who stole money to keep her (Carrie); one bore a rich man's illegitimate child (Jennie Gerhardt); one brother hung around hotel lobbies looking for easy money, got into trouble and ran off to peddle candy on trains (Clyde). His beloved brother Paul, the song writer "Dresser," ran away from the seminary where he was training to be a priest, spent some time in jail and lived off the bounty of a "madam" on his easy-going way to success. Without much in the line of theory, using only family materials, Dreiser could easily work out a view of life somewhat at variance with the conventional homilies of his day. More important, from the contrast between day-by-day life as it was lived by his brothers and sisters, and life as it was played out in popular melodrama, he devised a literary style that gave form, and even heroism, to the inarticulate.

Dreiser's triumph in this enterprise is Clyde Griffiths in *An American Tragedy*, the last novel published in his lifetime and the sum of his experience as man and artist. But from his first novel, *Sister Carrie*, he addressed himself to the problem of expressing the inexpressibles and, what is more, carried it off with virtuosity and delicacy. These two books are Dreiser's masterpieces. The *Tragedy* is in every way more profound, more complex in structure, more rich in suggestions. That is where we are to look for the tragic sense, the compassion and the sociological subtlety that have won Dreiser the respect, if not the affection of his readers. But Dreiser would never have been able to manage the complex architectonics of *An American Tragedy* without his abundant natural, literary gifts as a novelist, which *Sister Carrie* most patently displays. Like *The Scarlet Letter*, which appeared exactly fifty years earlier, *Sister Carrie* is one of those first novels that show off the almost shameless virtuosity of the novice.

Dreiser wrote *Sister Carrie* somewhat by accident, at the insistence of a friend. He was already, in 1900 (like Hawthorne in 1850), a mature man and an experienced writer; he was the author of so many competent magazine articles (many of them showing a verbal smoothness lacking in *Sister Carrie*) that he had been listed by *Who's Who*. He had also written a few short stories, also at the urging of his friend, but what he really wanted to write was plays, not fiction. "Had I been let alone," he told Mencken, "I would have worked out in that form." *Sister Carrie* shows it. It is, as no later Dreiser book would be, a novel of *scenes*, some of them so "gorgeous" that they remain in the mind like things in *Madame Bovary* or *Anna Karenina*.

There is, for example, the Hurstwood-Carrie love scene, acted out in a slow-moving horse-drawn carriage pacing along the flat, new, empty stretches of Washington Boulevard; the opening scene, Carrie's meeting with Drouet in the railroad car; Carrie's night of triumph on the stage, before an audience of "stout figures, large white bosoms, and shining pins" that includes her two blazing lovers; and the final stunningly illuminated scenes of Hurstwood in degeneration, one bum among many on a snowy night in the Bowery:

In the drive of the wind and sleet they pushed in on one another. There were wrists, unprotected by coat or pocket, which were red with cold. There were ears, half covered by every conceivable semblance of a hat, which still looked stiff and bitten. In the snow they shifted, now one foot, now another, almost rocking in unison.

Rhythmic effects of every variety (the train, the streetcar, the carriage horse, the shuffling feet of the bums, the rocking chair) are scattered through the novel so profusely that its lyrical quality becomes at times almost too rich. There are effects of light and color that point to Dreiser's early and lasting passion for painting and architectural decoration, which has hardly been taken seriously by his critics. There are contrapuntal effects with speech—urban and rural; common, middling and "cultivated"; slang and theatrical bombast—that very few other novelists (James Joyce is one) have ever attempted. To say that the best scenes in *Sister Carrie* are cinematic rather than theatrical is another way of saying that Dreiser was a born, virtuoso novelist, for the movies learned more from the novelist than from the playwright. But it is often helpful, as Robert Penn Warren has shown in an essay on *An American Tragedy*, to write of Dreiser's effects in terms of the "sweep of the lens," the "shift of focus," the "movie in our heads."

If there is a crucial scene in *Sister Carrie*, on which the success of the book hangs, it is the early episode in the downtown restaurant, where Carrie is "seduced" by Drouet. This is hardly one of the memorable showpieces of the novel, yet it goes far to set the tone of the whole. For here Dreiser must take a stupid, commonplace girl, whose only charm is her youthful prettiness (and a certain something else that must here be established finally for the reader) and turn her into a heroine—without letting her think or feel or behave in the heroic style. She must take the first decisive step of her life—down a path that she, her family, her world know to be morally wrong—without seeming to understand what she is about and without incurring the reader's exasperation or provoking his blame. For Dreiser has set himself the task of making Carrie sufficiently null to skirt moral criticism but vital enough to personify the creative force itself—to be, in effect, his Emma Bovary.

The writing in the seduction scene is careful to the point of finesse—a word I would like to bring forward in connection with Dreiser, if only because it challenges the old and worn-out complaints against his style. In one of the recent favorable statements about Dreiser (they are still relatively rare) Saul Bellow asked a useful question about the nature of "bad writing" by a powerful novelist, but moved away from the answer with the lamest recommendation: that "Dreiser's novels are best read quickly." The reverse is true.

"Fine" writing (some of James's or Virginia Woolf's, for instance) often fails on slow and close examination, while the coarse, dense, uneven language of the more subtle novelists (like Dickens) yields surprising rewards—and explanations of the art of fiction—to the careful reader.

Dreiser has brought the farm girl, Carrie Meeber, to Chicago, introduced her to the drab home of her married sister, sent her about the city looking for poorly paid, tedious work, and then had her fall ill and lose her job at the outset of her first winter in the big city. Now he sets the stage for temptation. Carrie is spending her fourth weary day of job-hunting wandering the downtown streets of the city with a borrowed ten cents in her pocket for lunch, when Dreiser confronts her with that delectable specimen of brainless virility, Drouet, the traveling salesman Carrie had met on the train but had not seen again since her arrival in Chicago. Four pages later Carrie has taken money from Drouet, and the loss of her virtue is in plain view. But the scene ends as Dreiser has it begin: unstrained, calm, inevitable in a comfortable, flat sort of way, even cosy. Here is the beginning, several pages into Chapter VI:

. . . Suddenly a hand pulled her arm and turned her about.

"Well, well!" said a voice. In the first glance she beheld Drouet. He was not only rosy-cheeked, but radiant. He was the essence of sunshine and good-humour. "Why, how are you, Carrie?" he said. "You're a daisy. Where have you been?"

Carrie smiled under his irresistible flood of geniality.

"I've been out home," she said.

"Well," he said, "I saw you across the street there. I thought it was you. I was just coming out to your place. How are you, anyhow?"

"I'm all right," said Carrie, smiling.

Drouet looked her over and saw something different.

"Well," he said, "I want to talk to you. You're not going anywhere in particular, are you?"

"Not just now," said Carrie.

"Let's go up here and have something to eat. George! but I'm glad to see you again."

She felt so relieved in his radiant presence, so much looked after and cared for, that she assented gladly, though with the slightest air of holding back.

"Well," he said, as he took her arm—and there was an exuberance of good-fellowship in the word which fairly warmed the cockles of her heart.

The literary clichés in this last sentence are ugly, but they have a purpose: to throw into relief Drouet's final "Well"—which is positively elegant. In this short passage Drouet speaks that homely Americanism five times; more than "Say!" and "George!" his other expletives, it is his trademark. Dreiser was a master of the use of senseless speech to establish character—and those who believe that mastery does not enter here need only examine the hundred different cries of inarticulate passion expressed by Clyde Griffiths's "Gee!" or compare Drouet's speech with Carrie's. In this passage, as throughout the novel, Carrie says almost nothing. Her short, primer sentences carry the flat twang without Dreiser's insisting on it: "I've been out home," "I'm all right," and "Not just now."

It is relatively easy for Dreiser to show why Carrie succumbs to Drouet, but much trickier to establish that this timid farm girl—naïve, compliant, decently conventional and without a notion of the seductive arts—can tie Drouet to the most permanent relationship of which he is capable, move on to a more complex lover, prompt Hurstwood to a crime of Balzacian dimensions and then move on again to solitary theatrical triumphs. Carrie hardly talks or thinks, but the warmth of her presence must be at the center of every scene in which she appears. To the men around her she must, without words, respond; here as everywhere, she smiles.

In this scene Dreiser first sets forth the idea that Carrie's fall is to be a triumph, that her sexual adventures stimulate the unfolding of her temperament, much as the sun's heat brings the plant to flower. The pervading atmosphere, the underlying sensual image of this scene is, in fact, physical warmth. It emanates from Drouet, who (in the passage I have quoted) is "rosy-cheeked," "the essence of sunshine" to whom Carrie is the "daisy" of the farm. His *geniality* and *exuberance* are the sun that *warms her heart*. Dreiser uses the word *radiant* twice at the opening of the scene to characterize Drouet, and the shining, gleaming, warming quality of the man is reinforced in the restaurant episode that immediately follows. Drouet summons the "full-chested, round-faced" Negro waiter with a hissing "Sst!" and his ordering of the meal, punctuated with the waiter's repeated "Yassah," turns into a little duet full of sizzling ss sounds. (It does not include the silent Carrie; but its last line is "Carrie smiled and smiled.") Drouet's apotheosis as a warming, radiating presence comes, again with intricate sound effects, as the waiter returns, bearing on his "immense" tray the "hot savoury dishes."

> Drouet fairly shone in the matter of serving. He appeared to great advantage behind the white napery and silver platters of the table and displaying his arms with a knife and fork. As he cut the meat his rings almost spoke. His new suit creaked as he stretched to reach the plates, break the bread, and pour the coffee. He helped Carrie to a rousing plateful and contributed

the warmth of his spirit to her body until she was a new girl. He was a splendid fellow. . . .

Now Dreiser has been careful, in the opening chapters of the novel, to show that Carrie, although momentarily unfortunate, is *not* in the grip of a massively malign fate. She is *not* starving; she is far from destitution; she has two decent homes to go back to. What is at stake is not Carrie's survival but her growth. Dreiser has therefore established the sense of spreading cold that grips Carrie, a cold which is seasonal and physical but also emotional, and to which this scene, full of Drouet's "radiant presence," provides a warm alternative. The whole cold-warmth pattern has been cued to the reader with a sentence about the difficulty of *transplantation* "in the matter of flowers or maidens," which focuses our attention on Carrie as an organism, significantly a plant rather than an animal, whose response to temptation will be less conscious than instinctive.

About a page before Carrie meets Drouet, Dreiser announces the arrival of cold weather with a few carefully composed sentences (the penciled manuscript, ordinarily clean, shows erasures and excisions):

> There came a day when the first premonitory blast of winter swept over the city. It scudded the fleecy clouds in the heavens, trailed long, thin streamers of smoke from the tall stacks, and raced about the streets and corners in sharp and sudden puffs. Carrie now felt the problem of winter clothes.

Carrie falls ill. "It blew up cold after a rain one afternoon. . . . She came out of the warm shop at six and shivered as the wind struck her." A "chattering chill" follows; "she hung about the stove." She recovers, goes out again to look for work, but hates to return to her sister's home at night: "Hanson [her brother-in-law] was so cold." This sort of preparation throws into relief the sunny radiance of Drouet and the answering, smiling warmth of Carrie. It also clarifies, in the most prosaic way, her acceptance of Drouet's money, which Carrie takes to buy the warm clothing she needs for the winter. But the whole cold-warmth pattern, and the accompanying suggestions of sun, heat and soft, young greenness, are there to be drawn on when, at the close of the scene, Dreiser makes the transfer of money a climactic act.

When *Sister Carrie* was new it was regularly denounced, even by the firm that published it, as an immoral and indecent book. Inevitably, later critics, even those so well disposed as F. O. Matthiessen, have reproached Dreiser for his timidity in avoiding sexual contact between his characters. It is true that Dreiser never removes Carrie's clothes or shows her in the act of love. (When, much later, he came to handle sex openly, as in *The Stoic*, the effect is breathless and not quite sane—directing our attention more to Dreiser's temperament than to that of his characters.) What I have called the seduction scene in *Sister Carrie* culminates in nothing more physical than a pressing of hands. Yet Carrie's acceptance of Drouet's money points clearly and richly to her acceptance of Drouet as a lover, not merely because we know that this is the way the world (and the novel) goes, but because Dreiser's language drenches the transfer of money itself with sexual excitement.

Here is how he does it. The food is served. The man and the girl sit across the table from each other, talking banalities. A sexual current arises, for the first time, between them, and is phrased by Dreiser with deliberation: a matter-of-fact, businesslike sentence, than a colloquialism Carrie herself would use, then a literary sentence, suggestively metaphorical:

> She felt his admiration. It was powerfully backed by his liberality and good-humour. She felt that she liked him—that she could continue to like him ever so much. There was something even richer than that, running as a hidden strain, in her mind. . . .

It is important here that our attention be focused on Carrie, and her wordless, actually thoughtless reaction to Drouet's masculinity. (Dreiser cut from the beginning of the scene a sentence about Drouet's liking for Carrie's "mould of flesh" that might have spoiled the tone of the scene.) Drouet looks, admires, and then acts; in two sentences rich with suggestion, he begins to fondle—his cash.

> There were some loose bills in his vest pocket—greenbacks. They were soft and noiseless, and he got his fingers about them and crumpled them up in his hand.

The first physical contact then takes place, in words that seem to do nothing but state a gesture, but the key suggestion of warmth is there:

> She had her hand out on the table before her. They were quite alone in their corner, and he put his larger, warmer hand over it.

Drouet "pressed her hand gently . . . he held it fast . . . he slipped the greenbacks he had into her palm. . . ." Carrie takes the money, agrees to meet Drouet again, goes out onto the street. The last sentences of the chapter resolve the play of hands of the climax, and refer back to the gesture ("Suddenly a hand pulled her arm and turned her about") with which the scene opened. They also resolve the underlying imagery of the whole: the exchange of warmth, the soft greenness of the farm warmed by the heat of the sun.

Carrie left him, feeling as though a great arm had slipped out
before her to draw off trouble. The money she had accepted was
two soft, green, handsome ten-dollar bills.[1]

What did Dreiser *avoid* doing with this scene? There is no sentiment, no moralizing, no foreshadowing of conclusions. Carrie's
charm for Drouet has been established without destroying her simplicity of temperament; and Drouet's masculine heat has pervaded
the scene without the element of lust. Drouet remains vulgar and
coarse, but not disgusting. The natural forces of growth and change,
the mysteriously casual interactions of creature with environment
that always roused in Dreiser the emotions of wonder and awe, have
been suggested by a metaphorical (but essentially novelistic) language which in turn gives a surprising eloquence to this tawdry
encounter between trivial personalities. The people, Carrie and
Drouet, are neither glorified nor idealized.

Two chapters and several days, perhaps weeks, later, Carrie
becomes Drouet's mistress. Dreiser puts off the denouement, and
indeed avoids presenting the event directly to the reader, not from
mere prudery but from a conscious desire to destroy the significance
of the act as action, to minimize the element of free will (in which
he was a strenuous nonbeliever) and to make credible the lack of
reflection in such a girl as Carrie. So we are given much detail about
Carrie's shopping and pleasure in her new clothes; about Drouet's
pleasure in her appearance and care for her material comfort; and
about all the practical problems arising from Carrie's move out of
her sister's home and into an apartment Drouet takes for her.

Dreiser's commentary insists, too heavily but never stupidly, on
the importance of money, the force of instinct, the significance of
habits—abstract topics that drain from Carrie's action the last vestige of moral or sentimental tone. He is particularly careful to keep
Carrie's mind blank, her speech halting. A thought of home brings
a gesture of despair and a query from Drouet: "What's the matter?"
Carrie answers with a line that is at once accurate American slang
and literal truth: "Oh, I don't know." Carrie recognizes in a crowd
of poorly dressed factory girls a face she had known at work, and for
the first time senses some of the consequences of her move from
decent poverty to comfortable disgrace. Her reaction is again a ges-

1. Dreiser thought at one point of using another transfer of money to prefigure Carrie's
capitulation to Hurstwood, her second lover. For very good reasons he penciled the passage
out of the manuscript, probably as soon as it was written. (The more subtle love affair
between Carrie and Hurstwood would not have been glorified by such a transaction; and
the climactic scene, Carrie's stage debut before both her lovers, would have lost some of
its effectiveness, for Hurstwood was offering Carrie money to pay for the clothes she would
wear on stage.) But Dreiser's choice of words for the discarded "money" scene is interesting. Hurstwood pulls out, not the loose, soft, noiseless crumpled greenbacks of Drouet,
but "a thin clean roll" of new hundred dollar bills. Taking off one bill, he "put it in her
little green leather purse and closed it up."

ture, a start, and Drouet's comment pulls us up with its irony: " 'You must be thinking,' he said."

Dreiser cut from the manuscript a long paragraph making clear how aware he was of the literary significance of what he was doing. The paragraph comes near the beginning of Chapter VIII, after Carrie has gone to Drouet's apartment but before she takes him as her lover. The book as it stands retains nearly all of Dreiser's original reflections on the moral implications (or lack of them) of Carrie's actions; but this excluded paragraph probes—in language so clumsy as to justify the excision—the stylistic problems of inarticulate fiction.

> We are inclined sometimes to wring our hands much more profusely over the situation of another than the mental attitude of that other, towards his own condition, would seem to warrant. People do not grieve so much sometimes over their own state as we imagine. They suffer, but they bear it manfully. They are distressed, but it is about other things as a rule than their actual state at the moment. We see, as we grieve for them, the whole detail of their blighted career, a vast confused imagery of mishaps, covering years, much as we read a double decade of tragedy in a ten hour [?] novel. The victim meanwhile for the single day or morrow is not actually anguished. He meets his unfolding fate by the minute and the hour as it comes.

So spoke the novelist who was, in every sense, the brother of Sister Carrie.

ROBERT PENN WARREN

[*Sister Carrie*]†

Under the pressure of a newspaper friend, Arthur Henry, almost on a dare, Dreiser began his first novel. He wrote the words *Sister Carrie* at the top of a sheet of paper, and his career was begun. He had no idea what the novel was to be about, but memory took over. He knew the old yearnings of his sisters and how they had been caught by the glitter of a world beyond them. So we see Carrie, a country girl on a train, on her way to Chicago to hunt work, full of unformulated desires and with no firm moral principles, and see her meet Drouet, a cheap lady-killer in flashy clothes. Dreiser remembered not only his sisters but himself and his own enchantment by Chicago and his

---

† From *Homage to Theodore Dreiser* (New York: Random House, 1971), 21–35. Copyright © 1971 by Robert Penn Warren. Reprinted by permission of William Morris Agency, Inc., on behalf of the author.

own experience as the yearning "beginner," the outsider full of the primal pain of wanting and not having.

Carrie, after a dreary round of job-hunting and then immersion in a dreary job, with the sense of lostness and depersonalization in the swarming city, is easy prey to Drouet. So, later, with her blind aspiration toward something more glittering, she is easy prey to Hurstwood—the manager of a saloon, a "way-up swell place," as Drouet puts it—who stands at a higher level than Drouet, closer to some mysterious center of power, wealth, and joy that poor Carrie cannot actually conceive but merely senses. And the crucial fact in bringing her to surrender is in this sentence: "Behold, he had ease and comfort, his strength was great, his position high, his clothing rich, and yet he was appealing to her."

But the great Hurstwood is, in a way, a victim, too—merely one of Spencer's chemical atoms. Even when Hurstwood takes ten thousand dollars from the safe of his employers (an episode based on the fact that the lover of one of Dreiser's sisters had stolen from his employer and fled with the girl), the event is, in a sense, an accident, a trap baited by fate into which Hurstwood falls. He is holding the money in his hand, debating the theft, when the lock of the safe clicks. Had he pushed the door? He does not know. In this brilliant moral and psychological study, what is the nature of Hurstwood's guilt? Is the slamming of the door an accident or an alibi, a trap of fate or a masking of the unconscious decision to steal?

As Richard Lehan points out in his valuable study, *Theodore Dreiser: His World and His Novels*, Dreiser kept revising this scene, apparently realizing that it was central to his conception, and the revision progressed from a scene of explicitly debated temptation toward one of moral ambiguity; the movement is from a decision to steal, which, in the first version, precedes the click of the lock, to the final version in which the "accident" seems to account for the act. While part of the general revision of the novel was to emphasize the nature of what seems to be "chance" in human life, another impulse emerges—the growing insistence, not on the role of "chance" in the objective world, but on the apparently indeterminate elements in the inner life of men. In fact, the main direction of the revision was to deepen the characters of both Carrie and Hurstwood, to modify the conception from that of the mere adventuress and the mere seducer, to increase the shadowy ambiguity in the growth of motive and the forming of decision. At the same time, there is a movement toward a sense of logic behind the ambiguity, but a logic which undercuts all moralistic debate—a logic that grinds on its relentless way in the unconscious levels of life.

For instance, as a structural, as well as thematic, parallel with the scene of Hurstwood, we have the scene when Hurstwood first calls on Carrie in Drouet's absence, a scene in which we find the same moral ambiguity. At the end of the call, which has been, in a literal sense, innocent enough, Hurstwood tries to implicate Carrie in an unspecified guilt by pledging her to secrecy. She "doubtfully" replies: "I can't promise." But as soon as Hurstwood is gone, we find this passage:

> She undid her broad lace collar before the mirror and unfastened her pretty alligator belt which she had recently bought.
> "I'm getting terrible," she said, honestly affected by a feeling of trouble and shame. "I don't seem to do anything right."
> She unloosed her hair after a time and let it hang in loose brown waves. Her mind was going over the events of the evening. "I don't know," she murmured at last, "what I can do."

At this point, Carrie has done nothing "terrible." The "terrible" unspecified thing lies in the future, but all the time, while she is experiencing the "feeling of trouble and shame," she is removing the finery bought with Drouet's money, and releasing her hair as though preparing to go to bed—with Hurstwood. Let us notice, too, that she is doing all this while staring, uncomprehendingly, at the image of the incomprehensible self there in the mirror—the self that will pursue its own fated way in spite of anything that she "can do."

Nothing is specified, nothing is clear, but how clearly and deeply we intuit in this little drama the nature of the complex process working itself out. Over and over again in his fiction Dreiser develops such moments of psychological depth. And in *An American Tragedy*, in Clyde at the death of Roberta, we find his masterpiece of psychological analysis.

It can reasonably be held that the sense of moral ambiguity is central for *Sister Carrie*, as it is central for *An American Tragedy*. In one perspective, the whole story of Carrie and her lovers is a study of the mechanical process of success and failure—a process that to Dresier appears as unrelated to morality as a chemical experiment. By inscrutable laws, some fall, some rise. Hurstwood sinks to ruin, Carrie rises to be a theatrical star, but success and failure are both aspects of a morally neutral process.

Sex, love, appetite, loyalty—all feelings seem to shrivel to meaninglessness before the cold objective law of success and failure. Stage by stage we observe Hurstwood on the "road downward" that "has but few landings and level places," and stage by stage, we see the changes in Carrie's attitude and behavior toward Hurstwood. From the first moment of boredom she passes to indifference, then to disgust, then to contempt and cruelty, and then to a coldly mechanical act of desertion, and all, in the end, passes into a blank forgetfulness. In other words, Hurstwood is, bit by bit, robbed of reality. Failure is a kind of death that precedes the mortal death, and the mortal death will be, ironically enough, merely the shadow of the "spiritual" death. Several years earlier, in the winter of 1896–97, in an editorial in his first magazine, *Ev'ry Month*, Dreiser commented on the current money panic and the suffering entailed by it: "In this world generally failure opens wide the gates to mortal onslaught, and the invariable result is death."[1] From this brutal editorial, with its underlying theme of the survival of the fittest and the idea of the "psychosomatic" relation between the hard world of economic competition and the physiological fate, we find a dramatic projection in poor Hurstwood; especially in the night scene in which Hurstwood, having decided to commit suicide, goes past the theater to take a last look at Carrie's name in "incandescent fire," and continuing on his way, slips and falls in the snow and slush outside the splendor of the Waldorf, where Carrie now lives. But long since, in the long process of the decay of their relation, both Carrie and Hurstwood have recognized the law of their condition, and both, in a deep unformulated sense, accept it.

The law of success and failure has, indeed, been long since demonstrated in Carrie's desertion of her kin for Drouet, and of Drouet for Hurstwood. The law is reasserted, toward the end of the novel, when Drouet, still the glossy skirt-chaser and now somewhat risen in the world, appears in New York and thinks he may recapture Carrie; but she is beyond him, his success is not in her dimension. By the law of success and failure, there is no place for him in her scheme of things.

From the opening of the novel Carrie has, in fact, been instinctively aware of the mechanism of success. Dreiser calls her a "little soldier of fortune," and that is literally what she is, an adventuress with an instinctive eye to the main chance, as undistracted by sex, or love, as by moral scruples. Furthermore, she instinctively reads the symbols of the world of success, and the first symbol is Drouet's clothes; in the end she is seduced, not by his manly qualities, but by the cut of his coat. Commenting on this, Dreiser says: "A woman should some day write the complete philosophy of clothes. No matter how young, it is one of the things she wholly comprehends." It was, too, one of the things the young Dreiser had comprehended: he had stolen twenty-five dollars for a coat that, long before he had attained any success, would serve as a symbol of success.

In Carrie's story Dreiser subtly develops the way in which commitment to what he would call "material" success could absorb all other aspects of life. The groundwork of this process, as we have remarked above, is laid by Drouet's clothes; and the next stage in the

1. See Kenneth S. Lynn: *The Dream of Success*, Boston, 1935, p. 24.

process occurs when, after her early struggle in Chicago, she again encounters Drouet, who takes her to dinner and gives her money. With her fingers touching the "soft, green handsome ten-dollar bills" (notice how the description endows the symbols, i.e., the bills, with intrinsic charm), she suddenly feels that she likes Drouet, and could continue to like him "ever so much."[2] And she does continue to like him until she meets Hurstwood, who opens her eyes to new vistas. But with Hurstwood, as with Drouet, what is remarkable is the cold-ness—the mechanical quality—of the sexual relation. On this point, at the moment of her marriage to Hurstwood, Dreiser is quite spe-cific: "There was no great passion in her, but the drift of things and this man's proximity created a semblance of affection."It is one of the moments of beautiful precision in Dreiser's writing. "Drift of things"—"proximity"—"semblance": could it be better, more suc-cinctly, put?

Here we may remember that, late in life, Dreiser, after his own bitter struggle for success and his years of compulsive promiscuity, could say that he had never loved anybody except perhaps his mother, that he had loved women merely in the abstract; that is, he had seen women as "mechanisms" for a certain pleasure, not as per-sons. As Flaubert is reported, perhaps erroneously, to have said of his great heroine Madame Bovary, that she was himself, so Dreiser, the soldier of fortune incapable of love, might have said, "Caroline Meeber, c'est moi." She is the first of the shadow-selves about whom Dreiser wrote: the first of the images that embodied his own yearning and struggle, and that, at the same time, endured the cold scalpel-edge of psychological analysis and suffered that vengeance for the outrage Dreiser himself had done to his own secret and incorrigible moral sense.

The feelings of sex, love, and affection do not prevail against the cold mechanism of success and failure that the story of Carrie delin-eates, but the novel is shot through with, even sustained and given life by, other feelings. There is the pathos of yearning, of wanting and not having, and the slow, grinding anguish of failure. The decline of Hurstwood—one of the great narrative sequences in American fiction—is rendered with almost intolerable imaginative involve-ment. It is as though Dreiser, even as he, the rising young journalist, began to taste success, became hagridden with the fear of failure; so, in his neurotically superstitious nature, he was driven to expiate the "crime" of success by realizing imaginatively all the pangs of failure and, by this expiation, to try to pay in advance for success.[3]

2. When Drouet gives Carrie her first pretty clothes, Dreiser presents a little scene of remark-able psychological insight. Admiring herself, Carrie catches "her little red lip with her teeth" and feels "her first thrill of power." Here the biting of her own lip, with its charge of narcissistic sexuality, is fused with the "thrill of power."
3. In this connection, to look ahead, it was after *An American Tragedy*, when Dreiser had at

Thus the very compassion in the novel may have a deep aspect of self-reference, and the poignancy may actually be the result of that self-reference.

There is, however, another range of feeling in the novel, also deeply related to Dreiser's own compulsive drive for success. Along with this drive there was—as there often is—a paradoxical criticism of success, even a rejection of it, a conviction that success is bound to be empty and meaningless, an unformulated awareness that success is sought so desperately only as a compensation for some fundamental and irremediable deprivation or failure, and that no success can, in the end, ever be a surrogate for what has been denied. So we find Dreiser, even in the full tide of his drive for success, suffering the shock of the encounter with Herbert Spencer, and saying of himself:

> Up to this time there had been a blazing and unchecked desire to get on, the feeling that in doing so we did get somewhere; now in its place was the definite conviction that spiritually one got nowhere. . . .

There is, then, a pathos of success as well as of failure, and as Hurstwood exemplifies one, so Carrie exemplifies the other—and this contrast provides, structurally, the poles of the action. As Hurstwood has been doomed to failure, so Carrie has been doomed to success, and at the end we see her in the apartment at the Waldorf:

> Oh, Carrie, Carrie! Oh, blind strivings of the human heart! Onward, onward, it saith, and where beauty leads, there it follows. Whether it be the tinkle of a lone sheep bell o'er some quiet landscape, or the glimmer of beauty in sylvan places, or the show of soul in some passing eye, the heart knows and makes answer, following. It is when the feet weary and hope seems in vain that the heartaches and the longings arise. Know, then, that for you is neither surfeit nor content. In your rocking-chair, by your window dreaming, shall you long alone. In your rocking-chair, by your window, shall you dream such happiness as you may never feel.

Carrie has everything, and she has nothing, and the rocking chair—motion without progress, life spent in mere repetition, a hypnotic dream without content—is a perfect image of the success that

---

last achieved fame and wealth as a writer and was living in an elegant apartment, employing a butler, entertaining lavishly, and playing the stock market, that he began to rail at the money-madness of the age, the tyranny of great corporations, and the nervous fluidity of American life. Dreiser, with all his memories of the old pinch of poverty, and with his aspirations to "social supremacy" that could be gratified only in a democratic plutocracy, began, in a final and contradictory irony, to regret the dissolution of the hierarchical society of the Middle Ages—a strange manifestation of his superstitious sense of guilt. But no stranger than the impulse that drew him to admire John Burroughs and to edit Thoreau.

"got nowhere."[4] It is the image of the pathos of success—and to sit rocking by the hour was one of Dreiser's own characteristic habits. To sit rocking while over and over again he would fold and unfold a handkerchief. The paradox of success continued, in various forms, to haunt Dreiser, as in A *Gallery of Women*, where, in reference to "Regina C—," he says of ambitious women that they draw "a certain kind of success or disaster about as plants draw a certain kind of insect." Success and disaster, success and failure—these can be convertible terms in the logic of life.

In *The Dream of Success*, Kenneth Lynn offers a very interesting account of the scene of Carrie in her chair. He notes a psychoanalytic account of the "gold digger" that describes the type as "invariably severely neurotic . . . capable of achieving their conscious aims temporarily, only to find themselves depressed, dissatisfied, bored." But he adds a sociological dimension to the scene in the Waldorf, for which, he says, Dreiser gives a clue in the fact that Carrie, sitting in her rocking chair, is yawning over Balzac's *Père Goriot*. Dreiser, as I have already said, had, only a few years earlier, discovered Balzac and recognized in his ambitious, success-mad young men the picture of himself, and de Rastignac, the hero of this novel, is a perfect exemplar of that cold-hearted breed. It would be a typical instance of that subtlety (for which Dreiser is so rarely praised) for him to put *Père Goriot* on Carrie's knee, as a way of identifying himself (consciously or unconsciously) with her, and a way of confessing, in the same fact, the emptiness of his own values, and, under the guise of pity for her, expressing a pity for himself as the ultimate victim. And connected with this self-pity outwardly directed, we may recall that when Dreiser saw the scene of the death cell in the stage version of *An American Tragedy*, tears came to his eyes as he murmured: "The poor boy, the poor boy! What a shame." But we may recall, too, the scene in that novel when Clyde Griffiths, finding his sister abandoned and pregnant, experiences, like circles widening out from the stone dropped into a pool, the pity for her, then for their mother, and then for the world; and finally, from under the guise of those objective forms of pity, the pity for himself bursts out, for he, too, is trapped in the mess.

4. As one of the various subtle structural "ties" or "cross references" in the novel, we find that when Carrie is left alone, after Drouet has made his suggestion that she act in the play being put on by his lodge, she sits in a rocking chair and indulges, for the first time, the flood of daydreams of theatrical glory—the anticipation of glory, and the discovery of the blankness of glory, both belong in the rocking chair. This scene affords another cross reference, here to another novel, *The Titan*, with the episode of Stephanie the actress. As we shall see later, the artist (specifically actress) lives outside ordinary sanctions and fidelities, for the obligation is to the "illusion" of art (specifically to the role, with the role existing out of time); so it is only the artist (Stephanie the actress and Berenice the painter) who can overcome, however briefly, the powerful Cowperwood, Dreiser's version of a Robber Baron. The parallel here is that Carrie's discovery of her "artistic nature" leads, first, to the betrayal of Drouet, and second, to her abandonment of Hurstwood.

Kenneth Lynn, however, is concerned to make a point somewhat different from Dreiser's identification with Carrie and the relation of pity and self-pity. He would emphasize the sociological aspect of the scene; referring to Alexis de Tocqueville, who, in *Democracy in America*, remarked that the interest of life to Americans consists in anticipated success, Lynn goes on to say that de Rastignac would not be bored as Carrie is, for in a society of birth and status like that of France the challenges to the *arriviste* remain infinite, while in a plutocracy, once the symbols of conspicuous consumption are achieved, there are no other worlds to conquer.

The observations of Lynn offer a valuable comparison, but it is one made by him, not by Dreiser. When Dreiser read Balzac, he saw a likeness, not a difference. For one thing, he was looking at the psychology of the deprived and ambitious young soldier of fortune and not at the society that offered the objects of his ambition. For another thing, even if he had had such an interest, nothing in his education, experience, or cast of mind would have equipped him to pursue it fruitfully. He did not even understand the complexities of American society except at the level at which he did treat it. Dreiser is as far from Henry James as Nigger Jim and Huck Finn on their raft are from Prince Amerigo, or the White Whale from Edith Wharton herself. Dreiser was not, and could not have been, a novelist of manners. He was, quite literally, a novelist of the metaphysics of society—of, specifically, the new plutocratic society of the Gilded Age. And this meant that he was, too, the anatomist of the guilt involved in the characteristic ambition of that age as well as the poet of the pathos of success.

This theme of Dreiser's, it may be added, lies at a different and deeper level from that of the novel of manners. Such a theme may, however, be sometimes found behind the façade of the novel of manners; for instance, Proust's *A la recherche du temps perdu* is a masterwork in the genre of manners, but its final power comes from the unmasking of the reality of the world Marcel had dreamed of entering and from his own re-definition of reality. Even if it is enacted in a world infinitely more complex than that of Carrie, the story of Marcel is similar to hers. Each, of course, has assaulted a "walled city," as Dreiser puts it, each has breached the wall, and each has entered to find a reality far different from what had been dreamed. If Marcel is not bored, it is not because the complexity of his world offers infinite challenge for the conquest of new forms of status. What challenges him is not in the sociological dimension; it is to find a new form of reality in the aesthetic dimension, in the telling of the tale. The point is that Proust recognizes the significance of that dimension, and has faith in it because he can distinguish it from the sociological.

And this distinction is precisely what Dreiser could never quite make. He was a powerful artist, but his artistic ambition was painfully intermingled with his ambition for money and fine clothes; in fact, he often saw his work as a mere instrument to satisfy his grossest aspirations. It is only natural, then, that success of the artist should, to him, seem as fragile and infected as that of Cowperwood, the hero of *The Financier*, or any Robber Baron. Let us remember that it is as an "artist" that Carrie succeeds, and it is an artist who, in the apartment in the Waldorf, sits in the rocking chair that goes nowhere. But Carrie is not merely "artist," she is also "artist as gold digger," and so, may we ask, does this image represent another level of self-scrutiny on the part of Dreiser—who had his own rocking chair?

When Dreiser wrote *Sister Carrie*, he had not yet breached the "walled city," he had merely invested the outworks. The great test yet lay before him. If he was, as he says of Carrie, full of "wild dreams of some vague, far-off supremacy," he, as the "mother's child" with the sense of omnipotence and of being chosen by fate that Freud attributes to one in that position, still had enough of his father's religiosity and bitter ascetic morality, and enough superstitious anxiety, to be fearful, as I have suggested, of his very dreams of conquest. More important, he had enough imagination to leap forward to the moment of fulfilling conquest, and ask himself, "What will I have when I have it?" *Sister Carrie* appears as the projection of his own secret conflict and self-scrutiny; perhaps not the projection of them, but the means by which he discovered them at all. It may well be, that is, that he could discover them only when they were embodied in Caroline Meeber and not in Theodore Dreiser.

I have been speaking as though *Sister Carrie* were important primarily as a historical and social document and as a record of the psychology of Dreiser. But it is more than a document, it is a vivid and absorbing work of art. In dealing with a novel, the most obvious question is what kind of material the author has thought worth his treating, what kind of world stimulates his imagination. For Dreiser this was the world he lived in—and the world he was—and by accepting as fully as possible this limitation, he enlarged, willy-nilly, by a kind of historical accident if you will, the range of American literature. The same kind of compulsive veracity (so strangely mixed with his compulsive lying) that made him record such details of his own life as masturbation and theft, made him struggle to convert into fiction the substances of experience at both the personal and social levels that had not been earlier absorbed.

The kind of realism that is associated with William Dean Howells had little relation to the depths that Dreiser inhabited, and when Howells, the editor of the sacrosanct *Atlantic Monthly* and dean of

American letters, encountered Dreiser shortly after the publication of his first novel, he felt compelled, according to a report that, if not literally, is spiritually true, to remark: "You know, I don't like *Sister Carrie*." Even though his eyes had long since been unsealed by Tolstoy to the degradation and pain of the poor and to the brutality of power in the modern world, even though he had courageously declared himself on the affair of the Haymarket bombing, Howells, however sympathetic and anguished he might be, still remained the outsider to that grim world that was Dreiser's natural home. And even if Frank Norris had shocked the country with the realism of *McTeague*, he had, in the end, gratified the moral sense of America by converting the novel of greed and violence into a cautionary fable.

Sister Carrie was different from anything by Howells or Norris. What was shocking here was not only Dreiser's unashamed willingness to identify himself with morally undifferentiated experience or his failure to punish vice and reward virtue in his fiction, but the implication that vice and virtue might, in themselves, be mere accidents, mere irrelevances in the process of human life, and that the world was a great machine, morally indifferent. Ultimately, what shocked the world in Dreiser's work was not so much the things that he presented as the fact that he himself was not shocked by them. The situation was similar to that of Dreiser's hero Machiavelli, who shocked his world not by unveiling the nakedness of power (the world knew all about that), but by regarding it with a moral detachment, by trying to delineate a physics, even a metaphysics, of power.

PHILIP FISHER

The Life History of Objects: The Naturalist Novel and the City†

✣   ✣   ✣

Work and Role: Acting

In the Chicago half of his novel Dreiser creates a hierarchy of work that rises to more and more directly involve selling the self while at the same time providing a sanctuary for the self within the more clearly acknowledged fictionality of its role. At the bottom of the

---

† From *Hard Facts: Setting and Form in the American Novel* (New York: Oxford U P, 1985), 162–78. Copyright © 1985 by Oxford University Press, Inc. Used by permission of Oxford University Press, Inc. Throughout this essay, page references to this Norton Critical Edition are given in brackets after Fisher's original citations.

scale are jobs in which the self is extinguished by toil. Carrie begins by actually making shoes—the poor man's train, carriage, and steamship, his only technology of motion. Her father, whom she pictures covered with the white flour of the mill where he worked, is the perfect illustration for the extinguishing of the self by the toil that produces such goods as flour and shoes. Hanson, who is the image of a lifelong toiler, is a silent man described as "still as a deserted chamber."[1] At the next level above these toilers is the salesman Drouet, connected to objects by selling rather than making them. He handles only "samples" and is not fatigued by the weight of things. What he sells is really himself, his exuberance and pleasure-loving confidence, but as in all sales of this kind a trick occurs at the last moment. The customer who has really bought the salesman finds that in fact he has bought a set of brushes, an encyclopedia, or a vacuum cleaner. The art of sales is the elision of the self and a product throughout the selling process, lending the salesman's personal glow to the object, then the severing of the connection after the completion of the sale so that the customer is left with only the object.

One step above Drouet is Hurstwood who, while a salesman, has no object to sell. As manager he, in effect, sells his tone, his presence and air to the nightclub. Standing around, the "dressy manager" rents out his personal approval. Objects have disappeared from the selling process, but the fictionality of social role is increasing. The customers do not *buy* Hurstwood, they purchase the right, by talking to him and being acknowledged by him as worth talking to, to believe that they are his equals. What Hurstwood sells, therefore, is not his personality, as Drouet does, but his air of knowing and making available the entire circle of which the customer would like to imagine himself a member. Drouet's personality and vitality would survive disconnection from the machinery of social life. Unemployed, Drouet would still be a lively and sought-out man. Because Hurstwood sells only his tone and services as an intermediary between figures in a circle, once severed from the social machine he is, as Dreiser says of him in New York, "nothing."

At the peak of the hierarchy of work that Dreiser has constructed is the actress. Her self, her inner emotional being, is what is sold to the ticket holders. The objects have vanished entirely. The personality and vitality alone remain to sell. Yet, this final identification of self and work is carefully regulated by the fictional shelter of the stage role: Laura, Katisha, the frowning Quakeress. It is only in Drouet that the actual self is naively present and in balance with the

1. Theodore Dreiser, *Sister Carrie*, Rinehart Edition (New York: Holt, Rinehart & Winston, 1957), 48 [37]. All further quotations from the novel will be indicated parenthetically after the quote.

objects that it sells and separates from itself in the act of selling. With Hurstwood, self and the fiction of position; with Carrie, self and the more profound split between self and role make more naked the renting out to others of the self, while sheltering the self within a "part." The world of New York is free of shoes, flour, and salesmen with their samples. The economic world is object-free. Transportation and entertainment, moving and acting are all that remain: motorman and actress. In Dreiser's Chicago hierarchy the two poles are paradoxically similar. At the bottom as a result of toil the self is exhausted by the objects that it produces, drained by shoes, covered with flour. At the top the self is not extinguished but fictionalized and costumed. The flour that covered Carrie's father is replaced by the stage makeup that covers his daughter.

What Dreiser has seized upon in his careful ordering of the world of work and its relation to the self is the privileged role of acting and the theater that had since the beginning of the Romantic Period been seen, on the one hand, as the central institution of the city and, on the other, as the most serious challenge to the romantic theory of the self. In the Seventh Book of Wordsworth's *The Prelude*, London, a world of performers, orators, ecclesiastical and political actors, and street performers like the blind beggar, has as its center the theater and the tumultuous fair. Wordsworth is only one of a set of 19th-century writers and artists that would include Poe, Baudelaire, Zola, and Manet to name only a few, for whom the theatricalization of life in the city made the theater or that theater of ordinary life, the street, the central spiritual fact about urban life. It is, however, in Rousseau's *Letter to M. D'Alembert On The Theatre* that the most profound analysis of the theater in its relations outward to the community and inward to the self is recorded. Rousseau's *Letter* has been explored by Lionel Trilling in his *Sincerity and Authenticity* and Trilling's main ideas deserve summary.[2]

Rousseau's concern is to denounce the theater and to prove its incompatibility with any acceptable and moral community. He sees three interconnected factors: (1) republican virtue, (2) the position of love in society, and (3) the sharp contradiction between the social role of women and their appearance on the stage as actresses. In Trilling's account a society that is republican, individualistic, and based on citizenship relies on a strong sentiment of self that each person must develop and protect.[3] Each must become himself, know

2. Lionel-Trilling, *Sincerity and Authenticity* (Cambridge: Harvard University Press, 1973), 62–67.
3. Rousseau's description clearly distinguishes the actor from the orator or preacher. "When the orator appears in public, it is to speak or not to show himself off; he represents only himself; he fills only his own role, speaks only in his own name, says, or ought to say, only what he thinks; the man and the role being the same, he is in his place; he is in the situation of any citizen who fulfills the functions of his estate. But an actor on the stage,

himself, and express himself in his public choices. Each must, to use the political term, *represent* himself, thus the intense civic importance of complete self-knowledge and sincerity. The essence of acting is, of course, representing what one is not, simulating anger one does not feel, weeping tears at twenty past nine night after night, convincingly representing one night a miserly landlord and the next a benign and courageous doctor. To value and foster the skills of the actor is to reward those able to not-be themselves, not feel what they in fact feel and, therefore, to strike at the heart of a social order based on full individual being and public self-representation.

As Rousseau pointed out, many consequences follow: the conversion of leisure from participatory to spectator experiences; the obsessive centralization of the feelings around the passion of love to the exclusion of more social feelings such as loyalty, friendship, and familial piety because of the dramatic suitability of sexual love; and, finally, the concentration of the theater on the actress.[4] This final consequence is due to the paradox of female virtue, in its ordinary domestic modesty and retirement, electrifying the theater with the energies of moral reversal.

The intuitive genius that Dreiser brings to his account of the theater and its central position as an image—like the rocking chair or the newspaper—for a description of American society is confirmed by the detailed interconnection of Rousseau's speculations and Dreiser's novel. To note only two characteristics here beyond those that are already obvious will suffice. Carrie's blankness, her lack of attachment or even mood, her easy forgetting of her family, her sister, Drouet, and even her disinterest in ever returning even for a visit, her passivity, and her ability to be almost hypnotized into acting under the gaze of Drouet, even her absence of desires as proved by her realization once she has a great deal of money that there is nothing that she wants to buy: all of these elements of blankness correspond to the assumption that Rousseau made that the more successful one were at acting the less one would have a sentiment of self. Secondly, the obsessive love interest of all of the parts played by Carrie, for which the best example is the harem girl that she plays in New York, goes along with a romantic deadness, a lack of erotic quality in her relations with men.[5] The audience's obvious fantasy

---

displaying other sentiments than his own, saying only what he is made to say, often representing a chimerical being, annihilates himself, as it were, and is lost in his hero. And in this forgetting of the man, if something remains of him it is used as the plaything of the spectators. What shall I say of those who seem to be afraid of having too much merit as they are and who degrade themselves to the point of playing characters whom they would be quite distressed to resemble." Jean-Jacques Rousseau, *Politics and the Arts: Letter to M. D'Alembert on the Theatre*, ed. and trans. Allan Bloom (Ithaca: Cornell University Press, 1960), 80–81.

4. Ibid., 82–92.
5. The role of harem girl exactly represents, in this case, the truth of the actress's relation to

of being in love with the actress that they pay to watch display her feelings is the relocated eroticism that has now disappeared from their actual lives. The most intense erotic moment of Dreiser's novel occurs when both Hurstwood, from his box in the audience, and Drouet backstage rise to a pitch of desire for Carrie beyond what they have ever felt in reality as they watch her play the part of Laura in the Elk's Club play. Similarly, as the frowning Quakeress in New York, Carrie faces an audience whose key can be found in the aging businessmen rich enough to buy the best tickets. "The portly gentlemen in the front rows began to feel that she was a delicious little morsel. It was the kind of frown that they would have loved to force away with kisses. All the gentlemen yearned towards her" (401) [313]. This erotic pleading, controlled and merchandized, is precisely what Dreiser had described earlier as Carrie's own relation to the clothes in department stores.

> When she came within earshot of their pleading [that of the clothes] desire in her bent a willing ear. The voice of the so-called inanimate! Who shall translate for us the language of the stones?
> "My dear," said the lace collar she secured from Partriges, "I fit you beautifully, don't give me up."
> "Ah such little feet," said the leather of the soft new shoes, "how effectively I cover them. What a pity they should ever want my aid." (94) [72].

The erotic helplessness and need is what both actress and audience, objects and shopper, court one another with across the barriers of sales and theater tickets.

The sexualized quality of acting, protected as it is by fantasy and the barrier of the stage that separates the beloved actress from the numerous fantasizing suitors in the audience repeats the paradox mentioned earlier that sheltered within the fiction of her role the actress sells precisely the vitality of her personality. Intimacy of self-presence and intimacy of sexual relation are both paradoxically present in the neutralized, stage-lit world of pretence. One of the first consequences of Carrie's success as an actress is that she begins to receive a regular stream of marriage proposals from men who know nothing of her but what they have seen in her performance.

Where Dreiser goes beyond Rousseau is in his refusal to contrast acting with sincerity, his refusal to oppose the representation of what one is not to authentic self-representation. Dreiser is the first novelist to base his entire sense of the self on the dramatic possibilities

---

the audience. As we see from the many invitations that Carrie receives, the rich men in the audience who date chorus girls consider them a kind of harem that is literally on display for the audience's choice while being fictionally on display for the vizier's choice.

inherent in a dynamic society. Acting involves primarily in Dreiser not deception but practice, not insincerity but installment payments on the world of possibility. In *Sister Carrie* acting is a constant social tactic. As a mockery of sincerity the words that provide Carrie's break into a speaking part in New York and therefore her rise to stardom are significant ones. To the Vizier past whom she is being paraded as one of the harem girls she says, in answer to his idle question, "Well, who are you?" "I am yours, truly" (387) [301]. In the very sassy pertness with which she improvises her answer she marks herself as a free and independent woman while her words (her part) declare her a slave. The final word "truly" caps the elegance of this paradoxical moment. To some extent acting in *Sister Carrie* always serves to preserve a freedom of the self from its appearance, and it is to that degree that it records a higher version of the possible or prospective self in defiance of the momentary "role" or "part" that it is compelled to play and be recognized in. When Carrie first sets out to find work in Chicago "she became conscious of being gazed upon and understood for what she was—a wage-seeker. . . . To avoid a certain indefinable shame she felt at being caught spying about for a position, she quickened her steps and assumed an air of indifference supposedly common to one on an errand" (18) [12–13]. She acts the role of one on an errand to avoid the collapse of recognition on the part of others that would freeze her into *no more than* what she happens to be in this momentary role of job seeker. Her acting is a protest on the part of the wider possibilities of her self. Similarly, Hurstwood in decline refuses to go home. "No, he would not go back there this evening. He would stay out and knock around *as a man who* was independent—not broke—well might. He bought a cigar, and went outside on the corner, where other individuals were lounging—brokers, racing people, thespians—his own flesh and blood" (330) [257]. It is the cigar that is the costume of this role. The ability to waste money on cigars proves that he is "independent" and not a destitute drifter.

Even when people appear just as they are they play their appearance as a role. Carrie "looked the well groomed woman of twenty-one." (286) [221]. This is exactly what she is. Nevertheless, a small distance occurs so that it is more accurate to say that she looked the part of a well-dressed woman of twenty-one rather than that she was. The diners at Sherry's restaurant act the part of diners, "all were extremely noticeable." What goes on in the restaurant is an "exhibit of showy wasteful dining." The word "showy" is used many times in the novel to mark the conversion of experience into performance. In Chicago Mrs. Hurstwood wanted to "exhibit" her daughter Jessica since it had become time for the part of encouraging suitors. The force of the term "conspicuous" in the phrase "conspicuous consumption" invented by the Chicago sociologist and economist Veblen in the early years of Dreiser's career is here interpreted with great nuance. However, it is not at all consumption that is conspicuous, but anticipatory states of the self.

The importance of clothes in *Sister Carrie* arises from the choice that one can exercise over them as a conspicuous performance of prospective being. Drouet seduces Carrie by buying her the clothes that would be the appropriate costume only for the role of his mistress. The clothes are ones that she could not even explain let alone wear were she to stay in her role of working girl at her sister's flat. Similarly, Carrie's first acting jobs in New York translate into the paradoxical ability to buy the clothes for the role of a young actress. On the other side, Hurstwood's shabby clothes *expose* his state, the opposite but equally conspicuous equivalent to the *display* of state that is the normal function of clothes. Because clothes can be changed more rapidly than apartments they become a more sensitive index to changes of state. Clothes are one's address. Finally, only hotels are places of living sensitive enough to the fluctuations of self to equal clothing as performances of the momentary condition of the self. In New York after they separate, both Carrie and Hurstwood move through opposite ends of the spectrum of hotels. This hunger for day-by-day accounts of the fluctuation of fortune records the need of a society in which money will be kept in the stock market so that its waverings of value can be represented in the daily newspaper rather than in land or goods which are, by comparison, subject only to year-long or decade-long readings of change of worth. As the rocking chair is to fortune's wheel, second by second rises and falls, so too are clothes, hotels, and newspapers to the long-term indexes of fortune and value.

The Plot of Decline

In writing *Sister Carrie* Dreiser made two profound structural decisions that are in fact related to the tragic ambitions of his work. *Sister Carrie*, like Dreiser's one other great novel, might have been titled *An American Tragedy* and in both novels there is special emphasis on the renewed meaning given to tragedy by the dynamics of American life. The essential structural decisions are: first, the division of the novel into two halves, the first taking place in Chicago, the second in New York. The second decision divided the New York half into a balanced and closely modeled double story that compels us to see and comprehend the rise of Carrie by means of the fall of Hurstwood.

In the Chicago portion of the novel we have a familiar 19th-century *Bildungsroman* of the orphan. Arriving in the city, relying only on the intangible energy of her nature, Carrie is the one dynamic, unsettled figure in a world where everyone else represents terminal points, places and levels at which she might arrive and stabilize herself. The Hansons, Drouet, and Hurstwood are the three alternative fixed destinations each soliciting, in effect, the orphan with the implicit question: "Isn't this enough? Can't you be satisfied to stop here?" They themselves are static (in Chicago) and only Carrie is in motion. Society is conceived of as a set of levels with different types and value systems. Chicago is a social comedy of mobility sketched between honest, hard-working immigrant toilers whose lives are decent and respectable, grim and pleasureless; and managers at the upper levels of a nightclub large enough to have five bartenders and the big men at the Elks Club. That is the complete social range. Drouet is the dead center of the scale.

New York is not an extension of this social scale into both higher and lower possibilities. It is an entirely new world, one that is a symbolic simplification into either-or choices. All processes are speeded up and an inevitable pair of slopes appear: youth and age, not-yet and has-been, celebrity and nobody, female and male, stage lights and total darkness, Broadway and Bowery. The second half of the novel is an absolute world, not a portrayal of a society of layers and alternative values. All that remain are inside and outside, rising and falling, fame and death. In New York not only is Carrie dynamic but she is seen against a social system which has only dynamic possibilities. There is no place as such in this world.

Like all tragic settings Dreiser's New York is a figuration of time and not space. It is composed of stages rather than locations. Here the *Bildungsroman* plot has lost all force, for it is a progessive, optimistic plot that is exploratory, comic, and essentially a plot of growth in which the central figure finds a concrete world that by means of marriage, work, home, and social position substantiates the youthful inner possibilities by solidifying them into the facts of a life history. Instead New York is governed by the decisive contribution of Naturalism to the small stock of curves for human action: the plot of decline. The plot of decline characterizes many of the central novels of the last decades of the 19th century. Hardy's *Jude the Obscure*, Zola's *L'Assommoir* and Dreiser's *Sister Carrie* are its masterpieces and Mann's *Buddenbrooks* is its intergenerational epic. These plots of exhaustion have as their central subject the realm of energy rather than value. They revolve around strength and weakness, not good and evil. Their essential matters are youth and age, freshness and exhaustion. Behind the plot of decline is the Darwinian description of struggle, survival, and extinction. Darwinism has the characteristic as a theory that it is more and more optimistic about larger and larger categories, more and more pessimistic as you reach down to more local or individual events. Species sometimes survive, individuals never, and even species often perish while the total balance of species, adapted to the facts of the environment, improves even at the cost of species, just as species improve even at the cost of individuals. The most acute pessimism arises from a consideration of the individual life cycle as one that rises from the helplessness of infancy to the capacity to ensure individual survival and then declining from that point to death. The primary question for the Naturalist plot is whether the division of life into these two stages (rise and decline) is one of a very long rise that reaches, as it often does in social or financial terms, to the age of sixty, and then follows a short decline. Or is the proportion reversed as it is in the body's strength, a rapid rise peaking at twenty and a long continuous decline that takes up the longest section of personal history? In Darwinian terms, this latter possibility would be a brief rise to the moment of reproduction in the twenties and then a long superfluous decline. The Naturalist plot of decline in Hardy, Zola, and Dreiser bases itself to a large extent on the history of the body and not that of social position. It is therefore a chronicle of subtraction and weakening based on energy, sexuality, and the conversion of freshness to exhaustion.

One of Dreiser's curious emphases is on Hurstwood's age. He is never able to sweep Carrie away emotionally.

> This was due to a lack of power on his part, a lack of that majesty of passion that sweeps the mind from its seat, fuses and melts all arguments and theories into a tangled mass, and destroys for the time being the reasoning power. This majesty of passion is possessed by nearly every man once in his life, but it is usually an attribute of youth and conduces to the first successful mating.
>
> Hurstwood, being an older man, could scarcely be said to retain the fire of youth, though he did possess a passion warm and unreasoning. (199) [154]

This older man is in fact 39, but Dreiser's point is a Darwinian one that refers to mating rather than to feelings or passions as they occur in the mind. The goal of the single youthful urgency is reproduction, not sexual enjoyment as an experience, and Hurstwood's early marriage led to children as his later affair with Carrie does not.

Only a few years later in New York, "he looked haggard around the eyes and quite old." At the age of 43 he is comfortably built and so "walking was not easy" (310) [241]. Carrie begins to draw away from him because "she began to see that he was gloomy and taciturn, not a young strong and buoyant man. He looked a little bit old to her about the eyes and mouth now" (300) [234]. His habits are those of a retired and sedentary man of sixty. He reads the newspapers all day, becomes a chair-warmer in the comfortable hotel lobbies and parcels out his money like a frugal pensioner who gives up the daily shave so as to have a cigar now and then. What might seem an exaggeration here is in fact a speeding up, a compression of effects much like the rapid rise of Carrie to fame. One component of a tragic rendering of events lies in compressing the inevitable and the incremental into a few shattering or magical events. Thus Hurstwood's theft, which might be viewed as the cause of his destiny in New York and so it would be if the order of Dreiser's world were a moral rather than a Darwinian and economic order, is in fact only a notation in compressed form of the inevitability, at some point, in his life of a balanced moment at which he teeters unaware that he is no longer rising but beginning to fall. The theft is a registration of the almost physical nausea, as on a swing or a ferris wheel, at that point where effort has ceased and in an instant gravity takes over to pull one towards the earth. Dreiser's theory of rise and fall is offered in the best long analytic passage of his novel, the opening three pages of Chapter 33, a chapter with the half title "The Slope of the Years."

> A man's fortune or material progress is very much the same as his bodily growth. Either he is growing stronger, healthier, wiser as the youth approaching manhood, or he is growing weaker, older, less incisive mentally as the man approaching old age. There are no other states. Frequently there is a period between the cessation of youthful accretion and the setting in, in the case of the middle-aged man, of the tendency toward decay when the two processes are almost perfectly balanced and there is little doing in either direction. Given time enough, however, the balance becomes a sagging to the grave side. (295–96) [230]

Dreiser continues by pointing out that every great fortune, made in youth and in fact representing the conversion of personal energy into money, would inevitably be depleted and lost by the weakened power of decision as the owner of the fortune aged, except that such men always conscript younger minds and energies and buy up their vitality. These words interpret precisely what happens as Hurstwood flees Chicago with the stolen energy that is represented both by the stolen money and by the stock of Carrie's vitality that he has also stolen from Drouet. Early in the novel Dreiser refers to money as "honestly stored energy" and it is to that extent the body's way of spreading out its stock of youthful energy throughout a life too long for its actual store. Hurstwood's theft is the exact double of his relationship with Carrie: in each he appropriates the energies of others. Neither the theft nor the affair is the cause of his fall, because the fall of which Dreiser is speaking is the inevitable fall of vitality over time. Instead both the affair and the theft are desperate attempts to stave off, once falling has begun, temporarily and by means of stolen energies, the rapid sinking that converts the hopeful into the hopeless.

Hurstwood's relation to Carrie is only the intimate form of the wider social fact represented by her relation to her audience: a social group of aging males whose stored energy in the form of money now disguises the actual exhaustion of their spirits. What they rent in the theater is her vitality and youth and not at all her talent or remarkable beauty. Dreiser is careful to give Carrie no particular talent, only the traits that are those of youth itself: freshness, hopefulness, confidence, the imitative skills that are those of children and the unclouded flexibility of those who have as yet no concrete world that they would not give up for the chance at something better. She is the "not yet" to which the only other term is "has been." In the theater these two feed off one another as actress and audience who exchange energy for the honestly stored energy of money.

In Dreiser's novel even Carrie's sister Minnie at twenty-seven looks old and used up. The division is that of the body which reaches its full height at nineteen or twenty and shrinks from then on to death. This life history is that of products and objects which are best when new or fresh and then become worn out and discarded. The life history of a shirt is one of continual decline. All goods are used up and replaced. Within *Sister Carrie* relationships, houses, cities, and especially living situations are discarded in the way clothing might be. Hurstwood himself is worn out rather than captured and submitted to moral or legal defeat. He is obsolete like a pair of shoes rather than aged like a man. He is left-over and a scrap. The Bowery of New York is a collective heap of discarded men. By the end of the novel he is not so much dead as extinct.

Hurstwood's decline is measured by the shrinking of his space from a Chicago mansion to a modest apartment to a smaller flat to a room to a cubicle, and it is measured equally by the melting away of his savings, or rather his stolen savings: $1300 when he reaches New York, $500 by Chapter 33, $340 in Chapter 36, $100 and then $50 in Chapter 37, then finally he is a beggar for dimes and beds for a night. An equation is made between the decline of his health, his eyesight, the amount of light in his world and the shrinking of his money.

Throughout his decline the single act that Dreiser repeats again and again is his reading of the newspaper. Reading becomes the partner term to the acting associated with rising, hopeful, prospective being. The newspaper possesses its reader with lives and events not his own in much the same way that a role does an actress. The newspaper is in fact a mediating object in New York. Hurstwood's only desire seems to be to go on reading it, Carrie's highest desire is to be featured in it. Breaking into the theater seems only a halfway point to breaking into the newspapers. The newspaper is retrospective, defining what happened yesterday. It is literally about what "has been." As Hurstwood reaches his nadir he is forced to root around for out-of-date newspapers to try to see if there is any news about Carrie.

Dreiser speaks of Hurstwood as "buried in his papers." On a park bench the newspaper is the blanket of the down-and-out tramp. When he no longer consorts with celebrities he reads about them in the newspaper stories. Once Carrie has gone she begins to appear in the papers and he can follow her there. The newspaper becomes a way of not quite dying to a life that he no longer lives. In one of those very lovely inconspicuous scenes that mark Dreiser's work at its best, Hurstwood, so cut off from the world that he would rather not look out the window, reads in the newspapers that a bad storm is due, then in later editions that it has begun, then that it is a record storm, then that it will end soon, and finally, that is has ended. To follow stars and celebrities who are in fact inaccessible is here put in its proper frame of meaning: the newspaper is the essential symbol of decline because it involves a preference for all experience as retrospective rather than lived, even the experience of a storm. The disappearance of Carrie from Hurstwood's life is brilliantly done, not by an article in the newspaper, but by the physical object of the paper itself. "He knew that Carrie was not there not only because there was no light shown through the transom, but because the evening papers were stuck between the outside knob and the door" (394) [307].

The resonant final third of Dreiser's novel does not link the stories of Hurstwood and Carrie by way of contrast, that is only the superficial social level of what is in fact a tragic inevitability, because Carrie's rise, representing as it does youth itself, and Hurstwood's decline, no more than a compressed account of age itself, are stages that magnify by means of "star" and "tramp" the inevitable small-scale rise and fall that together make up the life history of the self considered as energy. By means of two characters Dreiser can make simultaneous what is in actual experience consecutive, locating in two persons the prospective and retrospective phases of one life. To achieve this he carefully matches their lives as superficial contrasts connecting deep structural similarities.

Near the end Hurstwood lives at the Broadway Central Hotel. At this point they each live, as a favor, in a hotel where neither really pays. He lives there as a favor to him (a charity) on the part of the kindly manager. She lives there as a favor to the hotel (an advertisement). Carrie's meals are bought for her by men who compete for the privilege. Hurstwood's too are free at soup kitchens or as a result of begging from these same prosperous gentlemen. The public buys tickets to see Carrie and outside the theater they also buy tickets at the solicitation of the ex-soldier who harangues them to contribute the price of bed tickets for the hundreds of homeless men that he lines up like a chorus line, Hurstwood among them. Hurstwood marches down Broadway in an army of tramps and Carrie marches back and forth on stage in a harem of chorus girls. Carrie has won for herself a place in the chorus line and Hurstwood's life is made of calculations of his place in the soup lines, bread lines, and shelter lines.

Hurstwood's one final job as a strike-breaker is in fact described as a performance. We see him rehearse his role, practicing with the trolley in the yards just as Carrie practices her moves as a chorus girl. The strike-breaking "play" is performed by running the streetcar with two policemen on board through a hostile audience of strikers and their families who jeer and hoot as though at a bad opera. The streetcar runs are fictional and symbolic since their purpose is not to carry passengers but to break the strike by demonstrating to the public, via the newspapers that all of the strikers have lost their "parts" and have been replaced in their roles by new actors, men simulating drivers. Hurstwood spends a day rehearsing, then goes out to play his role on the city streets. He is pelted like a bad actor and runs offstage in mid-performance, abandoning his role as motorman or, as the strikers name his role, "scab." When he gets cold on the trolley "he shivered, stamped his feet, and beat his arms as he had seen other motormen do in the past" (382) [298]. His play is woven by Dreiser directly into Carrie's rehearsals, performances, and breakthroughs. He is pelted off the stage just on the day when she speaks for the first time and begins her rise to stardom. The strike is the aging performer's nightmare, just as Carrie's rise is the neo-phyte's dream. Dreiser's highly conscious repetition of elements in the two lives derives from his intention that they be seen as stages. Throughout his novel "Carrie" has only a first name and "Hurstwood" has only a last. They are first and last names that combine to make one life; first stage and last stage, rise and fall of fortune's wheel.

*   *   *

AMY KAPLAN

The Sentimental Revolt of *Sister Carrie*†

* * *

I

It is well known that *Sister Carrie* opens on two discordant narrative registers: the documentary description of a young girl's journey to the city, and the sentimental commentary on the moral ramifications of her venture. The first, most notable in the opening paragraph, details "her total outfit," consisting of "a small trunk, a cheap imitation alligator-skin satchel, a small lunch in a paper box, and a yellow leather snap purse."[1] The second casts her in a melodrama or sentimental novel, where "either she falls into saving hands and becomes better, or rapidly assumes the cosmopolitan standard of virtue and becomes worse" (p. 1) [1]. This narrative disjuncture follows a long tradition of the realistic novel in which the romantic illusions of the characters are dashed by their contact with the commercial reality of urban life. Stylistically, in this tradition, the dispassionate journalistic descriptions dismantle the black-and-white moralism of the sentimental commentary.

The problem with this reading, however, is that Dreiser's narrative proceeds not to debunk Carrie's dreams but to fulfill all her romantic and material aspirations of the first chapter, in which she is "venturing to reconnoitre the mysterious city and dreaming wild dreams of some vague, far-off supremacy, which should make it prey and subject—the proper penitent, grovelling at a woman's slipper" (p. 2) [2]. It is striking that this highly sentimental passage dubs Carrie "a half-equipped little knight," and in her first small success on Broadway she is promoted to lead the chorus line in the role of a "little gaslight soldier," complete with "epaulets and a belt of silver, with a short sword dangling at one side" (p. 290) [279]. The theater, the traditional symbol of illusion, becomes the vehicle for realizing Carrie's "wild dreams," and reencodes her romantic fantasies in a modern context when the city, in effect, does grovel before her photograph on a Broadway billboard. Even Carrie's disillusionment only

† From *The Social Construction of American Realism* (Chicago: U Chicago P, 1988), 140–51. Reprinted by permission of the author and the University of Chicago Press.
1. Theodore Dreiser, *Sister Carrie*, ed. Donald Pizer (1900; rpt., New York: Norton, 1970), p. 1. All further references will be cited parenthetically in the text. For the choice of this edition over the new Pennsylvania edition, see n. 5 below. [Throughout this essay, page references to this Norton Critical Edition are given in brackets after Kaplan's original citations—*Editor*.]

fuels rather than diminishes the force of her fantasies, which are expressed in the sentimental language that concludes the novel: "Oh blind strivings of the human heart!"—language which has caused much discontent among critics.

One of the most vexing problems for Dreiser criticism has remained how to reconcile his power as a realist—power that has been located in his challenge to moral and literary conventions— with his reliance on sentimental codes. Although sentimentalism has its own complex literary history, critics equate it in its broadest sense with Dreiser's notoriously bad writing: his cumbersome prose style, his high-flown moralizing, his investment in the tawdry dream- worlds of his characters, his melodramatic chapter titles, and his flowery endings; in other words, everything that seems the antithesis of a realism that directly portrays social conditions in lucid and unen- cumbered prose. Leslie Fiedler even relegated *Sister Carrie* to the tradition of popular sentimental women's fiction.[2] In addition, Drei- ser's sentimentalism is associated with elements of commercial pop- ular culture figured in *Sister Carrie* not only through Carrie's reading but through her spectacular theatrical career, first as an amateur in Daly's famous melodrama, then as a chorus girl on Broadway, and finally as a star in the Sunday supplements. These antirealistic ele- ments have been problematic to critics because, as I have suggested, * * * Dreiser has served as the test case for the viability of American realism—not only for detractors such as Trilling, but for supporters such as Alfred Kazin, who wrote: "It is because we have all identified Dreiser's work with reality that, for more than half a century now, he has been for us not a writer like other writers, but a whole chapter of American life."[3]

The problem of Dreiser's sentimentalism has been met by four major critical solutions. The most common solution privileges his lucid portrayal of social conditions—represented best by Hurst- wood's decline—and downplays the maudlin flights of Dreiser's prose—represented by the plot of seduction and Carrie's longings and cheap success.[4] Another solution is offered by the new Penn-

2. Leslie Fiedler, *Love and Death in the American Novel* (New York: Criterion Books, 1960), pp. 241–48.

3. Alfred Kazin, Introduction to *The Stature of Theodore Dreiser: A Critical Survey of the Man and His Work*, ed. Alfred Kazin and Charles Shapiro (Bloomington: Indiana Univer- sity Press, 1965), p. 5.

4. Early reviewers tended to single out Hurstwood's downfall for special praise and treated Carrie's story as a secondary theme. See Jack Saltzman, ed. *Theodore Dreiser: The Critical Reception* (New York: D. Lewis, 1972), pp. 1–52. For more recent examples of critics who privilege Dreiser's realistic qualities, see F. O. Matthiessen, *Theodore Dreiser* (New York: Sloan, 1951) pp. 52–92; Richard Lehan, *Theodore Dreiser: His World and His Novels* (Carbondale: Southern Illinois University Press, 1969), pp. 53–79; Mary Burgen, "*Sister Carrie* and the Pathos of Naturalism," *Criticism* 15 (1973): 336–49; Donald Pizer, *The Novels of Theodore Dreiser: A Critical Study* (Minneapolis: University of Minnesota Press, 1976), pp. 36–40.

sylvania edition of *Sister Carrie*, which restores Dreiser's original manuscript to what it was before his friend Arthur Henry revised it for the market: "Dreiser was composing a serious work of art," claim the editors, who retrieve it from Henry's "trying to revise it into saleable fiction."[5] Not surprisingly, the restoration of the "serious work of art" deletes the embarrassing chapter titles, which have been likened to Paul Dresser's popular ballads, and substitutes Hurstwood's suicide for the sentimental ending of Carrie in her rocking chair. A more compelling solution has been offered by Sandy Petrey, who argues that the straightforward narrative style of Dreiser's "social realism exposes sentimental posturing as absurd," as a hollow, outdated tradition no longer capable of attributing meaning to modern urban experience.[6] Other critics have shown similarly how Dreiser's plots and characters parody sentimental conventions to "controvert all the basic messages of popular fiction."[7]

These three different critical approaches recuperate Dreiser's realism by subordinating or deleting his sentimental qualities and differentiating his writing from the popular forms he employs. Another approach inverts his hierarchy. In "*Sister Carrie*'s Popular Economy," Walter Michaels, echoing Fiedler but disagreeing with his evaluation, claims that Dreiser is indeed a sentimentalist, or at least, in contrast to Howells, embraces the sentimental ethos of capitalism which values excess over restraint.[8] Philip Fisher, while not directly addressing the issue of sentimentality, makes similar claims for Dreiser's writing as a form of popular art, which rather than controvert or parody popular ideology makes its readers at home in a new world of consumer goods.[9] Earlier critics equate Dreiser at his most realistic with his critical "depiction of conditions" of work and unemployment, while those critics who privilege Dreiser's popular and sentimental side see his writing emerging from and embracing the consumer aesthetic of the late nineteenth century. This chapter argues that the critical opposition associating sentimentalism with

5. Theodore Dreiser, *Sister Carrie*, The Pennsylvania Edition (Philadelphia: University of Pennsylvania Press, 1981), p. 579. Although this edition is an invaluable source for scholars, I have chosen to use the edition which was published by Dreiser in 1900 and has been read by readers since then, because I believe that the revisions either made by or authorized by Dreiser are as much a part of Dreiser's final product as is his "original" draft. As this argument suggests, I think that the deletions show that more is at stake in the "new edition" than accuracy, but it reflects a longstanding critical desire to recuperate the great American realist, without his embarrassing sentimentality.
6. Sandy Petrey, "The Language of Realism, the Language of False Consciousness: A Reading of *Sister Carrie*," *Novel* 10 (1977): 104.
7. Cathy N. Davidson and Arnold E. Davidson, "Carrie's Sisters: the Popular Prototypes for Dreiser's Heroines," *Modern Fiction Studies* 23 (1977): 407; Daryl Dance, "Sentimentalism in Dreiser's Heroines, Carrie and Jennie," *CLA Journal* 14 (1970): 127–42.
8. Walter Benn Michaels, *The Gold Standard and the Logic of Naturalism* (Berkeley: University of California Press, 1987), pp. 29–58.
9. Philip Fisher, *Hard Facts: Setting and Form in the American Novel* (New York: Oxford University Press, 1985), pp. 14–21, 128–58.

consumption and desire, and realism with work and deprivation, is already generated by the narrative strategies of *Sister Carrie*, as a way of imagining and managing the contradictions of a burgeoning consumer society.

Although Dreiser starts by undermining the traditional locus of sentimental value in the virtue of the heroine and the middle-class home as a haven from the market, he does not thereby erase sentimental conventions; rather he reconstitutes marriage and domesticity as subjects of the market.[1] When Carrie steps off the train in Chicago to be greeted by her sister, the narrative dashes the conventions of the sentimental novel in which the middle-class home provides a shelter from the public marketplace. As Carrie embraces her sister, she loses the "affectional atmosphere" felt with the stranger on the train, Drouet, and finds "cold reality taking her by the hand" (p. 8) [7]. The Hansons' working-class flat not only offers no haven from the market but lies on a continuum with the workplace. In addition to inviting Carrie to live with them only to help them pay the rent, the Hansons distrust spending money for pleasure or for anything not related to "a conservative round of toil" (p. 10) [9–10]. Saving the little money they earn for a far-off plan to buy property, they spend money the way they work, hooked to a routine of delayed gratification. When Carrie leaves the Hansons, the narrative abandons the interrelated framework of domesticity and the work ethic which holds, in the Hansons' view, that "Carrie would be rewarded for coming and toiling in the city" (p. 11) [10]. As Dreiser was to articulate in *An Amateur Laborer*, Carrie soon discovers the absurdity of the notion of "earning your bread," and the greater importance of having "something which the world would buy."[2] To escape the dead end of the Hansons' home and the "round of toil" at the factory, Carrie finds she has only her self to sell in exchange for Drouet's "two soft, green, handsome ten-dollar bills" (p. 47) [45].

Although Hurstwood is a member of a different social class, his home serves as an extension of his work rather than as an alternative source of value. Just as his job requires that he act as an advertisement for the resort he manages, his family's conspicuous consumption serves as a banner for his own success and affluence. The hollowness of Hurstwood's home life is summarized by the chapter title "Convention's own Tinderbox" (p. 62) [59]. Where Carrie seeks an escape from the claustrophobia of working-class life by standing on the street outside the Hansons' apartment and then entering the

---

1. Davidson and Davidson argue that Dreiser exposes the failure of domesticity, as does June Howard in *Form and History in American Literary Naturalism* (Chapel Hill: University of North Carolina Press, 1985), p. 178.
2. Theodore Dreiser, *An Amateur Laborer*, ed. Richard W. Dowell (Philadelphia: University of Pennsylvania Press, 1983), p. 45.

world of the salesman, Drouet, Hurstwood escapes from the frigid atmosphere of his middle-class home to the warmth of hobnobbing with celebrities at his resort.

Domesticity in *Sister Carrie*, however, is never abandoned; rather it is reencoded as a marketable value. Like the readers counseled in *Ev'ry Month*, Carrie, at each stage of her life, recreates the conditions of domesticity in her makeshift homes and her play-act marriages. Dreiser describes the interiors she decorates for Drouet in Chicago and Hurstwood in New York in more detail than he does the sensuality between the lovers. Even these two men seem to value Carrie less for a risqué liaison than for a cozy domesticity. Drouet proudly invites guests to his home, and when Hurstwood flees to New York, he is especially gratified by his homey interior created with furniture bought on the installment plan. Hurstwood's final disintegration is marked not only by Carrie's abandonment but by his being forced to sell back the furniture. If sentimental domesticity is exposed as a convention in families at the beginning of the novel, it is reconstructed later in improvised settings, as though the couples were playing house. The reencoding of sentimental conventions in *Sister Carrie* can be seen further in the omnipresent rocking chair in the novel. Jane Tompkins has pointed to the rocking chair in the Quaker kitchen in *Uncle Tom's Cabin* as the seat of what she calls "sentimental power."[3] In *Sister Carrie*, the rocking chair mediates not only between motion and stasis in a mechanized society, or between private and public space, as Philip Fisher has shown, but between sentimentalism and realism, as the chair magically resurfaces, not in the kitchen, but in each rented room, from the Hansons' apartment to the Waldorf Astoria.[4] The rocking chair is the place where characters do not just observe the world outside their windows, but where they dream their sentimental fantasies of escape.

Just as domesticity is relocated in *Sister Carrie* from the stable home to rented spaces, sentimental language is divested of its traditional familial ties and reinvested in market-engendered values and consumer goods. Carrie's initial attraction to Hurstwood, for example, is described through a sentimental commentary on the inadequacy of words to "but dimly represent the great surging feelings and desires" that pass unspoken between two people (p. 88) [84]. When Hurstwood does speak, however, Carrie hears behind his words not feelings but, "instead of his words, the voices of things which he represented" (p. 88) [85]. This passage inverts sentimental signification, in which objects speak for the human heart. Dreiser attributes to the voice of "inanimate objects" more emotive power than he

---

3. Jane Tompkins, *Sensational Designs: The Cultural Work of American Fiction, 1790–1860* (New York: Oxford University Press, 1985), pp. 141–42.
4. Fisher, *Hard Facts*, pp. 154–55.

does to the words of any character. When Drouet, for example, takes Carrie to a restaurant for the first time, rescuing her from another job search, "as he cut his meat, his rings almost spoke. His new suit creaked." It is this voice, rather than his own incessant chattering, that "contributed the warmth of his spirit to her body" (p. 45) [43].

If things speak louder than both people and words, what language do they speak? They speak in the melodramatic cadence of seduction to a country girl bound for the city in search of work. During her train ride to Chicago, Carrie's dreams leave no room for the main purpose of her journey—a job; instead they revolve around the things she wants to buy. Whispering in her ear like the serpent in Eden, Drouet voices her desires and recasts the melodramatic role of seducer in the appropriate form of the traveling salesman. He describes the city as a vast department store for which his own appearance affects Carrie as an advertisement: "the purse, the shiny tan shoes, the smart suit, and the *air* with which he did things, built up for her a dim world of fortune, of which he was the centre" (p. 6) [5]. Like Hurstwood, Drouet is an "ambassador" for the things he represents.

Sentimental power in an earlier tradition lies in the home as retreat from the market; in this novel, sentimental power is reinvested in a market of consumer goods which serve as a retreat from both the home and the workplace. Carrie significantly enters the city at dusk, "that mystic period between the glare and gloom of the world when life is changing from one sphere or condition to another," two spheres governed by the opposing conditions of work and leisure (p. 7) [6]. As the narrative switches perspective from Carrie's first glimpse of the city to the people leaving work, her desires are joined to the general excitement of the "lifting of the burden of toil." The "soul of the toiler" speaks to itself in slightly archaic sentimental tones: "I shall soon be free. I shall be in the ways and the hosts of the merry. The streets, the lamps, the lighted chamber set for dining, are for me. The theatre, the halls, the parties, the way of rest and the paths of song—these are mine in the night" (p. 7) [6]. This desire, however, is labeled "the old illusion of hope," an illusion dashed for Carrie by her sister, whose "cold reality" is defined by the "grimness of shift and toil" (p. 8) [7]. Although Carrie moves to Chicago to work, her desires—marked by the language of sentiment—are invested in the escape from work. The opening of the novel divides Chicago into two cities not by space or even class, but by time—a liberated evening sphere of desire conceived of in terms of consumption, and the daytime confining sphere of work, in which cold reality is equated with the thwarting of desire. Most of the significant changes—or escapes—in the novel occur at night: Carrie's move with Drouet, her flight with Hurstwood, and her meeting with

Ames. In contrast to Hanson's work, which begins at dawn, appealing jobs take place at night and seem like amusement rather than work, as in Hurstwood's resort or Carrie's theaters.

The allure of the city at night inverts a familiar trope of "the mystery of the city," in which the threatening shadows of the city refer to lower-class haunts.[5] To Carrie on her first day, walking through the city as an applicant for a job, the "great streets" appear as "wall-lined mysteries" that exclude her from a world not of a dangerous underclass but of opulent objects of desire. Her first tour of the city in search of a job overwhelms her with a sense of her own powerlessness, "a sense of helplessness amid so much evidence of power and force which she did not understand" (p. 12) [12]. While new firms advertise their prosperity through large plate-glass windows, these windows are curiously opaque, as the labor that produces their wealth takes place in the back of the building, invisible from the streets. Carrie's small-town upbringing teaches her to read meaning on the surface of things. She interprets the windows as she would "the meaning of a little stone-cutter's yard at Columbia City, carving little pieces of marble for individual use," but she cannot fathom "yards of some huge stone corporation" (p. 12) [12]. Thus when Carrie finds her job, she assumes the identity conferred by this "goodly institution," with its "windows . . . of huge plate glass" (p. 21) [20]. Only when she goes to work does she see through the windows to the hidden factory.

Carrie does not remain passive before such overwhelming evidence of her own powerlessness. Like the Marches in *Hazard*, she actively creates significance out of the city's impenetrable facades. She scales down the vast city to a manageable, unthreatening size by translating its intimidating social structures into the sentimental language of consumption, transforming the city into a showcase for tangible commodities which speak to her. Unable to imagine people engaged in a social process of production, she does not question "what they dealt in, how they labored, to what end it all came," but instead imagines "far-off individuals of importance . . . counting money, dressing magnificently and riding in carriages" (p. 13) [12]. This desire for commodities and immediate pleasure provides Carrie with her strongest impulse to act, her "guiding characteristic" (p. 2) [2]; she is willing to argue with her taciturn brother-in-law to spend money on the theater, although in the same chapter she barely has the courage to enter a firm to apply for a job. Thus when she enters a department store for the first time, "she realised in a dim way how much the city held—wealth, fashion, ease—every adornment for women, and she longed for dress and beauty with a whole

5. On this trope, see Alan Trachtenberg, *The Incorporation of America: Culture and Society in the Gilded Age* (Hill and Wang: New York, 1982), chap. 4.

heart" (p. 17) [17]. The commodities in the department store speak the language of sentiment to the "whole heart" because they project in a "dim way" what is to Carrie an unrealized but desirable world that lies outside her current sphere of work.

The consumption of commodities in *Sister Carrie* functions in the novel to compensate for social powerlessness. Although Carrie and Hurstwood occupy opposite ends of the social scale, both are driven by their lack of social power. Despite Hurstwood's managerial position, he has no financial control over the business, and is not even permitted to handle the money in the cash register. His job is to act as though he were not working, to appear as the generous host rather than as the paid employee. He is described through the oxymorons of an "active manner" and "solid, substantial air," which create an image of solidity composed of the objects with which he adorns himself: "his fine clothes, his clean linen, his jewels, and above all, his own sense of his importance" (p. 33) [31]. Acting the role of host "lounging about," he transforms the conditions of powerlessness into a display of power through his studied pose of leisure. Yet clothes do not make the man, not because Dreiser opposes an interior self to an externalized masquerade, but because of the contrast between the display of status and the possession of social power. Hurstwood's precarious position as manager and husband is curiously similar to Lily's in *The House of Mirth*. At home Hurstwood is almost as powerless as Carrie at the Hansons'. His family surrounds him with an air of affluence and authority that ultimately lends prestige to his resort, but the discrepancy between his family's conspicuous consumption and its lack of social power undermines his authority at home. His wife and children long to enter the high society—families of bankers and industrialists—that they imitate. Thus Hurstwood's ambiguous social position spawns desires in his family which he cannot fulfill, and his impotence leads them to ignore him as head of the family. Although as a "man of authority" it "irritated him excessively to find himself surrounded more and more by a world upon which he had no hold, and of which he had a lessening understanding" (p. 153) [146], he never really had the control over his family he thinks he has lost (he had signed over all his property to his wife), just as he has no financial control over his work. Hurstwood's passion for Carrie can be understood less as a romantic rebellion against convention than as compensation for his lack of authority at home. One of her chief attractions for Hurstwood is her submissiveness: "nothing bold in her manner. Life had not taught her domination—superciliousness of grace, which is the lordly power of some women" (p. 107) [102]. When he first feels his control slipping at home, he consoles himself with the thought that "things might go as they would at his house, but he had Carrie outside of it" (p. 106) [101].

His treatment of Carrie as a commodity lies not only in spending money on her but more importantly in projecting into her the image of recovered authority he loses at home and at work.

The consumption of commodities in *Sister Carrie* not only compensates for the lack of power at work and at home but also expresses and channels a utopian desire for change, for the "good" which consumer goods promise.[6] Carrie's desire for change can be seen in her response to her first day at the shoe factory. She expresses her dissatisfaction most acutely walking home on the city streets which make her feel "ashamed in the face of better dressed girls who went by. She felt as though she should be better served, and her heart revolted" (p. 31) [30]. "Revolt" is linked to the voice of sentiment— the heart—and Carrie's sentimental rebellion turns not against factory work but against a discrepancy between the well-dressed girls and herself, a gap that could be filled by consumer goods. Later in the novel, when Carrie moves to New York, she has a similar reaction to her first stroll down fashionable Broadway:

> The whole street bore the flavor of riches and show, and Carrie felt that she was not of it. . . . It cut her to the quick, and she resolved that she would not come here again until she looked better. At the same time she longed to feel the delight of parading here as an equal. Ah, then she would be happy! (p. 227) [218].

Carrie translates the desire for change—for equality with other people—as she translates revolt, into the sentimental language of acquisition. This translation effaces any difference between dressing and parading as an equal and actually being one. Hurstwood similarly enacts his desire to become a celebrity by socializing with celebrities at his resort, where he in fact is hired to serve the people he treats as equals. When this position is threatened by his wife's ultimatum for a divorce, he worries obsessively not about responding but about receiving Carrie's response to his love letters. Carrie serves the same function for Hurstwood that clothes do for her; she promises magically to change him without his having to act.

The novel is interspersed with glimpses of alternative activities to the frenetic acquisitiveness of the main characters. Streetcar workers on strike, for example, attempt to gain power collectively by changing the conditions of their work. Later, as a strikebreaker, Hurstwood can no more join the strikers, when asked, than Carrie can follow Ames's advice to become a serious actress. "If I were you," says Ames, "I'd change" (p. 357) [342]. Both Carrie and Hurstwood share with Ames and the strikers the desire for change, yet rather

6. For the notion of utopian desire in mass culture I am drawing on Fredric Jameson's "Reification and Utopia in Mass Culture," *Social Text* 1 (Winter 1979): 130–48.

than actively effect that change, they seek to possess the object, or person, that promises magically to transform them. Carrie's conversation with Ames does not prod her to action. Instead it only makes her more acutely conscious of her lack of the "better thing" which Ames represents, and it increases both her "inactivity and longing" (p. 357) [342]. Wanting to be different takes the form of longing to have more, as identity is defined by the power to spend money. Thus, as Hurstwood loses this power, he becomes more and more anonymous. Although desire in *Sister Carrie* propels constant motion, it also becomes a substitute for actively changing either the social order or the individuals within it. This form of desire contributes to the paradoxical sense of stasis in the text at the times of greatest motion; Carrie is constantly on the move up the social scale—from one city, one man, one job to the next—yet she always seems to end up in the same place, as the final scene suggests, rocking, and dreaming, and longing for more. In *Sister Carrie* the desire for social change is channeled into the desire for novelty, the desire to construct a social reality in which change most often yields more of the same.

It has often been noted that desire, by definition, in *Sister Carrie* is never satisfied, that longing continually outstrips its objects, which lose their value as soon as they are possessed.[7] The characters always seem to be in pursuit of something that commodities promise but never quite deliver, because they seek in things around them an image of themselves. Unlike the Marches, who look for a familiar and stable self-image in an apartment, and Lily Bart, who seeks the outlines of a self in the eyes of others, the characters in *Sister Carrie* continually pursue an image of themselves as they might be—not as they are. Carrie is enamored of the theater for the same reason she desires clothes, because she believes that by dressing or by playing a part she can actually be transformed into the glamorous creature of her fantasies. Like Drouet, she hopes that the atmosphere of the fashionable resorts and theaters can rub off on the identity of those who frequent them.[8] Carrie desires things not for their own qualities or for pleasures they afford, but for the new self-image they seem to offer. Therefore, "seeing a thing, she would immediately set to inquiring how she would look, properly related to it" (p. 75) [72]. And Hurstwood's desire for her resembles Carrie's relationship to things, as he pursues in her an image of himself as he would like to be: youthful, powerful, and independent. Unable to fulfill this image by acting on the choices before him, he projects these attributes onto his ability to possess Carrie.

Dreiser's characters, however, look for themselves in things and in other people only to find what they are not. When Carrie observes

7. Michaels, *The Gold Standard*, p. 383.
8. On the importance of atmosphere in Dreiser's novels see Fisher, *Hard Facts*, p. 141.

the well-dressed clerks in the department store, she sees herself in their eyes "only to recognize in [them] a keen analysis of her own position—her individual shortcomings of dress and that *shadow* of manner which she thought must hang about her and make clear to all who and what she was. A flame of envy lighted in her heart" (p. 17) [17]. Carrie defines "who and what she was" by what she is not—by the fact that she is not as well dressed as the clerks. Carrie's only friend in the novel, Mrs. Vance, similarly serves as a yardstick for Carrie, who sees in Mrs. Vance all that she lacks: "the air of the petted and well-groomed woman. . . . She looked as though she was dearly loved and her every wish gratified" (p. 225) [216]. When they meet again, after Mrs. Vance has read of Carrie's stardom in the newspapers, Carrie looks down on, rather than up at, Mrs. Vance. It occurs to Carrie "that she was as good as this woman now—perhaps better. Something in the other's solicitude and interest made her feel as if she were the one to condescend" (p. 332) [319]. No two people in *Sister Carrie* meet as equals; one either condescends or is condescended to, is enviable or envies.

In a major study linking Dreiser's art to a culture of consumption, Philip Fisher suggests that commodities are projections of a collective psyche and that, in Dreiser's novels, the self is completely externalized in the surrounding city, which itself can be seen as a collection of commodities. "Far from being in any simple way estranged in the city," Fisher writes, "man is for the first time surrounded by himself. . . . Within the city anything outside the body is there only because it was projected there by will and need."[9] Consequently, identity is conferred on the self by the things around one. He therefore sees Carrie and Clyde Griffiths, the main character of *An American Tragedy*, as "blank center[s] engulfed by worlds" constituted by things, places, and the atmosphere they radiate.[1] Fisher, however, overlooks the contradiction exposed by Dreiser's novels in the structure of commodities: that they create common needs within a social hierarchy. Clyde may enter Gilbert's "world" by wearing the right clothes, but he has no foothold there because as a factory manager he cannot reproduce his cousin's position in the social hierarchy. Like Carrie, Clyde is trapped by this discrepancy between the desires evoked by commodities and the limits to his ability to fulfill those needs through his social position. Thus, the city does not only project human "will and needs" as Fisher suggests; it also projects the unequal social relations of power and domination. Fisher furthermore claims that "nowhere in Dreiser's novel is there the slightest trace of society, as that word is understood in nineteenth-

9. Ibid., p. 132.
1. Ibid., p. 147.

century novels. Instead there are worlds," and "worlds are neither economic, nor public, nor are they permanent centers of activity. Worlds are not generated by the webs of work because in Dreiser work itself is only one kind of atmosphere."[2] Echoing the romance thesis of American fiction, Fisher implicitly links the absence of society in Dreiser's novels to the lack of social classes structured by productive relations—"the webs of work." Yet in both *Sister Carrie* and *An American Tragedy*, the "worlds" projected by desire are generated by and continually come in conflict with a "society" constructed on relations of power located in the workplace. Work in Dreiser's novels is not reduced to atmosphere, but is the site of those power relations which fuel the desire for change that commodities promise but never fully realize.

It is this gap between desire and social power that reopens the space for sentimentality. Walter Michaels identifies Dreiser's sentimentalism with the excess of the capitalist economy, but the sentimental voice of commodities can also be seen to address the contradictions of a capitalist economy which locates desire solely in the realm of consumption generated by the power structure of production.[3] By marking the longing of the characters as sentimental, Dreiser shows how capitalism in the late nineteenth century gives rise to desires for "goods" that it cannot fulfill, and translates desire into the realm of the unreal.

*   *   *

ALAN TRACHTENBERG

Who Narrates? Dreiser's Presence in *Sister Carrie*†

> He is no philosopher.
> His only gift is to enact.
> All that his deepest self abhors,
> And learn, in his self-contempting distress,
> The secret worth
> Of all our human worthlessness.
> —Robert Penn Warren

2. Ibid., pp. 141, 142. A similar argument about the absence of society in Dreiser is made by Richard Poirier in *A World Elsewhere: The Place of Style in American Literature* (New York: Oxford University Press, 1966), pp. 235–50.
3. Michaels, *The Gold Standard*, pp. 41–58. For an analysis of Dreiser's relation to the culture of consumption that is closer to mine, see Rachel Bowlby, *Just Looking: Consumer Culture in Dreiser, Gissing, and Zola* (London: Methuen, 1985), chap. 4.
† From *New Essays on Sister Carrie*, ed. Donald Pizer (New York: Cambridge UP, 1991), 87–102. Reprinted by permission of Cambridge University Press.

1

Why has *Sister Carrie* so resolutely defied interpretation? Born into controversy when its original publisher tried to cancel its contract in 1900—the whole episode exaggerated by Dreiser into a notorious scandal of suppression—the novel has yet to free itself altogether from the fate of exemplifying a life or a cultural moment.[1] Few scholars dispute its importance—but as an event in the history of American mores and morals more than as a novel interesting for being just that: a work of fiction. Signs of change have appeared recently, including disagreements over what the novel may mean. Is the book for or against capitalism? Is it as sentimental as it often sounds? And the "bad" writing every critic, even the friendliest, has deplored—is it perhaps intentionally bad, Dreiser's effort at parody of the language of "false consciousness" to highlight a style of "realism" as antidote to the romantic pap, the "linguistic junk of commodified language" bred by consumer capitalism? What are the generic relations between "romance" and "realism" in the book? Recent readers have been prone to see the book as a battleground of styles, of genres, of ideologies, and to ask what *Sister Carrie* might mean for us today as a text of its own times.[2]

1. See the documents on "publication" and the "legend" gathered in Donald Pizer, ed., *Sister Carrie* (New York: Norton, 1970), pp. 433–470 [429–66]; all page references in the text are to this edition of the novel. [Throughout this essay, page references to this Norton Critical Edition are given in brackets after Tracktenberg's original citations—*Editor*.] I have found especially valuable for their integration of biographical and historical data with critical insight Ellen Moers, *Two Dreisers* (New York: Viking, 1969), especially parts 1–3; and Donald Pizer, *The Novels of Theodore Dreiser; A Critical Study* (Minneapolis: University of Minnesota Press, 1976), especially pp. 31–95. Two useful biographical studies are W. A. Swanberg, *Dreiser* (New York: Scribners, 1969), and Richard Lingeman, *Theodore Dreiser: At the Gates of the City, 1871–1907* (New York: Putnam, 1986).
2. I have in mind, in the order of my allusions to their themes, recent essays or chapters by Walter Benn Michaels, *The Gold Standard and the Logic of Naturalism* (Berkeley: University of California Press, 1987), chapter 1; Amy Kaplan, *The Social Construction of American Realism* (Chicago: University of Chicago Press, 1988), chapters 5–6; Sandy Petrey. "The Language of Realism, The Language of False Consciousness: A Reading of Sister Carrie," *Novel* 10 (Winter 1977): 101–13; and the exchange between Petrey and Ellen Moers, "Critical Exchange: Dreiser's Wisdom or Stylistic Discontinuities?" *Novel* 11 (Fall 1977): 63–69. The reference to "linguistic junk" is from Fredric Jameson's few remarks on Dreiser in *The Political Unconscious* (Ithaca: Cornell University Press, 1981), p. 159, which include the somewhat inscrutable obiter dictum: "The axiological paradox about Dreiser—he is best at his worst . . ." Sandy Petrey proposes a compelling but finally unpersuasive explanation, that the text of *Sister Carrie* can be likened to a battleground between discontinuous styles—the bad sentimentality of popular romance, and the good objective realism of the best dialogue and description. The former represents the "false consciousness" Dreiser wants to exorcise by exaggerating its irrelevance and parodying its destructive illusions, while the latter represents a Hemingway-like liberating honesty through which the illusions of consumer capitalism can be seen for what they are. There is much to recommend this view, but in the end it suffers from its own ingenuity and simplification. To divide Dreiser's writing in *Sister Carrie* into two competing styles is one mistake—the verbal discontinuities are multiple; to see the variety of styles as separable from each other is another—rare is the passage entirely free of authorial editorializing; and to valorize the Hemingway laconism as a novelistic style is yet another. See Gerard Genette's remarks in *Figures of Literary Discourse* (New York: Columbia University Press, 1982), p. 143, on the novelistic liabilities of the Hammett-Hemingway "purity" of narrative

The issue high on many scholarly agendas today is "representation." How does *Sister Carrie* portray its world, its characters, the springs of action within that world, itself as an action within the setting it projects in such extensive detail—what F. O. Matthiessen called "solid slabs of continuous experience?"[3] Critics of representation typically seek the revealing detail, the suspiciously self-contradictory passage; in a novel like Dreiser's they naturally focus on description—all those details about railroad journeys, city streets, department stores, Shore Drive mansions, the Broadway promenade, Bowery flophouses, elegant New York theatres and hotels. They seek patterns—of motion, performance, speech, characterization, and have opened the texture of the text to new meticulous investigation.[4]

Representation conceived as a description leaves unresolved the more difficult and opaque question of the novel as *narrative*, a *form* of action, the construction of point of view, a built arrangement of "scenes" and "pictures," to employ the Jamesian terms systematized by Percy Lubbock as aspects of the "craft of fiction."[5] Narrative also "represents," and *Sister Carrie* is before anything else a *story* told in a certain way—a way of story telling which shapes how we know what is being represented and how.

style. Finally, to see Dreiser as an implacable foe of consumer capitalism misses the positive value the novel sets upon Carrie's "false consciousness," for the things (commodities) which speak to her awaken precisely those desires commodity culture in the end cannot satisfy, thus advancing the process of her awakening. Dreiser's relation to the world he depicts is more ambiguous and dialectical than Petrey allows. I am indebted in my thinking about Dreiser's view of the positive elements within consumerism to a brilliant unpublished paper by James Livingston, "Form, Self, History: *Sister Carrie's* Absent Causes." Professor Livingston also sees the novel as a battleground—between the generic modes of "realism" and "romance"—a provocative historicizing and periodizing argument too rich to summarize here. Other recent works which propose useful reinterpretations of the novel in its history are Rachel Bowlby, *Just Looking* (New York: Methuen, 1985); Philip Fisher, *Hard Facts: Setting and Form in the American Novel* (New York: Oxford University Press, 1985); June Howard, *Form and History in American Literary Naturalism* (Chapel Hill: University of North Carolina Press, 1985); and Robert Shulman, *Social Criticism in Nineteenth-Century American Fiction* (Columbia: University of Missouri Press, 1987).

3. F. O. Matthiessen, *Theodore Dreiser* (New York: William Sloane Associates, 1951), p. 60. Matthiessen attributed Dreiser's method to his reading of Balzac. Writing in 1922 about his first encounter with Balzac's works in 1894—"It was for me a literary revolution"— Dreiser noted that the French author's "grand and somewhat pompous philosophical deductions, his easy and offhand disposition of all manner of critical, social, political, historical, religious problems, the manner in which he assumed as by right of genius intimate and irrefutable knowledge of all subjects, fascinated and captured me as the true method of the seer and the genius" (Pizer, ed., *Sister Carrie*, p. 402). The suggestion is strong that his reading of Balzac in this spirit contributed in a major way to the eclectic narrative method he devised for his own first novel in 1900.

4. See especially Fisher, *Hard Facts*, chapter 3, "The Life History of Objects: The Naturalist Novel and the City."

5. Percy Lubbock, *The Craft of Fiction* (New York: Viking, 1957), pp. 251–64. Lubbock's concern in these pages with "point of view—the question of the relation in which the narrator stands to the story" (p. 251) has, I believe, limited relevance to the characteristic interfusion by Dreiser (as by Balzac) of "reflective summary of events" (the Jamesian "picture"), the self-enactment of the events of the story ("scene"), and what Seymour Chatman, in *Story and Discourse: Narrative Structure in Fiction and Film* (Ithaca: Cornell University Press, 1978), p. 228, describes as "commentary" which can take the form of "an entire gamut of speech acts."

Is the form of *Sister Carrie* interesting enough to challenge analysis and interpretation? I think so; for nothing about the novel is more important, even culturally and historically, than its invention of a new way of telling a new American story—a new form for a new content. Of course a wall of prejudice stands in the way of a formalist (even a historically formalist) reading of this inaugural novel by a former newspaperman. Between Dreiser and the "craft of fiction" there has seemed to be little commerce. "Dreiser had no intention of creating anything like a Jamesian 'house of fiction,' " wrote Richard Poirier some twenty five years ago. "The shape of the material was the shape for the most part merely of his recollections. Writing for him obviously did not involve the 'building' of a world so much as reporting on one already existent."[6] More recent studies show that recurring patterns of images and actions—imagery of water, weather, doors, windows, rocking chairs, and acts of drifting, glimpsing, rocking—cannot be ignored as at least rudimentary signs of a motive to build rather than merely to recollect, as do more subtle foreshadowings, anticipations, and fragmentary but distinct elements of plot (coincidences, withheld information, deceptions, snatches of memory, even elements of crisis and *peripeteia*).[7]

Discussions of form in *Sister Carrie* have rarely ventured beyond the rise-and-fall pattern which dominates the New York half of the narrative (although Carrie's ascent and Hurstwood's decline begin their respective accumulations of momentum in Chicago), or the "plotting of inarticulate experience," by which Julian Markels meant, in an important essay in 1961, Dreiser's skillful method of arranging episodes "in order to dramatize with perfect coherence that absence of foreordained purpose in the universe, and its corollary, the hegemony of chance, of which he speaks so awkwardly in his 'philosophical' writings."[8] Markels concedes that Dreiser's "bad" writing (his "thick prose") coexists with his "good," and concludes that the author's "method of construction, which is his true source of strength," is "also his source of weakness," for it "disables Dreiser from portraying the emergence in human experience of moral consciousness and its corollary, literary style."[9]

Style has been the sticking point in efforts to pinpoint the narrative form of *Sister Carrie*. "Granted that he often writes as if language

6. Richard Poirier, *A World Elsewhere: The Place of Style in American Literature* (New York: Oxford University Press, 1966), p. 238. Subsequent page references in the text (WE) refer to this edition.
7. William L. Phillips, "The Imagery of Dreiser's Novels," *PMLA* 78 (December 1963): 572–75; reprinted in Pizer, ed., *Sister Carrie*, pp. 551–58. Also see Pizer on the novel's symbolism, *Novels of Theodore Dreiser*, pp. 31–95, and Fisher on its patterns of space and movement, *Hard Facts*, pp. 153–78.
8. Julian Markels, "Dreiser and the Plotting of Inarticulate Experience," *The Massachusetts Review* 2 (Spring 1961): 431–48; reprinted in Pizer, ed., *Sister Carrie*, p. 529.
9. *Ibid.*, p. 530.

itself were a bore," Richard Poirier remarks, echoing F. R. Leavis, "there remains the mystery of Dreiser's undeniable power over the imagination of even his severest critics" (WE 240). Talk of power and mystery, somehow connected with boring, slovenly writing, can still be heard in Dreiser criticism—a continuing sign, surely, of a still unresolved ambivalence toward this author and this novel, both from the other side of the tracks, so to speak, of the Jamesian house in which well-crafted fiction thrives among its other Anglo-Saxon and well-off inhabitants. Poirier himself provides a superb example, for as damning as are his remarks about Dreiser's disregard for writing good English and crafting fine fiction, the critic makes a dazzling about-face and finds virtue in all the alleged defects.

The view of Poirier's which I find at once most compelling and most mistaken concerns the role of Dreiser himself, or of his narrator-surrogate, within the novel. Dreiser refuses to give a clear characterization of *himself* in the book, Poirier observes—refuses to say where he stands in relation to his characters and his readers. The "fluctuations of voice" page after page represent a perverse self-fragmentation. Dreiser provides "no plastic coherence among the lurid varieties of self-characterization that emerge from his language." And all this is to the good, for "the fractured characterization Dreiser gives of himself as narrator of *Sister Carrie* is evidence of the integrity of his vision" (WE 240).

Poirier's views of the fractured narrator and of the integrity of vision are both, I believe, contestable despite their elegance. Contesting the first issue by showing a "plastic coherence" among the narrator's several voices will not be easy in a brief essay—indeed, to make the argument hold, nothing less than a page-by-page exegesis would do. My aim here can be only a suggestive argument, not a final one. The second issue inspires more confidence. Dreiser's is a vision, Poirier argues, "in which character—as a derivative of language and the power of language—is regarded as negligible" (WE 240). For Poirier the incoherence of narrative voice is the very sign of the coherence of the novel's asocial vision, its negation of the bourgeois ideology of the English novel, the vision whereby selves and societies are made by "characters" engaged in purposeful and self-reflective acts of language—in short, in conversation. Determined not to write a traditional novel, Dreiser "seems not even to care about achieving through language any shaped social identity." He simply rejects "those conversational involvements that imply that the self or society is formed by intensities of personal effort" (WE 240). More interested in "environmental force" than in "character," as the realists understood that fictive concept,[1] Dreiser is best—and

1. Leo Bersani, *A Future for Astyanax: Character and Desire in Literature* (Boston: Little, Brown, 1976), p. 53. "Behavior in realistic fiction is continuously expressive of character.

very good indeed—when he deals with "things," "the objects that fill what were the free spaces of America" (WE 249).

The challenge, then, is to see if the narrative voice of *Sister Carrie* does in fact make itself discontinuous and incoherent, and if it indeed treats character—in the sense of intersubjective relations mediated by language—as, in Poirier's word, "negligible."

Writing several years before Poirier, William J. Handy also argued that "the most immediate impression" of *Sister Carrie* "is that of the looming presence of Dreiser throughout the work."[2] But rather than fractured or incoherent, Handy sees Dreiser as an "unseen presence" who "integrates his own point of view with that of his characters" (H 523). How he achieves this—how, line by line, he insinuates his own point of view upon that of Carrie, complementing her limited self-awareness with his own more worldly knowledge, holds "the key to the effective artistic meaning of the novel" (H 525). "The ultimate effect becomes in *Sister Carrie* the expression of the powerful, omniscient presence of Dreiser, an integral part of every action, every attitude, every implicit and expressed value" (H 524).

Few critics have heeded Handy's extravagant but provocative point. Handy's most radical suggestion is that Dreiser installs himself as something more than or different from a technically omniscient narrator; he puts himself in the narrative as a subjective presence. The formal effect is to create for the reader a standpoint at once within and without Carrie's self-awareness—to hear and even speak her words in our silent mouthings of the text, while at once hearing and speaking another voice which comprehends what Carrie does not know of herself and cannot utter. And the final or totalizing effect for Handy is that the Dreiserian voice represents an "integration of self and art" (H 525)—what Ames helps Carrie realize, and which at the end Carrie moves tentatively toward.

Apparently random incidents carry messages about personality; and the world is thus at least structurally congenial to character, in the sense that it is constantly proposing to our intelligence objects and events which contain human desires, which give to them an intelligible form." The danger confronted by nineteenth-century realists such as Balzac, Bersani argues, is "a diffusion of meaning" threatened by excessive desire. "In a novelistic universe deprived of some governing pattern of significance, all events may be equally important" (p. 52). Although not directly cogent to the issue of the narrator's role in *Sister Carrie*, Michaels's debate with Bersani over desire, character, and novelistic form does bear on the question; see Michaels, *Gold Standard*, pp. 46–54. Fisher's characterization of Dreiser's characters as possessing a "self in anticipation" (p. 157) rather than one to which they might be "true" (p. 140) seems to follow from Poirier's observation about the "negligible" role of social selves in *Sister Carrie* compared to the world of articulate "objects."

2. William J. Handy, "A Re-Examination of Dreiser's *Sister Carrie*," *Texas Studies in Literature and Language* (Autumn 1959): 380–89; reprinted in Pizer, ed., *Sister Carrie*, p. 522: subsequent page references in the text (H) are to the latter edition. It is worth saying at this point that inserting himself as a "looming presence" was surely a deliberate choice (though not without buried psychic motives: see note 3 below). His competence in creating central point of view characters and in employing indirect discourse is perfectly evident in two stories written before *Sister Carrie*, "Nigger Jeff" and "McEwen of the Shining Slave Makers." See Howard, *Form and History*, pp. 106–107.

Handy's argument that Dreiser's narrative voice represents "authenticity as an expressive symbol" deserves to be cited directly:

> . . . the literary power lies in the singular way Dreiser's sensibility, as that sensibility inheres in every scene, acts to become an expressive symbol for artistic meaning. What is meant by Dreiser's sensibility is his felt, rather than formulated, values—those values which produce his own special responsiveness to the pathetic in life, his special kind of caring for mankind, his honest, his acute awareness of social cruelty, his sometimes reverential, sometimes bewildered, reaction to the way of life in America. It is this integration of self and art which produces the voice of Dreiser. (H 525)

The narrative voice presents itself, according to this eloquent view of Dreiserian pity and insight, as the needed alternative to the language of his "inarticulate" characters—to Carrie's especially, for she is Dreiser's own double, his shadow or surrogate.[3]

Handy and Poirier together help pose the problem I want to explore here: how the narrative voice functions in specific passages; whether fluctuations or discontinuities may be taken as facets of one voice, a controlling narrative agency which may be the main thing, the real point of interest in the novel. What *Sister Carrie* means, what it means in its own history and in ours, even what the novel is really *about*: these unsettled questions have quickened the contemporary life of this novel, especially in the present climate of historicist criticism. Character and society (or what constitutes "the social") are cognate issues, and throw open the door to historical interpretation of the novel, how it depicts its social world, how it understands the construction of character and of the social dimension of experience under the conditions of life it sets in motion. Analysis of the narrative voice, its distinctive role as a presence—its role in *socializing* the narrative—is what I explore here, with the prospect that reading the narrator back into the novel may help us read the novel itself back into its history, and make it more meaningfully available to our own.

---

3. The imaginative rapport between Dreiser and Carrie may well be the chief issue in the problem of the narrator's relation to his materials—one which I do my best to scant in this essay; it is simply too large, too dangerous for a brief discussion. Moers, *Two Dreisers*, is especially good on Dreiser's use of family experiences in the novel and suggests his ambivalence. The best insights into the narrative effects of Dreiser's doubling himself in his portrayal of Carrie as self-punishment for his own "wild dreams of some far-off supremacy" are in Robert Penn Warren, *Homage to Theodore Dreiser* (New York: Random House, 1971); Warren writes (p. 331) that "*Sister Carrie* appears as the projection of his own secret conflict and self-scrutiny; perhaps not the projection of them, but the means by which he discovered them at all." A full account of the sources of Dreiser's alternating closeness to and distance from Carrie must take the particular Dreiserian psychosis of his early career into account.

2

Toward the close of Chapter 1, as the train nears Chicago and Carrie tentatively responds to Drouet's gambit, "You'll be at home if I come around Monday night?" with "I think so"—they had just exchanged names and addresses and certain unspoken intimations—another voice, neither Carrie's nor Drouet's, enters the scene:

> How true it is that words are but vague shadows of the volumes we mean. Little audible links, they are, chaining together great inaudible feelings and purposes. (6) [6]

This is not the first authorial intervention in the opening chapter; recall the Balzacian observations as early as the third paragraph. There the author's narrative voice ironizes the familiar sentimental/ evangelical text, "the city has its cunning wiles" (1) [1], and sets up polarities ("better," "worse") which melodramatically predefine the possible fate of "a girl [who] leaves home at eighteen." These polarities present in the simplest, boldest, and apparently most sincere form the very terms the subsequent narrative will transvalue. Of course we cannot yet anticipate the narrative role of the better/worse syndrome, but it is not long (in the following Chicago chapters) before we realize that Carrie may well turn out "better" at the end for having been "worse" at the beginning—better, that is, in the transvalued perspective the narrative will meticulously, often laboriously, construct in the course of the novel. The method of constructing a new perspective upon these old terms of popular/ sentimental/evangelical judgment on country girls leaving home for the big city includes interventions such as this passage about words as vague shadows of meanings, to which we shall shortly return.

Early in Chapter 1 we cannot yet foretell the terms of a transvalued "bettering" process—though the direction is anticipated by the remark in the fourth paragraph, that "Books were beyond her interest—knowledge a sealed book" (2) [2], which we may recall at the end of the novel when we see Carrie, discontented in her success, reading *Père Goriot* (363) [349]. Balzac had been recommended to her by Ames, whose "ideals burned in her heart" (293) [281], and the effect of the story of Rastignac's pursuit of love and success in Paris was "That for the first time, it was being borne in upon her how silly and worthless had been her earlier reading, as a whole" (363) [349]. In the original manuscript Dreiser had made explicit the significance of Balzac to Carrie's own desires for an elusive happiness. The original passage has Carrie speak of the sadness of Lucien de Rubempré in *The Great Man from the Provinces*:

> "Yes," he [Ames] answered, "if a man doesn't make knowledge his object, he's very likely to fail. He didn't fail in anything but

love and fortune, and that isn't everything. Balzac makes too
much of those things. He wasn't any poorer in mind when he
left Paris than when he came to it. In fact he was richer, if he
had only thought so. Failure in love isn't so much."

"Oh, don't you think so?" asked Carrie, wistfully.

"No. It is the man who fails in his mind who fails completely.
Some people get the idea that their happiness lies in wealth and
position. Balzac thought so, I believe. Many people do . . ." (482
Penn)

These deleted lines clarify (perhaps too obviously) the significance
of the Balzac text Carrie reads at the end—a sign not just of superior
reading habits, but the beginnings of the habit of *critical* reading by
which she reflects upon her own experience by means of "serious"
reading. Her response to *Père Goriot* suggests that at the end she
had begun to unseal the book of knowledge.

In Chapter 1, however, Carrie's train ride to Chicago falls squarely
within the pattern of the melodrama of moralistic worsening. Like
the master of disguise in the evangelical ur-melodrama of "better"
and "worse," the cunning city "appeal[s] to the astonished senses in
equivocal terms. . . . what falsehoods may not these *things* breath
into the unguarded ear!" (2 [1]; emphasis supplied) The appeal of
the city *speaks* through *things*, and we are prepared at once for the
proliferation of "voices" in this text. " 'That,' said a voice in her ear,
'is one of the prettiest little resorts in Wisconsin' " (2) [2] is unmistakably a voice performing the role of tempter, the city's wiles in the
guise of a sweet-talking tongue. As soon as she replies "Is it?" Carrie's
career of conventional worsening has begun, and the narrator's self-
assumed task, implied by his ironic tone in the third paragraph, is to
subvert that judgment, to convert it slowly, painstakingly, cumula-
tively into another perspective, the complex point of view of the full
narrative as it unfolds.

The city has many wiles, and Drouet represents only the initial
voice that Carrie will encounter. His whisper in her ear suggests an
allegorical role; but Drouet is of course a fully actual person, a historical being whose role in the melodrama of the opening paragraphs
derives from an image of himself internalized from such images as
are available in his culture, an image of such a man as he imagines
himself to be. His voice in Carrie's ear bespeaks a historical character
expressed and particularized by those unconscious allegorical shad-
ings in his whispering voice. And her "unguarded" ear itself implies
a history, for it is only a partially innocent ear; we have already
learned in the fourth paragraph of Carrie's readiness to assume the
role of "half-equipped little knight," a role scripted by the popular
melodrama infiltrating an emerging urban commercial culture in just
the years covered by the novel, the late 1880s and 1890s—a culture

produced for mass consumption, of sentimental magazine fiction, costume historical romances, staged melodramas and musical reviews, popular ballads on sentimental themes (of which Dreiser's brother, Paul Dresser, was one of the most celebrated authors).[4]

The flirtation-seduction scene on the train replicates the conventionality of the sermon parodied in the third paragraph (we will soon learn how continuously present in the narrative will be allusions to the moral polarities, the "better" and "worse" of the evangelical-sentimental melodrama by which life imitated art in the middle regions of turn-of-the-century culture in America). After a few paragraphs of idle talk about resorts and hotels (Carrie's initiation into the *spoken* acknowledgment of such sites of pleasure), the narrative voice once more intervenes, this time in the guise of the social historian who will be available throughout the ensuing narrative not just to assure the reader that the story plays itself out on a ground of reliable fact, but more important, to sharpen the reader's attention to a dialectical tension between historical fact and theatricalized and sentimental illusion. The omniscient narrator provides social information—Carrie's mind and her social class, for instance, as "a fair example of the middle American class" (2) [2], or Drouet as "a type of the travelling canvasser for a manufacturing house" (3) [3]. These details help us see the flirtation in progress in historical-social as well as personal terms: a male salesman who is also a "masher" (another historical "type") playing up to a naive but self-interested country girl "quick to understand the keener pleasures of life, ambitious to gain in material things" (2) [2]—in short, prepared by an implied socialization already in process to enter the city as an eager consumer of the personal goods Drouet's vocation signifies: the flood of personal goods into the urban market which was one of the distinctive characteristics of the 1890s.[5]

4. Moers, *Two Dreisers*, contains an excellent, vivid account of Dreiser's own involvements with the emerging metropolitan mass culture, his relations with his brother Paul, who epitomized "metropolitan celebrity," and his own experience as a writer of magazine fiction. The essays in Richard W. Fox and T. J. Lears, eds., *The Culture of Consumption* (New York: Pantheon, 1983) contain relevant materials: see especially Christopher Wilson, "The Rhetoric of Consumption: Mass-Market Magazines and the Demise of the Gentle Reader, 1880–1920," pp. 39–64.

5. Livingston's unpublished essay (see note 2 above, p. 523) offers a valuable perspective on the political economy of the era represented by the novel. Other relevant works on cultural change and political economy in the period include Lewis Erenberg, *Steppin' Out: New York Nightlife and the Transformation of American Culture, 1890–1930* (Chicago: University of Chicago Press, 1981); T. J. Lears, *No Place of Grace: Antimodernism and the Transformation of American Culture, 1880–1920* (New York: Pantheon, 1981); William R. Leach, "Transformations in a Culture of Consumption: Women and Department Stores, 1890–1925," *Journal of American History* 71 (1984): 319–42; Kathy Peiss, *Cheap Amusements: Working Women and Leisure in Turn of the Century New York* (Philadelphia: Temple University Press, 1986); Martin Sklar, *The Corporate Reconstruction of American Capitalism, 1890–1916* (Cambridge University Press, 1988); Warren Susman, " 'Personality' and the Making of Twentieth Century Culture," in *Culture as History: The Transformation of American Society in the Twentieth Century* (New York: Pantheon, 1984),

"Lest this order of individual should permanently pass," the narrator adds to his account of the "drummer" and the "masher"—terms which had appeared "at that time" (we have already learned in the opening paragraph that the time is "August, 1889")—"let me put down some of the most striking characteristics of his most successful manner and method" (3) [3]. By the conventional literary politeness of "let me" the Dreiserian narrator plants himself within the text, becomes the implied "I" of the narrative ("I" will appear literally in Chapter 33 where the narrator distinguishes between "the higher mental development" and "the common type of mind" [241] [232]), thus qualifying, though inconspicuously, his claim to omniscience, to a privileged place in the narrative from which he might speak (as historian, for example) with unchallengeable objectivity. At this early stage of the narrative whatever ambiguity attaches to "let me" and the implied presence of a narrating *character* barely causes a ripple. The third person referent, "his," introduces a more immediately functional ambiguity. The pronoun clearly designates Drouet, but Drouet as a *type* and thus also not-Drouet. The voice in Carrie's ear now appears as both himself and not-himself, a person and a social type. His representivity as "drummer" and "masher" grounds his *personal* identity, places him in the reader's *social* cognition, recognizes him as a creature of a collective history (the word "type" implies that there are countless more like him). Throughout Drouet remains "the drummer," Carrie the "little toiler" and "the shop girl" or "that little soldier of fortune," and Hurstwood "the manager" and "the ex-manager." Introduced by the voice of omniscience—what the unobtrusive narrator can be assumed properly to know about his characters and their situations—social representivity and its historical origins becomes contrapuntal to the popular moral allegory in the narrative perspective, whose complication begins at once in Chapter 1.

In these early passages of intervention the narrator's point of view poses no problem. The narrator as historian fills in or documents social facts to be absorbed by the reader as signs not only of the specific social character of the individual named Drouet (his ontological dependency on the larger categorical name "drummer"), but as signs too of the social constitution of the entire fictive world in which the story unfolds: the fact that the immediate sensory world is a *society* in which individuals, at least from a perspective above and beyond their own self-realization (their roles within the internalized melodrama they imagine as their "real" and "free" beings), represent types or classes, countless absent others. As the narrative

pp. 271–85; and William Appleman Williams, *The Contours of American History* (Cleveland: World Publishing Co., 1961).

progresses, more inward meanings of "social" will appear, but here, in this early intervention, the chosen method, drawn from the repertoire of the nineteenth-century realistic novel, takes the form of an omniscient narrative voice exercising itself from beyond and behind the subjectivities of the introduced characters.

Not until the two sentences about words as shadows of meanings which appear as the train nears Chicago do we catch something significantly different in Dreiser's narrative voice—a commentary which establishes a new relation between narrative voice and narrative event. The opening sentences of a paragraph of reflection on the exchange of names and addresses and the tentative date for Monday night, the lines momentarily draw the reader's attention away, for the first time in the chapter, from the immediate scene toward an idea in the form of a general proposition, in this case an idea embodied in figurative images of shadows, links, chains. The rough meaning seems obvious enough: spoken words reveal only partially what people really feel and mean. That idea had been planted two pages earlier:

> There was much more passing now than the mere words indicated. He recognized the indescribable thing that made up for fascination and beauty in her. She realized that she was of interest to him from the one standpoint which a woman both delights in and fears. (5) [5]

In this case the narrator supplements the "mere words" of Drouet and Carrie by claiming his privilege of omniscience to tell us directly and authoritatively what, from the narrative point of view, *he* knows: what Drouet "recognized" (something "indescribable") and what Carrie "realized" (her ambivalent response to her perception of his "interest").

Now, as the train nears Chicago, Dreiser expostulates in a different voice coming from a different location upon the implication of "mere words," a two-sentence metaphoric discourse on language and meaning. Here he exceeds the normal privilege of omniscience. He introduces a voice as if from *inside* the narration (recalling the now silently implied "let me"), yet registered in a tone and diction quite different from that of the narrative proper.

It will be useful to pause here to clarify the technical features of Dreiser's rather sudden appearance in a different voice at just this juncture. We can call upon the distinctions between "narrative" and "discourse" Gerard Genette draws from the linguistic theorist Emile Benveniste, the "opposition between the objectivity of narrative and the subjectivity of discourse. Narrative objectivity means "the absence of any reference to the narrator," or as Benveniste puts it: "As a matter of fact, there is then no longer even a narrator. The events are set forth chronologically, as they occur. No one speaks here; the events seem to narrate themselves." If narrative is apparently autonomous, discourse is dependent upon a distinct speaker.

> In discourse, someone speaks, and his situation in the very act of speaking is the focus of the most important significations; in narrative, as Benveniste forcefully puts it, *no one speaks*, in the sense that at no moment do we ask ourselves *who is speaking, where, when,* and so forth, in order to receive the full signification of the text.

The relations between narrative and discourse, Genette observes, remain in balance in "the classical age of objective narration, from Balzac to Tolstoy," but change radically in the modern period.[6]

To ask "who is speaking" in the Dreiserian discursive passages is to find oneself wrestling precisely with the problem Poirier and Handy raise: the actual presence of a figure called "Dreiser" within the narrative. If he is there, then discourse has its clear, unequivocal source, its *someone*. If he is not there as such, then the voice of discourse is equivocal, a problematic posed by the "fluctuating voices" of the narrative. Although he seems to want to employ a signified authorial discourse—direct intervention in his own person—in a manner closer to that of Fielding than to that of, say, Howells, Dreiser remains essentially within the classical mode of "objective narration." He attempts to keep narrative and discourse separate, though his discursive appearances often also narrate or "recount," as Genette argues that discourse by its nature can do—that is, they can narrate from within the mode of discourse, in *someone's* voice (this identity of a speaker distinguishing discursive narration from objective narration proper). Dreiser's exploitation of the inherent impurity of discourse, as Genette describes it, indicates the hybrid nature of his narrative voice—which in turn suggests his attempt to accommodate his narrative to a new novelistic subject matter, a new point of view toward his material and his reader, and a new historical situation for American fiction. The unusual character of Dreiser's narrative in *Sister Carrie*, as both Poirier and Handy in their different ways apprehend it, derives from an innovative fusion of narrative and discourse, an equivocal and premodernist reordering of the priorities of the two modes—for the sake, it seems likely, of allowing the novice author greater freedom to make the story he recounts both its own and *his* own story: the story of his subjective experience of it mediating the story proper.

The discursive paragraph in question opens with two separate tropes which together comprise a strangely but not incoherently mixed metaphor. Then the passage returns to the interrupted scene

6. Genette, *Figures*, pp. 138, 139, 140, 142.

which is presumed to have remained in progress during the narrator's subjective commentary—that is to say, not so much interrupted but momentarily turned away from, as in a dramatic aside by a choric speaker:

> How true it is that words are but vague shadows of the volumes we mean. Little audible links, they are, chaining together great inaudible feelings and purposes. Here were these two, bantering little phrases, drawing purses, looking at cards, and both unconscious of how inarticulate all their real feelings were. Neither was wise enough to be sure of the working of the mind of the other. He could not tell how his luring succeeded. She could not realize that she was drifting, until he secured her address. Now she felt that she had yielded something—he, that he had gained a victory. Already they felt that they were somehow associated. Already he took control in directing the conversation. His words were easy. Her manner was relaxed. (6) [6]

The opening figures—words, shadows, volumes, links, chains—give the reader pause, require more than a quick reading to parse. As an ensemble of tropes they elicit from the reader an act of semantic analysis drawing attention away from the ongoing narrative they pedantically comment upon. Moreover, instead of clearly signified meanings we find ourselves amid ambiguous alternative meanings. What do volumes (material books? an immaterial quantity of space?) have in common with chains, which might imprison and isolate as much as join together? If volumes refer to books, do chains made up of word-links (whose relation to meaning is both shadowy and inaudible) imply sentences, lexical chains, of which books—this book we hold in hand, for instance—consist? Do the metaphors, then, warn us not to take the meanings of this very novel as exactly cognate with the actual words on the page, but urge us instead to attend to "great inaudible feelings and purposes" which lie somewhere beyond the written words yet "linked" to them, as shadows are metonymically linked or joined as traces (what Charles Sanders Peirce calls "indices") of their material source? The vague shadow of a meaning reveals at least that meaning is somewhere in the vicinity, if not exactly *in* or identical to the lexical signification of the exact word casting the shadow. Why does Dreiser introduce such apparent skepticism, which might well be taken as a reflection upon his own novelistic purposes, at just the point when Carrie's "I think so" expresses such an ambiguously indecisive response to the masher's advances—unless he wished readers to draw an analogy between the small but portentous talk passing between Carrie and Drouet and his own conversation, as narrator, with the reader?

One implication of the metaphoric figure is that words resemble or behave like *things;* they share density and mass, cast shadows, and possess autonomous force enough to combine themselves into chains. The metaphor thus plants an unconscious association we have already encountered in the fourth paragraph, where things breathe falsehoods into unguarded ears, and which we will encounter explicitly, in another passage of discourse, in a later chapter. True, the metaphors explain little about the logical or semiotic relation between words and meanings, except to imply that the relation is ambiguous. Words are only partial signs; their thing-like power lies precisely in this, in their imprecision—in what their ambiguity brings forth as absences, palpable half-disclosures like shadows, like those "little phrases" bandied back and forth between Carrie and Drouet the "real feelings" of which they are "unconscious." The discursive voice intervenes in order to translate that felt absence, not into precise lexical meaning, but into precisely rendered imprecision—what "he could not tell," what "she could not realize." (We will see later how the narrator makes his motive and function of "translation" explicit.)

The metaphoric discourse on novelistic language, on spoken words and inchoate meanings, coheres, then, into an observation absorbed back into the narrative proper as a discourse on conscious and unconscious meanings, chiefly on the failure of intention to achieve either silent or spoken articulation. It is striking, especially to readers accustomed to thinking of *Sister Carrie* as a "naturalist" narrative concerned almost entirely with "externalities," to discover how much attention in the opening chapter (and throughout the novel) the narrator devotes to what each character is "conscious" of, what each "knew" of the other's mind. The second paragraph in the original manuscript begins, "To be sure she was not conscious of any of this" (that the threads binding her to girlhood and home "were irretrievably broken" by the departure described in the first paragraph) (3 Penn). Just after Drouet appears as a "voice in her ear" we learn that "for some time she had been conscious of a man behind" (2) [2] and after their opening chit-chat we read: "All the time she was conscious of certain features out of the side of her eye" (3) [2]. We learn very early Carrie's capacity to dissemble, to pretend *not to be* conscious, to seem unconcerned and unaware—as she does again in the chapter's final paragraph when, in company with her sister, she exchanges a covert look with Drouet (8) [8].

The local relevance of the commentary is clear enough:[7] neither

---

7. Donald Pizer makes the important point that "The underlying function of many of Dreiser's philosophical comments . . . is less to establish a particular abstract truth which should guide our rational consideration of an incident or character than to elicit from us a sentiment which aids Dreiser fictionally at the moment in question" (Pizer, *Novels of Theodore Dreiser*, p. 87). The case might be made even more strongly that virtually all his apparent

of the characters possesses sufficient self-consciousness, powers of articulation, or wisdom to understand just what is happening in the little drama they are enacting. Both are engaged in the playing of roles, in small dissemblings, rehearsed performances; they are actors uncertain of their scripts (Drouet less so), though we as readers can plainly enough see a conventionally melodramatic flirtation-seduction in progress.[8] Both are "unconscious of how inarticulate all their real feelings were," yet they play at expressing or withholding feelings. "Neither was wise enough to be sure of the working of the mind of the other."

Unconscious, inarticulate, real feelings, the working of the mind of the other: they are key terms in the novel as a whole, terms Dreiser returns to again and again to confirm the narrative strategy initiated in the opening chapter, and to suggest, again surprisingly, that *consciousness* is precisely what this novel is largely about—a notion of consciousness which remarkably resembles that which William James developed in the same years. According to James, consciousness is (1) the *experience* of thought, rather than an abstract capacity as such, and (2) inseparable from the world of things which we speak of being conscious *of*. Dreiser's thingness of words and the wordness (or articulateness) of things, rendered by the narrator as voices, corresponds closely to James's argument that thoughts and things, rather than different substances, represent different functions, different experiences of the same nameless thing.[9] Thus Dreiser's typical discursive practice of departing from narrative proper at certain key points reveals a consistent motive: to provide in direct address to the reader (as discourse) an account (often figurative, in tropes of water, tides, weather, and so on) of inner experience, of intersubjective awareness of the other, which neither Carrie nor Drouet nor Hurstwood is capable of supplying in a conversational or meditational voice—yet which constitutes the form and content of each character's self-awareness. They cannot say so for themselves; it takes the narrator to say it to us for them.

* * *

digressions, when read with an ear to Dreiser's irony, have local before universal applications.

8. For an *almost* convincing account of how conventional a middle-brow sentimental-seduction novel *Sister Carrie* is, see Leslie Fiedler, *Love and Death in the American Novel* (New York: Criterion Books, 1960), pp. 241–48. See also Sheldon N. Grebstein, "Dreiser's Victorian Vamp," *Midcontinent American Studies Journal* 4 (Spring 1963): 3–12; reprinted in Pizer, ed., *Sister Carrie*, pp. 541–51, for a useful examination of Dreiser's making of Carrie into a conventional "love goddess," with "ambivalent sophistication and naivete" (p. 551).

9. John J. McDermott, ed., *William James: A Comprehensive Edition* (New York: Random House, 1967), "Does 'Consciousness' Exist?" pp. 169–83, and "The Notion of Consciousness," pp. 184–93.

KEVIN R. McNAMARA

The Ames of The Good Society:
Sister Carrie and Social Engineering†

1

Bob Ames has been getting bad press recently and I want to correct it—not necessarily by rehabilitating him, but certainly by seeing him for what he is. The electrical engineer in Theodore Dreiser's *Sister Carrie* who was for an earlier generation of critics like Ellen Moers an "intellectual midwesterner brought on near the novel's end to express Dreiser's own opinions," particularly opinions that suggest the "shallow[ness]" of the other characters' levels of "metropolitan success,"[1] is now something of a prude while Carrie, not Ames, is said to tell us the truth about the market.

Walter Benn Michaels has been most responsible for this reversal in Ames's fortunes. His essay, "*Sister Carrie's* Popular Economy," undoes decades of criticism of Dreiser's novel by rereading the relations between realist/naturalist literature, the self, and capitalism. It moves in three closely related directions. Against Leo Bersani, he argues that literary excesses of desire like Carrie's "are not subversive of the capitalist economy but constitutive of its power." They aren't— this is Michaels's larger point—because the essential, autonomous self projected by theorists of laissez-faire capitalism was only a mystification. In reality, he writes, "the capitalism of the late nineteenth and early twentieth centuries acted more to subvert the ideology of the autonomous self than to enforce it," since the economy of speculation that for him is the United States' economy in that period "runs on desire, which is to say . . . the impossibility of ever having enough money," that causes the speculator incessantly to risk what he has (is). In *Sister Carrie*, the representative self, Carrie Meeber-Drouet-Madenda-Hurstwood-Murdock-Wheeler-Madenda, is defined not by the properties she naturally possesses (the theory of possessive individualism), but by what she lacks but desires. At the heart of the self, then, is "a nothing of desire" that makes the self "speculative" because "in *Sister Carrie*, satisfaction itself is never desirable; it is instead the sign of incipient failure, decay, and finally death.[2]

† From *Criticism* 34 (Spring 1992): 217–35. Reprinted by permission of Wayne State University Press.

1. Ellen Moers, *Two Dreisers* (New York: Viking, 1969), 109, 103. Theodore Dreiser, *Sister Carrie* (1900; reprint New York: Bantam, 1982); page references for the novel will be made in the text. [Throughout this essay, page references to this Norton Critical Edition are given in brackets after McNamara's original citations—*Editor.*]
2. Walter Benn Michaels, "*Sister Carrie's* Popular Economy," *Critical Inquiry* 7 (1980): 386,

In a local but important argument in American literary history, Michaels opposes this speculative self to a self built on what William Dean Howells called "character" and Michaels, quoting *The Rise of Silas Lapham*, defines for us as something that "resists fluctuation; [it is] 'never the prey of mere accident and appearance.' " While crediting Howells's "commitment to social justice," Michaels produces a reading of Howells's moralized response to capitalist excess in order to place him at the head of a tradition that includes Bersani, but, more importantly, "a certain strain of American criticism, a strain that has by no means died out today," whose "gentility consist[s] not in being insufficiently critical of [its] society but in being scandalized by it." The literary history is important for my reevaluation of Ames's function in the novel because according to Michaels, "The closest anyone comes in *Sister Carrie* to articulating this Howellsian morality is, of course, the midwesterner Ames."[3] Ames is, so we are reminded, contemptuous of the sentimental tradition's emotional excesses, respectful of serious art, and a believer that one can occupy only one place at a time and should find happiness in it.

At the risk of placing myself among the scandalized, I want to contest both Carrie's status as a speculator and Ames's anachronistic gentility. Recasting Carrie is, I think, the easier task of the two, but also the less interesting, since we need only read the novel for signs of her speculative activity. What we will see is that Carrie engages in something less like speculation than magical thinking. Dreiser defines her "high-flown speculations" as "calculat[ion] upon that vague basis which allows one the subtraction of one sum from another without any perceptible diminution" (23) [21], and the imaginative exaggerations by which she "exercised thoughts of a thousand dollars" on a base of fifty cents (126) [112]. The closest she gets to speculation is when her roommate in New York, Lola, encourages her to demand forty dollars a week after she is promoted to a speaking role in a play. But Carrie instead asks the manager, " 'How much do I get?' " When she hears that she will make thirty-five dollars, she is too "Astonished and delighted" to demand the other five (342–43) [324]. We read that, in general, she has "little power of initiative" (244) [216], and that her self-regard is "not strong" (2) [2]. Indeed, in The Fair department store she does not desire objects; they make "claim[s] . . . on her" (18) [16]. Michaels himself notes in one instance what I would elevate to a general pattern: others help her to want. While Michaels calls it speculation,

388, 383, 382. See also Leo Bersani, "Rejoinder to Walter Benn Michaels," *Critical Inquiry* 8 (1981): 158–64; and Walter Benn Michaels, "Fictitious Dealing: A Reply to Leo Bersani," *Critical Inquiry* 8 (1981): 165–71.
3. Michaels, "Popular Economy," 380, 377, 390, 389, 381.

Philip Fisher describes Carrie's "anticipatory self," in whose inner world "The psychological notion of down payments, installment credit and commodity speculations is . . . entirely in place," and Amy Kaplan finds Carrie "sell[ing] her self in a repetitive gesture that constructs the self," I prefer to think of Carrie as a "speculum." That is, Carrie is a speculative instrument (she is "capital" [353] [313]) with which others enter the market—although none of them have anything near the speculative prowess of Frank Cowperwood, Dreiser's *Financier*—and a mirror reflecting her society, which makes her an instrument of reproduction, not production.[4] While in my reading she continues to have no stable identity, it is not because she is constantly producing herself. Rather, as she is made and made over by those characters who focus her vague desire, she becomes an example of how the self is produced through its position in the social and economic systems. Her success is offered as a justification of the new economic and social arrangements, and at great cost to the ideology of possessive individualism, but not in the way Michaels thinks.

Instead of retracing the path of Carrie's evolution to understand Dreiser's representation of the relations between self, market, and society at the turn of the century, however, I will focus on Ames's explanation of how she becomes, in his words, a figure for "all desire" (385) [342]. Ames's words seem at once to advertise and to contain an excess of desire. Yet, the excess in Ames's words is one that Michaels fails to contain. For, if Ames's advice to Carrie not to "wring [her] hands over far-off things" (384) [340] is advice born of "an economy of scarcity, in which power, happiness, and moral virtue are seen to depend finally on minimizing desire," as Michaels also notes, when Ames advises her "If I were you, I'd change" (386) [342] he comes to "represent to Carrie . . . an ideal of . . . perpetual desire" and thus becomes desirable to her.[5] Carrie, clearly, is not speculating in this passage; however, Ames appears to speculate with himself by speculating on the possibility of speculation with Carrie. To say that

4. Ibid., 382; Philip Fisher, "Acting, Reading, Fortune's Wheel: *Sister Carrie* and the Life History of Objects," *American Realism: New Essays*, ed. Eric J. Sundquist (Baltimore: Johns Hopkins University Press, 1982), 263; Amy Kaplan, *The Social Construction of American Realism* (Chicago: University of Chicago Press, 1988), 139; Theodore Dreiser, *The Financier* (1912; New York: New American Library, 1967).

   Were I to consider Carrie in depth, I would look less to how "Carrie's insatiability suggests that for Dreiser capitalism was just the economic transcription of a feminine biology" (Michaels, "Fictitious Dealing," 170), than to how she emblematizes what Luce Irigaray writes is the condition of "women on the market." For, from the " 'natural' body" of Carrie Meeber is created the desirable commodity, Carrie Madenda, whose "socially valued, exchangeable body . . . is a particularly mimetic expression of masculine values." Irigaray writes that this process "never takes place simply," but Dreiser offers the illusion that it does. (Luce Irigaray, "Women on the Market," *This Sex Which Is Not One*, trans. Catherine Porter with Carolyn Burke [Ithaca, N.Y.: Cornell University Press, 1985], 181, 185.)

5. Michaels, "Popular Economy," 376, 382.

Ames is having it both ways within the short compass of two pages may be to underestimate the potential of these lines.

As such, we would be wise to suspect the lack of reserve with which Michaels proposes, and Rachel Bowlby endorses, the notion that Ames proposes an economy of limited desire against nineteenth-century capitalism's Desire, Ltd. She has what would seem to be the last word on Ames according to the new reading: "Michaels is surely right to protest against critics who have seen a conscious authorial projection in . . . Ames, who impresses Carrie on one or two occasions [two-for-two is a good average] and persuades her to read Balzac. The solid literary values represented by the midwesterner are simply an anachronism."[6] "Solid values" drawn from an earlier generation of literary realists like Howells may be anachronistic. But there is a more fundamental anachronism in the now-dominant reading of *Sister Carrie* that I want to correct in order to reassess Ames's function in the novel. Simply put (although I shall spend some time substantiating it), by 1889, the year Carrie Meeber boarded a south-bound train for Chicago, the proprietary-competitive, or laissez-faire, market was virtually an anachronism. While it had defenders, these "old conservatives," as the legal historian Morton J. Horwitz names them, were a minority—albeit at times an influential one—fighting against the shift to a corporate-managed economy that was well under way, and the Sherman Antitrust Act of 1890 he labels "a last desperate and largely ineffectual effort to preserve an older America of small competitive businesses."[7] Thus, the insistence on speculation is not only inappropriate to Carrie's activity, it is historically inaccurate—an embarrassing oversight for critics associated with new historicism. More interestingly, the age of incorporation, combination, trust-formation, the period that social scientists from the turn of the century onward have identified as marking a shift in American social relations from autonomous individualism to social interdependence, produced new models of the self and a new class of professional men like Ames, who were called upon to transform and channel the desires produced by capitalism into forms that would serve the public interest.

Ames, I shall contend, is no prematurely obsolete engineer; he is becoming a *social* engineer and theorist of the self when he takes the final role in the creation of Carrie Madenda as a representative of her society, a representation that justifies the economy and Carrie's own evolution by reorienting her desire from economic to social production. In that scene, he preaches not the minimizing of desire,

---

6. Rachel Bowlby, *Just Looking: Consumer Culture in Dreiser, Gissing and Zola* (London: Methuen, 1985), 61.
7. Morton J. Horwitz, "Progressive Legal Historiography," *Oregon Law Review* 63 (1984): 681, 682.

but the careful channeling of desire and capital in directions likely
to benefit both the individual self and the larger social "organism."
His authority derives from his professional position as a businessman
and engineer in a world where combination has rendered the circulation of capital as carefully plotted as is the circulation of electricity among the streetcar lines that await the planned and
channeled growth of Chicago. "[C]onnected with an electrical company" when we first meet him, Ames disconnects himself after his
"little success" and opens a laboratory in New York's SoHo district
(252, 382) [224, 339]. His career move suggests a rise from a level
of practical action that facilitates the unobstructed flow of power to
a self-directed inquiry into the mechanics of power; in effect, he
moves from being a technician to becoming a theorist of what we
may follow Michel Foucault and call "pastoral power."[8] Like Dreiser,
the depicter of social conditions who in *Sister Carrie* mapped the
circuitry that constitutes society, Ames negotiates his way from prag-
matic, local activity to the study of the structure of nature's forces,
which the novel and the social theory of the time repeatedly assert
are the same forces that support economic and artistic endeavor.

2

Pursuing this line of argument takes me back to the origins of
American sociology as well as into economics and the early history
of antitrust law. I shall begin by recalling the thought of Herbert
Spencer, the English Social Darwinist whose influence on Dreiser
was remarked by an earlier generation of critics, but has recently
been ignored. In this, Dreiser criticism is consistent with recent work
in the history of the social sciences. Whereas in the Forties Richard
Hofstadter wrote of "The Vogue of Spencer," in the late Seventies
Thomas L. Haskell argued that Spencer's importance to the period's
social thought has been overestimated. Taking as his focus the more
voluntarist American Social Science Association, he writes that biological determinism was not "its mainstream. Most serious social
thinkers in England and America read Spencer with mingled fascination and horror, clinging hopefully to a far more voluntaristic and
spiritual view of human affairs." An overemphasis on its determinist
dimension may well be the reason that Spencerian thought can, as
David Hollinger wryly notes, "now claim a dubious honor: that it has
been shown *not* to have existed in more places than any other movement in social theory."[9] But Spencerian thought has more dimen-

8. Michel Foucault, "The Subject and Power," in *Art After Modernism: Rethinking Repre-
    sentation*, ed. Brian Wallis (New York and Boston: Museum of Contemporary Art-Godine,
    1984), 421–24.
9. Richard Hofstadter, "The Vogue of Spencer," *Social Darwinism in American Thought*
    [1944], rev. ed. (Boston: Beacon, 1955), 31–50; Thomas L. Haskell, *The Emergence of*

sions—and contradictions!—than is often allowed, and those contradictions extended its reach.

From *Social Statics* onward, Spencer defended individual liberty against all forms of state compulsion in the name of achieving "the greatest happiness." Unless one's pursuit of a desired goal infringes on the freedom of others, he argued, the state should not seek to curtail that pursuit or otherwise to affect the conditions of life beyond ensuring to all citizens an "equal freedom." Spencer's defense of laissez-faire still had enough currency at the turn of the century that in *Lochner v. New York* (1905), which ruled a statute fixing the maximum work week for bakers at sixty hours an infringement of their right to enter into contracts, not a protection of their labor power from exploitation, Justice Holmes dissented from the majority by objecting that "The Fourteenth Amendment does not enact Mr. Herbert Spencer's Social Statics . . . [A] constitution is not intended to embody a particular economic theory, whether of paternalism and the organic relation of the citizen to the state, or of *laissez faire*."[1] That Holmes wrote for the minority suggests that Spencer's idea of liberty had indeed insinuated itself into the language of the Fourteenth Amendment.

Thus, we find in Spencer a conflict between what we might call diachronic determinism and synchronic freedom. The model of individual free agents constantly negotiating to balance their own desires with a respect for the rights of other equally free agents fully supports laissez-faire ideology; however, the inexorable evolution of natural and social organisms to larger, more fully differentiated states equally entails that a corporate economy is the necessary economic form for a society that is itself a corporate body. There is also in his model of evolution what Donald Pizer has noted as a "built-in paradox" that adapts social evolution to both "a struggle-for-existence ethic" and "the realization of Christian idealism in man's personal and social life as evidence of the true direction of evolutionary progress," the position I argue Ames champions in a secularized form. Such are the paradoxes that Spencer bequeathed to the next generation of sociologists: equal freedom must be preserved at all costs, while social evolution toward a communal, cooperative state is inevitable; yet, poor laws, protections of the right to labor and other

---

Professional Social Science: The American Social Science Association and the Nineteenth-Century Crisis of Authenticity (Urbana: University of Illinois Press, 1977), 2; Hollinger, Comments in Symposium on Spencer, Scientism and American Constitutional Law, quoted in Aviam Soifer, "The Paradoxes of Paternalism and Laissez-Faire Constitutionalism: The U.S. Supreme Court, 1888–1921," in *Corporations and Society: Power and Responsibility*, ed. Warren J. Samuels and Arthur S. Miller, Contributions in American Studies 88 (New York and Westport, Conn.: Greenwood, 1987), 162.
1. Oliver Wendell Holmes, Jr., dissent in *Lochner v. New York* 198 *U.S.* 45 (1905) at 75.

legislative attempts to further this evolution are testimony "to the futility of . . . empirical attempts at the acquisition of happiness" because "Men who seem the prime movers are merely the tools with which [evolutionary change] works; and were they absent, it would quickly find others."[2]

When the novel was published in 1900, it was widely hoped in the United States that trusts and other forms of cooperative combination would bring the economy to "a comparatively constant state" that would be, in Spencer's words, "conducive to a better equilibrium of industrial functions" because unbridled (and often unprincipled) competition would give way to the steady growth of a well-managed economy. Many progressives and representatives of labor embraced the new arrangement as a rationalization of production. They saw the promise of corporate capitalism as "greater stability of employ- ment and better wages with higher productivity, as well as pensions, profit-sharing, recreational facilities, and even advancement from blue collar to white and prospective advancement up the corporate ladder," all of which would benefit those men and women with the least economic power. Sister Carrie shows us natural (as opposed to government-sponsored) market regulation, whose result is postu- lated as a dynamic balance between demand and supply in a "dependent moving equilibrium" like that maintained among the functions of a single organism. The novel's representative fortune, Fitzgerald and Moy's, grows under the stewardship of managers as the city grows. It is a predictor of the symbiosis of social and business interests that Dreiser, following Spencer, imagined as the inevitable outcome of individual fortunes being "conserved by the growth of a community" (260) [230]. Rooted in classical market theory, this sort of dynamic equilibrium was codified in Say's Law, which holds that "production and demand must generally balance each other at rel- atively full employment, with imbalances occurring only episodically and serving as corrective signals restorative of equilibrium."[3] Say's Law is allegorized in the novel by the balance between Carrie's desire and the opportunities at hand for its satisfaction, and by the ease of her movement along the circuit of success. Thus the novel is, I can- not resist suggesting, a "Spencerian romance" in which motive pow- ers are natural, not supernatural, and the heroine, a "half-equipped

2. Donald Pizer, *The Novels of Theodore Dreiser: A Critical Study* (Minneapolis: University of Minnesota Press, 1976), 14; Herbert Spencer, *Social Statics; or, The Conditions Essen- tial to Human Happiness Specified, and the First of Them Developed* [1865] (New York: Robert Schalkenbach Foundation, 1954), 11, 388.
3. Spencer, *First Principles*, 6th ed. (1900; reprint Westport, Conn.: Greenwood, 1976), 458–59; Martin J. Sklar, *The Corporate Reconstruction of American Capitalism, 1890– 1916: The Market, the Law, and Politics* (New York: Cambridge University Press, 1988), 23; Say's Law, summarized by Sklar, 54.

little knight . . . dreaming wild dreams of some vague, far-off supremacy" (2) [2], succeeds in her quest and thereby proves the virtue of the market rather than her own virtue.

However, according to Martin J. Sklar, by 1900 "no significant segment of organized opinion advocated a return to the old competitive market or the preservation of laissez-faire prohibitions on regulatory intervention by the federal government." The courts lagged public opinion until the "Rule of Reason" cases of 1911 made a distinction between reasonable and unreasonable restraints of trade, but the wider debate on combinations at the turn of the century centered on the proper extent of state regulation. In one of those cases, *Standard Oil Co. of N.J. et al. v. U.S.*, John Marshall Harlan partially dissented from the Court's decision by arguing that commerce "must be allowed to flow in its accustomed channels, wholly unvexed and unobstructed by anything that would restrict its movement." Much of Harlan's dissent takes issue with what he considered an act of judicial legislation in the new interpretation of the Sherman Act, but in this passage he invoked memories of an organic market even though such rhetoric was also used to naturalize the very activity he was contesting. Spencer, for example, had maintained that social progress is "part of nature; it is all of a piece with the development of an embryo or the unfolding of a flower [and] . . . must end in completeness."[4] Such, we are asked to believe, is the fate of Carrie Meeber (amoeba?) as she evolves from that flat-footed girl whose "hands were almost ineffectual" for any kind of work (2) [2] into the ultimate celebrity. Harlan's unrecognized dilemma was that if trusts and other industrial combinations were a new evolutionary stage of capitalism, then antitrust activity is a vexation and obstruction of the motion of the market.

In *Sister Carrie*, Dreiser followed Spencer by using the rhetoric of naturalism to conceal the conditions of social and economic exchange. The terminology is quite frequently borrowed from biology, but as Franklin H. Giddings, the first American professor of sociology, noted almost a century ago, "The basal theories of [Spencer's] sociological thought" in *First Principles* rest on "the persistence of force, the direction and rhythm of motion, the integration of matter and the differentiation of form." It is "At bottom . . . a physical philosophy of society, notwithstanding its liberal use of biological and psychological data." The novel's world is held together by electromagnetism: Chicago is "a giant magnet" that draws capital and people like Carrie to it; electric streetcar lines emanate from the city center like nerve pathways from a brain (12) [11]. The assembly line

4. Sklar, 180; Harlan, dissent in *Standard Oil Co. of N.J. et al. v. U.S.* 221 U.S. 1 (1911) at 96; Spencer, *Social Statics*, 60. On the three phases of judicial construction of the Sherman Act, see Sklar, 117–54.

on which Carrie works is a self-regulated circuit that keeps shoes marching along the path of least resistance, as the "complicated motions" of capital do for Spencer.[5] Characters are likewise charged fields. Drouet has a "daring and magnetism" that attracts Carrie (2) [2], while his "electrical, nervous condition" transforms her as "Laura" (143) [127]. When Carrie and Drouet dine together, an "interchanging current of feeling" "connect[s]" their eyes (49) [44]. Hurstwood "fixes" Carrie with his eyes' "magnetism" (94) [84]. Drouet bestows on Carrie her own magnetism: viewing herself in the stylish clothes he bought for her, she feels "her first thrill of power" (63) [56]; this physical attractiveness draws male theater-goers to her in New York. Clothing has an economic and magnetic power over Carrie: at The Fair department store, "[e]ach separate counter was a show place of dazzling interest and attraction" for her (18) [16]. Conspicuous by his absence from these circuits is Ames, whom I contend has mastered them.

Yet, as we know, economic and social change for the better at the turn of the century did not occur spontaneously because Say's Law does not hold true in an industrial economy. As the economist and monetary authority Charles A. Conant explained, the need to tie up capital in fixed plant creates a pattern of cyclical fluctuation as healthy profits and low interest invite an expansion of fixed plant that eventually leads to an oversupply of goods, then to declining prices and profits, higher interest rates, economic slowdowns, and, finally, depressions because investments in fixed plant are an immobile form of capital. The dystopic effect of cyclical slowdowns and the increasing concentration of wealth in fewer hands had been explored in Brooks Adams's *The Law of Civilization and Decay*, another "scientific" study of economic and social structures, which had been published four years before *Sister Carrie*. Adams shared with Spencer and Dreiser a scientific rhetoric and a sense that men's conscious actions played but a small role in shaping history; all three men thought that the major forces governing men were instinctual— that is, natural. But unlike Spencer, who thought larger economic "organisms" a sign of evolution toward better social and economic relations, Adams appealed to history in order to argue that centralization creates "two extreme economic types,—the usurer in his most formidable aspect, and the peasant whose nervous system is best adapted to thrive on scanty nutriment."[6] While Spencer was writing against state paternalism, Adams's immediate context was the Panic of 1893 and the contest between advocates of the gold standard and

5. Franklin H. Giddings, "The Theory of Sociology," *Annals of the American Society of Political and Social Science* 5 supp. (July 1894), 9; Spencer, *First Principles*, 218.
6. Brooks Adams, *The Law of Civilization and Decay: An Essay on History* (1896; New York: Knopf, 1943), 61. On Conant, see Sklar, 62–68.

bimetallism. Published as William Jennings Bryan and the "Silver Democrats" campaigned against William McKinley, the candidate of the banking interests, Adams's book was attacked in some quarters as a political pamphlet writ large, even though it never mentions American finance. It did not have to because Adams's final focus on the bankers of Lombard Street, who any populist could tell you controlled banking in the United States, made clear the nation's implication in the history he was recounting.

Had Dreiser followed Adams's "inevitable" cycle, *Sister Carrie* would have focused on the defeat of the Brooklyn Trolley workers by their bosses and the banks. But he let go of the strike when it had shown Hurstwood's fate: his inability to run the car along its track signifies the loss of his former managerial ability as much as the success of the strikers. The strike suggests that "new socialism," which Dreiser at one point reminds readers, produced "pleasant working conditions" in factories (31) [28], was widely resisted, even if he omitted events like the Haymarket Riot (1886) and the Pullman Strike (1894), which are directly pertinent to a story set partially in Chicago. While the headlines proclaiming "80,000 people out of employment" (267) [237] place Hurstwood in a larger context of economic crisis, they are counterbalanced by Carrie's thought after her quick success as a job-seeker that "no man could go seven months without finding something if he tried" (312) [277]. The competing theories of dynamic equilibrium and business cycles come into their most direct opposition in these contrasting observations, but the case for disequilibrium is undercut by the particular circumstances in which Hurstwood finds himself as an ageing felon. They make the problem he represents seem less systematic than individual, as the voodoo economists say of the S&L and junk-bond crises. By tying the workers' struggle against banks and corporations to Hurstwood's struggle against age and the inevitable "turning in the tide of [his] abilities" (260) [231]—a different tide from "the tide of change" (44) [38] carrying Carrie—Dreiser subverted the concrete reality of the strike. When the violence breaks Hurstwood, he leaves the conflict with a sense that the job is not for him, not that the strikers are right or wrong. We leave the strike without mention of its outcome, only the surmise of the already-defeated Hurstwood that "Those fellows can't win" because the corporations own the police (321) [285]. What might have been a critique of the use of police power by the corporations and of the ways social crises are (mis)represented in newspapers thus dissolves into ambiguities that reflect Hurstwood's private confusion as he looks out on a world in which he has relinquished his place by diverting the flow of capital.

3

Spencer counseled passivity in the face of social crises. The reader of *Social Statics* is urged to "look upon social convulsions as upon other *natural* phenomena, which work themselves out in a certain inevitable, unalterable way" (emphasis added). Spencer allowed that "We may lament the bloodshed," but he warned that "it is folly to suppose that . . . things could have been worked out differently." However, by the mid-1880s in the United States, Spencerian social evolution was being combined with a faith in human volition as an effective force for social change by such first-generation American sociologists as Giddings and Lester Ward, whose two-volume *Dynamic Sociology* (1893) was the first American sociology text. Ward's sociology employed Darwinism and physics, but he took issue with many of Spencer's arguments about social order. He rejected laissez-faire by arguing that abstract rights like the law of equal free- dom mystify the actual relations of power determining the extent of individual rights and the direction of history. While conceding that the history of meliorist intervention to date had been largely negative, Ward found cause for optimism in the fact that such activity has some effect and that it might be positive if properly aimed. Just as machines can be invented according to the laws of physics to do valuable work, Ward argued, so legislation must be invention and legislatures research laboratories for the ordering of society. Gid- dings likewise believed in the need for "scientifically-trained states- men" if social evolution was to progress as a dynamic or "moving equilibrium." While he defined the subject of this new social science as "the development of mind as a product of social activity and as an evolution of social nature," like Ward he argued that mental phe- nomena are also causes, and that the reciprocity of internal and external causes must be understood as part of an ongoing process of adjustment and adaptation of humans and the external world.[7]

Scientific rhetoric borrowed from evolutionary biology and physics to explain patterns of individual and social behavior was no doubt instrumental in the legitimation of sociology as a social *science*. The fundamental notion of "interdependence," which was used to describe postbellum social, industrial, and economic relations, was couched in a language of forces and vectors; as Thomas Haskell recently defined it, "interdependence" describes an objective "ten- dency of social integration and consolidation whereby action in one part of society is transmitted in the form of direct or indirect con-

7. Spencer, *Social Statics*, 388; Haskell, 203; Lester F. Ward, *Dynamic Sociology, or, Applied Social Science* 2nd ed., 2 vols., (1911; New York: Greenwood, 1968), 1:31–37; Giddings, 10, 74, 35. *Loewe v. Lawlor* and *Buck's Stove and Range Co. v. Gompers* ruled against product boycotts by unions; *Adair v. United States* upheld the yellow-dog contract. The Supreme Court decided all three cases in 1908.

sequences to other parts of society with accelerating rapidity, widening scope, and increasing intensity." The goal of these scientific studies of society was explained as "bring[ing] the social units into proper relation to one another, and to the society as a whole" by George G. Wilson, a professor of social science at Brown University who later expanded his scope as a Harvard professor, author, and agent of the United States government in the field of international law. The technocratic rhetoric of sociology not surprisingly attracted the attention of engineers, who were busy organizing their profession as a science, rather than a craft—although civil engineering had been a recognized profession before the Civil War.[8] Certainly, engineers were at home with concepts of transmission, acceleration, and intensity; they also thought of action as produced in increasingly complex and efficient circuitry.

In his history of American engineering during the progressive era, Edward T. Layton, Jr., explains the influence of Spencerian thought on members of that profession in the final decades of the nineteenth century by noting that "Spencer himself was an engineer. Engineers regarded him not only as a colleague but as an example of a new professional role: that of lawgiver and philosopher. Spencer was taken by Robert Thurston, the first president of the ASME [American Society of Mechanical Engineers], as having vastly widened the legitimate concerns of the engineering profession to include general questions of politics and economics."[9] If many, even the majority, of engineers during this period did not share the progressives' faith in democracy and the utility of government-sponsored reform, many engineers and laymen shared a faith in the applicability of engineering solutions to economic problems of producing and distributing goods at reasonable prices. In his 1895 presidential address to the American Society of Civil Engineers, George S. Morison declared that "Accurate engineering knowledge must succeed commercial guesses," and that "corporations, both public and private, must be handled as if they were machines." This sentiment informed the vision of progressive reformers and Franklin Roosevelt's creation of a "brain trust"; it perhaps reached its apotheosis in Thorstein Veblen's post–World War I call to replace the industrial managers and syndicates of investment bankers with a "soviet of technicians" concerned with the efficient production and distribution of goods, not with profit margins.[1]

8. Haskell, 28–29; George G. Wilson, "The Place of Social Philosophy," *Journal of Social Science* 32 (Nov. 1894): 140.
9. Edward T. Layton, Jr., *The Revolt of the Engineers: Social Responsibility and the American Engineering Profession* (Cleveland: Case Western Reserve University Press, 1971), 54.
1. Morison, quoted in Layton, 59; Thorstein Veblen, *The Engineers and the Price System* (New York: Viking, 1921). As the later chapters of Layton's study show, engineering asso-

It is in such a context that we must see Bob Ames, *Sister Carrie*'s engineer and sometime cultural critic. A representative of the social theorist as practical man, he uses his mastery of technical knowledge to improve his economic situation while criticizing "wasteful" excesses of "showy gastronomy" (254) [225], and he directs his criticism of literature and theater toward the social uses of fiction. Ames fits the University of Chicago sociologist Charles R. Henderson's description of the social theorist as someone whose "associations are with the refined, and his ideals of life are formed in the best company. But his professional pursuits compel him to weigh the claims of the entire community."[2] When Ames and Carrie meet for the second time, she, too, is moving in the "best" company. Started on her path by Drouet, she has been transformed by theater directors and the promotional apparatus into a star who lives in the best hotels and wears the finest clothes. She once dreamed that palaces and dresses would validate her worth; she now validates theirs.

Beyond Carrie's role of consuming and being consumed as a "delicious little morsel" (353) [313] confected by a succession of directors, and costume designers, there is another dimension to what Ames defines as her "representative" function (385) [342]. In it Carrie Madenda, the ideal object of male desire, becomes inseparable from Carrie Meeber, the proof of capitalism's liberation of the individual. An expression of the collective longing (385) [342] for fulfillment, of what Eric Sundquist calls "the age's own dream of success, its special romance,"[3] she is a figure for the imaginary potential that her audience can in turn ascribe to their actual social and economic lives. Carrie, too, was once nobody. As audiences recognize in her the reflection of their own desire and see in her fame the promise that the system of production satisfies desire, they may become reconciled to their present relation to the productive apparatus. In effect, she calms fears that industrial capitalism is producing the "two extreme economic types" Adams warned about by demonstrating that old-fashioned competitive individualism is no longer the path to success. Successfully managed, she shows that individual success in a corporate economy is the product of harmonious adaptation to the pre-existing constellation of social forces, something her naturally imitative behavior predisposes her toward.

Carrie performs this role well, but incidentally. She is not a

ciations in the Twenties and Thirties shared a predominantly conservative, laissez-faire ideology.

2. Charles R. Henderson, "Business Men and Social Theorists," *American Journal of Sociology* 1 (Jan. 1896): 396. Henderson appealed to the authority of economics and physics in representing the social scientist as a "practical" man who seeks "an exact balance between the debits and credits, the causes and results of social action" (396).

3. Eric Sundquist, "Introduction: The Country of the Blue," in *American Realism*, 20.

theorist like Ames, who "weighs the claims of the entire community."
He tells her that she will reach the goal he sets for her—making
private and public interest coincide—if she achieves great personal
success while at the same time renouncing her interest and agency
in favor of becoming the transparent conductor of the world's mute
desire (385) [342]. Recent objections to Ames center on this sort of
rhetoric, which recalls the language of Wordsworth's Preface to the
second edition of *Lyrical Ballads* or American transcendentalism.
Ames's comments and his practice suggest Emerson when he coun-
sels Carrie to use her "genius" to become "representative" (385)
[341] and live not only for herself. He reminds her that she can
"occupy but one [situation] at a time" (384) [340], but the implication of his advice is that she, like he, can comprehend the world
from her position. At the same time, his advice to her, "If I were you,
I'd change" (386) [342] names a logical contradiction ("If I were you,
I wouldn't be you") through which he makes himself desirable to her
and installs himself as her last director. What distinguishes his activity from Carrie's "high-flown speculations" is that he measures possibilities near at hand, while she passively dreams of what is far off.
Yet, the advice he gives is appropriate for Carrie, an actress who must
produce "selves" that are not her own and must remain alienated
from those "selves." It is advice that even we are asked to follow since
the desire that lures us to change is offered as the fundamental
mechanism of the economy and of our personal satisfaction if, as
Carrie, Ames, and Drouet do, we align ourselves with economic and
natural forces.

In fact, Ames's rhetoric is not out of place in a discussion of the
period's emergent economic and social relations. Howard Horwitz
has recently shown an overlapping rhetoric in the description of the
Emersonian self and "The dream of the trust, . . . to become a powerful person by not being an agent, or rather by being merely the
agent or instrument of transcendental forces." The trusts' defenders
decontextualized and recycled Emerson on agency and harmony to
cast as a benevolent "conver[sion of] the self to a transparent trustee
of the energy of production, seeing all, concentrating all, seen by
none, doing nothing," what detractors saw as activity in restraint of
trade. But Carrie does more than allegorize economic activity. By the
way she provokes desire or identification she *performs* what Ward
wrote is "The practical work which sociology demands . . . , *the organization of feeling*" into a well-managed economy of desire.[4] Ames,
then, cannot be dismissed as simply as recent critics would have him
be. As Dreiser's theorist of the ideal social and economic structure
of corporate society, he cloaks in a cultured rhetoric of beneficence

4. Howard Horwitz, "The Standard Oil Trust as Emersonian Hero," *Raritan* 6.4 (Spring
1988): 99, 113; Ward, 1:68.

technologies of power that were reshaping American society in far less utopian ways, even as he spoke.

Working the overlap in rhetorics, Ames makes Carrie a figure for everything as she becomes nothing herself—although as a product of the entertainment apparatus she, moreso than the Emersonian hero or the trust, is nothing but a point at which forces concentrate. When Ames proposes this future for Carrie, he in effect divests himself of the "trusteeship" he has gained over her. He invests her with an agency that she did not know she possessed and must now relinquish; as she does so, she enacts the relation of workers to the economy, wherein agency is surrendered for the promise of fulfillment through the consumption of the goods one helps to mass-produce. Her gesture is equally readable as motivated by a faith in the potential the productive apparatus has in store for the individual and as showing the process of interpellation, whereby one accepts as one's true self a representation that is socially produced. Ames's proposal occurs at a critical point in the novel, when it appears that Carrie's wanderings have been in vain because objects are losing their power to command her attention. She rejects the millionaire who promises "to gratify [her] every desire" (360) [319], stops running around New York with Lola, and lapses into melancholy. Her desire is reanimated by Ames's espousal of an essentially Spencerian altruism. What he urges can be glossed by a passage in *Social Statics* that describes the "ultimate man" as one "whose private requirements coincide with public ones . . . [I]n spontaneously fulfilling his own nature, [he] incidentally performs the functions of a social unit."[5] The means of producing this healthy mutual determination of self and society is precisely what the sociologists and social engineers were seeking.

Impelled and interpellated by Ames, Carrie will rise in the traditional hierarchy of drama, although I doubt that tragic flaws are reconcilable with the ultimate representation of Spencerian social equilibration—more likely it is high romance. But she is not consciously choosing in favor of a better channel for expressing her gift; she is intrigued by a man she does not understand. What Ames is doing as a stand-in for Dreiser is using the rhetoric of altruism to remake Carrie in the image of his more "cultured" desire. But instead of rejecting his role as a high-priest of culture on this account, we should consider him in light of Foucault's description of the modern state's pastoral power, a less-optimistic, more coercive version of the dynamic the turn-of-the-century sociologists were attempting to imagine. This power supports the state's "very sophisticated structure, in which individuals can be integrated under one condition: that [their] individuality would be shaped in a new form and sub-

5. Spencer, *Social Statics*, 397. Spencer used "Altruism" in *The Principles of Ethics* 2 vols. (New York: Appleton, 1898), 2:263–76, which he considered as superseding *Social Statics*.

mitted to a set of very specific patterns" that determine not just behavior within the law, but also normative behavior.[6] Because this pastoral power is dispersed through social networks and is not traceable to one or a few identifiable loci within or beyond this world, and because its use requires the preservation of the subject's freedom to act—it is an action upon the subject's action—Dreiser could cloak this power in the same misty beneficence that the trust's representatives used to characterize their production and price agreements. Rational, cultured, scientific Bob Ames is the ideal figure of pastoral power in the novel; he has mastered the three discourses that define enlightened society, and he indeed sounds like Dreiser's projection of an ideal self. As midwife of the new Carrie, and of the representation of the undefined class of "individuals" she stands for, Ames performs the pastor's integrative and restrictive cultural function.

This action makes explicit the paradox implicit in Spencer's theory that individuality is the product of social evolution and Dreiser's representation of the relations of production as naturally conducive to this individuality: the ideal form of individuality is not the speculator's radical individualism, which threatens the cohesiveness of the social organism through the disequilibrium he provokes, or even the Lockean individual; it is a human subject constituted by the structural forms and discursive practices of the society she "spontaneously" serves. Spencer envisioned as the subject's final stage, the "ultimate man," one who *a priori* conducts himself so as to serve society. His motivation is no longer divine example, but a principle of moralized Darwinism by which ontogeny recapitulates social dynamics: "As surely as the tree becomes bulky when it stands alone, and slender if one of a group; . . . so surely must the human faculties be moulded into complete fitness for the social state; so surely must the things we call immorality disappear; so surely must man become perfect."[7] This self's freedom, its "spontaneity," is immediately constrained by what "incidentally" has to be performed.

The individual in *Sister Carrie* is neither a molecular self nor a speculative desire; it is a culturally produced effect. It is a telling irony of the period that at the same time the individual was being reinterpreted as a socially constituted entity rather than a natural one and Reconstruction was giving way to separate but equal, courts and legislatures were rethinking the legal status of corporations and declaring them natural, not artificial, persons subject to constitutional protections including those contained in the Civil War Amendments.[8] Carrie Madenda serves to obscure these

6. Foucault, 422.
7. Spencer, *Social Statics*, 60.
8. See Soifer, and Morton J. Horwitz, "*Santa Clara* Revisited: The Development of Corporate Theory," in *Corporations and Society*, 13–63.

changes in the concept of personhood by creating the illusion that individual success is propelled by a superior "emotional nature" (398) [353], that certain unrepresentable something of self. She thus appears to rescue the notion of individual character from the cult of personality fostered by the very constellation of consumer capitalism, advertising, and the entertainment business that produced her. In fact, her "self" is doubly determined: it is objectivized by the agents of social and economic power that she serves, and it is the mirror of male desire. When Carrie left Columbia City, she dreamed of making the city her "subject." The world does not disabuse her of her dream since New York, Chicago, and their theaters are not revealed as sites of illusion. The narrative's illusion is that Carrie succeeds when the "mysterious powers" have made her their subject. Her final role is as a name and a face invoked to demonstrate that "natural" powers benevolently guided do important social work.

In *Sister Carrie*, Dreiser produced a novel whose art—both the art of the novel and the art within the novel—supports that vision. Its fiction of production suggests that the real production, even in the early stages of consumer society, is of representations. Through an artful use of the discourses of social science and romanticism/transcendentalism to represent the new economic and social relations, Dreiser erased the boundary between art and the market and made the prospect of serving the industrial apparatus appear self-actualizing by showing that desire, sublimated by imagination, is productive, and that its products are the things we should desire to possess. Art in *Sister Carrie* is, then, neither a critique of economics nor, as it appears to be within the novel, the transcendence of the economic and the completion of the social realm, even though at different times it appears to be offered as one or the other.

The allure of the novel is its promise that the strife between owners and workers and the social and economic dislocations of the nineteenth century—matters long considered the true subject of *Sister Carrie*—were subject to natural cures. This claim is different from, and more modest than, Michaels's claim to have uncovered in Dreiser's novel the secret "logic" of capitalism denied by the genteel tradition of oppositional criticism. Instead, I would say that Dreiser was responding to one historic phase of American capitalism. His response remains useful because the progressive heritage is still with us and *Sister Carrie* allows us to explore the power and limits of the progressive vision as it is offered by Ames. If subsequent history leads us to conclude that faith in technological rationalism was misplaced and the hope for an economic equilibrium beneficial to all members of society was driven by nostalgia for an economic rhythm that predated industrial capitalism, the novel's picture of the benefits of a corporate society was far from unusual in its use of that optimism.

BLANCHE H. GELFANT

What More Can Carrie Want? Naturalistic Ways of Consuming Women†

"Know'st me not by my clothes?"
—CYMBELINE

A recent magazine article evokes the perennial mystery of human desire by asking why a movie star who "has it all"—"a perfect body, happy marriage, wealth," and "success"—is "not yet satisfied" (Wilkinson). Beginning with a play of words, "Why Demi Moore Wants More," the article ends by finding the word *more* "elusive." This elusive *more* is the subject of my essay, which links a desire for *more* to determinism as a doctrine of causation common to literary naturalism, behavioral psychology, modern advertising, and consumerism.[1] Once consumption figures in a discussion of literary naturalism, at issue in this essay, the lines of argument move centrifugally in various directions to include such seemingly far-flung and unrelated matters as the Vietnam War, kleptomania, the "packaging" of American politics, women's fashion, material culture studies, fitness diets, images of burning bodies, the commodification of books, Jane Fonda's self-transformations, and indecent proposals to Demi Moore. All these matters converge at a single point of origin where a woman character, an American literary heroine, stands and looks. The consequences of this simple, ordinary act—which leads the woman to consume and be consumed—seem to me laden with literary and cultural meanings I must necessarily condense. To do so, my first tactical move will be to leap over an entire century in order to compare Theodore Dreiser's famous novel *Sister Carrie*, published in 1900, with a contemporary story that leaves one shaken by its brilliance and horror. I ask the reader to imagine the gap between the two texts as an ellipsis—a *dot, dot, dot*—filled in by decades of turbulent historical change that have redefined what an American heroine wants but not why she wants more.

A century ago, when little Oliver Twist said, "Please, sir, I want

† From *Prospects: An Annual of American Cultural Studies* 19 (1994): 389–417. Reprinted by permission of Cambridge University Press. The notes of the original publication have been condensed and reformatted for this Norton Critical Edition.
1. For representative studies of American literary naturalism, see Mitchell, Rahv, and Pizer, *Twentieth-Century*; for determinism and women's dress, see Prown and Roach.

some more," he was, in Dickens's words, "desperate with hunger." The child said "want" but meant "need"—a basic, biological need for food. As we know, Dreiser's *Sister Carrie* begins with a poignantly needy heroine, a poor working-girl without a job, skill, or money. The novel ends with Carrie Meeber, now a Broadway star, sitting in her luxurious hotel suite with a hundred and fifty dollars "in hand" and contemplating the meaning—or rather the meaninglessness, the "impotence," to use Dreiser's word—of money: "Her hotel bill did not require its use. Her clothes had for some time been wholly satisfactory. Another day and she would receive another hundred and fifty" (335) [321]. Dreiser's little actress now has everything she wanted: money, clothes, comfort, recognition, rich men proposing marriage. And still she thinks, and cannot help thinking, "she must have more—a great deal more" (335) [321].

What more, I wonder, can Carrie want? What is the meaning of desire that so exceeds the demands of need it seems insatiable? In the 1950s, the psychologist Abraham Maslow popularized the term *self-actualization* as a synonym for the human "desire to become more and more what . . . one is capable of becoming" (Maslow 4). Self-actualization depended upon an incessant satisfaction of needs that, Maslow believed, were hierarchical, ranging from the physiological need for food to a need for safety, love, self-esteem, and self-fulfillment. Each satisfied need released a new and higher need, making desire insatiable. Maslow was to complain that women who have it all soon begin "asking for more. . . . After a period of happiness, excitement, and fulfillment comes the inevitable taking it all for granted, and becoming restless and discontented again for *More!*" (98, xvi–xvii). The complaint was gratuitous, since Maslow, like Dreiser, considered desire genetic, a biologically determined component of a self driven to seek satisfaction.

As a naturalistic novel, *Sister Carrie* dramatized biological determinism through a plot that made every action consequential. No matter how casual a character's gesture, look, or comment seemed, it became the cause of an effect, the stimulus to a response that could produce a significant but unforeseen, and perhaps tragic, outcome. Determinism evoked Dreiser's famous comparisons of human beings to insects and animals, all subject to ineluctable drives that characters experience as desire. Desire is a natural force in the novel, but the objects of desire are socially constructed artifacts imbued with impossible dreams of happiness. Insatiability is thus ontologic and cultural, an innate human condition and the sign of social conditioning. Poor Carrie. Her desire is illimitable, but her imagination is limited to the world of goods. Carrie is always looking to see what else in the world she could want, and as Dreiser shows, she is conditioned biologically and culturally to want and buy—or buy into—

what she sees. I would argue that this simple sequence of seeing, wanting, and buying constitutes a deterministic structure of desire underlying naturalistic novels, like *Sister Carrie,* and advertisements psychologically programmed to motivate the modern consumer. In the 1920s, when creating consumer desire became a serious profession, the well-known behavioral psychologist John B. Watson left his academic chair at The Johns Hopkins University for a position with the J. Walter Thompson Company, at the time a leading advertising agency. Watson's departure from Baltimore uncannily reproduced the circumstances in *Sister Carrie* that surrounded Hurstwood's flight from Chicago. Both men headed for New York in disgrace, an illicit attraction to a young woman having cost them their marriage, their money, and their respectable positions.[2] Unlike Hurstwood, however, the penniless Watson had marketable psychological techniques that would earn him and the advertising firm a fortune— techniques of Pavlovian conditioning said to produce determinable responses to stimuli associated with elemental emotions—fear, pleasure, desire. Desiring a beautiful woman, one desires the Coca-Cola associated with her billboard image. Desiring beautiful clothes, Carrie yearns for something more she associates with money and material goods.

If we had a literary text devoid of the goods and advertisements associated with consumerism, a text that creates a world without department stores—the site and *sight* of consumption[3]—without restaurants, theaters, hotels, and the parade of fashion, an emptied world antithetical to Dreiser's Chicago and New York, would it be devoid of *Sister Carrie*'s pattern of desire? What, if anything, could a young woman see and want if she were suddenly transposed to a stark, empty landscape where there is no shop, no need for money, nothing to buy? This is the situation in my second text, a hauntingly resonant story that tests the possibility of escaping American consumerism and undermining the ways of consuming women.

First to Carrie.

As soon as she arrives in Chicago, poor desirous Carrie Meeber begins to dream and despair. Other women have what she, a poor working-girl, can never possess. Wandering through the city, she is a perennial outsider looking in at glamorous interiors through plate-glass windows that, Dreiser tells us, were becoming common in the city—office-building windows and the display windows of Chicago's new department stores. These glass windows revolutionized the relationship between insider and outsider by reflecting an image of the

2. For Watson's life, see Cohen; for his consumerist beliefs, see Buckley.
3. For consumerism and the department store, see Benson, Boorstin, Ewen and Ewen, and Leach.

outsider upon goods arrayed within. Just looking thus drew the shopper inside the store as she saw her image superimposed upon and
enhanced by dazzling things she was learning to desire. In effect,
plate glass changed the concept of shopping from satisfying to creating desire, and turned shopkeepers into "amateur psychologists"
delving into the secrets of human behavior. The Parisian shopkeepers who conceived the grand design of The Bon Marché, usually
considered the first department store, foresaw that glass windows
and cases would bring goods close to a woman who is just looking
and evoke in her desires "*she did not know she had until she entered
the premises.*" By linking consumption with women and evocative
desire with eroticism, department stores supplanted a longstanding
"commercial principle of *supply* [with] . . . that of *consumer seduction*" (Artley 6–7).

Carrie discovers Chicago's great department stores on her weary
quest for "a likely door"—a strange and wonderfully elliptical phrase
that suggests possibilities. When the door of a shoe factory opens,
Carrie enters hopefully only to discover, all too soon, that she should
have been looking for an *unlikely* door, a magical door to which the
key was money. Years later, as she anticipates her first hundred and
fifty dollars, she imagines this door finally opening: "What a door to
an Aladdin's cave it [the money] seemed to be. Each day . . . her
fancies of what her fortune might be, with ample money, grew and
multiplied. She conceived of delights which were not—saw lights of
joy that never were on land or sea" (334) [320].

Carrie sees what is not there except in imagination, illusion, or
desire, and she projects "the perfect joy" she cannot see upon
material things readily visible to the eye.[4] In this respect, she is not
unlike the writer of a literary text, who has imbued its material
objects with symbolic meanings, or the reader of the text, who
learns to interpret its symbolic codes. Carrie learns by studying the
semiotics of clothes, for she understands that "clothing constitutes
a generally understood language of society" (Ewen 126). To learn
this language, she becomes a willing student of her lover Drouet, a
salesman alert to distinctions in dress, and of women friends like
"the dashing Mrs. Vance," a fashion plate who arouses Carrie's
desire and envy (230–31) [221].[5] These characters fulfill the function of modern advertisements by associating commodities with
satisfaction and social class and by creating, in their well-fashioned
selves, enviable images for a shopper's avid eye to see. The city
itself is, preeminently, a place to see, as Drouet tells Carrie when
they first meet on the train to Chicago: "So much to see—theaters,

4. For the Marxist conception of commodity and fetish, see Leiss and McCracken.
5. For clothes and the concept of the fashionable during the 1890s, see Banner, Ewen and
Ewen, and Lurie.

crowds, fine houses" (5) [4]; "Chicago is a wonder. You'll find lots to see here" (7) [7]. Even Carrie's meager sister Minnie tells her, "You'll want to see the city first," and Carrie responds, "I think I'll look around tomorrow" (9) [9].

Carrie starts out looking for a job and ends up—rather endearingly, I think—looking around in a department store. Just looking transforms Carrie from a shop-girl, the term applied to her, into a shopper who sees an array of commodities she is learning to want. Commodities speak to Carrie in tender voices with erotic overtones sounded by the salesmen of consumerism and condemned by its critics. " 'My dear,' said the lace collar she secured from Partridge's, 'I fit you perfectly; don't give me up.' 'Ah, such little feet,' said the leather of the soft new shoes; 'how effectively I cover them' " (75) [72]. Through a typical Dreiserian inversion, Carrie is inarticulate, while little jackets, silk cravats, shiny buttons, and soft shoes speak in a seductive language structured by a grammar of difference, envy, and desire. Carrie succumbs to this language as she makes what Thorstein Veblen famously called "invidious distinctions" and "invidious comparisons" (Veblen). In Chicago, she compares her shabby, shop-girl clothes to the elegant fashion of lady shoppers who "elbowed" their way past her to buy the "dainty," "delicate," "dazzling" goods displayed in department store showcases. Invidious comparison lights a "flame of envy" in Carrie's heart, and envy arouses mediated desires. Carrie begins to want what she sees other women have—their clothes, and something more incorporated in contemporary definitions of consumerism: the self that is delineated by acquisition (Berman 107). In Carrie's mind, clothes make the woman, and in Dreiser's representation, clothes make the man, as the text immediately asserts in its description of Drouet: "Good clothes, of course, were the first essential, the things without which he was nothing" (3) [3].

The possibility of being or becoming nothing—a fear of anomie—haunts Dreiser's characters. Like Carrie in Chicago and Hurstwood in New York, they know themselves to be dispossessed faceless figures in an urban crowd, and they seek to fashion a distinctive self in the only way they can conceive—by wearing the latest fashion. In the theaters of Broadway, where Carrie will again look for a likely door, clothes obviously create the person: a gray suit transforms Carrie into a "little Quakeress," and a scanty dress, into an oriental harem beauty. On stage where all can see, fashion fulfills its promise to confer identity, though the self it creates is factitious and unstable, subject to fashion's notorious vagaries. Fashion used properly—that is, used up and discarded—makes consumption visible, especially in the theater, where consumption becomes inseparable from acts of seeing and being seen.[6] Intuitively, Dreiser's little actress links seeing with fashion, consumption, and social value. As soon as she sees Hurstwood, she evaluates his worth—his wealth, position, and sexuality—by his "rich" plaid vest, mother-of-pearl buttons, and soft black shoes "polished only to a dull shine." Dull is sometimes better than shiny in a text gleaming with "a thousand lights" (1) [1]. Seeing Drouet's shiny patent leather shoes, "Carrie *could not help* feeling that there was a distinction in favor of soft leather" (73, emphasis added) [69].

Somehow naive little Carrie Meeber has learned to make distinctions, the basis of personal tastes which, we are being told, reflect social class and cultural encoding.[7] Long before the term *distinctions* was to be given its current prominence in cultural criticism, Dreiser had translated it into dramatic action by having Carrie reject one man for another with superior taste, and into authorial judgment by finding Carrie's taste inferior to that of "the greatest minds" (like, presumably, the writer's). In reflective passages, the text comments upon the many minute but momentous social distinctions made by its characters—characters Dreiser views critically, but with a much-noted compassion. They are, after all, helpless creatures, driven by innate desire and "the lure of the material." In Dreiser's famous, and infamously clichéd, image, they are moths drawn to the flame—and Hurstwood is finally consumed.

The etymological root of the words *consume, consumer,* and *consumerism* is the Latin *consumere*: "To take up completely, make away with, eat up, devour, waste, destroy, spend" (*OED*). While economists define *consumption* as use in satisfaction of wants, the *Oxford English Dictionary* gives as its primary meaning "to use up destructively. Said chiefly of fire: To burn up." These contrary meanings suggest why acts of consumption elicit ambivalent feelings, attracting and repelling as *using* melds into *using up* or wasting, turning something into nothing. The end of *Sister Carrie* shows Dreiser's Hurstwood, once a man to be envied, reduced to nothing: he has no money, no clothes, no one, and, dangerously in a market economy, no exchange value. Ironically, the discovery of a likely door marked the beginning of Hurstwood's decline. By coincidence, it seems, Hurstwood finds the door of his employer's safe open on the night he feels most persecuted by his wife, most driven by desire for Carrie, and most befuddled by whiskey. Like Carrie later on, Hurstwood has stumbled upon a magical door and entered Aladdin's cave only to find its golden treasures illusory. The little actress came to see the

6. For consumption and seeing (or devouring), see Berger, Fenichel, and Friedberg; for the theater as perpetual spectatorship, see Garfield.
7. For personal taste and cultural encoding, see Bourdieu.

impotence of money, and the manager saw its evanescence. Hurst-wood's estranged wife takes the now ex-manager's small fortune, and detectives take the stolen money. Having lost his money, reputation, and natty clothes, the essence of his self, Hurstwood loses all desire, and his last suicidal words stand as Dreiser's last words in the Penn-sylvania edition of *Sister Carrie*—"What's the use?"

Hurstwood ends up "a nameless body" drifting to a pauper's grave in Potter's Field, and Carrie becomes a name used to advertise the pleasures of illusion: "At Broadway and Thirty-ninth Street was blaz-ing, in incandescent fire, Carrie's name. 'Carrie Madenda,' it read, 'and the Casino Company.' All the wet, snowy sidewalk was bright with this radiated fire." The source of the radiation is "a large, gilt-framed posterboard, on which was a fine lithography of Carrie, life size" (362) [347]. Poor Carrie. She wanted a real self and ends up a fiery figure of consumption. Her blazing billboard image holds her in arrest, as though she were "under the spell of one activity . . . to be sold"—which is how cultural theorists picture goods in a depart-ment store window.[8] As an image that promises pleasures only illu-sion can fulfill, Dreiser's little actress is as much a victim of deception as she is a deceptive representation among all the misrep-resentations sadly catalogued in the novel's much-quoted conclu-sion: "In fine raiment and elegant surroundings, men seemed [to Carrie] to be contented. Hence, she drew near these things. Chicago, New York; Drouet, Hurstwood; the world of fashion and the world of stage—these were but incidents. Not them, but what they repre-sented, she longed for. Time proved the representation false" (368) [353]. Today, influential cultural critics contend that representation itself has become an act of falsification as it "substitut[es] signs of the real for the real itself" (Baudrillard 4). I quote Jean Baudrillard, who argues, along with Guy Debord and others, that the evocative images circulating in consumer societies have no referents and that the representations these images bring to the eye are devoid of real-ity, as is the name Carrie Madenda. For Carrie Madenda, like Carrie Drouet, Carrie Murdock, and Carrie Wheeler, is a false name for Carrie Meeber which is, after all, a fiction.

I turn now to 1990 and a story called "Sweetheart of the Song Tra Bong" in Tim O'Brien's highly acclaimed collection of Vietnam War stories, *The Things They Carried*. The "Sweetheart" is an actual sweetheart of a young American soldier, Mark Fossie, a medic assigned to an aid station deep in the Vietnam bush, near the village of Tra Bong, an ideally remote place, Mark believes—and we are asked to believe—for his childhood sweetheart to visit. Mary Anne

---

8. For consumerism and the shop window, see Benjamin and Sohn-Rethel.

Bell duly arrives in Tra Bong, a seventeen-year-old blond with "blue eyes and a complexion like strawberry ice cream" dressed in "white culottes and this sexy pink sweater" and carrying a plastic cosmetic kit (105, 102). Thus begins a highly compressed story of initiation that describes a young woman's passage from innocence to experience as she assimilates the values of a new world and becomes a new person. To Mary Anne, Vietnam is as immanent with possibilities for self-actualization as Chicago was to Carrie, and as evocative of desire even though it offers nothing to buy. Mary Anne has been transported to a world without department stores, without hotels, restaurants, and theaters, a world beyond "the lure of the material," to recall Dreiser's phrase, and beyond the need for money. Mary Anne never expresses a desire for money and never appears, as Carrie does, with money in hand. Nevertheless, she begins to act like a shopper as she wanders about, just looking. Guarded by three soldiers, Mary Anne browses through the village, a dangerous place run by the Vietcong, looking with such burning intensity at "the wonderful simplicity of village life"—so different from the city's complexities—that "her pretty blue eyes begin to glow."[9] If the glow is that of a tourist appreciating the sights of an unknown land, it burns with the acquisitive desire of a consumer. For tourism, like consumerism, begins with seeing and often ends with shopping, getting something. "She couldn't get enough of it," Rat says of Mary Anne (107), and then adds cryptically: "She wanted more" (124).

What more, I wonder, can O'Brien's Mary Anne want in the dematerialized terrain of Vietnam? As with Carrie, clothes offer a significant clue. Mary Anne exchanges her pink sweater for "filthy green fatigues" which, like Carrie's little tan jacket, mark her initiation into a rite of passage. Short stories require a rapid transit, and Mary Anne falls almost precipitously "into the habits of the bush. No cosmetics, no fingernail filing. She stopped wearing jewelry, cut her hair short and wrapped it in a dark green bandana. Hygiene became a matter of small consequence" (109). Giving up deodorant, creams, maybe even soap, this "half-equipped little knight," to borrow Dreiser's phrase, equips herself with "a standard M-16 automatic assault rifle" (113). She learns how to disassemble the weapon, care for its parts, and shoot. She discovers "she had a knack for it" (109). Like the refashioned Carrie who sees a new and prettier, plumper self in the mirror, Mary Anne becomes a new and "different person." She develops "a new confidence in her voice, a new authority in the way she carried herself" (109), and new visions of her future with Mark, less definite and less conventional. When Mark, troubled by the changes he sees, mentions home, she tells him to forget it: "Everything I want,

9. For tourism and desire, see Pratt.

she said, is right here. . . . To tell the truth, I've never been happier in my whole life. Never" (109–110). Hedonistic desire keeps Mary Anne in Vietnam, Carrie in Chicago, and consumers in the market-place where, economists claim, they expect to purchase pleasure, the implicit promise of goods waiting to be possessed. In a single state-ment, Carrie wonderfully compresses the intention, desire, and future of the consuming woman: "She would be happy."

For Mary Anne, as for Carrie, happiness centers upon the self— or more precisely, upon self-actualization, a dream of *more* fostered by individualistic societies.[1] Mary Anne wants to actualize "possibil-ities" deep within her self that draw her to the "dark green mountains to the west." "The wilderness seemed to draw her in," Rat says, describing a helplessness before determining forces that links Amer-ica's sweetheart to Carrie as a naturalistic character. Driven by innate desire, neither can help being drawn to what she sees as sym-bolically charged means to happiness: clothes, comfort, and fame; or secrecy, violence and death. Through different means, each becomes a different person, different from her uninitiated self, out-wardly different from each other, and inwardly different from the real self each desired. Even the color of Mary Anne's eyes changes, turning from cheerleader blue to jungle green. "I saw those eyes of hers," Rat says, "I saw she wasn't even the same person no more" (117).

Mary Anne is changed by the Green Berets, who evoke her desire for killing, just as sporty men and fashionable women had evoked Carrie's desire for clothes and jewelry. *Made in Vietnam* could he the label on Mary Anne's new jewelry, a necklace strung with human tongues: "Elegant and narrow, like pieces of blackened leather, the tongues were threaded along a length of copper wire, one over-lapping the next, the tips curled upward as if caught in a final shrill syllable" (120).[2] Silent and yet eloquent, the eviscerated tongues speak persuasively, telling of seductions that leave a woman solitary after drawing her from one dream to another, one man to another. Carrie leaves Drouet for Hurstwood, and Mary Anne leaves Mark for the Green Berets. The mutual attraction between America's sweetheart and these lethally secretive men is inexplicable but irrev-ocable: Mary Anne follows the Greenies into the night to become a killer. Like Carrie, transformed into an incandescent fiery image of consumption, Mary Anne turns into a nocturnal silhouette, the res-idue of a consuming fire ignited by desire. She is consumed—and her killer self consummated—by a desire to devour what she sees: "Vietnam, I want to swallow the whole country—the dirt, the death—I just want to eat it and have it there inside me. That's how

1. For individualism and consumption, see O'Connor.
2. For the theme of regeneration through violence in American culture, see Slotkin.

I feel. It's like . . . this appetite . . . but it's not *bad* . . . it's like I'm full of electricity and I'm glowing in the dark—I'm on fire almost—I'm burning away into nothing—but it doesn't matter because I know exactly who I am. You can't feel that anywhere else" (121, original emphasis). O'Brien's narrator describes Mary Anne as "lost inside herself," but she believes she has found her self by incorporating into her own body Vietnam, the war, death. Like Carrie, she ends up the embodiment of the values of her world and, like Carrie, strangely disembodied. Carrie becomes a fiery image, and Mary Anne, burned out by fire, becomes an ominous shadow slipping through the jungle where she is now "part of the land." Wearing her necklace of human tongues, she spreads silence over this land, though she has given a voice to the narrator Rat Kiley and the writer Tim O'Brien, who ends by saying, "She was dangerous. She was ready for the kill" (125).

Mary Anne Bell belongs to a new breed of woman personified in recent movies and novels by the "hard body," so called in a 1991 article in *New York Magazine,* entitled "Killer Women" (Baumgold). In such movies as "Terminator II," these new women emerge as "combat-trained outlaws' who establish a "new standard of beauty" by appearing, like Mary Anne, without makeup, jewelry, or fancy clothes. For her role as terminating woman, the actress Linda Hamilton trained for months to transform her image—and her body—from that of the good, winsome, fashionably dressed Beauty she played in the television series "Beauty and the Beast." To become a Killer Woman, the Beauty who saved man from his bestiality had to release the violent impulses of the beast suppressed within her breast.[3] Drawn to the site of men's violence, she will transform herself through an act of consumption—a suicidal gesture of discarding or destroying her own self. In the movies, Thelma and Louise consume their socially formed selves by dying; in O'Brien's story, Mary Anne burns away into nothing. The Killer Woman has survived, however, to become a popular pinup in Desert Storm. Appearing originally in a jeans advertisement, she reappeared in the desert war zone: a "slim, lanky" figure, "tough, fit, cool, and lethal," she leans against a police car and casually dangles a carbine—a dream woman ready for combat (Ewen, 209).

The famous exponent of hard bodies, Jane Fonda, has said that *Playboy* images from Vietnam made her look at her body with "new eyes" (Fonda 20).[4] The softness of her Barbarella-self, she saw, had become complicit in the sexual consumption of Vietnamese women

3. For a psychoanalytical critique of the relationship between Beauty and the Beast in horror movies, see Williams.
4. For Fonda's changing persona in relation to warfare, see Dyer.

who were having themselves "Americanized"—eyes rounded, breasts enlarged—to enhance their value to American soldiers. Fonda's famous slogan to "go for the burn" thus traces back, through sordid images of consumption, to Vietnam, where O'Brien's Mary Anne Bell would carry out its mandate by "burning away into nothing." A simple but insatiable desire for profit ties this savagely exhilarating and anorexic vision of the burning body to a multibillion-dollar diet industry, as well as to books and movies.[5] Fonda turns the story of her self-transformation into a personal testimony that will help sell her aerobics *Workout Book,* just as countless products—face creams, perfumes, cigarettes—are sold through a movie star's endorsement. The *New York Magazine* attributes the emergence of "Killer Women" movies to the film industry's notorious pursuit of profit: "To appeal to women repulsed or bored by male action movies, they ["movie-moguls"] have created these woman warriors" (Baumgold 29). Killer Women sell. They have, indeed, become stylish artifacts used to sell designer killer clothes: black leather bike jackets, gold hip-hop chains, Chanel ammo bands—violence fashioned into chic (Baumgold 23–29).

This trajectory of an American woman consumer, traced with elliptical starkness by two male writers, raises aesthetic, moral, and cultural questions. Does the recurrence of the same deterministic structure of desire in stories set in different times and places point to static elements in human behavior, in the literary forms that represent them, and in the shaping forces of consumerism? Is O'Brien's Mary Anne, a woman wandering in a global village, continuing an itinerary laid out for Dreiser's Carrie? Chicago, New York and, eventually, Tra Bong—might this have been Carrie's progression if ninety years after *Sister Carrie,* Dreiser were to describe a young desirous woman following her man to Vietnam? There she would encounter a land seemingly beyond the consumer capitalism emerging in Chicago and New York, and yet a land that had become the ultimate *site* of consumption and the *sight* of an ultimate consumption—as it was destroyed and wasted, consumed by the fires of war. Indeed, Baudrillard (67) sees the Vietnam War as an insidiously involuted expression of modern consumer capitalism that functions as a society of the spectacle—to use Debord's phrase (Debord). In this society, as in Carrie's world, "it's all theatre" (Pynchon 3).

When O'Brien's narrator accused his fellow soldiers of having "blinders on about women . . . [about how] gentle and peaceful they are" (117), he apparently meant to clear himself of sexism. Nevertheless, I believe, his story redacts a stereotypical male fear of females who step out of their prescribed social roles. Drawn into the

5. For the relationship of the "culture of slimming" to late capitalism, see Schwartz.

heart of darkness that is war, Mary Anne rejects these roles to become, she believes, her real self, the killer woman who devours, wastes, and wastes away into a fiery image. Moralizing about a woman's fall, the narrator fitfully forgets that men created Vietnam, men transported Mary Anne to Tra Bong, and insidiously secretive men mediated her desires. As she enters a man's world and begins to want what she sees, Mary Anne seems sadly, if savagely, "a Waif amid Forces," to use Dreiser's words, a "wisp in the wind," a moth drawn to the flame.

Mary Anne's helpless submission to her surroundings dramatizes Dreiser's dictum that to see is to succumb. Defining the human mind as "a mere reflection of sensory impressions," and tracing impressions to the "flood of things" (203) [195], Dreiser made an equation between seeing and succumbing irrefragable. Carrie's mind is flooded by sensory impressions of the city's material things, and it succumbs; Mary Anne's mind is flooded by impressions of darkness, mystery, and violence. As in *Sister Carrie*, the most striking impressions in *The Things They Carried* are visual, and they are all of war. Another story in the collection states explicitly that war "fills the eye. It commands you" (85), a view shared by an *Esquire* article entitled "Why Men Love War." Written by a Vietnam veteran, the article traces men's intense feeling for war, a feeling fit to he called love, to a "fundamental [human] passion . . . to see things, what the Bible calls the lust of the eye and the Marines in Vietnam called eye fucking" (Broyles 56).[6] "Sweetheart of the Song Tra Bong" describes its heroine's blue eyes constantly looking, staring, narrowing, squinting, focusing, and reflecting the world they see by turning jungle-green. This physiological response makes visible the force of stimuli so driving and deterministic that they transform desire into a craving need, and the self into a helpless and atavistically craving creature.

Thus O'Brien's story displaces the biological determinism it reinscribes to the trope of addiction, a reality to countless American soldiers: "Vietnam had the effect of a powerful drug: that mix of unnamed terror and unnamed pleasure that comes as the needle slips in." Seduced and pleasured, Mary Anne "wanted more . . . and after a time the wanting became needing, which then turned to craving" (113–14). *Sister Carrie* had described the city as a powerful drug, producing upon the newcomer's "untried mind" the same "craving" that "opium" produced upon the body (214) [206]. In both texts, the trope of addiction coalesces with that of male seduction as a powerful man overcomes a helpless woman whose passivity requires a passive grammatical voice: Carrie is seduced by Drouet and that "inhuman" or "super-human" tempter, the city; and Mary

6. For the connection between looking, desire, and shame in warfare, see Wyatt.

is Anne "seduced by the Greenies." Social historians who describe "customer seduction" or commodities "wrapped in an aesthetic of seduction"—common and recurrent descriptions—place modern consumerism within the same paradigm of male power over a fatally submissive female.[7]

This submission raises complicated moral issues in both texts. In Vietnam, O'Brien's narrator says, everyone comes in clean and goes our dirty; how dirty is "a question of degree" and of moral integrity. In Dreiser's city, we are told, a young woman "becomes better, or . . . becomes worse" (1) [1], though the difference seems equivocal in *Sister Carrie*.[8] Would a poor working-girl have become a better person if she had remained in a shoe factory punching holes for four dollars a week? Did she become worse by accepting "two soft, green, handsome, ten-dollar bills"—perhaps the most sensuously seductive dollar bills in American literature? Should the blue-eyed sweetheart of Sigma Chi have remained untouched by the violence she saw in Vietnam and blithely returned home to await marriage and motherhood in a "gingerbread house" with "yellow-haired children"? Or should she have stayed to bear witness in her own being to the atavistic savagery of war by retreating farther and farther into its darkness to become its terrible realization?

Moral questions became legal problems when succumbing to the "drag of desire," as Dreiser phrased it, led to criminal behavior. Oliver Twist's innocent request for *more* evoked an awful, if comic, prophecy: "That boy will he hung . . . I know that boy will he hung" (37). In Victorian England, respectable middle-class ladies were lured into crime in glamorous new department stores where they suffered sudden attacks of kleptomania, a hitherto unknown disease of women overcome by an irresistible urge to steal. Women apprehended for department store thefts had a common plea: "I couldn't help myself."[9] Like moths drawn to the flame, they responded to glass showcases designed "to force people to possession." Victorian doctors explained that women "forced to steal" had been seduced by material things and victimized by their "sexual organs." Treatment of their "pelvic diseases" might entail surgery, to which kleptomaniacs swooning in Victorian courtrooms tearfully assented in hope of being freed from the blight of "biological determinism."

Critics of American consumerism, tracing back to Veblen and beyond, have described the deliberate evocation of acquisitive desire as conspiratorial, if not criminal, a secret attack by "hidden persuaders"—to use Vance Packard's famous phrase—upon an unsuspecting

---

7. For the concepts of the seductiveness of commodities and the seduction of the consumer, see Artley, Bowlby, Ewen and Ewen, and Hennion and Méadel.
8. For the impact of naturalistic determinism on the moral view of conduct, see Walcutt.
9. For kleptomania and the department store, see Abelson.

public. Discerning a businesslike "application of the wisdom of advertising, public relations, and behavioral science to . . . modern elections," historians have argued that the political "packaging and sale of candidates to voter-consumers" has resulted in an impersonalized mediated relationship of "packages to packages . . . shaped by managers who are themselves for sale" (Westbrook 145). In this view, everyone in modern politics is a salesman, like Dreiser's perennial Drouet, or like Hurstwood, a manager, or like Carrie, an actor— no one less so, perhaps, than our country's telegenic presidents. The vocabulary of politics has become synonymous with that of an advertising industry concentrated upon image-making, perception (as opposed to a putative reality), and selling.[1] Public policies, like brand-name products, have to be sold, and politicians, like traveling salesmen, energetically take to the road or to the shopping mall to buy a pair of socks.

Historians have claimed that the commodification of books, begun with the invention of the printing press, created an autonomous space for verbal advertisements. Books destined for a competitive marketplace carried the printer's own unabashed testimonials to their excellence. In time, these commendatory inserts were printed separately and distributed as publicity flyers, the precursors, historians believe, of modern advertisements and the endorsements still printed in today's paperbacks.[2] *The Things They Carried* contains six introductory pages of single-spaced excerpts from glowing reviews not unconscious of their incitements to buy. "If I can't get you to go out and buy this book," one reviewer writes, "then I've failed you." The profuse advertising of *The Things They Carried* contrasts with the lack of advertising that initially repressed the sales of *Sister Carrie*. The story of the novel's virtual censorship is famous in literary history both for its apocryphal versions, generated mainly by Dreiser, and its elusive truth.[3] In 1907, *Sister Carrie* was reissued by a publisher apparently impressed by a comment on the novel's appearance and quick disappearance: "In this country, the popularity of a book depends upon 'judicious advertising' " (Raferty). The publisher's ten-page advertisement recapitulating *Sister Carrie*'s infamous lack of advertising suggested that the novel had been considered too daring, too raw, for the American public. What better way to sell the book?

Today, the serious consideration being given to *Sister Carrie* attests to its sheer inexhaustibility.[4] Absorbing all the attention it has received, the text, like its insatiable heroine, cries out for more, the promise of a future that seems assured by its past. The future of *The*

---

1. For advertising and politics, see Rogin and Silverman.
2. For the commodification of books, see Eisenstein and Wicke.
3. For histories of the publication of *Sister Carrie*, see Brennan and Salzman.
4. For recent studies of *Sister Carrie*, see Howard, Kaplan, Michaels, and Pizer, *New Essays*.

Things They Carried remains to be seen. It may be bought and used and then used up. Or it may withstand the fickleness of fashion, critical and literary, and resist consumption through the strength of its highly praised style. Although clumsiness of style or lack of style has been considered Dreiser's weakness, *Sister Carrie* is a book that critics, in their insatiability, cannot consume. And yet unless it is consumed—bought, read, used, and used again—it ceases to exist. It needs for its self-actualization, its fulfillment as a work of art, the consumerist society that had depleted its characters, even the woman it enhanced, a rich and famous actress. Like Carrie Meeber, the novel must always have more: more readers, more appreciation, more sales—ultimately, an elusive *more* that represents the mystery of human desire.

"The ultimate meaning of desire," we have been told, "is death" (Girard 290), but the death of desire in characters who seem beyond consumerism—because like homeless Hurstwood they cannot buy, or like Mary Anne they see nothing material worth buying—turns out, in the two texts I compare, to be deadly. When Hurstwood comes to the end of desire, when he does not want anything more, he dies. When Mary Anne has everything she wants, she becomes an agent of death. Wanting more, Carrie goes on living, dreaming of a happiness that, fortunately perhaps, she will never know. Thus she remains, forever, the producer's ideally insatiable consumer.

I began by asking what more Carrie could want and ended with an unlikely sister to Carrie—a young woman who had found "everything" she wanted, so she said, in the violence of Vietnam. This kinship might have been anticipated if one believes, as various critics do, that Vietnam was as much the site of late capitalism as the modern American city, and that capitalism and a culture of consumption are inextricably intertwined.[5] In *Sister Carrie*, the mediation of consumerism through a woman's desire produced a sequence of seeing, wanting, consuming, and being consumed that I find reproduced in the distinctly different postmodern text of the "Sweetheart of the Song Tra Bong." Strangely enough, time has not altered the sequential pattern of desire inscribed in Dreiser's *Sister Carrie*. Nor has a drastic change of setting disrupted its design. Indeed, the ways of consuming women in naturalistic fiction appear to be static, impervious to the historical changes effected by a seemingly radical change of setting, of time and place. In a Vietnam bush as in burgeoning Chicago, a fixed relationship between stimulus and response determines female behavior and transforms an innocent young American

5. For postmodern capitalism and the culture of consumption, see Jameson.

woman, a small-town girl from the Midwest, into a consumer. Her desire, her insatiability, seems synonymous with a sense of lack she finds ineradicable. Seeing what others have and she lacks, this unconsummated and consuming woman believes that she must have more, and that having more will allow her to become (as Maslow put it) more and more the person she sees herself capable of becoming. This desire for self-actualization, a culturally inscribed individualistic desire, turns Carrie and Mary Anne into consuming women whose generic similarities should not remain hidden by differences in appearance. A fashionably dressed Broadway star and a camouflaged killer waiting to strike—in either guise, naturalism's consuming woman glows with a devouring fire. In *Sister Carrie*, the fiery image of a body that had been consumed with desire appears in an advertisement designed to ignite desire in others. In O'Brien's story, a burning body becomes the site of consumption as a woman is consumed by what she sees in a land wasted by war. There, as in America's cities, her fate, like her desire, is determined; in both settings, the place where determinism and desire intersect is the body of a gazing woman. The woman herself is a static figure, arrested in a pattern of desire, but she generates a vortex of forces that flow inexorably toward consumption and death. Men should fear this woman, for a man who gazes upon her may be doomed, as may be those upon whom she gazes. In *Sister Carrie*, Hurstwood becomes a nameless pauper who must die because his eyes once glowed at the sight of Carrie Meeber. In "Sweetheart of the Song Tra Bong," nameless others die because Mary Anne Bell's eyes glow with the green of Vietnam's jungle.

As for Demi Moore the actress—like Carrie, she ended up with money. In the movie *Indecent Proposal*, the actress portrays a woman who sells her body for a million dollars. One thing has changed in the last hundred years: a consuming woman's price and reward. In Dreiser's novel, poor Carrie Meeber accepted two soft, green, handsome ten-dollar bills for her desirous self, and when she had "in hand" a hundred and fifty dollars, Carrie Madenda the actress found herself rich beyond belief and, for a moment, happy.

Works Cited

Abelson, Elaine S. *When Ladies Go A-Thieving: Middle-Class Shoplifters in the Victorian Department Store.* New York: Oxford University Press, 1989.

Artley, Alexandra, ed. *The Golden Age of Shop Design: European Shop Interiors, 1800–1939.* New York: Whitney Library of Design, 1976.

Banner, Lois W. *American Beauty*. New York: Knopf, 1983, 17–27.

Baudrillard, Jean. "The Precession of Simulacra." *Simulations*. Trans. Paul Foss et al. New York: Semiotext(e), 1983.

Baumgold, Julie. "Killer Women: Here Come the Hardbodies." *New York Magazine* 24 (1991): 23–29.

Benjamin, Walter. "This Space for Rent." *Reflections: Essays, Aphorisms, Autobiographical Writings*. Trans. Edmund Jephcott. Ed. Peter Demetz. New York: Harcourt Brace Jovanovich, 1978.

Benson, Susan Porter. "Palace of Consumption and Machine for Selling: The American Department Store, 1880–1940." *Radical History Review* 21 (1979): 199–221.

Berger John. *Ways of Seeing*. New York: Penguin, 1979.

Berman, Ronald. *Advertising and Social Change*. Beverly Hills, CA: Sage, 1981.

Boorstin, Daniel J. *The Americans: The Democratic Experience*. New York: Random House, 1973, 101–09.

Bourdieu, Pierre. *Distinction: A Social Critique of the Judgement of Taste*. Trans. Richard Nice. Cambridge: Harvard University Press, 1984.

Bowlby, Rachel. *Just Looking: Consumer Culture in Dreiser, Gissing, and Zola*. New York: Methuen, 1985.

Brennan, Stephen C. "The Publication of *Sister Carrie*: Old and New Fictions." *American Literary Realism* 18 (1985): 55–68.

Broyles, William, Jr. "Why Men Love War." *Esquire* 102 (1984). 56.

Buckley, Kerry W. "The Selling of a Psychologist: John Broadus Watson and the Application of Behavioral Techniques to Advertising." *Journal of the History of Behavioral Sciences* 18 (1982): 207–21.

Cohen, David. *J. B. Watson, the Founder of Behaviorism: A Biography*. London: Routledge and Kegan Paul, 1979.

Debord, Guy. *Comments on the Society of the Spectacle*. Trans. Malcolm Imrie. London: Verso, 1990.

Dreiser, Theodore. *Sister Carrie*. Ed. Donald Pizer. New York: W. W. Norton, 1970. [Throughout Gelfant's essay, page references to this Norton Critical Edition are given in brackets after the original citations—*Editor*.]

Dyer, Richard. *Stars*. London: British Film Institute, 1979, 72–98.

Eisenstein, Elizabeth L. *The Printing Press as an Agent of Change: Communications and Cultural Transformations in Early-Modern Europe*. 2 vols. Cambridge: Cambridge University Press, 1979.

Ewen, Stuart, and Elizabeth Ewen. *Channels of Desire: Mass Images and the Shaping of American Consciousness*. New York: McGraw-Hill, 1982. Rev. ed., Minneapolis: University of Minnesota Press, 1992.

Fenichel, Otto. "The Scoptophilic Instinct and Identification." *The*

Collected Papers of Otto Fenichel, 1st Series. New York: Norton, 1953, 373–97.

Fonda, Jane. *Jane Fonda's Workout Book.* New York: Simon and Schuster, 1981.

Friedberg, Anne. "A Denial of Difference: Theories of Cinematic Identification." *Psychoanalysis & Cinema.* Ed. E. Ann Kaplan. New York: Routledge, 1990, 36–45.

Garfield, Deborah. "Taking a Part: Actor and Audience in Theodore Dreiser's *Sister Carrie.*" *American Literary Realism* 16 (1983): 223–39.

Girard, René. *Desire, Deceit, and the Novel: Self and Other in Literary Structure.* Trans. Yvonne Freccero. Baltimore: Johns Hopkins University Press, 1965.

Hennion, Antione, and Méadel, Cécile. "The Artisans of Desire: The Mediation of Advertising between Product and Consumer." *Sociological Theory* 7 (1989): 191–209.

Howard, June. *Form and History in American Literary Naturalism.* Chapel Hill: University of North Carolina Press, 1985.

Jameson, Fredric. "Postmodernism and Consumer Society." *The Anti-Aesthetic: Essays on Postmodern Culture.* Ed. Hal Foster. Port Townsend, WA: Bay Press, 1983, 111–25.

———. "Postmodernism, or the Cultural Logic of Late Capitalism." *New Left Review* 146 (1984): 53–93.

Kaplan, Amy. "The Sentimental Revolt of *Sister Carrie.*" *The Social Construction of American Realism.* Chicago: University of Chicago Press, 1988, 140–60.

Leach, William R. *Land of Desire: Merchants, Power, and the Rise of a New American Culture.* New York: Pantheon, 1993.

Leiss, William. *The Limits to Satisfaction: An Essay on the Problem of Needs and Commodities.* Toronto: University of Toronto Press, 1976.

Lurie, Alison. *The Language of Clothes.* New York: Random House, 1981.

Maslow, Abraham H. "A Theory of Human Motivation (1943)." *Motivation and Personality.* New York: Harper & Row, 1970.

McCracken, Grant. *Culture and Consumption: New Approaches to the Symbolic Character of Consumer Goods and Activities.* Bloomington: Indiana University Press, 1988.

Michaels, Walter Benn. "*Sister Carrie*'s Popular Economy." *The Gold Standard and the Logic of Naturalism.* Berkeley: University of California Press, 1987, 29–58.

Mitchell, Lee Clark. "Naturalism and the Languages of Determinism." *The Columbia Literary History of the United States.* Ed. Emory Elliott et al. New York: Columbia University Press, 1988, 534–49.

————. "Taking Determinism Seriously." *Determined Fictions: American Literary Naturalism.* New York: Columbia University Press, 1989, xii–xvii.

O'Brien, Tim. *The Things They Carried.* New York: Penguin, 1990, 98–125.

O'Connor, James. *Accumulation Crisis.* New York: Blackwell, 1984.

Pizer, Donald. *Twentieth-Century American Literary Naturalism: An Interpretation.* Carbondale: Southern Illinois University Press, 1982.

————. ed. *New Essays on Sister Carrie.* New York: Cambridge University Press, 1991.

Pratt, Mary Louise. *Imperial Eyes: Travel Writing and Transculturation.* New York: Routledge, 1992.

Prown, Jules David. "Mind in Matter: An Introduction to Material Culture Theory and Method." *Winterthur Portfolio* 17 (1982): 6.

Pynchon, Thomas. *Gravity's Rainbow.* New York: Viking, 1973, 3.

Raferty, John H. "By Bread Alone." *Reedy's Mirror* (December 5, 1901), quoted in Richard Lingeman, *Theodore Dreiser: At the Gates of the City, 1871–1907.* New York: Putnam's, 1986, 298.

Rahv, Philip. "Notes on the Decline of Naturalism." *Documents of Modern Literary Realism.* Ed. George J. Becker. Princeton: Princeton University Press, 1963, 579–90.

Roach, Mary Ellen. "The Social Symbolism of Women's Dress." *The Fabrics of Culture: The Anthropology of Clothing and Adornment.* Ed. Justine M. Cordwell and Ronald A. Schwarz. New York: Mouton, 1979, 415–22.

Rogin, Michael. " 'Make My Day!' Spectacle as Amnesia in Imperial Politics." *Representations* 29 (1990): 99–123.

Salzman, Jack. "The Publication of *Sister Carrie*: Fact and Fiction." *Library Chronicle of the University of Pennsylvania* 33 (1967): 119–33.

Schwartz, Hillel. *Never Satisfied: A Cultural History of Diets, Fantasies, and Fat.* New York: Free Press, 1986, 327–36.

Silverman, Debora. *Selling Culture: Bloomingdale's, Diana Vreeland, and the New Aristocracy of Taste in Reagan's America.* New York: Pantheon, 1986.

Slotkin, Richard. *Regeneration Through Violence: The Mythology of the American Frontier, 1600–1860.* Middletown, CT: Wesleyan University Press, 1972.

Sohn-Rethel, Alfred. *Intellectual and Manual Labor: A Critique of Epistemology.* Atlantic Highlands, NJ: Humanities Press, 1978.

Veblen, Thorstein. "The Economic Theory of Women's Dress" (1894). *Essays in Our Changing Order.* Ed. Leon Ardzrooni. New York: Viking, 1945, 68.

————. *The Theory of the Leisure Class.* New York: Viking Penguin, 1976 [1899].

Walcutt, Charles C. *American Literary Naturalism, A Divided Stream.* Minneapolis: University of Minnesota Press, 1956.

Westbrook, Robert B. "Politics as Consumption: Managing the Modern American Election." *The Culture of Consumption: Critical Essays in American History, 1880–1980.* Ed. Richard W. Fox and T. J. Jackson Lears. New York: Pantheon, 1983.

Wicke, Jennifer. *Advertising Fictions: Literature, Advertisement & Social Reading.* New York: Columbia University Press, 1988.

Wilkinson, Peter. "Why Demi Moore Wants More." *Redbook* (January 1993): 48–51, 91–92.

Williams, Linda. "When the Woman Looks." *Re-Vision: Essays in Feminist Film Criticism.* Ed. Mary Ann Doane et al. Frederick, MD: University Publications of America, 1984, 83–99.

Wyatt, David. *Out of the Sixties: Storytelling and the Vietnam Generation.* New York: Cambridge University Press, 1993, 182–83.

DONALD PIZER

The Problem of American Literary Naturalism and Theodore Dreiser's *Sister Carrie*†

The "problem" presented to the critic and historian by American literary naturalism has not been to describe the ideological origins of the movement.[1] Almost from the first, the philosophical roots of naturalism in America have been firmly associated with the pronouncements and fiction of Emile Zola, and especially with Zola's 1880 defense of literary naturalism in *The Experimental Novel.*

Zola insisted in *The Experimental Novel* that the principle of "the absolute determinism in the conditions of existence of natural phenomena,"[2] which science accepts in relation to physical life in general, should also be accepted by the contemporary novelist seeking

---

† From *American Literary Realism* 32 (Fall 1999): 1–11. Reprinted by permission of the author.

1. Although the title of my essay echoes those of Michael Davitt Bell's *The Problem of American Realism: Studies in the Cultural History of a Literary Idea* (Chicago: Univ. of Chicago Press, 1993) and Yoshinobu Hakutani's "*Sister Carrie* and the Problem of Naturalism," *Twentieth Century Literature,* 13 (1967), 3–17, I do not address the subject as do these writers. Indeed, the point of my essay is in part to reject their conventional critique of Dreiser and other American naturalists for not fulfilling the philosophical assumptions generally attributed to the movement.

2. Emile Zola, *The Experimental Novel,* in *Documents of Modern Literary Realism,* ed. George J. Becker (Princeton: Princeton Univ. Press, 1963), p. 163.

to depict the fates of specific individuals. The novelist should be an experimenter in the sense that he "sets the characters of a particular study in motion, in order to show that the series of events therein will be those demanded by the determinism of the phenomenon under study."[3] For Zola, in his twenty-volume Rougon-Macquart series, the tracing of this determinism took the form of depicting the history of a family negatively affected both by genetic defects within the family and by the destructive social environment of the Second Empire.

In addition to the assumption that Zolaesque pronouncements and practice had a major impact on late nineteenth-century American novelists, literary historians have also almost always held that the translation of deterministic ideas into American terms was a response by American writers to the rapid urbanization and industrialization of the country in the late nineteenth century and to the rapacious capitalism which accompanied this process. V. L. Parrington, in 1930, set the tone for several generations of critics seeking to discuss American naturalism when he noted of late nineteenth-century American civilization that "the bigness of the economic machine dwarfs the individual and creates a sense of impotency"[4] and that "the big city reduces the individual to a unit."[5] More recently, a neo-Marxist approach to the interpretation of late nineteenth-century America has resulted in a revival of the notion of the important role of deterministic social forces during the period, but now more often in the form of the victimization of the individual by a consumeristic ethos. In both Parrington's and this more recent explanation, late nineteenth-century American social and economic conditions are conventionally viewed as having confirmed to the literary naturalist of the 1890s the validity of Zola's emphasis on the deterministic basis of life.

The problem, therefore, has not been how to describe the origins of the naturalistic movement in America but rather how to reconcile what actually occurs in late nineteenth-century naturalistic fiction and these presumed ideological origins, since the fiction does not appear to coherently express the ideology. A number of explanations have been offered for this failure in coherence between a presumed ideology and its fictional representation.

First, there is what one can call the "literature as flawed philosophy" explanation. In this view of American naturalism, it is held that it is either impossible to write a deterministic novel because the philosophy does not correspond to human behavior, as E. H. Cady

---

3. Zola, p. 166.
4. V. L. Parrington, "Naturalism in American Fiction," *The Beginnings of Critical Realism in America, 1860–1920*, vol. 3 of *Main Currents in American Thought* (New York: Harcourt Brace, 1930), p. 327.
5. Parrington, p. 327.

claimed in a notable essay of 1971,[6] or that a deterministic novel is so inherently limited by its simplistic philosophical base that it cannot be a successful work of fiction, as Malcolm Cowley and Lionel Trilling stated in well-known essays of the late 1940s.[7] Both of these arguments begin with the presumption that Zola's deterministic ideas do in fact constitute the underlying intent or basis of American naturalistic novels and that these ideas can therefore serve to account for the inadequacy of works in the movement. Thus, on the one hand, the critic looking for a clear expression of Zolaesque deterministic ideas in fiction presumed to be naturalistic fails to find these ideas in the fiction and therefore concludes that this absence of an intended effect constitutes the weakness of the fiction, while on the other hand the critic who insists that they are present finds in their presence the source of the failure of the fiction.

There has recently been some revival of the effort to identify naturalism as above all an expression of deterministic ideas, as in studies by John Conder and Lee Clark Mitchell,[8] an effort which suggests the continuing vitality of the identification. But, as before, the connection either diminishes the fiction in advance of careful critical analysis of the work itself or is forced upon the fiction, and in both cases constitutes principally the continuing effort to establish a coherent center in an otherwise diffuse movement.

Secondly, there is what can be called the "divided stream" philosophical argument, a position associated principally with Charles C. Walcutt's landmark 1956 study *American Literary Naturalism, A Divided Stream* and echoed by many critics since, including myself to some degree.[9] Walcutt believed that naturalism has its origins not only in late nineteenth-century materialism and determinism but also in an earlier nineteenth-century transcendental faith in the spirit and in free will. This "divided stream" helps account both for the various seemingly irreconcilable themes in the typical naturalistic novel and for the inability of the naturalistic novel to find an adequate form, since novelists unconsciously undermine deterministic forms with anomalous elements derived from older kinds of belief. To Walcutt, this transcendental element in the divided stream is a kind of subversive force, unperceived by the novelist and

6. E. H. Cady, "Three Sensibilities: Romancer, Realist, Naturalist," *The Light of Common Day: Realism in American Fiction* (Bloomington: Indiana Univ. Press, 1971).
7. Malcolm Cowley, " 'Not Men': A Natural History of American Naturalism," *Kenyon Review*, 9 (1947), 414–35; Lionel Trilling, "Reality in America," *The Liberal Imagination* (New York: Viking, 1950), pp. 3–21.
8. John J. Conder, *Naturalism in American Fiction: The Classic Phase* (Lexington: Univ. of Kentucky Press, 1984); Lee Clark Mitchell, *Determined Fictions: American Literary Naturalism* (New York: Columbia Univ. Press, 1989).
9. Charles C. Walcutt, *American Literary Naturalism, A Divided Stream* (Minneapolis: Univ. of Minnesota Press, 1956); Donald Pizer, *The Theory and Practice of American Literary Naturalism: Selected Essays and Reviews* (Carbondale: Southern Illinois Univ. Press, 1993).

therefore preventing him from achieving his announced aims. Thus, despite his hugely productive insight that naturalism is not a "pure" product of late nineteenth-century scientism and materialism but rather combines old and new ways of thinking, Walcutt still engages in a comparison of discursive naturalistic beliefs and the putative fictional expression of those beliefs and thus still finds the fiction flawed in its failure to coherently express those beliefs.

Finally, there is what I have named the "naturalist hoisted on his own petard" philosophical argument. This recent tendency, derived from New Historicist and Cultural Studies methodologies, as in the work of Walter Benn Michaels,[1] rejects the naturalist's assumption that he is writing as a critic of his society in dramatizing the determinism inherent in the crushing of the individual by social forces. The naturalist, as a bourgeois functioning in a bourgeois society, is in fact, and unaware to himself, held captive by the very social values he believes he is criticizing—held captive both in his response to market conditions in the production of his work and in his unconscious endorsement of a consumerist ideology. Often cited as evidence for this position are Theodore Dreiser's revision of the first draft of *Sister Carrie* under pressure to make the work more saleable and his powerful identification with Carrie's response, in the opening portion of the novel, to the material splendor of the department store as an institution. The attraction of this approach is that it seems to "rescue" the naturalistic novel from inconsistency by finding both the novel and the novelist irresistibly enveloped by the society of which they are the products. But it also, as we shall see, often misrepresents the work in its effort to trace within it a uniform reflection of the social values the critic claims for the period as a whole.

To move on to the relationship of Theodore Dreiser's *Sister Carrie* to the general issue of the failure of connection between the ideology and fiction of American literary naturalism, it may well be asked why I have selected this specific novel as a basis for examining the issue in concrete form. One important reason lies in the centrality of Dreiser in any discussion of American literary naturalism. This centrality arises from his personal background in a poverty-stricken immigrant home, his immersion in late nineteenth-century thought and his effort to reflect the ideas derived from this reading in his fiction (he is far more the ideologue than his contemporaries Stephen Crane and Frank Norris), and his public role as lightning rod for the movement given the length and prominence of his career. Furthermore, of all of Dreiser's fiction, it has been *Sister Carrie* which has conventionally served as an introduction to his naturalism and thus to American naturalism as a whole. *Carrie*, as his first novel, reflects

---

1. Walter Benn Michaels, "*Sister Carrie*'s Popular Economy," in *The Gold Standard and the Logic of Naturalism* (Berkeley: Univ. of California Press, 1987), pp. 29–58.

his effort to shape material derived closely from his own difficult early life, and that of his sister Emma, into an expression of his basic response to experience. It also contains many of the characteristics traditionally associated with literary naturalism, including, in connection with the portrayal of Hurstwood, a brief glance at a biochemical explanation of behavior and a close account of the decline of a character in the context of an urban setting.

How, then, has *Sister Carrie* served the purpose of the various interpretive schools I have noted which seek to discuss naturalism in America as above all a flawed movement because of its failure to express a coherent naturalistic ideology of determinism?

First, it is argued that Dreiser in the novel either thinly or confusingly depicts the sources of character within a genetic or environmental determinism. Very little of Carrie's background is available, for example, as a basis for understanding the origin of her nature or actions, since we are told almost nothing about her parents or of her life before she comes to Chicago as a young woman. She is thus more a blank to be written upon by her adult experience than a figure fully shaped by her origins. As for Hurstwood, we again know nothing of his early life. Dreiser does make a weak and minor effort in the infamous passage about anastates and katastates early in the New York portion of the novel to offer a chemical basis for Hurstwood's decline in that city, but he undertakes this explanation briefly and almost casually and then forgets it.

A second conventional reading of *Sister Carrie* as flawed naturalism is that the city as environment plays a seemingly contradictory role in the lives of the two principal characters. Thus, it is argued, Carrie is portrayed initially as almost a cipher; she is just another immature and untrained figure from the provinces to be overwhelmed by the overpowering destructive conditions of a modern metropolis. But she in fact survives and rises through a Horatio Alger combination of luck and pluck, relying on her inherent qualities of perseverance and sexual attractiveness and on her desire to achieve success. Dreiser's point, one that runs counter to expectations inherent in a naturalistic ideology, is that the right kind of temperament can capitalize on the possibilities for personal gain in an otherwise threatening environment and thus advance rather than be crushed.

A different but analogous problem arises in any effort to interpret Hurstwood in deterministic terms. He does indeed appear, in the New York portion of the novel, to be a clear indication of an individual determined by his environment in Dreiser's depiction and discussion of him as a figure bred in the comparatively small pond of Chicago and thus unable to compete and survive in the more competitive New York ocean. But Hurstwood is far more than this, since Dreiser's characterization of him in the Chicago portion of the novel makes clear that whereas Carrie's initial position disguises her underlying strengths, Hurstwood's disguises his weaknesses. The lengthy initial description of Hurstwood, for example, as a minor functionary whose only importance lies in the trappings of his role, and his lack of foresight in his dealings with his wife and of decisiveness when faced by the temptation of the unlocked safe—all characterize a man who may appear prominent and strong to Carrie and Drouet but who is not the man he appears to be. Thus, the adverse conditions Hurstwood encounters in New York do not, in fact, determine his fate but rather serve to bring to the surface characteristics already present in his make-up, characteristics which now become dominant in the shaping of his life.

As I have already noted, yet another attack on *Sister Carrie* flawed naturalism is present in the claim by recent cultural critics and New Historicists that the novel expresses its determinism not as a coherent body of dramatized authorial ideas but as a largely submerged web of representations of cultural agency at work whatever the beliefs of the author. This form of criticism shifts the emphasis in a deterministic reading of the novel from Hurstwood to Carrie and claims that her drive to success within the consumerist ethos of a capitalist culture is an instance of the powerful conditioning effects of that culture and thus constitutes the significant participation of the novel in literary naturalism. Often cited as evidence of Carrie in thrall to her culture are her admiration for social display of any kind, her capacity to adapt her mimetic ability to the marketplace, and her discarding of Hurstwood when he becomes an obstacle to her advancement.

Critics of this persuasion, however, usually ignore Dreiser's own clear depiction, especially toward the close of the novel, of the limited impact of Carrie's culture on her underlying nature. Ames stimulates in Carrie both an interest in the life of the mind and in a less profitable but more meaningful theater, both of which, it is implied, she will pursue. In addition, Carrie herself is not satisfied at the close of the novel with the material advantages which success has brought her, as Dreiser states with considerable emphasis in his final apostrophe about her continuing search for happiness. In short, Dreiser depicts Carrie's early whole-hearted pursuit of the material principally as a condition of her economic and social need at that time, not as a permanent element welded to her character by her culture. So here, too, a deterministic reading fails to account for Carrie—in this instance, fails to account for her in relation both to Dreiser's portrayal of her development and to how he wishes us to understand her at the close of the novel.

A final attack on *Sister Carrie* as incoherent naturalism focuses on Dreiser himself in his role as Balzacian commentator on the meaning of the action he depicts, and holds that Dreiser in this role seems to vary in his conception of the philosophical nature of that meaning. So, in an often cited passage, Dreiser, in an apologia for Carrie's sexual fall, claims that "man is but a wisp in the wind"[2] because his free will has not evolved sufficiently for him to resist the pull of instinctive needs. But not long afterwards, again in relation to Carrie's fall, he announces that there is more to the subject of morals "than mere conformity to the law of evolution" (68) [65], since the human desire for beauty creates its own moral sanctions. Here, too, then, in the shift from the discussion of Carrie as but another "wisp in the wind" to that as a figure in full pursuit of the "beauty" of life, there is a significant change in emphasis from a deterministic ethic to one permitting and even endorsing the agency implicit in the imaginative seeker.

What is common in all of these critical readings of *Sister Carrie* is not only the stress on the presence of a significant strain of determinism in the novel, but also the discovery of equally significant elements which compromise or contradict this strain. We return via this criticism, therefore, to the problem posed initially: Is there a way of reconciling a reading of *Sister Carrie* as naturalism with the failure of the novel to fulfill the principal criterion for naturalism implied by the origins of the movement and still held by most critics as one of its essential constituents?

Two points in relation to the history of this problem which should be obvious by now are that there is no clear-cut answer to this question, given what actually occurs in the novel, and that the failure to readily find an answer in the actualities of the novel has often been used as a sure sign of the limitations of the work. But the failure of criticism to produce a clear-cut philosophical reading of *Sister Carrie* as deterministic fiction does not mean that the term *naturalism* cannot offer a productive approach to the novel, both for what occurs in the novel itself and for the relationship of the novel to other works of its literary moment. This continuing role for the term can be achieved by a greater recognition of two major ideas: first, that meaningful fiction can seldom translate general or abstract ideas into character, scene, action, and dialogue without muddling these ideas as ideas—that is, without rendering them as a kind of diffuse, complex, and sometimes inconsistent reflection on the human condition rather than as an indisputable finding—and, secondly, that despite this inevitable tendency toward philosophical fuzziness and incoherence, the general drift of represented ideas in a novel can still be

---

2. Theodore Dreiser, *Sister Carrie*, ed. Donald Pizer, 2nd ed. (New York: W. W. Norton, 1993), p. 56 [54]. Subsequent references to this edition will be cited parenthetically. [Throughout this essay, page references to this Norton Critical Edition are given in brackets after Pizer's original citations—*Editor*.]

described, analyzed, and given a name suggesting the nature of this drift.

Of course, the academic critical mind, trained as it is to examine for logical consistency both between various representations of belief (for example, between literary manifestos and the work of art) and within a specific structure of belief (that is, within the work of art itself) has difficulty accepting this premise. But, I would argue, when the object of study refuses to accommodate to a particular way of examining it, it is more productive for literary history to shift the basis for examination rather than to dismiss the object because of its failure to accommodate.

What kind of naturalism, then, in the sense of a drift or tendency toward an expression of a large-scale view of human nature and experience, does *Sister Carrie* express? Let us look at three major ways of characterizing this drift.

The first is the central role of inherent qualities of temperament in achieving success. Dreiser, as I have already noted, only vaguely or thinly suggests the origins of specific kinds of strength or weakness in a particular temperament, but the nature of these strengths and weaknesses and their role in the fate of the character are major centers of attention in the novel.

Thus, Carrie's will to survive is posited by Dreiser as a largely inarticulate quest for beauty and happiness which eventually translates into her artistic strength. She exhibits throughout the novel an ability to accommodate to what is demanded of her in fulfillment of this goal, including the capacity to be at the right place in the right time for the advancement of the goal, to violate social and moral norms in its pursuit, and even to be cruel if required. So, for example, during the Chicago portion of the novel, she is unwilling to accept the drab life of the Hansons and its industrial corollary the shoe factory as her destiny; she makes an unconsciously shrewd use of Drouet's and Hurstwood's interest in her; and she seizes upon the opportunity offered by the Avery Hall amateur theater production to define for herself and for others her capacity as an actress. She may be, in several senses and in Dreiser's oft-repeated imagery, a waif upon a stormy sea, but she is also always paddling toward port.

Hurstwood, on the other hand, is the true drifter, one whose weaknesses are initially disguised by his position, by Carrie's admiration for him, and by the vehemence of his desire for her. But his basic limitations, which are indirectly revealed to us in several ways during the Chicago half of the novel (as I have noted earlier), come to full expression in New York in response to the city's pressures and his own isolation within the vast swarm of the metropolis. Unlike Carrie in Chicago, who had faced much the same conditions, he cannot find a course in the face of these conditions and so truly becomes what Carrie was truly not, a waif on a stormy sea.

A second major drift toward naturalism in *Sister Carrie* is that of the significance and power of social circumstance. This tendency, I hope it is clear, is not to be confused with a clear-cut attempt to achieve an effect of environmental determinism, as in Stephen Crane's *Maggie*, with its depiction of the residents of a slum as fully imprisoned within a slum culture. It is rather more a matter of the close and powerful link between states of mind and feeling on the one hand and social setting on the other. The Hansons are an obvious example of this link in Dreiser's depiction of their dreary lives and their corresponding dullness and emptiness of spirit. But in a less obvious but more significant sense Carrie is also deeply responsive to the emotional resonance of her social world. So, early in the novel, she feels herself sinking in spirit to the level of the Hansons but quickly rises in spirit in response to the fine restaurant Drouet takes her to. Throughout the novel Dreiser will seek to show her capacity to seek out a better world for herself, but he is careful to show as well that her stimulus for doing so is in part the response of her spirit to her surroundings when she finds these inadequate to the needs of self—initially a response to the limitations of the Hansons and the shoe factory, but then to those of Drouet and their apartment after she has met Hurstwood, and then to Hurstwood himself and their middle class flat in New York after she discovers a more opulent world there. In other words, her fate is not determined by her surroundings but her surroundings nevertheless can be said to play a powerful role in her life in that the deep response of her nature to the specifics of her immediate world prompts the direction of her life. As Dreiser assures us at the close of the novel, lest we confuse Carrie's longing for the trappings of a better life with a superficial materialism, "not them, but that which they represented, she longed for" (368) [353].

Hurstwood offers a somewhat different version of the same relationship between an individual and his surroundings. As with Carrie, he is not determined by his conditions but rather, in his case, given the absence of an inner man, he is the sum total of his conditions. Thus, he is initially content in the role of successful middle class functionary and family head within a smallish world. However, he is shaken out of this role by a danger inherent in it—that of the reawakening of sexual desire—and is eventually cast in the role of a criminal escaping to another city where he will live in an adulterous relationship. He thus eventually sinks to the emotional state of the outcast and penniless bum that he has become. In other words, though Carrie has the capacity to push beyond her immediate social world and though Hurstwood is more defined than created by that world, both characters share a powerful responsiveness to their worlds, a responsiveness which helps shape the direction of their lives.

A third and last major instance of a naturalistic tendency in *Sister Carrie* is that of the novel's open acknowledgment of the great role of the sexual in human affairs. By the "great role of the sexual" I do not mean a depiction of sexual need as an uncontrollable gross animality, as occurs several times in Frank Norris' *McTeague*, but rather as the writer's recognition of the vital role of sexual desire in shaping a destiny. This theme is most clearly apparent, as I noted earlier, in Dreiser's portrayal of Hurstwood. It is Hurstwood's longing for Carrie which precipitates him into the downward plane of his life. Love and romance are not involved in his response to Carrie; he is drawn rather by what an attractive young woman represents to a middle-aged, sexually-jaded husband—an opportunity to regain his own youth and freshness by the sexual conquest and possession of a fresh, young girl.

Carrie presents a more complicated instance of the same theme, since except for a brief period of responsiveness to Hurstwood's attentions in Chicago she seems to lack sexuality in her own inner nature. But in fact she projects a theme of the power of sexual desire in ways other than its exhibition in her own behavior. So, her desire for the things of life can be seen as a sublimated sexuality, as a desire for possession taking the less risky and more immediately fulfilling direction of things. Also, Carrie's instinctive recognition that a man's desire can be channeled into a better life for herself, as is revealed most obviously in her relationship with Drouet, dramatizes the significant role that male desire has conventionally played in a woman's life. Along the same lines, Carrie's ability to mimic, during the Avery Hall performance, the emotions of a heroine who is the victim of a man's desire represents her awareness and responsiveness to this traditional depiction of a woman's tragic fate. And, finally, Carrie's recognition, at the close of the novel, of the danger of further sexual relationships in view of her awakened realization of the direction she wishes her life to take, is a confirmation of her awareness of the often powerful role that male sexuality plays in a woman's life. In short, whereas Hurstwood acts out the conventional role of the man brought low by desire, and Carrie the instructive role of the woman who acquires the ability either to use or to escape from the consequences of desire, both live in a world where sexual desire is often the most significant force in the shaping of an individual fate.

Now, a few final comments on the critical issues raised by this effort to reconcile *Sister Carrie* with a traditional view of the nature of American literary naturalism.

It has long been observed that Dreiser in *Sister Carrie* is not interested in confirming conventional moral ideas. His fallen heroine does not bemoan her fate or become pregnant but rather builds on her fall, at no loss of character or self-esteem, to achieve a better life. And his adulterous criminal declines not as a direct consequence of his criminal and sexual acts but because of what can be called natural causes—that is, because he is weak and cannot cope within a social scene where he is not protected by a secure social role.

What is necessary now is to accept the corollary premise that Dreiser is also not interested in confirming the conventional idea of the naturalist as determinist. The premises are corollary because in each case Dreiser wishes to reveal that life itself, as he perceives it, is far more complex (and thus perhaps ultimately less solvable) than the clear readings of the nature of existence present both in traditional and (in his own time) more recent systems of belief.

Nevertheless, without offering a clearcut endorsement of the naturalistic premise that man lives in a fully conditioned universe, Dreiser buys into a qualified acceptance of portions of that premise. His characters do survive or go under on the basis of specific aspects of personal strength; they are deeply responsive to the social conditions of their existence; and they live in a world in which sexual desire colors almost all human activity. In short, more than most novelists before the turn of the century, Dreiser questions the notion of the autonomous self by testing it within such concrete and often unyielding contexts as the irreducible givens of temperament in a specific self, the social setting within which the self functions, and the sexual nature of selfhood. Thus, while not writing a deterministic novel in *Sister Carrie*, his portrayals of Carrie and Hurstwood reveal his acceptance, with significant qualification, of the notion of a conditioned existence.

And it is indeed this complex qualification of a simple premise, rather than its coherent and consistent endorsement and representation, which constitutes the power and permanence of *Sister Carrie* and which also suggests the great usefulness of the novel in any attempt to understand the nature of late nineteenth-century American literary naturalism.

CRISTINA RUOTOLO

"Whence the Song:" Voice and Audience in Dreiser's *Sister Carrie*†

Theodore Dreiser's connections with the music business in the years leading up to the publication of *Sister Carrie* have yielded little in the way of new approaches to his first novel. Scholars typically treat his editorial stint with a Tin Pan Alley magazine as part of his more general training in journalistic writing and his relationship with his songwriter brother, Paul Dresser, in terms of their differences in personality and cultural language.[1] But a closer look at Dreiser's turn-of-the-century writings reveals a sustained and insightful examination of music's presence and importance in American cultural life. Indeed, during the period when Dreiser edited *Ev'ry Month* for music publishers Howley and Haviland (1894–96), American musical practices were in the midst of dramatic changes and expansion. From his perspective as an employee of Tin Pan Alley, as brother of a famous songwriter, and as cultural critic, Dreiser published several illuminating essays about the state of American music and its shifting values. This article will consider these works and offer them as a way into some new thoughts about the place of music in Dreiser's first major novel, *Sister Carrie*.[2]

In the voluminous critical discussion about Dreiser's first novel, a good deal of energy has gone into recognizing and analyzing its representations of the visual culture of commodity capitalism. Rachel Bowlby has offered the most compelling analysis of how Dreiser's novel registers in impressive detail commodity capitalism's leveling of being and experience into the dynamic of seeing and being seen. Bowlby considers Carrie "an image *par excellence*" who epitomizes the "new consumer capitalism" in which " 'things' are inseparable from how they look."[3] In this primary focus on image and visuality, however, Bowlby and others risk obscuring the already hard-to-see place of music, sound, and hearing in turn-of-the-century "consumer culture" and Dreiser's novel alike. *Sister Carrie*, while short on

† From *American Literary Realism* 35 (Fall 2002): 39–58. Copyright © 2002 by the Board of Trustees of the University of Illinois. Reprinted by permission of the University of Illinois Press.

1. See *Theodore Dreiser's Ev'ry Month*, ed. Nancy Warner Barrineau (Athens and London: Univ. of Georgia Press, 1996) for a discussion of the impact of Dreiser's position as editor of a Tin Pan Alley magazine on his subsequent fiction.
2. See Dreiser's articles on the arts at the turn of the century in *Art, Music, and Literature, 1897–1902: Theodore Dreiser*, ed. Yoshinobu Hakutani (Urbana: University of Illinois Press, 2001).
3. See Rachel Bowlby, *Just Looking: Consumer Culture in Dreiser, Gissing, and Zola* (New York: Methuen and Co., 1985), pp. 65, 62.

scenes of music-making per se, is in fact rich with what might be called musical "affect." The spirit of sentimental songs pervades this novel, from the chapter titles, which, as Sandy Petrey notes, might be mistaken for Tin Pan Alley titles and lyrics,[4] to the language of the novel's many sentimental moments, to Carrie herself, as one particularly "affected by music" and at crucial moments both propelled and limited by her aural sensitivity. These moments are particularly significant when considered in relation to the often heated debates about the role of music in American urban society at the turn of the last century, debates that often focus on young women's relationship to new musical styles and venues. Besides engaging questions about turn-of-the-century music, a focus on the novel's aural register also generates new ways of thinking about Dreiser's ambivalent perspective on modern urban society and the inconsistent style in which he represents it.

While some regret *Sister Carrie*'s occasional sentimental moments as lapses in his more properly "realist" mission, others read them as significant expressions of his relationship to consumer capitalism.[5] Petrey, for example, claims that Dreiser's sentimentalism functions ironically to underscore the "false consciousness" of mass cultural forms and styles, thus supporting his novel's realist critique of the social conditions of capitalism.[6] Walter Benn Michaels, on the other hand, argues that Dreiser's sentimental voice unironically indicates his novel's fundamental "endorsement" of commodity capitalism by in effect positing unquenchable "desire" as the engine of human nature.[7] In spite of their different takes on Dreiser's attitude, both assume a seamless link between sentimentalism and consumerism, and fail to acknowledge a resistance to consumerism that, I would argue, emerges from *within* Dreiser's sentimental moments, as a defining element of their appeal. Indeed, Dreiser's sentimental voice seems to signal, as Amy Kaplan has noted, a form of desire that commodities appeal to but cannot fulfill given the social conditions of turn-of-the-century capitalism.[8] *Sister Carrie*'s representations of musical "affect" and the resonance between the novel's sentimental prose and Dreiser's essays about music in the 1890s suggest a tension within sentimentalism and within turn-of-the-century commer-

---

4. See Sandy Petrey, "The Language of Realism, the Language of False Consciousness: A Reading of *Sister Carrie*," *Novel*, 19 (1977), 101–13.
5. The earlier critics include Alfred Kazin in *The Stature of Theodore Dreiser: A Critical Study of the Man and His Work*, ed. Kazin and Charles Shapiro (Bloomington: Indiana Univ. Press, 1965); F. O. Matthiessen in *Theodore Dreiser* (New York: Sloan, 1951); and Donald Pizer in *The Novels of Theodore Dreiser: A Critical Study* (Minneapolis: Univ. of Minnesota Press, 1976).
6. See Petrey, p. 112.
7. See Walter Benn Michaels, "*Sister Carrie*'s Popular Economy," *Critical Inquiry*, 7 (1980), 373–90.
8. See Amy Kaplan, *The Social Construction of American Realism* (Chicago: Univ. of Chicago Press, 1989), pp. 140–60.

cial music, as both propel their audiences towards but also away from the new flood of goods competing for mass attention.

Numerous factors combined in the 1890s to complicate assumptions about the relationship between music and identity and, more specifically, between music and desire. Chief among them, particularly for Dreiser, was Tin Pan Alley's newly aggressive methods for producing and promoting songs that would sell, methods that seemed both to appeal to and to create what Dreiser would call the public's "desire to hear." One of the industry's new marketing strategies was a growing appeal to women. Many women, no longer satisfied by their Victorian role as domestic parlor pianist, experienced emotional freedom at the cabaret or concert hall, while conservative critics loudly voiced concern that women's growing public exposure to certain music would lead to their moral degradation. For leisure-class women attending Wagner operas as for working-class women frequenting dance halls, at issue was the nature of a listener's response to certain musical elements. Was a person "affected by music" in danger of being remade by that music? Dreiser's own ambivalent answer to this question joins his ambivalence about consumer capitalism itself, as he seems at once thrilled by the promise of freedom and authenticity he associates with the new musical culture and concerned that this culture might constitute new forms of servitude and delusion.

"Things Breath'd into the Unguarded Ear"

Dreiser's autobiography describes his first impressions of Chicago, when he arrived there in 1889, as distinctly musical. Characterizing the young Midwestern city as a "roaring, yelling, screaming whirlpool of life," Dreiser shifts his metaphorical ground from nature to culture with images of the city as symphony and song:

> It is given to some cities, as to some lands, to suggest romance, and to me Chicago did that daily and hourly. It sang, or seemed to, and in spite of what I deemed my various troubles I was singing with it. . . . How I loved the tonic note of even the grinding wheels of the trucks and cars of the Chicago of that day; the clang and the clatter of its cable and electric lines. Its great beer and express wagons, its lurching surge of vehicles in every street. All had a tonic, rhythmic, symphonic import. . . . Chicago, as I viewed it then, was symphonic. It was like a great orchestra in the tumult of noble strophes. I was like a guest at a feast, eating and drinking in a delirium of delight.[9]

9. Dreiser, *Newspaper Days* (Philadelphia: Univ. of Pennsylvania Press, 1991), pp. 22, 20, 3, 4.

Dreiser thus figures his initiation into a modern, urban subjectivity as a function of a particular kind of musical experience, one that quickly transforms the anxious newcomer into a delirious listener/ singer. But the city-as-symphony promises the migrant a new kind of agency at the same time that it threatens to submerge his selfhood into something large, tumultuous and overwhelming, albeit civilized by tonic and noble strophes. Dreiser's metaphorical shift from symphony to feast—and from listening and singing to eating—hints at the possibility that the urban audience can become subject to appetites beyond its control.

At the beginning of his novel, Dreiser similarly figures Carrie's first impressions of Chicago in terms of music, but without the ennobling metaphors of symphony and feast and with greater emphasis on the newcomer's vulnerability.

> A blare of sound, a roar of life, a vast array of human lives, appeal to the astonished senses in equivocal terms. Without a counselor at hand to whisper cautious interpretations, what falsehoods may not these things breathe into the unguarded ear! Unrecognized for what they are, their beauty, like music, too often relaxes, then weakens, then perverts the simpler human perceptions.[1]

The narrator's cautionary voice here warns against the effects of the city's sounds which, "like music," might corrupt an "unsophisticated and natural mind" like Carrie's (8). We quickly find, however, that neither Carrie's mind nor her perceptions are so easily classified, and that these words of caution represent notions of femininity and truth that begin to seem things of the past.

Dreiser's focus on the sounds of urban experience not only reflects the fact that cities were noisier places than the smaller towns from which he and his heroine traveled, but also suggests the qualitative changes in music's social presence that were taking place in cities like Chicago and New York toward the end of the nineteenth century. Before writing *Sister Carrie*, Dreiser himself became familiar with new means of producing and selling popular music when he was rescued from unemployment during his first months in New York City by the publishers of Paul Dresser's songs. With Dresser's encouragement, Howley and Haviland set Dreiser up as founding editor of *Ev'ry Month*, a women's magazine that would promote the company's sheet music by offering previews of three or four new songs with each issue. As principal writer as well as editor of *Ev'ry*

---

1. Dreiser, *Sister Carrie* (Philadelphia: Univ. of Pennsylvania Press, 1981) p. 4. Unless otherwise noted, all quotations from the novel are from this edition.

Month, Dreiser found himself both supporting and, in a sense, competing with this burgeoning industry. Particularly at this early point in his career, before he had any real success as a journalist or fiction writer, Dreiser's enchantment with the immense popularity of his brother's songs was tempered by concern that his own more serious and important authorship still lacked any significant audience.[2]

While recording technology and radio would bring about dramatic changes for American musical experience after World War I, changes that are receiving growing scholarly attention, Tin Pan Alley's modes of production, promotion, and distribution preceded these technology-driven changes and in a sense paved their way. Magazines like *Ev'ry Month* were perhaps the least conspicuous of the new marketing strategies developed by the music publishing industry in the 1890s to create a sustained market for new popular music. Named for the cacophony of piano strains emanating from the windows of one block of 28th Street in New York, Tin Pan Alley centralized the work of composing, arranging, printing, and marketing popular music. Rather than wait for minstrel and vaudeville performances to generate a song's popularity and marketability, music publishers now worked to create instant demand and what might be called "brand loyalty" to publishers. To help this process along, songwriters sought out celebrity singers to advertise and popularize songs and hired boys to sit in vaudeville audiences and join in at the song's refrain, to give the impression that the song had already "caught on." Beyond the vaudeville stage, publishers filled urban spaces with their product by hiring musicians to play and sing on street corners, from moving trucks, in music stores, department stores, and restaurants. Like the planted audience member, these performances would advertise a song's attractiveness by staging its irrepressible ubiquity, its already-being-part-of the urban soundscape.[3] Like commercial culture generally, the new music publishers promised to satisfy audiences' desires, a promise captured by the sign in the office window of Charles Harris, who in 1892 wrote the first multi-million copy hit, "After the Ball." Advertising "Songs Written to Order," Harris' sign puts the listener's desire as the object of songwriting as well as advertising.

Tin Pan Alley's growing presence at the turn of the century particularly influenced the emerging venues and rituals of urban "night-

2. Ellen Moers writes that Dreiser had "mingled shame and admiration" for his brother's success. See *Two Dreisers* (New York: Viking, 1969), p. 69.
3. I got this important word—and concept—from R. Murray Schafer's *The Soundscape: Our Sonic Environment and the Tuning of the World* (Rochester, VT: Destiny Books, 1994). Schafer sees his research as an attempt to answer the important, but typically unasked question: "what is the relationship between man and the sounds of his environment and what happens when those sounds change?" (3–4). For a good discussion of early Tin Pan Alley, see David Ewen, *Tin Pan Alley* (New York: Funk and Wagnalls, 1964).

life." Cabarets, nightclubs, and restaurants combined popular tunes with alcohol and food, a synergy of pleasures that, as Lewis Erenberg and Kathy Peiss have demonstrated, were the site of new social experiences and the focus of new anxieties.[4] Musical theater was on the rise, benefiting from the influx of black composers and performers to the city, and with them new "ragtime" styles of music and dance. While these changes drew people into new forms of entertainment and leisure, they also inspired anxiety, and at times protest, about their social effects. Many feared that these new musical venues and styles might destroy the innocence and virtue of young unmarried women, who made up the majority of the new audiences. According to Erenberg, critics of nightlife "believed that too much expressive pleasure in a risqué environment endangered young women" and warned that once women allowed themselves to enjoy music in a public setting—such as a restaurant or cabaret—they would be "easily led to prostitution and away from the traditional role of home and mother." Peiss recounts newspaper stories "filled with dramatic accounts of innocent daughters tempted by glittering dance halls, seduced and drugged by ruthless 'cadets' or pimps, and held against their will in brothels."[5]

Tin Pan Alley was not alone in generating new musical sites and experiences. The leisure class was also "steppin' out" more frequently, spending their evenings at the opera or symphony rather than in the home. As music critic and novelist James Huneker wrote at the turn of the century, "passed away is the piano girl"—gone, in other words, is the amateur female pianist, who now would rather go out than stay in her parlor and entertain the family.[6] Joseph Horowitz has noted the "protofeminism" inspired by leisure-class women's growing passion for Wagnerian opera (which Theodor Adorno names the prototype of twentieth-century popular music), as it seemed to arouse and encourage female erotic experience not only outside the home, but also in the company of other women.[7] No longer fixed within the private space of home, where music once served to strengthen the emotional bonds of family and the boundaries of

4. Lewis A. Erenberg, *Steppin' Out: New York Nightlife and the Transformation of American Culture, 1890–1930* (Chicago: Univ. of Chicago Press, 1981); and Kathy Peiss, *Cheap Amusements* (Philadelphia: Temple Univ. Press, 1986).
5. Erenberg, p. 82; Peiss, p. 98.
6. James Gibbons Huneker, *Overtones: A Book of Temperaments* (New York: Scribners, 1904).
7. See Theodor Adorno, *In Search of Wagner* (London: Verso, 1991). For a fascinating discussion of American women's devotion to Wagner at the turn of the century, see Joseph Horowitz, *Wagner Nights: An American History* (Berkeley: Univ. of California Press, 1994). Willa Cather's several stories about opera singers, her novel *The Song of the Lark* (1915), and Kate Chopin's *The Awakening* (1899) represent music, and particularly classical music, as an important modern force in breaking Victorian conventions and reshaping or "awakening" female sensibilities. On the opera audience as homoerotic space for women, see Terry Castle, *The Apparitional Lesbian* (New York: Columbia Univ. Press, 1993), p. 203.

bourgeois femininity, music's growing presence in these public and anonymous arenas threatened no less than to remake women's emotional economies: to turn potential housewives into fallen prostitutes.

"Words and Music"

While on the margins of debates taking place in music journals and general periodicals, Dreiser's early journalism includes several insightful reflections on American musical practices. In particular, Dreiser's perspective is interesting for its focus on the apparently growing contradiction between music's subtle and powerful effects on listeners and its increasingly rationalized mode of production. In two articles written at the turn of the century, Dreiser targets the music industry for, in effect, turning songwriting into an assembly-line process at the same time that he asserts a kind of sentimental faith that popular songs and their audience might nonetheless transcend the dehumanizing effects of this new musical economy.

"Birth and Growth of a Popular Song," which appeared in *Metropolitan Magazine* in 1900, begins in a celebratory tone as it describes the "methods by which all songs are given publicity and an opportunity to appeal for the good favor of the public." Illustrated with several large photographs of stony-faced men and women laboriously translating songs into rows of "pins" at a piano-roll factory, the article soon gives way to more sober descriptions of a division of labor that turns even the songwriter into a kind of factory worker. After attracting the attention of a publisher, which requires having the right connections more than anything else, the aspiring songwriter signs away most of the song's future profits to that publisher; the manuscript then makes the rounds to an arranger who makes it "the best for general piano purposes," to the printer, and, finally, to the marketing division, which disseminates it among a host of "pluggers," including hand and street organs (whose own hierarchical business Dreiser elucidates in some detail). As the narrative progresses, the song which had seemed accessible to "almost every one" and romantically intangible in its appeal at the beginning of the article becomes an objectified and manipulated commodity, overshadowed, like the people in the article's accompanying photographs, by the machinery of the music industry.

In "Whence the Song," published in *Harper's Weekly* in 1899, Dreiser similarly emphasizes the human cost of an increasingly profit-driven enterprise but, at the same time, insists on music's potential independence from the material process of its production, as well as its capacity, paradoxically arising from its new market-driven ubiquity, to generate new forms of national sentiment. He begins by describing the unstable life of the songwriter who, even after striking gold with a successful song, can never depend on continued success and typically returns to the obscurity from which he came (as would Paul Dresser himself). Highlighted in his cast of temporarily successful though ultimately exploited characters is an African American songwriter whose catchy tunes are earning the company big profits while the writer himself seems content to forgo his own enrichment. Though a version of the "happy darky," Dreiser's black songwriter serves as an example of the successful songwriter: both naively oblivious to financial matters and victimized by profit-driven publishers that exploit all songwriters alike. Indeed, Dreiser implies that those most likely to write good songs are, like his African American songwriter, least likely to be thinking about profits while writing them and thus most vulnerable to the market.

In spite of this tragic undercurrent, however, Dreiser concludes his article with a highly sentimental image of music detached from its origins and spreading outward to "circulate" through American spaces: "It seems wonderful that they should come to this [pauper's burial], singers, authors, women and all; and yet not more wonderful than that their little feeling, worked into a melody and a set of words, should reach far out o'er land and water, touching the hearts of the nation." As it follows the journalistic realism of the article's first half, this rhetoric seems to challenge his own critique of Tin Pan Alley culture industry. Dreiser's sentimental voice even suggests that the industry itself enables national expressive culture: "We have heard the street bands and the organs, the street boys and the street loungers, all expressing this brief melody snatched from the unknown by some process of the heart. Here it is wandering the land over like a sweet breath of summer, making for matings and partings, for happiness and for pain."[8] While one might, following Petrey, read this ending and its sentimentalism as ironic exposure of false consciousness and commodity fetishism, Dreiser's sentimental rhetoric about music's power of transcendence nonetheless throws into relief the capacity of music, even at its most reified, to defy its commodity form and fill social spaces as immaterial, intangible sound that cannot be contained by the marketplace.

Dreiser's idea of successful music (as a mysterious language of the heart defying material and social boundaries) also marks his writings about classical music, whose growing commercialism in American culture he also condemns, even more harshly than Tin Pan Alley. In a review of a recital by African American opera singer Sissieretta Jones (touted as "the Black Patti"), Dreiser broke ranks with his editor and other critics by insisting that the black singer's voice inspired

---

8 "Whence the Song," *Harper's Weekly*, Christmas issue 1900, pp. 1165–66a.

"rhapsodies" and reminded him "of the beauty of nature." Reproducing the racist plantation nostalgia of his day—she "brings back visions of the still, glassy water and soft swaying branches of some drowsy nook in summer time"—Dreiser's preference for Jones also anticipates a modernism that celebrates the authenticity of "primitive" peoples and cultures as a kind of corrective to the modern urban commercial context. (That he favorably reviewed an African American artist purportedly led rival newspapers to accuse his editor of being a "nigger lover."[9]) Like the black songwriter, Jones seems to represent the pure musician, undistracted by but vulnerable to an increasingly commercialized industry.

Dreiser tended to be highly critical of the concert establishment, particularly the technically dazzling virtuosi that his contemporaries flocked to hear.

> There is a difference between playing soul-stirring strains, and the rendition of flowery, classical passages which require ceaseless practice, lightening energy and a sort of wizard juggling of limbs and muscle, to perform. It is a far cry from a brilliant piano recital, to the rendering of a sympathetic melody. As a matter of fact, pure music has nothing to do with the instrumental performance of it. If it came borne upon some breeze from nowhere, it would be doubly sweet for then it would be freed of all earthiness and would have nothing to do with strings and keys and fingers.[1]

By insisting on the "difference" between the "wizard juggling of limbs and muscle" and "pure music," Dreiser insists on music's potential, and desirable, independence from body, instrument, and—by extension—the entire material and social apparatus of its production. As he implicitly criticizes (and instructs) the typical concertgoer who seems to prefer the "brilliant piano recital" to "pure music," Dreiser is harder on the classical audience than the common listener, whom he trusts to know a good, truthful song (like Dresser's) when he hears it. And yet even here, he suggests that, rather than deficient in their listening, American concert audiences are merely disingenuous in their professions of taste: "There is considerable evidence that the United States are largely superficial in their knowledge of music, and that as for their love of it, they have none—that is, none for the kind of music they profess to love."[2] In other words, all of those who pay high prices to hear the latest virtuoso would really prefer a sympathetically rendered Paul Dresser tearjerker.

9. See Yoshinotu Hakutani, *Young Dreiser: A Critical Study* (Rutherford: Fairleigh Dickinson Univ. Press, 1980), pp. 80–81.
1. Quoted in *Theodore Dreiser's Ev'ry Month*, p. 90.
2. Quoted in *Theodore Dreiser's Ev'ry Month*, p. 89.

At times, Dreiser saw his own work of writing as unable to compete with music that, like his brother's, seemed to express "the spontaneous mirth of the heart." In an *Ev'ry Month* column, Dreiser characterizes the urban population—his potential readership—as much less interested in reading than in the more visceral experience of hearing. After decrying the failure of "newspapers, magazines, pamphlets and books" effectively to reach their audience, he proclaims:

> Everywhere, on every hand, come . . . signs of the but ill-suppressed excitement and *desire to hear*. Everywhere are those who seem *half hungry to hear* a man once more endowed as the orator; everywhere those who would gladly be thrilled by the sentiment of an impassioned voice.[3] (emphasis mine)

The public's preference for impassioned voice gave rise to some anxiety for the aspiring writer of newspapers, magazines, and books, who clearly wished to see himself in a position not only to *reach* an audience but to shape its tastes and values. In a short poem written for *Ev'ry Month* entitled "Words and Music," Dreiser conveys in no uncertain terms his sense of the secondary status of text and authorship to music and songwriting: "I being but the words and not the song,/None cares to hear,/Till wedded unto music sweet and strong/Divinely clear."[4] That his own audience was probably more interested in "music sweet and strong" than in his words is suggested in a letter he received from his sister (whom many consider the model for "Sister" Carrie): "Thee [nickname for Theodore] I wish you would send me and Ed every month regular as Ed plays the violen [sic] and I would like it for the music there is in it. Sister Emma."[5]

In a tribute to Paul Dresser after his death, Dreiser elaborates his sense of the distinction between words and music by insisting that his brother's songs move their audiences not through their lyrics, which he finds banal and sentimental, but through their music, whose character eludes concrete definition:

> And what pale little things they were really, mere bits and scraps of sentiment and melodrama in story form, most asinine sighings over home and mother and lost sweethearts and dead heroes such as never were in real life, and yet with something about them, in the music at least, which always appealed to me intensely and must have appealed to others, since they attained so wide a circulation. They bespoke, as I always felt, a wistful, seeking, uncertain temperament, tender and illusioned, with no practical knowledge of any side of life, but full of a true poetic

3. Dreiser, "The Prophet," *Ev'ry Month*, 3 (February 1897), 4.
4. *Ev'ry Month*, 3 (February 1897).
5. Quoted in *Theodore Dreiser's Ev'ry Month*, p. xvi.

feeling for the mystery and pathos of life and death, the wonder of the waters, the stars, the flowers, accidents of life, success, failure.[6]

While the conventional sentimentalism of Dresser's narratives misrepresents "real life," their "music at least" contains something else that "appeals" and "circulates," and speaks a kind of truth about human experience in their very refusal to offer "practical knowledge." Indeed, it is their uncertain, wistful and seeking qualities that give them "true poetic feeling." These qualities, for Dreiser, mark music's inherent power not only to exceed verbal forms of representation, but also to resist the market forces that are quickly absorbing its "appeal" for the very "practical" purpose of generating profit. The future of Broadway musical theater, as he writes in an *Ev'ry Month* column, depends on whether or not "our composers will come to understand that the people want the spontaneous mirth of the heart, and not mirth to order."[7]

As the lyricist of at least one verse of "On the Banks of the Wabash, Far, Far Away," which has become Indiana's state song, Dreiser briefly experienced the relationship to audience that he imagines both songwriter and orator to enjoy. In an introduction to his brother's songs, he describes his first hearing of the lyrics as they were sung in the street outside his New York apartment:

> At first I could not make out the words, but the melody attracted my attention. It was plaintive and compelling. I listened, attracted, satisfied that it was a new popular success that had "caught on." As they drew near my window I heard the words, "On the Banks of the Wabash" most mellifluously harmonized.
>
> I jumped up. A part of the words were mine—my careless, indifferent gift to him. But made by his melody and labor into something so much more appealing than I could ever have imagined. It was Paul's song . . . And they were already singing it in the street. In three months more it was everywhere—in the papers, on the stage, on the street-organs, played by orchestras, bands, whistled and sung every place.[8]

In spite of his words, at whose recognition he jumps, the song is "Paul's," and its power of attraction is its mellifluously harmonized melody which seems in turn to harmonize its mass audience.

Dresser's songs, of course, managed to satisfy the people's desire for spontaneity while also generating profit (and, some would insist,

6. "My Brother Paul," in *Sister Carrie, Jennie Gerhardt, Twelve Men* (New York: Library of America, 1987), p. 910.
7. Quoted in Nancy Warner Barrineau, "The Second Issue of *Ev'ry Month:* Early Roots of Dreiser's Fiction," *Dreiser Studies*, 22 (Spring 1991), 27.
8. Dreiser, "Introduction" to *The Songs of Paul Dresser* (New York: Boni and Liveright, 1927), p. ix.

sticking with successful formulae). For Dreiser, his brother's songs succeeded not because they were made "to order," but on the contrary because Dresser never allowed himself to be anything but spontaneous and emotionally genuine. "Asinine" as they may be, the lyrics to Dresser's songs are inextricably tied to his catchy sentimental melodies and harmonies, and it is worth reflecting on how both their words and musical style are echoed in *Sister Carrie*. While Dresser wrote songs in most of the popular genres—including "coon" songs and patriotic airs—his most popular by far were nostalgia-filled sentimental ballads. Called the "weepiest willow of them all" by Isaac Goldberg, Dresser captured the ambivalence of new migrants to the city who, like himself, held memories—real or imagined—of the simpler social world left behind.[9] Songs like "Just Tell Them that You Saw Me" and "The Letter that Never Came" derive their pathos not only from their sentimental recollections of "gray-haired mother" and abandoned "sweetheart," but also from the alienation of the songs' narrators, usually speaking from the position of urban migrants who, like Carrie, wistfully experience moments of "repentance" or regret, and a "longing" for a past that can never be recovered.

In "She Went to the City," for example, both narrator and female subject of his title have become strangers to the cozy rural life of their youth. When the narrator returns home to "the village, where I used to roam," he learns that his old sweetheart "went to the city, far, far away" and is thus lost not only to her mother, "hope ever burning in [her] breast," but also to him. "The Letter that Never Came" similarly, if more tragically, describes a nameless melancholic who waits in vain his entire life, and even after death, for a letter from a distant intimate. The absent letter seems to stand for the absent sociality of his past, something that the city, full of anonymous souls like himself, cannot reproduce, except as the object of nostalgia. Even Dresser's most famous and celebratory song, "On the Banks of the Wabash," memorializes the brothers' home state from a perspective "far, far away" in space as well as time, as its narrator nostalgically recalls river, landscape, mother's face, and sweetheart, who died without knowing that he really loved her. Sentimental songs of the 1890s like Paul Dresser's appealed so widely in part because they invited their audiences into an imagined community that shares both an irrecoverable provincial past and a lonely urban present. As Mark Booth argues, the songs' principal subjects are defined not only by their lachrymose nostalgia, but also by an implied

9. Isaac Goldberg, *Tin Pan Alley: A Chronicle of American Popular Music* (New York: Ungar, 1961), p. 112. Dresser, it is important to note, did not move with the times into writing ragtime songs, and in this sense represented a kind of resistance to modernity, although I would argue that both sentimentalism and ragtime responded to and reflected modern circumstances.

urban heroism, as survivors of migration and its accompanying traumas and as pioneers in a modern individualist world.[1]

Dreiser began writing *Sister Carrie*, then, at a moment when he was highly aware of music's commercial ascendancy in urban America. While others worried that new musical forms and styles and new venues would morally corrupt innocent audiences, Dreiser was more concerned about music's growing commercialization, which he paradoxically saw as both a threat to and agent of music's power to gesture towards the inarticulable desires that all presumably shared and to create sympathetic connections between increasingly alienated and distant populations. If read in terms of its musical context and Dreiser's musical commentary, *Sister Carrie* can be seen to engage this paradoxical relationship between commodification and authenticity, as well as to raise questions about music's role in the life of unmarried young women.

"She Went to the City"

On the novel's first pages, just after the narrator describes the potential hazards of the urban "blare of sound" for the uncounseled, Carrie, on the speedy train to Chicago, is addressed by a more private voice. The "masher" Drouet first enters the scene, in fact, as a "voice in her ear," an intrusion that challenges her "maidenly reserve" and undermines her "sense of what was conventional under the circumstances" (8–9). Drouet's bold display of "daring and magnetism" initiates Carrie's aural relationship to her new urban environment and signals this novel's departure from any stable idea of conventionality.

As he occupies the position of serpent seducer taking advantage of her "unguarded ear," Drouet appeals to Carrie in a way that nonetheless echoes Dresser's songs, as do many "voices" in this novel. Both his hackneyed language and his less than virtuous intentions are here overshadowed by the fact that they tap into a shared place of authentic emotion:

> How true it is that words are but the vague shadows of the volumes we mean. Little audible links, they are, chaining together great inaudible feelings and purposes. Here were these two, bandying little phrases, drawing purses, looking at cards, and both unconscious of how inarticulate all their real feelings were. . . . Now she felt that she had yielded something—he, that he had gained a victory. Already they felt that they were somehow associated. (13)

1. Booth, *The Experience of Songs* (New Haven: Yale Univ. Press, 1981), p. 168.

As only "vague shadows" of and "audible links" to the emotional reality lurking within, words here lack signifying power, acting more as conduits between pools of "real" but "inarticulate" feeling. Rather than mutual understanding, the pair's conversation achieves their sense of being "somehow associated," of their feelings being "linked" together. Drouet's seduction of Carrie is clinched when, later, Carrie "relaxed and heard with open ears" his seductions and "could not help but feel the vibration of force" emanating from his presence (79). As a metaphor for communication, the relaxed and vibrating ear here appeals to the distinction of aurality from the other senses as a form of "open"-ness to external "forces."

Like Drouet, Hurstwood secures Carrie's attention by a "vibration of force" that arouses response without communicating anything in particular: he "seemed to radiate an atmosphere which suffused her being" (114). A richer and classier man than Drouet, Hurstwood wins Carrie's affection through his even stronger appeal to the "great inaudible feelings" behind words. While critics tend to focus on the fact that Carrie is drawn to Hurstwood's clothes rather than his character—seduced by the superior quality of his leather gloves and shoes—she is at least as responsive to his voice. Dreiser even suggests, provocatively for our interests, that their conversation is analogous to background music in a play: "Such conversation as was indulged in held the same relationship to the actual mental enactments of the twain that the low music of the orchestra does to the dramatic incident which it is used to cover." Again insisting on the inadequacy of words—"they but dimly represent the great surging feelings and desires which lie behind"—the narrator concludes, with a sentimental flourish, that "when the distraction of the tongue is removed, the heart listens" (115).

The following exchange between the two, then, draws particular attention to Carrie's "listening heart," a metaphorical aurality that underscores a form of understanding and connection that eludes signification and transcends moral implication:

> In this conversation she heard, instead of his words, the voices of the things which he represented. . . . She did not need to tremble at all, because it was invisible; she did not need to worry over what other people would say—what she herself would say— because it had no tangibility. She was being pleaded with, persuaded, led into denying old rights and assuming new ones, and yet there were no words to prove it. (115)

Carrie "hears" the "voices of things" rather than their meaning; invisible, intangible, and nonrepresentational, Hurstwood's pleadings persuade by their vocal quality alone, drawing Carrie into "new" and inarticulable "rights" that, by virtue of their inarticulability, can be neither defended nor challenged.

As it draws Carrie further away from a more conventional feminine selfhood, girded by "old rights," this scene also thrusts Hurstwood into a central role in the novel, as someone who, like Carrie, becomes associated with musicality. Hurstwood seems "capable of strong feelings" that distinguish him not only from his more capricious friend and rival Drouet, but also from his "cold, self-centered" wife (109). This emotional capacity seems to account for his professional success as well as his downfall, representing a structure of feeling, shared by Carrie, that both strives for upward mobility and remains unsatisfied by its material and social rewards. Like Drouet's desire, Hurstwood's emotions are revealed in his voice, but his vocal qualities seem to bear a mark of distinction: "his feelings and his voice were colored with that seeming repression and pathos which is the essence of eloquence." As he declares himself to Carrie, "his voice trembled with that peculiar vibration which is the result of tensity [sic]. It went ringing home to his companion's heart" (123–24). As it "drop[s] to a soft minor," Hurstwood's voice becomes distinctly musical: "He was striking a chord now which found sympathetic response in her own situation." Finally, Hurstwood nostalgically caps off this exchange with an actual song, as he "whistled merrily for a good four miles to his office an old melody that he had not recalled for fifteen years."

Dreiser extends such musical scenes of seduction beyond their conventional resonance with sentimental romance and suggests that susceptibility to certain qualities of voice might lead one not only into extramarital dalliance, but also into the thrall of department store commodities. A chapter entitled "The Persuasion of Fashion" figures Carrie's famous consumerism as yet another relationship between voice and ear: "Fine clothes to her were a vast persuasion; they spoke tenderly and Jesuitically, for themselves. When she came within earshot of their pleading, desire in her bent a willing ear. The voice of the so-called inanimate! Who shall translate for us the language of the stones?" (98). This "voice of the so-called inanimate" becomes the very substance of the commodity's desirability as Carrie's desire is figured as a condition of active listening, of openness to sound.

But later in the chapter, the narrator insists that Carrie is not simply a "passive creature," wholly bound to the "trivialities" of shopping (and, in this case, of the "conventional" attitudes of her gossipy companion Mrs. Hale): "her own feelings were a corrective influence. The constant drag to something better was not to be denied" (102). As she sits "wistful and depressed" in her apartment, these "corrective" feelings are roused as Carrie overhears a neighbor practicing the piano:

> Now Carrie was affected by music. Her nervous composition responded to certain strains, much as certain strings of a harp vibrate when a corresponding key of a piano is struck. She was delicately molded in sentiment, and answered with vague ruminations to certain wistful chords. They awoke longings for those things which she did not have. They caused her to cling closer to things she possessed . . . As she contemplated her new state, the strain from the parlor below stole upward. With it her thoughts became colored and enmeshed. She reverted to the things which were best and saddest within the small limit of her experience. She became for the moment a repentant. (101–102)

The music she overhears—whose "wistful" harmonies could be anything from Frederic Chopin, a favorite among women pianists at the time, to Paul Dresser himself—arouses in Carrie, more than anything else, longing for things. But unlike the desire she experienced earlier in the day for the pretty objects displayed in store windows, this longing is not only for "things which she did not have," but for things she already had, and for "things which were best and saddest in her experience." In other words, what might be characterized simply as "consumer desire" becomes, during her moment of audition, a kind of resistance to consumerism, in effect a desire for a different time and place when she was perhaps content with what she had. The word "things" during this musical moment shifts in reference from the crassly material to the more abstractly experiential.

Beyond highlighting Dreiser's sense of music's ambiguous relationship to and role in consumer desire this moment also represents a distinctly modern scene of musical production and reception. An earlier historical (and literary) moment might feature a parlor setting in which sisters play sentimental music at the piano for one another, sharing a "wistful" moment that brings them closer together. In this case, the pianist is an aspiring professional who, like many young women at this time, has moved to Chicago to study; Carrie remains an isolated listener, a consumer, lost in her own thoughts.[2] By associating Carrie with harp strings, Dreiser invokes domestic femininity, but only to underscore the difference between rented apartment and traditional parlor: Carrie resonates sympathetically to an anonymous piano, and to a pianist whom she might never, and indeed never does, get to know. Distinct as well from a nineteenth-century image of

---

2. For another prescient scene of music-making, see Edward Bellamy's *Looking Backward*. Bellamy constructs an imaginary future where music is piped from its lived performance into the individual homes of a community.

woman as man's instrument (in which case Carrie—as harp string—
would be played upon by some male artist)[3] the image of Carrie as
resonating harp string instead invokes a naturalist social model of
individuals unwittingly driven and pulled by anonymous and invisible
biological and social forces.

But Carrie's listening is also, as I have already emphasized, a "corrective" experience, a space and time apart from the urban context
that is otherwise so effectively sucking her in. It is upon this scene
that Drouet enters and establishes his own inability to resonate with
Carrie by revealing his difference from the more porous and intense
emotional economies of Carrie and Hurstwood. Suggesting that they
"waltz a little to that music," and thus treat it as conventional entertainment rather than the very "color" of her thoughts, Drouet "made
clear to Carrie that he could not sympathize with her. . . . It was his
first great mistake" (103). Here and in the following chapter, music
becomes a trigger for both the desire and the dissatisfaction aroused
by Carrie's new urban context: "What, after all, was Drouet? What
was she? . . . She was too wrought up to care to go down to eat, too
pensive to do aught but rock and sing. Some old tunes crept to her
lips, and, as she sang them, her heart sank. She longed and longed
and longed." Feeling as if "all her state was one of loneliness and
forsakenness," she "hummed and hummed as the moments went by,
sitting in the shadow by the window, and was therein as happy,
though she did not perceive it, as she ever would be" (113–14). Humming, like the piano music that preceded it, expresses Carrie's resistance to convention or stasis of any kind at the same time that it
bespeaks the loneliness of her increasingly fluid urban existence.

Carrie's wistful humming also prefigures her eventual transformation from hearer of "certain strains" to the producer of her own
"voice," more specifically her own sentimental strains on the stage
of musical theater. Her inspired performance in "Under the Gaslight" is often discussed as the culmination of her commercial self-
construction, the moment when she most obviously becomes the
"image" of herself. But her "innate taste for imitation" has found her
not only "re-creating, before her mirror, the expressions of various
faces" but also recreating actresses' voices: she "loved to modulate
her voice after the manner of the distressed heroine" (150). After a
shaky start on stage before an audience, her moment of recovery is
specifically tied to her finding just such a voice. Still nervous, Carrie
initially delivers "lines" that "were merely spoken . . . in such a feeble
voice" that "came out . . . flat" (170–71). Her talent reveals itself

---

3. The classic example of this gendered relationship is that of Trilby and Svengali.

only when she is able to infuse her voice with a new kind of energy: "Carrie listened, and caught the infection of something—she did not know what," and only then "her voice assum[ed] for the first time a penetrating quality which it had never known" (174–75). She quickly overshadows her fellow cast members as she engages more with the play's musical accompaniment than the spoken lines: "scarcely hearing the small, scheduled reply" of the other actor on stage with her, Carrie put "herself even more in harmony with the plaintive melody now issuing from the orchestra" (180).

Foreshadowing the inversion of power that is to come, Carrie's voice now seduces a "listening" Hurstwood and sets into motion the chain of events that leads to his demise. After he too "[catches] the infection" that prompted Carrie's inspiration, he finds himself "almost deluded by that quality of voice and manner which, *like a pathetic strain of music*, seems ever a personal and intimate thing" (177, emphasis mine), and ultimately, "deluded" or not, he makes the decision to leave his wife for Carrie: "He forgot the need of circumspectness which his married state enforced. He almost forgot that he had with him in the box those who knew him. By the Lord, he would have that lovely girl if it took his all. He would act at once" (180–81). The "infectious" emotionalism of this moment seems to promise a kind of freedom from the hollow conventionality of his marriage and social position, and, though doomed to fade like the emotions roused by a sentimental song, suggests that both Carrie's success and Hurstwood's response are more authentic alternatives to their everyday lives and selves.

Once Carrie and Hurstwood leave Chicago and arrive in New York, references to music and aurality virtually disappear as the novel becomes increasingly preoccupied with Hurstwood's demise. This demise is marked by his retreat into reading, as the newspaper's representational distance protects and abstracts him from an increasingly hostile urban reality. The revised ending, however, brings Carrie's musicality back into focus. Rather than simply indicate once more her unquenchable longing for "things" both material and intangible, Carrie's musicality is given new significance through the perspective of Ames, whom some take to be representative of Dreiser himself. In her final encounter with Ames at a dinner party, Carrie finds the young inventor sitting by the fire and listening to music being played in the background:

> "Isn't that a pathetic strain?" he inquired, listening.
> "Oh, very," she returned, also catching it, now that her attention was called. . . .
> They listened a few moments in silence, touched by the same

feeling, only hers reached her through the heart. Music still charmed her as in the old days.

"I don't know what it is about music," she started to say, moved by the inexplicable longings which surged within her; "but it always makes me feel as if I wanted something—I—"

"Yes," he replied; "I know how you feel."[4]

While Carrie is "still charmed" by music that reaches her "through the heart," Ames is able to sense the "same feeling" through differ- ent, and presumably more intellectual, means. After claiming to "know" how she feels, Ames attempts to diminish the power of this "inexplicable" desire by insisting that it is inevitably frustrated: "It doesn't do us any good to wring our hands over the far-off things" (440). He then, in this and a subsequent conversation, tries to get her to focus on her power articulately to represent longing, rather than mutely to submit to it: "Sometimes nature . . . makes the face representative of all desire. That's what has happened in your case" (441).

This exchange effectively leaves Carrie where she has been most of the novel—"the effect of his words was like roiling helpless waters"—but it also raises important questions about the function and status of art and artists in the new urban society, made up increasingly of subjects like Carrie. One reason Ames seems so out of place in this novel is that he affirms a too-neat distinction between representation and reality: good art, for him, is that which "voices [people's] feelings" for them, which represents emotional reality to those who remain inarticulate about it. But Ames doesn't seem to understand that inarticulateness is inextricably linked to Carrie's experience of desire, that Carrie would rather be moved by the "great inaudible feelings" than represent them. Indeed, what has moved her to act throughout the novel has not been her ability to re-present but rather her resonance with the "blare" of modern energies often figured as musical. Her stage performances, in this sense, are no different from her experiences as audience—in either case, she is a resonant harp string.

According to his close friend Richard Duffy, Dreiser's breaks from writing Sister Carrie, as he was struggling to bring it to some sort of conclusion, found him relaxing not only in talk but in music: "[Drei- ser] always sat in a rocking chair, if he could find one. . . . If he was not talking he would be humming the refrain of 'On the Banks of the Wabash' or of some other popular song. He had hundreds in his

4. Sister Carrie (Oxford: Oxford Univ. Press, 1991), pp. 441–42. The references to music in this scene do not appear in the original version of the manuscript, before Dreiser revised it for Doubleday.

head."[5] This image of the author immersed in song, unable to finish his novel, suggests that Dreiser was struggling among other things to distinguish his own work of writing from the musicality that permeated his own as well as his heroine's imagination. Would his words, like those of Ames, have the effect of "roiling helpless waters"? Would he, like Ames, seem like an outsider to the world of his readers? Will music always seem more "real" than the most realist fiction? In his early essays as in his first novel, Dreiser presents music and responsiveness to music as powerful aspects of an urban consumer society threatening to reduce the individual to his or her desire. Arousing genuine emotion, music seems capable at once of trapping the "helpless" consumer in an endless cycle of frustrated desire and elaborating a space of resistance to the materialism and isolation of commodity capitalism. Dreiser's withdrawal into rocking and humming recalls Hurstwood's rocking-chair retreats from urban realities, as well as Carrie's rocking-chair musings, including the final scene of the novel that finds her "singing and dreaming" about "that radiance of delight which tints the distant hilltops of the world" (464). Titled "The Way of the Beaten: A Harp in the Wind," the novel's final chapter suggests that, for the moment at least, sentimental song reigns supreme in this heroine's sense of self and of her place in the world.

---

5. Quoted in Richard Lingeman, *Theodore Dreiser: At the Gates of the City, 1871–1907* (New York: Putnam, 1986), p. 269.

The Chronology of *Sister Carrie*

Dreiser's chronology in *Sister Carrie* is historically both exact and inexact because of his indecision in dating Carrie's arrival in Chicago. In the holograph version of the novel, the date cited in the first paragraph of chapter 1 was originally 1894, but it has been erased and 1884 written over it. In the typescript, 1894 is the typed date, but it has been written over in pencil with the date 1889. This date, 1889, appears in the published version. As has often been noted, 1889 is the only specific date in the entire novel and therefore is the "key" to the documentation of social detail in the work.

Dreiser's revision of the date of Carrie's arrival probably took the following form. He initially used 1894 but soon decided that 1884 would be a more appropriate date because it is close to his own first impressions of Chicago and to Emma's affair with her architect lover. (In the holograph, there are a series of questions at the close of chapter 3, not in Dreiser's hand, quizzing Dreiser on the validity of his Chicago details. All of these questions refer to the date 1884.) As Ellen Moers has suggested, however, Dreiser settled upon 1889 as a working date when he wrote the New York portion of the novel because this date permitted him to synchronize Carrie's and Hurstwood's experiences with his own knowledge of New York life of the mid-nineties. When the typescript was prepared, the typist misread the almost illegible date in the holograph as 1894, but in revising the typescript Dreiser recognized both her error and his own need to have a later date than 1884 and corrected 1894 to 1889.

The principal effect of Dreiser's lack of certainty about the date of Carrie's arrival is that though the novel gives the impression of detailed accuracy in its rendering of social history, this impression is in fact "true" only for the New York material. Dreiser's Chicago in *Sister Carrie*, with its horse cars, newly developed department stores, specific theatrical performances, etc., is Chicago of the mid-1880s rather than 1889–90.

August 1889:	Carrie arrives in Chicago.
Fall 1889:	She begins to live with Drouet at Ogden Place.
Summer 1890:	Carrie and Hurstwood elope to New York and take a flat on Seventy-eighth Street.
Late 1892:	Carrie meets Ames, who is visiting New York.
Mid-1893:	Carrie and Hurstwood move to Thirteenth Street.
February 1894:	Hurstwood loses his Warren Street saloon.
June 1894:	Hurstwood is down to his last fifty dollars.
Summer 1894:	Carrie gets a job in the chorus of the Casino Theatre.
October 1894:	Carrie moves to the chorus of the Broadway Theatre.
January 1895:	Hurstwood participates in the Brooklyn street car strike; Carrie gets a speaking part in her show at the Broadway.
Early spring 1895:	Carrie leaves Hurstwood.
May 1895:	Carrie opens in a new show at the Casino and is a great success. She moves into the Wellington Hotel.
September 1895:	Carrie's show goes on the road; Hurstwood is living in a Bowery lodging house.
Fall 1895–February 1896:	Hurstwood works at the Broadway Central Hotel until his illness.
Early May 1896:	Hurstwood is discharged from Bellevue Hospital; Carrie's show returns from the road and is at the Casino.
June 1896:	Carrie goes to London with her show; Hurstwood works at odd jobs.
Winter 1896–97:	Carrie returns to New York in a new play: Ames is living in New York; Hurstwood commits suicide in January or February 1897.

Selected Bibliography

• indicates works included or excerpted in this Norton Critical Edition.

THEODORE DREISER

Novels

Sister Carrie. 1900.
Jennie Gerhardt. 1911.
The Financier. 1912; rev. ed., 1927.
The Titan. 1914.
The "Genius." 1915.
An American Tragedy. 1925.
The Bulwark. 1946.
The Stoic. 1947.

Short Stories

Free and Other Stories. 1918.
Chains. 1927.

Poetry

Moods: Cadenced and Declaimed. 1926; rev. eds., 1928, 1935.

Plays

Plays of the Natural and the Supernatural. 1916; rev. ed., 1926.
The Hand of the Potter. 1919.
The Collected Plays of Theodore Dreiser. Ed. Keith Newlin and Frederic E. Rusch.
     Albany, NY: Whitson, 2000.

Autobiography and Travel

A Traveler at Forty. 1913.
A Hoosier Holiday. 1916.
A Book about Myself. 1922; rpt. as Newspaper Days, 1931.
Dreiser Looks at Russia. 1928.
Dawn. 1931.
An Amateur Laborer. Ed. Richard W. Dowell. Philadelphia: U Pennsylvania P, 1983.

Sketches, Essays, and Reportage

Twelve Men. 1919.

Hey Rub-a-Dub-Dub: A Book of the Mystery and Wonder and Terror of Life. 1920.

The Color of a Great City. 1923.

A Gallery of Women. 1929.

Tragic America. 1932.

America Is Worth Saving. 1941.

Notes on Life. Ed. Marguerite Tjader and John J. McAleer. University: U Alabama P, 1974.

Theodore Dreiser: A Selection of Uncollected Prose. Ed. Donald Pizer. Detroit: Wayne State U P, 1977.

Selected Magazine Articles of Theodore Dreiser: Life and Art in the American 1890s. Ed. Yoshinobu Hakutani. 2 vols. Rutherford, NJ: Fairleigh Dickinson U P, 1985, 1987.

Theodore Dreiser: Journalism. Volume One: *Newspaper Writings, 1892–1895.* Ed. T. D. Nostwich. Philadelphia: U Pennsylvania P, 1988.

Theodore Dreiser's Ev'ry Month. Ed. Nancy W. Barrineau. Athens: U of Georgia P, 1996.

Art, Music, and Literature, 1897–1902: Theodore Dreiser. Ed. Yoshinobu Hakutani. Urbana: U Illinois P, 2001.

Theodore Dreiser: Interviews. Ed. Frederic E. Rusch and Donald Pizer. U Illinois P. 2004.

GENERAL BIOGRAPHY AND CRITICISM

Books

Cassuto, Leonard, and Clare V. Eby, eds. *The Cambridge Companion to Theodore Dreiser.* New York: Cambridge U P, 2004.

Dreiser, Helen. *My Life with Dreiser.* Cleveland: World, 1951.

Dudley, Dorothy. *Forgotten Frontiers: Dreiser and the Land of the Free.* New York: Harrison Smith, 1932.

Eby, Clare V. *Dreiser and Veblen: Saboteurs of the Status Quo.* Columbia: U Missouri P, 1998.

Elias, Robert H., ed. *Letters of Theodore Dreiser.* 3 vols. Philadelphia: U Pennsylvania P, 1959.

———. *Theodore Dreiser: Apostle of Nature.* Rev. ed. Ithaca: Cornell U P, 1970.

Gerber, Philip L. *Theodore Dreiser Revisited.* New York: Twayne, 1992.

Gogol, Miriam, ed. *Theodore Dreiser: Beyond Naturalism.* New York: New York U P, 1995.

Hakutani, Yoshinobu, ed. *Theodore Dreiser and American Culture: New Readings.* Newark: U Delaware P, 2000.

Hussman, Lawrence E., Jr. *Dreiser and His Fiction: A Twentieth-Century Odyssey.* Philadelphia: U Pennsylvania P, 1983.

Kazin, Alfred, and Charles Shapiro, eds. *The Stature of Theodore Dreiser.* Bloomington: Indiana U P, 1955.

Lehan, Richard. *Theodore Dreiser: His World and His Novels.* Carbondale: Southern Illinois U P, 1969.

Lingeman, Richard. *Theodore Dreiser: At the Gates of the City, 1871–1907.* New York: Putnam, 1986.

———. *Theodore Dreiser: An American Journey, 1908–1945.* New York: Putnam, 1990.

Lydenberg, John, ed. *Dreiser: A Collection of Critical Essays.* Englewood Cliffs, NJ: Prentice-Hall, 1971.

Matthiessen, F. O. *Theodore Dreiser.* New York: Sloane, 1951.

Moers, Ellen. *Two Dreisers.* New York: Viking, 1969.

Newlin, Keith, ed. *A Theodore Dreiser: Encyclopedia.* Westport, CT: Greenwood, 2003.

Pizer, Donald. *The Novels of Theodore Dreiser: A Critical Study.* Minneapolis: U Minnesota P, 1976.

————, ed. *Critical Essays on Theodore Dreiser.* Boston: G. K. Hall, 1981.

————, Richard Dowell, and Frederic E. Rusch. *Theodore Dreiser: A Primary Bibliography and Reference Guide.* Boston: G. K. Hall, 1991.

Riggio, Thomas P., ed. *Dreiser–Mencken Letters: The Correspondence of Theodore Dreiser and H. L. Mencken, 1907–1945.* Philadelphia: U Pennsylvania P, 1986.

Salzman, Jack, ed. *Theodore Dreiser: The Critical Reception.* New York: David Lewis, 1972.

St. Jean, Shawn. *Pagan Dreiser: Songs from an American Mythology.* Madison, NJ: Fairleigh Dickinson U P, 2001.

Swanberg, W. A. *Dreiser.* Scribner, 1965.

Tjader, Marguerite. *Theodore Dreiser: A New Dimension.* Norwalk, CT: Silvermine, 1965.

•Warren, Robert Penn. *Homage to Theodore Dreiser . . .* New York: Random House, 1971.

Zanine, Louis J. *Mechanism and Mysticism: The Influence of Science on the Thought and Work of Theodore Dreiser.* Philadelphia: U Pennsylvania P, 1993.

Articles and Parts of Books

Aaron, Daniel. *Writers on the Left.* New York: Harcourt, Brace, 1961.

Gelfant, Blanche H. "Theodore Dreiser: The Portrait Novel." *The American City Novel.* Norman: U Oklahoma P, 1954.

Hapke, Laura. "No Green Card Needed: Dreiserian Naturalism and Proletarian Female Whiteness." *Twisted from the Ordinary: Essays on American Literary Naturalism.* Ed. Mary E. Papke. Knoxville: U Tennessee P, 2003.

Kazin, Alfred. "Dreiser: The Esthetic of Realism." *Contemporaries.* Boston: Little, Brown, 1962.

Lynn, Kenneth. "Theodore Dreiser: The Man of Ice." *The Dream of Success.* Boston: Little Brown, 1955.

Martin, Ronald E. "Theodore Dreiser: At Home in the Universe of Force." *American Literature and the Universe of Force.* Durham: Duke U P, 1981.

Mencken, H. L. "Theodore Dreiser." *A Book of Prefaces.* New York: Knopf, 1917.

Phillips, William L. "The Imagery of Dreiser's Novels." *PMLA* 78 (December 1963): 572–85.

Pizer, Donald. "Theodore Dreiser." *American Realists and Naturalists.* Ed. Donald Pizer and Earl Harbert. Detroit: Gale, 1982.

————. "Late Nineteenth-Century American Naturalism" and "Nineteenth-Century American Naturalism: An Approach through Form." *Realism and Naturalism in Nineteenth-Century American Literature.* Carbondale: Southern Illinois U P, 1984.

Poirier, Richard. "Panoramic Environment and the Anonymity of the Self." *A World Elsewhere: The Place of Style in American Literature.* New York: Oxford U P, 1966.

Sherman, Stuart P. "The Naturalism of Mr. Dreiser." *Nation* 101 (December 2, 1915): 648–50.

Trilling, Lionel. "Reality in America." *The Liberal Imagination.* New York: Viking, 1950.

Vivas, Eliso. "Dreiser, an Inconsistent Mechanist." *Ethics* 48 (July 1938): 498–508.

Ziff, Larzer. "A Decade's Delay: Theodore Dreiser." *The American 1890s.* New York: Viking, 1966.

SISTER CARRIE

Armstrong, Tim. "The Electrification of the Body at the Turn of the Century." *Textual Practice* 5 (Winter 1991): 303–25.

Bowlby, Rachel. "Starring: Dreiser's *Sister Carrie.*" *Just Looking: Consumer Culture in Dreiser, Gissing, and Zola.* New York: Methuen, 1985.

Brennan, Stephen C. "*Sister Carrie* and the Tolstoyan Artist." *Research Studies* 47 (March 1979): 1–16.

Burgan, Mary A. "*Sister Carrie* and the Pathos of Naturalism." *Criticism* 15 (Fall 1973): 336–49.

Corkin, Stanley. "*Sister Carrie* and the Industrial Life: Objects and the New American Self." *Modern Fiction Studies* 33 (Winter 1987): 605–19.

Davidson, Cathy N., and Arnold E. Davidson. "Carrie's Sisters: The Popular Prototypes for Dreiser's Heroines." *Modern Fiction Studies* 23 (Autumn 1977): 395–407.

Farrell, James T. "Dreiser's *Sister Carrie.*" *The League of Frightened Philistines.* New York: Vanguard, 1945.

•Fisher, Philip. "The Life History of Objects: The Naturalist Novel and the City." *Hard Facts: Form and Setting in the American Novel.* New York: Oxford U P, 1985.

Freedman, William A. "A Look at Dreiser as Artist: The Motif of Circularity in *Sister Carrie.*" *Modern Fiction Studies* 8 (Winter 1962–63): 384–92.

•Gelfant, Blanche H. "What More Can Carrie Want? Naturalistic Ways of Consuming Women." *The Cambridge Companion to American Realism and Naturalism: Howells to London.* Ed. Donald Pizer. New York: Cambridge U P, 1995.

Hakutani, Yoshinobu. "Sister Carrie: Novel and Romance." *Theodore Dreiser and American Culture: New Readings.* Ed. Yoshinobu Hakutani. Newark: U Delaware P, 2000.

Handy, William J. "A Re-Examination of Dreiser's *Sister Carrie.*" *Texas Studies in Literature and Language* 1 (Autumn 1959): 380–89.

Harmon, Charles. "Cuteness and Capitalism in *Sister Carrie.*" *American Literary Realism* 32 (Winter 2000): 125–39.

Hochman, Barbara. "The Portrait of the Artist as a Young Actress: The Rewards of Representation in *Sister Carrie.*" *New Essays on Sister Carrie.* Ed. Donald Pizer. New York: Cambridge U P, 1991.

Howard, June. *Form and History in American Literary Naturalism.* Chapel Hill: U North Carolina P, 1985.

Humma, John B. "*Sister Carrie* and Thomas Hardy, Regained." *Dreiser Studies* 23 (Spring 1992): 8–26.

Humphries, David T. " 'The Shock of Sympathy': Bob Ames's Reading and Re-Reading of *Sister Carrie.*" *Dreiser Studies* 32 (Spring 2001): 36–55.

•Kaplan, Amy. "The Sentimental Revolt of *Sister Carrie.*" *The Social Construction of American Realism.* Chicago: U Chicago P, 1988.

Katope, Christopher. "*Sister Carrie* and Spencer's *First Principles.*" *American Literature* 41 (March 1969): 64–75.

Lehan, Richard. "*Sister Carrie:* The City, the Self, and the Modes of Narrative Discourse." *New Essays on Sister Carrie.* Ed. Donald Pizer. New York: Cambridge U P, 1991.

———. *Sister Carrie.* Detroit: Gale, 2001.

Lewis, Charles R. "Desire and Indifference in *Sister Carrie:* Neoclassic Economic Anticipations." *Dreiser Studies* 29 (Spring–Fall 1998): 18–33.

Livingston, James. "*Sister Carrie's* Absent Causes." *Theodore Dreiser: Beyond Naturalism.* Ed. Miriam Gogol. New York: New York U P, 1995.

•McNamara, Kevin R. "The Ames of the Good Society: *Sister Carrie* and Social Engineering." *Criticism* 34 (Spring 1994): 217–35.

•Markels, Julian. "Dreiser and the Plotting of Inarticulate Experience." *Massachusetts Review* 2 (Spring 1961): 431–48.

Michaels, Walter Benn. "*Sister Carrie*'s Popular Economy." *The Gold Standard and the Logic of Naturalism*. Berkeley: U California P, 1987.

• Moers, Ellen. "The Finesse of Dreiser." *American Scholar* 33 (Winter 1963–64): 109–14.

Petrey, Sandy. "The Language of Realism, the Language of False Consciousness: A Reading of *Sister Carrie*." *Novel* 10 (Winter 1977): 101–13.

Pizer, Donald, ed. *New Essays on Sister Carrie*. New York: Cambridge U P, 1991.

• ———. "The Problem of American Literary Naturalism and Theodore Dreiser's *Sister Carrie*." *American Literary Realism* 32 (Fall 1999): 1–11.

Riggio, Thomas P. "Carrie's Blues." *New Essays on Sister Carrie*. Ed. Donald Pizer. New York: Cambridge U P, 1991.

• Ruotolo, Cristina. " 'Whence the Song': Voice and Audience in Dreiser's *Sister Carrie*." *American Literary Realism* 35 (Fall 2002): 39–58.

See, Fred G. "Dreiser's Lost Language of the Heart." *Desire and Sign: Nineteenth-Century American Fiction*. Baton Rouge: Louisiana State U P, 1987.

Shulman, Robert. "Dreiser and the Dynamics of American Capitalism." *Social Criticism and Nineteenth-Century American Fictions*. Columbia: U Missouri P, 1987.

Sloane, David E. E. *Sister Carrie: Dreiser's Sociological Tragedy*. New York: Twayne, 1992.

St. Jean, Amy Ujvari. " 'Blind Strivings of the Human Heart': Existential Feminism in *Sister Carrie*." *Simone de Beauvoir Studies* 16 (1999–2000): 135–44.

• Trachtenberg, Alan. "Who Narrates? Dreiser's Presence in *Sister Carrie*." *New Essays on Sister Carrie*. Ed. Donald Pizer. New York: Cambridge U P, 1991.

Walcutt, Charles C. "Theodore Dreiser: The Wonder and Terror of Life." *American Literary Naturalism, A Divided Stream*. Minneapolis: U Minnesota P, 1956.

Witemeyer, Hugh. "Gaslight and Magic Lamp in *Sister Carrie*." *PMLA* 86 (March 1971): 236–40.

Zaluda, Scott. "The Secrets of Fraternity: Men and Friendship in *Sister Carrie*." *Theodore Dreiser: Beyond Naturalism*. Ed. Miriam Gogol. New York: New York U P, 1995.

Zender, Karl F. "Walking Away from the Impossible: Identity and Denial in *Sister Carrie*." *Studies in the Novel* 30 (Spring 1998): 63–76.

Sister Carrie: The Textual Controversy

Brennan, Stephen C. "The Two Endings of *Sister Carrie*." *Studies in American Fiction* 16 (Spring 1988): 13–26.

Dowell, Richard W. " 'There Was Something Mystic about It': The Composition of *Sister Carrie*." *Biographies of Books*. Ed. James Barbour and Tom Quirk. Columbia: U Missouri P, 1996.

Hayes, Kevin J. "Textual Anomalies in the 1900 Doubleday, Page *Sister Carrie*." *American Literary Realism* 22 (Fall 1989): 53–68.

Pizer, Donald. [Review of the Pennsylvania Edition of *Sister Carrie*.] *American Literature* 53 (January 1982): 730–37.

———. "Self-Censorship and Textual Editing." *Textual Editing and Literary Interpretation*. Ed. Jerome J. McGann. Chicago: U Chicago P, 1985.

West, James L. W., III. "*Sister Carrie*: Manuscript to Print." *Sister Carrie* [The Pennsylvania Edition]. Philadelphia: U Pennsylvania P, 1981.

———. *A Sister Carrie Portfolio*. Charlottesville: U Virginia P, 1985.